★ ★ ★ ★ ★

"This Book is amazing! It's a very interesting blend between christianity and epic fantasy. There are a lot of spiritual and philosophical discussions that makes you reconsider values and thoughts you take for granted. It has a VERY good language. It's in my opinion the fantasy book with THE best language."

J. Lennquist,   Goodreads

"I enjoyed this book so much. The setting is detailed and lived in, pulls you into the story. You truly worry and feel for the characters and their mission, and at the same time you think you're reading a lost and forgotten tome of Christian history... I would recommend this not only to any fantasy fan that's been burned out on the genre to get a new perspective on it, but anyone looking for a great book.

Cory P, Oil City PA

"...its already the best book I've read in a very long time.
Love the writing style, its fantastic."   **E. Martin. Colorado**.

"...it combines The Divine Comedy, The Lord of the Rings, and the City of God."
L. Tarleton, Grand R, MI

"So there was a book I got for Christmas, and it was amazing, and I wanted to share its existence with all of you. It's called Never Leave Your Monastery by H. G. Potter. It's a world similar to ours except with a whole lot more magical menaces–it's a dangerous world out there, which is why the novice Jacob Magister is cautioned to never leave the monastery he calls home, but does he listen? Nope.»

Emerald@
myturntotalkblog.wordpress

★ ★ ★ ★ ★

. . . I don't generally read books of fantasy, but I found myself pulled in from the beginning. The writing flowed and made the many different names and places easier to absorb. . .the rhythm and dialogue gave the saga the feel of the Middle Ages. I liked that Jacob always stayed faithful to his Christian beliefs. . .the truth--applicable today--stood out. It was an exceptional thought-provoking tale of good versus evil. Father Harry also has a wonderful sense of humor evidenced by some of the parenthetical zingers peppering the book..

Kathryn O'Donnell

NeVer LeaVe YOUR MONASTERY

H. G. PoTTeR

H. G. Potter

Never Leave Your Monastery
second edition 2016
third edition 2018
fourth edition 2019
fifth edition 2020
sixth edition 2022

CODEX INTERMUND
ISBN 978-1-7325499-4-4

Interior illustrations by author

Batang 9
(space 10.3-11)

TOMUS PRIMUS

Never Leave Your Monastery

ABBOT CROMNA temporal & spiritual head: Abbot of Whitehaven
BROTHER JONAH elder monk, Yahoran
BROTHER ABEL elder monk, Kilurian
BROTHER ZADOC Elder Monk and Theologian, Mahanaxaran
BROTHER ENWICK Novice Monk, best friend of Jacob, an Ael
BROTHER FORMOSUS Teacher of Jacob, former professor of Whigg
BROTHER ULCRIST Master Trainer of Guardian combat Monks, Aelic
BROTHER OSSICA Abbey Tribunal, master librarian, Mahanaxaran
BROTHER FRAGGA Abbey Tribunal, caretaker of Abbot, Kilurian
BROTHER JACOB Novice Monk, Guardian monk in training, Kilurian
BROTHER LUCIAN Monk leader of the opposition faction, Kilurian
BROTHER AMOS: Monk and Abbey physician, Mahanaxaran
ANHERM OF WHIGG, famous writer, ex-wizard, deceased
BROTHER YULLA Guardian Monk, opposition faction, Yahoran
BROTHER SAREK rival monk of Whigg, couselor to King Graham
DROCTULF dwarven captain, most experienced of all Valraphs.
STORMRAKER champion, elf-blood of Ayrs, best fighter of the valraphs
BUCKBAR LANCELAS valraph footman, part-time philosopher
DAUFIN NERILETH valraph hornsman, of Plathonis
CORYDON ELETUMAL valraph footman
THINGLE MARSYAS valraph scout
FINCH KELPEIROS valraph scout
JACKTHORN SYLDEIN valraph ranger
TELPERION GRANOC H valraph ranger
GRIMBLE FORKBEARD dwarf of the blue mountains, fighter
MARAGALD: old hermit, who dwells within Whitehaven, Kilurian
GUY OF XARAGIA: Encyclopediac writer of Gandolon
KRUTH (KRUTHENDEL) of the Hermit Hills, Lore-master, Arcavir
KNIGHTS GREY, WHITE, BURGUNDY: Last of Ammouric Knights
KING GRAHAM: Feudal Ruler of AEL LOT, last Kingdom to resist
BROTHER ORBIAN: exiled from Monastery of the Weeping Brotherhood
DUKE IKON of Gorre, legendary Adventurer of the ancient continent
ARIZEL (BANNOCK): self-employed Wizard of Gohha, much unknown
SAHKAH mercenary Lizardman
NIMRUL, DIRE OF MELANCHOLY: Archdeceiver and Dark Lord of two
epochs, fell King of Nzul, also called NORTHING, NAZAGEIST, Archdruid, and
BALECROWN, origin and race unknown.
INFERNAL MONK cell-mate of Jacob, name remains unknown
NOROCH son of Arundek, the Gargoyal
MULG: horgoth Warlord, hobgoblin henchman of the Dire.
THE FURTH HIGH KING: The King of Kings whose World-Throne is on
Argunizia

Certain monks of ancient time, whose names are forgotten, built the amazing Abbey of Whitehaven. They designed her architecture by means of a mysterious art. She appears to cling to the massive rock of mountainous crag that rises upon Vastess Ocean. How exactly mere men could have constructed so enormous a dwelling in so impossible a place the annals do not say.

An elder monk patrols the monastery at the rising of the sun. His task is to admonish the brethren and exhort them to faith. One monk never failed in to do so, save for once. One bright day Brother Zadoc did not patrol. He was in a terrible hurry, and everyone knows that monks should never be in a hurry, especially not an elder.

The wiry monk crossed the shafts of light that break into the cloister garden in the early hours. He turned and went down twisting steps of worn stone, and across creaking wooden parapets, then down through a dark corridor and up into the various bright hallways.

Other monks were bent down repairing ancient stonework. They recognized the shuffle of his sandals, the ruffle of his habit, and the rattle of his beads. He said nothing. They certainly thought it strange, for he usually greeted them with words of faith.

This time he did not even send a glance at them. His gaze was down low and his arms folded in his long grey-dark sleeves. He would allow no distraction on his way. The complex of passages and stairs in Whitehaven is not easily navigated, not even for a monk of many winters. Zadoc had seen many winters, as his shaggy white beard testified. That is why Abbot requested him. A serious situation had arisen: a monk had gone missing.

At first just a few monks had noticed the absence. They deemed it of no consequence...an empty spot where a monk should be, an irregularity at the rear of pointed hoods lined up for evening chant. It was something altogether minor. The monk must have fallen asleep in his cell.

When he did not show for anything the next day, his fellow novices became alarmed. Young men do not skip meals, not twice. At once they alerted Brother Zadoc, who after all, was novice master. He bade them check the monk's cell again. He was not there.

They sought him but they did not find him. They did not find him in the library, nor the infirmary, nor anywhere else in the sacred confines. Zadoc widened the search. They did not find him lingering in the Caves of Penitence and no one had seen him in the town Whilom below. Although confessed by all to be a star novice, he must have traveled off somewhere.

But who would be so foolish as to leave a monastery, the best of all possible lives available in the midward-age of the world?

The matter was about to become serious for Abbot Cromna. If they did not find the novice, there would be an accounting before both God and King.

Abbot was on the floor of the Grand Chapel, prostrate before the altar, his face to the tiles. Being overseer and spiritual father, he had suspected that it must somehow be his own fault. He was a good Abbot, never neglecting duty. With all the preparations for the feast day of St. Ambrosius the Nephilid, the empty spot had escaped his notice. When at last he found out, he at once ordered all the monks to pray...

A cloud of incense floated in the air above the altar. It had been lingering from early in the morning, the fragrance etherial and unearthly, not sweet and flowery. It drifted down and settled over Abbot.

He grabbed his crutches and set them upright, and pushed and pulled himself from the floor. It took some strength, but he was middle-aged and his arms were in good shape.

Zadoc arrived. He went and steadied the struggling Abbot. Abbot nodded to him.

"You got lost in our labyrinth of a monastery?"

"Only for a moment...it is not as bad as the maze of the world, where our stray novice wanders out there...out there somewhere."

"I would say he is lost in the labyrinth of the mind, rather... Tell me, did you perceive him unhappy here?"

"No, Abbot...I did not percieve that. I would guess that he became weary as novices often do, for their spirits are frail. He must learn perseverance. As you know, what the brothers do here profits little. . . helping not even monks themselves, unless prayer be continuous on their lips. All is vanity without the favor of the Most High. The monks are assuredly not perfect, not even one. I dare say that it is your formidable task to shepherd them...but God favors you."

"I think he must. Angels whisper many things to me. Many hours have been spent praying for the missing novice. I have been offering thanksgiving. The Good Shepherd heard our prayers, wretched though we are. He's brought back the lost lamb to us already. Just last night before dinner we intercepted the lad. He was attempting to return unnoticed, as if his escapade were nothing. Monks cannot just come and go as they please. We shall hear his answers. Now be at hand and advise me. We must learn if he yet has a mind submitted to our Rule. If he does, you will let him in on our plan. It may turn his curious eyes back here to his home."

Abbot gripped his crutches and began to work his way beneath the ten Maurobic arches. CLICK-clock went the shafts that struck against the stone tiles. Altitudes of crenelated ceiling and pine gables echoed the sound.

Brother Zadoc went along beside him. A monk of certain sagedom, his face was worn and wrinkled, his hair white as snow but with eyes glancing about sharply like an eagle. He caught sight of his prey: the wayward monk.

"Novice Jacob!" he called out in his old raspy voice. "Abbot Cromna will speak with you now...!"

The fellow in question was sitting alone in meditation. Under his monk's cowl he kept himself hooded. He had hoped to remain unnoticed after the others left the chapel. It did not work.

Abbot and Brother Zadoc reached the aisle. Zadoc genuflected as all monks do, but not Abbot. He could not. Even with crutches, the injury in his knees prevented him. Instead he bowed a deep bow, a slow and careful reverence.

The young monk maneuvered out of the choir stall and hurried over to them. He doffed his cowl and bowed the cursory bow. The gesture of respect revealed something. Bruises decorated his tonsured head on account of the recent misadventure.

Abbot noticed the bruises, but said nothing.

The three monks stood there in front of the sanctuary: Abbot Cromna, old Brother Zadoc, and the wayward novice. Somewhere far above in the intricate stonework of the ceiling's galleries pigeons were cooing.

Abbot spoke. "Brother Jacob, the brothers have been looking for you. May God who is All-knowing dismiss your waywardness. We should discuss things, you and I. -Not today however, but do stick around... will you? You may speak your mind freely with your Abbot and with Brother Zadoc here."

Jacob did not dare look at him.

Abbot leaned on his crutches. He gazed a ponderous gaze up into the spaces above.

Jacob lowered his eyes. ". . . Master."

"Whatever you were doing in those woods, my son, you will explain to us, aye...but later... not now. The mind of a monk should always return to God first. Do you understand?"

"I understand, Lord Abbot."

"Therefore return your thoughts with us. Although you are far from perfect, admittably, you are nevertheless accomplished in learning for your age. Therefore Brother Zadoc and I would know your mind on something... a bit of a mental puzzle that we have been pondering lately... A young monk with fresh mind like yours might be of assistance, wouldn't you agree Brother Zadoc?"

"Even saplings have been known to yield worthy fruit, my lord...on occasion."

Abbot took a deep breath. "We wonder about this: it seems that most folk do not accept anything "far-fetched," especially what they cannot see, namely, see with their own eyes."

"—what I saw in the woods...the brothers must be calling it far-fetched, but—"

"Keep focused...Jacob. Whatever went on out there will be addressed later. Put it aside for now. We have, in strict, an inquiry that is critical. And I think it is something that will interest you. Consider it a kind of *in promptu* quiz. Are you ready?"

"May I prove ready, master..."

"Then I will lay it out before you. It's about seeing...and believing. The proposal is this: everyday people require that if something extraordinary is to be believed, they must see it "with their own eyes" or they will be quite slow to accept it ...especially things that sound far-fetched."

"–if something extraordinary be believed...hmmm. There's no doubt men are skeptical about many things outside the range of everyday, and will refuse to believe anything too far-fetched. Master, the great part of my life, and now my submission-years, have been here, up on these cliffs, thinking monkish thoughts. I am unfamiliar with the everyday thoughts of men."

"Well, Jacob, monks are drawn from the ranks of men. So take an example from common life. Even monks use the expression: "When I see it with my own eyes, I'll believe it...""

The novice pondered a moment.

"See it...all glory and splendor of the world? Shouldn't a monk be happy enough to read of it in books? That's what must have thrown me off. Desire to see the world, with my own eyes...all the mundane things that will vanish away. I chased after earthly glory, passing fancies, forgetful of THE glory everlasting. A knavish thing, what I did, going off like that...abandoning all the brothers. Permit me to remain a monk. Let me make up for my offense by the lowest chores and penance."

"Yes. . .you remain a monk...and we'll see that you make up for it soon, be assured. But you are slow to follow my instruction. I repeat: our question has nothing to do with you. Right now something of high state vexes us. So consider the proposition squarely: most folk, even monks, rely too much on the visible, as they say, "seeing it with their own eyes?""

Jacob paused, suspended in thought for a moment.

"You want an answer from me, master, because of my abilities. I already have come up with something, but am surely too..."

"Then divulge it, but remember humility."

"As you say, master. Yes, I do grant the proposal, that such must be the case. How insightful the race of men –and how NOT! Most folk trust whatever is right up front...and that only. Most see nothing beyond that. Is not that how a magician gets away with his tricks? ...and they see little of what's really going on. Recently the old purblind hermit reminded me of something....what's most valuable in life human eyes do not see."

"The old hermit? Then rightly spoke that old raven..." Abbot said, "Heaven has a crystalline wisdom...and a contradiction. Physical sight is a lesser prize. Faith is the blessed way.

Blessed are they who have NOT seen, and have believed.

Do you fathom the meaning, Jacob? They are the words of the Lord himself.

"Visible proof: something for the physical sciences and mundane learning. That's all good, but as my Abbot knows, not what Heaven rewards."

"Right... Now then; check this proposition: recall the individuals whom our Lord first called, who sojourned with him. They were men of faith...no? They were blessed in faith...but we wonder if less so than often imagined. We propose this: they had faith, Jacob, but not so great as we monks."

"Master, do you speak in riddles? The Apostles walked with God himself, and He lived in their midst."

"We know that," he answered. "...but listen here: take something that is visible: any particular action that is a visible action. Men view it and usually know what is going on. Does such viewing require anything of faith? Not at all; nothing special found there. The same is true for those who actually saw the Christ and his miraculous works, back in the days when He walked the earth. Was great faith necessary for them? No, they saw miracles and they accepted what revelation teaches. We, on the other hand, we have NOT seen such things in our time; but we do believe nevertheless. So then: were the Apostles themselves, although blessed, more blessed than we monks, today in this last age of the world? Not at all! We have NOT seen. *Blessed are they who have NOT seen.* That's us! We possess a blessed faith more than they! How can that be? We have learned to *walk by faith, not by sight.* The insight, I fear, leads to something of a paradox."

"Yes, my Lord Abbot... a paradox: defiance of common wisdom. In this matter it goes against the common notion *seeing is better than believing.* However, may I dispute with you on the Apostles? I say this: they also must have had greater faith than at first supposed. For they saw a man, outwardly a typical carpenter who eats bread, toils, sleeps, and all the rest, but they were informed that the same human was in fact the one true God: the invisible become visible: The Incarnation. It must have seemed ludicrous to most folk in those days. Even in our time it is still "a mystery." Wouldn't such a thing, seeing God in the flesh, take just as much faith, if not more? The Apostles were at least equal to us in faith."

"How true...you have made an excellent counterpoint-well said...but careful, boy...with us monks you are safe. The great clerics would take insult at your gainsaying. Better to feign ignorance with them. You would easily match even them with that little mercury in you. Pray ernestly lest you pride yourself on it. We wish to use your monkhood. Hold those thoughts, and turn now with us to another matter...

Monks and all servants of the Lamb should not esteem miracles without some caution. Wonders do arise that cause people's eyes to widen; the visible miracles men often claim to witness, all the commonly known and famous ones: impossible rescues, complete and permanent healings, levitations and invulnerabilities, telepathy and bilocations, solar and lunar phenomena, future visions and apocalypses, and many others. Monks in due time accept and recognize them

...provided that the Soothfold does not object. Correct?"

The novice did not respond. Why did the Abbot treat on these things, being so obvious an instruction?

Elder brother Zadoc, who had been listening, suddenly interjected. "Abbot himself has become privy to amazing news, Jacob. —news of a great miracle." Wrinkle-faced with many winters and his faded habit hanging on his wiry frame, Zadoc's eagle-eyes were stabbed with wisdom.

Abbot nodded to him, giving the go-ahead. The old one fixed his gaze upon Jacob.

"Ready your mind again, Jacob. Of this you may speak to no one. Hear it: raising the dead is no longer something we may dismiss for saints of legend..." There was a sudden flapping of pigeons rushing off somewhere above. "*Mirabile dictu*, a simple priest has found the power in his hands!"

"A priest...raising the dead?"

Abbot now spoke in a whisper, as one who wonders. "With chosen prayers, with incantations long forgotten, a certain priest performed a resurrection *ex monumentis*. Through his hands Heaven restored someone who had been in the tomb over a year!"

"Were it a trick of some sort," remarked Zadoc, "our experts would have detected it."

"—nothing else can explain it!" said Abbot. "Other resurrections were done as well, everything in the presence of infallible witnesses. They have testified to what they saw."

"By the saints, a priest can do that?" Jacob asked. "Which priest? Is he one of ours?"

There came no immediate answer, only a reluctant pause. Abbot glanced over his shoulder. He was nervous about something. "The priest remains anonymous. We admit that he is prudent to do so. He has shown his work to few others, to the Soothfold in strict."

"My lord Abbot...that one of our Ammouric priests can raise the dead...I need to see it to believe it. He must be a holy priest indeed."

Zadoc interjected to make a correction on that point: "Dutiful...he is said to be as dutiful...but holiness of a noteworthy sort his superiors never reported. Heaven-above knows why the power is granted him. Why should so obscure a cleric be chosen for so famous a miracle?"

No answer was offered. Abbot gazed off somewhere to interior distances. The pigeons cooed a soft cooing.

"There is something else," Abbot said, furling his eyebrows and frowning. "There has been a proposal. It is something strange, something...diabolical!"

He leaned in close to Jacob. "Listen to me, Brother Jacob. You have heard of the Friars of Whigg on the continent, have you not?"

"I have, master. They are our brothers in Christ."

"Indeed they are, Jacob, but they are also proud and bitter rivals. May God shed his mercy on them. Some of them have unhealthy obsessions. They say this miracle-worker of a priest...they say...that he should use his power to help the endangered realms of the world. The Friars say: let him raise certain deceased personages, men who know how to draw upon mysterious forces. Let him raise men of famous repute."

"...famous men...you mean; from long ago, from a previous age?"

"Yes, but particular men, powerful lords. They want him to use his miraculous hands on the wisemen and wizards of Nystol!"

At that exclamation the whole flock of pigeons in the dome above was stirred to a panic of flapping flight.

"What? I doubt that Heaven would ever approve that! Raise up wizards long extinct?" Jacob exclaimed. "Nystol's many towers were desolated. Flames consumed them all, their libraries and all magic scrolls. It was Divine Justice!"

Abbot and Brother Zadoc exchanged uneasy glances.

"—not all wizards...and not every scroll did the fires destroy." Zadoc warned.

Some shadow just then passed over the three.

Was it a cloud drifting over?

Jacob looked, but could not determine the source.

Abbot hesitated. "This priest—" He turned and whispered to Zadoc. The elder nodded back. A theologian's mind was needed on such matters:

"...it is written," Zadoc said in his dreamy yet precision-voice, "both the righteous and the wicked must rise at the Resurrection. That's right, the wicked also shall rise. You see, Jacob... there are certain gifts, that, when Heaven bestows them upon frail mankind, no conditions against their usage are decreed. Heaven freely gives them. Freely may they be used, be it either in wisdom or in folly. A priest may, with this power given, restore whomsoever he wishes. He could wake the wizards from their pagan sepulchres, the sweet incense of Heaven drifting across their boney nostrils."

"—ushering them back from the abyss!" Abbot turned away so as not to show his consternation.

"Unto what possible end...?" Zadoc said. "Yes, you are wondering." His eyes flashed a stare that penetrates souls. "It would be this: with their powerful spells the wizards could not only restore civilization but also push back the troll-horde. Once and for all they could overthrow the creature of the North, the deathless master of the black realm."

"You mean all that heresay about the ghost-creature in Nzul?"

It was no mere halfling's fable. The Dire of Melancholy, a powerful Archdruid of an unknown race, ruled the distant feudatory of Nzul upon Northernmost Whitehawk. He was the dark lord of our time. The ancient wizards had countered him, and though they had driven him back, he had proved impossible to destroy. Rumour had it that he slept in his impregnable fortress. The wise knew that he slept not.

Abbot was searching Heaven with his eyes. He glanced around in suspicion as if his words were too loud.

"Several high level prelates have agreed to the plan. It sounds reasonable, but I warn you, there is something profoundly unwise with this sort of "practical" thinking. I am amazed at how many monks and clerics have consented. How can they even think of abusing a power that the only Lord can give? If He gives power to raise the dead, would He not also grant the authority to banish that apostate creature, and drive him back to the pit without resorting to ancient magic?"

"The Friars do not realize," Zadoc added, "how awakening long-extinct wizards of the hopeless epoch would be...catastrophic... achieving much worse than that creature of Melancholy could ever himself do in the world. They must be corrected."

Abbot declared: "As Godmouth and Eldane of every Whitehawk Kingdom and all the Furthlands beyond, I must act." He paused in the carefulness of a grave command. "You Jacob, will be our voice. We bid you write a philosophical tract; use all your first-hand knowledge. Spare no precise language, nor couch cozy words. Spill as much ink as you need, tearing into the demented theologies of those Friars."

The Abbot and Brother Zadoc disclosed other things to Jacob as well, things that most novices would not comprehend. I cannot here divulge all of it. Suffice to know this: I was to write out a detailed argument against the folly. They considered me the right pick, eventhough I had left the monastery and come back. You see, among all the monks, I alone had encountered an actual wizard of Nystol.

"Get to work on it; that will keep you out of trouble." Abbot abruptly turned away. He and the theologian Zadoc made way back across the Grand Chapel, crutches clicking as they went.

The pigeons were no longer cooing.

Within days I completed the tract in Latin and submitted the pages to Brother Zadoc. He looked it over for errors. It was published the week I left for Hordingbay; my first and only divine treatise: Jacob of Whitehaven: *De Resurrectione Magorum*. Two winters have since passed.

The wool-frocked Friars of Whigg, our theological adversaries, of course got a hold of it, as we intended. They have opposed my admonition as a quarrelsome display, angrily scratching out in writing that I am a heretic. These brothers profess that there is nothing at all wrong with disturbing the dead...not if its for a good cause. They are quite out of their depth. Do honest people imagine that such an ingenious and evil spirit may be overcome with a little magic?

The ancestors titled him "the Dire" for a reason, you know. True, many tales men have told of that ghostly creature who sits upon the Throne of Melancholy, but does anyone know the real story on him? Contrary to the presumption of the Friars, against him not even the wizards of Nystol ever dared, not as far as the histories indicate, and that was back when their magic was at full measure.

Let the wizards remain condemned to oblivion; their restless sleep beneath desolated Nystol.

We who are believers need not their magic.

Could we ourselves not move mountains with but a mustard seed of faith? I myself went against that mirthless lord of Melancholy, and without magic. Not only have I been to his court, but I have returned to tell of it. The Friars, the "great intellects" of Whigg, sit all safe in their own library of seven ivory parapets, fattened on sumptuous fare, reminiscing holy poverty in woolen frocks. They have never actually espied that unholy minion, nor the troll horde.

They have no clue what's out there.

Months away and miles across unforgiving wildernesses and icy wastelands, there is a place accursed,

where civilization's exiles stalk the night
beneath the aegis of an infernal archon.

It is the frigid region beyond the Northern forests, where is bounded the not-very-hospitable principality of Nzul. There, overlooking all, stands the impregnable fortress, the dreadnought known as the Arc du Baffay.

To get there, you must traverse the outlands that "forgive no traveler." The trees of that forest are tall and magnificent. The primordial form of those pines hint that they are from a time beyond human knowledge.

You can even see the swaying tops from here, not so far from the monastery. They are the entrance to a vast and true wilderness.

Those who have never been through it politely call those pine-forests "The Timberhills." But from of old the expanse was called "the Lokken," a name that has persisted in several languages even to this late age of the world.

They extend even to the remote Northward shores of the island. So before I tell of the hellish dungeons of that villainous overlord, or speak on the long-robed wizards of Nystol, let me admonish the monks who are new. Go not into that forest. Take it from someone who knows. Seek no familiarity with the charm of the woods. Do not think to be going in a just little ways. It is no place for a monk's meditation, only his doom.

Doom found me, my friends, a doom that is worse than death. We monks, more than anyone, know that there are things worse than death. Doom was the price I paid for my folly, a folly begotten by Pride. To have left this monastery, without permission, was indeed Pride. To go where angels fear to tread was folly, and to journey blindly across tangled horizons was doom.

The truth entire I now dare present to you, brothers, be it with or without your pardon, omitting nothing; knowing full well that I could burn at the stake for what I am about to divulge. But it is the best way to furnish you some peace of mind, for in your hearts lingering doubts over me must certainly remain.

My mode is plain, not flowery or embellished with fancy words and high rhetoric, or with clever descriptions of sunsets and landscapes. This is how the words of a monk should be; unadorned, just like the simple habit and rope he wears. He views all created things as of less worth.

I exhort you therefore in telling of these things to weigh not only our common weakness, but the sad end of all things unless we monks, each one of us, accomplish some worthy reparation for this world so forgetful of God.

So it is with due warning and the earnest appeal to Heaven's mercy that I now tell the tale..

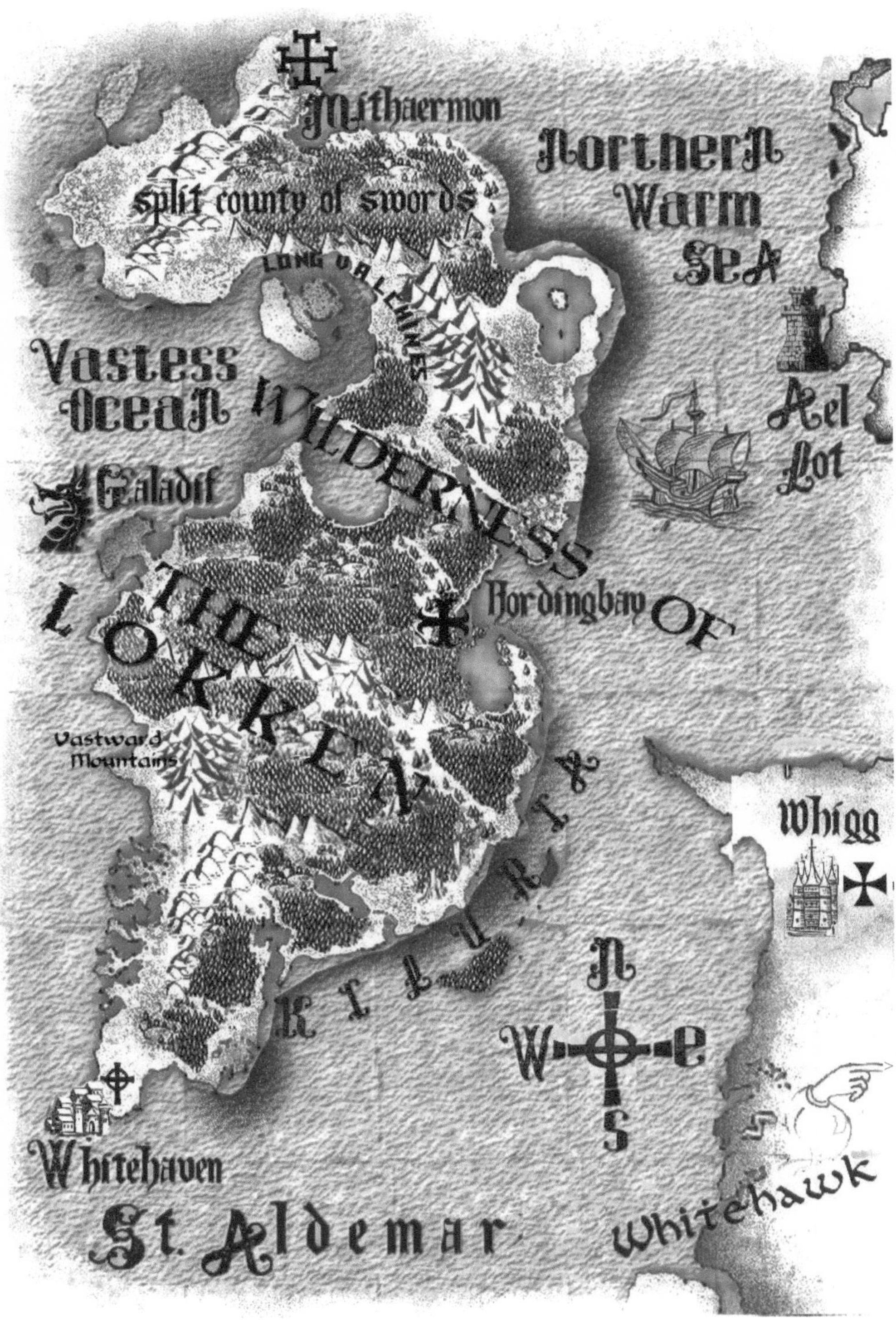

Mithaermon
Northern Warm Sea
split county of swords
Long Vale Mines
Vastess Ocean
Galadir
Ael Lot
Nordingbay
Vastward Mountains
Whigg
Whitehaven
St. Aldemar
Whitehawk
N
W
E
S

The storm was heralded by an angelic vision of the great *Agathodaemon* Ambrosius, the lion-headed, who stood on the summit of a mountain in command of the winds and recited the seven hundred seventy-seven unwitten verses.

Thannato Excorpus
Contra Prophetias Mercurii Yod

A Storm Approaches   I

The testimony of the wandering monk, masterful at the quarterstaff, who traversed territories treacherous and unknown, entering mysterious realms, the camps of savage armies and lairs of many fantastic beings. It was not for treasure, or fame, or some earthly endeavor that he went. The Spirit from on high drove him into the wilderness, there to oppose the very chamberlain of Darkness, the ancient creature within the impregnable Arc du Baffay.

Tell, o traveler of worlds long vanished, tell of that great contest, and everything the monk endured to get there, and fail not if some call it outlandish, for you will convey a light to those who cannot see, a lantern to those in dungeons dark.

Start with the terrible storm that blew from the Vastess Ocean and battered the monastery in the fourth winter of Abbot Cromna, the morning after the feast of St. Placidus. Massive black billows gathered upon the horizon and blocked the rays of the rising sun. Hulking thunderheads overtook all the Westward shores. Within the hour they were looming overhead. Above the monastery the fleet of juggernauts rushed like pirate ships, black sails unfurling, hurling hailstones and thundering like giants. It was a tumult unexpected. The dark billows did not drift, but moved as if by will. All the sky was in revolt.

Flashes of lightning shocked the air and cracked out thrilling rumbles. Some suspected that such tumult indicated the disapproval of Heaven. The tempest blasted the Orchard of Catafrax with frost and ravaged all the countryside. It took heavy toll on the peasant's farms in particular. Nor was the property of any free lord spared.

After that it decimated the ranks of the gardens, tearing down branches. Glistening sheets covered all the landscape. After the wind ceased a pale shroud of mist blanketed the ground. A creeping whiteness moved across the landscape, as if a thing alive, searching.

Strict justice was exacted upon the weak. Was it not that mischievous spirit, come to pour out trials and temptation upon everyone, even rope-girded monks?

But with all that, in the darkness just before first light, monks mustered in peace, cloaked in shadow.

Let nothing hinder monastic duty. So enjoins the Rule.

In that primordial dark, as every time, monks assemble, stepping from shadows into the partially lit choir rows. A thunderclap rattled the sacred vessels of the sanctuary. Candles flickered. They covered their heads with their cowls. The chanting began.

Monstrous blasts shook the air. Outside lightning blinked across the umbraged sky. Far away in the hills the pagans came out of their caves to study the tracts of lightning and discern the pedigree of the forgotten gods.

The thunder passed over until the storm moved off.

Monks pushed back the hoods. *Magnum Silentium,* the Grand Quietude, had not been so quiet.

Enwick, a sturdy and earnest new monk, some sixteen winters, now entered the chapel. He was mature for his age in speech and bearing. A wholesome and well-built fellow, and he was bright, a sure bet to become one of the Christ-crowned priests.

He stood before the assembly of monks. He must be scolded for failing to rise for prayer. He knelt down before the elder monks, doffed his cowl, and bowed his head.

"I missed the first hour... I ask for penance... it was not for oversleeping that I missed." He bent all the way down to touch the floor with his head.

Brother Ossica, the *disciplinarius*, was required to do a brief interrogation in the case of novices. Ossica was a black-skinned Mahanaxaran, a formidable man for his sharp gaze, but always squinting and coming off as slightly amused.

"You say you did not sleep in? Why did you miss? Spooked by a little thunder?"

"—a distraction held me back, a thing strange: I spotted something outside hidden in the dark, but lit up by lightning flash... something not of our understanding... a creature moving through the woods....I seen it from my cell window, a supernatural beast....monstrous..."

"How interesting, Brother Enwick."

The monks became all very interested at this. Enwick did not look at them. His eyes were fixed on Ossica.

Enwick added: "...it must have crawled up from one of the caves: a dragon. It froze me up in fright.

"a dragon...."

"Yes...they burn down whole cities you know. Who hasn't seen the skull in the Regulian library? ···they do exist. They snooze in the deep for an *aeon*. The earth herself, burdened with the sins of men, awakens them. The thing is out there."

Silence of incomprehension followed, then a burst of laughter; laughter echoed in the chapel where monks must beg high Heaven to overlook innumerable transgressions. Was there any monk who was not amused? Such an imginary excuse was at least worthy of gaining a dispensation.

"Enwick...the only snoozing going on was in YOUR bed!"

More laughter···So this monk, without failing in the tone of respect, raised his voice. "The city of Galadif worships the image of a dragon, a dragon instead of the one true God, dont they?"

The monk-laughter faded away. Galadif had been Whitehaven's biggest failure. We had never suceeded in bringing the gospel to those ignorant folk.

Enwick was a red-haired Ael. Ossica thought it better to treat any Aels with leniance, having no kindred of that nation himself. The monks of Whitehaven dwell upon the grand island St. Aldemar, called Kiluria of old. The Aels had conquered not even a generation past.

Ossica squinted. Ael or not, Enwick must learn not to contradict superiors. Enwick's repeated faults had gained him anything but credibility.

"In that town of Galadif the pagan imagination never rests, Brother Enwick. If you imagined the thing a danger, why did you not come at once to WARN your brothers? Enough then of childish stories, you are a monk now. Even were such a beast yet alive to crawl up here, *quid refert nobis?* What is that to us? Does a monk fear a created being, a merely finite being? Or does he fear THE uncreated and infinite being? Or, in your case, did you fear the beast so much and God so little that you would let it hinder your sacred duty?"

Enwick kept a humble posture. He contrived no answer where no answer was possible.

The disciplinarian assigned no penance. Enwick lifted himself from the floor to depart. He turned about and stepped away. But with sudden start he lifted head and wheeled back around —a wordless protest.

With this boldness Brother Ossica's eyes widened. "Be not one to contrive idle stories, Enwick! Such fantastic stories! ...excuses that bring triviality to these sacred halls!"

Enwick stilled his tongue. He remained and bowed again.

Ossica warned, "Well...have you anything else to say?"

"—they are NOT lies, by my own marrow. I have only this; there is some great monster out there... and all you who laugh: climb up to the crow's nest and spot the horned beast with your own eyes! The thing is creeping around the woods!"

With cheerful satisfaction all monks went off to their day labors, some to remove ice, others to look after the animals, others to copy the manuscripts. They had been well pleased with Enwick's imaginative outburst. Several curious monks however, surprised that Enwick did not retract, wondered if it were more than entertainment. They wanted to take a look.

Novice Jacob Magister was also curious.

Seven ascended, a line of monks went, moving spiralwise, upon step and stair, circling many levels.
At last they filed up to the highest area;
into a narrow spire where, far-seeing as at sea,
for a ship's vantage, a "crow's nest" swayed.
One may view all points on the horizon.
Looking downward one sees, beyond the sandals of monks, the enormous vessel of ancient wood and rock: the stone-crafted ship called Whitehaven monastery. The founders built her high on a crag overlooking the Vastess Ocean; a natural defense against ever-menacing sea-raiders.

To the North lay the Orchard of Catafrax.

One scans to the South and beholds all the salty sea, and spots tall sails of many-masted ships breeching the horizon.

To North and East the busy fishing-town Whilom hums below.

Not much farther beyond town broods the primordial Timberhills, that wilderness reaching every shore of the grand island. It stretches across the Northern horizon without any apologies, without hosting a single comforting sight of human dwelling.

Of this my journal keeps fresh the words:

There in the crow's nest we all stood, seven monks.

We peered into distances from the crow's nest, and let the drizzle of the cloudy morning cool our cheeks.

Brother Zadoc was the first to speak: "Something astir I do see beyond... I can just spot it···barely. It does have a creaturely look...as Enwick said. Through the forest branches....do you see? To the West and North...just below the thicks and fogs. Anyone else mark that?"

"Over that way? I do not see anything," another monk said. "The mist upon the wood is just too thick.

Of course who has eyes sharp as yours, Zadoc?

Your eagle-vision can sight ghosts through thick clouds."

Brother Formosus saw something. "Aye, there stirs something out there ...true, I grant that much....something moving...reddish segments; and what could be golden fins. One can see how Enwick mistook a dragon..."

"You have never seen a deep-dwelling dragon, have you?" Jacob said. "So you cannot tell. Therefore it might not be a dragon, or again it might be; and if so, one which outlived the centuries." Being just a novice I should not have added in a simple opinion to demonstrate learning. But I continued my vain dissertation. "In the bestiaries some of those are depicted, some others having *segmenta*, and in the encyclopediac manuals of Guy of Xaragia it is described..." I finally realized what I was doing and cut short my report. Monks care little to answer or add to the scholarly notes of novices...

A certain old man was up there in the crow's nest with us. He also made the long climb. All the way up to the top he had trusted his spindle-legs. In a tattered black robe he sat and kept his peace. This mysterious one was from the ancient Kilurian city-state Mithaeron. He was after the appearance of an old raven, perched and ponderous. Older than Zadoc, he was nearly blind, his whitish eyes aglow with unearthly vision. And hoary was he, his beard being like frost on forest hemlock. The other monks out of routine politeness awaited his word.

He had taken a narrow place on a little bench of that high porch.

"All ye monkish tongues, keep ye them still now. Be ye silent a spell." he said. A seeming protracted series of moments slipped by. The thin furrowed lips at last parted and moved. "Ye brethren cannot say what goeth 'neath the eldark trees," He spoke as in an utterance. "Hark well; it is, in sooth, a beast, perilous indeed. The novice was right; a wyrm of the intermundane world, and the devil's spirit. She comes disguised...few would guess it. Rickety wagons come, aye, wagons rolling in line. Squeaking wheels, do ye hear? Those who have ears let them hear it... and hear me: a traveling troupe of players and actors cometh, the dragon's servants, cunning folk. They are the troubadours of Galadif. Once before came they hither, many winters ago, in the days of my heathenry. A danger for souls be they, as much as the dragon Vorthragna herself!"

The many-headed dragon Vorthragna, hydra-progenitor of all dragons, according to lore···but how could he possibly know it were actors? None could hear sounds of wagons.

This old one was not like the rest of the elders. He was not a rope-girded monk like the brethren. He wore something like dark sackcloth, being a penitent man who sometimes lodged with monks: he was the hermit Maragald. (now, brothers, long since garnered unto the Lord).

...keep far from them, and from all that carnival, beloved of God. Weigh you these things I say: for the sake of bread and circuses entire nations have floundered. Do ye few monks, mere bellies, hope to resist such worldly entertainments by your own strength? Already some of you salivate. It is the Devil's long preparation... Fast and do penance instead. *Resist the devil and he will take flight!"*

"—entertainments?"

"Amen I say to you, beware of them. Of entertainments few are there for helping souls. Most are for hindrance. The clans of Galadif will put on a show for you to purvey the cult of the dragon. Meditate on God's holy laws instead. Enter not the confines and tents of the wicked.

Blessed is the righteous man, who is like a tree planted by flowing waters."

"Old raven, how is it that you, who are near blind, can know it's circus wagons?" I asked. "Even keeness in eyes like Brother Zadoc's could not. No, the thing seems something of a ..."

"Hold your tongue, boy," warned another monk, a professed. "We weary of your questioning and hapless mental display. You have not yet learned to act as a proper monk. Have respect and advance not against your elders."

"I do not advance against the old one," I countered. "...and I do not fathom why you jump on me like that."

"You just did it again," noted Brother Zadoc. "A novice should not even dare speak in defense of himself."

"Enough..." Maragald said. "Scold not a novice too much; your Rule warns. The young monk Jacob is a brave soul, although sometimes he strays like a little lamb. Right well is made the alarm. What novice Enwick saw was not vain fancy. I say to you, he saw in earnest a fire-breathing dragon...in spirit. Fire-breathing, yes, not physic fire, but the scathefire; that is, Hell's doctrines that scorch the soul. You will shortly discern what I mean. They seem to be merely colorful wagons, happily decorated, golden fins. They are not what they appear —aye, just like a lavish marble sepulchre, or the works of the pagan poets: beautiful outside, sweet to hear, but all corruption within, fraught with decay and dead men's bones.

Amen I say to you: here is the great beast faining with clever disguise.Come, be not fooled, ye monks.

Do you think that because a man blind that he cannot see? Not only is this old raven able to see all round, but by the power of The Ancientmost I see many things that come to pass,

for I utter this and say that, and the days unfurl it all

like some fateful scroll... Heh? The Angel has touched my lips with the burning coal. Ancientmost uses them as an oracle, that he may give warning to wayward souls.

So harken well, all ye: ware be thou, each one, of that serpentine idol; pray lest empty curiosity present you her temptations, and you be swallowed alive, just as a snake swallows a sparrow that by stealth it has seized."

Maragald often gave such warnings. At that moment the Eastern sky, murky with the retreating storm, rumbled its last thunders, as if to confirm his words. The wagons advanced nearer from the Western forest.

The old hermit continued.

"Learn, you monks...the eye of the spiritual man catches sight of things visible to the spirit...for by grace does the veil of this terrestrial world thin, and not by human will. I say to you, the smoky magic of a dragon's breath clouds a mystery.

The sun blotted out of the sky! There! A lethal mist drifts across the landscape. Only the eye of a right-living monk can penetrate it. You new-made monks and you novices, heed my council: do not doubt the power that you have been given. Vouchsafed, did ye not, to use Heaven's gift when you donned the habit? Swore you not, to war against the eldest enemy of both God and Man? If eyes of the flesh hinder a monk to see only wagons and horses, then by disbelief that is all ye will see, no more."

"...and that is all we can see, Maragald," commented Zadoc, ready to counter anything irrational. "...and all that we should see. Forgive me, venerable one, but you bring too much caution. You are overzealous. We accept reasonable things, and we are not to be afraid....strong in the spirit we have blessedness in our vision."

Maragald seemed to frown, but he let go a slight smile under his beard. He lifted his mystical raven-eyes heavenward. Eventhough he is the "raven," and "mad," all could see that an unearthly Wisdom lit up his face.

"You are not so keen as you suppose, Zadoc! Careful; lest tainted human reasoning foul your divine science. Blind monks...*blind are ye who say that you can see*! Brothers, does not attachment to the flesh blind a monk from the truth ever-abiding? Use your spirit-eye. The mist of the forest conceals a gruesome terror, a great dragon, DRACONEM! conjured up out of the dark places of the world. It is nothing less than *Vorthragna*, mother of all dragons dwelling-deep.

She makes way along the threshold of the great forest. The horned power will turn to approach the town walls. Not satisfied with devouring the king's deer, and bored with burning the peasants' crops, she will instead go creeping about the orchard.

She hopes to surprise the unwary, or to seize and devour idle townsfolkand to tempt rope-girded monks with magic."

So he warned. Was he right? Monks should be vigilant after all. They should take seriously the rambling sermon, even of an eccentric old hermit.

The beast moved in wavy motion like some serpentine hunter, a sphinx leaning close upon the new Jerusalem. The red wagons trundle along the rolling path, bobbing like a line of fishing flotillas as they passed through the swells of mist. Here was an ancient mischief wrapped in mist. Seven wagons in number were they, and seven horses drew them, their heads sporting decorous gear, crowned with golden fins. It was the seven-headed dragon of prophecy. The haggard hermit lifted his hoary head and spoke again.

"Inside those wagons sit enchanters.
Just as in the prophecy you monks have heard.
They wear the diadems. Like the secret army that waited
in the belly of the wooden gift-horse for the Trojans,
they will not appear until they are within the outer walls.
And the Harlot of Babylon sits upon the scarlet Beast,
crowned with a display of brass horns.
It is a troupe of those who go about plying cunning tales,
and with shameful masks they hypnotize souls.
They do the work of Hell, wandering through the world seeking whomsoever they might ensnare. From beyond the great forest they come and will pitch their tents in the yards of Catafrax."

Brother Ulcrist, master trainer of guardian-monks, a dark-eyed dark-haired Ataluran, had also come to the crow's nest. He spoke up. "What possibly could be diabolic or cunning with a band of actors and performers?"

"Are you not an adept of fist and staff, Brother Ulcrist? How then can you be so unlearned in the spiritual contest?" Maragald spoke a plaintive speech. "Do you not teach the new monks of such things anymore? Do you forget *the Sapphire Instruction*? Do you monks let down your guard and welcome now everyone here, even the pit-borne devils, in order to please men and their ways? These performers are like sorcerers, they have a way of summoning spirits, the extinct gods raised up anew as demons.

Whether or not they be wise to it, they are doing it: tools of Hell are they, like the ignorant men who crucified our Savior, even venerable brother Anherm admitted as much." (Anherm of Whigg...that was my former tutor of Latin, one just recently fallen asleep in the Lord, our famous and most beloved brother, envy of the Friars). The old raven continued: "Anherm agreed on this; the actor is an illusionist who beguiles with drama, and wears the unholy masks of old demon-gods, reviving by artful display their manipulations and mischievous tales. I ask you, would a true Christian wear a mask? Be it not the contrivance of old vine-crowned Bacchus and his goat-riding revelers, a demon-god stirring up the maniacal imaginations from erstwhile pagan time?

Ah yes; we welcome the actors and gaze in fascination upon their glamour. Will the thorn-crowned King of Kings have anything ado with such a libidinous herd of goats?

Rather, He will say to them *Depart from me, ye accursed, for I never knew thee.*

Indeed, when he comes he will not delay, but he will separate the goats from the sheep..." With that sermon, the brethren who were here and there and had heard all, with haste departed from the crow's high nest.

Ye monks of future time: should you find this tome in some forgotten corner of the monastery, then I prophesy that rather has it found you. Thumb through the leaves, but do not dismiss it as just another fantastic yarn. It is not an idle tale fabricated by superstitious men fading away. Treasures are stored herein that monks have made earnest labour to preserve. I say to you: they communicate many mysteries, and just as the sunlight scatters the dragon's mist blanketing the lands, so too may these words clear away your doubts.

Brother Jacob's translation of *The Black Book*

THE DARK PROPHECIES

Of the dragon and her entertainers we would soon learn more than enough. Town-boys bounded up the monastery steps with the news.

They reported that the circus-guildsmen were "unusual," the sort of characters heard tell of in old rhymes: quick-fingered jugglers, some rakish elf-kin and dwarfish folk, lanky half-giants, together with stalwart men: "Sons of Hercules," well-hewn wrestlers and shaven-headed boxers; horsemen and cavaliers, gallant experts at jousting, (they were rumoured to be true knights, no actors), and fencers acrobatic, with a pair of jesters. Even sultry dancers from the East gave a show. And, as destiny would have it, a magician lurked about, sable-robed and mysterious.

Tents were erected, and colorful banners; the bait prepared.

A musical introduction began...the organ triumphal.

The strangers waited for the townsfolk to come running, which of course they did, and without delay.

No monk of the monastery came running.

Twelve elders counsel the Abbot of Whitehaven, concerning the governance of the sacred enclosure, and they advise him on any question respecting divine teaching for all the churches of the Whitehawk league.

That day, word came to the twelve of the circus invasion.

Can any news bring an elder monk to become alarmed?

The twelve proceeded into the stone-piled hall of councils with Abbot Cromna to discuss the matter. What should be done about it, if anything?

They do not run, but slowly process in. They sit on ancient stone benches and each elder may speak without interruption. Abbot presides.

He sits not on a high throne but a stonework bench, equal in level to the others. After Abbot involks the help of God, Eagle-eyed brother Zadoc, mercurial theologian, worn but sturdy elder, was first to speak.

"In keeping with our sacred custom, my brothers, I propose that monks descend and explore this uncommon thing, this tournament-circus, but permit them not to attend displays of acting. I admit that Maragald is right. Let not any of you lambs stray near that many-horned beast who salivates, and who calls away the townsfolk with fantastical allurement."

The elders all nodded. Beards hove down and back up. This counsel, agreed, was a stern one, but was thought best. Younger monks like myself were there as well, who may only listen. But they also hummed in approval.

Elder brother Jonah, a man from Yahoros, as Abbot, sounded soft words like a dove giving warning.

"The serenity we keep here, this remote perch
in its contemplation should not be taken for granted.
This peaceful watch upon skyward crags;
it is a haven set by the churning shores of the sea.
So let it remain. The world's vexing must not disturb us.
Nay, when it comes to men of the world...
you cannot deny them their entertainments and daily mirth. No one can help that, but it is written: *Woe to you who laugh, for you shall weep and mourn*. We monks are not men of the world. Our duty is to guard these sacred precincts, a place for men to seek refuge after the world drinks down their lives.

Whitehammer of Uriel Archangelus guard thou these poor souls! Therefore I bemoan, let no unworthy contamination of false gods outrage this place,
where the Kingdom of Heaven falls tangent upon the terrestrial sphere."

Again the elder monks affirmed, humming in concord and stroking their beards. All seemed decided on this...but were not all decided.

Outside the drizzle began to slaken; clouds opened for the beaming sun and scattered the grey. Someone in that chamber, not an elder, made a proposal for reconsideration. It was crane-like brother Formosus, wise in book learning but not in years, and nevertheless granted leave to speak.

"Let the elders come to agreement. Will the beast and musical horns enchant our townsfolk as was done with the men of Galadif?–beguile them from their fiefs or from their families, only to yoke them into idolatrous submission? Who will prepare the harvest? Who will feed the children of Heaven?...who will feed the monks?! Nay, trusted brothers should be sent down to shoo away the overbold adversary."

Consternation was set on the brows of those elder monks as they sat on those stone benches.

"It will pass," Brother Zadoc said. "On second thought, there is much that is praiseworthy in the old dramas, and the peasants or townsmen do not trespass in learning from the old pagan wisdom. By seeming disinterested in the whole affair, we are preaching: something else captivates monks; the wisdom of what is immeasurably sublime, the ever-abiding Word. Our prayers, therefore, and the unending worship; these protect Whilom-town and Whitehaven, monastery-upon-the sea."

The theologian's learning was beyond question. He was an example for all. In his youth he had stolen a pear from the sacred orchard of Catafrax. He had requested a stern penance. So many years under harsh conditions he had worked at the monastery windmill.

Next a certain monk set back his cowl, and lifted his chin. He was one who was ancient, and whose look I had imagined to resemble a pelican, (a joyous fowl that feeds her young plucking at her own chest). Brother Abel was a native of the distant sacred land Vesulum, whose ancestors had been desert nomads. In a raspy voice he gave confident utterance.

"*Inítium sapiéntiæ timor Dómini.* Remember, you monks, it was the Lord our God who made heaven and earth.

Eve was our first mother.

It was curiosity that drew her and distracted her from garnering the acceptable fruits. Had she instead been not so anxious to sate her hunger for something new, as much as we monks are anxious about dazzeling our eyes, she would have ignored the climbing serpent and kept working.

The fall of our race would not have transpired.

It has brought all the evils of the world, my friends."

(Brother Abel was truly old, the oldest, over one hundred years). He added, "Aye, true enough...but then the story of Man

would never have been told, the beast never confronted,

Man never redeemed,

and the Lord may never have opened our way into even greater revelation...fellowship with the divine.

In the end how beneficial was the mistake of Eve!"

Abbot Cromna paused and stroked his beard over and over.

Brother Abel's remarks were enigmatic and meant to go either way. Did it make Abbot nervous? All were hush. All awaited his word. His watchful owl-eyes glanced to interior spaces. Finally he spoke his mind.

"Think about it, all ye monks. Long have we regreted what has become of Galadif. We failed to *convert* the men of that city. What shame before the Lord. So it was, but I will not have those idolatrous cannibals come here and *REvert* the men of Whilom!"

So the decision was made. Eventhough it did not seem like so dangerous or crucial a thing, when it comes to sacred matters, one must never assume. The Abbot picked a few monks, including Formosus. Of course why he nominated Jacob Magister, a novice, must be ascribed only what destinies a mysterious God designs.

Abbot blessed the convoy of monks and addressed them. "You monks go into the yards of Catafrax and warn souls. If you find any peasant, townsman, or noble, otherwise upright, but who of a sudden is forsaking duty, the sweat of the brow, in exchange for glitter, for glamour, whom the empty display has captivated, rebuke him. With gentle word do so, as behooves the monk. Remind him of the Judgement, and thereby deliver his soul and preserve your own."

So Formosus and Jacob were off together with two others assigned to the minor expedition. (Those two I do not name, to save them a little embarrassment).

The custom of entering the world below in pairs must not become extinct amoung us. It makes our presence unmistakable, and is best for spiritual protection. The Rule insists.

Old Maragald the purblind hermit who had spoken of the beast had not given up so easily. He was waiting by the gate for us. When we approached, he did not fail to admonish.

"You monks in your exalted learning will not be persuaded

by what a blind man can see. So be it...no man is steered away easily from a worldly course, but as you go at happy pace

to your spiritual demise, measure ye this:

The ancient earth is not so hush. Therefore unto thee I prophesy

and do not shirk the power of what is told through me: now cometh the times long foreseen in holy visions and of which the saints warned: *The dust of the ancients shall rise!*

These years be named by our furth-ancestors

as The Time of The Harvester: It is come, I say.

The Furth High King will soon return to rule all, to rule with an iron rod. Behold! He finally quells the old dragon, that is to say, *drakodemon,* the devil's consort loosed on the wide world. That is how it must go. However, before that great day, many things must first transpire—and much travail. Learn that even now many demons are released; they patrol the lands on featherless wing. Entire kingdoms—royal courts seduced by their whisperings—woeful days near for the race of men.

There is already upon us what is called The Great Abandonment.

The greater part of souls shall turn from the faith handed down by our fathers. Many talented writings are now filling the void left after Nystol's burning; writings that teach

not what is godly but a liberty that is false. Charity and kindness

—forgotten! Altars they leave empty. Common men deny the dogmas.

The good are barely able to speak with any conviction.

Not so the wicked, not so. The wicked fill many pages

with passionate zeal for their cause. Even more must I prophesy.

When the inferno of carnal desire and hedonism has scorched souls,

borne fruit and become ripe, a Dark Shepherd appears.

He will be elected Eldane of all Whitehawk Kingdoms,

and Godmouth, assuming the Grand Abbacy,

in our own beloved Whitehaven, monastery-upon-the shore!

This one is no feudal prince of the world,

but a shepherd, a dark shepherd; a bishop.

On account of an outward display of piety

he will seduce many and win praise.

On his command Ammouric clerics introduce novelty

to our sacred rites, so that little by little, he inspires churches and even kingdoms to embrace customs not worthy of God. Only certain righteous will not be deceived, those elect whose liege-lord is The Furth High King, and they must resist; those few who do resist will be righteous and true, strengthened by the yearly pilgrimage to Lamb's banquet hall on the sacred mountain.

But they must surrender up their lives in the end.

This chastisement for the kingdoms is fitting;

the innocent pay for the guilty.

Men have indulged themselves with rotten heresies, carnal dramas,

and howling entertainments, denying the authority of the keys.

Then suddenly the war-wind blows,

shaking the thrones of Kings. Cruel wars blossom in procinct.

These wars leave not a meadow of Whitehawk

unsoaked with blood nor any kingdom neutral.

The old hegemony renewed, faithful kings

harry the archonate power, only to strengthen it.

An empire of shadow is born, and the kings all die
drenched in crimson spillage. This is the All-war,
a chastisement on the godless nations.
Kingdom shall war against kingdom, brother against brother.
Every crown of Whitehawk tips under anxiety great, and countless
feudal lords die by sword and bow, for there will be a slaughter and havoc
on the plain of Gederon as never before seen. This chastisement from high
Heaven is overdue, recompense for the uncharity of Men.
Peace will seem impossible. Then, from out of nowhere:
a mysterious peacemaker arises; a man of high charisma.
This is Inversus. He will be a man, have no doubt;
but will seem a god. Loved by many, he claims the Imperial diadem,
and he installs a lying peace among the kingdoms.
He declares that he is come to enlighten all,
but he will fault the terrible war on the old believers,
and many shall be put to the sword. In the spirit of the Archdeceiver,
he works wonders before all the Ammouric princes.
It must be accepted, this chastisement.
Pride has stiffened the knees and kept the folk away from church on
Sunday. Greed bids them toil by the sweat of their brow even on the
Sabbath day of rest. Against the Inversus none shall dare stand. Then he
will do the unthinkable: he restores Nystol and is seated upon The Eldark
throne of The High Magistracy, founded of old by Satan.
He is to be worshiped by all as divine, as a god, the Supreme Magus!
The Dark Shepherd will preach in his name, causing all, from the
greatest down to the least, to bow down in adoration. This chastisement is
given because men have not opened their ears to the Truth Nor their
hearts to His divine love.
Whosoever has ears let him hear!"

So he prophesied. Brother Formosus then spoke. "What scripture can
you cite for such outrageous prophecy, Maragald? For example, what you
say of a Dark Shepherd?"

"Study closely my teaching. I claim it from St. John's vision, for there
it is written: *And I beheld rising up out of the earth another beast, which had
two horns like a lamb, and which spoke like a dragon …and it maketh the earth
and all the dwellers therein to adore the first beast.*
The beast is *like* a lamb; but is not.
Two horns are a bishop's miter, a tall hat having two points, and he is
like a lamb, as it were, *like* a Christian, but is not. He speaks *like a dragon,*
that is,
he speaks and pours out the dark smoke
disguised as sound doctrine, obscuring the true light.
Confusion comes instead, not understanding;
for he is a *dark* shepherd, and a *gnostic.*

If you have an ear, hear it: the Inversus will obtain the scrolls of
Simon Magus lost beneath desolate Nystol, and so will he perform many
works and great marvels before all. Be not deceived. The Dark Shepherd
is but the herald.
He will cause all to fall down and adore one who madly boasts divine
origin.

Were it not for the elect, all would be deceived.

Remember what has been prophesied, for they know not the Lord;
He who became dead, and lives.

And I shall prove more. Concerning the Great Abandonment, the complete loss and final repudiation of right faith in many Whitehawk kingdoms...

it is Christ himself who prophesies
Yet the Son of man, when He cometh, shall He find, think ye, faith on earth?

Many will follow the Dark Shepherd who will possess the High Abbacy, and with teachings that disguise sin as virtue he shall be midwife of evil, he brings forth the Whore of Babylon! The yearly pilgrimage will be abolished! Fear not, in that time God himself will feed you from the Tree of Life. Monks,

Be faithful unto death, sayeth the Lord, and ye shall win the crown of eternal life."

Formosus shrugged. "Maragald, old raven, the brethren will always have recourse to the divine teachings of the Lord in the gospel,. Let the square-hat scholars who have learned the deep and hidden meanings in this world be the interpreters of the sacred books. Do you imagine His Word would be destroyed?"

"Not destroyed; no they cannot, but be not so simple, Formosus. It is also written that He prophesied, *in those days the Sun shall be darkened...*

"Maragald, did Our Lord not also say, *I am with you all days, even unto the consummation of the world?* Then why fret you so? The Sun is faring quite well, and soaring high, venerable fellow."

"What I have said is a prophecy uttered by Christ himself, the Furth High King!"

"I do not recall him speaking of The Inversus."

"He did so; against those who rejected him, Christ warned, *I am come in my Father's name and you receive me not. If another will come in his own name, him you will receive.* The Confederacy of Ammouric Kings has already done this!"

"Hmmm...it is unknown what he meant...but to say that so many of those who have been faithful will turn away in abandonment...that is high imagination indeed. Christ was merely opening a question to purvey us faith; such is the interpretation of the learned Friars of Whigg and the *Soothfold."* [1]

----

[1] *Soothfold:* The conciliar body of Ammouric Sages in the Furth, they must be present for the election of the High Abbacy, the Abbot of Whitehaven, Primate of Aldemarz, The Godmouth and Keeper of the Bachal Dsu, Staff of God, Solitary Eldane of All the Churches. For two centuries the Primacy was reserved for the Patriarch of Vesulum, and the Soothfold meet in the holy city Vesulum, where the sacred texts were kept. Later they were asked by the order of Magi to come to Nyzium (Nystol) in order to limit and govern the usage of magic, as a neutral arbitrator, but after a century

"Formosus, why would he ask such a question were there no danger of so great an abandonment? I tell you, Christ warned,
in those days the Sun shall be obscured.
He means not the physic Sun, but the metaphysic Sun, the very light from the East! It is the gospel light of the risen Lord, but it shall be darkened by the dragon's smoke. Mischievous heretics with counterfeit faith pervert the divine teachings, teaching men to seek after secrets. Their itching ears will heed any alien doctrines instead, the work of Gnostics!"

"Nay, Maragald...the Gnostics long ago have set down their heretical pens. Joy-clothed saints silenced them with the truth ever-abiding. We do not fear their devious writings."

"Fear you may not, but wrong you are if you dismiss them.
The Gnostics are NOT done; they did not scatter like the other heretics, but underground they went. Gnostic monks never cease to ply their pens for hellish tracts, publishing alien doctrines of the Abyss in monasteries beneath the earth. Soon they will obtain the accursed scrolls of Simon Magus."

"Maragald, where in thunder do you come up with such imaginings, such dark prophecies?"

"The Ancientmost has given me the sight. That is why I warn you as He did, *The moon shall not give forth her light and the stars shall fall from the sky.* Do not suppose that these events are far off in the future, brothers. By "the moon" is indicated The Church. She has already grown dim in my own span of years. The Time of the Harvester; it is near. Repent! Awaken now to the deceits of the dragon or you too shall succumb —struck down by the swipe of his tail. All the earth will be convulsed!
When wretched men do not expect it, a sign above appears.
Shines forth a light, and lo, the master has returned.
Those who have chosen Darkness will flee into the caves
to hide. But those who have believed, who have endured,
and done what he commands, see Him coming on the clouds in glory, for *there are shouts of joy and victory in the tents of the just.*"

So went the conversation, if that's what you want to call it. Few monks took Maragald seriously; not in those days, brothers. That old raven, who had retreated into the woods for many winters, claimed many things instructed him. And mark you, he claimed it not from angels, but directly from The Ancientmost. You see, unlike all of us, the hermit was

---

they moved to The Monastery of the Weeping Brotherhood in the Dry Blood Sea for the wickedness of Sorcerers had come to full fruition. It was in this time that the Patriarch chosen was ever thereafter an Abbot of a monastery. Finally Nyzium was burned down in what the Soothfold claimed was "the Wrath of God". In a later century they migrated to the West on account of the Arian threat, and in the fifth and sixth age the meeting place remained at Whitehaven, although the Soothfold was no longer an influential council in world affairs.

different, robed not in fine grey-dark frock, but an old tattered *darfurque* habit, blackish, to signify holy renunciation of all things. Secretly would he burn hours upon hours of late night oils in the library, combing the texts for some hidden heresy. Once, having discovered a number of heretical books in our modest library, he had appealed to the Abbot to have the books burned.

All the brothers were appalled at the idea. "We are makers of books, not destroyers of books!" exclaimed the Abbot. Many pointed to the importance of keeping them for a record of human experience.

But Maragald would not agree. He argued well; let such books be annihilated, the memory of them completely erased. What value is a handsomely bound book, he argued, compared to some perilous instruction stored up in its pages, doctrines of dark Hell, and fraudulent wisdom for a future monk: an unwary and naive monk, a poor soul who, fed lavishly their curious and colorful lies, might adopt such a vain theology and be deceived unto final impenitence. Upon his last day, near judgment, having trusted in a mere counterfeit, failing to pray like many souls, willfully is he formed against all truth, which he foolishly designates untruth. Lost he would be; for all eternity.

After all, the hermit asserted, real faith is from The Ancientmost, and is orthodox, whereas heretical faith is a faith given from the Devil. What is that acheivement? Aye, faith do the wicked also boast. It is written, *even the devils believe, and they tremble.*

In order to be saved, he reminded, all great masters affirm that one must hold the truth passed down without defilement. Even were one to make all proper judgements in theology, numbering in hundreds, save for just one improper that was fiercely clung to, being from the devil, and adhered to defiantly, then one would be lost.

Remember the words of Our Lord: *For truly I say to you, until heaven and earth pass away, not the smallest letter or stroke shall pass from the Law until all is accomplished.*

To go against the truth by assenting to false belief is a mighty sin indeed. Maragald had unfolded his worry over bad books: he said we monks who preserve such devilry must answer; must give account. We must explain why, when we percieved a trap set for the loss of a soul, we made copies anyway. Did the preservation of human record win anything in such a case?

What he was proposing made plenty of sense in some minds. Afterall, the fiercest temptation for monks is forbidden knowledge. In tears Maragald fell to his knees upon the floor of the abbey at synod and begged the Abbot again, lamenting aloud, revealing true devotion, asking that all souls, repenting, turn to God. "Will such books be available to read in Heaven-high-above?" he asked. "Do we not pray, *thy will be done on earth as it is in heaven?* And would Heaven in merciful goodness will that any young monk be put in jeopardy by happening upon such writings?"

The Abbot was quite at a loss, and reluctantly agreed to have locked away certain books, that only appointed librarians may refer to them, or special permission be gained.

This was not enough for Maragald.

He wanted them burned. Consuming flames are the only appropriate justice for such parchments. So sixteen noteworthy books were, in fact, burned.

Maragald returned quietly to his cave in the woods.

Many of the learned monks resented him for the new limitations put upon their researches. Word of the incident got to the wool-frocked Friars of Whigg, who decried our "barbarism." They used it ever after to discredit our theological publications. It was soon thereafter that Maragald began to go nearly blind and returned to live at the monastery, unwelcome though he was. Some tried to humiliate him with gossip, saying that Heaven punished him with blindness for not appreciating the artful writings of men.

That curse he turned into a blessing however; the blindness was Heaven's gift, he claimed, lest he be tempted to read what was profane. He did have an unforgettable appearance; long strands of grey hair, features earthy and honest, but raven-like, and an unmistakable aura of otherworldliness aglow in pale and unearthly eyes. He had seen things in the woods, things, he claimed, that should not be seen by mortal men; heard things that must not be uttered.

Many monks were curious for his interpretations, and all his similar sermons rambling. Should the ancient hermit be taken seriously? Could anyone weigh rightly if he were mad or honestly inspired? He was afterall, rather learned beyond all others in the prophecies of The Lamb. Raw was he, and genuinely so; not like some presumptuous scripture scholar from Whigg, some friar trafficking in isolated, academic, and hollow interpretations. even full bereft of vision was no curse. So abased was he and for the better afterall, for in suchwise God spared him the sorrow of viewing the many sinful deeds of men.

His words I kept to myself in peace, neither rejecting them nor affirming. Perhaps it were best to let other monks adjudge him mad. Should those dark prophecies be found rightly understood, they would sting the comfortable monks too much...The popular brothers did not cease to deride the hermit. He no longer tried to persuade, save but to repeat a single phrase: *Numquam relinquas monasterium tuum.* "Never leave your monastery."

. . . neither the scribes of Atlantis, nor sooths of Egyptian Karnak, neither the contemplations of Neoplatonian Dragons, nor even the monks of Kiluria could save the wizard. He was unable to shun the desirable nemesis Lazaria. Wherefore unto profane love did he woefully succumb.

The Book of Bloody Battles

III   THE WAGONS OF BABYLON

The mission he gave: shoo away the circus. With the blessing of Lord Abbot, nothing should worry monks. Such a dragon is like any other minion. Give it a swift kick and it will flee, no?

In fact we should worry. Any dragon would be less dangerous than this kind. Most dragons cannot hurl down star-monks with a swipe of the tail. Dealing with a metaphysical beast will not be as easy as shooing away a stray dog or feral cat. Four monks, including myself, filed down the steep descending steps and after a lengthy descent arrived in the terrestrial places.

The way leads from the bell-tower and Cromna's crag into the deep grove. Carcass-seeking vultures perch by the crag, watching and waiting. Those who pass below the winged lords are subject to a looking over. The wrinkly-headed birds are particular to the willow's dead branches for their sun-bathing. They stretch out their wings against the azure sky, surveying the landscape for a fleshy feast. The monks did not eschew the avian scrutinies which reminded them of the futility of carnal life.

We arrived at the outermost gate, the boundary of monastery's sacred ground. The watcher-monk was at his post. That week the post was assigned to Enwick. According to custom, the gate-keeper quotes aloud the famous psalm for anyone departing from the monastery, adding nothing else: "*if ever I forget you Jerusalem...*"

Having heard that reflection the squadron of monks resumed the march. The winding way transects the orchards and tumbles on through the walls. Over the bridge of St. Mercurius we strode and arrived down at the streets of town. Having passed the many local establishments and guilds, we at last came to the orchards and yards of Catafrax.

We reached the place and saw those "wagons of Babylon," the carts adorned like a red beast. They were indeed a sight: colorful, ornate and delightfully novel, how unlike the ever-present grey stones of the monastery.

Brother Formosus glanced around.

"Now that he is not around to hear me say it, Jacob: I admit the old crow Maragald may not be at all wanting of true sight. The devil never sleeps, no, not ever. He tempts us not just with minor delights. No, Jacob, you are yet a novice but you will see. Beware; he wins us over with what is attractive, then he's got us. Or else he presents what's forbidden as a solution to a problem that he himself has set up! He does not play fair cards."

"What dandy wagons, even so, master Formosus!" I said, most terribly anxious. "...but now what are we to do?"

"Keep in mind the warnings of Maragald. Eventhough he sounds like a raving lunatic, truth sometimes issues from the mouths of madmen. Abbot has entrusted to us silver crizets, some charity for the performers, encouragement to speed their travels away, certainly no premium for entertainments. Abbot desires a quick departure of the actors and wagons. Of course, Jacob, that's no realistic expectation.

"Even Abbot knows that it's not nearly enough coin. Say nothing, if the peasants get wind of our plan to deprive them of fun, we might see Heaven-above sooner rather than later."

The presence of the monastic-squadron was unmistakable; especially that rope-girded monks were entering such companies. The Circus-master approached and greeted the monks.

How could we monks be rude to the fellow, or tell him to take his crew and get out of town? He said, "You Christian monks were sent, I wager, to drive us away. But all the circus will be doing is a bit of naught, save eleviating the monotonous life of the peasants."

It sounded honest enough. But these men were the idolaters of Galadif, that castle and town which had rejected Christ, and some men had insisted that they should be treated as dogs.

Monks however cannot do that.

Instead we yielded to "common sense." A certain brother, (I shall not say who), carried the crizets. He addressed the Circus-master:

"Does God so require that? Here; a gift from Whitehaven for you; not to bribe you to leave, but for your wayfaring."

No other monk there dared say anything. Monks do not like to be rude or unwelcoming, and surely not against a celebrity like the Circus-master. We smiled at him. He took the crizets and granted free admission.

How different were the monks of the past.

On fire with truth, they always rejected gifts.

They besieged Galadif with the gospel, or else preached on divine wrath, and they smiled not.

Soon we would be drawn into a species of idolatry. And I ask you, what is the favor of mere men after all? It is no assurance of Heaven. Should monks care if the townsmen get angry and cry out against us? We are striving to keep their souls from temptation!

Such were the thoughts swirling through my head. A monk should care less if men brand him unenlightened! For sure, it is a piety to allow oneself to appear ignorant, even superstitious, a fool in the eyes of the worldly-wise; to be thought rustic; to defy all learned but godless niceties.

The Lord says, become like children.

Do not fret if your are defamed on behalf of God: no, speak your mind; be a stumbling block to the sophisticated.

Into the dragon's maw: we saluted the Circus-master and moved on, like "captives from Jerusalem," conquered and led to Babylon.

Conspicuous, we navigated the crowd, the colorful carnival: so entrancing, a landscape of fantastical curiosity, all those wagons painted like the rudy idol of the dragon, and great actors and festive players—the orchard of Catafrax no longer resembling a new Eden, but now a valley of earthly delights. Distrust and aversion should arise in a monk,

but we gazed gladly upon the festivities...

The dragon was about to digest Brother Jacob.

The sweet acid of various spectales and plays, or songs, and every cunning amusement will digest him! And into the belly of the beast I went: *in bestiae stomachum intrare*. The rope-girded monks went off to different entertainments, like curious chickens, looking askanse, stepping carefully, as the dull-feathered fowls that step carefully through a barn filled with various animals.

An hour passed. The carnival was like a dream. I preferred not to wake from it. Any sense of time was lost to me. I saw engrossing charms and sights: marvels and tricks, and feats of physical wonder, or at least seeming so. There were the hilarities of the mute jester, the hypnotics of the gypsy girls and their flaming torch-dance, the strange and awful daring of the strongman and the ju`gglers, acrobats, the renowned boxers, and, of course not least, the gallantry of the tournament. The combat-entertainments thrilled me all the more. Where did all this come from?

I detected the odor of meats roasting, wafting through the air; and smoke of something delicious. A kind-hearted believer, a pious and monied burgher, fetched for me some portions of roast and a draught of ale as well: It was lunch time already...and various morsels to be had after that: dried fruits from far away, and the delights of bakers.

I now turn my testimony to another matter ...having slipped away from the other monks I indulged in the carnival for over an hour; afterall, the others too were gazing at all those frivolities. I even became a bit overwhelmed with all of it. No matter, a fascinated mind will not relent. By means of the eyes does the tempter have an entry. I was quite conscious that I had let myself fall into danger. I could pray the beads. I should pray at once. The circus is run by wicked men. The men of Galadif, they say, climb to a high place and they offer human lives to the dragon, of which they themselves partake.

So I was about to pray the beads, but just before the fingers touched the beads dangling from my rope,

I spotted the tournament.

They were readying horses for the joust. To this I have to get close; I thought. I will view all this! I must slip away and wait for every round of it. I cannot fail to view it! So nearly passed all the afternoon...

So do I confess my worldliness.

The novice went adrift into the sea of onlookers.

It was Brother Formosus who finally went to look for him. Formosus was the teacher of Greek, and in particular the Greek of philosophers. He had gained the confidence of Ulcrist, headmaster and trainer of guardian monks. "The novice Jacob is not a logical pick for your training in combat," he had warned. "So distractable is he, barely able to keep his mind on what's in front of him, not enough to train as Guardian of Sacred

Relics." Ulcrist could not but help take up Formosus' challenge: "You are not as skilled a teacher as I am, Formosus. I will make him focus, and he will learn to work his body as a guardian. Then will he appereciate your philosophy."

Formosus at last found Jacob. He glared at him. Jacob looked away, pretending not to notice, instead watching the preparations for the joust. No smile of relief or amusement broke through Formosus. He seemed indifferent, displaying little frustration that one might expect from a normal human being. Under his cowl he retained inward composure, his voice measured and monotone, but his heart was wroth.

"Novice Jacob, come along. Let us return to the monastery. Everywhere I have been looking for you. We are now to be climbing back up the monastery steps. It is not as easy as coming down. We must hasten at once. It is your day to help in the kitchen...remember."

"Yes, I... I will...by and by, brother. I don't like to say it, but this is so much better, better than kitchen...and better than monk-life. Every day is the same, master, too much so. Only guardian-training excites me, and that is nothing compared to these sights. Stay; watch a while longer. I should, Ulcrist would want me to, to see more on fighting techniques."

"Obey...and come at once, Jacob Magister,
and dare not again contradict. Come, or risk this freedom not soon permitted again...now, Brother Jacob, NOW!"

"It is a necessary lesson to watch fighting men fight. Who knows but that someday I must protect the monastery from the like, from pirates or other sea-raiders. I tell you..."

"Your resistance has just assured that you will do extra kitchen duty ...besides, these are not real fighters, They are actors."

"Not so, brother, not so... They are real! It's a rare thing."

"I cannot leave you here alone, Jacob. Monks traveling are to keep each other focused, wardens against the solicitations of tempters and worldly-wise. Even with that precaution, no one can protect a monk from himself. You have been sneaky. You slipped away at a moment when the crowd went thick."

"You never said that I may not wander."

"Beware, Jacob Magister, some corrupt brothers among us wait to hold something against you; they will seek to bend you to their will in return for not informing on you. A young monk must be without reproach if he wishes to evade the hyenas. There is something deadly that entraps a monk, it is called disobedience."

"Then will I inform the Novice-master myself and make it known. Brother Ulcrist would approve. It will not be counted against us if we stay here for a while, or if it is, then I say the crime is worth the punishment."

"*He who does not work should not eat.*
Do you wish to go without food for a day?
How daring you are... An undiciplined monk cannot serve as one of the combat-trained guardians.

I will request of Brother Ulcrist that you be dismissed from your training."

Formosus was right. Training in the weaponless combat requires strict discipline—it graces a monk for overcoming the body's natural sloth; sloth that is begotten by the pride of life. There are numerous humiliations to which the flesh is subjected during workouts, "mind over matter," as they say. This is an ancient "way of combat." The trainee must always remain in spirit obedient to his masters, above all to be humble. It also requires resolution against destructive action, never taking delight in blood-sport, no, not ever delight, nor look upon it for entertainment, like the tourney. Formosus reminded Jacob of these things, and added. "The LORD trieth the righteous: but the wicked and him that loveth violence his soul hateth."

Guardians are never to use deadly hands for selfish motives, as for sport, or in anger. Weapons in fact are forbidden us, save for the quarterstaff. It is in keeping with the warning of Our Lord, For *all who live by the sword will die by the sword*. The admonitions of the Lord meant that monks should refrain from war.

Even so, over the years the monasteries of Whitehawk had grown weary of the constant raids from those bloodthirsty rovers of the Southern Seas, massacring both monks and townsfolk, loading sacred treasures and golden reliquaries onto their dragonships. Some monasteries decided to fight back. So God sent us certain deliverers.

The Shang-di monks, masters of combat,
sojourned from the far-Eastern realm.
They were exiles from the kingdom Anshan, the Eight Tigers Monastery. Originally the monks there had renounced all violence. When the Bandit Wars were ending...
some monks would not consent to the emperor's command:
for he bade the monks: do not continue the wars against the bandits. Resume the discipline of peace. The monks did not heed him. Indignant at the taunts of their enemies, they marched into to the neighboring feudal village which the bandits were occupying.
They slew them all to the last. Everyone heard of the disobedience.

The Golden Emperor refused to execute the monks for it,
since monks are consecrated. Into exile he sent them instead.
Far they sailed their fan-ships,even all the way to Whitehaven
of the seaward cliffs. Eight of them, "the eight tigers"
lived out their last days with us.
The virtuous monk-general Tien Joshur became our Servant Master-trainer and bequeathed us his sublime techniques in *the Sapphire Instruction for Campaigning Monks*.

Since we are Christian monks, we did not adopt all their methods, only the open-hand and the quarterstaff. That was established all the way back in the days of Abbot Elenchius.

In those days all monks became adepts at the martial art.

Then word got around to the King, and he wished to enlist our monks in his wars. Eventually the monks became influential and held sway in politics. They forgot the monastic way.

So Abbot Aonas put an end to it, allowing only select monks to keep the training.

The prohibition caused a virtual civil war within the cloister.

Abbot Cromna was the election of compromise.

It is therefore not permitted that the guardian monk enlist in any earthly army. We are not to pursue bloody war, or initiate a fight, but we may engage in defensive combat. The goal is to render the opponent frustrated and unbalanced, and wear him out. It is not for entertainment.

"But this here is sport," I argued. "....this jousting... it was never condemned. You yourself, Formosus, taught us that virtue can be found in violent sport, as the Shang-di monks believe, and as the philosopher admits."

Formosus had an answer.

"Even the wicked practice virtue, Jacob, but they do so for their own purpose. It is a fallen purpose. Also, in that other matter are you unstudied, novice. The joust was indeed publically condemned. The regent had the decree nailed up in the first year of the Abbot Aonas. No, it has not been taken seriously by the subjects. Even so, it was never revoked...so monks are bound to it. You see, our consent does not matter; nor does it matter that anyone else observe them. What matters is that we observe them.

"In time may you learn the wisdom in this. I warn you, you can get caught up in all the martial glamour: like a sea urchin in some fisherman's net. It may be the failure of your novitiate—the price you pay. Do you not wish to continue our study of Greek philosophy? Frock and name alone make not a monk. It is study and prayer that makes a monk...

"Jacob, return to reason. The peasants and guildsmen, our townsfolk, they have naught to look forward to but another season of plowing, sowing and reaping, or hard labouring in town.

"So this bedazzling tournament easily ensnares them, as novelties are wont. It is our duty to make up for this before Heaven, to pray on their behalf, because they know not the mysteries. They don't bother with us monastics these days, unless they must. They do not prize us. They do not venerate the tassels of our ropes as in days past. Its because we monks are no longer simple and God-fearing. The tempter drives them against us with these entertainments.

"Is it not the case, in this age of the world, that fervent monks and priests-anointed are held as altogether despicable, while robber-knights and cunning wizards are praised and greeted with high honours? I've seen it myself, often the marketplace. When some wizard or snake-oil peddler comes through he is given free apples and nuts, even sides of bacon and flagons of wine. Monks and priests are always ignored."

Formosus stared at him. I stood waiting, ashamed to look directly at him, but thinking over what was next, the coming attraction: the tournament.

It had already begun. A loud cheer went up at the CLANG of the heavily armoured cavaliers. They smashed one another's shields with the stern smiting of contrary lances. The men rocked on their mounts and almost tumbled over.

"Even you, brother, are now getting interested!" I said. "I am sorry that I must stay so long. But you can see why. Sell me to this circus if you wish. Since I was a boy nothing has thrilled me like this joust."

"You are still a boy, Jacob. See what you have done? You have drawn me into your folly!--a short thrilling this will be...you are a stubborn one. Now I will undoubtably end up concealing this from the novice master. But there are monks that you will anger by not showing up for kitchen duty.

"THEY WILL sell you to this circus, since you like it so. Certain monks have for several summers already resented your presence, your free spirit, and now you give them just cause to act."

Brother Formosus tarried a bit longer to watch another round. The knights again failed to unhorse opponents.

"Bah, 'tis mere show and pomp..." Formosus proclaimed. "Now, Jacob, observe how a real monk with spirit rips his eyes away from all exciting and worldly things."

The monk Formosus shook his head, sighed heavily, lowered his gaze, and promptly departed without his student.

Our Lord, the good shepherd, always conveys a messenger to warn straying sheep. My novice ears were not open to hear it. I harkened instead to the clangor of lance and shield, the pounding of horse hooves. That the youth did what he wanted to do, instead of what the superiors wanted...that might sound like a little normal rebellion in youth, but risky for a monk, especially a novice.

The day was coming to a close. The lances were put up, both knights retired. The entertainers gave a last bow and went their ways, back to wagons and tents.

wick had made a sandwich for himself in the kitchen and had pocketed it. He now extracted it from his habit and was unwrapping. His day- task was to watch at the lower gate. From him Jacob could keep nothing, eventhough he try terribly, not a thing.

On the way up returning to the monastery, Jacob walked alone. Upon reaching the lower gate he saw Brother Enwick.

"Where have you been?" Enwick asked. "Why did you not come back with the others? Hours passed since they went back. You missed chant."

"...what now?" I replied, half out of wit. "I just looked for something different to do. I can longer endure the monastery. Your "dragon" burned some grand dream into my head. You see...now it's my new plan... Want to hear it?"

What plan is that...? Say it, and I'll show you its folly."

"I am going get away from it all, Enwick, I be itchin' to leave fer good, tip-toe away."

"Tip-toe away? But you are doing well here, and have a full belly. Your life is like a nobleman's. We are friends, and kin as well. Why would you leave and go off and take up miserably in some town? You will fetch only lowly work and innumerable hardships. You will have no brothers, no mother, and your spiritual father will be far away. Are you the kind of solitary bird that lives on his own, on some housetop? I don't think so."

"It seems I am ill-matched for monkhood, with all the "humiliation." Have you not pondered what is it like to be a man who freely chooses his own dinner? That's what this traveling carnival has taught me. Life can be good, exciting. There is honour and fame to be had, instead of monastic obscurity. Must one spend all years in somber penances?"

"I have my ham sandwich here," he noted. "I chose this for myself without the others knowing. There is enough freedom in the monastery. You are just distraught because you want something else, anything else...but it will pass. Nothing is better than being a monk." Enwick's brow made a stern wrinkle. "Or else you've been devil-turned. Look here now, this be pure wreckage, a thing resorted to only when a monk becomes dead-minded. A monk says that he is escaping the life —no happy ending guaranteed, or likely. What if some dreadful turn leaves you wretched and alone in the world? Our townsmen would never let an ex-monk put up in the houses. You will have to go off to some other town far away, be an outlander. And if you rue it and seek to come back, the return alone is an extreme risk. First you must cross back through unforgiving wilderness, those Timberhills. Then you must convince the Abbot and the other monks that you are worthy to be re-admitted."

"The circus is for me, the tourney. It was awsome to watch. My training is the best. I am ready for any trial."

"Are you really? I hear that your training has left much to be desired. If you are so foolish, go. But remember that the founders of the order set down warnings long ago, Jacob. The innumerable pines, the ancient hills, and untouched lakes of the Timberhills are confusing and treacherous, a veritable labyrinth. Lost wayfarers starve to death. Even during the summer days, they say, keep out. The paths, yes, do appear safe, but something treacherous and unknown lurks there. Some say it's the dragon of Galadif, others say the wild men, and still others say demoniacs, the Wyrmheld. Do not venture into that vastness, not unless a Ranger takes you. I remember the written words, "*if you would pilgrimage through the Lokken on your own, keep to the wagon-roads, but plan for the worst and pray for deliverance. Her denizens will enchant and are not of God.*"

"Come now, my friend. The founders exaggerated in order to keep young monks from running away," Jacob suppressed a laugh.

"No monk who has ever left alone has returned. Do you not harken at table Jacob? The monastery annals confirm the warnings every year at Candlemas, when the reader recites the general dooms at supper. He reads for all to hear. Each word he clearly annunciates: ...*verily, o monk, enter thou not the eldark wood solitary faring, lest thou be overcome by spirits, and thy soul perish withal.*" They even add a bit of silence for rope-girded monks to reflect. Seven monks were sent to convert Galadif in the last year of Abbot Elenchius. They all vanished in the wood. How grave be the admonitions!"

"Heaven-above sees my thoughts," I said, thinking to undermine his reasonable fears. "I know the warnings, and I know not how I shall do this. But it is destiny. Heaven's handmaid guides me."

"She will not give you a hand to accomplish folly," Enwick warned again. "Let the higher monks speak for Heaven's will. Act honorably and open your plan to the Abbot."

"What would happen then?" I countered. "Were I to do that he would require me bid farewell to each monk. They would start asking me why. Tell me, how does one unfold such dubious meditations, harboring so worldly a new purpose? As you know, certain monks will employ incontrovertible knowledge—convince anyone to their own view. Sound right well it might, but be it real help? —not even. You know how it goes. Among us lodge certain righteous monks, men upon whom The Ancientmost bestowed deep minds. They hear of your dreams and take you aside, quelling your intentions by their spiritual reasoning, and they steer your neck to view the vanity of your plans.

"Still, let's say I cling to my purpose of leaving. Say that I rebuke them, claiming too much prayer and not enough work has distorted them, their minds—diminished what's practical. So I get away from them, but then come the slothful monks, (many of that kind). They too know of my weakness; and rushing to my cell they protest losing me; but it's really because they have been using me as their fill-in whenever they need someone to cover for their unauthorized naps.

"In this way, first the mind is made uncertain and then the thoughtful monks breech it, and the complaints of closer friends like you plunder the heart. Added to that, Enwick, wicked monks will not fail to remind me of what I owe. That I shall miss their steady supply of contraband comforts: flagons of Vanic wine, strong leaf for my pipe, soft pillows, hardly ever had by serfs or a rare luxury for the busy townsmen.

"So breaks apart resolution, and the plan for earthly glory is comprimised. I shall obey them and retire to my comfortable bed, less of a man. So it would happen with you as well, brother."

"Your point; and I am wise to that," said Enwick. "But God purposely discourages monks from leaving. I suspect that a life of stern integrity in the world, as you propose, is not for you. The wide world is a wretched place. It is not at all happy-go-lucky like your day at the circus, going off to see whatever is the next show. Sure some folk get along swell, make good coin, harbour a beautiful family *et cetera*. Not you though. You will spend your days ceaseless under some ruthless taskmaster, like a woodpecker, constantly pecking, but rarely finding a worm."

"And how would you foresee that? You have the same count of winters here as I. Or did you train under Maragald?"

"True... I should not hope to convince you. I am but just midward of the novitiate. Say, maybe you are right; afterall, if being unselfish you decide *not* to run off, perhaps you will miss some terribly vital adventuring. Hmmm...maybe you should go then afterall!"

"What? You change your tone already now?"

"I must not be selfish, as you have said."

"You wish you could go, Enwick. Stay here and pray for my success. If I am to succeed, my escape must be accomplished in secret, acting with shrewdness. Say nothing, I beg you."

Dawn was opening her preamble of light. A monk grabbed the thick rope that drops down from the tower-bell and yanked it. The massive hollows resounded deep bellowing. Again I watched my rope-girded monks begin filing in. Two monks lite the altar candles; all other monks go to the benches and stalls. The enormous prayer-tomes are checked for the right page.

Abbot goes to his seat; the choir master intones with the organ. All monks are standing. The chant fills the air and the smoke of incense lifts to the nostrils of the Lamb standing on throne. We sit down and resumed orizons.

Monks have a role just like anyone else in the world. They appeal to Heaven, begging the Father of All to overlook offenses and grant protection; for the King, for Abbot, and for all. The supplications are wrapped in *aroma mystica*, incense revealed to Whitehaven alone: a certain resin imported from far away, from the outlands of darkness and great danger. When morning light filters into the grand chapel, the sanctuary-gate creels open. The *selva* enters and spoons bits of the incense into a golden censor. He lets the tiny nodules tumble onto the hot coals. Up he carries the smoldering vessel. He executes exact lustrations before the altar.

The chain rattles. Rivers of smoke pour out. The fragrant cloud permeates the spaces around and above. Large plumes expand out of the nebula. Angelic beings hover over the sacrifice. Rows of monks turn a page of chant notation in unison. Demons take refuge in the narrow cracks of the monastery masonry.

When the chant is completed, the monks receive the All-blessing in the old tongue. Each will go off to his particular monkish work. He does not wander about. The monk sees to his daily labor; he cherishes the way of life, he is without complaint. He is accepting of whatever Heaven assigns him.

Later, after the prayer-tomes were closed and quiet returned, Jacob overheard some monks whispering news on the carnival...in town for another day. The jousting cavaliers who worked the tourney knew that an old friend was near. They refused to leave until they had gone to him. Jacob took this to be a sign of favor. (enough time to make sufficient preparations).

The Ammouric gospel depicts Christ as a feudal King, and the disciples as vassals, his oath-sworn knights.

The Deeptracker's Guide

IV   KNIGHTS OF THE AMMOURI

hese knights of the tournament sent up a request to see Abbot: a great prize for them. Whereas typical ***Knights of the Realm*** or vassal cavaliers seek after honors, and glory, and gold, these were lords of the cross, Ammouric Knights that serve Heaven. They do not ride for their own purpose or aggrandizement. The manualist Guy of Xaragia writes that a consecrated knight, that is to say a paladin, radiates protection from fear in a 100 foot radius.

Such lords are protected from many forms of magic and enchantment. Illusion spells, for example, cannot deceive them, for their eyes are blessed with true sight. Such protections are conditional: paladins must not pile wealth or covet spoilation, they maintain no castle or lands, but every other gold peice won must be given as alms or to the Church.

They retain only maintenance for horse and squire, for lodging and daily fare. Otherwise they are pious and simple-living wayfarers.

Jacob intended to become a squire for the knights, or somehow sign up with their order. Most of the crowd he had not caught on to the reality. They were real fighters. Only other fighters like me could catch the professionalism of their moves during the tourney. The comical stumbling around and antics left few suspecting that they were anything more than actors.

They are also like the trail-finding Edolunt Rangers, those woodsmen who patrol the Whitehawk *incognito.*[2] These perigrine cavaliers normally achieve but minor fame because they too are obliged to disguise themselves and never boast. Often must they find such work in years of truce or peace.

In fact, Abbot was both liege-lord and long time chaplain for the long-journeying knights. Abbot had often fed them the sacred bread. He satisfied their hunger, not just with mortal food, but with immortal nourishment.

The knights took to their thundering mounts

---

[2]*Edolunt Riders*: Rangers of the vasts forests of the Furthlands. Appointed by the Emperor, they patrol the frontiers of the civil lands on horse, guarding all kingdoms from intrusions of the dark hordes from the north.

Their horses pranced up the many steps, hooves click-CLOCKing, and they entered the sacred enclosure.

Weapons are forbidden in the peaceful monastery, except for our own wooden monk-arms. When i saw the knights that morning I wondered why Enwick would admit these warriors without confiscating their weaponry. It had to do with their official and formidible appearance. They were clad in hauberks of chain; combined with well-polished shoulder-paulder like argent suns...so appearing as angelic beings.

Reflected beams of light poured out from these metallic chrysinauts.

Their majestic helms were each of a unique form. Each depicted in olden style some aquiline wings or leonine claws, iron sculptures that stretched to the sky like a conquering power.

They dismounted and took steps, their armour like a gurgling creek of steel. They sported a heraldic tunic matching the field-color for each fighter, for each a double tincture: the burgundy, the white, and the grey. The charge of the Whitehawk emblazoned their shields, and athwart the field the metal of their military order, the seven points inaurate of a heliacal rising; the new day of the Ammouric faith upon the horizon.

The morning air was chill on my cheeks. In the sky's distance of blue eternities the solitary planet *Calduin* was setting in remote solitude.

One of the cavaliers, whose arms-color was white, addressed me. I stood there in the cloister in my habit holding a broom.

"Not you, monk, but your brothers will stable them. You go inform the Abbot. Pray, go now. Announce that guests have arrived."

I put the broom aside and hurried off.

Abbot's study had a cedarwood frame which gave off a relaxing scent. A small window of stained glass provided a mystical glow. I appeared and motioned to Brother Fragga who had been strolling nearby. Brother Fragga, for those of you too young or new to recall, was a rather ponderous giant of a monk. He was peaceful and slow of speech, though quick to the service of fellow monks.

It was he who attended the lame Abbot Cromna.

The door was open, and the Abbot saw them and saw excitement upon Jacob's face.

"They are come already?" Abbot asked, (but not to me did he seem to speak, but as it were to himself). "Hurry then, come... Oh, yes...you... young Jacob. Come here then, both of you; help me."

Brother Fragga Slowtongue and Jacob went to Abbot and helped him, hefting him up from his seat. The great one was not lightweight. They got him on his feet with the two crutches under his arms. The elder also had some soreness in his bones that stifled his movement and pained him when he walked.

Brothers, you have heard many things of this now famous Abbot. He was a distinguished lord. Long curly locks of grey hair fell resting behind shoulders. Sometimes they would dangle athwart his oval face and kindly rounded owl eyes.

The breezes sent upon the balcony above would often stir the mane when he stood addressing us, and he seemed like a Jove.

But also, in dealings with the brethren, he radiated the divine presence to me in a different way, strange to say, like a comforting and serene grandparent, although he himself was but in middle years.

He was the only one in the monastery whom ancestral right required to grow the long hair, in accord with his descent from Maceonid royalty, for he was also a feudal Aelic lord who had spent his boyhood as a hostage among the Yahorans.

I was about to hear a conversation which few could well reckon with any real comprehension. It was just Fragga and I (out of some fifty-two monks) who were the ones in the monastery to hear the strange talk. We were about to bring Lord Abbot out of his chambers, when we heard the chainmail-clad lords approaching within the cloister, their armour and spurs clanking; echoing oddly across the stones of the monastery.

In but a moment they were already at the door.

They each grasped the Abbot to embrace him; and one of them, (I do not recall which one), spoke first.

"Abbot! We must come to you, not you to us. You know that any help in the service of God we always take up for you. You should have not troubled yourself to get up."

All three of the cavaliers knelt down, and bending low, kissed the scapular of the venerable one. The Abbot appeared stern. He frowned and lowered his head.

"—No? Do you think I will just sit when lords must be greeted? You are the ones that need help. So you durst appear before me, after so many years of wandering about?! Errant Knights!" he sighed with indignation. "Dare we even call you lords anymore?"

The cavaliers looked at one another with dismay and perhaps a little fear, but a smile formed on Abbot Cromna's face.

"Have you no answer for this preacher? Are such warriors timid around him? See, the winters have not slowed me down, my sons. Looking at you now I am reminded of the freedom of the sons of God, and praise be to Him who has preserved you, who keeps your vigour undiminished. As for me, not every part is lame: my heart is right gladsome today. And beware, my mind also remains quick enough."

"A fair rebuke masked as a compliment. You were always good for that," the White Knight said. "We have been away twelve winters. We have for many passings of *Calduin* hoped to make it back. To return to our high teacher and patron."

"Each of you, welcome. And we admit this reunion is less happy than it should be. It must be bittersweet after all that's happened...so many of your brother-knights perishing in the wars." The Abbot looked at each knight closely. "And your expressions betray something else. The great quest we charged on all religious thanes, it remains unaccomplished, for had you achieved it a burden would be lifted from your brows."

"It came undone as you say," replied the White Knight. "We have failed. The ways of men hindered us

···so availed the evil power. The genius of shadow secretly consolidates his empire. Cunning doctrine and melancholy writings are in the hands of every court's counselor. No spook, but clever is that Dire indeed, employing certain minds, other geniuses like the famous Professor Naza.

Cunning is his deceit and his influence is unrestrained on the continent. Sin and Doom ride the pale horse freely in every kingdom of Whitehawk, and lawlessness, and hungry war, and cruel plague: The Red Death, *maegolot*, spreads unhindered. As for ourselves we have been caught up in the Wars of the Heresies, finding little time for the peace of God, or the quest.

None of us has even found the circling river of which the legends tell, that torrent twisting down to the Yule Queen of the fourth world." (I had scant knowledge as to what lore the noble lord was referring. Once I had listened to a bard sing of the "Queen of fourth world." Was all this about a fairy-queen some vain imagining? She was said to be a lady of transcendent luminosity and passing fair, depicted as a crowned mistress clad in fey-armour. Her palatial fastness stands somewhere in the extensive mesolithic caves, the intermundane expanse).

The White Knight continued. "What in earnest improved? Seasons pass and many things change, and one war ends and another begins.

When so many long-journeying knights never returned and law was never restored to their castles, there came another contest: the Wars of The Pagan Uprisings. Those wars have not yet ended. Now we also see a *War of The Heresies*.[3] The teaching of the **Red Ascetic** has overwhelmed all the Whitehawk League, and is all but lost on the continent. We can no longer travel safely there.

But even here the mischievous vine of *elfshade* clings to your monastery walls. Thier fronds are the ears of the evil one."

"Our monks tear it down and burn it." Said Abbot "But within a few weeks new vines have returned. Is there left any place where the listening leafs are not found?"

"They are everywhere. We had to take up jousting, passing as guildsmen with the traveling actors out of Hordingbay. We have good fare and go unsuspected as well, hoping to overhear tidings from tradesmen, or some song-gifted bard, or some far-searching wizard."

---

[3] *The Wars of the Heresies*: also called "*the time of three wars*". After the first efforts of the unholy war had failed, extremists were recruited by the warlords of Arraf (the desert-East), so there arose a new warrior-cult of the *Arian* heresy known only as the "Cult of the Veil." They made vows of absolute loyalty to Lord Synostocs of Atalur, namely to conquer all the western kingdoms or die trying. So a subsequent generation of crusaders again had to go East to protect Vesulum against the threat. The Ammouric knights held the city and pushed back the Veil. For a full treatment see appendices *Veil, Cult of.* Also NB *The Red Ascetic* an epicurean philosophy adopted by the later emperors and finally made into the state religion by the Inversus.

"Cunning wizards do seek far and wide for their spell components,' Abbot replied, "even in our times, but be assured my sons, as I told you before, trust not their report."

The second knight stood forth. His visage was august, with beard white as snow, he being the first, the elder lord; his arms-color was grey, a Grey Knight, and he sported a distinctive golden medallion of three miniature hounds leaping, linked nose to tail forming a ring.

"What a good sight to see!" he said, beaming. "—our great lord and chaplain still keeps guard...! We sailed and rode many weeks, and weeks turned into months and months into years. We searched the furthlands far and wide, to the edges of the Chronian Sea and the Northern tundras of the Hith, through the deserts of Yezez and Setet and the closed kingdoms. Even to the ends of the furth we rode, to Anshan and Sippar. We have not heard even rumour of that for which we sought. Rather we learned only how all of our brother-Knights of the Ammour are now stretched out upon a gory defile, unburied. The ambush of Stormring people call it, our companies overcome by the scimitars of darkness and axe-blades of chaos."

Abbot's gaze drifted over to the next knight, a knight of burgundy field.

"You knights must not let that dampen the burn of your faith. Search the other worlds, entering even into the netherlands. Yes, all your comrades are fallen, only you three outlive all the Ammouric chivalry. Only you three remain to retrieve the key to the Voraganth. Your devout comrades have gone to imperishable glory and shall see what cannot be seen or spoken.

They cannot return hence. Nor shall we with mortal eye look upon them again in this life. But there is one of you, one who has not yet spoken...you, one whom some thought dead. You conceal your visage, and only let us see your eyes.

Why not remove the coif and show your mind?"

This third knight arrayed in a burgundy mantle looked up.

He had a dark scarf wrapped around his head and face.

He lifted his chin and pulled back the chainmail coif.

Nothing he said in reply but unraveled the dark linen.

Scars stretched across his nose and cheeks in hatches.

Some ruthless butcher had carved deeply upon the flesh.

Even so, with all these cuts, the visage was not hideous to look upon.

Even the contrary, one did not wish to look away.

Abbot spoke to Fragga and I. "Look upon this face, you monks, He was captured by the Troll horde, the tribes of shadow." Abbot whispered. "Even the gift of speech has been stolen from him? To have been elevated so lately to the *selvad*! Alas, were our monks of a higher discipline and ardent zeal, there is no doubt that we might lay hands upon you and heal you. Yet where there is so little faith scarce anything can be done."

"No matter," the Grey Knight said. "This lord is our companion and our crowned priest, one who has little element of earth or water remaining in him. His heart is a soul of pure fire. In his resolve to find what is sought, he went even farther than ourselves. As far as the lost cities of the East, Khnum and beyond he rode, and Southernmost wastes, even unto the ancient rises of desolated Nystol. It was there that butchers took from him his speech."

"Aye, Nystol...and it is not the only place.

At every edge of the Whitehawk continent do occult powers await," Abbot recalled. "In the Orient brood the ghostlands of Setet and Hills of the bloodthirsty Khalu-kim, and here in the West corruption now sits on the imperial throne, and in the far North the hinter-evil waits, the Mind of Melancholy; the crown of Nzul,[4] girded within that impregnable fortress the Arc du Baffay;

And there is known another place where now awakens great mischief.

Away in the southern deserts there stand the ruins of Nystol, a mortal glory of nine towers once, which in time yielded immortal infamy: a haunt of sleepless wickedness. Few explorers have returned from that woeful place of abomination and desolated ruin." Abbot paused to search some distant memory.

"There, in that place, dwell the *shedim*, the shades of wizards who harry the living and have no rest.

Only Ammouric *selvas* can banish them, something no other power can do....but let us speak this day no further of Nystol, for our reunion should be a glad one, and we must take care lest the elfshade vine pick up whatever the stone echoes."

"May we be given guarded cells here, venerable Abbot?" the White knight asked.

"You are barely safe here, but I shall post guardian-monks for security. The brothers keep watch upon the horizon and sentry the monastery walls... Take comfort then; remain for a few days, each of ye, or as long as needed. Withdraw from struggles of the road. Our rope-girded monks shall pray. Be refreshed with a good rest, with bread and our own ale."

The White Knight said. "Before this talk ends, Abbot, some grave tidings: Know that we have observed how the planets are moving in sequence of the *Hyperlyptic Alignment*.[5] Some time ago the high

---

[4] *Nzul, Banzu (alt. Banzaul, also Baffay):* The region of the spirit-creature Nazageist (The Dire) located somewhere in the Crach mountains. The Arc du Baffay is said to be a horrible place of smoke, iron furnaces, black towers and unthinkably colossal architecture, a typical dwelling for any master of evil. No one save King Argoth and a few survivors of *the Bladetongue*, (a famous epic poem), have ever returned from there, so there is little else to report. It was built by Nimrul the Archdeceiver designed to be higher than the throneroom on Mt. Argunizial. Legend asserts that its library is a horrible maze of book-stacks whose texts curse those who read them with insanity. Further descriptions were recorded in the final chapters of *the Bladetongue* but the unholy powers have managed to destroy those chapters.

[5] *Hyperlyptic Alignment:* an alignment of the seven planets well known and used by Arcanes but the exact time of which was no longer able to be determined.

prophetess announced to the Ammouric Soothfold that there would be a sign of celestial aligning, that it would mark a great one in the Western isle to pass...then *it* would begin; the *Maceonid Kingdoms*[6] slowly but surely begin to slip away from righteousness. Is that a trustworthy prophecy?"

"I have heard of her utterances," said the Abbot. "Aye . . . it may indeed now become so, in sooth. Keep it privy, the simple believers are easily discouraged. Portray not too much credence in that dark lore if they ask."

"Of course...but when we arrived at last on these shores," the White Knight continued, "we received report that the venerable Anherm of Whigg, servant of God, most pious and knowledgeable, has indeed passed from this world. Will not his life as a monk—"

"It cannot bode well for the kingdoms of Whitehawk that so virtuous a soul may soon be forgotten. He was the last of the *Magi.* There's a sadness in it; but his was a happy death.

His years of humble laboring in the vineyard vouchsafed him that. In the blessed obscurity of a monk, God at last garnered him unto himself. Anherm ended his earthly pilgrimage as someone rarely seen, a rope-girded monk
and no famous wizard."

A silence hung in the air a few moments.

"Also, master, besides the load of incense, we carry these three lesser gifts, gifts we kept for you, things we acquired during our endeavors in the Arraf. We meant them as gratitude for the monk's prayers, and as seeds of hope for some recruits.

Now I think, let them also be a commemoration of Anherm's service, and wayfaring into the world above, the kingdom far beyond human sight."

"—Gifts? Bless you. All this right now drains out the dregs of melancholy. A light and peace is suddenly with me. It must be wisdom when a soul sees things from God's perspective. Believe it: Anherm had wisdom, and I wager he will stand with the just."

"Only a few saw that he was just;" replied the Grey Knight. "His words were iron and his works penitent...

Only the best instruments should be supplied for the preservation of his writings." The knight proceeded to extract from his satchel two medium containers, cylindrical in shape.

---

[6]*Maceonids:* The descendants of Maceon, survivor of the great deluge of the first age. They became kings throughout the Whitehawk continent and ruled from age to age, although at times they lost their sovereignty, such as under the Atalur, and the Aideen and later Regulian empire. The Maceonid League of Kings was sometimes formed to fight against such overwhelming powers. Not all Maceonids became Ammouric, "white-robed" kings, but some, such as the Maharim and the King of Kargiwall, and a few other apostates, remained heathen.

"This is gold leafing for the page's gilding, and powder of *lapis ceruneali* for every celestial field. The deeply-mining dwarves of the Eastern mountains mined these ...to adorn his masterpiece as finest illuminations."

Abbot took the container. He opened it and gazed upon the contents. "The minerals of earth purvey us so many fine things wherewith to render the prophecies of last codex, the harvester codex, the seventy-seventh tome. May Allfather reward you for it."

Abbot passed the cylinder to Fragga.

The Knight of the White Cloak was the next to present a gift. He drew forth from his baggage a large book with a white binding bearing finely-tooled ornament, worked on a strange whitish hide, something like vellum, and silver braces in eld tracery.

"This codex of untouched parchment is ready to be filled; it has been fashioned by the brethren of deep and hidden *Vorsalir*,[7] the holy cliff-city in the great twisting canyon, deepest land of the Whitehawk continent.

It has been designed especially for the sacred tomes. Accept it, honouring the memory of your master scribe. It is bound in the rarest skin, the white herd of Ambrosius in Arahom,

a sacred material for a sacred work."

"Take it lad..." Abbot gestured to Jacob, who didn't notice at first, being amazed and standing agape. I was trying to take in the meaning of all this. "Haul up a great and cumbrous gift, boy. . ." Abbot said, "Open it."

Jacob brought forth the massive codex from the cavalier's arms and opened up the pages for the Abbot to examine.

Abbot touched them with the tips of his fingers.

"May these pages be a throne for wholesome words.
May they not tear nor grow frail, and may the figures of sin
never be found in them, as in the other tomes.
How precious a sign of devotion is this.
Now may the brethren begin the labour
for which Anherm had hoped..."

Next, the Burgundy Knight reached into a leather satchel at the baldric. He drew out a vial of incarnadine liquid;

thin black streaks and tiny globules darted about within.

---

[7] *Vorsalir* (Northlung speech) *Vesulum* L.: a cliff-village hidden away in the lower *canyons of Hermius*, known as Vesulum. Vesulum became a training ground for kings and a place of study for *selvas* (priests). It remains the only city that can rival wicked Nystol (Nyzium) in spiritual power. Although no Ammouric monastery was ever established there, it did boast the greatest library of sacred works from the ancient world. The city remained pure from corruption and heresy until the usurpation of the cult-master Shahi Nuzzib. Further description is found in the appendix entry for *Vesulum*.

Somewhere out in the distant Timberhills we could hear howling, a wolf's long, lonesome howl.

"The metamorphic gall of Gnotus the bronze dragon,[8] noblest of dragons deep-dwelling," the White Knight said, "...mixed together with his brazen bile; to yield the ink of knowledge. For ages was it kept, for an *aeon-rest*, unopened in the library of Morpheus Memnos,
    the last Archsage of Nystol;
    before flames consumed her towers
    and the dark smoke filled the heavens."

The Abbot's lips hung open. He was almost in disbelief. "I do not know what to think of this... how do we express worthy gratitude for such a gift?" His jaw under the hoary beard slackened as he touched the glass and took hold of it. "Spirit of Anherm," declared Abbot. "May you never fade from our memory. To obtain this must have come at such cost! With this blessed ink we shall render a translation of Anherm's writings, whose profundity merits it; the first writing to be placed, at last, in the seventy-seventh tome, the final age.

The Wars of the Heresies rage. Even our sister house,
the Monastery of the Weeping Brotherhood in the *Dry Blood Sea*,[9] I am told, is infected. Reports tell that the monks there weep no longer for the profound joy of Christ's rising.

No, instead they shed tears of woe on account of vile heresies overwhelming their own cloister.

The Ammouric Church must be purified. Know this: if Heaven has appointed the great day, He has also granted to Hell an hour of Darkness prevailing."

Abbot continued, "And now, cavaliers, our monks and this lad Jacob here shall secure these wonders in the sealed place of the *scriptorium*.[10]

---

[8]*Gnotus, (alt. Notus):* The wisest of dragons, first of the "Neoplatonian dragons", this creature repented from oppressing the earth and warring against Allfather after hearing the teachings of the Neoplatonic philosophers. The bronze dragon Gnotus sought to bring this illumination to his own race. So attempting persuasion of the other dragons in the Aeonic gathering in the Chasm of Yaa, he was ostracized and pursued by the wicked dragons. The dragons defeated Gnotus in aerial combat over the vast southern desert.

[9]*Dry Blood Sea,* (Dunes) A vast desert of reddish dunes which dominated the center of the Whitehawk continent. Tradition holds that the sands became reddish in colour during the second age. The story claims that the bronze dragon Gnotus lay upon the sands bleeding for nearly a century. The sage Morpheus Memnos recorded the wisdom which the dragon whispered in song, the mysterious Vortex Poem, also called "*the meta prophecies*" which the great one recited, a grand Neoplatonian contemplation, which is said to be lost somewhere in the nine thousand and ninety-nine pages of the *Black Books of Melancholy*.

[10]*scriptorium:* Hall of a monastery in which monks do the sacred work of the copying down, writing, and illuminating of manuscripts.

Go, brother Fragga; I can manage on my own a while... Bring these gifts to keep in the place we spoke of before. I must now speak in privy to these chivalrous thanes, my spiritual sons...We have rooms for each of you, but first I must ask of you knights an question...and it is an iron one."

"Anything, my lord."

"Good lords, I was shocked to have heard that ye were working the traveling carnival. I did not think it true report. Did ye not know that the circus is funded by the idolaters of Galadif? Even women and children are forced to bow down to the beast. There is not a Christian soul left in their whole town.

The performing in such tournaments is given to the spread of that low heathenry. No?"

The White Knight apologized for the seeming scandal.

"The King of all the Aels has discovered how great is become the cult of the Dragon in Galadif. He sent his own cavaliers, ten *Knights of the Realm*, and thirty-five pikemen, to hunt down the beast.

They failed to find the dragon's lair, and only a handful returned. The survivors reported cannibalism, and witnessed diabolical rites performed upon unholy altars. A mob of rustics, in fear of the dragon's vengeance, burned the king's soldiers asleep their tents....and they cleverly blamed the blaze on the dragon. Now His Majesty sends us to investigate, but disguised."

"Then you do well, but ware be thou. With the dubious exception of Hieronymus Pike the dragonslayer, St. Arsacius, and a few others, men cannot prevail *contra draconem*.

Only the courtly Elves of ancient times could ever hunt and slay dragons. Men by mere natural virtue are incapable of such feats. I have written as much in a letter warning King Graham: only dispatch saintly heroes to such a trial.

May Almighty and merciful God deliver the souls of Galadif.

So, you knights, you must take your rest. Come, good lords, we shall show you to your quarters."

awn painted puff-clouds into red roses. They scudded along the Eastern horizon. The light touched the monastery the shadows fled away. The cavaliers were up and saddled their mounts. Down they rode into the town again and prepared jousting show for the circus-crowds.

A few rope-girded monks, guardian-trainees, followed. They were given leave to observe the expertise at many kinds of arms. They watched and were amazed, and would thus pass the entire day.

After the knights had finished and the sun was declining from its zenith, I called the two brethren and they conducted their horses upward.

No talk passed from their lips.

Back up they all went to the monastery. At vespers Jacob praised God with his lips, but his heart was elsewhere. The carnival supplied him many memories of colorful sights and spectacles.

The knights went to pray in the crypt. Many large monastery candles were blazing, and the shadows were near. They spent the night-hours before the image of the Radiant Lady in the presence of the Lamb. Upon their knees they spent themselves in ever-calling prayer. They placed their swords, in the brass-studded sheaths, at the foot of the glowing shrine. Each of these knights hauled out from their sachels a prayer-shawl of Ammouric weave and drew it overhead as they knelt down.

Their most fervent prayer was that they might never shed innocent blood during the havoc of war.

I had never witnessed such "Knights of the Shawl" nor heard anything of "chivalric enterprise." It was all a mysterious thing. They did not pray as ever-chanting monks pray. Theirs was in a different mode.

They softly sang their own martial hymns. These cavaliers reveal their true names to those of their own order alone, so secret and dangerous is their work. They forbade us to record their actual names until dead. Lest this work fall into the hands of the enemy, I shall continue to refer to each by the tincture: the White Knight, the Grey Knight, and the Burgundy Knight).Jacob discovered them at the shrine in the crypt where adoration to the Lamb is made whenever the stars glow bright. All novices and elders venerate the blessed head of Ael, son of Maceon, the original king of the Aels, and of all Kiluria. There too resides the image of *the Lamb who stands as if slain*, among the remains of the brethren asleep in the Lord, the dead who live forever.

After an hour, two of the shawl-knights withdrew to retire, but the White Knight remained; when he finally arose he began turning away to take leave, but I stood waiting. The candles flickered.

Would I, a novice monk, be so audacious as to break the absolute silence of the dead?

"Excuse, your lordship. Pray relieve of me a certain question with which a lowly monk is burdened."

"What do you require, monk? What be high critical as to break silence?"

"That a certain critical inquiry in mind be entered, for this I."

"You choose a time and place not wise. Be thou quick and ask planely."

"My thanks, my lord. Enlarge on that endeavor of which you and the Abbot made discourse earlier."

"Of that I may not, and will not, further speak on't. You, boy, as it seems, are about to become a monk and vow obedience. Recall that The Rule enjoins a monk no exchange of words during the Grand Quietude of the starry hours."

I bowed and moved away. You would think that the dead must have awoken. The cavalier stepped away into the cloister, opening the door off retiring to his chamber. Even then, the I would not restrain myself.

"I think it must well please God that you are so patient with me, knight..."

He looked back at me with the glare of disbelief at this effrontery.

"Admittedly, I am but the least taught of sound manners," I explained, ". . . but do tell... how is it obtained—the knighthood of your Ammouric order?"

"Observance of ancient discipline is the start... And we do not feign humility with self-deprecations," the knight replied, brow wrinkled.

"... but since knights are rare visitors here, God allows that I speak of great things. I am not one who exalts many reasons; therefore will I, in turn, yield but few. Warfare and expedition are perilous occupations. Do not suppose, monk, like many folk do, that a fine sword, a horse, and expensive armour are all that the rank requires. Manly virtue is required....and for our Order, the authentic invite of Heaven. We are devoted to the Radiant Lady; it is she who supplies our needs. She is our honour."

After a silence the magnanimous lord spoke."A search long, and as such, a life-consuming labour, –it is not a man's daily bread, not even a monk's.Of the many things one may do with one's brief days, the sworn crusade is among the worthiest, but also the most dangerous. Sweat and blood it means, and it usually ends in death. How many of my brother knights lay unburied in some remote glade, or washed up on some beach, rotting within their armour as the gulls pick away at them...?

It is not some easy sport and privilege. We enter the dark places of the world and even maneuver the fiery cisterns of hell.

We fortify ourselves with the heavenly bread. Earnestly we pray. If he campaigns without first winning divine aid, the Ammouric Knight will end up lost, his powerful work undone, and he will be likely forgotten.

Secrecy forbid that I unfold any more. Too much I have already spoken..."

"If you cannot treat more on all things; then your knighthood..."

Again he turned and was going.

"My lord, sir, pray, answer but one extra thing for me.
What exactly is meant by the words *chivalric enterprise*?
Is it a seeking for some treasure in ages ago lost?"

"Answer you?" he said. "May the throne on Argunizial spare us. We will not break further the holy silence of heaven. And besides, you know not what you are asking—such a question is answered with not a few words."

"'Tis quarter hour shy of Grand Quietude. The holy hush is not yet commenced. A few words, that's all I am asking from you."

He looked closely at Jacob. Exactly whom would he be teaching. Was the youth prepared? He took a breath, and stepped back in the room; turning about he knelt down again. "Is it now? You do not hear well, do you...? But very well...

You have been of avail in tending the horses.

I have supplied a hint. Quell your mind and think. The answer will come. We do not become cavaliers in order to be admired, boy. Our martial splendor awes you, easy guess...all this arrayed mail of splendid luster. Be not so simple, lad. Rather try to picture it, imagine this armour burnt and bloody, or fraught with deeply-sent bolgoth arrows, or hacked by the scimitars of the Veil-knights.

That is where imperishable glory lay. A long-suffering cavalier is forgetful of his own welfare.

This avowed purpose delivers us from human folly. Our word holds us to what we are promised. No wife do we take. Our time is devoted to skill and quest, so stern is the purpose of focus and detachment needed. Off the trail, if on occasion we dismount, our knighthood is not suspeneeded. This means passing the hours not in rest or trivialities, but in the crucible of prayer: the shawl. Do you think that our life must be exciting? So it is, but not in the way you suppose."

So he spoke, frowned, and left.

I awoke in the middle of the night.

How deep had dreaming sunk me under the spell of *Melancholia*.

The world offers no guarantee of success, no warrant against disastrous overthrow or enslavement, or harsh poverty. One does not live forever in this world. If I resisted my curiosity, like monks must always do, and did not go, I would never taste the mysterious wine, the momentous enterprise to which the three knights were vowed.

I imagine my future as a monk: forgotten and obscure, like so many others before. Blessed obscurity is something a monk should earnestly crave! Fair enough...one could live a long monastic life....but if so, what else was omitted in life? I had to just stop debating the whole thing in my mind. Will I be some lukewarm fool?

What sleep could close his eyelids? In the cool evening Jacob watched for the moonrise. He scanned from his little cell out across the boundless night sky. A sign was given, there in the gloam. The full-phased lunar disk was up. A dark and vaporous mist obscured her, but she cast her beams on the cloudy stage above as to portray some far-away furnace of fairy, or patch-eyed dwarves to forge axe and sword enchanted. A blast of air shifted the shapeless and vagrant torrents, which sank unveiling that mysterious orb, soaring in spectacular display.

Suppose thou that straightway without deliberation
one should my path assume?

The Deeptrackers Guide

V   QUO VADIS?

ew light touched the monastery, the shadows fled away. Jacob threw on his habit, wrapped round his cloak, and yerked his belt. He packed his few "possessions," and slung a wine skin.

So he was to tip-toe away....

I slipped into the monastery kitchen, made sure none were watching, and loaded my sack with apples, bread loaves, and strips of bacon.

Already before dawn the knights had set out, but this time disappearing into the forest. Their horses were nowhere in sight. As I was approaching the stairs going down, the cock crowed —Say, was that a warning from the patron saint of unhappy denials?

The old purblind hermit, Maragald, was kneeling there in the garden. He looked up and paused, listening. He went back to work. He had detected someone. He might not see every flower and bush, but he could smell them all and any nasty buzzing bugs. He also knew the unique step-patterns of each monk.

"What ho! Who goes there tip-toeing past? Brother Jacob?" he called, grasping a spade.

"I know thy vestigia. Whither goest thou, boy, quo vadis?! Why tip-toe? Who or what hath roused thee from slumber so early?" The elder stood up, expecting an answer.

"Where? Why...I must be going off to fetch milk, blessed one. I am to help with the cows again."

"Thou dost no such thing, young brother." he asserted, suspicion gathering deep furrows beneath hoary eyebrows.

"Can anything be concealed from you, venerable Maragald? I follow wherever these feet lead... I must be...on second thought...I must be sleep-walking... for I dream and walk about in my sleep. So long, brother... I shall awaken by and by." Jacob started for another route out of the cloister.

"He who dreams is not aware," the hermit said sharply.

The young monk turned back around. The hermit had warned me. "Do not answer with fictions, Brother Jacob, if you value your immortal soul. On holy ground you stand. The monastery is sacred, a terrestrial inn for those who are wayfarers to the region of light.

Awake to the light of day, my friend. Here is not a hideout for those who maunder. Boy, what is wrong?"

"Nothing is wrong...nothing at all."

"Speak nothing less than truth if thou art even yet a Christian!"

"I confess that I am awake, but my spirit dreams. My body is walking about, but I fear it is my spirit that is doing the wandering. Monks do not shudder at dreams. A dream is just a dream."

"Not always...some dreams are important. Some dreams are sent from The Ancientmost. Tell it, lad; I'll keep confidence."

"The actual matter...(and I was not going to tell anyone)...perhaps you can help me. I have decided that this rule of life is not for me. I am tip-toeing away from this place to go off and see the world. Some fair maiden heralds a destiny from afar, appearing in my dreams. I say she is no phantasm, but real. So I must search. Don't worry yourself; I shall be fine. There is no cause to alert the others. Please give them my regards and thank the Abbot. I should find work in the big city Hordingbay." (I feared to mention those wagons to him again).

"Tell me more on your dream—a maiden appears? It may be the succubus under the appearance of angelic loveliness. Have I not always been trustworthy with the things you tell me?"

"Very well....in this dream there comes a passing fair maiden, fairer than any I could have imagined, and quite real I insist, not just an imagination; she comes from the Furthsea to meet me in some place that is familiar but somehow unknown. In her arms she holds the white gift-book, a tome, one like the long-journeying knights had, or a book similar, unwritten. I try to explain myself to her, but she looks upon me for a time and then at last speaks..."

". . . and she says:" Maragald added,

"Here is the book you seek, a book written within and without. Open it; you can open it. It is the book of what was, what is, and what is coming to be..."

"By the saints above, how is it you knew her words?" Jacob cried, amazed. Maragald answered not, but continued:

"...You look at the maid and then glance again at the book, and again at her, and at the book...and still again. You keep wondering as to what its pages should contain. You finally reach out your hand to open it, but it is too late. She has turned and stepped away, and wraps the vellum within the folds of her white gown.

Into distances she drifts away. You try to follow her but cannot. Then you awake and see that you are in a cell, in a monastery, in a place where no terrestrial woman is permitted."

"You also have had this dream."

"No···some of the brothers have had such a dream, or vision, and even some of those brothers whom the incarnadine plague will someday take; and this dream has been a phenomenon known for many seasons now. As to what it portends, no one can say for certain. Suffice to say that it is a dream, and in some ways not a dream at all."

"Then who is the maiden? Is she the Radiant Lady? The Queen of Heaven- above is the only female that is allowed in the corridors of this sacred precinct...and she wisely keeps her distance."

"She who appears is not the Radiant Lady. Perhaps some other spirit in this world, but not "of" this world."

"In that case I esteem her more than terrestrial, but some celestial lady from afar, some ethereal maiden. She is for me no illusion, not a mere image of fancy."

"Aye, she is real; that is certain, else others would not sometimes have the same dream. Spiritual beings are permitted to enter into the dreaming imagination.

Angels are known to do so often, including the fallen ones.

I do not say that this is the case for every dream-character. Nevertheless, remember: The Evil One may represent himself as an angel of light. Listen now: I do not say she is an angel; neither do I deny it, for she is a messenger. Whoever she is, or whatever she represents, she must come from one of the three created worlds, or from intermundane spaces. It avails the monks little that she disturbs their already scant sleep. After a monk has this dreaming vision, he looks up at the ceiling of his cell and turns the mystery over in his mind again and again wondering at what it might portend. He cannot fathom it. She may be a cure for Melancholia.

Perplexed by the sickly imbalance of bile, the monk turns back over and returns to the hushed oblivion of sleep."

"Not me, I stay awake and wonder. In order to understand the mystery of this dream, I must go and find her."

"I cannot see if you are judging rightly in this. However the dream is yours. Do not think that because the others have had the dream that her words meant the same to them. She may be a haloed saint seeking some high work of charity, requesting something that they ignored."

"It must be done, whatever it is⋯" Jacob said. "She is a fair maiden whom some deep-dwelling dragon holds hostage perhaps, a challenge unforeseen, something unpredicted. I do not really like that we must part, but the very air is crying out for me to leave from here."

"That is quite a weighty decision." the hermit said. "Is not the Pearl of great price found here? Many things are imparted to you, but perhaps you interpret them wrongly. You are about to grow your first beard.

In some secret place of your mind you must be hoping

that she is in fact lovely and awaiting rescue...and more than just rescue. You must decide for yourself, as it seemeth to me."

"So it is as you say. But I must slip away now."

"Do not. The Divine Will shall be made known to you in time. She is a power, and maybe sent from The Ancientmost, but not for your desire.

To serve the Ancientmost

...that is the greater good; obedience is a greater task than any self-willed faring."

"I must not stay in monastery any longer."

"You are upset by something. Your training with the quarterstaff is not yet complete, is it? Many and violent are the dangers of the wide world, many enemies. I am old and blind. Perhaps I am also wrong, after all, I myself lived in the forest alone many a year.

Aye...perhaps it be better then. It is not for me

to hinder you further. After all,

He who seeks to preserve his life shall loose it."

The old raven knelt down again in the soil and continued the gardening. Autumn was already come and much winter preparation was to be made. The hermit's sudden indifference about everything had surprised me.

"What mean you, venerable brother?" I said. He paused his work, holding fast the spade. "I mean, Jacob, that...this life is not for you. You live for your own. Here we live not for ourselves, but for others.

Your brothers may not treat you like a king, but you are dear to them nevertheless. Do you think you will be honoured on account of succeeding in the world?

Your interest should be as brother for your brothers, to love them as Christ commands,

not chase some nebulous sense of destiny, worldly glory or fair maiden. It seems, though, that you have already determined this change of course.

Beware: *Arcus ianua mox clauserit."*

"Better to be cautious and fear the taking of sacred oaths," I remarked, now troubled. "Soon I must take final vows."

"As it is written, terrestrial life is drudgery, but in our way a man can live free of fear, in the blessed light from...Ah well...I must not burden you. Lift up thy head, boy. The sights of the circus overwhelmed you.

You hope become one of their fold; no? that is my guess; a celebrated fist-fighter or jousting cavalier adorned in martial splendor..."

"The circus will take me in as a worthy fighter, a hand-to-hand fighter who has some moves, monk-moves not many have seen."

"Who has bewitched you? Will you now, having received the Spirit as a monk, end in the Flesh? Pluck out your eye if it causes you to sin! What will you do if the circus masters say 'no'?"

"The knights are in need of helpers. I shall work for them, perhaps as squire, even someday become a knight."

"Those knights are peculiar indeed, not mere entertainers. Perfection of living righteously is their way, serving The Ancientmost in battle, in quest. Holy poverty they prize even above skill in combat."

"To live perfection? Is that not also the effort of the monks here?" I asked.

"These knights you saw...they are not like other knights. They are single-hearted paladins devoted to prayer. Aye, in a way, they be much like rope-girded monks. They never retain piles of wealth, keeping only enough to fund horse, armour, squires, food-wagons, and all needed for the ever-calling pathways. they give a tithe to the Church, and anything extra they pass to the poor. Plunder and loot holds little interest for them.

In exchange Heaven-high-above grants them certain powers: *telesthesia*, that can detect evil up to 60' distance, and immunity to all pestilences, and the laying on of hands.

It includes even the ability to turn the undead. All these are needed for the quest. Purity gives them advantage in hazardous battle, a blessed sword and sturdy mount are granted them to this end.

Regarding all this way of life Guy of Xaragia, the famous manualist, has made exact record."

"And if they are like rope-girded monks...do they work?"

"The ever-calling road IS their work, the toil of battle and the long expeditions." said Maragald, sternly. "God suspends their weak humanity in hardships and provisions them with unmatched fortitude."

"Then even an able monk might be taken under their tutelage, the retinue of a questing knight....?"

"Are you fit to be a rope-girded monk even? They were monks first, each one. One must be invited to it, a life of constant journey as the questing knight is wont. To take up so intense a striving is not done for mere vainglory. Some knights have spent their entire lives seeking the elusive Chalice of the Last Supper.

Nevertheless, if you long for such an employ, you might try it, and start off serving as a baggage-boy among them."

"I will crusade with them, and even find the chalice, or fight against Veil-Knights. Those men have seen the wide world; and even though wisdom counsels me that I should remain in this place of peace, I will not.

As long as this craving is in me, I shall not be at peace. I have no choice but to yield to it."

"No choice? Certainly there is freedom, and always a right way." He declared. "Think over it, monk; You will exchange your woolen frock for constraining armour, your prayer beads for brutal iron ball and chain...Perhaps it warrants a try anyway, if only to learn of its hardship."

Maragald put down his spade and stood up again. He gazed earnestly. "Know that when the time comes, you should listen for The Ancientmost's voice, and ask of His Will above all else, and also this: be thou true to thyself...I have always esteemed you.

You will find the sacred mountain and the alabaster corridor of heavenly stairs, and you may ascend those stairs to the palaces of light. But first, Jacob, you must descend, and take the axe to the root." Maragald paused for a moment; his eyes luminous with unearthly aura, his wrinkled brow as one in deep places. He suddenly froze. "However, with all these future things said, Jacob,

the Spirit moves me where it wills.

There comes a sudden hindrence in my counsel to you. I must increase my tone. By no means should you abide here. Instead, I say: flee this place, now while you have the stomach for it:

The Beast lurks about this place; the dragon's smoke

has entered the sacred halls. For the sins of monks,

the cloister is become the haunt of pit-born devils.

Hear this: an angel once in a vision communicated something to me: it was Heaven, you see, that left me this way, near blindness

—not as a curse but as a blessing! The angel said that The Ancientmost allowed this so that my eyes might not behold the great temptations that would one day afflict our beloved rope-girded monks."

"So you now advise me to leave instead?" Jacob said, "How can you so change your counsel at once?

You are truly an old raven tetched with madness, Maragald."

"At first concern for the good of your soul urged me to haul you back from a rash decision," he said, "as is customary when dealing with a wanderlusting monk.

We are to dissuade with dire warnings. That has always been the first tactic with any new monks whom either the devil deceives or whose own flesh drives them out. We persuade them to stay. But I am grey, and I keep assuming that things are the way they have always been.

They are not...things here are no longer that way!

You see, the poisonous monks are becoming bold as of late.

If I could, I would return today to my cave in the forest.

Why, one monk even scolded me and rebuked me yesterday

because I found him in some mischief he was after doing,

in flagrante delicto. Now the viper acts injured

and outraged at me, as if I am the evil-doer!

Many who were pious have fallen away

...no longer have they the fear of God!

More and more the monks are making less and less progress in righteousness. They comfort themselves that they have made enough progress and will stay on that same level. On the contrary, they unwittingly "sink into the waves of damnation's sea," for like a tree there must be

either the growing of spirit or else a mouldering.

Many have benumbed consciences and do not even realize how deeply in the mire of uncleanness they writhe; how like hordes of termites their sins have eaten out the innards of the monastery-tree, even though some leaves up high still appear green of hue.

Don't you hear the din of iniquitous laughter during meals?

...All serious-minded monks in aforetimes were wont to be harkening to the writings of the fathers read aloud.

In those days, most monks honoured the Rule, more in the observance than in the breech. No man was given leave to talk, not during meals, not until Abbot began. Now all are prattling, laughter as soon as the prayer is done. It is an outrage hazardous to monkish souls, to Heaven distasteful, a selfish routine adopted from the urbane Friars, as if they were our betters!

Many so-called "wise" monks, in truth, should be better described as clever. Of sacred wisdom and discipline they only know how to skirt it.

They have altered the order of things, and lenience under the guise of mercy has little by little brought forth luxury and worldliness.

With what shall the salt be seasoned if it has lost its savor?

It is of no benefit and must be cast out.

Of monk's discipline whatsoever here remains is used instead to exact harmful recompense on those who dare correct the wicked!

Even the good Abbot is threatened: beware lest you make reforms, they say. An air of oppression hangs over the choir-stall when all sit down at chant of morning. Is that not so?

So Jacob, after re-examination of the state of things, I stood,

and there came over me just now thoughts

of the Lord's Great Accounting,

and so I now fear for your salvation

if you stay in this place. You are young and have not the perseverance in the face of persistent corruptions, a thing that must be learned. Even now as we speak I am having a vision, child. No, I cannot believe my eyes, what a tremendous marvel of woe,

this highly-perched monastery—a house of iniquity,

the headquarters of all mischief, a whore drunk

upon the blood of martyrs! The beast trampling these very stones! Desolation! Flee from this place Jacob and seek another perch if you can, although there are few...

...or else live a Freeman's life, offering your tithes at church.

I myself would also leave if only my eyes could see well enough to fend for myself. These are evil times. The Inversus has sent his unholy apostles even unto the sanctuaries.

Be watchful on your pilgimage. Trust no one. Beware of The Red Death: the Incarnadine Plague, a blast which sins of the flesh transmit.

I did not mean to alarm you.

Make some good thoughts for yourself now.

Now tell me, how obtain you that big town, Hordingbay? It be a-good-ways beyond the great and haunted forest."

"Tis a-ways indeed, master, and I cannot sail upon the Vastess Sea, but I am stalwart and ready for the labour of feet. I am certain the circus will hire me for good pay, but if not I recall a shortcut through the Lokken: Ringwood, and the Timberhills that pass ultimately into the Chestnut Vale and Hordingbay."

"Son, dare you follow that forgotten route? Stay away from those infinite lands of conifer, the Timberhills, which our ancestors called the Lokken.

Perils: passing strange and unusual things transpire there."

"I must go that route if I mean to intercept the wagons. Be it nothing to fret over. I have strolled a little ways into those woods several times already in the past few moons.

The place is not too wild.

Has any report come of ever-lurking robbers?

Sniffing wolves find no prey there, nor do any other life perils prowl for that matter···nothing that I cannot take care of myself with the trained fists of a guardian monk."

"Not so well trained are you as you imagine, so mind yourself. Certain forgotten kindred lurk up there. They are the perils I have in mind, unmindful one. Have you not studied how, in the world-age when bronze was prized, the days when the cromleths were raised, the demon-gods held sway? The mountain-kin ruled our kind with dreadful hands.

The ancient Kilurians of St. Aldemar, savage cannibals

...they worked strange magics, and they were flesh-eaters as well, of human flesh. The idolaters of the dragon are among their descendants.

We who are monks know that the years are but days,and we plumb the centuries as if years, "for an age quickly passeth and is gone." The elder races also await their coming time, eager to again vex the civil lands. Consider the men of Galadif...a whole town living in fear and consenting to human sacrifices on high altars.

Keep to the path and do not stray out of it, not for a moment, lest going aside some eld enchantment ensnare you, and thoughtless, you lose an eternal destiny."

I could not really heed so many of his warnings, intent as I was to abandon myself to destructive folly and in such great hurry to do so. I peered through the gate and saw the shadowy eaves of the forest not far off. The sun was already upon the horizon rising like a titan.

The friendly abbey hound, a fine tracker with long fells of fur, now came sauntering up and nudged me, as he also were meaning farewell.

"Farewell, Lars...such a worthy creature you are..." Jacob said.

"He is a perceiving one, that dog; and mindful," Said Maragald. "He once led me out of the labyrinthine woods when I was lost at night, one black night. Eventhough I hollared angrily at him that his direction was the wrong way, and rebuked him; he refused me, he would not follow.

He knew I was lost. I would have been dead at the bottom of a cliff if he had let me go on... Swift-footed he is yet, formerly a cavalier's dog, even with years upon him...he is most loyal and ever-watching...a beast with seeming wit. Not all dogs are so.

He always returns to this gate, for he is awaiting his master's return... Mantayl Yordrusil, an Osring-cavalier who came to usfor lodging...some eight passings of *Calduin* since."

Now I said nothing. For already I knew about the dog and suspected that Maragald had retold these things about him to stir up some feeling in me. Even so, sadness for leaving came over me, but I had made the decision and wanted to be a man about it. I must resolve and stick with it.

"That Sir Mantayl, the dog's master, he had been marked with a sorcerous curse in the Wars of the Veil," the hermit continued. "When he returned, none durst come near to him, save Lars here. So he came to us for a time and the stay should have benefited, but the lord claimed that the curse was still upon him. The man prized a magic ring left over from the world of ancient magic. It had a side-effect: a kind of maniacal overconfidence to venture into dangers alone. He disappeared and was never seen again. This dog often goes to his master's pathway in the Lokken and waits for him to return, but an empty belly drives him back here every day."

"Right..." I said, knowing nothing else to say (a right monk would say "I shall pray for the soul of noble Sir Mantayl"). Instead I hoped to cut short the discourses with Maragald. "So I'll be off on this long trek now...dream though it be."

"Brother Jacob, this dog, hear me, can sense things. His nose can tell when the wisp of Hinter-evil is upon the wind. He can also scent the nearness of the Elfshade vine that overhears the talk of men," the hermit whispered.

"—wisp of Hinter-evil?"

"Mind the wake of your words, man. I should not have mentioned it, but you've not been through the wide world and must learn the furthlore. Jacob, you have not just one enemy.

There walk many. And also the unearthly thing, a famous being brooding in the Northern barrens of the Outreaches;
   a creature that lingers in forgotten chambers;
   its tormented intellect here and there surveys the realms
   by means of servants. Intense is the spite within its soul,

even against this dog, a mere beast...hated for closeness to Man! This ancient spirit of fairy is a wicked thing, and he still creeps upon broad earth: the Dire of Melancholy!"

"Thanks for the warning, Maragald, but heedless of moonlore and crusty old spirits I must hazard it anyway, like a questing knight. The dog should stay here with you.
My journey will be an arduous one."

"This dog always returns here, but he will know if you require him, so well he knows those Timberhills...if you get lost.
Let him go with you a-ways, till dinner. But you also need a guardian that can go a distance, so follow me."

Into the monastery courtyard I followed the purblind hermit, eventhough I would rather not.

We went over to the central pool and grand fountains where three swans floated in serenity. The old hermit signaled kindly to the largest one, and to my amazement, he perceived not a swan, but a white goose come paddling up...yet by the look one would estimate a half-swan.
Them the brethren never approached. These, "*semi-cygni,*" were exquisite and calming to watch, but *feroces*, wild and dangerous. One of them was obeying the hermit, and this was just the beginning of wonders! There in the early light, Maragald leaned over the pool toward the half-swan and moved his face close to the graceful creature. He whispered some words.

The blind hermit stood up and addressed Jacob Magister. "Does the bird nod —indicate agreement?" He asked.

"The bird did make nod, *constat* Maragald!"

At that point the animal leaped upon the rim of the pool, paused, hopped down with a couple of flaps; came and stood beside us.

"Have you not heard that it is even given to some of the faithful *loqui cum animalibus* —to speak with animals?" he explained. "Sometimes they will come right close and follow along, as to give at least some comfort of companionship.
Aileron is the name. Treat him well, he will do all to protect you from above—when danger comes...and come it will, he will return to you at once."

As we left the courtyard the half-swan went along beside me, but soon took to wing. The companion-swans, remaining in the pool, sounded out to him. I gave him thanks, but considered it an unecessary help. I wanted Maragald to hinder me no further, but he insisted; tarry but just another moment.

"Brother, you do confess that your soul groans under some fatal sway of Melancholy...correct?" he asked.

"No, not fatal...if by that word you mean fate inescapable. The philosophers say each may claim a blessed path.
We can claim it or not claim it, 'tis a fair choice. Even so, I say that I must do this and not contest its power over me."

"You imagine that you are going to freedom, because it is a new enslavement that constrains you, Jacob. It was holy baptism that once freed you, and you entered monastery with gladness.

But now in these years your spirit little by little has consorted with melancholy, returning you to spirit-bondage, as most other monks. That is why you crave escape, getting out before its too late. So do some others crave, secretly. Unlike them you have the intestines to actually tempt it. But know that you can not escape melancholy by a change of place. You must fight it."

"By the way," I interrupted. "Can you secure a load of iron rations for me from the cellar?" I was feigning that I had not really heard a single word. Maragald frowned.

"To you I offer insights profound, keys to freedom and life, but the howl of the belly is too loud for you to hear it..."

I stared at the old man, as if puzzled. Oh the vanity of my ways.

"Yes I have rations, child. It will not be enough to last long. Come follow me, Jacob, I have something best to procure for your pilgrimage, something to help you get by at first. Not a kind place is the world...Alas, mere belly...revelations cannot avail you quite yet..."

He led the young monk over to the inner gate around to the outer wall and the little shed where all the gardening tools were stored. Maragald was the only laborer to enter it. He had constructed it himself, and it also served as a minor seclusion chamber for him when he missed the hermit life of tranquility.

"Just wait but a moment, and don't go away quite yet. Need you something..:" He disappeared into the shed and he must have opened up the boards of the shed floor. He returned carrying a substantial purse.

"When I was your age, my mother, a noble, had amassed a great deal of wealth, some of which was even used to maintain this monastery. She left me an inheritance, these gold coins. I never could discover how to be shorn of these as a hermit wanting for holy poverty.

One must always have a little prudence for a grim day of sea-raiding parties or cruel brethren. I would be happy enough to leave the coins to the monastery upon my parting from this world. No longer...They are of no use to the unhappy monks now. Our monks enjoy more wealth than even Heaven can account. The Age slips nigh unto its consummation. What is the good of saving when you know that the Creation is about to be rolled up just like a scroll all at once? So the rope-girded monks have not any need for tawdry gold anyway, plenty of chinkers comes their way. It was not always so. Take you these and keep them hidden.

In the world you will need monies to survive.

If you fear bandits are approaching, toss the purse in the woods and mark the spot in your mind. This will do you well, *pro itu et reditu*. Quickly now, bury it away under your belt."

"Yes, bury it away!" A voice said, coming from the cloister, along with the laughter of several. Someone had been listening to the conversation. It was Ulcrist, Yulla, Lucian, and Formosus, all together and come suddenly. They approached, cowls partly concealing cynical expressions. Formosus addressed me.

"You take advantage of the purblind Maragald, as it seems, unbeliever!" He rudely grabbed the sack of crizets out of my hands, and he passed it to Brother Lucian, who opened it, looked inside, and displayed the contents to the others.

"Why at such early hour would monks disturb someone's meditation?" Maragald asked, indignant. "The sack of coin is for emergencies!"

"It matters not. We know it to be an emergency for this doubter here," said Ulcrist. "...a wee amount of change compared to what we will fetch..."

"Tell me, you disobedient and doubting novice," Formosus said, turning to me, "how many crizets do you suppose your sale would win us?"

"Is there something wrong, Formosus?" I answered, "How much a man is worth is beyond reckon. Didn't you teach us God's wisdom: how Man, made in the image and likeness of The Ancientmost, is of unestimable worth?"

"I did teach that. However it turns out to have been only partly true, for such is how it appears in the eyes of God, not we men. Christ was sold for but thirty pieces of silver. The seller should have known better and required a higher bid. You yourself, Maragald, but an old-timer, might be worth a weighty sum to the right buyer. That was my meaning."

Maragald then looked to Ulcrist. "Are you also so intent on gaining lucre? Why did make a vow of poverty?"

Ulcrist had no answer, so clever Forrmosus gave one. "Poverty can be spiritual rather than financial. Certainly tis true that Our Lord had little else than what he could carry. But we who are spiritual monks know not to adhere to so simple an interpretation of divine perfection. We understand the Rule as spiritual, as an ideal, not something to be expected for everyday. We are right in this."

"What possibly mean you by that?" Maragald asked with a less polite tone. "The supreme-sophist! The *diabolus*! I see each one of you, even those two others; Yulla and Lucian, rope-girded monks, my brothers.

I have known you since you were mere strapping lads learning the chant, but now you are muted by shame. You cannot hope to remain unknown in doing something wrong...I know you by your footsteps."

Now it was Brother Ulcrist who answered the venerable hermit. "What brother Formosus means, old crow, is this:

They know this one is trying to flee the monastery, to shirk obligation. Right well enough...but why not profit a little from it? In this way they help the fool get what he wants: work in the circus. The search for this misfit in the crowds yesterday morning was the last bone for these brothers who had to do his share of kitchen work. The latest insubordination has sealed it. Formosus and several other spiritual monks are weary of unspiritual behavior. He will never be a satisfactory monk. I did not want this for my student, but I am under oath."

"What sort of oath?" asked Maragald.

Ulcrist ignored the question and continued his discourse. "We went back down to the circus and went about asking, and discovered that they could indeed take another hand to work the wagons, a healthy beardless youth like this one. They would not take on stragglers. We may sell him to the circus for a reasonable sum and split the taking. Not to worry, mere belly. The circus will feed a hand who is bought and paid for much better than they would some tag-along. The misfit will be thankful for this favor. Both parties win in this case."

"By all the halo-made saints, you would not sell a rope-girded monk?!" cried Maragald.

"Keep your voice to a whisper, old man," warned Formosus. "You would not let the trouble-browed Abbot discover you helping a monk break vows, would you? Enough trouble with Abbot has come your way as of late."

Ulcrist hove chin high, as in judgement. "Misfit monk...that he is, and we are going to sell him. And you Maragald will earn a coin for keeping your mouth shut. And just in case he tries to wiggle from our grasp or assay his trained-hand against us, we have enlisted these two, strong-armed brothers who would also earn a little extra bread themselves."

At once together they seized Jacob by the arms. They had an iron grip.

"Unhand the boy!" the outraged hermit shouted. "You are monks, not savages. Ulcrist Dretch...!"

"I am trained in open-hand combat," I warned. "You know my abilities, and I am the admitted best. I could easily wrest out of your hold and damage you badly, all you monks, if I really cared to. No need for such smarting grip."

Formosus said: "These two are also trained, brother Jacob, so unless you are confident against both...but I wager you do enjoy all this little drama. Tell you what; Maragald, you keep also your mouth shut and we will let this one hold onto a few kine
—the unauthorized sack of coins you gave him."

Maragald lowered head —disbelief.

"Brothers, I beg of you, do not commit this sacrilege before the Lord. For your own sakes, do not trespass in this way. Formosus, what has gotten into you lately? This goes against everything you have ever taught. Did not even the first philosopher, a mere goat of a pagan, say that it is better to suffer evil that to do evil? Let the boy go. Be patient with him. He will, in time, change."

"The Grecian philosophers set my feet upon the path of knowledge. But we are beyond that now, Maragald," said Formosus. "Smarted off for the last time he has. Life as a slave—it ought to humiliate him well enough.

In some future year; the circus returns, we take him back and make him a slave of Christ again. Then he will appreciate. See, the fool does not even struggle against us. He wants us to bring him out from here."

"It is an honest call that he wants to go, yes." replied, Maragald. "To flee—from us, my brother Formosus, *from us*... but knows he little of what he is after doing. He would change mind within a couple of days and return here, back to the safe and cozy monastery. Don't you see that? Recall how desperately you yourself once tried to flee the life when you were near final vows. We had to sit you down and persuade you. Stay, don't leave here, the Lord needs you, we said. But you resisted, 'let me teach at the university again,' you cried and you would not listen."

"Enough said, Maragald," warned Ulcrist. "Any more and I will find a way to silence you. Misapplied pity like yours—it's no fix for things!"

"Just one consummate question; Formosus," said Maragald. "How is it that you, a philosopher and humanist, have stooped to this?"

"I shall tell you how, Maragald, if know you must, and let the boy listen well. Everyday I remember my old life, before I became a monk. My life was good. I was a lecturer at the University of Whigg. Do you monks never consider the life that you left behind?

I had an excellent career, and I had achieved considerable academic notoriety. For a time it looked as if I would even marry a worthy and fine lady. Then the Christ appeared one night, his heart burning, and called me to serve him—not as prestigious professor, but in this way, as a monk— invited to years of renunciatory Christian living, penance, and obscurity. How does one resist Christ? At first I refused; denied it. But I found peacefulness whenever I saw monks.

How could I bear such a low state? I could not reason my way out of His sublime calling; the chance to truly help the human race.

Yet my earthly desires did not fade. I had to deny them, or deny God. So I yielded. I knew it would be hard, but I would no longer be tormented in mind.

Yes, you might say that I now prefer to return and gaze at the shadows flickering on the proverbial cave's wall, entertaining shadows. Comfort would have us never turn our eyes away. That was before the full light of the revelation of the Son of Man dragged me out of the cave to this monastery.

Now, because I have heavenly knowledge, I really can't go back. Ignorance did have a certain…bliss —the philosophers never realized. I long for my good life, the ease of my flesh—not constantly under trial of ever-calling prayer and fasting. Weary am I; the monastery-responsibilities, the walking by faith, the holy poverty.

I cannot now escape this place, this miserably tranquil monastery. Even if I dared, I am too old to make a change. I still long for what I have lost. Therefore I have made alliance with Ulcrist and these others; to change our way of life here, to improve it, and to make it more tolerable and humane."

"Formosus, you entered this monastery —freely! *He who puts his hand to the plow and looks back is not worthy of the Kingdom of Heaven!*"

"Enough, old raven! You have your answer. Do you not see? We are doing the boy a favor! Nothing more…"

By the tone Maragald understood it —a final warning.

Ulcrist said: "They are off then to the circus-master. They will make our transaction. Remember Maragald, if any of this gets to the others, or to Abbot, we will sell you next. No need for us to worry, every rope-girded monk of Whitehaven knows that your many moons alone in the hermetic groves of Ringwood left you quite unhinged of mind. No one would think it alarming if you were said to have maundered off into the labyrinthine Lokken. You would instigate us further into uncharity; make us leave you deep in those woods, old raven? But enough sins are upon the soul of each already. No one will give heed to your ramblings. Now say your farewell to this one."

"You betray your very souls!" replied Maragald unperturbed. "Knowledge I have about those arcane woods more intimate than any wild-eyed witch or trail-seeing ranger. So take your chance, unless you wish to poison me, like the monks who tried to kill the great St. Benedict. Otherwise do not threaten with idle threat. Your sin of sacrilege is what shakes me. I do not fret over how shall go my last hour. As for you, Jacob: these unkempt servants now do this dastardly deed, and you, deluded, care not about it."

The reproach fell but faintly on my soul, my ears made deaf by the excitement of escaping the monastery.

Did Jacob not care that he was being sold as a slave to the circus? He did not know what it meant to be a slave. Like some mindless ghost, he was dead to Maragald's words or the fact that his brothers were committing sacrilege. He was concerned only with himself, and with obtaining the object of his idolatry.

Why did you slip away, o wanderer, boy who esteemed yourself a man? Were you trying to make it through the wilderness of this life? Will you regret abandoning the paradise of your cell? Will you be refreshed at the empty wells of the incomprehending world with all its curiosities?

Maragald dismissed him; made the sign of the cross, using the minor exorcism:

"*Vade Satana.*"

Of supernatural adversaries the initiate will number many, all of whom seek against thee unceasingly. Is not the most vexing of these all too familiar? Be it not thy own self?

Morpheus Memnos
Utterances of the Dragon Gnotus as-he-lay-dying

VI   Per Silvam Tenebrosam

nto the Timberhills the wagons rolled, and with them I went trudging. I was already certain that I had made a terrible mistake. O profound reversal! Jacob Magister a slave!

And what could it profit rope-girded monks to have sold their own? What meagre prize could induce them to auction off their own to a traveling circus? What shamelessness to so diminish the monkhood! And all for filthy lucre!

The brothers contracted for a handsome sum. At once they distributed the hosts of their god Mammon between themselves, and how unclean was the feel of slippery silver.

Off to the market they hurried to purchase sweet dainties, liquors, pillows, silks, and various meats.

How often did the circus get someone who claimed that they *wanted* to be a slave? Jacob Magister had so claimed. Therefore thralldom commenced at once. He was made to hoist provisions—tools and many other things for marching with the circus that very morning. Work was grueling; there was never much pause and they rarely stopped. There were few breaks. If he did not obey: beatings would ensue. But otherwise a sufficient dinner was had, provided that he finish all tasks. The circus version of supper, porridge and roots, although it would have been turned down by a Whitehaven monk for being of insufficient palette, was become precious. Jacob now gobbled it up ravenously.

It was shortly thereafter while finishing his allotted gruel that he realized something. Let it be attributed to the selfishness of youth, but it had never dawned on him how common folk must labour all the day; that they do not expect yummy dishes, nor the study of higher things in the afternoon. Neither have they access to books, nor manuscripts, nor a cozy cell into which to retreat, let alone a sumptuous dinner.

These realizations were disturbing enough, and added to his new found consternation was a certain trepidation: the knights were nowhere to be seen.

The next day was a day of unrelenting and punishing travel on the muddy wagon roads, as he was often finding himself pushing the encumbered vehicles; the otherwise colorful wheels slowed by the deep mud of the earth. They would even yoke him to the wagons for a pull. Later there was no rest, but painful burdens were again piled on his back.

In a remote glade of the Timberhills the carnival finally camped. The men lit fires and served up the gruel again. It was a most tasteless porridge they provided, these strangers who now owned Jacob. How he missed the various and filling victuals of the monastery.

Jacob slept on the damp ground. Almost slept, that is, being extremely uncomfortable—no bed, and only one blanket.

In the murkiest part of the night he awoke out of an awkward but heavy sleep. A strange and eerie sound resounded through the night air of the forest. An owl hooting somewhere out in dark wilder expanse...

Jacob lay listening to the strange sound never before heard.

After a time the nocturnal avian flew away and then, after a few moments, the peculiar creature again hooted, farther off in the dark. A strange place the forest at night, and more than spooky.

He was about to fall asleep again, as the others, but there was another sound. It was the sound of persons conversing in some foreign language, whispering. He looked up and spotted several of the indentured hands slipping through the dark, older boys intent on becoming woodland bandits, so it seemed. Why else would the boys simply leave the carnival--troupe in the middle of the night, sneak off into the dark hinter? They moved between the tents and wagons. They had packed up their supplies on their backs and were tip-toeing away from the camp. They went easily through the tall grasses and disappeared into the tangled trees of the gloomy Lokken.

Jacob thought of the extra work he would have to do, and so fell back asleep right away, for his weariness was great.

The ever-traveling carnival packed up early on the next morning. It went unnoticed however that some were missing. One of the men on horse marked this first as they went along the wagon line for inspection. Others were informed. Another rider rode forth and cried out.

"But where went those new acrobats! Where now have they scurried!!?" It was the one who was the magician, a man in sable raiment of the kind worn by wizards of far-away Egyptian Gohha.

He turned horse about and went up and down the wagon line calling for whomsoever may have seen "the mountaineers, the acrobats that dangle from ropes and poles." He had a few words with the circus master and continued to demand an answer. It was a roiling scene. The whole caravan halted.

"Spotted them going, myself, I did," Jacob shouted. "They slipped off in the dead of the night... So tired I fell back asleep before I could manage to cry out."

"Thrall, in which direction?" asked the magician.

In answer Jacob pointed to the West.

The magician again spun his horse. He drew a horn from his saddlebag and lifting to his lips sounded it. The blast resounded throughout the forest. He waited...all halted and were still...and no one perceived rightly what was going on.

After a few moments the tall grass ruffled round about. Several creatures were coming towards them through the woods. These at once were revealed to be dogs. They circled the magician. Clearly he was their master. He placed his horn back in the saddlebag. Had these dogs been with the caravan all along, following at a distance? Where did they come from? He spurred horse. The dogs, some eight or nine of them, (an eastern breed, it seemed, with bushy tails), followed him into the murky woods.

This was more than a middling entertainer-magician. And no more was he found again about the caravan.

Just shy four days passed with the caravan encamped in a fen by a little brook. Jacob Magister's thralldom had become quite miserable, quite intolerable for him.

"...They slapped me around quite a bit they did. One good thing came of it; namely that I recovered my sense, at least partly. What a life I had in the monastery! How possibly could I escape this?

The headmasters of the circus were pagans. One night I watched the idolaters erect an image of the beast and light bonfires to worship.

The huge DRACO came to them that night and stirred in the woods, snorting. Everyone could hear it lumbering about, snapping branches in the dark, moving on the perimeter. Had they summoned him to hunt the deserters? The beast did not come forward to show itself. No one ever actually saw the creature.

How with no supplies could I survive the wilderness, let alone a dragon? Would that dragon track me down and devour me? The wagon roads were in many places overgrown, so only those who knew how could follow them.

Could one find the way back alone? If some hungry beast doesn't take you, you can get lost in dark woods and soon die of starvation.

My new masters had at least provided a woolen cloak. I kept it wrapped around at times, save for when working. I had prayed to God to protect me. One day, while fetching a bucket of water down at the brook, I took note of something delightful, something uncommon.

A goose landed upon the smooth flowing waters.

Was it the same great half-swan of recent complement?

Was this Aileron, the battle-goose who was sent to me as a protector? The bird drifted near. He did not scare away.

Suddenly right close, he was looking for a morsel. A bit of stale bread was in my pocket.

There was now no doubt that this was the half-swan Aileron. I had not been abandoned. Perhaps now escape *was* possible. Hope was what Aileron now lent me, hope.

Each time the creature approached the camp during the day, men seeking to make a meal of him would chase after the poor bird and it would be off flying away.

Now it was the nightly routine that bullish workers would come and fasten my neck and hands with a noose. It was a precaution, lest, unhappy with relentless toil, new circus-slaves run off under a moon's light. This noose was loose but impossible to undo, and it was attached to one of the fat taskmasters who would awaken if he felt any movement. This was always a most uncomfortable way to sleep. Several times already I had tried to unfasten the noose, and failed, only to be kicked by the brute master.

Who knows, it might be possible get back home. I would go to the Abbot and beg for pardon. If the Abbot agreed, there would be easy work with monks instead; although surely they would never allow me to return to my former state wearing the habit, not without years of penance. I would work for them instead, even if just lugging buckets of water. Better to be a slave for them, for heaven's sake, than these unrelenting circus masters.

Now, I tell you, Heaven caused the half-swan Aileron to perceive this situation, somehow, with animal mind. The creature would approach silently at night and peck at the rope in a single place.

Soon the night came when the rope was severed in feazings. The goose deftly took to wing. I crept and quietly disappeared into darkness of the forest.

How dark is the Lokken at night! That is why the old pagans called it the Lokken. My only light was a misted crescent-moon.

To locate the wagon trails I circled round and found them leading back towards home.

The long Night continued, with drizzle and drifting fogs. At least the wool cloak was a minor protection from the bite of cold air.The tracks had somehow faded into a deer path under a swell of fog. I sat down and rested for a while. Sleep never found me. Instead came shivers, for coldness penetrated all under the cloak on the cold ground.

My half-goose was somewhere nearby, watching, and that gave me confidence.

The next day things did not look good. The morning greeted me with snow flurry and I determined that I must have mistracked farther from my destination.

The morning I spent trying to find a new path back to the tracks. What great regrets I had. Cold and drenched in my own sweat, now hunger and weariness set in. Snow, otherwise a charm, fell all around in vast sheets. Even the trees now whispered, albeit peacefully, as if to sooth my nerves, for surely I would soon perish, overwhelmed by chill and fatigue. I heard only hoots of owls in those thick forests of serried pine, and the occasional lonely and haunting howl of a distant wolf...a signal to his brothers that I am weakened, ready to be taken?

I picked up a well-worn trail at last, It passed through glen and dale, through spindly vines and over fallen timber, beneath crooked branches and over marsh grasses, thickets and glades. This trail had been well used, but by what denizens? Tree branches had grown into an archway to pass under. This was Ringwood, the most enchanted groves of the Lokken.

Below the crests of those old pagan hills the orange sun dipped into ocean's horizon like a titanic soul downward falling. After he was gone the confusion of grey mist took his place. Every direction looked both correct and doubtful and one clearing appeared the same as the last. I stood still: a dismal moment, the realization that I was truly lost...

Some say a night in the Timberhills will leave a man bewildered for years. I pulled the cloak more tightly round me. That deep bewilderment of the Lokken was real. Fear coursed through my limbs like a frost. Barbed and needled branches struck my cheek as I made way through the thick places.

eaven sends messengers. They fly between the worlds. These messengers, otherworldly men to be sure, are monks. Swift of mind, their messages are sealed with true knowledge. Some say there are as many kind's of monks as variety of bird, and therefore the features of each monk can be likened to the variety of winged species; their look corresponding to a certain habit of bearing. The monastery's wide-eyed owls hover over ancient texts when the hour is late. Eagles awaken at sunrise and take to wing at once upon the upper airs of the gospel, soaring, (like Saint John the Evangelist). Then again, some monks seek solitude apart, the cranes and herons. Also many like pigeons poke about. They eat and make messes and their true purpose is a mystery. Many monks are peaceful doves. They must have the protection of hawks, the warrior-monks.

I was remembering a conversation I had with a certain hawk: the master trainer for guardian monks, Brother Ulcrist. It was my monkish work after all, to train so as to strike against sea-raiders. We trained everyday, although we never expected to actually use it.

I thought of one morning after training: a feirce glance from master Ulcrist restrained me after the dismissal while the others went off to lunch. I expected to be chastized for my laziness.

"I wish to speak with you," Brother Ulcrist declared, rather dispassionately but with a fierce countenance. I remained in my spot awaiting command, like a soldier, unmoving, eyes fixed, staring straight ahead.

"You are not my best student, Jacob. You clearly desire the perfect form, so we keep you. Therefore you must get your sleep. It is obvious that you have not...and as of late, you have displayed little mirth...so seems it to me. Why is this? Come now, unfold it."

"Sleep, master...?"

"I shall not repeat the question. I am your brother and someday war-companion. You can tell me of anything that troubles you."

"Last night I could not sleep."

"Yes, go on⋯"

"...in my cell, I was thinking, I was philosophizing. I have been questioning all behaviors and thoughts. I want to make my own decisions. The Church calls it Pride."

"Pride? The tomes of physicians name it a symptom of *Melancholia*...speak thou more on't."

"As you wish master. It were to me as if I were invisible, or hosted a forsaken and mischievous power in my mind, trapping me in a kind of bottomless pit of my own contrivance where I am my own lord of real or unreal."

"Wishful but dangerous dreams...sounds like to me, as stirring yourself into *Melancholia*. Neglect of discipline is a most common symptom, it's from a lack of humility. And, my dear hyperion, that yields excess of black bile. Perhaps you have been neglectful of discipline? The undisciplined soul drifts into a spiritual morbidity—when a monk does not look to what is required daily...Therefore instead you will drown your worry in prayer, not in the abysmal recesses of vain fantasy.

Ask the physician, Brother Amos, he will agree I wager:
failure to trust in divine providence; languor. Does the diagnosis fit?"

"It does fit, I think. Before dawn I was at least given to open my eyes, but I would not otherwise stir. It is like a fantastic but alien thought, a weed taking root within me. I barely made way to morning chant."

"You must realize that the fault lay within. It is not alien to you. It is you. But somehow I suspect you have not yielded to the weed of Melancholy entirely."

I said nothing, not with words. Brother Ulcrist, master trainer, was a hawk, and as it were; with a hawk's eyes he could see.

"You are an Ael," I said. "Your race conquered our folk."

"FORGET THAT. You have my full confidence, Jacob.

Races of men rise and fall, but trust among warriors cannot be replaced. I will speak of these things to no monks, nor to anyone. I am your trainer. You must trust me. Admittedly you are not the best guardian monk, but there is promise. Do not veil your mind from me. I can tell when you are doing that. So be straight with me, and be not suspecting.

–tell what brings you back from Melancholy?"

"Master...last night I was in melancholy thoughts. for a long time in the dark I sat, as if the dark could comfort me. Some angel must have come and driven away away the demon, but still I did not sleep till the last hour.

Light pryed open my eyes as a new day poured through the window. I was glad to awake in my cell. Some days I do like being a monk.

I rose up, clothed myself and girded the rope about my waist, my beads with satchel slung at my thigh.

Melancholy thoughts fled like shadows.

The light, a new light; seemed to me brighter
and more excellent; less diffuse than other days."

"You therefore wish to be counted among the brethren of the light, even though you know we monks are wretched sinners all? Have you ever known lightbeams to be not casting some shadow somewhere? Some monks, hear me, feign piety, as if their souls cast no shadow. On the outside they seem as daylight, they do polish the cup's rim, but within their hearts they covet melancholy and darkness. Could this be the case for you?"

"No...I do not think so."

"Then I can only help you by training you as I have already. Do not forget what I have shown you this morning; can you tell me?"

"The shadow which the fighter-monk is casting himself...check it often. You showed us how to check our fighting stance by the shadow it casts. We must learn by it how we are supposed to look."

"Jacob, do not forget it. Make the break while there is still time.
Heaven admits no confused and unhappy monk."

Brother Ulcrist looked long at Jacob. He looked with the scrutinous eyes of a hawk, expressionless, as if saying to Jacob, "You are not good enough."

He wanted an explanation, an accounting. I had given him not much. That was good, he would be one to join the others in profiting at selling me. He did not see fit to counsel me then. I will forgive him.

y mind returned to present troubles as I continued the sightless woodland trek. Ulcrist, although not a friend, had trained me well, establishing in me the knowledge passed on from Tien Joshur. But I was not therefore less afraid, certainly not less afraid of the wolves. They must have picked up my scent, but they have stayed away...so far.

And who knows if that dragon of Galadif also has been sniffing around as well...or likely some other fur-clad tooth and claw beast lumbering around as well...I could drive off one beast certainly. But a stealthy pack of wolves would indeed be formidable. They would, if hungry, risk taking a monk, and if persistant they would get the better of me. Wolves take many travelers in the Lokken.

God even protects his wayward serrvants. I made it through another night, although never quite sleeping.

The light of morning revealed to me now a wilderness terribly unfamiliar. I was deep in unknown and mysterious regions.

I traveled that entire day, venturing in directions unknown, and all the more weakened and stumbling. There was a sturdy vine branch hardened by summer rays, something useful for the haphazard and pathless tread, or to use as a quarterstaff.

When I recovered a roadway, after some half a mile, I spotted from afar someone else on the road: a man, one who was stout, short of stature, but he registered otherwise undeterminate from a-ways off. The rush of snowflakes falling obscured the details of his features from my sight.

–a forest ranger? Even if just a woodsman, that's a relief.

The relief was not long lived. I glanced down to step over a fallen log, the road not being maintained. When I looked up again the stout figure was vanished, lost from sight.

By the time I reached where I had last marked the figure, I could detect a presence. A grand oak was beside the way where I had seen him, an oak taller and more eldritch than all others round, like an ancient sentinel. With a tremendous trunk, zigzag stretched the course of many branches. It was a Half-Oak, a tree sacred to the Aels.

I examined the path where footprints should have been in the snow, but found only deer tracks.

Then at once, there appeared from behind the massy trunk,

a plump little man, a dwarf, with great curly orangish beard

and mane, and burgundy cape. An axe was tucked in his wide belt. In the one hand he had a sack for carrying. He marked me not, but was busy gathering wild chestnuts and putting them in his sack. When turning about he spotted me, and startled.

"How now there, fellow! –Didn't catch sight of you on the road.

What brings ye into Ringwood and the Chestnut Vale?

An outlaw be you...roving the lands? I suspect it. Don't take my purse. I might appear downright harmless, but I am a vicious nibelung dreadfully skilled with cutting instruments, trust you. Some did learn it unfortunately too late, for many I've slain, not giving them a chance...but aye, otherwise fairly harmless."

"How nice to meet you. I am...or I was...a monk of God;" I said courteously. "no roving marauder-but a monk lost in these woods. I walk in peace and have never harmed any man. I am looking for shelter and some decent fare. My supplies are forfeit to they elements. I see in your hands that you've found some supper."

" *Was* a monk, you say? Then I wager now an outlaw monk, for a monk vows to always be a monk and never leave. But that's none of my business. Aye; decent fare I have found: on the forest floor. They are tasty troves, and plentiful. You would have some?" He stretched out his stubby arm with wild chestnuts in his palm.

"Certainly; but I do just now remember; the chestnuts of the Half-Oaks are reserved to the King. It is unlawful even to touch them."

"Heard you that?" he replied, smiling. "Not even to touch? You have lodged too long in the monastery, monk. The law does not forbid you to touch them. Seriously, you look hard pressed. Take one, and eat. The druids were wont to say that one of these would help make strong a good heart, at any rate."

"No thank you, I shall not. Perhaps it is for dwarves; not me. How gracious that you have thought of my health. I would be best helped if you might point the way to some friendly encampment."

"Hmmm, maybe I know one...but please; treat me as a fellow man. I am man, and only a half mix of dwarf. Everyone is half something or other, no? And heed not those forgotten half-regulations. The reason that the king's law was kept for this wood, makin' like the whole forest as forbidden, in fact, is because...back in those days, the kings, jealous of their power, condemned the place as enchanted.

If men came in here their eyes would be opened to the magic free for all, stored up within the fruit of these trees.

How else did you think the wizards of the first age acquired their powers; back in the days before Nystol? Certainly you have heard that.

But I have never heard of anyone getting sick from eating these."

Closer to that dwarf I stepped, intrigued. The dwarf did not lack charm but his wit was attuned to ways of the wilderness and the world, and he was someone of earthly power.

He held out his hand, generously offering the chestnuts.

"Go ahead. Most folk but half-recognize those forgotten dooms anymore. These be wholesome to eat; the easy kind; you can eat them whole without having to crack them in half. See; cooked or raw."

He took a bite out of one and smiled. "Nothin' like magic chestnuts; hits the spot. I am particular to them even without roasting."

So I took some from his hand, half-convinced.

How foolish. Not even the squirrels of the wood take them, for all creatures have wit of the prohibition.

"What does it matter anyway?" I asked myself as I placed one in my mouth. "Not bad..." Would the king's men even find my emaciated corpse out here if I died from hunger? It was tasty indeed. So I ate a few more. Would the great crown take notice of such minor infractions? Is a forgotten law to be always and absolutely upheld?"

"Your words betray you to be brightly prudent lad.
I am Grimble, half-dwarf of the Mountains. I will tell you,
if you just follow this road down, taking no turns where there is a cross in the trail, you will come to a crescent-lake and to our hunting encampment on a wee isle.

I'm with a few like-minded fellows. We will serve you some hot cider, warm rocks and a blanket. Now I must run along fast-footed before it gets late; it is unacceptable for me, being a dwarf, to be seen publical with a human. You will find a little boat, so just ferry that to the isle. You will find it. We shall await you."

"There be a dragon in these woods." I said. "Heard you that?"

"I heard." He replied. "...Don't fret.
That wyrm comes out only at night for what is offered him.
He does not bother with human flesh just passing through. The wolves be a greater threat, but they went North.
Mind you, I hear that those particular chestnuts make humans sleep, because the toxins do have a soporific effect. Take a nap under the eldark tree here before you set out. We shouldn't have you take the wrong trail for drowsiness. I shall leave some cider-pressed liquor in my boat for your headache. See you soon?"

I nodded agreement; for all seemed a good enough bet.

The dwarf turned and went off speedily down the trail, limping, as from some old wound.

At once a mysterious narcolepsy overcame me. I made for the huge Half-Oak, for there by the ancient trunk was a clear place where no chestnuts had fallen and moss provided a dry place from snow to sleep. Before the onset of evening I awoke.

What an awful headache. Although the snowfall had melted, the fogs and shadow seemed worse.

The chestnuts had provided a little strength. Even so, they were bitter to my stomach. I remained beneath the Half Oak and for a while did not stir, thinking for a time.

At last I got myself up and followed the trail, pulling my cloak again tight round. Passing some minor lakes and I spotted that magnificent winged half-swan; he was still near, a lordly but dangerous denizen of both air and water. He had been appearing now and again, sometimes even coming close in order to check my safety. But I was still rather famished.

If things got desparate enough, could I catch and roast my animal friend? Oh wretched flash of a thought! How shameful if perhaps the noble animal in some way might somehow detect these new meditations, alas my selfishness!

If the grand bird had been sent, it must be what Heaven planned, but not for a personal satisfaction. Our Lord fasted forty days and nights in the wilderness, to give example, did He not? Could not I go without fare for but a few days, making some recompense for my trangressions?

Afterall, those birds make assault with their beaks and webbed claws. To have one as an ally in dangerous places is a irreplacable help. Too bad he could not help me find my way.

So I went on. Through tangles of branches I spotted something: a campfire some ways off. This was certainly the camp to which the dwarf had invited me. I gave thanks looking upon that fire.

Flakes of snow dropped from the needle-clusters and pine cones and bounced on my shoulders.

In such a time the most basic elements of civilization bring such releiving sense: I imagined the flames were roaring; the fierce power of nature tamed by Man, it glowed as when the orb of the sun hurries below the rim of ocean and snatches the last moments of day. What hope for stiff limbs, especially after more than an entire day of traipsing through thick hills, fell and fen and through many a rocky and misty vale.

From a forested hill I looked down on a wilderness-lake. The fire was on an islet in the middle of the lake, a lonely shelter serried with fir trees.

Sweet were the fumes of the burning tinder that wafted my way. Descending, I went on hurriedly.

The lake was small enough to see the opposite shore, but large enough not to say it was small, being in the shape of a horseshoe. By the time I reached the shore a low cloud of mist obscuring mush of the shore began to move off. From the mid-waters to the brink of the shore the motionless water was a smooth crystalline surface of reflection. Starry night sent up the moon and the clouds above scudded away.

So clear and still was the surface I think it must have mirrored galaxies far above.

I climbed across slimy stones and narrow sand rim testing the way with the vine branch.

There was the cheerful little boat of which the dwarf had spoken. It was not moored. He had left a wine skin in the hull for me so I quaffed the all the liquor at once.

Away on the islet the fire was blazing. The campers were probably hunters and had taken some prize game and were preparing it. It smelled so good.

Without second thought I took the oar and pushed off.

Strange things transpire in the woodland dusk. Dusk; that time between the worlds of day and night when things are obscure and enchantment goes forth. The oars dripped lazily each time I heaved them up from the water.

The nautical design of that little boat was masterfully wrought. She was carved out of some whitish wood. So many kinds of wood there are, having learnt them in my training for fashioning quarterstaffs...but this wood I could not identify. The prow was finely carved with tracery of a delightful damask pattern, and her smooth bearing across the dark surface barely left a wake.

Finally I was close and called out in raspy and weak voice, "Hello up there! No alarm, a wayfarer requests help, being unarmed. I am a in need of some provision; the invitation is from one fellow, the half-dwarf Grimble..."

There was no reply.

That fire was suddenly extinguished. All the woods of the isle went dark. Danger was near with that unwelcome turn. Not enough danger however to turn back. When one is hungry boldness increases.

Perhaps they were not hunters. Perhaps they were travelers, or other dwarves. Certainly they had heard me. They must have heard me, but why did they not understand. Did the dwarf neglect to give them notice of my visit? Or did he not return to camp? It would make minor difference anyway, When I arrive and they see me approaching, having a cheerful face, and being a monk, they will not be afraid, Hopefully that dwarf was even now explaining that I'm no threat...and certainly they will not miss my torn habit. "He is a pious pilgrim." They will say, welcoming me and having me stay the night, with blanket no doubt.

And, if they do not offer it first, I will charm them for some fish, or a strip of fatty meat, perhaps a cup of gleaming cider, as the dwarf told.

Crashing through overhung brambles and over submerged branches, I rowed into islet's overhung shore. I looked about and saw not a soul, only the smoldering fire near, a sign that someone or something had just been there. The words of our Abbot came to mind:

"*Ware be thou, that wilderness is a place where demons dwell...*"

I stepped over the lichen-covered rocks and went in. Approaching a minor clearing, I could even see the shore opposite, for it was a island not half furlong width. Below on the ground the little campfire was yet smoldering. Where went those who had been tending the fire?

"Anyone there...? Hello...? You have a guest. No need to hide...one Grimble invited me here..."

Consider, brothers, that even according to simple peasant manners, one does not assault a wanderer in need, no matter how bothersome he might be. Although the world went through many mortal wars for centuries, hospitality was always the first rule.

It is true. In our time the love of men has grown cold.

As far as a wolf from dogs does an elf stay clear of men. Saga-sayers make a mistake in depicting elves riding horses, and purchasing books from scribes or potions from wizards, or even coming into town for the tavern or some other civil venue. They require none of those things, and seek no magic, nor have they any thirst for ale. Other kindred will come hither, aye, mayhap, but never elves. Rather do they remain deep in the woods or underground. Learn thou whatever lore they wish to impart and accept whatever is wise. Tell of your quest and win their favor, but avoid challenging them, for slayers of dragons the elves once were...

Entry for Elves in the *Intermundane Bestiary*

So I was in on a remote pine-forest island in the cold night. Dark ilhouettes began to take shape in my perception, silhouettes of armoured warriors, shadows against the moon's pale light that filtered into the camp. They of slight build, somewhat gangling warriors. As they stepped out from behind the great pines, eight of them I counted, armed with various weaponries, axes, spikes, swords. Their horned helmets resembled demons to me, especially in my half-delirious state. Moments went by as they remained poised. They were studying me, perhaps waiting to spot others with me. A drifting swag of smoke from the extinguished campfire slipped in and obscured them, but certainly I could tell these men were no hunters, nor cheery entertainers with the circus.

They shifted, moving into position, every step was cautious.

They advanced quickly and hemmed me in. Neither forward nor backward was advance possible, nor was there an opening on my flank—my fighting strength was all gone anyway. I might have at them with certain maneuvers which Brother Ulcrist had taught me, but I could not sustain a backlash. Even might I risk it, and the vine-staff would flash, yes, successfully fending off reprisals, but they would recover for more rounds and I could not gather the strength to continue, not in this condition.

Added to that, a sworn moral rule hindered me.

Heaven forbids monks do combat unless a sacred relic must be defended. True, we monks may fight to defend innocents, even sinners if need be. So commands scripture, but we must never defend ourselves, even when dishonoured.

Ropes at once slapped against my all too delicate skin. The sheer pain resulted in me dropping my spiral branch. Sets of hands grappled my legs from behind and I went down. It was easy for them to jerk me up and fasten knots, labyrinthine knots, which constricted me in such awkward ways.

...an easy catch. Had I just a smoldering of fire in my belly I could have taught them some lessons, (so I imagined at the time, but it was not really so, as it turned out that they were seasoned veterans. Eventhough they were not as sturdy as the great knights, these seemed much more formidable, like "demon-men," possessing unnatural strength and ability).

My cheek drew up the pine needles from the forest floor. They bound me fast by the ankles and then by wrists. The only answer to my groaning was an echo from the infinite forest. The echo, returning from that wilder mystery devoid of human habitation, groaned in a vastness of untamed beasts and primordial lakes.

Now these horned warlords had a commander.

The one who had that responsibility was disinterested in taking part in any further ruckus. Stepping away he went to rekindle the campfire.

The new masters of my life, these demonic warlords, began to sing some verses in their own tongue...I could not tell what language right away.

The campfire soon was blazing and the flames lit up everything with an orangish hue, and it made them all appear all the more demonic. Who were these terrible lords?

One warrior placed his hands on his ancient helmet and slowly lifted it off. The camp light defined part of his face.

He had pointed ears and capriform facial features, all which marked a considerable difference from your everyday Ael or Silurian. Was this an elf of some sort? My memory searched through images of the various races listed in the manuals. There are many races of men, races of various skin hue and comportment, and also races of various spirit, such as dwarves and elves. Is that right? Who can say.

The chainmail was an old make, and the helm as well, together with axe and shield from centuries ago. They had more the look of vikings out of some old northern saga. Certainly no gentle forest dwellers were these. A rare breed for sure, neither elf nor man; but what seemed a conjunction. "Half-elves" men loosely title them. But not as the "Courtly Elves" the *Sindar* of the extinct kingdom Plathonis, (Nigh two-hundred passings of Calduin since anyone in Whitehawk has had contact with that race). And these kind laugh, unlike the elves of the stories. That's because they are half men. When has a courtly elf of the old sagas, pure-blooded elf, ever been described as laughing?

There is a certain legend proposed for these mountain-dwelling half-elves. They themselves profess that it is no fiction, but I cannot accept it. Apparently the legend proposes on whence issues their kind. It is from an unnatural generation, resulting from an artificial hybrid: the union of elves with the daughters of men. Unlike the courtly Elves of the stories, these kind actually do grow beards. "Mountain men," or "elfbeards" the townsfolk call them, One who is observant might even spot them combing their beards or concealing their ears as they sneak into some town for supplies. They call themselves "*valraphs.*"

A frightful conversation in their native tongue commenced. As a monk I had learned a variety Whitehawk languages, some extinct for many ages. I had studied even a bit of elvish. Certain scholars of Whigg insist that elvish is merely a fabrication of bards. Elves, they arrogantly insist, do not exist. But these my captors spoke a kind of mongrel tongue anyway, so I got the gist of what they were saying; it was a mix of our own language, some elfish words, and something else, perhaps antique Osril.

Bound fast by the ropes and lying there on the forest floor I listened. At issue was cooking, namely, how to prepare human flesh, whether roasting or boiling is better. Were these mountain-men actually wild-men,? Or would elves really crave human meat? The old legends have little hint that wood-elves or mountain-elves take human meat. In my mental state I could not quicken the translating of their talk further, so I missed some things. I could tell this: whatever they were planning certainly wasn't to my benefit. After cooking me, this terrifying demonic crew planned to set my bloody head on the rocks...a macabre sign to scare off intruders.

Mercy! Vile goblins and bloody trolls do such things, but elves and half-elves? Not at all...
Or were they actually just a degenerate tribe of men after all?

Would they have any taint of pity in them? What has the hand of Darkness been preparing? For what purpose grim has that black claw-hand sent these demons down from out their remote sleep in mountainous caverns?

I was like one *having eyes but who could not see, ears but could not hear,* one who had refused to mark into what brambles his own feet were leading him, what thorns and thistles.

It is unwisdom to seek escape from oneself,
or from the sight of the God. Verily is it written of the heavenly ones:
Where can one go to hide from their gaze, or the gaze of him who sees all?

These captors said many mysterious things, but for your comprehension I place here full record of their heated talk:

"Well done, ye Valraphim...and now we have a prize.
...some youth exiled from the clans of men
...but see, clearly he be no arms-ready fighter.
He must be a scout, I would say.-could be a clandestine stalker for that wizard's crew that's seeking after us with dogs."

"If this one be a noble youth as you say, Storm, he is not a chitty-faced one." Another said. "Look close. The wretch be near first-beardling. It may be that this human gave ear to the whispers of fairy treasure, and he roves the wood. It's a good bet that he is come to make a play for it."

"He carries he no arms, having nar bow, nar axe, nar hauling spear?"

"—nar even a knife," another answered. "Just a stick has he. And by the look of him...can't guess for what mischief he is come. But look close, no beard, trimmed about the head, his crop harvested...some sort of thrall."

"Nay, 'tis cropped as a monkish cropping," said the other. "Aye, that's it! A monk count ye this one. Of that I declare full certain now.
The townsmen of Whilom do have monks to make worship."

"A monk?" said someone else. "If he be a monk...don't rough him up now or it will mean ill omen for us. He must not be marred."

Another said. "Naw... but let me look after him. And I give all you this warning. You don't touch him either. He is perfect for what is needed."

The one who spoke those last enigmatic words was the one whom I would soon learn was Thingle. The judgment he was about to announce was quite a surprising thing.

This Thingle stepped over me, and he stood there astride, eyes bright with excitement, horns sprouting from the helmet, eyes glittering with coldness.

Pine tree-tops swayed to and fro against the blackness of the night air. The warrior glanced about at his brutish fellows.

There was no response from them.

"Think on this, Valraphim; if we have captured a monk indeed, we who rarely ever encounter the likes of such servants, then something in the stars be afoul. Rope-girded monks never appear in the high legends sung o' dwarves nur elves. Stormrake, you keep away from him.

If he be one who carries some plight on 'im, then I announce this: the song of the enchanting lady be ABOUT TUH COME TAH PASS. 'Twas a prophecy of mis'ry that yur pythoness uttered:

the one consecrated to the Nazarene will repair the rift and summon the evil day. Somebody must therefore be ruthless and cut 'im tuh pieces; one-a-us has to be the nasty goblin, and right quick.

We must put blood 'gainst the curse."

"You got her utterance mistook, Thingle." warned the one is called Stormrake. "I heard that enchantress. What she said was, not "*one consecrated to the Nazarene will repair*," but that the one consecrated will "*make the Nazageist despair against an evil day*"...she was saying that a Christian monk will finish off the Balecrown. Our Song-lord himself has written a letter to recruit an extra monk"

"Not only that, but it were bad omen to off a monk," added another, (in the confusion I cannot now recall which), "...prophecy or nay. If we off 'im, then we be cursed under Heaven...hmmm... but if we do not, then we risk that he will fulfill prophecy. 'Tis a vexation, I do declare to the contrary."

"...Right..." Thingle said, "but do not fret. As a favor to all you fellow soldiers, I, Thingle, will do the grim work myself, as it seems best. Now observe it exactly, all of you, how I shall do it. Watch close and take careful note in yer minds how such a thing must needs be done. Observe his blood to squirt out in a certain rather excitin' way, a bit of crimson artistry, all for good laughs..."

This "Thingle" extracted a shortsword from his baldric and brandished it on high for showing all, his eyes twinkling. He gripped with both hands and summoned all his might.,. to pierce as a singular thrust.

On the verge of the abyss, and dark Hell opened its ravenous jaws... There was a length of moment before the self-appointed executioner, this elfbeard Thingle, jerked down his cold battle-blade. I attemped to jerk away.

Someone pulled back on his arm however, someone reaching from behind. The would-be executioner tottered. The aimed thrust was left unfinished. Another voice spoke.

"Hold off from carnage not yours, darn fool Thingle!"

It was that friendly one, the voice of Grimble the dwarf! How I was exceedingly relieved! Grimble would explain my trespass to them surely.

"The only curse this one knows," he said "is the curse of virginity. I just remembered, Thingle: these monks may never take a wife. He is a half-man, a virgin. How disreputable is that? To spill his blood is a duty. It is come now time for Grimble, the son of Olofas, to render what offering is due to the gods! It is not for you, Thingle. Get back."

"No. It is my work."

"What? No? Thingle, how now do you dare say no to me?"

"I shall do as I wish, Grimble. The blood-lettin' to be acheived is mine honor. It is mine!" Thingle was deeply agitated, his breathing quickened.

"Are you gonna to go against ME?" The red-haired dwarf warned him in a loud whisper. "Careful, Thingle. Watch your words, Thingle! This is not your claim. Stand off, I say. Only one may shed blood; you learned the ritual. I am priest and shall do it when ready, when the moment is right.

This one be consecrated to another god. Tis a special case."

Another helm sported brass wings outstretched, a champion with them, "Stormraker the Beardless.":

"Neither of you will spill his blood...he will fetch a glad ransom, and plenty of it. I, Stormraker, claim 'im as hostage of the Valraphim, so the code warrants me. I outrank you both. Besides, he is not the one prophesied, the one foretold by the enchantress. He is too young. He could not have learned the tongue of the ancients over many years. He cannot be the one.

Did you think the flames were to roast him?

I know you are hungry, but eatin' humans,

that is in no wise lawful. Stop regarding your bellies always."

"Its me-head, not me-belly." Thingle shouted back. "'Twas my idea to light up a good fire to draw 'im 'ere, and a high cleverness that be, for townsmen get chilly when winter comes. You all got logs-a-burnin; like gleeful goblins. But all this was my idea. Since you get hungry like me, you also have plans to chew flesh tonight.

Nobody here has made pact to not kill.

Our pact was to harness no magic, 'gainst that we swore solemn, aye."

"Naw, Thingle, naw Storm," bellowed Grimble. "Here now...he is my catch. I seen 'im first and said the luring words to reel 'im in."

They glared at the dwarf Grimble. The elfbeard Thingle was defying Grimble the dwarf. He would defy also Stormraker, who was a superior officer.

Thingle spoke again: "I no longer reckon it be high wisdom, Grimble: doin' whatsoever you want of me. See, I have my own mind still this night. Honor is owed me by right...and there's been much cogitatin' in my brain lately...it's my turn to offer sacrifice, and yur bellies have had enough of bein' empty!"

"And who again be YOU exactly?" Grimble asked, indignant. "What a vainglory of words you belt out tonight, and from so unaccomplished a rank! Else you are sick with cave-rot. Think what has been done fer yer hide, the debt cha owe the old ones, yer submission, Thingle, whats gotten into ya? Remember, you've been trusted with somethin' rare!"

Fitfully I glanced around hoping to find some sentiment of pity in the other soldiers. The one named Stormraker stepped in to end it, pushing away Grimble. "The monk is "hostage of the Valraphim, by law free from the death strike." Stormrake stood there unmoved, guarding, and waited.

"Thingle, you are me partner," Grimble continued, "...and so you get your chance another time. Hold back, else my deadly dagger slice it twain. I found 'im first...and you, lawful Stormrake, you have no claim either. You know the law. This human I found me-self, and he came by mine invitation. Also I readed the boat me-self and happens me-self owns her. 'Tis a thing fatal and weird. The spirits led the boy across the forest and he took in mouth the forbidden chestnuts...so my cleverness brought it about. It was meant."

"Aye, the witch will not be refused," remarked one of the others, sternly, as a protest against him.

"Let the captain decide it," another interjected. "It is the code: avoid the quarrel with higher rank, but let top rank determine what be fair. Captain, what determine you on this matter?"

The captain was watching. He was also half-dwarf nick-named Drocwolf, short for Draug Dhu-nibelung which means "wolf-berry dwarf." He had been standing apart by the fire listening. He had a patch-eye and a steady, sure voice, being older and experienced, of wrinkled brow and many battle scars. This was a true veteran fighter judging by the glance of his single predatory eye. "What controversy now? Step away and keep down your cries.
Grimble, stand off, I say!"

Grimble grunted fitfully. He lowered his weapon and stepped back, pouting. It was an immature complaint; much like one who cannot obtain that for which he yearns, and therefore bitterly prays for the world to end.

Drocwolf the captain declared an explanation for the decision.
"We don't crave human flesh, all ye, blasted goblish knaves!
You know the law. Can you not see that he is one of the rope-girded monks from Whitehaven, monastery-upon-the churning shores? Do you not recall him there, watching, when we played our gig in the show?"

Drocwolf bent down toward me and peered directly with his one good eye. "This is an obscure location, monk. Here is a lake in hilly northlands, hidden away by the Ringwood, nar even any woodsmen venture so far. It's been a secret, slumbering in stillness and quiet for hundreds, nay, perhaps even thousands of winters, untouched by men and their saw-blades. Monk, harken to me. For sure the lake has changed shape since the day the divine hand drew back the Deluge.

Look up there above. Her swaying pines are high-reaching, sentinels primordial, I say of a purity preserved from Time's dawn. Few ever this beauty will see. Here is serene simplicity, monk, and those towering trees are more than trees, but a mystery for your mortal eyes. Be glad you are here."

"Enough poetry!" grumbled Grimble. "As all rightly suspected, his be no disguise. He be then in truth a monk. I have warned ye all; the witch— her eldritch prophecy cometh soon to fulfillment, even this night! I will put a stop to it."

"I was the one who first warned on that," said Thingle.

He stared at Grimble. His face was also purple with rage. He stepped athwart me, the bound monk-captive, with intent to end any further parley by a definitive use of his short-sword...

> "Unless you have actually seen an angel, you will not appreciate the severity of our penances."
>
> *heretical monk of Vath*

Something transpired next that no one expected. A sudden terror from above, an onrush from on high, Terror flying that swooped down with a blur of feathers flapping like the onslaught of some avenging angel.
Twas no angel, rather a lordly animal was this terror.

The half-goose Aileron worked this valour, the winged guardian which the hermit, servant of the Ancientmost, provided me.

O humbling power of destiny! I owe my own life to this fowl. I owe it, friends, believe you this: to a mere animal God has indebted me.

How did that famous winged beast perceive my plight in so timely a manner? The creature had days before abandoned me. That was of course prudent. Now, oh to my astonishment, he appears back at service to go at odds for me against my captors.

Do you recall how the blind Hermit communicated to the bird such a task? The bird was to be loyal, a deadly guardian.

The white blur of flapping wings and webbed claws perched on Thingle's helmet. The nervous half-elf was startled and taken by surprise. He removed several paces backward. The wings flapped and the black beak snap-snapped for the greater part of Stymphalian havoc.

These mountaineers would never have guessed it. A bird was bold enough to have at them, unafraid of their bows, battle-axes, spears, even had their short-swords been swiftly unsheathed.

The great winged-one was deadly and fast.

After confusing Thingle he assailed one elfbeard and went right on to another, snapping at their faces in rapid succession. Confused, they did not upraise their weapons. The soldiers withdrew seeking some distance from the fray. At last the magnificent creature stood fast between, squawking fierce threats, wings outstretched. I were one of her own chicks.

"What accursed flapping thing is that?" said Stormraker. "The thing bit me, nasty bird! Tore at my cheek it did! Lucky it didn't pluck out me eye. The monk has unnatural allies!

So we were right...our hostage is not of the usual strain!

Aye, consecrated to the Nazarene he must be."

"It matters for little," said Thingle. "As soon as my hands find oppurtun-ity to chop the hose-neck of that flapping fowl, your bellies will be thankin' me, and we'll be tasting bird-meat, a fat supper, both bird and human flesh. Such honour is mine. No valraph may tell me what to do anymore, not Grimble, nar any be he high nar low."

No half-elf had the grit to go against the great half-swan, not even Thingle, whose declarations fell empty. The fighting fowl is well renowned for precision smiting.

"What be wrong, all ye? Be ye all craven crotchers?!" the captain Drocwolf bellowed.

Still they held back.

"I'll report to all back home, trust it, that each of you were chilled by that fat bird, not one of you even producing the intestinal fortitude of nasty goblins. Ye are nar Valraphim, afraid of a feathery fowl with webbed feet.

I cannot believe me-eyes. Chop off the top of that spooky flapper!-and you had best make quick work, if would ye sup tonight! Marshal up! Advance together, smite and maime the wings. But mark this: don't damage that monk it is fending. For the monk we will fetch us some heaping coin as ransom. Close in all ye now!"

All at the once the elven mountaineers with readied blades stepped toward the great goose rampant with wings rising.

The creature held ground, valiant, a thing hard enough to imagine. He did his feints so well that it seemed almost if the staff-master Sodd Bloodman himself had trained him. After a few rounds he tired.

Through the trees and branches he flew and circled the islet, searching for another passage.

Then he was gone, aloft upon the western breezes of night.

"Supper slips away from our grasp again!" cried Grimble.

"It would have been a tasty one," remarked the captain Drocwolf. "...roasted nicely over our flame, meaty and juicy. But keep all ye a nervy spirit. We are Valraphim, we can take any turn."

"And the hostage? How do you judge, Captain?" asked Stormraker. "The Crown will reward us well for saving him; a right monk is worth something, if he is rightly right. We shall see. If we do not obtain that for which we invest ourselves, then he will be our only profit. Otherwise the nobles of Thulez or Hyrcanth might have plenty o' coin for a learnt servant...bah, but we cannot sell a monk.

...but if the rations run out before then...we may need to boil his flesh,..an arm or a foot at a time, perhaps the law will permit it. We shall ask the Song-lord."

Stormrake gazed at me, grinning, as if Captain Drocwolf spoke in jest, but I found little humour in it.

"This one be ours now. So, Grimble, away with yer complaints, and—"

"What say you if he be indeed the one prophesied?" asked Grimble, interrupting, cross at the decision. "We can hazard no chance if he be. The fate so uttered must not come to pass in any way."

"Grimble, cast off the false prophesy which that the sylphan enchantress simulated," said Stormraker, "—that old hag. Her words are damned. She wove a spell in your mind, she did. Think hard on't: if it be in the stars that some virgin-man bring about the unthinkable, that the ancient citadels of Nyzium should rise again, then it cannot be avoided, no matter what you or I do! It is fate. Only by fulfillment of the law can any hope to escape such a plight. So why risk shedding a monk's blood and angering the Ancientmost?

Do you think he believes in stars? He put the stars!

Now go after yer duty, keep watch on the shore..."

"Keep watch... Oh not again. Say...the lieutenant has the watch now. It is not my hour!"

Droctulf the patch-eyed dwarf cleared up the matter. "Then if it is the lieutenant's watch, he should be already lookin' after the duty. Enough murmuring...we must have strict silence. There may be other monks of his ilk about. The goose's echoing blast will have perked up ears."

"Right, captain," replied Stormraker, "So then it is my watch. Stormrake will get ready for keeping the watch." The soldier stepped away to gather furs. It was Stormrake, the champion, only one of them who did not have a beard, and who had preserved me. I earnestly did not want that one to leave the camp.

"According to the protocol," said Grimble. "a captive should be interrogated. Let us do so. Then we shall know for sure if he is the one."

On this point the entire band together concurred.

"Right..." said Drocwolf.

The captain came close to me and leaning down peered into my sullen visage."Cry out again," he said to me in a low voice, bulging fiercely his eyes, "and we will be havin' supper tonight for sure..."

He untied the gag.

"Now...What were you after out here...?" he whispered. "Why out so deep in these woods, at this hour, manling?"

I was discombobulated from the tumult, and far too spent to fabricate a decent explanation. "—I went and got myself lost, sir,... so now seeking a little provision... The dwarf Grimble told of cider, and warmth of crackling fire."

"You be indeed into the fire now, lad. Ye should have kept yerself in that frying pan ye call monastery." Grimble glared at me with wild eyes. Drocwolf looked straining again, with his one intact eye, jerking about in its socket.

"Craved he a little cider? I say he is too much the fool," said one of them, "–or knows how crafty lies are passed."

"He is a beardless one, and young." remarked one of the others. "...and too wary of us elfish mountaineers to speak squarely."

"That may be..." remarked Drocwolf with admonition. "...there is said a well-known saying; *all who wander are not lost.* "Aye, he is easily a run away wanderin' monk. But we must have hush now, and put off any further talk." He gave orders in a loud whisper, "Keep the flames low...Stormrake, watch you fast upon the western shore. Tread quietly; all quiet."

Stormraker the Beardless nodded and disappeared into the mists.

"You others, keep your peace now and listen...another like this one may tread nearby."

"All quiet, Valraphim." they whispered to each other.

Those cold forests are eerie in the hush gloam of late Autumn.

There was a prolonged silence as these mountain-men stilled and listened for sounds or voices echoing in the misty and murky woods. A grinding windmill away far off in the town of Whilom could be heard. A few moments passed in silence, and still more time. A drip-drip of droplets tapped upon rusty forest leaves.

"I says it to all ye again," Drocwolf said in a loud whisper, "and weigh it well, if you're smart hell-raiders you'll see clearly that we can win ransom for this one's hide.

But you remember why ye valraphs came here, do you not?

Do you, Buckbar? Do you, Corydon? Not for loot, mind ye,

but rather a higher cause. Keep ready, the Song-lord will show soon enough. I reckon those hunts and the doggards that we heard at sunset are even now close on his trail."

"The minstrel will show soon?" said Grimble with cynicism.

"—incarnate fiend, he! Fie! Arrogant "pure-blooded!"

Now see, I be weary o' lingering here in these damp woods.

We came to put down an intermundane wyrm, haul away its carcass and trove, not tarry in the nowhere like nincompoops." Grimble frowned, added more provocation, "How long then, Drocwolf, keep we on this blasted isle without pies or mead, and not a taste o' roast?"

"Yank back the reins on yer murmuring, Grimble," Drocwolf warned. "You will be found a malapert, with a lashing due.

We cannot hunt a dragon if we ourselves are being hunted."

"Just shy ten days have been spent." Grimble snapped bitterly, "...we rot away to bones, keepin' for that minstrel of yours to arrive...and he's not even a valraph like us, but the blood of more mischievous fairy runs in his veins. He's probably havin' his fill o' nectar even now.

Consult your wisdom; the purpose of our holding this ground

he keeps to himself, a secret, not trusting the rightly-sworn.

All the while we must heed of your corrections.

Well now, some have had enough o' this, livin' off

chestnuts and berries. I need a goblin's meaty fixin's

...and so I am ready now to fix you straight...!"

"What meanest thou? Have you gone mad?" said Drocwolf. "Do you not cherish the oath of a Valraph?"

Grimble grinned, and his eyes glinted like the breakers on the cold Northsea. There was indefinite silence. He straightway turned over his boar spear and couched it, opposing the point to Drocwolf. The dwarf was round behind me. I remained bound and kneeling.

"Valraphs! Ha! ...hear it, ye dogs be all mongrels. But nar am I pure nibelung as of old. I be a half-blooded dwarf, scion of the human Olofas; as was me-great uncle long centuries past, the Dwarf-Emperor Nergalf. Therefore be afraid."

He cast away his spear and unsheathed a deadly dagger. He whispered in my ear.

" 'tis a vorpal weapon, monk. Don't even budge unless I say."

With his other arm he locked me and readied the wavy-serpent blade at my throat. Now the others saw it, and their blades and war-weapons they hefted ready, and faced opposed. Thingle turned about and stepped over behind Grimble. Two were on one side and many others were glancing back and forth, not being clear whether to side with Drocwolf or with the other.

Their faces were writ with alarm, and the valraphs glared most uncharitably at one another.

"Mutinous ...Grimble!" bellowed Drocwolf "Who be you now to take a hostage to yerself? It is worst defiance yet made of right conduct. Would that the Song-lord had announced his suspicions early on. He should have spoken up. You've been naught but bad talk and mischief!"

"So he told you his suspicions? Who cares what he thinks. Suffer me to pour this human's mortal blood upon the earth, right now. Then I'll forget grievances—namely your perilous captaincy. If agreed, I'll do whatsoever Droctulf requires. This human is, know it, me own catch!"

"What is this, Grimble?" said Drocwolf "Why do you require spillage? So you can appease extinct gods with innocent blood? Not under my watch. We observe fair conduct in this company. Yield up your arms! I had you a heathen-style dwarf all along;
you cannot play me for a fool!"

"Do ye even now fail to realize how the fulfillment of doom is written out plainly before us?" Grimble said. "This is the very one; the grey sisters put him right into our hands: an innocent monk! Even the fates are eager for us to escape the ancient doom, the wizard city Nystol rising from the dust!"

Drocwolf, captain of mountaineers, right away couched his spear with a flash of his hands. The controversy magnified to a high tension, and panic seemed upon the company of armoured soldiers. Each watched another's threat, glancing with baleful eyes. Would Grimble snatch away my life by a sudden pull of his dagger? If he did move to do it, the captain, Drocwolf, with a sudden lance poised, could lunge against him...but it would be too late.

At any rate, I was precariously caught between sharp iron points about to unleash. Now I remained there on the cold pine needles, kneeling. My cloak wrapped about me keeping from worse exposure. I should right quick make some review of my life, and reckon my misdeeds, *peccata innumeribilia...*

So do I divulge to my brother monks the encounters with those beings, the Valraphs.

I confess vain curiosity about the world. All is made more clear in my *diarium*, the fault-journal. I place below an entry.

We will for the moment turn from the tumultuous scene, the elphic fighters and grim deeds, for a few leaves. We must return soon enough. Weigh now instead the words of my tutor Anherm. That beloved elder monk left a letter for me, as he was expecting to depart soon for the next life; Now in the face of my own death, my thoughts turned to the words in this letter.

Brother Jacob,

A few more days are granted me to sojourn in this terrestrial plane. Therefore I will have you no longer unknowing, but have you instead know things even if without you comprehending them right away. It is you I have chosen, albeit your mind is ready, but yet undisciplined.

Keep this close: powers, both visible and invisible, seek to hasten my demise. They are afraid of me, not of my power, but of what I represent. Wolves in sheep's clothing are preparing it. They are so shrewd that they will not leave a trace of foul play. They have even dared to don our holy cloth, our habit! They will act in due time.

Even Lazarus, whom Christ raised from the dead, could not escape the brutal assassins who later came for him. Before its too late, I must point you to the strange circumstances of how Nystol fell.

The Archscribe Morpheus Memnos was the first to record the story of Nystol, centuries ago, but he passed from the world before he could complete it. The work is known to be extant, but is almost impossible to find. Brother Orbian of Vath wished to make a summary of the events for memorization, since the papyri were in terrible condition and would soon become extinct. His work, The Great Burning and Banishment *is a worthy treatment, although only a poetic sketch. School children in Authapis, Regulum, Ulthor and other cities on the continent used to memorize it. But now the text has been outlawed in all lands save that of the Aels! Find these writings in the tome I am leaving, for it has the true history.*

Who is trying to suppress this awful truth, and why? The frailty of my flesh and bones humbles me now. The dark past is forever gone. I longed for what I did not understand, something beyond sight, some secret of the western horizon, things only vaguely sensed, hidden in rock and stream, oak and vine. So in my youth I admit, I did become a wizard. The circling years passed. When at last by some miraculous grace I found what is truly precious, the old longing soon faded.

Some time ago, I now recall, a certain wise man warned me on this. He was a devout woodsman with whom I shared fellowship. The man had a vision. He told me that I would pay the price for my faith. If I cling to the truth, he said, keeping my vow against all magic, the devil himself would in time come after me, the one who is "a murderer from the beginning."

Only you have the mindwise tools to use the tome I am leaving.

Beware. The translating skill I have taught you; the kings and princes of the earth will seek after you for it, and even the powers of the Netherworld. Fare thee well, good soul. Remember humility, for it makes a man worthy of God.

Please, cease not to pray for my poor soul.

Thy brother in Christ, Anherm

The mysterious "tome," the tome which he hid away and which he commended to my use, was a treasure. I would not let it slip away. Unfortunately older monks reached Anherm's cell and extracted all writings the very hour that he died. There is left only this letter, which he handed to me, not two months before his last day. I was to unseal it only after his passage.

As a child, when my father was still alive, I obtained scant degree of bookwise learning. We did not go into the towns often, because the folk did not speak well of my father. Telling tall tales of magic does not make one popular with those who depend on the favors of angels in order to survive.

My father had known Anherm in the time before the wizard Anherm forsook being a wizard and became a monk.

There was a time, you know, brothers, in the age before ours, when the word "wizard" evoked not thoughts of charm, but of terror and sacrilegious outrage.

Anherm would to persuade my father turn away from pagan darkness, like he himself had. *Repent, and believe the gospel.*

As far as being merry friends they had much to be at odds over.

Neither would he dare a truce or compromise. My father was one who indulged in strange company: cunning wizards and pagan priests. As for me, I could not explain why I admired Anherm and the peaceful monks more so.

Eventually my own father noted this, and came to resent it, calling my church-going conformist and elitist. I became estranged to him. A swineherd by trade, he forced me go and submit to the blood-painted warlocks in the hills who beat on their great drums. He demanded that I conform to the old pagan ways.

Worship the dragon.

I refused and cited the All-law. In obedience I went into the hills anyway and appeared before the warlocks to hear what they had to say. They did teach a certain wisdom, but they were themselves lacking instruction regarding the most important wisdom, the one eternal God.

It was not long before I yielded to the demand of integrity. I refuted the warlock's troll-lore with only those few lines of sacred verse to which I had been exposed. After all, *What fellowship does light have with Darkness?*

The warlocks saw dishonor for their kind in keeping with me. They returned me and poured shame upon my father for his son. "Insolent, questioning behavior will not make for magic instruction," they said. As for my father, they pointed to the fact that he was a friend of brother Anherm, who for them was a traitor.

They confronted my father over these things before the bonfire at summer solstice, and the High Warlock rebuked him and stripped him of his power, and of his magic robes. This was a profound shaming. The life of a Warlock, in my father's mind, had been the highest possible honor.

After a time of pleading, he decided to forever disown me. He abandoned my mother and me. He went to live in the caves. He never returned to our village. A year later the king's soldiers reported him captured and executed in the Arcane Wars of the pagan uprisings.

My mother could not support us both, since I was growing and required more and more sustenance. When the time came, she made me a warm wool cloak and sent me off to the monastery to sue for admittance, to live with Anherm, whom she knew would look after me.

The monks accepted me as a novice even though I was unmannered and uncultured.

Even after a period of fasting, when invited to dine, monks do not partake of victuals until first Abbot has tasted. That being observed in a postulant, he should then be invited into the life. Right manners quell base hunger, a sign of good preparation.

As a boy I had been almost entirely working with the swine!

Several boys craved admittance. Enwick and I were the only boys not to taste the soup immediately after the bell was rung for orphans. Eventhough we had not had any fare in days, we watched and waited for Abbot to put his fingers to the spoon. Even with the sweet steam of hot vegetable soup reaching our nostrils, we did not move, We did not give into lower impulse. The others at once picked up their spoons and, dribbling, rushed to fill their bellies. Perhaps it was the Lord's permissive will that one so unworthy as I unfairly learned the secret, cheating some other poor lad out of the Lord's inheritance (as once did a young lord in scripture). God's will is inscrutable.

After several seasons learning the ways of the sacred fold, my life as monk-in-training had become happy.

I was going along rather straight and narrow.

There had been nothing of wars to concern us, save for the wars of the pagan-uprisings. Galadif was the only Kilurian town left outside the All-law and the Christian sway of the King. Monks today are removed from the war-council, eventhough the Whitehaven abbot once held a voice of power in the king's hall.

After the Arcane Wars ended, the monks of Whitehaven no longer engaged as political councilors. Only the Friars of Whigg have such prestige. However at the king's request our guardian-monks may be drafted in wartime.

I am now many more winters and, although without a full beard, I am said to be one who is highly educated and can even teach Latin. We monks have clean bedclothes all the time, warm bath-water, a monk-physician to attend to our every ailment, and our meals are hot, the excellent work of trained culinary monks. Although our daily tasks are base, we do not work too much and even sleep during hours when we should be busy. Of course, and it need not be said, this luxurious state of things does not favor a monk's penitential purpose.

There walk many badly behaved monks, monks who refuse to repent, who are only in it for the comforts. Have any of us been in danger of praying too much? Our hands are soft as were once the hands of the wizards of Nystol. We live off the sweat of the peasant's brow, filling our bellies. My friends, as it is written, who will teach us to flee the coming Wrath?

To the old gods I used to offer the most exacting and devout worship, libations to powers graven of wood and stone, *idolons* fashioned by human hands. This went on for years. All for nothing it proved. What help in battle did the old gods ever furnish my men?"

Duke Ikonn of Gorre
The Book of Bloody Battles

Return of the Minstrel   IX

Aileron the goose had displayed a kind of animal virtue and courage, so it seemed. Yet the great bird was outmatched.

All things seemed a blur that night.

So the captain had decided that I should live, to be kept for ransoming. The rebellious and crazed dwarf on the other hand could endure no more. Grimble had advantage, a vorpal dagger ready at the my neck. A cold parley went between Drocwolf and the mutineer Grimble. Within a flash all drew blades and couched their spears; fixed one against another, their faces purple with alarm, eyes lit up. Are these "valraphs" men tainted with fairy blood in their veins, or are they elves tainted with human blood?

Was there ever such an unseemly contention among those courtly and noble elves of legend? These were hybrids, these "elfbeards," more familiar to you as rough men than fine elves. And they were mountaineers who could scale any sheer surface or stern erthwerk, hardened outdoorsmen were they, but quick to the steel.

Now many other things were murmured in their mountaineer's jargon of which Jacob had only scant usage.

A flash of blood-letting was close. All the turns of his life in mind he was reviewing: how he had acted, things he should have done instead, the evils not done, weighing so lightly the counsel of monks, and a myriad of other failings.

To leave a monastery without permission, that was nothing to boast. Even so the good Lord does not forget a straying soul. As it is written, *he shall send send his angel before you*. Angels, after all, neglect not even a minimal prayer. Presently hooves were heard thumping through the islet's wood and obscuring fogs.

Some beast was entering upon the scene.

A figure mounted on an animal appeared and halted in shadow 'neath the fir branches. There, in the murk was a white stag, and a rider mounted thereon.

"Who goes there?" Stormraker called out. "Show yourself. Be it the Eloniah?"

"—He;" replied the mysterious rider.

I looked and the stag trotted forward, his antlers exalted out of the wood.

The rider was of a presentation fantastic.

His wavy mane and great beard were white as snow.

Though he was of minor stature like a dwarf, his presence was colossal. He was a being similar to a valraph, or some sort of elf, but much refined in noble dress. Wisdom was writ large upon his brow. His flashing eyes surveyed the scene like flowing waters. He rode upon a glorious white beast.

He held fast in his hands "the Chyldeshire," a famous double-horned bow not easily acquired in the legendary forests of that name.

The being was a gnome. He was not churlish
and certainly not puny as little creatures imagined
in silly tales or garden statuary. This one was much like a courtly elf, in radiance or aura I mean, not in physique. He eminated a luminous and wise presence. So as among the Elves long ago...

Therefore estimate this "gnome" somewhere between an elf and a dwarf, and were you to actually stand him betwixt each of those kind, you could not determine from which relation the gnomes mostly draw.

I looked again. The features resembled what surely suggests noble issue, but his voice had a certain carefree tone, at once both of gravity and levity. Bright but ghostly eyes conveyed something of the mystical. His locks of gold-white hair braided in barbaric style rested upon scaly armour. He wore a magical kind of hat, silvery corded, whose double cone pointed toward the heavens. The elfbeards were in awe of this deer-rider, but the dwarf Grimble had no time for him.

"The Song-lord returns!" proclaimed one of the elfbeards, "The Arcavir!"

"Oh, the minstrel hath returned! Oh boy!" Grimble muttered.

The gnome directed his mount right into the commotion. His presence at once caused break-up of the skirmish.

"Return yer arms to yer belts, Valraphim!" shouted the Captain. "This endeavor is under the warrior-poet, the Song-lord."

This was not obeyed by all, and Drocwolf kept couched his spear, and of course, Grimble pressed his dagger against my artery.

"Lay aside thy weaponries," the rider himself commanded. Finally they all obeyed, save Grimble.

The mysterious being at once ordered that role-call be announced.

So the captain, unmoved from his battle stance, listed them all: "Oath-bound Valraphim report!

Telperion Granoch, valraph ranger "-Aye!"

Thingle Marsyas valraph footman," "-Aye!,"

So too answered each of the following: *Buckbar Lancelas* valraph footman, *Daufin Nerileth* valraph champion, *Corydon Eletumal* valraph footman, *Finch Kelpeiros* valraph scout, *Jackthorn Syldein* valraph ranger, *Stormraker* valraph champion, *Drocwolf* dwarven captain, *Kruthendel* gnome bard,

and Grimble Forkbeard dwarf fighter...

"We caught this monk snooping around camp," the Captain explained. "But Grimble has mutinied. He has taken a monk as his own hostage, and threatens us with devilry and bloodletting."

"Why so long away, minstrel?" asked Grimble resentfully. "You are idle, coming around not when asked, and paying no heed when called. Mind you, a deadly strife is now uprisen among us."

"Mind yourself; to you I am not answerable, but rather are you answerable to me, dwarf. My ears caught unworthy talk just now, a felonius plot stirring. You and Thingle have a score to settle?"

"You come just in time for it, gnome."

"Grimble, are you had with excess of wine?" said the gnome. "Your own tongue betrays you again. Or did you contrive this in view as the skins have been empty for days?

Bad blood there is indeed if you seek a victim.

Why did you delay this so long? Don't answer; I know why: it has something to do with the ghost to whom you have turned back, like a dog to its vomit. I have already been suspecting it. We could have avoided many mistakes, so why did we NOT avoid them? Some malice blocked our foresight.

Now hear it: You and Thingle both must quit this resolute company tonight, or else learn its deadly limitation."

Grimble looked at Thingle, who returned a glance of uncertainty. "There is no way out now," he said. He glared at the minstrel. "Thingle, you swore a blood-oath." Grimble shouted. "Remember the fair witch's prophecy!"

"That "prophecy" was given by no witch," explained the gnome, "but an ethereal lady, a saintly woman that appeared to us down in the dark, sent by heaven, no doubt.

Both Storm and I agree, she prophesied no doom for men, but that a monk of God must be used against the wicked lord of the North, whose influence spreads over every land.

Why she appeared to us I cannot fathom.

We are no army to go against him."

There followed a silence that lingered.

"....and what of you, Thingle," said the gnome. "I never guessed you to be one to disgrace the elven house of your noble issue."

Thingle, a young soldier, froze. Nothing was spoken for an entire *tempus*. Tears formed in his eyes. Thingle doffed his helm and bending his neck down let his face be covered beneath dangling locks.

The resonance of the Song-lord's voice and words had moved him. He let go his weapon and dropped to his knees.

"You do most honestly and rightly ask, Song-lord. I beg all you, Valraphim. What Grimble has involved me in I cannot longer bear. May I not serve those fatal ghosts, shades infernal, anymore.

I did want much respect, I craved the rank of a glorious lord.

Not anymore..! I swear it off."

"Now what brings this unseemly turn!?" bellowed Grimble, incredulous.

"When I gaze upon the visage of the Song-lord," said Thingle, "and hear his voice, wicked thoughts quit me...and there is new hope of a sound deep to heart, and sleep without nightmares...I cannot go this way; instead I have a chance to fight out of it.

Become worshipful again I will...and a rightful soldier.

I renounce fantastical gods! Let Kruthendel, master of song, be my overseer! Have mercy on this sad goblish grunt!"

Grimble, who was looking upon this submission with contempt, spat at his fellow conspirator.

"You grovel then? Burn and blast your bones, Thingle!
The old ones have already claimed your spirit.
That's all you are, a goblish grunt, no Valraph. You don't care.
You would let all beings suffer again under the sway of Nystol.
You're a knave, and quite empty in yer head.
You could have been a hero like me,
and you would have won imperishable glory."

Grimble sighed as one sighs who is dismayed at all things. He said; "And this one here, this monk...for sure this is the one of which her utterance warned. A follower of the new god would do the deed, she said, like this one. Now the world is closely doomed!"

"I yield no more to any doom-say," said Thingle. "Nor to your old gods any longer, the prophecy I say is false.
The many gods are demons!"

"Don't you care what will become of the wide world?" said Grimble, "Don't you remember the feats of your great kin, and of mine, the delving dwarves whose hands built Nystol and then rightly desolated her? You self-pleasing elfbeard, Thingle!

I would rather end my days by starving, alone, in this grim wood, eaten by the dragon, than fall in battle beside a traitor like ye. Even I, a dwarf, cannot bear ye. Mark me, this question of loyalty calls some answer argued in blood. I'll venge me when the chance comes."

"It is you who speak with traitorous lips, Grimble," said Drocwolf. Neither Thingle nor Grimble responded.

"Enough of unworthy talk, Grimble," said the gnome.
"You have heard the law, and you tremble not.
Evil be you found. Leave us therefore and go serve alien gods.
Thingle, however, yields to our clemency.
I allow him to stay and to him will be assigned just penance as for any man...by the way, the hostage is not yours."

"So let it be done," replied Grimble. "I'll be finished with all ye now, and break off. Go my own way. But first I take *The Black Book*. It be mine by every right. I was the one recovered it from the dead. Give it me now, else the monk dies!"
Grimble tightened his grip around my neck.
"Do not think I will settle for something less."

The gnome sighed. "To surrender any of *The Black Books* would jeopardize our endeavor and extinguish hope. Outside the All-law nothing will light the way for you, nothing. Grimble, I warn you. We could arrest you for trial and execute you simply under the old code which has been long in force.
You forfeit the help which the true deity provides.
Is this what you choose for your final hand?"

"The minstrel speaks squarely, Grimble," Captain Drocwolf added.
"You cannot translate the text anyway. Even if you could, the secret lines are buried somewhere in over a thousand pages.
Why covet what is beyond the reach of your mind?

I think that you are looking to take glittering gold for it,
trading the codex into the paws of the jackels,
the Remnant Arcanes: Icloharius, or Zuphagen, or Oevius Flammonar.
Devious minds they. . .or perhaps some other Arcane?
They have been conniving centuries for a switch such as this."

"Not them..." replied Grimble. "Do they even yet walk the earth?
   Mercury-minded Arizel Apholulius certainly does, by means of magic no doubt. Other men have informed me of these things, noblemen not often seen.
   It concerns the prophecy of the old gap-toothed hag we all heard. Listen again. I memorized it word for word:
   "*The disciple of a new god shall know the spell and convey a blackened book, and Nystopolis shall rise again.*"
When we heard it, none of you Valraphs knew much on it.
   I, however, knew it to be fateful. But I admit that I cannot read the codex." Grimble was thoughtful for a moment, weighing something in mind. His eyes lit up. The Lokken wind howled.

"Aye, there are many *black books*, and I am not so foolish.
The eldritch prophecy must come to pass.
Could a mere mortal throw off how lay the crossing of stars?
Other reasons press me to keep the black book with silver-braces.
A few things in my clever mind I have from the Arcanes.
I am wise to what their fixin' to use the book!"

"That's because you met them and relayed them the hag's accursed words." Drocwolf said with indignation. "You even withheld this from the Valraphim. This day the darkly clad rider and his magic dogs nearly found us out, had not the monk, inadvertent, pitched off their scent.
   We have it that Arizel, that same wizard whom the Aels and all Maceonids call Bannock, poses as a princely guest, having infiltrated the noble houses.
Today he was out hunting all of us
on this sea girt island, that cunning mind.
So Grimble claims to know the reason of the pursuit?
Then lay it before us."

"First hand thou me the codex," snorted Grimble. "The old relic is a worthy treasure for my keeping!"

"Not at all, excepting you answer me."

"So then I will. They covet the book because they fear
what is writ therein: a great incantation."

"And how is it that you know, Grimble?" Drocwolf said.
"Did the demon-gods confide their purpose grim to you?
What was the price for this knowledge, Grimble?
Was it the flesh and blood of a sworn comrade?
Was it...the blood of the old dwarf Ginnar?
Why did nearly all the dwarves of this party meet their dooms?"

There was a guilty silence. Grimble looked askance.

"So it was as I suspected!" cried Drocwolf. "Does an honorable soldier let his compeer fall in combat without first taking painful injury to himself?

Rather he fights. He is a lion despite wounds, even if only to secure claim on his companion's corpse. Ginnar did not fall to the black arrows of the *bolgs* that hour, did he, Grimble? You finished him yourself and let his dark blood pour out for the lips of demon-gods."

At this revelation all the valraphs gasped in horror.

"We learn of the guile..." another said, "and how it was that a darkly clad hunter was able to reconnoiter our progress, even being able to reach this isle here, before us."

"Ye knavish spouts all!" bellowed Grimble, purple with fury and twitching with shame. "What I have done was for ye own good. The dwarf Ginnar was an old general and useless, but he put up a goblin's nasty fight. I slew him,
I did, on his knees. I sent my own kin back to dust.
Why wear such doleful visage? I had to see to it:
No one else would dare; he was weak and feeble.
The foolish codger stumbled about and found me calling upon the old gods. Bah, that's none of your business.
True, I accomplished an evil deed, but I would do it again, and again, a thousand times more; let horror come! Every Valraph swears to thwart the resurrection of the accursed Nystol. If none of you have the stomach for it, then I myself alone will do it, whatever the cost, even if, in the immortal name of great—" Grimble cut short the name of his secret demon-god.

He had now confessed the secret execution of his own kind
and so grinned with a grin full of daggers.

"...Look now, I do not in any way rue it," he said happily, "save only this: that dwarf Ginnar was once a passing hearty friend. You poor fools, the mountains embrace old Ginnar.
The berserker's draught of the eldritch mead
taught me how; it worked the very deed
by these hands. I put him to an honorable end, and did it
while his boots were on. He went not sick in some bed,
his war-deeds forgotten. He would have surrendered his own life anyway had he been wise to how much he slowed us down."

"But you are far from his style, Grimble. You offer not your own life as heroes do."said Drocwolf. "The great oathfold of the Valraphim, and the roots of the earth, cannot stay silent against you now, Grimble of Urahaus.
Yours is now to taste the bitter bread of banishment,
a thing worse than death. In the end your spirit, so benighted, must rove the wailing shores of the outer darkness."

"Banishment? I'll style each of you a traitorous marauder
when I return alone to the halls of the Valraphim.
Then it is you who shall be banished from memory, not I.
None of you reckon the power of the eldritch gods.
You have all lost your ways, a new god bamboozles you.
Your minds are weakened and unable to see how the fates
measure every step of us all. Only I can complete this quest.
You others do not measure up to the elves or dwarves of old. I shall do it alone if I must! –the book, minstrel, if thou wouldst continue thy earthspan."

That lordly being, "the gnome," and stag came up to me. He leaned and peered right at me, searching with strange grey eyes as to see within.

"Keep yer distance, gnome," warned Grimble. For moments there was nothing else said.

The gnomes pupils glinted like stars.

"By the look of his tonsure, I'd say you have a monk there, Grimble," the gnome said. "but one who is too young and has scant knowledge of ancient texts. He is not the one."

"Do not hope to defer the matter, Kruthendel, you crafty gnome. We dwarves did keep a few silver-braced books, whereas the elves did not keep any books, not-at-all. And you gnomes cannot live without them,
or at least sweetly-sung song.
I make consequent on what I say.
So what say you on this trade: the codex for the monk?
A monk is, after all, worth many books, and can make more besides."

The gnome leaned back, stroked his beard and sighed.
He frowned and breathed in deeply.
"There is a tome in Ginnar's old pack, but Stormrake has been loaded with it. Corydon, go fetch Ginnar's luggage and haul out the silver-braced book, that gloomy tome." Corydon was an otherwise jesting and rambuncious warrior, but in such moments he always went silent.

"Don't satisfy him any part," warned Finch Kelpeiros, "...it is evil come. We will all die steeped in gore against the reprobates if needs be!" Finch, an elfbeard identifiable by his particularly bulbous nose, was actually raised from childhood to work as a burglar, but coming near death in the dungeon he was adopted by a curious and clandestine organization, *the Guild of St. Dismas.* They take oaths to employ their skills only under rightful authority. Kruth chose him to be one of the Valraphim, using his old roguish abilities for operations against the powers of Darkness. He and Corydon were best friends, inseperable.

At his word Corydon Eletumal halted before going to fetch the luggage pack. He looked to the gnome for any change of order.

" 'Tis my decision." The gnome assured him. "Let the dwarves record it in dragon's gall, setting the mark in their annals. As Arcavir I command it."

So Finch nodded and Corydon went and looked after the task. The gnome from his mount glared at the mad dwarf. He spoke aloud:

"Now weigh ye closely all this: At any time during our journey Grimble might have cut our throats, just like camp-sausages severed, easy to do whenever long hours of quest usher in slumber. But he needed us to protect himself against other enemies.

Guileful, he has used us well. You were to cook his meat and look after things and haul cumbersome provisions.

He planned to heist the silver-braced book once we reached a town and bargain it for a fat price. Not often it has been...not often indeed, that *elphim* must answer so strong a demon-magic. Why do you not teach us how dreadful are your hands, even right now, Grimble? Instead you would make trade for the Acheulian book. Could it be that you are not so confident of that berserking power as you would have us credence?"

Grimble did not answer. He looked about. He was nervous.

Corydon, a moment later, returned lugging one of those cumbrous packs, dwarf-made, the kind adventurers strap onto their shoulders. I had never seen such a curious bag for lugging with many pockets and straps and danglestuff.

Corydon frowned and buried his arms in the pack.

He hauled out, with considerable effort, a rather substantial codex bound in dark grey elephant hide, with silvery braces, adorned with several mysterious glyphs.

He passed it to Finch.

"Master Kruthendel, we must not give this great relic over to a traitor!" Finch warned. He treasured the book, gazing upon its cover.

Kruth quickly steered his mount over to Finch and whispered so that the rebel could not hear, but I heard them.

"Bide your own counsel now. It is my task to measure these plans. The monk has some mysterious part. Give the dwarf what trove he bargains...tis too much encumbrance anyway"

"It be all of madness," Finch asserted. "We should fight him instead."
"Do not question. Obey. . .
You yourself have witnessed the bloody onset of the Wyrmheld.12
Who will deny that infernal possession rules them,
ones who move like the flashing of sky-fire.
Such a blood-thirsty spirit can possess a dwarf like him as well. I have no doubt he could send every one of us to the halls of twilight by his own mischievous hands, hands which the enchanted frenzy of the demon has quickened."

"What whispering keeps your plots privy?" bellowed Grimble. "Are you two lovers? Just put the codex back in the dwarf-sown pack. I claim it all, the whole pack." Grimble snarled and pressed his weapon at my throat again. "I'll need the remaining rations of dry meat, and the roots as well, all the dainties I can lug; in exchange I'll add some truthful wit."

Finch, reluctant, re-packed the cumbersome book. Corydon brought the food demanded. They lugged the full rucksack over to Grimble.

"Now Grimble, you have what you require, so just let the human go, and exchange the knowledge you bargained you would."

"Untie the monk; he will be coming with me a-ways, perchance you try somethin' you would regret."

---

12 *Wyrmheld*: fr. *The Intermundane Bestiary* "Of the men from Galadif, and others descended from the Atlanteans, ye may meet warriors who are intoxicated with the awful vice of battle lust. Scripture calls these berserkers *Anakim*. Ye cannot address or reason with these for they will assail thee at once. Mind ye, give them no quarter. Among the worst of this brood of vipers is none other than the Wyrmheld. The venom of the *drakodemon* has entranced them and they drink it down in loathsome rituals. They are consumed by that evil spirit entirely, and they have surrendered their humanity and even their personality···entirely."

"Do it, Corporal," said the gnome to Thingle. "...since you also had a hand in all this."

They unraveled the knots quickly. Insane Grimble lifted the rucksack and fastening it on to me stepped away from the circle. His blade was no longer fixed at my neck. The reputation as a berserker was enough of a threat.

"Be wise," the mad dwarf warned. "...in a rush these hands could catch each of you...and me bodkin run ya through, even to the hilt all drenched in blood. You know it be no empty boast...you'll die like dogs if any of ye challenge me. There be no more tradin'; just attend to what I require and all you may preserve your earthspans."

Thingle stepped aside. Grimble turned me around for Thingle to access the remainder of the knots. Grimble taunted him as if privately:

"Now behold it: Thingle son of Olofas unbinds a mortal fool, but he himself is found a fool scorned, a shameful thrall again!"

The brigadier Thingle in turn gazed back at Grimble.

"Woe cometh to thee, Grimble. Repent of this. Who among the rightful soldiers does not make service his foremost goal?"

"Careful, Thingle," the one-eyed Captain Drocwolf warned, "and all you Valraphim; set not your face against Grimble. He fights like a devil."

"Forced hallelujahs might be milk for you," declared Grimble,
"but I reckon things more as fits the heroes of yore
. . . along with them I say: better off below as a powerful lordling,
even in the gluttering furnaces of Dis, than a servant cowering, a servant chosen. And remember this: that it was Nergalfin, a dwarf, his sword vouchsafed Nystol's ruination all those centuries ago, so in the same way a dwarf will keep it from rising again."

What he said was true enough. You see, the dwarven engineers first built Nystol for the dark-robed wizards at the end of the second age. So, when at the end of the Third Age cunning Nergalfin the dwarf-emperor, sternest of all, obtained the Holy Lance, he sealed the destruction of that city.

Nothing, not even fear of hell's after-torments could ever keep Grimble from extolling that famous legacy on behalf of his hero Nergalf. It must never be continenced that Nystol rise again, no matter the cost for Grimble. It was a question of honour.

But Grimble also feared a widely held belief:
only a demon-god could see a fate warned about in prophecy.

"Aye," Grimble admitted. "Things were said. Now you, Thingle, are found worse than I; at least I shall make a proud catch for death, if that forsaken power come. And though I die, my rank deeds will remain infamous till doomsday. Remember, I hold fast to my word, evil tiding though it be. Now keep smart; hitch the pack onto the manling." He whispered harshly to me: "...and in case you, mortal, have any thought of running off with your long legs, remember this, Grimble the Quick won his council-seat by a consecutive bringin' down of twenty hares; by axes hurled."

After a few backward steps down to the islet's narrow shore we boarded the boat. Stormraker had come up from the watch and was at the rear of Grimble and myself. The warrior could have surprised Grimble, but the gnome signaled him to stand down.

Grimble said more: "And of the self-righteous "Arcavir," who is really just an elf-inbred and book-thief and lyin' fairy-bard

—regarding whatever might say he about me—I want all the Valraphim to know: I honor the bargain and will exchange what I know...even outlaws can have honour...I shall let the monk go by morning...but I will not speak truthful wit until I am in this icy lake and on the fey-hewn vessel."

Grimble tugged me toward the boat, and I nearly stumbled backwards. My boots splashed into the cold water, and I almost slipped on a mossy rock, for the rucksack unbalanced me. It was much more cumbrous than one would expect from a pack of dwarven-make. At last we were both aboard, after much effort. Grimble had to keep his eye on those he was betraying. He pushed off from the shore with the oar.

"What usage have you with a monk, Grimble!?" Drocwolf called out from shore, mockingly. "Will you have him for workmate in the circus?" Grimble had me paddle, and did not answer.

The Arcavir, wise to his purpose, instead answered Drocwolf's question:

"It is already past the winter solstice. Is he tracking Saturn instead? The planet will not be in position again until midnight next. Grimble must therefore wait to offer the hostage as a sacrifice to the old dragon-spirit... but he knows that we can track him down and catch him if sleep comes, or that I can easily employ some bardic charm on him. He would not risk waiting a day. He must be after something else. I do not know what he is up to. It was just a trick? Or if not, he may trouble to keep the lad until after the next twilight."

"This morning at breakfast he said he had climbed up that mighty Tor risin' above the treeline just yonder," added Stormraker. "Said he would go climb it again and snag some eagle-eggs. Then he said something else I did not full reckon.

That there was a giant's seat up there he had seen.

He wants to see it again. I say he was lying again."

At this remark the gnome turned and looked. Something had just opened to his mind. He said nothing.

Grimble spoke out from the middle of the lake in a gleeful vaunt. He did not have to shout. The still and gleaming surface carried the sound. He spoke of an intonation to stir the vortices. An Outhapian astronomical tract claims to mend the Hypostatic Rift,[13] thought impossible, and so to bring

---

[13] *Hypostatic Rift:* This was a world-changing rift in the fabric of the Kosmoid which occurred on account of space, time and causality idealized beyond the metaphysical determinates of the known. Voethius claims it was the result of a conspiracy. It first took shape in two opposed camps of Arcanes on disagreement over how matter and form combine in a substantial (and corresponding superstantial). -full treatment in index

about Nystol's restoration: a spell preserved somewhere, possibly in one of *The Black Books*...a spell authored by Simon Magus, genius of Sorcerers, archenemy of St. Peter. I wondered over it.

"Do the remnant Arcanes look to resurrect Nystol the old college of wizards?"

"No," Grimble said, "they want to extract some written spell for something else. I'll sell the Arcanes the silver-braced book, but it will take them a thousand seasons to translate."

The gnome directed his mount trot up to the lake's rim. He said, "Be all such spell-force drawn from the vortex, Grimble. How could a spell repair the Rift, if no spell these days can extract force from the vortex *because* of the rift? How? T'is not possible —unless one could mediate the planetary alignment

...but that is unheard of, not to mention life-devouring.

What's more, not even the most wizened of would-be-wizards in our time can even translate those words... especially not an astronomical tract, not one writ by Olophyxus.[14]

Think over it, Grimble, what if that monk manages to escape you, seizes the old tome and escapes you...?

If he is the one, as you suspect, he will indeed translate the words.

Then that fair witch's prophecy will be fulfilled

...by reason of your knavish score! The monk will mend the rift.

Nystol will rise again. Leave off the monk with us instead; don't take such a great risk with wizards."

"Wizards, aye, and of many other things in the wide world besides them men should be wary," said Grimble. "I keep my own council, lovely minstrel...

I advise you, and every valraph, endeavor not to trick or spook me... Now then, human, a steady going, mind you. Keep course where I direct. There's no escaping my swiftness. You have heard the others; I have me some deadly demon-gods for friends."

I meant to speak, but the crazed dwarf cut my words off.

"Keep any words barred behind your teeth, monk, if you mean to ever speak again. We go ashore exactly where I point. The Ataluran edge of a vorpal weapon15 is at yer neck. Mark thou that lofty tower of rock jutting there yonder arisen? That's where our heading must be.

Just opposite the Tor with the henge altar.

There the alignment of planetary influence will perfect the offering. Do as I instruct and who knows, you may yet learn something of honour before death...aye, death, lad. I bargained with the gnome to return you in

---

[14]*Olophyxus:* A famous Rumilian astronomer who wrote prophetic treatises at the end of the third world-age.

[15]*Atalur:* A land of many small fortresses or western principalities in the East founded of the Atlantean colonists in the second age. —full treatment in appendix.

I do so.
The Wyrmheld are berserks; and much worse than Vikings. Their witchery bestows upon them a sort of unnatural speed in combat.

Entry on WYRMHELD
The Intermundane Bestiary

X   THE MUNDANE SACRIFICE

ne morning, a couple of years before all this tumult, I went on a stroll outside the monastery walls below the cliff of Whilom. Distracted from prayer I happened to glance down since areas of mud must be navigated when entering the yards of Catafrax.

I took not another step. Something sent shivers up my spine: on the moist ground were unmistakable imprints of large cloven-hooves. Alarmed, I ran away at once and returned through the gate.

I hurried to inform the head grounds-monk that a devil had taken material form and lurked in the vicinity.

But could that be possible? Not long did I wait for his answer. He explained that it were no hooved devil, but a cow must have been passing through at night. It sounded reasoned enough, but something did not sit right for me in that answer.

They keep neither cows nor goats, the men of feudal Whilom-town...

My years in the monastery have supplied me with not a few haunting accounts of angels and demons. Surely the Devil's legions invisibly besiege the sacred walls more than anywhere else. Throngs of bat-winged demons sue for entry day and night. They are admitted only if a monk sins.

I know what some of you younger monks are thinking.

You think that our story is merely a fable, a fantasy made up to fill the doldrums of doing chores. So it would seem.

Your profound mental dependence on the rational tolerates not the witness of a dwarf possessing super-human speed and strength. You profess that you have never heard of such a foolish thing. You say that it is against common science. Brothers, can you not perceive that this dwarf's ferocity was a demonic enthusiasm? Take for example the type IV demon. According to Guy of Xaragia, the entity can grant to his servants superhuman strength and speed for at least twenty rounds of combat. We understand this to be an unholy restoration of preternatural faculties.

Let me provide you with a true account of similar possession, or influence if you will. It occurred at the monastery. This was not twenty winters ago.

At that time the Holy Ghost bestowed a great desire in our monks to help the poor. The holy fervor was on account of the preaching of Abbot Aonas. The monks wished to provide the poor of the land with better nourishment during the winters. In that season the peasants often found that they had not saved enough of theirs to share. The extra supply of the king's stock would run out.

A certain beloved monk hails from the distant tropics of Mahanaxar: Brother Amos, the monastery cook and herbalist. He went to study medicine in later years under the Friars at the University of Whigg, at last returning to become our physician.

When he was young, back in those days, he worked in the kitchen and had developed talent at preparing delightful morselsknown as *succords*. Eager to do this for the poor he saw many days raising the miniature fowl over the summer.

When Christmas passed and the snows came, he would spend hours frying up succord bits for the poor. These were to be dipped in special sauces of his traditional Mahanaxaran recipe.

It was an economical, but addictive snack.

Soon crowds of hungry vagrants from the town of Whilom were lined up outside the monastery steps. They were looking for the tasty succord wings on Church feast days. Now this monk Amos was a robust young man, and well built. He would stand out there with an assistant monk in the frosty air with his pots and pans and fires.

He would cook up these hot delights for starving folk.

It would get chill sometimes in the snow, so we built for him a little wooden shack, and a fence through which he could pass the food. This kept secure the morsels also, since crowds would grow thick, and sometimes thieves would slip in. Quick hands could seize the share allotted for the poor when the monks had their backs turned toward the stove. After some time the folk learned to come only in daytime hours.

Now it came to pass that a particular woman from the outskirts of town would saunter up on horseback. She was mad to obtain these tasty succord wings with special sauce. She was not so poor, having a well-sized pony, yet was she neither fat nor of ill-habit; at least not evidently so at first.

But she always seemed cross or melancholy.

On more than one occasion she was heard to make unsavory remarks. Rumour had it that she was somehow unclean, and had been seen gathering herbs in the forest. This rumour we monks thought not worthy of any concern. Otherwise she seemed frail in physique and of little account.

On the feast of St. Agatha, Brother Amos was standing outside in the evening after the succord wings supper had been passed out and was putting things away. The fire-pit had already been put out, the utensils and crocks were already cleansed. Suddenly this woman rode up on her pony bareback. She was expecting to have the succord wings given to her even without dismounting. Her hair seemed wild and out of control, as did the fierce glance of her eyes. The exact altercation, which occurred between her and brother Amos, is here recorded in the annals:

"I am here for my succord wings," she declared in demanding tone.

"I am sorry, ma'am," said Amos, "the monks are not serving at this hour."

"What?"

"Supper has already been served." He said, "We have no succord wings at this hour. Perhaps the monks have some bread for you—."

"Don't give me any of your tongue!" she shouted, "unless I have the succord wings in my hand—"

"Please, calm down," said the monk, now worried. "The monastery does not serve the succord wings at this hour."

"Yes...you do!" she screamed.

"NO —WE —Don't." affirmed the monk.

"Why not?" asked the woman, on the verge of rage.

"Because...-we don't." replied the monk, incredulous. He was unwilling to yield a rational explanation to someone so clearly irrational.

The woman glared at him with ferocity. She suddenly hissed out at him from upon her horse, almost like growling beast of some sort. The monk Amos, unaccostomed to such behaviors, and proud of his exalted station as a newly-made full monk, stood there unmoved,(he was not long practiced in meeting hostility with calmness, nor arrogance with humility).

He pointed at her and asked indignantly:

"Did you just hiss at me?"

"Yes, go ahead, c'mon!" he said, now incensed that someone could be so bold. "Get your skinny *hiney* down from there!"

The woman dismounted. The pony moved away from the shack's fence, or from her. She approached where he was standing. Now certainly this was no way for a monk to respond; however, when it comes to sudden aggression, few monks are different than anyone else.

Gaining control of himself, Brother Amos backed away from the fence.

"Don't you back away from me, you porcus!" she exclaimed. "I will end you!"

There was with him an assistant monk, a youth who in later years became Abbot Cromna. He came in to see what was going on. He too now presented himself before her.

"What's going on here?" Cromna asked. She did not answer, but in a fury struck at him with her fist through the aperture.

"What in the--!" cried the assistant who also backed away at once. He tried to close up the little door but could not, for she held it with a strong grip. Brother Amos, completely unfamiliar with such onslaughts, nevertheless got his dander up and moved forward to assist Cromna close up the door. They tried to hinder her entrance, as she was endeavoring by brute force to get in. They did so, but not without receiving grievous wounds from her rapid blows. Then, as if it were the demon himself speaking, she warned him screaming (in curse language I do not record):

"DON'T MAKE ME ASSUME MY ULTIMATE FORM! I WILL UTTERLY WRECK YOU!"

Brother Amos had her by her locks for a moment, but she yanked away. The assistant monk, imagining he could somehow communicate with pure rage, begged her to cease, pleading, "Whoa, whoa, please ma'am."

She looked at him with eyes black as black hell-fire and growled, "DO YOU KNOW WHO I AM? I will tear your head off!"

She hissed like a leopard a few more times, assaying to smite them both with strong flailing as may the sorts of wild hill women or warty witches. It was no act. It took both of those stalwart monks pressing with all their might to stop the door of the cooking shack to keep her from forcing the way. As this great contest was going on, the warty hag described in exacerbated tones at the top of her lungs the horrid tortures that awaited those who dare defy her:

"I'm gonna eat your swarthy face off and digest it in front of you! Then I'm gonna spit it out into the ditch!"

Locked out, she started slamming her body up against the door. The monks were both stupefied.

"DO YOU WANT A PIECE OF ME?!" she growled. "I shall become as greater than Satan to you!" The woman ripped off her gown. *Mammae suae revelatae et nudae*-swung about savagely and she spread her arms as to fly. She went back to her horse and rode a short distance, screaming lewd profanities. Remaning in sight, she obtained a piece from an old plow. At once she returned and used the iron head to smash through the flimsy door shaft and fence of the shack.

She entered in and seized Brother Cromna.

What happened from there one can only speculate, for the monks described it as transpiring with such speed and ferocity that all was a blur. Cromna bade Brother Amos run for help. The enraged one pinned Cromna on the floor.

She attempted to chew his face, but found it somehow not possible, (perhaps because she had so few teeth). Instead, with awesome strength and speed she proceeded to break both of his knees. She struck them with smashing blows from her small fists, all the while cursing in the weird and pagan language of the hills. How a little woman could do this to a fully grown man is beyond my understanding.

Brother Cromna, it is believed, being a superior Christian in so many ways, was given the grace not to fend against his torturer but instead, on behalf of Christ, (whose knees were not broken at the crucifixion), to yield to this intense pain for the salvation of souls, thereby making up for anything lacking in the agony of the cross. So does the Apostle exhort us all to do the similar works.

Brother Amos was later asked why he did not intercede to hinder the hag. Both he and Cromna claimed that Amos had run out of the shack to the monastery steps to cry for help, which he did.

At once he returned, within timing, at most, thirty-three chant notes. The hag noted the sizable Amos re-enter, but her assault of fury was fomented. She took off on foot into the obscurity of the winter woods, howling her intention to bash them all, her hair twisting in the wind and her savage breasts fouly swinging.

Into the mysterious Lokken she disappeared. (Even her little pony had fled the scene of mayhem; for the poor beast understood that he no longer served a mere mortal.

The monks found the horse the next day seeking hay at the monastery stable.)

Cromna suffered from the injuries. The knees never healed.

But I wonder if the works of the wicked are so powerful as that. The crushings of the hag, or demoniac, if you will, were accomplished as she uttered a curse over the action. Why should Heaven let such injuries go unhealed? Would not the healing of them be a testimony of God's power?

Afterall, how much stronger is God's blessing

than the Devil's curse? It is a worthy question,

and I shall repeat the answer. Abbot Cromna himself credits this as the explanation, namely, that Heaven left his knees less than fully healed. This is a testimony against those conceited with misbelief regarding supernatural agencies. For some men do assert that "the Devil is not," or that if the Devil does exist, "he may bestow no abilities or powers."

Some insist that there are no warty witches or cunning wizards, or if they are among us, they are merely "earth-worshippers, or forest folk." It is impossible, they say, that someone be possessed of an evil spirit.

Such reasoning is quite popular as of late,

so high Heaven has seen fit to confound that intellectual pride. Let one man henceforth need crutches, and this man let be witness to the truth: that the devil's servants are not without real power.

Cromna, having retold the story from the pulpit, gave the brethren the following commentary in his sermon on the incident, after he became Abbot:

"Brothers, some of you, some whom Heaven has chosen, and are here today, have secretly adopted the "rationalist" way of thinking, supposing that it is not good for peasants or even nobles to hear that there exists a never-sleeping Devil.

Little preaching is done on this regard. Yet I ask you,

if there be no Devil, if there be no Hell,

what is it that we must be saved from?

If it is enough only to love God and be at peace with all,

then why did our Lord warn us of the unquenchable flames?

Would he terrify men with an empty threat? Why did he become flesh and redeem us by dying a cruel death on the cross?

If there be not drooling demons and pit-borne devils, or if Hell be merely some nebulous place of mind which the flesh need not fear, none of these extreme measures would have been necessary.

Out of hatred and envy the Devil seeks the deception of souls, and our ultimate demise. Those neglectful of ever-calling prayer he cunningly uses; be it crook-weilding bishop, long-robed priest, rope-girded monk, or square-hat scholar, nay, add even the untaught. All are candidates for that unhappy end. The Devil needs but one unhappy apostle."

He and Amos were glad to escape with their lives...and their faces. The wild woman has been spotted on several other occasions in the forest, but the authorities have not yet to this day apprehended her.

The service to the poor continued, but the fear of her remained, and when the poor heard it, dread of threatened retribution from her magnified.

They called her the "Lethal Lady of The Lokken" and "Hecate."

No more came they for the succord wings, preferring to remain hungry in body rather than risk a nocturnal attack from a hag.

In their superstition they believed that even the succord birds had been claimed by her.

So goes the account, no fiction, famous even up to these last years, but is now in danger of being forgotten, so I could not neglect it.

ow with credulity return thou in mind to Brother Jacob's account of the bizarre occurance, and all he underwent as Grimble's captive in the Timberhills: —Grimble, using the dagger's threat, took me his hostage to keep his new enemies at bay, and forced me to haul a rucksack filled with supplies of the Valraphim, and a mysterious tome. He made escape in the little boat and had me row him away from the islet to the shore of the horseshoe lake.

After disembarking, we went up to that place where a massive stony Tor thrusts up steeply from the forest floor. We ascended it on rock-hewn steps. Probably those poor souls enslaved of the heathens had chiseled them relentlessly in some forgotten era of the furthworld. I lugged the pack up the steep incline in the moonlight.

The terrible way up those primitive stone steps hefting that pack, neared the last flight. Several times it brought me to a halt, not able to go at all, but just cling to wet surfaces. If I happened to take a mis-step or lose balance, I would plummet to the jagged below.

With his vorpal blade the mad dwarf pointed the way. Then of course I lost balance and slipped, and was falling to certain death. The dwarf reached out, grabbed the pack and hauled me back in a flash.

"Careful, monk...we'll have no wasting of your blood-"

We pulled ourselves at last up to the final precipice after
a most fearsome effort. I unstrapped the rucksack from my burning shoulders.

The dwarf looped me with rope immediately, in an unnatural flash.

There was no longer any doubt that Grimble's boasted power was true. Within moments I was belly-down on the cold rock,
hog-tied again, and much more tightly. The wicked one
dragged me and leaned me up against a primordial henge-altar.

"—Just in case you try something. Don't cry out or I'll gag you. No one can help you now anyway. We stay here, for I have prepared the offering."

We were on the highest point in this forest. Only the tops of the firs were neighbors here. There were three mighty henges, and a stone altar not sighted from below.

"Keep hush and be still, monk, like they taught you," he whispered in a menacing tone.

He took out *The Black Book*. After paging through it, he became frustrated at his inability to read it. To the rock's edge he pushed it aside.

"Accursed gnome and his stolen books...!" he grumbled.

Grimble gazed up at the dome of stars. A long time, perhaps an hour passed. It was getting colder. My joints ached me something dreadful from that awkward position. The twilight had completely vanished. I stared at Grimble. Under his beard he returned a frown, a kind of frowning only dwarves can frown. In the dawn rescuers would surely arrive, hunters, or brother monks.

"Now mind your own soul and pray to your savior-ghost.
If you are hoping that the minstrel might come for you, you be disappointed. The old fool imagines –that I am offering to Saturn.
He does not know Vorthragna.

Her eye is the moon's dark side, when it passes the Goat Galaxy,
that most gladdens the celestial beast when stained with mortal blood.
A monk's blood will please them even more."

"...but I am not a monk any longer!" I said. "Or if ever I was once a
monk, I have run away! I am less than a man. No good for sacrifice!"

"Not quite a monk? Then why have you the tonsure?"

"I have disguised myself as a traveling monk," I explained. "Hot meals,
a place to sleep were my rewards...and learning besides."

The dwarf was far too worldly-wise to put credence in such a tale. "It
doesn't matter: a mortal's life blood is all they require.
If you are the one foretold in the fair witch's doom-say, then you must
die anyway. Better quickly done and done well by my hands. If you are the
one whom them stars choose to set back up the throne of wizardry, and
open Nystol of many towers, then see: I will reach out and haul down
those stars, and vex the worlds; I am defiance! The dwarves must never
again see such dishonour. Do you fear?"

"I cannot change the age or put it under the rule of some forgotten
wizard-towers," I said. "If you do hold that some fate must come, then by
your own word it cannot be bypassed, so your efforts will be in vain.
Therefore just give up now. Don't fight something you cannot stop.
The divine hand will shield me against harm.
His arm reaches down from his holy mountain.
If instead he wills my end, then I end justly...
for I am a faithless monk."

"All the more reason to suspect that you are the chosen one
foretold, for only a faithless monk would cast an ancient spell.
You talk too much, when you should fear more.
We shall see. Sorry that your last moments be so unworthy.
I do rather need be of strict focus to make perfect the offering. Preach
your final words, monk. Tell me, satisfy me with the curious teachings of
your curious deity. Tell if I shall be punished in the next world, having
sought to right this one by rightful force. If so, then what punishment will
the divine master inflict? Nay, for to me He seemeth to punish without
rhyme or reason."

His question gave me an idea. Fear of God's wrath was the only sort
of preaching left to give Grimble, so I should use it.

"You expect me to be your teacher, and then become for you the
blood-sacrifice? It will avail you naught. The rope-girded monks taught
me that there are things worse than death, so I suppose you should be
warned. It is true. When sinful deeds are done, they must be punished, for
God is just.
Sacred scripture, teaches what sort of retribution might come, be it
either by Nature's justice or by God's own merciful hand, whatever is
appropriate and fitting. Different kinds of punishments for different kinds
of sin..."

"Even the nebelung-priests of the elder gods profess as much." said
Grimble wryly. The dwarves were betrayed at Nystol, cruelly locked away
in darkness. After they designed and built her towers, they were betrayed.
"My kin were locked within the Tower of Ru to starve, lest they reveal the

secrets of Nystol. Where be the justice for them? And what of crowns and nations who knew and looked the other way? What vengeance for them?"

I answered him: "It is written in Ecclesiasticus, *Fire, hail, famine and death, all these were created for vengeance*"

Storms, earthquakes, and giant waves are stored up for wicked nations and cities. And look at what happened to Nystol. Overwrought with learning, the unlearned burnt her down. Or if catastrophe fall on some monastery or city, a city which men otherwise esteemed harmless, like Gandolon, then God's all-seeing gaze must have been seeing a people secretely hardened in some sin. *Those whom He loves He chastizes.* But say the people are innocent and continue to suffer, then we should suspect that they are paying for the sins of some other wicked city with whom they have league.

Grimble, every man gets some justice. The frightful claws and gnashing teeth of four-footed animals are particular for terrible or violent sinners.

Can anyone calculate the variety of enormities against the Ancientmost? The sages agree there are two kind: many terrible sins fall under the violent sort. That's not all. Count many more among the fraudulent. Yes, deceit and cunning earn fitting punishment as well: what punishment? For liars and frauds He returns not the attacks of four-footed beasts, rather "two-footed beasts," other men who employ scourging tongues against them."

The mad dwarf laughed a mad laugh. He was peering at the stars again, sensing something in the air. There was a change in the wind, and a coldness stirred, a grey traveling mist.

The mist moved around us in menacing manner. It formed some ghostly shape, a far-cast reflection or phantom. It drifted between the dolmens: lo, a humanoid shape, tall, frightful, with terrible fangs and blackish eyes. The dwarf went pallid of flush. The phantom seemed an astral projection of some sort, nebulous, decarnated, such as a wizard might send.

"Master!" Grimble exclaimed, addressing the apparition. He prostrated in idolatrous homage.

"Why do you call me master?" the ghost whispered in deep dreadful tones. "We both know who is your master now, and she has many heads. You have betrayed me, Grimble."

The crazed dwarf was agape.

"No master, they lie to you, this sacrifice...be for—"

"I understand well enough." hissed the shadow. "The vine of elfshade does not misreport. You make sacrifices to the old dragon

in exchange for beserking power.

But you once swore fealty to me, and I granted you knowledge."

The apparition stretched out a boney hand in accusal.

"You have made yourself into a liar. Now I declare, you cannot touch this monk. He is mine. But upon you a dooming retribution I convey."

Grimble got up and turned his back on the apparition,

with bitter expression. The phantom dissipated, leaving a dark polluted spot in the air.

"What in thunder was that?" I begged of him, now even more terrified, hair standing on end.. No longer would I be inwardly fighting doubts to confirm the existence of spirits. I had seen one.

"What was that; you ask? Rather ask who.

That was the forsaken fey himself, the Balecrown; Nazageist, whom men call Northing, heinous and vile, the so-called 'Dire of Melancholy,' Archdruid of the groves of hell.

He fancies himself highest of archons, because he has a monopoly on the little magic the world has left.

Forget him, that vain creature."

"What did he mean when he said: "The monk is mine,'...?"

Grimble gave a sardonic look. He responded with the most antithetical of all possible responses.

"What care be it of yours? The spirits say that only a monk can defeat my master. It'll not be you. You're about to die anyway. As for me, I no longer play his games. So fie upon 'im! Make right with *your own* master, monk!"

The dwarf stretched out his arms in supplication, uttering words in some infernal tongue. It was similar to certain dialects of the Gohhan valley or the Setet and the other closed lands of Arraf, but even more alien then those. From his baldric he drew an ancient obsidian blade. It was the shape of a crescent moon. He went to his knees and readied the knife under my neck. He would have me bled like a bull or goat. I was about to die. I struggled to free myself, but to no avail; the ropes were too firmly knotted, labyrinths of chord...

The sinister nibelung continued to pray his infernal prayers, monotone and droning. He breathed deep and gripped for a blood-letting strike.

But from somewhere above there came a sudden flapping and swoosh of beaten air. As a war-cry upon wind it shocked, like a trumpeting alarm of a creature enraged, and flash of claws and feathers.

All bore down upon Grimble.

Stunned by the mighty Aileron, flapping and flapping, and pecking, that dwarf stumbled backward and fell on his rear. The sacrificial blade bounced from his hand and clanged on the rocky ledge.

The flash of white feathers now was just as quickly away. The hermit's great gift had not been in vain. The bird had been watching at a distance, had perceived the diabolical aggression, and remembered me. The half-goose vanished beyond the pine tree tops.

"That accursed winged-devil again! A hell-guard of yours, monk!" Grimble tore off his mask and slid over to fetch his sacrificial blade.

Now other sounds they heard, voices, coming closer. But Grimble stood up, alarmed and awakened out of his ritualistic trance.

He stepped over toward the cliff's edge. I stretched upward as much as I could to see below and saw nothing at a distance below the tree line.

"—wretched valraphs! Curses...!" Grimble bellowed angrily, "the goddess will not brook a hasty rite mixed with many distractions. This is not what Grimble foresaw.

How is it that they are now beware? It must have been the bird, or perhaps it is mercury-minded Bannock; his little nasty spying homunculus. What will Grimble do now?"

"How possibly can you spot anyone so far down in this darkness?" I asked.

"I am no valraph. I am of the race of dwarves, knave. Infravision; to 60 feet penetrates blackest subterrene...my sight does me well. You should have known that..."

All of a sudden there was another interruption.

On the rim of the lower rock on the opposite ledge gnome and stag appeared, The Arcavir was armed and mounted, ready for a fight. This time he had a bow, braced, the string taut, housing a fast-flying arrow.

He guided his antlered servant; the stag trotted and went by the precipitous ledge, to my amazement, and his hooves click-edy-clacked like doom on the top. Turning the stag about the gnome leveled aim from the opposite ledge. Grimble's eyes widened. in a singular movement he leapt upon the trivault threshold of the henge altar. Before I looked back, the gnome had let go a shot.

The shaft lodged in the place where Grimble's helm guarded the cheek bones. This sudden impact took him off guard. Although it had not pierced the armor plate of the helm, the hit knocked him back. It did not teari into his face. He did not cry out, but fell bestride the altar.

This was not the end. He lay there on the rock surface next to me for a heartbeat. His incredulous eyes turn to me, and cry out and so he sees my eyes. I gaze back sternly into his eyes. There, in the swirling trance of madness, I glimpsed of an unspeakable fury. It was alien, like something abominable creeping up from the pools of souls long condemned

The dwarf's face goes flush. An owl hoots somewhere in the distance.

Grimble arises with a new rush of unholy vigor.

As soon as he stands up, another arrow whizzes through the night air. This time Grimble with his unnatural speed was ready. He reached and snatched the deadly shaft out of the air. It never met its target. This was done in the same way a nimble dog might catch a buzzing fly in its snout.

He sternly cast the arrow down to the stone ledges. In his defiance he stood "The fletcher of yours, although commendable in skill, must set in swifter feathers against me, gnome." said the dwarf. "but kindly relay his guildname to me when all is done."

"I fletch my own shafts, dwarf." Kruth replied, astonished.

Now at the end of this interval other valraph soldiers had climbed up the tor. They were watching warily. The one they called captain, Drocwolf, battle-chief, took the responsibility for opposing the traitor hand to hand.

"Even quick arrows will not bring him down," declared Drocwolf. "Someone must go 'gainst him hand to hand. I am the choice among those who remain; I must go. Grimble, you like to boast that unlike other dwarves you can match me in daring, strength, and speed. Come then, let us together at last measure steel, axe to axe, or sword if you like. Let us see if your words were sober."

Moments slipped by as Drocwolf and Grimble glowered at one another and circled each other with ready blades, the henge-altar between them. The engagement did not last long at all. Immediately, with blinding dexterity, Grimble darted round and guided his battle-blade in a low upward slice.

Drocwolf's parry would have been quick against someone like me, but was far too slow against Grimble. He found himself on the stony surface bleeding, not but a step away from me. Wounded badly he could not move. Grimble could have dispatched his adversary at once, but he spared Drocwolf. He backed away a few steps, limping, not because of pain, for he seemed not to feel his wounds, but he could not work his leg muscle.

The Arcavir guided his stag along the opposite edge of the summit-precipice, keeping a safe distance. Grimble feared the "fairy-bard" too much to hazard a direct assault. Anything could happen, and did happen.

"So now you know," Grimble warned bellowing. "Had you not once saved my life, Captain, I would have finished you.
Beware, I will send you all, each one, trouping down
to the lower hells if you do not keep clear of me!
...hark and listen. Do you catch that...?
Maddened men with dogs and torches are nearing!
The townsfolk will burn you men at the stake. Haste, therefore. Recover your injured captain and avaunt!"

"We will be taking the monkling too, Grimble..." said Kruthendel sternly. "Let us listen then, and hear what can be heard."

There was quiet, and silence in heaven above; where galaxies turn in their undetectable turning. Only the nimble dogs far below could we hear, and those beasts were yet on the far side of the echoing crystalline lake.

Kruth's arrow slid against the hollow bow. He drew taut the string.

"Why rely on that shameful and unmanly weapon, Kruthendel? Come, exchange blows of axes instead, and show thyself an unmitigated warrior, as reputed of old." Grimble spoke great taunting.

Kruth did not answer. So further accusal poured out.

"Yer ancestors never-ever did employ such instruments. You're an example of what that baseborn and hybrid race of yours has come to. —so it achieves against you fair justice for denying the assembly of the many gods. You abandon a noble tradition for mad fanaticisms, and the gods reprise themselves by bringing shame to yer kind."

Grimble, was standing with his back to the ledge, and his boot rested on *The Black Book*. Somehow the arrow had not much disabled his leg. He snapped off the shaft.

"An arrow shaft lodged in me leg was hurtin' a tad. Never leave behind a magic help, that's me prayer, and not the lucky shield either." Grimble was being at once sarcastic and sincere.

"That wisdom excites no mirth in us. You must be melancholy. Be you done this blood-letting now."

"I—blood-letting!? Which of us now is after doin' that? But why haven't you aimed for me heart? You had the advantage, minstrel. You'll not humour me; lest I die honorably, or at least bravely, in battle? All here know how you can dole out closer elfshot than that."

"Ye Wyrmheld, Grimble." the gnome said. "You have lost yourself in a demonic dream. I have provided some due pain to awaken you. We rather want to keep you. A court marshal would require you pay a life-worth, and do public penance, but we would bring you back to virtue, for a day of righteous glory. I wager that pain might awaken you to your fault. My purpose is to turn you from further mischief, you melancholy dwarf."

"What arrogance had in your excuse! I have no quarrel with ye valraphs, and I am not under yer command anymore, minstrel. You have no threat of discipline for me. Now it is you whose violence breaks the teaching of All-law."

"...you make point on that, maybe. The havoc is part mine, aye. But do not doubt my love for you. Even after many centuries I have again slipped into the old fault: too quick to battle.
Too anxious to load the slender bow.
If for a day of glory...pain might awaken you to your fault, tis' my wager: turning you from further folly and mischief, melancholy dwarf."

"You do not convince. I'll not make any peace with you, minstrel, by the noble blood of my race, never!"

"If, like me, you had been down through all the hells with Duke Ikonn marauder of worlds, and glimpsed what awaits the damned, even dwarves...aye, your soul would be all hallowed by the tale I could relate of it. Then you would understand why I have resorted to this. A bit of pain in this life is trifling compared to the tortures that await the unrepentant in the next. Still, I have no—"

"Vainglory be concealed in yer sour talk! Now thrice I declare it, never will I even truce with you, minstrel. As an example for Valraphim to remember: a soldier free from your fold, and still a soldier, and one with honour, no servile surrender. It is your violence that trangresses."

"I've always had a stomach for war, and tasted much of it.
Of old, in the years before the revelations
...Oh the tales I could tell. But these limbs are tired from a thousand years of war. There is no fair match 'gainst you with axes. Let me answer for it; these shafts answer you for now, to help you kneel."

"Force me to kneel? Your God-king will approve you on that? Would the mild Shepherd favor that? Aye, you are no less war-weary than I, and so employ even a lazy and cowardly weapon."

"It's an easy thing to point out shadows in a face lit by grace. I must do this, you leave me no other option. The code obliges to protect the innocent by dint of pain, if need arises."

The elfbeards stood there watching Grimble closely.
What ploy might he launch next?

"Take the monk then already," The dwarf said begrudgingly, "Grimble will vouchsafe the prophecy comes not to pass, the old gods will help at last. But I retain the accursed *Black Book*. If what they seek is somewhere

in these thousand incomprehensible pages, no disciple of the new god shall have it."

"Granoch!" called Kruth, "Cut loose the monk, but keep spry...Grimble, let him come, for we know you are fixin' do the world right and win fame. The elf-kin of old... fool though you be to heed some old beldame's doom-say."

Telperion Granoch, a valraph ranger, named after the famous tree of legend, was older and very keen. He unsheathed his shortsword and stepped cautiously.

At last free from those cruel bonds I crawled carefully away from Grimble.

I heard myself praying: *"In iustítia tua edúces de tribulatióne ánimam meam."*

The crazed dwarf stood fast on the ledge, the other side of the altar. Grimble did not seem the least diminished nor did his injuries hold his attention in the least. He seemed the more powerful and dreadful. Against this stature, of a sudden, Thingle stepped forth from the line of opposing elfbeards.

He hefted his axe and readied his shield. He shook his head in dismay. The fir-tops shuttered in the night breeze upon which drifted pine needle scent. Again far away the owl hooted.

Thingle advanced on Grimble keeping the battle stance, ready to swing. His eyes peered fearfully from behind the iron helm's visor.

"Stand down, I say, brigadier," roared the captain Drocwolf who lay there bleeding. "It is the command of your captain.
The Valraphim have charged me with keeping discipline,
a thing blessed by the Arcavir's song.
You are not making up for your fault this way.
You want to live, don't you?
Help us root out that wyrm under Galadif and win glory?
Obey me and you will again be called Valraph...Thingle!"

....but the elfbeard had already determined his mind and was closing in on Grimble cautiously ...not cautiously enough.

The gnome, knowing Thingle could not be persuaded to hold back, instead tried to persuade the opponent.

"The hour is never too late, never too spent, Grimble." the gnome said. "They deceived you; your own guilt has not all the ponderance. Spare foolish Thingle, like you did Drocwolf just now; that is worthy. Then return to us, and with tears receive pardon, and peace. By Heaven's mercy you could someday stand with the just before the first born of the dead."

"I'll not forget the gods of my forefathers, gnome.
Someday the dwarves will rise in glory again,
feared warriors upon the broad earth, as of old.
Chosen valraphs will march with them,
for gods dwell in the hollow hills!"

"But even those now know that they are not gods.

And how will dwarves, elves or any of us elder races sing of Grimble in days to come? Who among the Valraphim will not become sour with the remembrance of this?

Will they sing well of betrayal when Grimble's clan is mentioned in the mead hall of Neflheim?

You have given ear to many untruths, Grimble. The Whitehawk ancestors knelt on the sacred mountain and heard utterances from the first born of the dead. It was the prime way of things, until the wicked tread upon the young earth and filled the folk with the lies of the hollow ones,

declared many gods instead of one.

We are to serve men, not sacrifice them.

The Furth High King has charged us with the task.

He has delivered the humans from the power of shadow, and from the dragon. Hear the sacred warnings."

Thingle was passing around the altar and ready to open on Grimble.

There was a thunderous splitting of air as Grimble spun about and swung at his opponent in one move. Another shot from the bow simultaneously whizzed by, but the maniacal dwarf was quick. He crouched to dodge it.

"No...Thingle!" cried Kruthendel.

He started praying in a strange tongue. Unearthly was the sound of his voice...his elphic language; there was something sweet about it; it were as angel-speak. Thingle swung but his axe sliced only air. Grimble stealthily ducked from the blade's course. Eventhough Thingle had presence of mind enough to maneuver in such a way with shield, to fend a double strike of swinging sword and deadly dagger, there was little doubt who had the game.

Another round of hazardous battle ensued, and yet another.

Thingle somehow skirted the lightning strikes of his opponent, and made feints to aggravate, but could not expose his flank even for a split second.

This angered Grimble the more, and his eyes jiggled in their sockets.

In his rage he bellowed terrible curse words.

"You have enthuzed this one with the magic of the All-blessing, haven't you, gnome?...you-weak and forgiving!"

Grimble swung wildly dagger and sword, and missed Thingle again. The onslaught pressed him back upon the henge altar.

"It seems that I shall offer a sacrifice yet!"

Grimble cast away his dagger and griping the pommel and hilt with both hands raised his sword above his head. He was intending to cut Thingle in half. Before the murder stroke was complete, the young soldier, just shy of a hit, evaded rolling away.

The sword of Grimble struck clanging on the stone altar. The blade shattered, the tip broke off, and shards flew.

"Ah...my sword...Gamazung–it has been broken!" the dwarf cried out. "The sword of our ancient house, the blade of Nergalf!"

Grimble stopped and stood stupified. He gripped the hilt of the shattered blade and stared at it. Bafflement was his expression.

Thingle heard this, stepped away, and withdrew his assault. Grimble continued his lament:

"The metal battle-blade, the hallowed edge, the eld bronze hilt forged
    of the furth-orein far off Atalur, so it came to be in days of
unremembered lore. . . at last, by my fatal hand, only the hilt and shard.
It has always been at my side, this fine blade
. . .now there surely be no turning back."

There was an unquiet silence. The crazed dwarf's mind drifted off to some other place of weird revelation. His iron gaze became hollow one. He spoke aloud words to himself.

"Aye, but a broken blade has yet one last surprise stored in it!"

With the flashing speed of a seeming singularity,
Grimble spun round and lunged, with a deliberated swing reaching,
with the jagged broken base, tore the throat of Thingle.
Kruth gasped at the sight, and Thingle staggered.
His battle axe and oaken shield dropped to the rock surface
and echoed a hollow ring. He held tight his torn neck
as blood-poured through his fingers. It was to no avail.
Grimble gripped the broken steel for an interval, peering into the eyes of Thingle. He lowered the broken weapon. Scarlet blood flowed down over the metal scales of the corporal's armour. At once, with the dagger in his left hand, Grimble pierced his helpless opponent again, in the heart.
The slayer withdrew and stepped away.
Thingle dropped to his knees and fell forward.
The coat of mail jingled and rang when it slammed.
His blood poured out and seeping spread silently
like a serpent athwart the black rock-surface.
His frame moved no more.
And so his spirit fled away to the next world.
The owl in the unknown distance hooted a third time.

"Just comeuppance for ye, fair weather fellow. Thy span has duly ended, " Grimble declared. "Where is your messiah-ghost now? Your All-blessing must not always take.
The stars of fate prepare the retribution theirs. To a stern plight
    men must yield. Not so troublesome a change, dear ox-tails; go thou to dwell among the dead, and learn of their faring, for they are senseless and in shadow. May the blue mountain embrace you."

Hazardous battle is a hard thing to see.
There was a gloomy silence, and all stood watching. Grimble, staggered, drunken with bloodlust, vaunted aloud accursed pagan sayings.After sating his rage there came tormentive quiet.
The gnome, from his mount, began singing softly.
My words could fittingly describe the mysterious tones. It was a song of a most peculiar and melodious sort, as from some long forgotten memory.
The translation matters not much, for the meaning seemed to be in the melody. I came across the verse years later in an old rimestock, a compilation of Fomorian poets plumbed out of murky centuries. You of

course prefer to learn what was sung. 'Tis a cynical thing to translate a poem or song, but human vanity requires this vain attempt:

> *Ye are gods, and, behold, ye shall die, and the waves be upon*
> *you at last. In the dimness of time, in the fathoms of the*
> *years, in the changes of things, Ye shall sleep as a slain man*
> *sleeps, and the world shall forget you for kings.*

The dwarf let out a crazed and mocking laugh, as it were to himself, or perhaps to fend himself from the bardic charm.

He broke the sweet sounds with dissonant and raucous abuse.

"Eldritch doom-verses hedge no power—" but Grimble's own voice cut short his speech at the throat. Something else took his words away. He looked up to the vast sky-dome and depths of boundless space. His mind must have entered an even deeper lapse. His eyes glistened with what seemed like scales, and these fell upward and moved rapidly away, toward some strange and distant galaxy.

They watched looking up as the spirit fled away.

"No! ...no! ...goddess!" Grimble shrieked with guttural terror,

"Do not abandon me! I shall answer the debt, the mundane sacrifice." Grimble seemed to be entreating
some external, perhaps astral, power.
Much diminished in stature, goblin-like, he stood there
as with the stillness of another dimension.

"Indeed it be the *drakodemon*," said Stormraker. "See, he's different now...the eyes no longer glisten.

She was amongst us all, hiding within the shadows of Grimble's brain, all that time, ...listening, working dissemblance."

"Aye, I had a demon...so? All the same, I'll come 'gainst ye
all the more merciless now, be it bare hand or broken blade."

Grimble bellowed his threats with maddened resound, brandishing his broken sword Gamazung.

"See, that new god of yours incensed me so,
that I am reckless to spite the world
...this shattered heirloom will make a quick end of the quarrel,
and ye all see I need no berserking help!"

He stooped and picked up *The Black Book*, stained with the blood of Thingle, and he braced it close to his chest.

"I'll yet drink mead with the feudal lords of old,
in the Hall of the Erlakings, in the blue mountains.
We who are bold taste death but once.
The powers will uphold me."

Grimble turned about. He drew the loop of rope that had been used to tie me and gripped close the tome, and in a sudden dash he bounded off the edge, hurling himself into the murk.

From the exalted precipice of that Tor he plummeted, plummeted into damp and misty airs below. He vanished from sight. The fir tree tops shook, and right away was he gone.

The elfbeards, those who could, sped over to peer down into the gloomy forest far below.

"What see you, valraphs?" asked the gnome.

"We see nothing...but shadow and mist," said Corydon. "and the tree tops, swaying in the breezes of night. But hark."

The forests have an echo, and secrets all their own,
but how to interpret their warnings few ever learn.
Moments passed. We stirred no more, but listened intensely.
Stormraker, having excellent hearing, went and stood on the opposite edge peering off to the West. The famous fighter whispered loudly in alarm.

"The dogs of Bannock! Can you hear them? They are sniffing out our trail! Torches come near, torches held in the hands of men!
–the idolaters of Galadif! They have discovered our purpose."

"They are no clever foe compared to Grimble." grumbled Drocwolf, who sat up on the rock, holding his cut. "Never was I glad to have that dwarf along. His seemed to smack more the soul of a goblin."

"What supreme wreckage!" declared Stormraker. "Our crucial work lay in doomed course, and not only that, but this turn of events endangers every realm. The Sorcerers will control the arcane writings of that *Black Book*! Now surely the realms of men will go the way of Galadif."

Drocwolf dropped back to the ground, exhausted, disgusted.

"Not quite, my dear." said the gnome. "I admit it is become critical.
But the dotard does not have the prize he imagines.
Grimble's service to a base nature clouds his wits.
I yielded to him a different volume, the forty-fourth tome.
The Sorcerers are seeking the thirty-third tome.
Nevertheless, it is a devastating loss,
for it contained the *Seed-songs* of Parthalon.
A great host of other valuable knowledge recorded by the *Eldari* [16] is found there, only in the forty-fourth volume. We will never see it again."

"The glow of torch fires, they are turning away,

---

[16]*Eldari* (in elven, *Elthildor*, also *adj.*; Eldark, Eldrist): The foremost authorities of wisdom available before the revelation of the All-law. Their theology was henotheistic, positing many gods emanating from a non-personal deity, a supernal force. This group cannot be pinned down to a certain location or culture, and many believe that it was a secret society who has preserved lore from the first age, even tracing their name back to the race of Elthildor. Their religious system was based on a philosophy having many similarities with Neoplatonic theurgy. Later, certain Arcanes adopted the system and kept to the old wisdom, (eventhough it was thought defunct by the latter day Archsages). Such throwbacks were called the Eldari and they gained a reputation for great transcendental magic. Some of these survived the great burning and later came to embrace the All-law, Anherm of Whigg being the most noteworthy of these.

heading north again," Corydon observed. "At least we have stalled the enemy again for a time. But, Kruthendel, what do we about this hostage?" (The valraph mountaineers were peering into the murk beyond the ledges, hoping to espy Grimble. They were debating whether he might be hiding in a tree. One of his kind could actually survive such a fall; perhaps he had somehow used the rope, something common among dwarves. Quietly I moved myself near the altar, but a few steps.)

Before Kruth was ready to expound, I had Thingle's axe ready in my own hands. I was determined to get out of this bizarre situation.

"Keep a distance, all of you," I warned. "I'll not play the hostage again, nor be a victim offered to some spirit.

I know the smiting o' this here long axe.

So dare not one of you hurl your fairy magic on me, or think to put me under some enchantment. It will not work anyway.

I am a monk, rope-girded. Heaven-high-above protects me even tho I wander. I can fight a deadly fight with my hands too. Against you all, reckless carnage if need be then...or if you must see me fall, who among you will die first in order to test my battle frenzy?! Your airy magic cannot check this brutal axe."

I was not trained at combat with a long axe. Yet I was capable of a raging fight, but that would be contrary to our code. Somehow I still wanted to go by the code? Perhaps a mere show of explosion, thats it.

I could yet gnash and grin and growl through my teeth anyway, like a war-hungry savage. Thusly did I do that.

The elfbeards looked at one another and at the gnome, uncertain of what to make of the sight.

The gnome said: "The grey elves from below you have in mind, monk; these mountaineers are not like them.

Diabolic or unclean magic rife with side-effects never do they use. These are pure as billy-goats or ledge-foxes. Certainly a monk knows how God has provided every living denizen of the mountain forests with certain powers. Are not billy-goats quite invisible to the eye when looking at a mountain? Doesn't a fox have many tricks?

The half-elves know many mountain paths, the rustle of each pine, the cromlechs, and the secrets of different stones. As for me," he continued "Gnomes employ some harmless natural magic, magic without all the nasty side-effects. I am a woodland denizen, usually keeping in a cozy remote tower in Whitehawk, Torgrith tower in the secluded hills of Chyldishire forest. You need not count me an enemy. What is your descent, war-monk?"

The gnome leaned forward on his stag as to determine some new found challenge. "What interest to you, weird being? I am Jacob Magister of the house of Escorvus, originally the house of Rumilian royalty, my mother was a Kilurian. None of that matters. But these fists will matter."

"The boy does have him some spunk," said Stormraker.

Know ye this work to be in seven volumes enclosed and titled *The Black Books of Melancholia*. One of these volumes I myself examined and this I know: preserveth they writings which date back even before the revelation of the celestial wheels.

Kruth Eleusinion
The Deeptracker's Guide

ven a miniature poodle can deliver a nasty bite.

Would they persuade and fool me?

Would he beguile me into trusting them but then keep me hostage? Would these raiders abduct me, hauling off into the nether-caverns, or even deeper into the eldritch forest, never to be seen again?

"My monk-brothers will be going about looking for me," I warned. "They have banished and even slain fairy and hesitate not in venging themselves. Keep then a good distance.

I heard the singers tell of what you denizens did to King Herla.

Some dwarf deceived him and now he roves the world hopeless, in time-bent swells of nethercloud. It's a peril to have any doings with the elder races. To me you are all demons corporeal; that is my resolute judgement."

"What men report on King Herla...it is a rumour! You just settle down there, human," said Drocwolf, strong enough now to stand, with the help of Corydon. "We've meant what's lawful and delivered you from being bled like an animal sacrifice. Dismal ghosts would have drunk their fill of your blood!"

I turned round his words in my mind, holding the axe ready. Right he was. But I wanted no more of fairy kind, or even half-fairy.

"Much obliged..." I muttered, resentful that the whole thing transpired in the first place. "Now I am going to climb down and go home.

If any of you follow, I'll deprive you of your rakish limbs with this."

"Hold, son of Escorvus," The bright-eyed gnome said. "These will not let you go with the war relic of their comrade.

You must leave the war-axe. Their honour is at stake.

The relic be a matter of honour to them."

I stepped toward the climbing place within the ledge.

"And what is more," added Drocwolf, "you hold one of the eight Axes of Tmolion, hallowed heirloom of the Erlakings who braved the Axecut Trail of old, a thing that Thingle received as a family-gift.

It be of unknown antiquity, in the forges of the nibelung."

"I'll be off now, going along my way. The axe is to protect me in the mirkwood. I'll not tarry here anymore among you spirits."

"Spirits? We are flesh and blood. Were we but spirits alone, that axe would not deter us, but it would slip right through ethereal forms.

Did you not witness the half-elf Thingle fall and pour out a pond of blood, never to rise again?

So now take you heed to calculate matters aright.

We have fey-blood, but it is scarlet, same hue as yours, for we are more near the race of men than is acknowledged. Don't hold anything against us."

"So it seems...and that well may be." I answered warily. "Still, I am done with you all...now I foot it homeward. If they want back, I'll leave it in the stump at the lake's edge, where the trail turns toward town."

"So then go, but do not forget us. We need provisions," Kruth pleaded. "Do not suppose that these soldiers, though half-elves, can live off tree-bark like deer, or like woodland sprites do.

These too have bellies that go empty.

We do plead for a few rations. Will you fetch us some goods?

These roaks crave roast and wine. They have not even seen a squirrel in days. Soldiers like these cannot hold out much longer. The Crown bade us hunt down the dragon of Galadif. Only valraphs can take a dragon...or else holy saints. Regular soldiers always get burned or devoured. We are trapped as long as the hunter runs his dogs every day and every night. He used a crystal ball or some other device to learn where we are encamped. Now he circles the lake with his canines, scaring off squirrels and deer. Is there any other place where we may hide safely on this sea-girt realm of yours, large as it is. He is starving us out. He knows we can't last long on berries. They are hardy mountaineers, not wood-elves."

How unkind was my reply. "Go back and work the circus, they will feed you. Whatever you do, don't slaughter the stag there," I spoke angrily. I looked down and backed away to climb down to the steps of the tor.

"You leave us little choice than to butcher it. White stags are divinely favored, everyone knows; their horns be sacred relics; like the branches of the first tree. —most graceful of creatures. Soldiers have no other choice without supplies."

I looked back at them. The stag stood there. The creature was staring motionless, almost with a kind of knowledge in its eyes, as knowing the words! And there is no doubt in me how such a rare and graceful animal must be treated, for it is special.

"Why don't you wait with us until the dawn." said the gnome. "Don't venture into that wood at this hour. If the dragon does not first find you, the hunters will. We will not be there to help you. They'll declare you an imposter and hang you, What's more, the dwarf Grimble is possibly yet alive, for the demoniacs are strong and die not easily. Somehow, through some eldritch magic, he likely survived his jump. You saw how he tore those arrows from out his own flesh..."

It was a point not easily challenged. Enemies, or the dragon, or mad Grimble awaited down there in the mirkwoods. Perhaps he was even raking the woods for me already. With his infravision the nibelung could easily capture me, only to offer me as a sacrifice in some other secluded grove.

He would be obliged to seize some human before Saturn passed, or the New Moon, or the Goat Galaxy, or whatever celestial conjunction to his demoness consecrated.

To make the trek through the woods at this hour would render any monk an easy take. Kruth's soldiers would not again risk losing more of their comrades to salvage me.

"Fair points..." I admitted, "...but if I yield to that wisdom, then I should move at first light." I stepped back up to the stone ledge. "But afterward don't imagine I might have any part of your adventures. Meals are best taken warm. The monks are strict over the kitchen so I cannot help in that."

"You will have change of heart," The gnome said as he dismounted the white stag. "But first we should rest a while as the night is no longer young. We must mourn the dead and tend to the injured. Corydon, fetch the blankets."

Kruth went to where commander Drocwolf lay propped up against the dolmen altar. He outstretched his arms and raised them. He began praying in a strange and unknown language. He beckoned me come near, approach where they were attending Drocwolf.

"Please supply him the monk's divine healing," the gnome said.

He took my hand and guiding with a prayer he brought it down on Drocwolf's bleeding cut.

This was healing of the miraculous sort, *thaumaturgic.*[17]

On the cool and smooth rock surface of that stony rise I sat back down and watched. The Song-lord ended his song. Confused, I asked this question:

"And what is this place, gnome, the cromlechs and altar? Is it for idolatry of men in earlier times?"

"These liths the giants reared in early ages; they, the first of idolaters. An enchantment these have, and you are not far from reckoning their purpose."

"The early world-ages? Can any living creature speak of them with certainty?"

"No, men cannot. Nor can even gnomes. Certain knowledge even of our own time is not easily come by."

"Tell me all you know, and I shall listen well. You know things that are lost to men. I will not sleep a wink."

Some things Kruth did remember, and bade me to keep safe this lore. The epochs of Man he taught, and many mysteries divulged to me, of

---

[17] *Thaumaturgic* Gr. lit: "wonder-working," it is not wizardry, but similar in outward trappings, in that it invokes sacred power with scrolls and specially prepared books, amulets and symbols, vestments and incantations, as well as wands and staffs, holy swords and miraculous invocations.

seven world-ages of the Furth. I have recorded much for monks in the *Encyclopedia of Whitehawk*. Suffice it here to know this: The Arcavir counts ages. Three ages are past, one is now, and a last "The Time of the Harvester" is yet to come. Many things concerning the mysterious reckoning of ages I did seek of him over and over, and Kruth told me, On this and many other legends Kruth had seen many things, for he had sojourned among men even since the third age.

Our first parents dwelt in the earthly paradise, Dilmon, as sacred tradition teaches. The first age was called golden. After disobedience, the Archsin, a less happy time succeeded for men; for men strove against giants, and giants against heaven: the gigantomachy, the contest of the giants against the angels to seize Argunizial the sacred mountain. The dark Princedom of Nzul was established in the icey North.

A thousand years later the city Atlantis drowned in the great waters of the deluge. The survivors found a refuge here on the Furth continent, when only the scattered descendants of Maceon, son of Noah were living in the cliff-side huts of Vesulum. The Atal built huge Atlantean fortresses in their midst, in the land they called Atalur, and they pressed many into slavery. And being desirous of the many Egyptian commodities they had once enjoyed in Atlantis, they invited the Egyptians to settle nearby, in the land Gohha, whose flooding river reminded the Egyptians of their homeland. This was the Age of Bronze weaponry, when the megaliths were raised, and for a brief time great heroes tread the lands: Duke Ikonn, Elkomenon the Mage, Godiun Fout, Arcesilea, Petrozeon the Thick: the men of renoun.

When those were gone from the world a third era commenced, an age of Iron. The Greeks and Romans arrived, but having fiercely independent minds they would not submit to the Atalurans; and they founded their own cities: Azerdon, Gandolon, Orusca, Yahoros and Regulum. Great learning commenced and soon wizards grew powerful. With their experiments they fashioned abominations, monsters, too dangerous for the cities of men. The five kings banished all wizards far away to the desert plateau of Sardu. But the wizards did not sleep. They built there a many-towered collegium of mages, Nystol.

After she defeated the cruel Atalurans in war, Regulum became the hegemon of the continent. but it was only with the consent of Nystol, whose power was steadily increasing.

In time Regulum waned. Dark years followed, the Platinum Age, an intermediate era of wizardry. Nystol tyrannized over the souls of men: many came to a sad state under that occult power, but she was finally destroyed by the Scourge of God: the barbaric Maharim, and the treachery of one wizard. Such was destiny, the era of faith commenced, and the Ammouric kings established the Whitehawk confederacy...The Fourth Age.

The elfbeards were standing about and sitting on the rocks here and there. They sent nervous and sad glances at the corpse of Thingle.

Finch, Corydon and another were looking after various tasks. He came up to me and covered me with what seemed an elf-woven blanket, of a strange weave that no man can identify. It was surely the warmest of blankets. It kept me as warm as if near a furnace.

Shortly I passed into a light sleep...

lpha and Omega the disciple sees, whose lamps are standing golden in the vision, and these are seven in number.

Seven seals and seven angels with vials; so is it writ in St. John's book of visions. Seven times a maiden appeared to Jacob Magister on seven separate nights; for what purpose high he did not yet clearly see.

The maiden appears before him again, similar as before, in the white gown and holding the gift-book of the knights.

She utters his name, as before, saying "Open, Jacob Magister, open the book and learn the story within."

In the same way, the monk stands befuddled. She turns and walks away down the arches of corridor with the book, and she turns the corner and disappears. Jacob reaches out to accept her invitation, but she is gone.

"...some hours later I awoke from that dream, I awoke to an unusual hum, a humming of words.

The overcast night, iron in its hue, was beginning to end.

It was just before the stars flee from the first light.

At first puzzled as to where in thunder I was, it was not long before I remembered the bizarre altercations which had recently ensued. The hum was elfbeards chanting in unearthly tones.

I turned and looked. They had placed Thingle's body on the rock's surface. They were honoring his remains. The stag was gone off, but the gnome was there standing in the same place.

The one whose name is Buckbar Lancelas had brought out pots and the others had gathered tinder. He was the Valraph's camp cook; sometime battle-hand...and also a philosopher: before long he had stirred up porridge. He passed me a bowl. Dare I partake of elfish victuals? Might they have some fairy herbal mixture? I was too hungry for such caution.

There was something about these elfbeards that impressed. They were really fairy? They treated each other as brothers, sometimes even more compassionately than monks. The forest of the world was violent and selfish, and yet these warriors looked out for each other.

To be alone in the world, for someone like me, was not wise.

Was I wrong to have judged my brother monks? Sure, a few bad apples...

The solar rays penetrated the dome of sky before the last hymn. They toasted bread and procured for me a hearty slice smeared with butter. All were gazing with troubled brow at the never-to-wake Thingle.

"We who fight must eat, even as we mourn for the dead," Drocwolf said. He looked at me, he glanced about, and announced "...only light breakfast this morning, ye men. Now look close. Observe your companion Thingle, his remains slowly transform into rock. Here his shell must remain. He was not quite fine enough for the quick elements of air or fire, or even water. Earth shall claim his remains."

"What do you mean by that?" I said. "Will you not give Thingle your elfish burial?"

The valraphs paused from breakfast. Several looked over to me askance, some frowned. Drocwolf gestured and took me aside. Apparently I was not to call them elves. They liked not that designation. Men were they, they insisted, aye, for sure... albeit with fairy taint, but men; the human stock of valraph. What is born of flesh is flesh, and do they, like other men, go to dust when they die? *Elphic* blood flows through their veins. Valraphs are a hybrid pedigree. They are not natural.

Nature consents almost never to mix diverse species, as oil mixes not with water. Nor may anyone blame Allfather. He would never confuse spirits. What is born of spirit is spirit. Many call it science to say that dogs derived from wolves, yet it is altogether an unstudied assumption. for in spirit they share too little.

No, the race of Valraphs is the acheivement of man's contrivance, the perverse will of wizards.

The ingenious alchemist Rebus Pecequiohr authored their kind by his science of *metagenesis*, (along with many other intrigues for which wizards are famed). At Nystol, they sought to design a race of superhuman warriors, beings powerful enough to destroy the monsters that wizards had foolishly fabricated in the previous age. Even more importantly, the Arcanes of Nystol hoped to assemble an army to defend the libraries, for magic cannot master the art of war. By that time the collegium Nystol had become infamous. It was shunned by all. They could not even hire mercenaries from other lands. So in desperation they captured a cave-elf, Gulathar. Upon his flesh they performed research cruel, extracting the secret spindle and spark. Somehow, by some unthinkable magic, they sewed it within human seed. So is reeped a whirlwind, the valraphs, hybrid men, like mules that cannot breed. Not buried like men, they return at once to rocks and streams, forest and dale, like fairy. Of their spirits who can say?

"See there, his feet and hands already transform into the colors of the mossy rock," exclaimed Drocwolf. "Nature has her rules despite the designs of men. In a few hours he will be indistinguishable from the rest of this crag."

"Does your kind not have eternal souls?" I asked in dismay.

"Even hybrids do have souls, monk. Doubt it not. Does that cause you wonder? Our race is become even more mysterious than the elves themselves.

First our kind dwelt among men, in villages and towns of the world, but that did not last. We were easily spotted and meanly teased because of our visage and our pointed ears. They mocked our noble look, calling us "elfbeards." The human civilization distrusted us, and we were seen as misfits and outsiders, even as harbingers, bad omen. Soon, on account of many fictions, our kind could not live among men. We were hunted. So retreated the valraphs to the mountains and caves to build our own habitations far from other men, remote, not unlike what you rope-girded monks keep.

Sometimes into human towns we go, but only rarely, and for a brief visit." So he spoke and taught me the lore of valraphs.

They all left from that blood-stained tor; and I followed them down the narrow ledge-steps to the forest below, tired and confused on account of the night passed. It would not be far to the path where I could part and bid farewell to the elfbeards. As we made way down a forested slope, some of the elfbeards fanned out and were picking little red wilder-berries.

"Be quick," said the gnome. "The dark hunter and his dogs will soon come. Take care, Grimble is unpredictable; one doesn't know what a dour-soul like him might be up to—"

Why did the gnome cut short his sentence? As they were turning the corner round the little deer path, there in front of them, horribly suspended, dangled a pair of worn bluchers. They were Grimble's half-boots, and in them the notorious traitor himself! His body was swinging from the rope wrapped around his neck off a long, leafless branch. The squeaking line caused the lifeless oak to groan like a ghost as the corpse slowly turned in the damp morning air.

Whether it had been the dark hunter or the other humans who executed Grimble, we shall never know for certain. It seemed that having jumped from the ledge, perhaps he cast the rope, which caught in a tree and spun him around by the neck, cutting off air. He did have a rope draped around his neck when he leapt. However it seemed tied, hastily. Kruth ordered they rake over the entire area for *The Black Book*. They took a considerable interval searching around the base of the craggy promontory and elsewhere. They found nothing save Grimble's broken sword, the hilt. The Arcavir called them all to assemble around the hanging body.

"Look now, all ye. Closely inspect this pitiful sight.

See what the despair of idolatry teaches when joined with the artifices of the devil. Now then, *The Black Book* lay nowhere around here, nor a rent leaf of it. Enough proof then to conclude that someone else hanged Grimble

and made off with the codex. A possibility, but problems
...things not quite in sorting..."

"So it does seem," Stormraker affirmed. "How could anyone capture the enraged Grimble and bring him justice? We could not. Look, he used his own rope, and his hands are unbound. Even when he was not under the berserking spell, it was near impossible to bring down that deadly killer."

"Perhaps he turned the blood rage of the *drakodemon* on self, affected in his mind," The gnome explained.
"When the proper blood sacrifices are neglected,
the insanity becomes acute. The mind of the devotee enters
into an unholyb *mania* of the worst manner. The afflicted is convinced that he has no other path than blood; he must kill."

"...a *melancholia*?" I asked.

"No, not a mood nor disposition...but a *mania*
...he envisions horrors indescribable, bombarding his imagination with bloodworks elaborate. But know that most of the dragon's servants have survived this ordeal and have not been driven to such a length as this. Were this to happen each time a sacrifice were missed,
the *drakodemon* would have few adherents left.
At some point the she-beast departed him. Now again, there must be something more."

"What drove him to this? Despair was it?" I asked.

"From the ground the blood of Thingle cried out.

So the stony heart of Grimble was maddened, guilty all the more, since he would not lay aside the imperishable glory of his famous ancestors. He learned a pernicious shame.

He had betrayed a sacred trust; he had sworn oaths of loyalty and submission ...in the sight of all he had accepted it, and, like the rest of you elf-kin, had sworn off the use of magic.

The terrible reality of his betrayal grieved his heart secretly,

and his soul capsized, alone down here in the mirkwoods

...believing that Allfather was his adversary. Did he harken to the she-beast's threat? Would a despairing shame carry him to this extreme, and then some moribund spirit urge him? It was the easy way out, as he reckoned it. Already his spirit must be paying for his crimes."

"And he will pay for this as well..." remarked Buckbar, who was the youngest (and not smartest) of the valraphs, having not yet a grey hair.

"Perhaps not for this crime," remarked someone.

"Know that it is a worse killing than other kinds." I said. "Afterall, a man knows better his own self, and so has every reason to be merciful; what excuse can there be? Only insanity can excuse self-slaughter...but he was not insane, not in earnest. He could express clear thoughts, albeit evil and twisted."

"A mind magic had enfeebled. But he chose that for himself;

he knew the magic carried side-effects, and he accepted idolatry," explained the gnome. "Even so, it is not ours to judge if his final place will be endless frost-scalding in abysmal Vlogiston, or instead some refuge."

"Vlogiston?"

The Arcavir paused his gnomish thoughts. "It is a dread river of liquid cold for *elphim* at the very edge of the cavernous world,

an intermundane region."

"Do you mean the inexorable prison of flame,

of dark fire?" I said, trying to reckon accurately the lore.

"It is like the place you imagine, but Vlogiston is not so deep,

it is yet intermundane; between the worlds, in the region of the great drops or canyons...a place to imprison natural spirits, and to scourge with punishing cold."

The other hell, according to him, the one I had in mind, is similar, yes, but different than Vlogiston. It is not the same, not the hidden place, near the earth's center, prisons of woe girded by molten seas, where black-scaly servants administer tortures for wicked humans. That Hell which I learned is the second sphere that God created, being much lower than Vlogiston,

originally a prison for apostate angels exiled from Heaven.

The *Erelim*[18] guard the doors against them.

---

[18]*Erelim*; Akaratic term from the 2nd world age, indicates those created of pure light, deathless beings, the spirits otherwise known as holy angels

That inferno is inescapable. An abysmal desert of raining fire, lava rivers, and noxious gases. Of physic humans, some souls do achieve the nadirs of evil reached to warrant entrance into the scalding pits. So it is justice done, for such refused divine clemency when offered.

That is much worse, a burning blast never quenched.

"You elf-kin also heard of the torment to last forever?" I asked.

"That is something monks say Christ has taught, and they pass it down, but I could never fathom it. Even the learning of the Anherm did not supply proof on that. How can someone do anything so atrocious as to warrant that?"

"I am but a gnome, but it reminds me of a little incident once. A deep-sieger I once knew died a telling death. Returning from a raid on a dragon's lair loaded down with loot, the man stumbled and got trapped in a cave-pit.

His comrades hove down a life-line. He grabbed the line to get hauled up, but he was too heavy. Regardless of all the persuasive arguments they offered, he clung fiercely to the weighty bag of silver and gold he had seized, and could not be hefted out. They begged him, but he refused to part with so great a haul. Soon the dragon returned to his lair. The beast picked up the scent and angrily searched the pits for the treasure gone missing.

The dragon found him. A change of mind was no longer possible. The breath-weapon roasted the poor soul thoroughly, quite to a crisp.

The Almighty is your Lord, but he will not force you to save yourself. There always is a choice that must be made.

Let us speak no longer of it. Come now, we shall commit Grimble's armour upon his earthen grave, far from peaceful Dilmonath."

"We cover him now," ordered Drocwolf to all. "If I guess right, the earth will not transform him, but he will be rejected and spit out...so we cover him,

the same way as we would other rebel-fairy, glow-eyes
or weird-feet, all the black-hearted horgim
butchers or nasty goblins. Let him be counted
among the host of Mulcifer."

The half-elves attended to this task. As they gathered rocks,
I stood there with the Arcavir at these funeral rites.

At this point I could have left, perhaps should have left, and sought the path again through to Hordingbay. But I thought it best to learn more of these strange circumstances, and these valraphs.

"You had best foot it back to your cell, monk..." said the gnome. "and...perhaps heeding kindness (to which religious devotion calls every monk...) you will not forget bringing a few rations for us, in Christian kindness?"

---

created at the beginning of time. Many were led into rebellion by Lucifer, and "there was war in Heaven".

"I must learn first one thing from you, Kruth fairy-bard,

and answer well if you would have some help. Why do not you and your valraphs just go into the hollow hills, or into mountain caverns, going down steep paths to the intermundane region, or from wherever you hailed?

How is it that you are left stranded? Can you not build you a many-masted ship and sail across the furthsea to the lands from which you've hailed?"

"You seem an honest human. If I impart answers to these you must keep it close, and speak not on these matters lightly for they are grave indeed. Give word not to speak of these things without iron cause. Remember, one gives not his word lightly to the elder races."

"You have my sworn word; these matters I will not speak without gravity...not to anyone...unless at your bidding."

"So let it be sworn. And what I am about to disclose will also to these valraphs have something new as well: to learn why they have waited here these ten days, obeying my command as to an absolute will."

"Yes, it be high time we learned as much," said Stormraker interrupting, "why so forced on empty stomachs to endure abuse of wind and rain?"

Kruth paid no heed of his remark, but continued.

"A dark hunter, as you know, patrols these hills and lakes daily, trying to starve us out. He knows that I await the translation of a certain book: the *codex* known as the thirty-third volume of *The Black Books of Melancholia*, trove of the extinct Achuleians. I had been wary over the whole enterprise, because we had already suspected a traitor among us. Now at last we have learned his identity. That's why I did not disclose our purpose of holding up on this murky islet to these other valraphs. I could not tell anyone which exact *codex*, since this intelligence could inspire the unknown traitor—(be he valraph or nibelung—and I had my suspicions), for the capture of that crucial heirloom.

My sense of things was close indeed: one of ours did not really fall in war against the bolgs. A cold murder was accomplished within this band of war-brothers. The dwarf-lord Ginnar was found cut down, and now we know it were by treachery, indeed Grimble's, on his own kin too.

How stony the heart that can accomplish such a deed."

"But your traitor Grimble used the tome as it were some sort of prayer book," I observed, "or perhaps a grimoire, and paged through it looking for a spell or fallen prayer to render me as sacrifice, but he could not read it." Kruth explained many things on this matter. Clearly the work has records of sundry spells and prayers, but it is a work written by humans, of researches and ancient legend. Also, the *codices* preserve in the *bzebus* leaves record of all the sinful deeds of men, and the betrayals found in all the furth-races. Rumour has it that there is a secret page that must be found and examined for portentous reasons. It is a vortex-poem, something which if translated, could be dangerous for the future of Whitehawk. Apparently Grimble was not deceived on that point. These books, he insisted, must be gathered and sealed in a vault.

However, one cannot just leaf through the tome like other books to find the right passage, since the elder Latin is quite arcane. Nor is the reading of this thirty-third tome something which the gnome, smart as he is, can accomplish. Eventhough the being is of *elphic* stock, the ventricle of failing memory taxed his ability at the ancient tongue. There was thought no one from our lands who knows the Saturnian-Age Latin well enough to read the many hundreds of pages quickly, for, as he claimed, so little time be left in the world. With all the ability of monks at Latin, most would only read, we reckon, a third of a column per day, especially given many other responsibilities. But the Arcavir marked this one exception: there was dwelling here, on the beloved island St. Aldemar, a mind who can read ten or twenty pages in a sitting, an extraordinary amount, though a single leaf might host as many as three thousand words...

"You must understand," Kruth continued, "that the ancients included no chapters or indices in their compilations.

It is impossible just to look something up and go to the appropriate page. Therefore the entire *codex* has to be read through in order that the desired section be discovered and copied.

That is why we wait.

"Every day Allfather keeps us safe, for the dark hunter has been unable to find us. When I blow my horn, this stag comes to assist us.

I ride him, and we jargogle those distractible dogs, luring them away from our camp."

"And what length is this book of melancholy?" I said. "How many days will it take for your translator to finish?"

"How long it will take is unknown." Kruth said. He went into detail. According to the gnome, the complexities of the Saturnian-Age syntax create a mental labyrinth. Sometimes the main verb does not appear until the end of a three or four hundred word sentence. Roughly a thousand pages be sown in each of the tomes, of which are seven tomes verified.

A brilliant translator was being secretly employed, a man who lives near, and Kruth was banking on him coming across the sought passage any day. Everyday the gnome checked the hill to spot the lamp-signal from the translator. The needed passage might be at the end of the tome, or, hopefully, somewhere closer to the middle, if God favored. He said his reader had surely finished the first hundred pages by now.

"It is past twenty days;" he added. "Therefore, I reckon the key passage is not to be found in the beginning of that volume, else he would have left out the happy lamp."

"A thirty-third volume is found out of a seven volume series?" I asked. "You have ceased to make sense. You must think me drunk not to notice. You also spoke before of a seventy-seventh volume..." (Who would not challenge this oversight?) The gnome provided even more detail. Each particular volume of these seven volumes is titled, for unknown reasons, not the second, but rather the twenty-second, not the fourth, but forty-fourth. So scribes call them an *elyenthine* set. Holy men say it is a symbolic numerology, because the terrible deeds recorded therein men must forgive, not seven times, but as the Lord instructs, *seventy times seven times*. Others have proposed that the Eldari did write seventy-seven volumes, filling them all with rubbish save for each eleventh volume. The tactic was perhaps meant to confuse those who might plan some mischievous usage. Each extant volume, it is thought, covers an entire age of the world's writing, roughly a thousand pages each, corresponding to the seven world-ages.

"And exactly what passage is your translator seeking?" I asked in amazement.

"We do not know. However, we trust that our reader is also wise, and when he sees it he will know it to be the passage that must be destroyed, or perhaps kept and preserved; our knowledge is too incomplete to predict what should be done. We know a few things on the passage: it must be an Ammouric passage dating from the third world-age. There do remain a few further clues, key words, fragments and such, but that's all."

"All this just for a passage in a book?" I asked. "How could that be? And tell me, who is this black-robed prince, a wizard of old perhaps? Why is this one after hunting you?"

"A wizard of old certainly, so count him not so steeped in evil as some practioners. He is Gohhan, said to be the last of the Magi, but boasts that he is a sorcerer. Perhaps he merely styles for himself a cunning reputation. Anyway, he is a powerful prince who covets the silver-braced book for his own purpose deep, also unknown to us. Grimble knew why. He took that information with him to death, to Vlogiston...till the end of time.

We guess that it may have something to do with his role in an ancient conspiracy, the prophesied "War of Iniquity" dating from time immemorial. We cannot know for certain now, but if the passage is found, much will it reveal.

We have acquired the services of this translator, a monk working in your monastery.

Disguised as circus entertainers we hoped to contact him again, but have not yet spotted his lamp-signal, careful not to bring alarm or compromise his secrecy. We thought all monks would want to see the circus. He did not show up.

One thing we do know for certain: the recovery of the thirty-third volume has awoken many powers. A tempest is stirring, one that is cosmic in magnitude. The dark prince seems always one step ahead of us. He was even in the circus, though we recognized him not. . .until too late."

"And his magic...?" I was thinking aloud, "It be the more powerful than yours, minstrel...?"

"As it appears, at least on the surface of things.
I am bound to follow the law, whereas the dark prince,
if he is a Sorcerer, wants of limitation and law.
The consequent absence of discipline, is itself, I believe, his weakness and eventual downfall. We have seen him consulting another book, the copy of Kruthendel's own work, something that the famous writer set

down long ago involving advice and strategy for underground expeditions, the *Enchiridion de Rebus Subterraneis*!"19

"I have heard of that famous writer, the Eloniah," I remarked. "He also wrote in the obscure tongue."

"Many have heard the name," replied the gnome.

"But few know anything about him. Did you know for example, that he is not even a man?"

"Not a man? Is he a creature like you? Or a man of elfish stock?"

"Can such be called a kind of man? Certainly he is not greater than man, nor warrants being called less. The gnomish race from which Arcavirs come is secretive, but from its origin is subterraneous. Our songs however are of the trees and the sky and the worlds above.

This famous author is older than the forest. I hope to see his writings again; after all, his writings are mine, for he is me, or I am he, to use proper grammar. So I have been told and I don't doubt it. Kruthendel is my name among dwarves and gnomes, and elves. Men simply call me Kruth, or "The Eloniah.

The histories say that I was dragon-tamer a thousand years ago, but I remember it not."

"You are that famous writer?"

"I am he...Arcavirs are lore-keepers, guarding the land itself with learned songs for all men to learn."

"That is remarkable. Should I expect anything less of enchanted beings? So why do you seek him, I mean your own, writings? You said his writings, your writings, are for underground expeditions. Do you wish to descend into the earth?"

"We have already. However, my handbook *De Rebus Subterraneis* was written for humans.

Human explorers must keep some instruction ready to describe for them the dangers of deep-world travels.

They have no natural magic after all. I have my own reasons for this expedition as well. You see, my own copy vanished centuries ago. It obliges a re-publishing."

"But why should humans want to go traveling beneath the earth?"

Kruth explained at least three reasons. Travel is much swifter than surface-going if one knows the way. Secondly, the infernal brotherhood has its monasteries down there, bases of operation for fallen powers. And this: that for magic-users seeking rare spell-components, vital clues and relics are hidden away in deep libraries. And a third: that the stability of

---

19*Enchiridion De Rebus Subterraneis* translates "*Handbook on Subterraneous Matters*." However since the fire of 1666 the title is widely known from Thanato Excorpus printing as *The Deeptracker's Guide*.

things in the upper world is linked to what transpires below. Take the Yule Queen for example.

For five centuries she waged mortal war against the *horgim*,[20] and the dark elves, (who are worse than goblins), their various allies, and against other fel kinds and vampires, such as the trolls, spiders, and attercaps. She is keeping absolute chaos at bay down there. Now, however, a new sinister power has brought the Yule Queen to near abandoning her subterraneous lake and castle.

"A Yule Queen?" I asked, ". . .would that be the same monarch who is titled the celestial queen of the netherworld? Is she your matron?"

"You have heard of her?"

"I have learned something of her as of recent. Just these days past three Ammouric Knights sojourned at the monastery, having arrived with the traveling carnival as if for tournament. From the greater Whitehawk they came, refugees from the Wars of The Heresies. They spoke of a quest, and of the celestial queen below, but further on't divulged they nothing more of knowledge, fore-vowed by some silence of high import."

"Ammouric Knights...?" said Kruth the Arcavir. "That cannot be...the last of Ammouric Knights lay all together in a common grave: the narrow defiles of the Aramtha Gorge. They have, every one of them, fallen in the Ambush of the Stormring some seventeen winters past, in Kargiwall. Not one of the righteous was captured alive. Not one surrender. You be surely mistook, as they fought to the last. What device of heraldry was blazoning the shields of these knights?"

"The white hawk above, and below a sunrise irradiated of seven wavy points in horizon," I said, "upon a crossing argent and colored ground, burgundy or white."

"True, that be the device common of the order." said Kruth, stroking his beard thoughtfully "It could happen that some long-journeying knights roamed far across Whitehawk continent, and were unable to return in time for that doomed march."

"They were Ammouric Knights, by my life. In such wise did the venerable Abbot name them without error, and I heard them answer with

---

[20] *Horgrim (pl. of Horg)*: also, *Bolg*, alt.= *Horgrim, Bolgrim* spelling widely varies (adj.= *horgoth, bolgoth*): shortened form of 'Hobgoblin". The Hobgoblin Empire is found throughout the subterraneous world of the intermundane caverns. Their strongholds are found in every major expanse and they patrol the great caves constantly, continually threatening war against elf-kin and human adventurers, or any other "unlicensed" travelers. Hobgoblins are athletic, rather sizable compared to a mere goblin or an elf, often larger than a man, and they are always trained footsoldiers, well armoured, and bred of a warrior society. They are quite morally deficient and violent-tempered, always looking for a fight, filled with hatred against other races. They are never seen on the Earth's surface on account of a strange sickness that overwhelms those who have gone up.

my own ears. He said that they must continue the quest...even into the netherworld."

"Humans descending into the intermundane caverns? No living mortals can enter the fatal bowels of the deep, not on their own, at least not without a copy of my handbook. They be surely wise to this lore. Did they disclose whither next they would sail?"

"Methinks they abide on St. Aldemar awhile, for they have not been landed but two week. Perhaps they have ridden back to the shore. And for what do they search? Do they also seek one of your *Black Books*? Our Abbot knows why they ride, but he guards close that secret, too high a matter it is for my low station."

"Be assured, they do not seek that Achuleian tome," Kruth the gnome said, "for such men heed little of book-wise learning, a thing they would rather leave to deep-minded clerics and well-taught monks. What they seek is audience with the celestial Queen below, to convey some message or recover some relic, and it bears high on this mystery. Iniquious forces are arising. The knights will not succeed without the aid of *elphim* like us. Even were they to somehow enter into that profound depth, they would surely not find a way through the mazes of caves, canyons, and perils. Few are the mortals who have ever survived it. Few ever can see the celestial Queen. Few have heard her song. They durst descend there anyway, bravery teaching them folly. If only I might provision them with my *Enchiridion de Rebus Subterraneis*."

"I shall find them in forest or town and introduce you to them."

"No. It is too dangerous for us to be seen in the halls of men. Only if a comical company conceals us, like the circus. In any other appearance we are not remembered with affection and said to be bad omen. We cannot at this time aid them; we have our own work to do. Let them be, and pray Allfather accomplishes what is best in their regard."

"I would myself swear to the quest and fight beside them."

"You will have lived a brief span then, for your frame is stalwart, but your heart is not suited for the cruelties of modern combat."

"You are not the first to have said so...it is regretful, but even be that honest counsel, I would shrug off such a harness...I'll shun fighting other men, and haul back a dragon's head instead."

Stormraker the Beardless, watching the others pile rocks, also heard the conversation, and could not help but to speak.

"A seer has affirmed it, and she has said that dragons are awakening deep in the earth."

"Dragons...dragons deeply-dwelling?"

"...they are not passed from the world!" the one named Daufin exclaimed. "No one but the heathen priests of Galadif have seen a dragon for some three hundred of---"

"Keep your talk shy of a whisper, and that includes you, Stormrake," warned Drocwolf as he stood overseeing the rock-piling elf-kin. "The enemy has many spies in these mirkwoods...Actually it now be only two-hundred and sixty-two solar years since..." the patch-eyed Drocwolf added. "Kruthendel and I were the last to spot one in the upper world, as far as any lore remembers. In the second age the dragons crawled down deep to hide below: the aeon-rest. If any subterraneous explorer has gone down far enough to find one slumbering in lair, he has not lived to tell of it."

The woodland gnome looked at Jacob, looked at him stern-like. He solemnly addressed the wayward soul, "...and now, monk, you are privy to much news that even great monarchs of the earth have scant heard. So then,...are you game? You will throw in with us? Come with us, and we shall do the fighting, and you can heal our wounds."

"I am not yet sold on the endeavor. ...my father told many such tales, slumbering dragons, a Yule queen, sorcery, mostly fictions. The righteous soon held him suspect. Tell me, who is this monkish reader you claim you await in view that some rare passage be extracted?"

"He is a monk of Whitehaven abbey," answered the Song-lord, "Anherm of Whigg. His ability for arcane reading is renowned even on the continent."

"Anherm? He was my own tutor in the abbey! Anherm of Whigg; an elder monk he: the brethren affirmed that he reached shy two hundred winters in good health. It was in the days after I first arrived at the monastery when his health diminished. Nevertheless, I was able to study under him for several winters. What is more remarkable was that he was able to teach a dullard like me. Now here I must pass along some woeful tidings to you: you have reason to sorrow, for hark thou this: of Anherm, your translator, know that he has passed into the next world, breathing his last just a few days ago. Our good brethren buried him with solemn Ammouric rites."

"How now?! Our reader is no longer! Unsay your words. Poor Anherm, gone so far away. How shall we learn your wisdom? Now we may never discover the warp of the conspiracy. Now there is no one who can open the book for us, no one to translate the mysteries!"

Kruth was deeply troubled; he wept bitterly. For several moments this lasted. Was he to become inconsolable? The other valraphs also wept, and those who did not weep attempted to console the others. They seemed not so much to mourn Anherm, but because Kruth wept, added to the fact that they could never obtain that for which they quested, for it was sealed shut in an arcane and obscure language. Wiping away his tears Kruth said,

"The Remnant Arcanes may at last have within grasp means to accomplishing their dreadful designs. Now a fear and a Darkness may truly overwhelm the earth."

"Remnant Arcanes?"

"...A clandestine society of Arcanes who survived Nystol's fiery desolation, and who were also responsible in part for it. They saw with their own eyes the fall of the magian towers, and by sorceries breathed they long past the normal span of mortal men. Most agree that it is mere legend. None turned save Anherm."

"Nystol? Of those ruins you speak with a fear on your lips."

"It is a place desolated," Kruth explained. "Anherm of Whigg was indeed the same wizard of erstwhile repute, but not one of them, not a user of sorcery. He put away the study of the new magic when he witnessed the side-effects. Even so, their dark teachings soon became vogue. For that he was banished from Nystol along with *the Elthildor*, in what has been remembered as "the exile of the Eldark sages," one of the greatest of betrayals.

The experience profoundly changed his life. Later, realizing the vanity of all things, and the mischief of worldly minds, he begged Heaven to serve God as a monk. Many things are now transpiring at once, and I have seen in my dreams how the unholy forces have advanced simultaneously, coordinating their moves. We believe that the Sorcerers have contrived a most diabolic conspiracy to revive an ancient evil of unimagined proportion, perhaps even to seal the *hypostatic rift* by utterance of some doom-spell. They are seeking something mysterious, and they must have the tome."

"Aye, that tome...those strange *black books*, seeking them out in the lower world has cost me many of my own soldiers," Drocwolf interrupted sorely, "and some were kin."

"We all have wept; we miss them mightily," Stormraker reminded him.

"I have gleaned much on Nystol," I said, "but it is a place forgotten, some says accursed. What manner of conspiracy do these Sorcerers weave?"

"That is what we hoped to reckon by locating the mysterious passage of the thirty-third volume. There is an obstacle: no well-taught monk or deep-minded cleric is known who can read the Eldark text fast enough to be of any help. But hold, did you not just say that the eld monk himself tutored you?"

"I did. Anherm never spoke of a codex similar to the one Grimble took."

"Of course not. Anherm could not mention the book's existence. As he himself unfolded to me when we last spoke, your monastery has been infiltrated by evil-minded monks."

"Perhaps bad monks, perhaps doubtful and rotten, but conspirators? I doubt it...I never heard him accuse anyone thusly..."

"He would never accuse other monks," said the gnome, "Anherm was of too frail an age to take on so great a contest of accusals. Surely it would have resulted in counter-accusals, and possibly misidentifying imposters or conspiratorial monks."

At this point, a lanky valraph, Daufin, one with whom I had yet to make greater acquaintance, was climbing up the leafless oak tree from which Grimble's body hung. This elf reached out and, swinging his long axe, cut the rope that suspended Grimble's corpse. It dropped and hit the earth with a hollow thud, not like a heavy human body, but light, like an apple falling.

He added his part to the lesson:

"Anherm was laboring through our codex, *Liber Melancholiae* Tomus XXXIII, reading in the late hours of night, desperate and raking through every line. I now see, in view of our predicament, that he drove himself.

He was most relentless. He knew the stakes and how close the nexus of the Hyperlyptic Alignment, how crucial our mission. His health suffered, and his body could no longer sustain his massive brain. That is how deeply our ever-calling quest possesses us, once the knowledge is known."

"Just knowing something from books...what's the use of that?"

"Knowledge, not just information. Knowledge is like the sunlight that causes leafy branches to pivot upward to heaven. It can turn humans, their clans, cities, entire nations. But men themselves must reflect it if they wish to scatter the Darkness. And don't be fooled: human sorcery is lying knowledge, a great threat, wreaking soul-damage on the user, being even more powerful than our native magic of fairy."

Daufin Nerileth did not cease his dissertation there. He was a knowledgeable and experienced soldier; a quiet and cautious man, the most learned fighter of all Valraphim. "Also know, Jacob Magister,' he continued, "that human sorcerers employ not the benificent magics of yore...the eld charms of brook and dale, as you see in the gnome and fairy-bard, but his magic must be rather the work of demons, intruders from beyond the terrestrial sphere. You saw the berserking magic of a demon in Grimble, no fairy magic 'twas. Fairy magic does not have those insane side-effects. So in his frenzy he miscalculated the Hyperlyptic Alignment. He wrongly reckoned it. Aye, it is past, it was last night..."

"The Hyperlyptic Alignment?"

"It is an alignment of Saturn with Mercury in the Goat galaxy," the Arcavir said. "It is the only time in which the vibrations are correct for the restoration of the hyperlyptic integrity within the celestial vortex, opening the universal source-fonts for manipulation and making possible again the forbidden magic of Nyzium. It is this we hope to thwart."

"Aye, lest that witch—what she let pass her velvet lips...come to pass." said Corydon.

"Talk only well of that ethereal lady and her prophecy, Corydon," snapped the gnome brusquely.

"A strange fill of lore that you fey-creatures talk up," I said. "Those old magics will never return, and most of them were just rumour. The Sorcerers whom you have told, they are some foolish men dreaming dreams. The many gods are extinct, just as you have sung, gnome. If things go awry in the wide world, Lord God will straighten them out with the justice of his hand."

"Sure enough, Ancientmost will protect tribes, gold-crowned kings, mortal men, even so..." the gnome added, "but he does not force loyalty. Certain obstinent lords he cannot keep from destroying themselves and others... freely chosen is the ordeal you humans must take."

"If Anherm were so burdened, why didn't he assign me or some other monk to do the translating work?"

"It is because, just as he told me, monsters lurk in your monastery. It is unsafe. There you will find housed infiltrators, agents of the evil one, infernal monks trained to deceive the faithful. Anherm trusted only himself with arcane knowledge. Whomsoever he may have suspected, we can now only guess. He took that knowledge to the grave. Anherm could have sought your aid, but he knew: even the most trusted peers fall to the interests of a loose tongue. He confided to no one, save the venerable Abbot."

The elfbeards bore up the corpse of Grimble and lowered it into the shallow pit. They folded his pale hands and within stiff fingers placed the murderous hilt of the shattered sword, a once great heirloom.

"What you claim on monkish gossip is so." I said. "...and I confess, that is, I have seen it, or rather heard it. Those kind of monks: wolves are they, in sheep's clothing."

An agent so disguised, I admit, is most difficult to detect. The *diabolus* employs many schemes. And there is human folly to add. An undisciplined monk, judging himself upright and holy, even though mindfully he would not intend it, can do harm. Even in a monastery renowned of great charity, no monk can keep hush any secret long. Words fly about like a monstrous rooster from one pair of lips to another; many-tongued rumour, a demon for sure. A monk has no refuge from other monks. More than anything else, temptation for a monastic is this: to reveal failures of other monks or gossip. Who would be thought a fool to have left them? Enough said of these things. I had set my heart on the happy wonders of worldy life, since I supposed Heaven was far from reach now.

"Do not attempt to dissuade me. It is true: I do read the Saturnian-Age Latin better than any other, having been taught by Anherm himself. However, I've made up my mind; and I shall continue my travels; not return to the highly-perched monastery. To my own command I consign myself."

"You wish to escape all this, what your own eyes have seen and ears heard?" Kruth asked.

I did not answer. Such struggles were beyond me. I esteemed myself a mediocre monk at best, and seeker of the good life...one who would not be a target for demons, having already been wrecked. A simple freeman let me be; no threat to the Dark empire. Unmasking spiritual deceptions and untangling conspiracies, that's just too much. Let holy monks or adventurers like the valraphs save the world. Life as a townsman I would surely appreciate, a simple faring, and a predictable one!

"You flee from the sanctuary and embrace the world of men, hoping for something better?" the gnome asked squarely. "Ha! And you seek freedom from wicked tongues? You deceive yourself. Say it is not so...stay and help us, for in short time the conspiracy of a thousand years will ferment, and we shall not possess the knowledge to answer it.

You should be able to locate the thirty-third volume in the monastery; Anherm must have hidden it somewhere.

Almighty God had you stumble onto us, the very monk whom Anherm chose to pass on his rare skill, a blessed inheritance, ere he went into eternal rest. No coincidences...

If you, the monk we need, sent by God, turn from this, I foresee great peril will shortly cover the civil lands. Men unperceiving lulled into complacency...the wide-ranging scythe of spirit-death follows; Red Asceticism whelms all, minds dumb and hearts numb, and in the end every last soul shall enter into fateful bonds.

If a dragon wishes to restore his diminished reputation after a thousand years of aeon-rest, the vain creature must arise from his bed of gold and search the hollow earth for enemies, even take to wing upon the surface. He must once again prove his fury.

The Intermundane Bestiary

XII   OF NOBLE DEEDS AND WICKED

The valraphs piled cold stones upon Grimble's cold corpse.

The sky above was shrouded with clouds of deep iron hue, The sunrise pierced them with yellow streaks. Dapple bled through the greyness below. An odor of decaying soil and leaves permeated the dank air.

Stone after stone they tossed; CLINK, clack, clink.

When it was done the elfbeards marshalled.

...It was not terribly cold, but chilly enough. I had to wrap my cloak tightly. Kruth uttered strange sounding gnome-prayers over the site. The wet pile kept sliding apart.

"Why pray you over the grave of a traitor?" asked Stormraker the Beardless in a bitter tone. "What law or custom recommends that? The lout slew Thingle, a soldier, and my long-time companion. See, the stones will not stay, but slide off; not even the earth submits to cover him."

"That is right..." said Kruth. "What you say, Storm, we all know how he was after doin' a fair share o' murderin' and witchery."

"He was a black-hearted one alright," remarked Buckbar. "Fell, as any nasty goblin."

"...but could he have regretted his act," Kruth added, "somehow repented in his end, nay but for a moment? He also was a good brother to Thingle once. Nor do we know his last act for a certainty. I say let us err on the side of mercy. Let us not judge what is hidden from us. He was dearly mistook. It is not ours to say more. He was under a demon spell. We will administer the usual rites"

Stormraker at once retorted with passion. "—not judge what was clearly done before all? His actions were black, but still his own.

I, for one, no longer expect fair decisions. This oathfold, seemingly drunk with draughts of the sprite's mead, is beyond any sober help. Does anyone contest how the expedition has cost too many Valraphim already? We let slip away nearly a entire year locked up in the basements of that miserable tower-prison of Zenops the wizard. It was he who had built the singlar colossal tower in Kithom's gorge, thinking to rival Nystol. Boy monk, record this in your books: the Tower of Zenops was originally meant to shame Nystol's towers, for the Arcanes of Nystol had exiled the old fool. So he built a colossal tower of his own. Its roots stretch down even to the grand caverns.

"We escaped it...but for what? How many fatal ends can be counted now, hapless comrades lost from traps and deadly creatures, plying the deeps of intermundane earth? When we departed from the mountains of Ayrs we were fifteen of us sworn as The Valraphim. Mysteriously, it were but one valraph lost, and one hycman, whereas all who were dwarves perished. Now we are left six elf-eared mountaineers and have just one sturdy axe-hafting dwarf, just one to estimate our depth, no second opinion."

"Why hoist up the memory of past woes, Stormrake?" asked Drocwolf, ". . . is the present melancholy not enough?"

All looked at Stormraker for a moment. Kruth ignored the rash words, but a defense based on proof was expected by all. So Kruth began a eulogy:

"Many are the ways doom unfolded when we trekked through the great caves and grand galleries.

Many a righteous dwarf, plus a hycman, did not avoid doom. Let me recount them, starting from the beginning.

The Horgoth Empire lays claim to a vast under-region indeed, and hobgoblin patrols are ceaseless throughout the caverns, where pellucid mists and lambent fungi illumine.

The horg warlords even fashion massy tombs down there for their heroes, with traps guarded. We found such a tomb, and went in out of curiosity.

That was when the mischief started, for soon the hobgoblins were alerted.

Hauk the Trollwise died there in that place.

Some of us caught a glimpse of the spike come hurtling out of seeming nowhere. The powerful mechanism impaled him. We could not dislodge his body.

We could not reach to take him down, affixed as he was to that dooming mechanism, bleeding in the corridor of the vault. And not so trollwise as Hauk were any of us, not at all. We lost a sure guide.

What a devilish irony!

The audacious horg-slayer received no rites, and has this only commemoration: his bones hang on display in the tomb-labyrinth of the very foe his ancestor once smote down, the gruesome hulk Mulgeron, Anarch and hobgoblin-chief. We had to leave Hauk there. His corpse made wise a hobgoblin patrol. Later, we could hear the echoes, black-hearted horgs hunting us somewhere in the corridors not far off.

They were hot on our trail. Why look for an excuse?

We should have quelled fear and taken the risk.

We should have held up there a spell and sang a song of power, honouring a fallen warrior's funeral.

Mursa of Hanningdeep also had his last hour, when a horgoth arrow blackened with poison lodged in his back. So fell he to his knees. The butcher Mulg and his fiendish detachment of black-hearted horgs, from afar upon the ledge of Idha, caught sight of us fleeing across the white sands of Hell-gap, the grandest of caverns, and he bade them pluck a far-sent volley of vulture-winged shafts. By some unlikely hazard one missile actually found its target. No one even noticed that it struck Mursa, not until the horgs were already overtaking him. Some of us turned and saw the dwarf on his knees, the arrow lodged in his back.

From afar we all saw how Mulg, son of Mulgeron,
himself finished Mursa off... they caught up to him.
A Kalaran scimitar Mulg uses, in his bloodlust brandishing it.
We could have fought to the last to venge ourselves.

"Then was taken Tory the Harelip, nimble hycman-thief we purchased from the Othgog prison.
He never had much chance to earn his liberty.
The infernal monks caught him the time we sent him in, when he slipped into the shadowy deep-world library and saw the collection of volumes bound in human skin.
Who knows what evil he suffered? Who durst accompany him? He spoke of those monks and their library as "an easy job."
We did wait for him and wait, and no more could wait.
He left a few mysterious thieving tools, keepsakes.

Ginnar of Tuskaland, the white-beard general, also was lost.
All have now learned the truth of that veteran's demise,
and whose iron it was opened his veins
to let pour forth nibelung blood in red streams.
It was no hobgoblin's shaft which got him,
but a blade turned from where a sworn Valraph would never expect,
from his own oath-brother Grimble. Not long after,
the foe tracking us came across Ginnar's abandoned corpse.
Those bolgrim surely offered not even a grunting funeral for him, but rather they did a thing which they always threaten in taunts: rites which they claim involve roasting the enemy's flesh for a camp meal.
Another strong hand was soon lost in the lands of the everdark, Duri the Tall. A glamorous nymph, a sylph of the mushroom forest, lured him into her lair. A few of us caught a glimpse of her unearthly beauty. We all heard the song of wonder that the charming witch sang,
the whispered prophecy on Nystol
that echoed through the dim forest of mushrooms.
You all mistook that fair witch for the ethereal lady that appeared.
It was not her. That ethereal lady was pure and gave words of hope. But the fair witch lured in Duri. He committed an unwise act and let his desire rule his feet. Who knows for what purpose foul the enchantress has used his bones?
If only he had known what the old crone really looked like.
Then the crafty hand, Faxi the gem-wise, embraced a useless end.
He slipped from the ledge while ascending the spiral stairs
of the world-bridge, the mountainous stalagmite called the Vanith.
We watched, helpless even to reach out a hand as the poor dwarf plummeted down through volumes of cavernous air and clouds of flapping bats. His only funeral Muse was the bubbling of the mud pits into which he plunged headlong.
At last count include now these two valraphs,

Grimble the Treasonous and Thingle the Penitent
who lay in stillness upon earth. Only six elfbeards have skirted doom,
plus a dwarf, and a gnome. Only two of us are trained warriors.
But would you have us leave Grimble's body to wild beasts?
And have you ill-will even against his soul?"

"Do what you must, small man," said Stormraker. "I will be going my
own way soon. You are, in fact, quite crazed yourself. How many times did
we have a happy chance to seize gold from the tombs of kings? You called
it an impiety and forbade it...instead compelling us to lug around enormous
black tomes and rimestocks that no one can read. What right-thinking elf
or valraph would give up a tranquil dwelling in the whispering trees or a
cool cave in hollow hills, working as an artisan or metallurgist?
    –To hazard this business instead? Follow a leader obsessed?
    I would rather join the circus. Indeed I did enjoy my week with them:
the fair wages and tasty morsels: succord wings. Permanent position in
such a musing company is far the wiser."

"Is that so?" replied Kruth. "Remember, you are oath-bound to the
quest. Oath-breakers never finish with honour. Will you be faithless?"
    The Arcavir spoke in righteous indignation. He pointed to Grimble's
corpse.

"Persevere, and though we perish withal, right shall prevail in the end.
This glorious endeavor will be imperishable and never fade.
Shrink away from this matter, and the lamps of the sky will totter,
and the earth begin to sink into a darkness unending.
Shame will haunt your eternity."

Stormraker said, "So that you will see your errors, Arcavir, I shall
answer your accusals. Hear me teach how justice was worked in all deeds
done down there, and relate the actual causes whereby fell those named of
Valraphim you've recounted.
    First, as for this knave under the cold stones here, Grimble: everyone
knows that he was a shameful fellow, with a soul of a madman–, given to a
life of greed.
    Sadly, he was ever counting his coin, even going so far as to purchase
his friends, vanity's comrades. Perfidious bonds of pact, never
understanding authority, true fellowship, loyalty, or sacrifice. Thingle
relented and turned from idolatry, but as for the other, may divine Justice
be upon him.

    As for the rest of them...I start with the last you counted,
    Faxi the gem-wise who slipped and fell from the world-bridge, the
Vanith. Why did he stumble?
    He had been under a hypnotic daze, or rather, entranced, and he let
himself adore the gleaming gems he was collecting, constantly taking them
out and looking them over.
    Admonish him I did; said he was placing mere stones above all else.
    Why he fell from that spiral ledge has more to do
    with the strange inlaid gems he found on a golden amulet.
    He wore it around his neck. That dwarf constantly examined it
    while we marched, turning it over and over again,

and he kept staring into it, as into some fatal gyre.
He said it could inform him of things that no one else knew,
save the *Erelim*. He stumbled several times,
tripping over himself, not watching where he was going.
I warned him: put the amulet away, keep it out of sight.
His gleaming and crystalline paradise had his attentions
rather than careful steps on that narrow stairs to the world above.
The poor wretch slipped and dropped through volumes of air;
was anyone surprised?
And recounted you of the dwarf Duri, brother of Faxi.
Who here proposes that his hour was unforeseeable?
At every settlement or deep-tavern we stopped by, he went in to
charm some nymph into pleasure. His desires were low enough indeed, for
he would even stoop so far as to pay for unclean embraces.
It was no trouble at all when, not long thereafter,
that sylph of the mushroom forest bewitched him
with an illusion of her unearthly beauty, and so consumed his life.
She is now for sure trafficking his bones for her craft,
for such a sin embroils the sinner both body and soul.

Add the not-so-old, white-haired general, Ginnar; indeed a great loss.
He had too much confidence in his own men, trusting to them every task
that he should have looked after himself.
At every opportunity he voted for rest and camping.
His excuse was old age, though everyone knows
that dwarf-kin do not grow frail when the beard whitens.
So by his own laziness the not-so-old man slowed us down.
No one dared slight him with correction.
He was a distinguished veteran, but self-satisfied with his fame.
Grimble, treacherous in heart, marked him like a wolf that sees a weak old
stag, and takes advantage of the right moment.
When Ginnar had fallen behind and the hobgoblins were close,
Grimble fell upon his prey.
No one was going to jeopardize his designs.

Nor did you neglect to mention Tory the Harelip,
the hycman whom we ransomed from the massive prison of granite.
A master thief like Godiun Foute; and was he not brave,
a stern fighter as well? Yet who among us
does not count his purse safe now that the red-hand no longer eyes it?
Corydon tried to bring him around: take the thieves' oath
and join the Guild of St. Dismas. He would have none of it.
Instead he went alone into the underworld library,
hoping to fetch something precious.
—I wonder if his leathery skin now serves as the binding
for some strange tome in that underworld library
...terrible thought, heh? Tis' too bad.
We esteemed his skill, not his character.

Raud the Strong as well...
You forgot to count him, didn't you, Kruthendel? —
One of my own dear friends. He too was lost.
He was consumed in just a few hours

by a devouring pestilence, *maegolot*. And how unexpected
...afterall, dwarves do not get infections. Who can describe
with words the misery of his groans? ...a blight of horror...

Who dared to stay by his side? How did he contract the contagion? I never ceased to warn him of the dangers of every strange delicacy we came across, every underworld berry or subterranean shellfish, every exotic fruit or unusual mushroom, and every little grey deer or reptile egg he salvaged for cooking up at dinner. Like Tantalus teased in hell; never obtaining the longed-for taste.

Raud thought it unworthy for a dwarf to heed the advice of elf-kin like me; after all, he would say, dwarves have tougher stomachs than elves. His days were numbered regardless of whether he lived beneath the surface or upon it.

Only the day passed he had given me his oxen mead-horn for safekeeping.

Then, 'ere that, there was Mursa...a talented warrior, young,
champion of the Valraphim. To rein him in was a constant effort. He was always for humiliating the miserable company of black-hearted horgrim that pursued us.

He kept trying to get them riled, and that was not easy.

The enemy were following orders and had no real fire for the chase, nor did they care much if companions were forfeit. Mursa would make sure that the foe was tricked, getting them to do something stupid,
and he would have a laugh at them.

A little respect for the enemy could have served him well.

He was a show-off, thinking himself cleverer and more capable than the rest of us. He only associated with those Valraphim whom he deemed of high enough rank. That cost him, having too few friends to counsel or to correct his behavior.

When we were fleeing across that subterrene plain,
he spotted Mulg and his crew behind us in pursuit.

They were still high up on the cavern cliffs, coming out
of those tunnels. And they also could see us.

Mursa took the opportunity to mock them, and he called out
in the fell tongue, "Tell the horg host that it was Mursa the Nibelung who made a fool of you!" So he vaunted aloud. The rest of us were fleeing farther off, but we all heard it.

That horgoth detachment let fly black-winged shafts from above, all aimed at Mursa. When he saw the whizzing doom on its passage, he turned to run. It was too late. A black shaft had found its target.

A few moments later Mulg's cudgel, not a scimitar, cut short his day. Kruthendel, with crazed fixation, roared that we must continue to flee, and flee we did, rather like lions from deer.

At last there is the question of Hauk the Trollwise, first of valraphs to fall, and of how, or rather, why, he forfeited his span.

Hauk was infuriated at the foe.

He could never rest, always planning some way to ensnare them. He hoped to pour his foaming cup of wrath down their throats. Certainly what these horgrim had done in the past was an evil thing, and the base and cruel acts were many.

However, it goes against every custom of war and every code of honor to disgrace the tombs of the fallen in the way he planned.

Blacker hearts than they know bravery.

Even a sense of honour does not escape the horg.

Hauk well knew that even those brutes honour their own fallen, protecting the tombs and treasures of great chieftains with terrible traps.

The hidden spike impaled him; it was not a mechanism too difficult to detect, but he had become sloppy. His fury had eclipsed his better judgement, but our own fear eclipsed ours, and no one checked Kruthendel's command to flee.

So we fled, again, aye, like lions from deer.

Let Hauk's demise be a lesson for all, that we often be too wroth against a foe. We call them dishonorable and blameworthy, but in truth mishaps befall more often by reason of our own careless swagger.

We must never work evil upon any, but only justice.

Some of this company murmurs against that; would rather a furious desire be realized.

It is true; fight we must, and a fight against black-hearts is best when many of the foe lay still upon the cold earth justly slain. If ever you do so, dreadful recompense might be opened to you. These black-hearted horgim, contagion of the world though they be, are given leave to thrive not by their own power.

By the permission gained they thrive, a chastisement for the sins of men, for the unjust and corrupt kingdoms in Whitehawk.

When we dared into their forbidden everdark territory,

we were entering danger for ourselves,

and these enumerated fallen now testify to it...

So take care to revise your tale, Kruthendel. They deserved it in strict justice."

"And who uttered this plan?" I asked.

Kruth was glowering at Stormraker. The warrior looked away, unwilling to make further challenge... enough said. The gnome had heard my question. He answered it in full:

"Stormrake has valor but little tolerance. Yes, there was a voice that called us. Let me tell in full how the endea*vor began*

...*it is something I cannot unfold without first giving* word

on the supposed origins of the book: A voice from another world prophesied many things. When the men of Kutaal[21] in the second age first

---

[21] *Kutaal:* This region is also the name of the great race sprung of the youngest son of Maceon, Kutaal, who refused to leave his brother go alone into exile. He was given reign of the vast region of semi-arid grasslands that in the north borders the desert of Kithom (Kathon) The capital of Kutaal was the coastal city Namaliel in ancient times, until it was devastated by successive raids of the Atalur, Kalar, Dark Orkhan and the Imperial Armies. The Kutaal were originally nomads and do not mix with other races. Droves of various foreigners in their beloved city made it too

received *The Black Books of Melancholia*, the bindings were not black, but white, and easily recognized as the fine skins from the sacred elephant herds in Kithom.

Nor were they of "Melancholy" titled. These were first rumored among us to be compilations kept by the *Elthildor*, whom men call the Eldari, the wise of old who were the first dwellers in Achuleia, most ancient of civilizations.

In these silver-braced books they had recorded many of the sacred mysteries, hymns, and prophecies from the beginnings of the ages. They included written directions from Allfather himself on how the books should be filled. As time went on and men listed many things in their annals, these were to be sent to the Eldark for sacred recording, and a new entries were prepared in Nystol every twenty-two years.

As centuries passed it was noted that dark splotches appeared on the covers of each volume. Scribes attributed this to great age. However, other books with the similar bindings and equal age did not darken so. Many attributed the phenomenon to an increase of sins, the sins recorded and condemned in the volumes from which the human kingdoms had not repented.

The books became dark grey and even blackened entirely by the third age. By then, however, few could remember how to read the lost language and the *Akaratic*[22] script, the ancientmost kind of writing, a skill kept only by the *Elthildor*. During the close of the fourth world-age, even fewer could remember. Large portions of marginalia were created by Latin commentary and translations in various languages, like Oruscan Greek, the common tongues in those centuries. As time passed, even that language changed so as to forget its original structure. The books at last came to be dismissed as writings of impossible difficulty. They were regarded as of little value even by the righteous men of Ulthor.[23]

---

dangerous for them to live there. But another city would arise for them, Vesulum.

[22] *Akaratic*: glyphic writings left over from the first world-age. These are thought to be the oldest of all writings in the Furth, representing a celestial language used by God himself.

[23] *Ulthor (Ulthork, Ulthuring):* The great kingdom of men which became the seat of order and civilization in the northern regions after the waning of the *Regulian Principate*: Bordered by the Sea of Goldyndol, its principle city, Yrbath, relies on the fishing industry. Maceon planted the Ammouric faith in old Ulthor in the time of his passing, and it has not weakened since, as it has in the other kingdoms of the upper world. Ulthoran minuscule is the principle script of the fourth age. The Ulthorings were great kings, such as Argoth the Good. It became a province of the Regulian Principate in the third age but finally broke ties with Regulis when the Red Ascetic came to power. The rangers of Ulthor protect many places in Whitehawk sacred to faith, such as Mt. Arguzinial and Vesulum, and The Edolunt Riders, still patrol the civil lands of the old empire.

The order of Ammouric monks in The Dry Blood Sea, the Monastery of the Weeping Brotherhood, remained secluded from the world. They kept the tradition of preparing *The Black Books* even after Nystol was desolated.

Word came that several of the oldest books had been found. They had been preserved in the foundation tunnels of distant Nystol. A reckless party of sand-pirates had somehow made way through the terrors of the desert wilderness.

They had entered into the sub-corridors of the ancient cliffs.

There they found a library, books in near mint condition, and an excellent but incomplete collection of these.

Most notably missing, however, was the eleventh volume.

Now each man can haul only one cumbrous tome at a time.

Eight explorers had gone but only three of them returned back alive from the desert trek. Only three volumes were therefore recovered, the twenty-second, thirty-third, and fifty-fifth.

Word of this recovery somehow came across the sea to our mountains.

The shrewd dwarf Mimir, wise to the immense but unearthly value of the tomes, sailed from Telemark

across the Inner Furthsea to Hermopolis

and traded his arsenal of elf-forged weapons for the silver-braced books.

On his return voyage Mimir became ill and did not recover.

Two moons later, perhaps from exhaustion in his mad attempt to read through the volumes and learn all knowledge, his dwarf-span in this world ended.

It was at this time that a voice called each one of us. Each heard a voice, according to the spirit, as each has testified: a divine whisper, bidding us to guard 'the books that men's misdeeds have darkened.'

Old Ginnar, thinking himself alone with the burden, was first to speak of his visions to fellow dwarves,

(just like someone who, driven by melancholy or revelation, lapses momentarily and utters enigmas aloud to himself). But news came of the mountaineers claiming like experiences. Much was revealed at the grand *elphim* assembly, the Vatheng.

Where in thunder begin our search for the silver-braced books?

Uncertain, like a pack of wolves detecting

a strange and unfamiliar scent, we tarried too long and lost the initiative. Weeks passed waiting for news from the dwarven kingdom.

We failed to seize moment and train. As we were preparing to set out for the halls of the Nibelungs, where Mimir had lived, there came strange news. Among the treasures of Mimir's lonely chambers the dwarves recovered the mysterious texts. But they had vanished again.

"How had they vanished? -certain well-versed Archscribes

among the dwarves. They were teachers who wanted these texts safe and gleaned the importance. Unlike us they acted at once. These did not know that certain dwarves and valraphs had already been divinely chosen as the sacred guardians.

They were eager to make plans for the preservation of the texts, wishing that the human race not be lost to wickedness on account of ignorance.

So on they set out on their own, by leave of the Nibelung council. Two gnomes and two dwarves were to transport the books to **Vesulum**[24] secretly. They did not want to risk news of their pilgrimage brought

to the attention of evil minions, so they did not notify the Vatheng or seek a military escourt, such as the Edolunt Riders.

Instead they planned for a clandestine operation.

The volumes could be quietly transported to the treasuries

of the temple complex, sacred halls of the Ancientmost in Vesulum...

"On their pilgrimage way, however, the hell-hounds of a bolg-horde picked up the trail. The scribes were pursued and overcome near Zenop's colossal keep, the Tower of Wyrdd. The bloody army of the great skull-standard, the mighty Mulg, horde-chieftain of the horgim, by chop-chop deprived all four scribes of their tops and seized the sacred treasures!

"There went about confused reports of the plight of that crew. Hycman scouts had witnessed the nasty deed from afar. They confirmed the capture and execution of dwarves and a gnome. Mulg himself did the deed.

"After the rash act, he and his bad boys realized something.

By this bloody work of terror they had interfered with pilgrimages of the Ancientmost. Strange to say it, but from this fact alone

the perpetrators themselves were fraught with dread and terror.

They grabbed the relic-books.

Mulg and his band fled from the scene

to hide themselves away in the deep and dark,

(as if concealment from Ancientmost were possible).

The brutes carried the mysterious **codices**

into the fatal bowels of earth, far down into the vast intermundane caverns. There they received good coin for the items from monks, the infernal monks, whose law is inversion. It must have been afterwards that the three surviving volumes somehow got split up.

"The Vatheng decided to act. Our spelunking party

of axe-bearing dwarves and sure-shot half-elf mountaineers assembled: the Valraphim, sworn by oath to the quest.

We went with the stout dwarves down there, into the dark and stony places below, home of the fel grey-elves and nasty goblins, even farther into the world-caves of intermundane earth.

Our purpose: recover the sacred relics.

"It was a matter of honour, for these books had been given

---

[24] *Vesulum (Vorsalir): a holy city* and training ground for kings and a place of study for *selvas* (priests), spiritual stronghold in a little cliff-village hidden away in the lower *canyons of Hermius*. Certain areas were established for prayer with guidelines requiring spiritual clean-ness. Many great monks, priests, and clerics came from there. It remains the only city that can rival wicked Nystol (Nyzium) in spiritual power." Although no Ammouric monastery was ever established there, it did boast the greatest library of sacred works from the ancient world. The city remained pure from corruption and heresy until the usurpation of the cult-master Shahi Nuzzib. Glossarium includes Aetholus' description.

into the custody of the *elphim*. Although they be the heritage of Men, we *elphim* were marked by unmentionable power to intercede on behalf of men and preserve them.

The books tell the saga of the divine shadow-warrior, and of the sins of men who betrayed him. They also recount the history of the tribes of Ammouri. They are encyclopedic compilations of sacred chronicles and many other tracts, including spells and poetry.

Albeit, the books were memory incarnate for the human race."

Kruth took a long draw off his horn pipe.

"For the race of men easily forgets what the past has taught." Corydon added, a sudden spark of insight. "Men do not recount from one generation to the next; they forget how the hinter-evil and other powers many times deceived their ancestors.

The new generation hopes to forget history.

We can remind them anyway."

"We resolved to carry our torches farther down into the dim corridors," the gnome continued, deep in recollection.

"We captured one of the horgs and by interrogation learned that all but the twenty-second volume had been sold to the infernal monks, Gnostics who worship the demon Abraxas.

Zenops, one of the wizards who has dealings beneath, had paid a high price for the twenty-second volume.

He was enraged to discover himself unable to read it.

We decided to make the trek to his tower before heading to the dark monks. But we caught the attentions of his patrolling centaurs, (as it now appears, perhaps through Grimble's signal, for the *drakodemon* was already long at work through him).

The centaurs captured us.

They imprisoned us for what must have been many moons in the subterraneous root of the colossal Tower of Wyrdd.

The Sorcerer himself interrogated us, and not delicately.

He learned of our purpose grand, eager to obtain knowledge of some obscure passage from the books, to his own design. By means of such a passage he hoped to find a precious talisman that housed a gem, what was called "The Nagamaud Amulet" We could not help him; we ourselves could not even read the books.

The ordeals did not end there. Yet neither did help from above.

When we were doubting possibility of ever being freed from that dungeon, there was an apparition, some luminous power revealed to us. We think it an ethereal creature of the *nephilung* order. The being had what seemed a lion's head, sporting seven horns like a star. This entity broke apart the iron locks of our various subterrene cells. Then he faded back into the ethereal without explanation. At once we gave thanks and infiltrated Zenops' study, put him out with some old-fashioned fairy tricks, and grabbed our silver-braced book. We snuck away, escaping notice of the centaur-guards, to continue our quest. As you have heard us recount, even though all the dwarf-kin escaped the tower-dungeon, they did not survive the perilous trek through the lower world. Many dwarves, Valraphim, were left in stillness upon the silent and stony floors of the grand galleries."

"So many mishaps you have endured..." I was thinking aloud again, wondering at the marvelous struggles.

"In those remote caverns," added Drocwolf, "battles must be fought, yes, but how hazardous the circumstances of the everdark regions. Survival is never accomplished by skill or talent, rather do unseen perils and butchery unrestrained take both the wise and the foolish, the seasoned veteran, and the overbold younker...aye, the dented axe as well as the one never whetted. Survival would seem a stroke of mere luck, had we not faith. Even so, you could enter into league us, swear an oath, and give us a monk's blessing every day. In the face of mischief, or monstrous onslaught, you could utter ominous curses against trolls and demons. You could read holy words of power out of monkish books, employ the quarterstaff in your hands. It would tip the scales in our favor. Your monk-hands could heal our battle wounds, and the divine protection of the *Erelim* would extend to us."

"Does it not extend already?" I said. "–do you doubt it simply because some have been lost? You said that the Ancientmost himself called you on this quest. He may not have been interested in protecting selfish participants."

"We did not survive because of an excelling righteous life. Yet are these remaining wastrels. But your power of ever–whispering prayer might cover even them."

"Is that not superstition?"

"Of a reckless and untaught deep–sieger's crew I am captain," Drocwolf replied, "but also have wit on things more akin to philosophers.
The prayer of a rope–girded monk or long–robed priest,
and the work he joins to it, may not appear significant
to the naked eye, but mark ye: dread its power."

"That may be, but who takes grace must have an open hand, even though he be but a wastrel" I said. "These elder races, gnome, do retain yet enough faith, unlike me. Consider this: a powerful monk would have known better, not lost his way, his soul coming so close to perdition. Besides, where there is little faith, healings and holy protections, even of a priest–anointed, will have little effect. Even if powerful words are incanted with skill, celestial war is not granted to a wandering soul.

Therefore I refuse. I renounce pride and avoid further presumption. I cannot face dangers with you, since by leaving the monastery I have lost divine favor. I would only become a burden. Then I would be hunted down and finally forfeit my dear life like so many of your crew already. Before long, no doubt, worse evils would befall you as well on account of unlawfully recruiting a monk.

I am going to resume my hope and go about my business as an ex-monk, unknown and bothering no one. I shall pray and Heaven high–above might grant me some minor consolation: a wholesome life...perhaps a fine wife who can keep a splendid home. So I'll grow old, dying in my bed supported by children who care for me. Martial glory is not for me, rather it would end with this head of mine end up planted on the end of some goblin's pike or hair–tied to a giant's belt.

Take care. With what little faith I retain I shall pray for you and your Valraphs...but now I say farewell."

A true master discourses on staff-method and enlightenment in the same breath. He is a tiger that tracks down his prey and pounces on it. He will fight tooth and claw, but leaves the catch of meat untasted, unmarred

Tien Joshur
Summer Instruction for Campaigning Monks

XIII   *O Ye of Little Faith*

Jacob now saw everything in his mind: "Scant wisdom in this..." he said to himself "keeping with such not-entirely-human types, troll-creatures and elven-hybrids, a mysterious gnome, hot-headed dwarves, and every fairy, all the elder races. The old warning is not too hard to keep—shun them..."

He declared to them: "You all know that I am a run-away monk. But I'll not be all beholden to any of you, despite these occurances."

"Will you be heading back to the monastery?" a valraph asked.

"I am free. I am alive. It is thanks to your help, and God's. So thank you and fare you well."

"And you also fare well...but mark this counsel: stay clear of the Ringwood, those eldritch woods."

"The Ringwood and Timberhills... all part of the Lokken. Is there anywhere there to walk without dangers? I think not. It's a large expanse...but I can hazard it alone anyway."

"Monk," cried Stormraker. "We valraphs perish for lack of food. These roaks here who delivered you from the knife will starve without some square meal soon! I have nothing to cook them. Can you help...?"

"Lush beds of mushrooms grow here and there on the forest floor," Jacob answered, "and there is small game.

You will take some squirrel no doubt. Are not elf-kin superior with the bow? Thank you for saving me from Grimble, but not for making me hostage in the first place.

I shall send along something if I can. Good luck!"

Off he went and did not even look not back at them. It was really for the first time that he ever weighed dangers against his eternal soul, calculating rather that someday this life will end for him. He went along in a hurry to make distance from any fairy magic or strange enchantment, or any witch or other weirdling they might attract.

He jogged until out of their sight. His heart beat a rapid beat. They had saved him from Grimble's ritual blade and deserved a fair turn. But down he sped through pathless woods, as if flying from devils. Back to the rust-colored trail in the pine groves he arrived, glad to put distance between himself and madness.

Soon Jacob slowed down. If he lost pace he would need to pause for breathing. His plan did not allow for loosing pace.

"Without any breakfast, or but a few spoons of porridge from the valraphs the morning before, I was eager for the monastery hall. A cozy nap in bedafter a square meal would be splendid, then getting ready, washing up for the noon meal with the brethren.

First say nothing... Feign no ignorance, but later tell the whole true account."

The "real" world was clearly brutal and chaotic. He was sure of that: all the combat in which real warriors engage, witnessed for real when Thingle fell —all too ruthless and fast.

Along at a cautious pace he went and over each hillock and peered far ahead, as much as the coniferous thick permitted.

The sun came out beaming on his course. Jacob was fretting to himself. "Could I return and stay living as a monk, and not see the world? But the world's bloodshed witnessed was all very sad: real fighting and death, not just jousting, or sparring like monks. . . no, rather a mortal trap from which straightaway to recoil."

Woodland birds chirped their own noonday chant.

So he was returning... returning to forfeit the nice vanities of an earthly life. He was decided. Miss out on many troubles. Remain an obscure and unknown monk in Whitehaven-upon-the-sea.

"And thanks be to God I'll be sure of supper.

On the road I paused and listened often, and not just for thundering horse or barking dogs.

The Lokken has weird woods, as all confess. Listening turned out to be a prudence. A horse was galloping not far away. Soon from a fold in an overlooking hill:a black-robed lord, mounted on a black horse."

The rider neared enough to see: it was the long-robed mage from the circus, with the bald head, famed as most exceptional in his art. On a black horse a dark prince rode, clad in black raiment over which hung a mysterious sable cape.

Jacob had seen him demonstrate his magics before the incredulous crowd. Was this then that mercury-minded "Bannock" of whom the valraphs told? He did not doubt it.

The rider rode alone. Where were the dogs, where the hunting breeds about him, tracking through the fens?

Jacob slipped away and concealed himself within the massive trunk of a fallen gondo pine.

He scrambled up a steep incline off the road, the banks, into the hollow pine athwart the road's earthen walls, its bark shrouded over by emerald lichen. "His deadly dogs," he prayed, "if they come hunting about here; dear Lord, deliver me. Let them not pick up my scent, give me not into their jaws, or into the hands of a ruthless wizard."

The rider directed his horse forward into the defile.

Perhaps the animal was weary, or else the rider sensed a presence. The rider urged on the slow-moving animal, and she reluctantly climbed the steep road.

Suddenly, an impish little squirrel on the tree's branch made an outcry, and did so with much noisy harass.

The long-robed wizard noticed it, but took only slight regard. He did not investigate, nor even turn eyes in Jacob's direction. He passed right beneath the monk's concealed position, below the tree's trunk, his horse nimbly navigating fallen bouldersand saplings. After some moments he relaxed, and halted his mount. He was listening.

Not a muscle did Jacob move, poised like a leopard. The rider dismounted. Had he detected him? Hauling out a little pouch from his dark-robe he produced several diminutive stone figurines. Holding these he rubbed them. For some time he stood still.

What he was doing? His hands drew something out from his saddle bag; a wee book, the title of which was impossible to read from above.

The wizard briefly consulted this, and placed it back.

Jacob himself tells it:
He waited a few more moments and slowly raised his arms.

I tell you, from his fingers issued smoke! That is what I saw! The white wisps suddenly formed in the surrounding air, or perhaps it was a mist. Through its curling I discerned a disturbing and fantastical transformation:

His dogs leapt forth out of the mist, as if born *ex nihilo*. Hunting dogs they, the oriental breed with bushy tails, the kind that you see imported from distant Anshan or Cathay and sold in the markets of Ael Lot. Was I seeing things?

They dashed out, bushy tails wagging, pointy ears. The rider seemed to suspect that someone was watching.

Immediately each bushy-tailed dog hurried and greeted the master, trotting about in circles as if just let out of a gated yard.

Such dwimmer-craft do monks like us never imagine.Needless to say, I was pale with dread, and froze in the hiding place, my mind racing, calculating how they could easily sniff me out.

The dark hunter, the wizard, would find me and punish me for spying his wyrdding hands at work."

Reckoning but a farth to his flank: Jacob saw a swift-footed doe. She also stood and watched, ears twitching, wise to this event.If the deer were to bolt in the opposite direction, the nimble dogs would not come my way but make for the opposite way to chase her instead.

The gentle creature stood still and looked right at the monk, but could not herself see the dogs below or their master; only detecting a commotion. Jacob greeted the deer with a whisper.

How strange, the deer seemed to understand, and consented.

The graceful creature bounded away in a direction the canines could easily detect. She leapt over the hidden monk and right onto the massive tree-trunk bridge, and darted across to the other side of the road.

Many canine attentions were distracted. They sped off to pursue the game. A couple of older dogs however did not give chase, but halted to watch the master. This pair went about nose-to-earth, wagging tails, and up the incline neared Jacob's concealed position. They sniffed the air. One dog stood gazing in his direction; ears pricked.

The monk budged not, nor even bent more into the tree stump. His heartbeat lowered, his sweat and odor withdrawn. Deep concealment is part of a monk's masterful skill.

The other canines returned from their hopeless chase and the wizard mounted again. All moved quickly ahead as a pack. The two canines now re-joined the others. He waited, not moving for many breaths.

Something made the wizard give up his search and put distance.

"I reflected during my protracted concealment. "It must be him, Arizel, the famous sorcerer. But he is not an antichrist, no, just a powerful magic-user. The dark prophecies which Maragald recounted —are they even now coming to pass? The hermit professed as much was yet to come."

He let his thoughts wander and soon his eyes closed. Sweet sleep settled upon him, and the monk curled up on the soft moss of that massy trunk...

eave that youth have a spell now in his dreamy slumber. He must filter the many things that were rushing upon his mind, brother-hearer.

His world was but small. Only a few tradesmen regularly make it through the Lokken with wagons each year. They are merchants and fur traders. They brave the great forests and haunted wildernesses to get here. Once, a new fur trader and his retinue of guardsmen arrived at the village and displayed furs. The trader had obtained the furs from almost every corner of the northern lands.

After the monks had purchased a selection of leathers and vellums for the monastery, it was the townsmen's turn.

There was much chatting and shuffling about the merchant's tents on that bright day. The smell of festival roast was hanging in the air.

Yet even with that, Jacob's boyish curiosity was the greater appetite.

The fur trader, whose wrinkled eyes had squinted upon many horizons, smoked his horn pipe in the open tent.

His helpers presented the furs to the townsmen.

Jacob went near to him, and after the presentation ended,

asked him to speak on a particular pelt of a large animal...

"The fur of the wolf..." the tradesman pulled a fur from the pile, "and you still have a few of those beasts traipsing around your Timberhills. But these are pelts from hulk-wolves, much larger and dire. This one stalked the barren wolds of Kargiwall until a half dozen of my arrows were lodged in his head. The creature would have swallowed me whole. Some bards tell how the ancient heroes slew them hand to hand, or hand to paw, rather."

"Where is the land Kargiwall?" the boy asked.

"Had I a worthy chart I could show you.
Your island St. Aldemar is far from Kargwall indeed, lad
...but I have been there. I took this wolf myself.
No one without skill should dare go up against one."

"Can I get there from here to hunt one?" Jacob stroked the wolf fur.

"Nay...lad," He laughed. '...it is East across the sea.
Even were you at last to arrive at the ports of the Furth,
to Ael Lot the walled city faring on the salty sea,
where the continent reaches closest to your own shores,

many moons of rugged journey..."

"So I should cross the sea."

"To reach them you must traverse places of deadly peril, for the lords beyond the frontier cannot restrain the many bandits, there are no Edolunt Rangers to patrol, and, as this pelt attests, there lurk huge hulk-wolves that would swallow you alive in a single gulp... me as well in two gulps. A land bitter, of rusty sands and jagged rocks, no grass, only purple and red lichen."

"Why did God's hands fashion such a land?"

"Perhaps as a warning...who knows?"

" —A warning?"

"The land was once lush and green, like so much of this isle.
Two feudal Kingdoms arose, and brothers were the kings. But the ancient inhabitants of Kargiwall abandoned the All-law and worshiped instead false gods, in fear of the dragon.
When the judge of the living and the dead took his seat on Argunizial, neighboring Ulthork he blessed, but not the land of Kargiwall.
On account of God's disfavor, few green plants ever grew there again."

The boy's expression was a puzzled one.

"This is what men tell who have kin there," he said "and some have seen the chronicles writ in ancient tomes and rimestocks, but I have known few who learned those lost volumes."

"—And what of the dragon?"

"Of that I know little. Some say it was not a dragon,
but just a spirit, a melancholy angel. Others say that the dragon has now come here to your island. So have I heard."

"Have you ever seen a dragon?"

"Hope I never do... You might find one sleeping upon heaps of treasure under the surface of earth, but it's the last sight you will ever see. If they come up here, just run away. You can't trap 'em, and they have neither pelt nor fur." He looked upward and pondered. "No, I don't imagine they have fur..."

Jacob's childhood thoughts were quite easily distracted from one thing to the next. "What is the spotted fur here, this one, so soft..?"

"That is from Nathycanthe of the many lovely hills, warm kingdom of the north, in gorges and misty rains. The pelt is had from a leopard, a fanged four-footed beast which stalks the mountains."

"Yes...Who is the king of that land?"

"That mountainous range has no crown of Whitehawk,
only druidic priests, and no Christian ones. The old hegemony never stretched into those savage precipices."

"old hegemony?"

"Aye, the Regulian Confederacy, boy...? Know you so little?
...founded of old by the ancient king Tarquin
    ,...all lands called the Whitehawk in our time, the league of Christian kingdoms. Now the wind blows echoing war again for them. A great contest will the white-robed monarchs see to, but this time not with swords."

"—a fight without swords?"

"It is complicated, but if you listen close I shall tell you
    some things that others fear to mention.
    Cunning men, men whose love has grown cold, hold sway in the world, lad."

"Will they come here?"

"I do not think it. In this land there is not enough wealth for them to plunder. Here your clans are still occupied with pagan uprisings. If the heresiarchs came here, they would have to settle with the pagans, and they would not do that."

"Why?"

"I do not know, boy...I am not learned in all things. I do know that these master-disemblers fashion a counterfeit church. They have brought entire nations under their sway."

"Why do not wise men stop them?"

"Only true men of God who do have real faith can hinder them. You see, boy, many passings ago, before your grandfather lived, the great college of high learning, Nystol, thrived in the furthreaches.
    It burned down in a single day and night.
    All that was written, the learning of books and scrolls,
    all were lost. So men could not consult vital lore,
    how to watch stars, how to record laws, what sacred days to keep,
    what plants to use, which magics are helpful and which baneful,
    what side-effects for each, and what sacred doctrines to expound
    and what alien ones to condemn.
    All this went extinct
    and the civil lands were in peril, for an evil archon
    got wind of the catastrophe and planned to take advantage.

During that age of magic, when so many were entranced with all the glamour, they did not see how a mischievous power, unwatched, was rising. The power that was and does now remains a baleful mind.
    He conquered the Hithgroth in the Northern wastes
    and the kingdom of Nzul, building an impregnable fortress
    with the accursed stones of Sennoch.
    With the civil lands severely weakened, this abomination
    and enemy of men sought to dominate all.
    He mustered a huge army of Darkness; of dower elves and trolls, of horgim and giants, led by robber knights, and they invaded the civil lands. Only one righteous king, Argoth the Good, keeper of Ulthork, resisted.
    He smote down that undead lich in the dismal hall.
    But the spirit-creature himself was not destroyed,
    for spirits cannot be. So the great king locked him away

in the cathedral Hall of Melancholy within the mountain,
imprisoning the dark druid in his own fortress.
So were the civil lands saved.
But it did not end, for the undead spirit of the thing, in its malice,
perdured. There incarcerated, it waited for an age and has developed a
new plan. The thing cannot escape from there, but his publications go far
and wide.
He is seducing men with words rather than compelling them with the
sword and axe.
His conspiracy is to deceive men unto abandoning the Furth High King
and undoing all Whitehawk, that all men will come to woe.
But what am I doing? Why tell these high matters to a boy
who will not remember? Look now lad, you don't repeat this to anyone.
If you must tell someone, tell your hound, but mention not me; Promise
me."
The fur-trader sent a serious and fearsome look upon his face. Jacob
knew he was dead serious.

"Must I promise not to tell?"

"Bah. A promise rarely keeps silent a tongue! No more of that. I will
speak no more of kings or of balecrowns or of anyone else on that
continent. It is dangerous business. Ask what you will, but not of that."

"One more question only: what animal does this fur belong to?" Jacob
said, stroking another fur, thirsty for more knowledge, "this strange grey
fur, much like the leopard fur, spotted, soft, but darfurque. What land is
that from?" Even as a boy my thirst for knowldge was unquenchable.

"That, good lad, is from no land that knows the sun. It's a pelt from a
cave lion. The Whitehawk continent is ancient. All kinds of amazing things
dwell in the vast caves, grand galleries down there below, creatures of
which few hear, from before ever it was called Whitehawk.
And now this conversation must end, for I have said too much.
Go home to your mother, boy..."

f a maiden passing fair he dreamed, (was she not more than
an image the mind conjured?) Surely of an actual person,
or astral projection of a real spirit? Wondrous her raiment,
a white gown flowing like the soft moonlight. She cradled a
sturdily-bound book, a tome as those bound from the white
elephants of the sacred herd in Kithom. The maiden spoke
and addressed the monk, asking him,
"Chosen monk of God, be there not one wild-spirited
elf of the mountains worthy of trust, nor any of their kin,
the honey-sapping gnomes or stout dwarves?
Were not such beings given for the help of men?"

Now Jacob Magister pondered in his dreaming and was about to
answer, but his dream was to be interrupted —a wisp of smoke, a familiar
sleeve of a robe —brushing his face.

"Open thy mouth. Eat this, boy. Heaven gives thee strength."
Maragald, the old purblind hermit had found the boy.
He found him near the point of irretrievable weakness.
He had a set down bundle of sticks and ignited a small fire

to fend off the cold mountain airs.

"...the living bread Abbot has consecrated; Amen.

And when you are done have these. These shiny acorns I am roasting...acorns, yes, quite tasty. You would have ended your days here under this tree had I not learned to track game with more than what the eye picks up. The dog Lars here went far ahead. He found you hours before I did, warming you up at a crucial hour. You owe your life to a dog. What a gladsome thing —yet alive! I brought Smoked salmon and cider as well. Eat and drink, and let us get your belly full!"

"Please, hermit, leave me rest for another hour here. On my way I'll be going." Jacob said, barely alert, but yet proud, "Strange and melancholy adventure has turned upon me: robbers. Your gold, I flung it away somewhere, I did. Under a stump, I cast the purse just as you told me. So it's not here." Flames fluttered and sent smoke into Jacob's face.

"That is not why I have come. You should know better. This chill for another night could take you. Nor is there time to rake about for the nook where you flung that purse. We are to the monastery tonight, and prayers whispered. You repent of this knavery and quell your unholy disease of melancholy. Bide for another night to rest, and then a week, a month, a year, or decade, as long as you please. Before you know it, you'll be an old monk like me, ready to greet Christ in rapture and clouds with gladness."

"No, I can stay here and challenge the night, and be on my way, free from holy obligations. This little fire is warming me enough."

"No more be had of your insolence, boy.

I shall plant Christ's iron rod upon your head!"
(Maragald's threat, a hermit's threat, is never to be lightly dismissed. They do, after all, live in the wild).

"Only of yourself think ye?" he asked sternly. "You will not abide here. By my life you will not. You have heaped enough worry on us all.

You will go along with me or else you will perish tonight from the frost, forsaken of God, unforgiven. The Theologian says that hell-fire burns but does not destroy, nor even give off light! Will that then be had for keeping you warm tonight, and for all eternity? You will know never any rest, tortured without end by the devil and his apostate angels!

...No, you are not as important as you imagine. It is the monastery that is important. Therefore let us hurry back. Come, follow me."

Far above the pine-tree tops some broad-winged bird of prey patrolled the dome of heavens. A high-pitched screech echoed —a sign not to quarrel more.

So Jacob accepted the augury.

The discussion paused and by late morning Jacob was following him, old Maragald with his staff in hand, and the canine trotting besides. They were on their way through the leafy paths and pine-needle narrows, shortcuts which the old hermit knew so well.

"Maragald, I have turned away from Heaven, and am an apostate. Why haul me back into the high haven of the Lamb?

In the sacred scriptures Judas betrayed our Lord

and sold him for thirty silver pieces. By allowing myself to be sold to the circus have I not done the same? ...and it was for the exact same amount! but he is called "the lost one." In fact you yourself called me "lost one" before I left."

"That is something I honestly said; I did call you that, boy."

"Then I am lost, and there is no hope for me."

"You were lost, indeed, but in mind, and on account of a confusion. Now you are found. I do not say that you committed sin. In the young, like yourself, malice is not easily found. But Judas' knew better than to propose to help the messiah by handing him over to the Sanhedrin. Judas was worldly wise, and well instructed. He knew that whatsoever good a man may strive for, it must never come about by evil agency. He chose the evil turn anyway. The end maketh not just the means whereby it cometh.."

"Still, I am a monk, and I had the lights of God's teaching
in my soul; but I fled for sinful fascination."

Maragald retorted: "Is there anyone else besides the Christ whom you know of or have heard of, boy, who is reputed NOT to have sinned? Therefore are there any who do NOT deserve Death and Hell? "*if we say that we have not sinned then there is no truth in us, for the wage of sin is death*:
STIPENDIUM PECCATI MORS EST!
And it is also written "*It is appointed for all men to die once, then comes the judgement.*" Allfather may punish men,
but it is far from to how greatly we deserve.
Yet if there walk any men who have not sinned,
how could death be justly warranted them?
Only the Radiant Lady was provided such a favor.
The Archsin did not touch her.
Be not fooled by the devil's deceit and say that you are unworthy to re-enter the monastery. Of course you are unworthy. Come, trust your God. The worshipful brothers will intercede for you before the Furth High King."

"I think of Formosus. If he sees me again, he will surely do something worse against us."

"*Noli timere*, be not afraid. Formosus was to be a wise man but has compromised himself into a man of follies, and teaches instead not divine wisdom but the theologies of Man.
His flesh has eclipsed his reason
and he teaches one thing but does another.
He has become one the sophists, hypocrites over whom his erstwhile hero Socrates once grieved. Formosus has been swayed, Jacob.
He recently obtained some "wisdom" works of a certain Grecian word-smith, and even will betray his philosophical father, preferring the clever reasoning of on earthly things
to the sublime realm of eternal forms.
Ulcrist is no better, for he has...but no, I shall not speak it.
It is not lawful to tarnish a good reputation, even if the good reputation be not deserved. I say do not mind the wolves in sheep's skin, but keep away from them. Do not engage them.

Have faith! Listen to this, Jacob: do not fret over any monks.

For on account of my ever-whispering prayer Heaven grants you a help. Here, take this sacred stone,a wonderstone, and wear it always. I prayed for you while you were gone, and God showed me this stone.

See, it is alabaster, the stone of the heavenly steps.

Wear it around your neck with faith.

It will detect the presence of wickedness...anywhere in a 50' radius."

Jacob took the small white stone and placed the cord around his neck. He thanked him and made a minor bow.

"You need no pagan or eldark magic, spells and sacrifices.

You now possess this stone and there is a name inscribed upon it which Heaven gives you. It is a divine protection.

You will be known only to whomsoever you wish to be known and only true friends can recognize your name, and that you are Jacob Magister.

The wolves in sheep's clothing you cannot avoid.

Yet by a second power I protect you.

A sacred mist will enwrap about you to conceal your identity. Just as the Ocean-born dragon conceals himself in misty smoke, so we also may use mist, a holy mist. They will not percieve your identity, you whom they once sold into bondage, their own brother.

At least not by sight will they recognize, blinded by sin as they are.

Be careful however. Like wolves they can sniff you out.

Let their noses pick up from you nothing else save the odor of sanctity. So mind you your religious obedience.

Always keep honestly the commands of God, and the Rule of St. Benedict. In so doing the holy talisman will not fail.

When the time comes you will unmask yourself.

Then by proof you will reveal their iniquitous crimes.

They are the Synagogue of Satan!

We must hasten. Tomorrow is the Feast Day of Saint Ambrosius the Nephelid Now let us be off, you and I.

We follow the morning star.

"From many worlds come many fantastic beings, but pray ask thyself, which of them can honestly expect to escape the final day?"

Morpheus Memnos
Utterances of the Dragon Gnotus-as-he-lay-dying

XIV   ET IN ARCADIA EGO

Up high omewhere in the Lokken a Wyrmheld was watching from a hilltop. He saw two travelers move through the forests below. The Wyrmheld himself did not move. He simply watched, and waited.

Late in the day, when the sun was in descent, Jacob and Maragald arrived at the hoped-for destination.

When they reached the top of the many steps from the monastery gate, they stopped to catch their breath. Abbot, who happened to be moving about the cloister with Formosus and Fragga, spotted them. Immediately he hurried toward them, even though he could barely make good on his own.

The crutches clicked against stones.

Jacob saw him coming and knelt at once.

"Please Master, have mercy.."

The Abbot sighed with gladness. "You have tried to fly away, little chick, before you have grown wings, or can even walk. But Heaven has returned you! So thanks be to God!"

Abbot became a bit tear-eyed. He motioned to Jacob to get up. "We imagined that we had lost you for good. No one thought to see your return."

He embraced his recovered lamb. Abbot turned to Jacob's companion,

"The monks thank you sincerely, Maragald. May God reward you, and tonight you will have a good supper."

"Maragald, have we here a guest from some other monastery?"

"What is wrong, Formosus? Have you been drinking?" said Abbot. "Don't recognize him, or don't want to? Go and tell the others that we will have a big supper tonight, with beer for every monk. No mere water and soup, no monk's fare: The salmon for tonight! We command a feast to celebrate! Music as well, so notify them all."

"Lord Abbot," replied Formosus, "your new guest, I am sure, is noble. . . but today is not. . . not that sort of a day. That reception is rather what a bishop is given. We have been low on supplies as of late. For salmon we would have to send rope-girded monks all the way to the other side of town—"

"Is it not the Lord's day? Do as we command," Abbot said sternly. "Do you not see that he who was lost has been found?!"

Formosus raised his eyebrows at the words. The Abbot looked at Jacob and said, "Go say your whispering prayers now, monk. Give thanks to Heaven for your deliverance. After it shall be time for supper and all shall feast and hear glad sounds."

Jacob bowed and Maragald bowed, and both departed for the echoing chapel.

On the way through the courtyard, Jacob noticed horses stabled. They looked familiar. They were knight's warhorses.

"The knights have returned?" Jacob asked. Brother Maragald paused to determine some answer.

"For them some trouble is brewing it seems," he said. "They have come back from the forest. I wager that the robbers or some other lawless band such as you encountered has injured them. The forest is home to many dangers. The knights had to hurry back here immediately. They know of our herbal medicine and healing chant. Let us learn what exactly it was. . . and so we shall...after supper."

"Can our bellies not wait?" said Jacob. "Do not fear to go with me now, old one; I do cherish them and I must visit them before the sun sinks below the horizon. You should be there with me."

Maragald and Jacob stepped through the inside gates which moan and clang more coldly than wrought-iron should. Passing through the courtyard they moved about the echoing corridors and long shadows of the cloister. They came to the cavernous infirmirary where the brethren had the bandaged cavalier on cushions.

It was the Burgundy Knight who had had fallen. A bloody pile of chain, straps, and plates, his armour and sword lay in a corner. The herbalist and physician monks were there tending to his wounds. More candles the monks brought in. Shadows flickered along the walls.

Two other monks were kneeling and the other knights standing watched. When Jacob approached, the White Knight recognized him. Jacob knelt by him and he glanced, saw the monk, and spoke.

"This great lord is nigh passing from the world."

There was silence for a time. One of the monks softly intoned the *Clamavi*. The odor of the sacred myrrh of Xasbur wafted through the air.

The White Knight arose. Prayer shone about his brow. He gestured; bade Jacob step into the archway entrance.

"Keep still now and listen," he said in whisper, "Abbot says that you are the novice Jacob Magister. You are the same one who stood and greeted us with the Abbot and carried our gifts, are you not?"

"I am the same. What concerns you on it?"

"Do not question us in such a way. Remember your low station, and that we are knights, and we are highly placed.

You have not yet even proved yourself as a monk. But even so it is this irritating quality in you that is of interest to us. The knights have spoken of your inquiry...albeit without scruple, with which you hoped to learn of our grave enterprise. Our brother, whom you see here, will soon leave this world. He has lived a life making sacrifices for the quest. This knight has spoken of your kindness to him, and-"

"May the heavenly angels favor and attend his way. What befell him? I saw him strong, just two days ago. He has been attacked?"

"Do not interrupt. A riotous crowd struck him down in the forest...just this past night."

"Also have I been knocked around in the Timberhills, a bit," Jacob said. "A deranged band of woodland-folk waylaid me yesterday. They released me."

"Perhaps a wandering remnant of the throng we encountered?" he wondered aloud, searching his thoughts.

"Why did he not escape on horse?"

"I shall tell you, but do not interrupt me again
if you wish to hear all. We were encamped in the vale of Ringwood.
He went alone and led his horse down to the stream's bank
under the starry evening, to water the beast.
It was not a quarter hour after that, when we heard,
above the crackle and hiss of our campfire,
the barking of nimble dogs coming our way.
Our companion had not yet returned up from the river.
The two of us rushed to fasten one another's scaly mail
and gird our blades for some deadly encounter.
Through the trees we spotted hundreds of torches nearing,
a mob of armed peasantry. So we led away our horses
and hid in a nearby cave on the low cliff wall of the basin.
At least there, if they fell upon us with assault, we might, in a narrow area, hope to prevail. Fearing that our brother knight might not be able to adequately conceal himself in the wood. We made ready.
He mounted his palfrey and sought to ride back to the encampment.
It was then that a night-rider, some sable-robed prince or cleric on a black steed, appeared and directed the peasants to surround him. The throng harried him grievously, struck at the horse, and at last yanked our knight down with hooked spears, weapons not permitted by honorable code.
The one mounted cleric in particular we recognized,
garbed more a sorcerer of some sort. Was he was the one
who had cast a spell of dissent upon the untrained minds of the folk? The smell of burning torches was not the only odor in the air. Every restraint it took for us not to sally out to rescue him
...offering the rebelling mob justice by steel. We could not take the risk, being greatly outnumbered. We heard the rider.
He bade them offer only punishing blows, but fear his wrath
if they slay a knight. We are the last and only Ammouric knights who remain. We alone must fulfill the quest, and we vowed that not even the saving of our lives should jeopardize it, so great is it an accomplishment for good. Not many are the things which we could permit
against its hopeful accomplishment,
lest the world entire be swallowed in Darkness.

But even so, we felt as cowards. We did espy the mischief.
Would that the Lord not forbidden vengeance!
Our brother fell to stony earth from his mount.
I bit my own lip in stunted fury at this; tasted the salty blood.
We could no longer endure the sight and rushed out
from concealment to offer resistance, for it is written
 in the Leviticus of God's Holy Word,
"Thou shalt not stand idly by whilst thy neighbor's life is imperiled."
The rider, he, a sorcerer I suspect, first saw us coming at a distance
with sword and shield, and therefore loudly warned the throng to shed not
the blood of a noble. He was surely, brothers,
either a coward, or a noble keen not to be afoul of the law;
but the mob he could no longer control. In wild frenzy,
they dragged our brother, struck him cruelly with grisly pitchforks,
and cast him all weighted with armour into the ever-flowing river. We
stormed their position, but too late. In river's shallows we went swinging
and splashed thunderously before the mob.
With savage bellows of battle rage, brandishing our weapons, we
drove them all off, fleeing for their lives.
We recovered ourselves and returned to shore.
We retrieved him, still living, caught on the shallows of the bank
–his life blood ebbing away."

"We must discover the identity of this dark rider... " said the Grey
Knight, arisen from his prayer. He has puzzled us before, and
continues to elude us, but there is something of nobility in him which might
bring him round. He tried to check the mob."

The man stepped over to Jacob and gestured his wish to speak more
words apart.

"I have but few good things to say by him," said the White Knight.
"Some illusion-maker he, I reckon, but at the time I thought him a cleric.
Closely I looked again and recognized him to be the same black-robed
man who had just days before taken up with the carnival.

He was mysterious and alone.

On the same day we ourselves had joined, and he had been observing
us. He disappeared after only a few days. I say he is an upstart, who, by a
lying tongue, has roused the local peasants with rebellious talk...a worker
of mischief and spreader of discontent. After the attack, the throng went
off to accomplish other misdeeds.Sought they nar wealth nar gold, but to
harry men of stern faith.

One hapless follower lagging behind the others we captured.

We offered him what he could not refuse and it yielded much."

"It seems that this dark prince has plans other than mere mayhem,"
continued the Grey Knight. "After appearing in the church, he mustered a
band of compatriots by rabble-rousing, accusing the Ammouric clerics of
living off the fat of the land, the sweat of another man's brow, and of
corruption and vice.

Nay, some recent reports of vice found in men of the cloth must be not
fictions. He made sure all knew it. Who would doubt that there walk such
villians clothed with the holy cloth? We humans are weak, even the kind
and the honest."

"The war-wind blows," declared the White Knight. "The Red Asceticism already spreads to this otherwise merry isle. But this one seems not that, but of foreign origin."

"The dark rider of which you speak," I explained, "if he be the same who has vexed the mountaineers, the elf-like roaks whom I encountered, then no cleric is he, nor pagan priest."

The Grey Knight responded with amazement.

"Elf-like men, and mountaineers...? Elves, if it's valraphs you mean, half-breeds, they are said to be bad omen, although some men swear that they do avail powerfully for travel in mountain hall or cavernous land. You did then certainly spot half-elves in the wood?"(Suspecting that if such a report got around he would not be free of trouble, Jacob replied with cautious words).

"So they claimed. But they were like mad dogs.
Are not such folk the stuff of mere chilren's tales?
At any rate, they were wary of the hunting canines which that dark rider employed. By the look of his company at hunt, passing me on the trail, he is among nobles. The commoners must suppose him to be a deep-minded cleric, some prelate of the sacred councils. They say his name is Arizel, whom the Aels call Bannock."

The White Knight returned from some deep consideration.

"If they say that—if it truly be Arizel, the Master of Planets, of infamous name, then we are at once both fortunate and in great peril. He aided our fathers in the Wars of the Veil, but also he is said to have brought much of the known world to chaos by seeking to fix things with strange magics."

"The remnant Sorcerers have interest here?" the Grey Knight asked.

"I wonder over this...what would they be aiming at here? This one, Bannock, Mercury-mind, I have heard his ancient name in other lands: Arizel, a name spoken with dread. He is a master of illusion.
Has he shrewdly disguised himself as a cleric?"

"I saw the same one, in garb not unlike a cleric," Jacob said, "but only marked as a wizard by those with discerning eyes.
He is dangerous, a dissembler and persuader with words.
He has the power... " (he halted his treatment here, brothers, not daring to speak further on the things he had seen).

"What? You have heard on his power?"

"Tell us now, man." The White Knight looked at Jacob with troubled brow. "Don't leave anything out, no matter how strange. It stays between us."

"I espied him on the trail; I witnessed his magics with my own eyes.
He summoned a pack of magic dogs."

The Burgundy Knight cried out in agony from his bed.

"We do not doubt you," said the Grey Knight.
"It is a slight trick compared to what we have seen of other Sorcerers. Our brother needs us now however. We will speak more on this."

"Our brother groans in final misery," said the White Knight, his attention diverted. "Go now and pray for him, monk. We should even pray for the right turning of that dark prince, that he may fetch his justice soon, penitent in this life, lest fire in the next. We shall say more on this in hours come by and by." The two knights turned to attend their fallen comrade.

Maragald and Jacob departed and heeded the knight's request.

The story of Jacob's first adventure in the forest has passed into the things to be remembered.

enoliths are certain standing stones, cromlechs of immensity, raised by unknown dwellers long ago down in the mega-caverns of deep earth. Deeptrackers call the stones Xenoliths. Some say that they restrain the Netherbeasts in deeper regions below, but Kruth in *de bestiis subterraneis* says that Xenoliths are meant to be signs of hope for travelers. Hope, after all, may be all that is left a traveler-soul.

After chant of evening monks take their supper. (As you know, holy brothers should have meals in silence).

This time, the rope-girded monks brought forward the pitcher and bowl and poured water over Jacob hands for washing. This washing is always done for guests in accord with the Rule.

Who can enter the holy place? The man with clean hands and a pure heart.

They saw a monk, but the thaumaturgical veil prevented them from rightly noticing which monk. So they recognized him not, but the master did. In the short time at the end of supper when monks are permitted to speak, Jacob spoke of the adventure. But he did so without revealing himself. He had assumed the name of a rumoured traveling monk: Brother Orbian of the Monastery of the Weeping Brotherhood in The Dry Blood Sea, "having come to make copies of precious and rare tomes found only at Whitehaven." Brothers, could anyone recognize Jacob as long as Maragald's veil of mist concealed his identity? Even though he sat in his usual place, across from Brother Enwick, no one guessed it.

Inquisitors might list this disguise here as a *culpa*, brothers,

which I humbly confess to you. The scrupulous would count it a deceit, aye, not to announce one's true identity.

Jacob apologizes. But in defense I offer this: did our Lord who is perfect did not require the leper to announce all he knew

"tell no one who it was who healed you..."

"Orbian" told the monks that he had met up with a certain Brother Jacob in the town of Hordingbay in his travels, and that the wayward monk had described in full his thralldom to the circus, as well as the mishap of wild elfbeards capturing him in the forest. So "Orbian" told them all, only adding that the monk Jacob, who claimed to have experienced these things, would not divulge where in thunder he was heading. Certainly that was a mostly true statement.

"Orbian" added how the monk in question intended to return one day with authority to witness against all mischievous monks.

At first no rope-girded monk believed the story.

They smiled, treated it like a quaint fairy tale.

When Jacob became vexed, the monks offered to explain it away, affirming how easily the *diabolus* can trick the mind.

"If what you claim is so, Orbian," said brother Aisa (the heron), "then I would say that Jacob must have become delusional for lack of daily faring while he was lost...He has been harkening to the hermit Maragald too much!"

Then an elder, thickly bearded brother Zadoc, the theologian, munching on bread crust, smiled and spoke.

"Clearly something odd has transpired....and there is a fear which the devil inspires....but I wonder....how is it that Jacob Magister, when he was with us, a monk who did not tell tall tales like Enwick here....how is it he would he make up a story of having been attacked by half-bred elves? Or else the wild men of Lokken? We know Jacob. Indeed our poor brother must have suffered some kind of adversity. The description you give, Brother Orbian, sounds real in certain parts....except the part where Jacob is being taken by the hands of mythical beings, elves or dwarves or the like...that is quite a fantastic thing. You should not believe that. We admit many mysteries in this world wrought by Divine Providence, more than the philosophers can count. But elves and dwarves? And a "gnome"....

what in your wild imagination does he look like? Where does he live?

Come now, it is best to first propose a rational explanation:

Brother Jacob got famished and ate the morulent mushrooms, or sacred chestnuts, and the pagans found him."

"Orbian" turned this argument over in his mind many times. Surely it was not impossible that his mind got tricked. He had, afterall, at the behest of a dwarf, eaten forbidden chestnuts. Perhaps the valraphs were just backwoodsmen who had fun at his expense. Later a thought,—perhaps it was Jacob's angel

—reminded him of something. There is a warning
which St. Benedict added into the monastic rule,
which monks may resolve to obey:

And let no one presume to tell another whatsoever he may have seen or heard outside the monastery, because this causes great harm.

Therefore Jacob wrote everything down and kept it in his journal from that point onwards:

"...finally, one hour, while in these thoughts, a way of proof dawned on me. The beings had entrusted to me knowledge of the accomplishments of our brother Anherm of Whigg, before he passed into the next world. He had been translating *The Black Book*.

The mysterious book therefore I should be in his old cell, which had not yet been passed to some other monk. In accord with stipulation, Anherm would not have left the silver-braced book in the *scriptorium* to be shelved with other books. Anyone could acquire it there. He must have kept the work close, watching and guarding against the eyes of unworthies; surely it was there hidden in his cell. I went moving through the dark corridors of the abbey hooded and alone. I raked through Anherm's empty cell, but found nothing...

At daybreak I awoke in the cot reserved for guest monks.

The warblers of Catafrax were singing
and the smell of pancakes wafted about.

It was good to be back in the monastery.

Now it was also during this short interval that Abbot Cromna approached for instructing Jacob in the chapel one afternoon.

He brought along Zadoc the theologian, the eagle-eyed brother.

There transpired the conversation in which Abbot tested Jacob's philosophic ability, and also assured him that he was still a monk. Then they spoke concerning a miraculous power of resurrection found in the hands of an anonymous priest. This conversation, you may remember, is the first thing I described and quoted for you at the opening of this tome, in the *prologus*. Private news came that the wool-frocked Friars of Whigg on the continent had planned to employ this priest, a *selva*, to resurrect certain wisemen and wizards of Nystol. Their purpose hollow: to use the ancient magic, overthrow the Dire. So desperate and ignorant a plan Abbot piously rejected. He is The Godmouth of the entire Whitehawk and all the furthlands. Certainly that is to the great annoyance and resentment of the wool-frocked Friars. Will they not obey their own Eldane? Now Jacob tells:

A knock on my cell door... I opened: The Grey Knight: "Fear not;" he said at once. "I know who you are; that you are not "Orbian." You are Brother Jacob, scion of the Escorvan house of Rumil. You have somehow disguised yourself from the wolves who dwell here.

Listen: our companion, an Ammouric *selva*, wished for many years to have a son, but he had vowed to the quest, never to marry, and now he is near his final breath and is about to go to glory.

He has spoken of a great hope to make you his son by adoption; someone who might carry his quest. It be not likely that he shall last. What say you?"

Astounded, I stood agape. Realizing that further gaming was vain, finally I spoke.

"I am too unworthy of such a thing. Let another."

"Good, you answer humbly, as a monk should. The great and chivalric lord speaks. God has granted him speech in order that he might bid farewell and give final instruction to his companions."

"A man cannot speak without a tongue!" I retorted.

But he did not answer my lack of faith. "Come!"

One does argue with such a lord. I followed him through the shady pillars of our porches. The knight of the burgundy mantle lay in a bed in the *sanitarium*, an air-chamber hollowed out of a stone protrusion of the cliff complex. Many candles placed about revealed the mystical splendor of the healing cave.

When I came to his side, I perceived great weariness upon his face, a face which bore the many wounds of torture. His eyes however were peaceful, and though barely able to move, he looked upon me. I had never seen a man dying before, and I had always imagined that such a one would be crying out in fear and consternation. It was not so, but he seemed at times to be peering beyond the veil into the next world."

"My blessing" he said, "Even now I seek a son, one who will inherit my quest, for I have nar else to offer. Will you accept? Know that if you do, this quest requires your sonship...and may also require your life as it has mine."

"Noble knight," I said, "if you wish it, name me your son; My own biological father has long disowned me anyway. I shall be your son by your word, for you will have spoken it. It is the least I can do for such as you. I cannot however take your quest. I am a monk and must live my days in ever-calling prayer and abstinence for Heaven."

"The quest cannot be separated from the inheritance.
You cannot swear my pursuit? You will become a quest-knight.
There is no youth else, none right suitable otherwise.
I know things of you. You are the boy I entertained years ago
when Anherm was still with us. In those days
we disguised ourselves as fur-traders. Surely you recall me?
I told you of the wide world which God has made
and man has corrupted. Anherm chose you
because destiny is written all over you.
I helped him to see that. It was in hope of this moment
that all your learning and training has been done,
that you might swear the mysterious pursuit passed from me."

"Not well do I recall those years, but as you say. Even as it was, it cannot come down to me. I am not able to swear an ever-calling crusade in this world. Even were I not a monk, a voyage to some far-off destiny would not be completed. Whatever great relic you seek, I warn, Heaven wills it be not accomplished."

At this the Knight's eyes grew wide, as alarmed, and grabbing me by the with the remnant of his strength he pulled me toward himself and put his face near mine and staring powerfully into my eyes spoke in a gruff whisper.

"You are young, our last hope. Receive the quest, else all be lost."

"Be at peace," I said, "I shall not deny you then.
I do promise and accept it."

"Accept all of it...to yield never, not to comfort me a dying man, but accomplish or die. Lay claim to it...by your word...You must not feign worthiness to comfort a dying lord."

There was a pause. In the stillness of things I knew that it had to be.

"I claim and accept all by my word to accomplish, by all my power."
He leaned back down, then wrapped his burgundy scarf ceremoniously over my head.
"Why you are chosen you may never understand.
Destiny is upon you; you were chosen from above.
Do not merely accept this sonship; you must fulfill it."

"I shall do you as you require."

He whispered the secret words of the quest.
It is a part of divine wisdom which I do carefully provide
in this journal set down for you, brothers.
Lest unworthies learn of it,

it is done by means of symbols and signs. If your mind be trained and your heart true, then you will perceive it soon enough.

"Say that you will recover it or die, Jacob."

"I shall so do as you bid...or die."　　　　　– "Swear it. "

"I swear it."　　　　　– "May Almighty God help you."

"I do not understand this secret," I said. The knight was fading. His speech shortly became broken.

"I have vaguely understood only a few things myself," he said, for there was no interpreter of the words. To even...find a proper entrance to the lower world we have failed to do. You must do it, and...find the elven lady, the intermundane queen whose castle is besieged....She knows how...and point the way..."

"And if this thing is not accomplished?"

"A seething shadow is already upon Whitehawk, and flowers of evil blossom in the minds of men.

A fearsome cleansing too shall come. The proph—ecies affirmed that it would come in your own lifetime. It shall last three days and...three nights. In this passage of spiritual darkness, only....the righteous shall live, only the penitent if they understand what to do, and all the wicked of the land shall perish in it."

"Is that not a happy thing?"

"Not if everyone has become wicked. All things from God's hand are good. In the death of no creature is He pleased. Yet know this...when the time comes, who will slow justice?

Once wickedness and cruelty become the universal good, justice ...returns. The time allotted of mercy is nigh spent.

Shadow has already overwhelmed some feudal kingdoms entirely.

We could avert it ...through...our effort, and salvage...many souls. If the quest...is not accomplished,and the key of sacred doctrine forgotten, vast numbers of beings shall be deceived, especially we ...who are men. Many in ....darkness of mind... shall...carelessly...follow the path of ....the wicked. Narrow is the way...that leads to life. You...must open...the gate and you must blow the siege-horn.

Do not falter. Wield that worthy brand when the moment comes."

The knight pointed to his great sword set there
near the foot of the bed.

"What gate do you mean. . ?"

"—It is not unfolded through spoken words, but...in time you will...perceive. And now, my son, I must ask you to just stay here with me, at my side...for a while, since your presence is a great consolation...to me. I say to you: use that great sword I give you. In years long passed that brand was forged in the accursed smithy of Mount Abaddon for the campaigns of a dreadful Warlock in Kargiwall, a man so wicked, whose soul so dead...but one who vanquished many kings with his mischievous magic.

This Warlock was finally overthrown in battle
by the Ammouric Grand Knight Norgonce

...I cannot much longer speak...for...I am weak..."

He was hush a few moments, but suddenly continued.

"...dire magic in the sword....arcane power....was drained out along with foul spirit....the condemned soul of unholy witch-lord who fell in battle holding it. But the blade itself, the matter, was taken, and it was presented to the Church to examine. They found it to be a highly subtle metal, a vessel for spiritual force...they said it can harness the spiritual might of its user, what is called a pneumatic blade.

The Church has cancelled the evil and blessed the brand.

In the hands of a righteous soldier it becomes an unparalleled weapon of righteousness —a holy sword. Its powers: not only to warn of the attacks of wild-eyed witches and blood-painted warlocks, but to track down heretics and menace them and their ilk, since most heretics are also magic-users."

"I am a monk; not trained for a sword, only a staff."

"Keep it close. For many years I tracked down heretical outlaws and brought them to the Prime Interquist to learn the truth. Then came the call of my quest, the sword has also availed in that.

It is Witchbane.

Ware be thou, you must be lawful to even touch it."

Over I stepped and took up into my hands the enormous two-handed blade. The hilt curved upwards toward the keen edge slightly, and was engraved with a design of thorns. The pommel was crown-shaped, masterfully proportioned. It was truly an exquisite blade.

"The ones who forged the blade engraved the thornweave," he continued, "...they must have been thinking to remind the warlock of how God cursed the earth after the Archsin, that only thorns and thistles might come forth for the race of men. Conjuring such an ancient memory would stir the warlock to fight even more hotly against those 'neath the banner of the Lamb. They did not foresee that the cursed blade would become blessed. They could never guess that a *selva* holding the sword would think of thorns and it would remind of the crown worn by Our Lord, that true humility earns victory in combat. You may strike if need be, but the battle-blade will not accomplish a murder-stroke, not even on any witch or wizard. Only drive them back it will; instill divine fear. Wield the sword when the day comes... "

"Tis a fine blade, my lord," I replied. "Thank you for this gift, father. Abbot will keep it safe as one of our treasures—"

" —NO! It is more than a mere gift to be hung on the wall.
You yourself keep the sword and guard it well!
You alone...Witchbane is your blade now.
He who quests must not fear to wield the weapon.
May Abbot give you permission.
You must have it, have it at hand
...to WIELD it! "

"I am a monk, not a knight. I do not match with blades that sever flesh."

"It is a spirit-cleaver. Why do you reject my hope? You must not reject...you MUST not ...!"

The knight's gaze drifted away from me, to look into the distance beyond the veil. I could not let my scruple worry him.

"I shall keep well the sword."

"Son, take care of my horse Burgundius, he has been loyal..."

Not an hour later and the noble knight shut his eyes to this world for the last time. They covered him over with the purple.

Et in Arcadia Ego.

Sadness came and lingered awhile. To my own cell I returned and into the late moon sat on my stool gazing

upon the brand Witchbane. The hilt and haft were stained from the knight's blood-soaked gloves. At what did the metallic riddle hint?

The rope-girded monks mustered for noontide meal, during which no talk is permitted. However because several monks, whom you have known, were living without restraint, wherever they arrived they induced the weaker monks to ignore the rule, even if the Abbot were present. There was, not surprisingly, little care displayed among the brethren at the news regarding our fallen knight, as far as I could tell.

The knights themselves as guests take their meal in a separate hall, in accord with the custom.

Among the monks there was feasting and talkativeness, even hilarity. Contrary to the rule flagons of wine were brought out at a time unwarranted. I overheard one monk, not even whispering it "a relief it is that we must look after the dying horseman no more. "

What cold words. *In labóre mortálium non sunt et cum homínibus non flagelLántur. Ideo quasi torques est eis supérbia.*

Yes, he wore pride like a necklace.

That monk, pleased and encouraged that none corrected his insolence, brusquely stood up. He made a shameless toast for all.

He turned to Abbot and uttered further outrages for all to hear.

"May I be the jester a little? Look at you there, Abbot,
all satisfied with your share of the meat,
belly rolling out and not a care, you middle-aged old fart.
Assign me not again duty nursing one of your   guards,
grown old and miserable, a veteran from some unjust war,
hands unclean with the blood shed of many foes.
He earned the dark cloudy death he got, I wager.
As for me, I have other counsels.
Watch closely the way you shepherd monks from now on,
or you will never be convinced that your supper is free of some deadly thing, a witch's poison which some resentful monk used for seasoning roast. -Just some practical, albeit unsavory, advice, my good abbot.
Take care that you heed this jest.
Nay, embark on your fishing boat at sea without a care.
Not one here is slow to obey you. Just make sure that you assign light work from now on and all will be well."

This monk, Lucian, laughed a fake laugh. He sat back down at table and scratched his beard as a sign of contempt. Glad applause burst out from some other monks. The conversations continued. No monk dared protest the overbold words and the abuse he heaped on poor Abbot. Abbot hanged his head and did not eat. A Christian of such high station should not defend himself when so many other subordinate Christians are near enough to do so.

Enwick was there and although he was speechless at first,
he would not bear this insult disguised as jest, nor let it go unanswered.

"Lucian, you whining and sorry excuse for a monk!
I used to hold you in high regard. But now look at you,
sore over the hard task you were given, that's understandable
...but your bold words have disgraced our father
and all the monks who for ages dwelt in this monastery.

How can you, a servant, seek to upbraid the rightful lord before all? Do you not know that he sits in the seat of Christ himself?

You arrogant man, scratching yourself like a shameless dog; oblivious of all respect for Heaven, mocking, with no sense of authority, filled with pride and self-rule. I tell you, the Lamb will not let it go unpunished."

So frowning he spoke with indignation. Brother Yulla stood up. He was a monk with an undeniably sturdy frame, not someone to be taken lightly, a trained guardian-monk who had perilous hands.

"Keep the peace, you monks. Without peace, I tell you,
this monastery will tomorrow become a museum!
Heaven will tolerate your contention no further.
Imagine no more monks to pray for themselves and the townsfolk. Enwick, you novice, what you say counts for naught, you don't know the issues; you have not enough winters as a monk to speak with knowledge.

Every mouth should stop moving, every tongue cease now.
Rumour travels swiftly and it has many bent beaks,
the folk will learn the scandal of this quarrelsome talk.
They will stop piling our tables with meats and handsome feasts. If we are lucky we will have to go back to lentil soup,
that's it, for every meal. Monks will flee
and the place will get deserted. The only one left will be
that old fool hermit ever-praying for apocalypse.

So then, let's make a truce. No one cares for the shepherding of Abbot Cromna here, save for a few overly-zealous monks, feigning righteousness. That's something! You cannot guide a flock of sheep if they will go each their own way, Abbot, especially those who know elsewhere greener grazing. You are wasting your strength.

So then, I counsel you now, let yourself at peace,
and leave these monks at peace. Stop trying to reform them.
They will not change. They can't change. Don't kill yourself
over their wretched souls. You need to consider your own salvation. Do the right thing and resign. Then you can do all the fishing you like.

Convey monks under sail to the castle Ael Lot
where they might beseech the King: let His Majesty assign some keener monk the abbacy and all the shepherd-work."

Abbot answered the charge, and did not hold back:
"Heaven knows that your lordship is well to be free
from this burden of governance, grave as it is. Brother Yulla,
for not glad was I of the news that the Lord had so chosen.
But should human reputation succeed to check His Holy Will?
God alone is responsible for my elevation to this office, not
the King, although divine mystery employs royal power for the
appointment. Some situations are beyond a man's ability to fix, try as he
may. If he keeps at it, the man will tire, even come to grief.

It may not be that way in the world, where a man who is untiring
prevails, wins some betterment of things for himself and his peers, but not
so here. More often than not such things go otherwise in the Church.

A monk cannot alter his state. He is one vowed to submission
to Heaven and to his own superiors.
So why do you encourage me to resign? Remember:
whoever shepherds these monks also must safeguard the teaching of
all the Ammouric Churches, he must not be timid as The Godmouth, and as
Eldane must preach crusade. No light work is that.

It is not my plan to deny God my service, to give up the crook without
divine nod, not without a sign good enough to convince all, even the King. I
know my request that you follow the Rule is a tough one indeed. But think,
you have not many years in this life. So do not just act like busy bodies.
Earn your bread and your fish.

Better to spend our years as monks trying to live out sacred discipline,
even if we can never master it; better to try, not living easy, but working
hard. I tell you, better that than go before the Judge on The Last Day show
not a single coin of interest earned on what he left in your care."

So spake the Abbot, and several monks there were convinced at
hearing such a defense: let the Abbot be, make oneself useful as a monk,
wait for the reward on The Last Day. Not Brother Yulla however. Looking
askance he continued his pressure.

"Your talk is fine talk, dear Abbot, hoping to excuse your misrule with
wise-sounding words, alluding to the gospel.

Well done. Now that you have had your say, let us, you and I, reason
together. You know that certain monks here will not want even another
month of your shepherding.

Can you bear it yourself? Disgruntled monks do not go to Heaven,
nor do they avail anyone else in getting there.
You have kept enough time as Eldane. Do not covet the post.
The churches are delinquent and the monastery lifeless.
Others more capable would like to try the work:
Ulcrist, for example, or even me, if the monks demand it.
Abbot Cromna, understand, you cannot bring round
the better part of us to your idea of how things must go,
what a monk's life should look like. So then be humble
and at least set a date for your retirement which Heaven will ordain.
That would give the disgruntled monks some hope.
But if not, then know that after they leave
you will need to do their work. No one else here will do it,
not if he likes to be able to use his fingers to count his sins.

I can guarantee that. Not a threat, it's just
the way of the world, Abbot. A stern lesson, but worthwhile."

To these bold threats Enwick gave stern reply.

"Do not think that I shall fail to oppose you, Yulla,
regardless of your threatening frame, or that you are a guardian monk.
Will you contend with the God of gods,
like the titans contend 'gainst the thunderer in the ancient world?
From what abyss have you reeled up such evil words, monk of God?
Truculent, unbecoming of the sons of God;
or where in thunder thinkest thou art?
Or with whom do you imagine that you parley?
You treat of what Heaven has divinely ordained
but deny the power thereof. No, I am not fearful.
My angels protect me from the likes of you,
chaff to be burned when the great one appears,
his winnowing fan in his hand, about to thresh the grain.
Aye, we will see who stands strong and tall
on that day. But before then, take care to guard your tongue
and not incur the wrath to come, you and all your brood of vipers:
think hard on't now. Abbot Cromna is sacrosanct.
Anyone who pressures him to resign or harms him
will answer to the King. Of that I have already vouchsafed! "

With that Enwick sat down. He ignored reactions and was eating again.
All were stunned at his striking words and what had transpired
unexpectedly. There was no easy talk after that.

The careless words of my brother monks were regretful, but it taught
me a critical lesson. I resolved to speak to the Abbot regarding my own
issue. If anyone could help, surely Abbot could. Although weak, he did not
pale at the opposition, but was a man intoxicated with the Divine.

Orbian of Vath appears to have been a heathen, one who sought to write a history of the entire conspiracy, in hopes to expose its origin in ancient times. He even "became a monk" in order to gain access to sacred scrolls in the desert library of Vesulum.

Monastery Annals of The Weeping Brotherhood
25th of Elentari,
fourth year of the reign of Echecratides

Jacob must be *wise as a serpent* now. Should the good Abbot detect in him a continued *melancholia*, or even a slight *mania*, or suspect him to be demon-possessed, he would be obligated to hinder him and restrain his activities.

So he tried to convince himself that the elven-hybrid mountaineers surely had been less than real. Rather were they phantasms or dreams. He must have eaten some fabulous woodland mushrooms, or weird chestnuts; things which cause hallucinations, things wizards must acquire for the making of mysterious potions. He should no longer take seriously the lore he had heard; not anything from anyone who had anytime in that forest, such as Maragald. Were not his dark prophecies wrenched out of scripture? No, enough with that, Jacob must recover and reclaim the good life of monastery living.

Jacob presented himself before Abbot in his study. Abbot gazed at him with puzzled brow, and gestured for him to come forward and sit. The solar rays of morning beamed through the stain glass of his den. Somewhere in the unknown recesses of the monastery a dove was cooing.

"Where have you been? We had you kidnapped or dead. It came to my ears that you took leave of our beloved way of life? Why?"

"Please, master, please ignore the vanity of a feverish monk, a monk led astray by his own imaginings."

"I am Abbot, not master. Nothing we ignore, nothing. Unfold these things in full. Do not fret, Jacob. Suffer not over being concise; as is wont of your age.
On faith I, your Abbot, command it. There is nothing that a soul undergoes, be it suffering or be it sin, that Allfather has not permitted in order that we might learn."

"Then I think it is this: that I should have the blessings of my holy masters before making grave decisions, such as leaving. It is obvious that the beings were sent by the devil to destroy me, for I left my spirit unprotected. Will I be sent away now? Will I no longer be counted a monk?"

"Do not pretend that we are so strict. Was your dream of elves from the devil, or from yourself?"

"I do not know, but it were real enough by way of pain not to have been a dream. Could it have been something else? Could it be some state between sleep and wakefulness? I remember eating a mushroom."

"Mushrooms grow in the forest, and the town-herbalist Thyestes has kept record of each kind, but there are rumoured to be others. Many wizardic ones are mistaken for edible ones. If indiscriminately eaten, they can cause the mind to become bedeviled, to perceive horned demons, or pointy-eared elves; where in reality one is in the presence of only men."

"But could the elves have been phantasms from outside the one's own vision? Or shadows, of which I am not the author, sub-real beings who had enchanted my mind? For I do not think that I mistook. "

"Did you eat anything else?"

"Chestnuts... But certainly no danger, are they?"

"This is a proper inquisition. We alone will ask the questions.
Certain powerful chestnuts which the Crown has forbidden to eat. But you need not them. The imagination is powerful enough, and can make something seem exactly as real to the dreaming senses. Roving spirits also traverse the intermundane thresholds of dream-vision." He then explained to me how the experience was prepared by the agency the demon, and that our tradition has certain rules of detection. Beware, exterior phantasms can easily be represented to the sleeping brain and accepted by the unwary. Angelic beings, include the fallen ones, have been known to penetrate into a lucid, half-waking sleep. This you may observe in those treated for ailments by the administering of certain fungal derivatives. So this is why the brothers pray not only for the sick who terribly need prayer and spiritual protection, but even for wholesome souls, for they only seem safe. Rope-girded monks we instruct to place a crucifix in the cell, over the bed, to protect from melancholy.
Otherwise Nightmares will arrive with fire
in their nostrils snorting to take the unprotected on a hellish saunter through regions intermundane," Abbot warned. "With such knowledge said, how esteem you the eldritch visions now?"

"Then....I say....aye, it were the demons."

No quick response was forthcoming from the Abbot. Jacob took it to mean that Abbot was open to that as likelihood, but reserved judgement. After some thought, the Abbot had an explanation.
"The rule prescribes that if a monk harkens to the suggestions of the devil, or of some other wandering spirit,
and so leaves in haste, he should be taken back,
even several times, since he is oppressed. Therefore you shall stay and learn to resist, fight spirits, and persevere. But take care not to be so quick in certitude of what you saw.
The old adversary will master tricks over an isolated monk in order to spread confusion."
Abbot continued to explain. Even other agents may be detected for such dream. Even God himself may allow such if it would further his good purpose for souls. Of course, he said, once elder races dwelt in the world,

certain rarified beings of legend. Not to speak of angels... Such races are gone, never to be seen again. In the same way are many other things.

"Vanished are the great lizards and the winged dragons that once traversed the globe of the wide world." He remarked.
"Their colossal bones are displayed in the grand libraries.
I have seen them..those beasts dustward gone,
like the elder races, to the oblivion of ages past.
So you can be assured that this was an illusion."

"Yes, I am certain, master...an illusion. And I am certain
that, were it not an illusion, or a dream, I would not be here
talking about it, for the fairies would have taken me.
I remember sitting in the woods under a chestnut tree
to rest a bit, and after that were these experiences,
a series of visions that I now suspect were manufactured
by my imagination, or demons, and these were so realistic that anyone might be fooled. Perhaps it were sent by Allfather, to drive me back
to this monastery where I belong."

"Do you really believe that, Jacob?"

Jacob's gaze slowly fell. "Something else of it, something unfinished, does remain."

"Hmmm. We must ponder it. It is right that many dreams have been known to stir the soul, in a kind of simulation, not only vision, but auditory and tactile sensation, as well as olfactory..."

Abbot explained how the demons are permitted access to the imagination and may manipulate it, and even stimulate the nerves in such a way that the entire experience develops as if it had actually been lived out. This is a warfare. Type IV demons begin by tempting souls into longing for a different pursuit or position, whatever the heart nurses for a long time, some hidden envy and ambition. The victim of this sort, so deluded, is then convinced that time is running out, that he is in danger of never attaining the envied position. The demon resurfaces, feigning to be an angel of light, or else the wisdom of human nature, and supplies some saving plan or bold words to thwart a monk's sacred resignation.

"If religion becomes only private, it has has lost its salt." he said. "It will soon blossom into the flowers of distorted vanity, or delusion. The farmer begins to believe he will become a wealthy baron, the king is imagines that he can become pious as a simple hermit, the undesired maiden mistakes herself for the prince's paramour."

"...And the obscure monk deigns that he must leave" Jacob added, "on some purpose grand?"

"Perhaps, since to wander is the opposite of the monastic way.
You must be completely honest with me, Jacob.
Is there any part of you that suspects that you were not maundering, and the phantasms not just dream?"

"There is not any doubt that it was a dream...save for one thing."

"What is that?"

"Somehow, the work of master Anherm. It was brought up in conversation by the fairy-bard, the gnomish man called an "Arcavir" who had bookish lore and was leadrer of the elf-kin, a kind of deputy for them."

"That is most unusual." Abbot stroked his beard (Abbot had but a short beard then, not a long one as the reliquary depicts, brothers). "Were the elves really demonic, they would shun mention of so saintly a man as Anherm, a man who became the foremost sign of an interior victory against evil. What else did they tell you?"

"That Anherm was busied in the translation of a strange book."

"What book is that?"

"They called it a tome, one of an encyclopedic series bound in dark elephant hide, a series entitled *The Black Books of Melancholia.*"

The Abbot, whose eyes had been lazily studying the desk he was sitting behind, now looked up with a look of controlled alarm.

His voice became unusually stern; Jacob had never known him thus. "Soft, and shut thou the door, Jacob." He hastily did as Abbot commanded. "Sit here down before me. Many things has this world of which you know naught, Jacob, and though by Anherm you were quite well taught, I am certain he never told you of those works. No, we fear that it were no dream you dreamed, Jacob, an enchantment perhaps, but an honest experience.

This now has become something of exceeding gravity.

What else did they tell you of those books?"

"That they were near impossible to translate, though Anherm could do it. I think I might even try my skill at it, were it possible."

"Did they tell you of the whereabouts of the tomes?"

"Only that they had been searching through the lower world, in subterraneous monasteries that....uh...."

"We bid you tell all. Nature has no chastisement to be met where there is no sin."

"—monasteries that house monks, bad monks, monks who make book bindings with the skin of trespassers. "

"Never mind that....Which volumes of *The Black Books* did the half-elves possess?"

(Now I in earnest worried, brothers; how did the Abbot know so much regarding the tomes? Or that they were half-elves? Had he also made contact with them?)

"There was a thirty-third volume, which they claimed Anherm was translating for them," Jacob explained. "The forty-fourth volume they yielded to the demoniac Grimble the Nibelung for a wergild, payment for my life. Of the other volumes I know little.

How do you, good Abbot, know all this eldritch tome-lore?"

"Your place is not to question. I fear that I know fewer things than you, Jacob, other than it was something of crucial and momentous issue.

Anherm ruined his health in an attempt to translate the volume he possessed, and he was certainly not ready to die, having not finished his work."

"Rumour has it that Anherm was once a wizard."

"Of that I may not speak, for we are bound by the seal.

We can however tell you this —and keep what I tell you secret; I bind you under obedience. The great soul of that man was from an age long passed, and he was famous throughout the Whitehawk continent. In truth, Time's steady march counted him thirty passings of the planet *Calduin*,[25] that is roughly over four hundred passings in solar age, not just a fanciful tale derived to explain his odd manner of speech."

Abbot proceeded to relate the following account.

After Nystol burned, so profound was the calamity,

that Anherm, though a powerful man, began to see life differently. He learned from the Eldark, and finally submitted himself to the Ammouric Soothfold. He turned to God in penance.

He became a rope-girded monk, content to live his last years

in hush contemplation of the sacred mysteries.

Something happened however to disturb his retreat.

Anherm bade Abbot come to him as he sat in misery taking his last breaths.

There in the *infirmarium* he begged Abbot to hinder any secular, be he noble or common, from acquiring the tome. He said that he translated a crucial passage, but there, before his eyes, he rose from his chair and tossed his translation into the fire.

Abbot rescued the book and cried out, "Brother Anherm, by the Saints, why?" Anherm spoke of deceivers in the monastery, voracious wolves in sheep's clothing, who were working among us in hopes to win the obedience of monks, monks who can make books.

So you see, Jacob, before God took him

Brother Anherm relinquished the original into my possession.

He warned that if anyone approached me seeking the tome,

that I yield it not up to any unless a certain riddle be solved.

Now Jacob, if you can loosen the riddle's knot, we shall surrender the tome for you to translate, for we do not think it should remain here."

"I will try my best, but I am not the most clever monk."

"Here then is the riddle. I memorized it; listen, it goes like this: '*Called a traitor, yet even so, how popular I am! Kings and bishops pay me well. And men of learning extol my works, and my crimes even the wise overlook. Only the poets spite me, and title me the murderer!* ....hmmm."

Jacob paused in thought. "I do not know; it is too difficult."

---

[25]*Culduin:* probably the planet Mars, watched by all Whitehawk sages for time calculation especially underground travelers of the intermundane lands.

"Turn it over for a while. I wonder why Anherm did not tell you the answer; after all, you were his sole pupil of Saturnian-Age translations. Take the flat beach-stone there
and keep it in the book's seam so that it will not shut.
By *thaumaturgy* I will lock the silver-braced book with the riddle. If you shut it again, you cannot open it without saying the answer."

"The old man thought more highly of me than he should have." Jacob said, disappointed in his failure. "He must have thought me clever enough. I esteem myself rather dense, eventhough I can translate the Saturnian-Age tome, and betray any author's meaning."

"Very well then, I am going to pass it along to you anyway.
Somehow you will find in yourself. I can no longer keep it here."

"Why not; is it not secure?"Abbot turned to a large oaken chest in the corner of his chamber. He opened it and drew out the large tome marked on the spine LIBR MELANCHOL XXXIII.
Elaborate was the silver bracing shaped like crane feet
and it was well fastened. For such an old bookit was in rather good condition. He set it on the table between them.

"The things written in these elephant tomes, whatever they be, will never be forgotten. Jacob, I am being watched, by whom I am not sure. I fear a secretive faction of dark-minded monks is plotting against me, not-so-secret anymore after yesterday; they suspect I have it, and hope to seize it. But if I passed it along to you, even were they to kill me, they would not know where to fetch it."

"You fear for your life, my Abbot?"

"Some forces in this world are beyond human influence, Jacob. One thing alone gives the monk prevalant hand over them; it is this: that we especially among men know worse things one must fear besides death. So we do not fear death. Whereas other men can only boast such an attitude, we live it out. Whatever knowledge is in this book, men are ready to kill for it. No one will suspect a common novitiate to be entrusted with it. How much did you tell the brethren concerning the half-elves?"

"I spoke only of the brawl, the goose, and a mad dwarf named Grimble."

"Nothing of the codex?"

"They could barely swallow my insane-sounding talk as it were. To add some description of apocalypses found in an ancient codex would not have been taken seriously by a reasonable monk."

"And you spoke to no one else?"

"No one else, but...there was the hermit; I also told him."

"—very well. Maragald, the old raven, is thought to be mad himself anyway. Of the half-elves and that gnome, be they assaying to contact you?"

"They may indeed. They know that Anherm is dead, Perhaps they will endeavor to infiltrate the monastery in order to take back the codex.

However, under the leadership of the gnomish Arcavir they are unable to commit so great a sacrilege as to steal from a monastery."

"Continue as you are, but while you are here you must translate the book and continue Anherm's work. That will be your penance for having left the monastery without permission. Anherm more than any other knew the mysteries of this world, and of desolated Nystol, where is the throne of Satan himself."

Anherm had been most trustworthy and wise. He would not have helped the adventurers had he thought them up to mischief. Abbot bade Jacob keep the book always near; never let anyone have it, even just to touch, for unearthly powers seek its lore. They hunt relentlessly for it.

Soon Abbot would require Jacob to depart from the monastery, for the spies of the infernal powers were about, and it would not be long before they might find him. Jacob, he said, must be cleverer than they,
    and one step ahead, relying on the help of angels
    ...and must tell no one of this.

"Let me be quite clear:" said Abbot "if anyone learns of this other than those who are chosen; it could jeopardize the very monastery, and if this monastery, then all the Whitehawk lands! Even the king is not fit for such knowledge."

"What you command I shall not fail in. My Abbot, certain monks have done me injustice, even though I myself in my sinful folly did not resist them.
    They do lurk about this cloister, and are highly honoured.
    Perhaps they are the ones you also suspect. However because I did not fight them but even wanted them to sell me to the circus, it would be wrong for me to not forgive, to point the finger at them. After all, as a monk I must live with them many winters. The Lamb himself will chastise them."

"You judge rightly and are a worthy monk, Jacob Magister. However their plotting to destroy you will not cease. They would do so before you can expose them. No doubt even now they prepare your demise. We must keep you under guard. *Be thou clever as serpents...*"

"There is no need, Abbot. By faith I know that Heaven conceals my identity from them. I am understood to be Brother Orbian, a guest-monk from the Dry Blood Sea.
    A concealing mist has been placed over me,
    the prayerful work of Maragald's *thaumaturgy.* "

"So walk you unrecognized by them, as "Orbian?""

"So do I walk unrecognized, like an angel."

"May Holy God, the worker of every miracle and wonder,
    be praised forever! Go at night into the *scriptorium*
    where no one will interfere. When the translation is finished
    or the passage Anherm sought is found, you will bring it to me. Then we must decide what to do next. If you are found out
    and the brethren wonder, do not let anyone know

that you have permission from me. You must be prepared to take chastisement for it, and be ready to flee at any moment."

It was decided. Jacob spent three days translating the thirty-third volume, entering his translation in minute letters within the wide *marginalia* of the ancient leaves. After his flesh wearied of study he would practice the staff techniques of Joshur. He was improving.

It was at last determined that he was ready to finish his training and fashion his own quarterstaff, as is custom for guardian monks who have reached the mastery. So he took two synd axes, breakers, and a cardine saw; and his brother Enwick, and went down to the subsanctual forest where there grow ash pollards and walnut beneath the cliffs.

After searching for an hour they found a blackthorn that was ready.

They toiled all day until vespers.

A new day came and brought unsought blessings from God and rope-girded monks led a team of pack-horses to transport the trunk into town.

That whole week Jacob worked on his quarter

and finally the wood yielded a smooth and remarkable staff. He named this staff "Reckoning".

Abbot now requested that Jacob spend some time writing down

what he knew of Nystol and her perils, not only from what he heard from Anherm and his own earthly father, but whatever he could glean from his encounters with the Valraphim. Together with brother Zadoc they put together a damning tract against the folly of the Friars.

Our monks published it.

nto a great enclosure of rock the ancients carved out our *scriptorium*, a hidden place where once there was an open cave. Following a short passage into the rock one finds a door to the separated chambers of cave. It is a place where the brothers sometimes gather for solemn initiation into the mysteries.

This is the chamber where the founder of our monastery, Blessed Clement Ammouri, originally lodged, doing legendary penances for the villagers below, involving freezing cold water and always sleeping on the cave floor. He was a Rumilian who had teleported into the afterworlds, accompanied by the *Erelim*. He saw with his own eyes the Archangel Uriel appear on the crag, and brandish his white hammer to defend the souls of wretched men drained by melancholy, saying

"build here for your brothers a house of the Lord!"

But he also saw the fires prepared for the wicked, those souls who do not renounce melancholy. Uriel guided him through all the afterworlds.

When he at last returned from those distant planes, it is said that he spent every day doing penances. "There be not much time left for us," he would say. "Let us endure happily what we can in this life, brothers, for many souls there related to me how they wish they could have their time back for the doing of penances. The goodness of God is beyond human understanding."

The monks have adorned the cave now with many fine frescoes depicting scenes of C. Ammouri's holy life, and these are visible when lit up by tall candles. There also is a salubrious fountain of living waters, *aquae vitae*, three-tiered, spilling into pools we call the purification. It is not permitted that the waters stand still, but they must be kept flowing by means of mechanisms and pumps.

Our Ammouric fathers consider these sacred waters to be of high importance, and it is the custom of the monks to protect and guard them. When an initiate seeks entrance into the order, he asks for the water, quenches his thirst, and washes away his impurities, a sign of entrance into true life. They are the result of collections of dew, condensed from our living earth, that is, the blessed mosses that glow, and form on the cave walls and whose phosphorescence lights up the chamber with an emerald hue. This is moisture arisen from the waters of the deep, the inaccessible places far below, and this drips down the cave walls and flows into the fountain's wide lower pool. It was fashioned a couple hundred years ago. Monks crafty at such things made it, the three tiers is an arrangement representing the three worlds, or as some have noted, even perhaps the flowing of the great fresh waters (and that is wisely excluding the last world, the prison-hell of spirits, also called Anghar, brothers, a dry desert of a place where not even a drop is dripped from Lazarus's finger).

A fortnight passed and Calduin was upon the Western horizon.

One night Jacob was working in the scriptorium under candle light, translating some poetical verses in *The Black Book*. The section had been provided by an Archeologue, that is, one who studies the ancient world. The poem was epic, just the opening fragment from something much longer, titled *Katabasis Synostoxou*, The *"Descent of Sinostox"* which, (may Heaven forgive me), I here translate, albeit unlawfully.[26]

> *Recall what Ages have forgot, holy muse, what songs did chariots a thousandfold thundering forever drown, before the world was waxen old, when blades forged of Atlantean smithy overturned the thrones of kings, heralding the mighty empires.*
>
> *And tell the passing of those heroes into stone-hewn halls descending; where lords their bright treasure-haul stored, relics from the wide world, the ages of battle, guarded by some grim Netherworm, booty for monstrous foes and powers dreadful; huge tombs bound and inexorable, sorcerous glyphs that doom the raider. So echoes the hollow warp of the worlds, doors sealed to the vaulting deeps where adamantine blade once rung, the clangor of contest mighty.*

---

[26]Throughout the old Furthlands, in the time of the five kings, it was decreed that no one should dare translate any poem. All translations smack of impiety. To translate a religious text was unthinkable.

For thither came Tithonus' son Sinostox of fierce aspect, who
unleashed anew fell spirits from their dismal lairs such kinds as are
unnamed and unsung, enemies of both God and Man, who in vain
revolt against holy power and divine dominion broke forth, and
planned to unchain the defiant titans long in Erebus bound, spirits in
subterraneous wastes letting slip a thousand circling years: to strive
in combat invisible.

And bards of distant origin come might tell you of her day, How it
was in that bronze cradle of time, as the last clouds of Vulcan's
black fury still lingered upon the rolling sea, and did swag over
great billows like a ghost, that prince Sinostox, scion of the
Atlanteans, sought to cheat the gods and withhold the promised
gold, the time when Apollo and his uncle had ended long penance of
mason-work and set the last hewn rock of Troy's mighty walls.

And with the coin he paid the dwarven smiths to fashion
Elmethodon, sword to shed the blood of myriads, putting many cities
under its edge and at last to strike the untouchable seal that so long
sealed the abyss.

In the far away and terrible place of this oneiric poem

Jacob took his time and pondered, translating the Greek *secundum spiritum*, wondering at that strange and forgotten world. The poem continued, but prayer called him. The monk cannot finish the translation.

One name, however my brothers, did stick to his memory.

This was the name Prince Sinostox.

The name is remembered through all Whitehawk, but shoudn't be, nor in the intermundane realm, for it is a name of great infamy.

Perhaps you have heard it sung in an off-mode, for that prince was truly lawless, of chaotic path, the great antagonist of high legend who opposed and struck Duke Ikonn and entrapped the Ammouric Knights. It was Sinostox who first brought the weapon of great and cruel danger into the furthlands, the accursed brand Elmethodon, a wormslayer of the seventh power. It was Sinostox who unleashed the unholy Beast from the bottomless pit. Here before me was in full the grand epic in its entirety, original and unchanged!

Suddenly the white wonderstone under his habit, that rested on Jacob's chest, Maragald's mysterious gift, seemed to shift itself. It just went a little to the left.

It was communicating something—detection of evil?

Jacob happened to glance at the portal. One of the brothers had entered and was slipping about through the hall-columns and shadows. He headed to the southern door which attaches to the craggy caves. There also is stored some of our salt and meats.

His cowl concealed his face and Jacob could not guess which of the brothers. The monk noted him sitting at the scrip-desk as he was about to pass; he halted and turned to Jacob.

Forgive me brothers for failing to address many troubling things about him. You no doubt have some memory of him, so why tell anything else wrongful about him? His deeds will be known at the Judgment, but as he still lives, let us pray for him to turn from his ways. For we do not point out the speck in our brother's eye. Nevertheless, in this case his deeds cannot not go untold, even if we would have it another way. Just as the evangelists did not fail to note the errors of Judas, so I will tell what he admitted with his own words.

Chaos, not order, was at work in the soul of Ulcrist Dretch, a Yahoran whose only absolute law was self-aggrandizement.

He was feigning to be a lawful monk, but all was ambition, and satisfaction at seeing things fall apart. Then raw power takes over. Whereas ambition mixed with studied revenge impurely excited some opposers long past, as they did the marauder Sinostox of old.

But how pure was the ambition that drove Ulcrist!

As I learned later, his own secret masters had taught him the alien dogmas that extol "freedom from the illusion of both good and evil." Supposedly he joined them for his own advancement. Clearly he was uncomfortable to obey even the pit-borne devils, but did so only out of unworthy craving for power.

It seemed that he was aiming at some high teaching appointment in the Whigg university. (Some of the less forgiving brothers would have applauded such a move for him). Yet since all new monks we instruct to overlook the faults of others, Jacob therefore greeted him:

"Peace of Christ, Brother." Jacob whispered.

"There be no longer time for conversation, monk," he answered, (but a rude assumption, for Jacob only meant to be courteous and not make conversation). "*Magnum Silentium* must be observed," he said piously, "But I thank you. Do I interrupt your toil, monk?"

"Not much...but will you allow me to continue my labors, even if you wish you speak only necessary words? The candle is low."

"Indeed...but pray, know that this *is* forbidden until Advent...but wherefore you are a guest, unfamiliar with our customs. We permit no toil in the *scriptorium* at night, expending so much quarion-wax. I am Ulcrist, once a friar at Whigg, but called to these shores instead."

Had Jacob restored to silence at this point, he might have saved himself much trouble.

"I must translate this text secretly, so I beg forgiveness. It is a gift for my Abbot. Are you on your way to the fountain for a meditation?"

"I am. And you are preparing a gift? For what occasion?"

"If you will not betray the secret..."

"I keep privy many things. You have my word."

"After I finish, I will be on my way from this abbey, brother, as you may have expected...to return something precious to someone highly placed, and the dangers are great indeed."

"I shall pray. It sounds adventuresome."

"So does it sound to those who have not tasted of adventure," Jacob remarked. "As those ruffians themselves do attest, who captured Brother

Jacob in the forest··· They be witnesses—such excursions may lead to an early demise."

"May Heaven deliver him. Fear not, the Lord will *send his angels before* him. We now return to silence...What of your life back in your own desert monastery?"

"It must wait until this labor is accomplished. Then will I return there if the Ancientmost wills it."

"Then perhaps I should keep it safe for you, this elephant-hide tome here, which you rightly consider precious. I see that it is the same text which brother Anherm, of venerable memory, we often saw laboring over. It is a famous one indeed. I have seen you holding it close, grasping it and not suffering others touch it. Understand that you are a guest, brother, and that although the Abbot has given it to you, it is only on loan. Certainly the disciples shared all things in common, and did not act in such a way with a mere book.

You heard the dangers of the wilderness here, how of late
it has even taken from us a dear brother monk?

Our Brother Jacob was young and foolish, so he wandered out to see the wide world. The forbidden forest snuffed out his life. Why, even one of the long-journeying knights has also died

while riding through, attacked by an enraged throng of heretics.

Be careful, friend, and before you travel, consider also this:

were you to perish in the wilderness like him, perhaps by bandits or some other calamity, your translation would be lost, and the irreplaceable tome as well. Or, it might be destroyed on your trek back to The Dry Blood Dunes, as was a precious volume borne on the back of the donkey Atlas in the mountains some years ago, famously slipping off in a tempest and washed away in a mudslide. Easily this too might get lost or water-logged or somehow destroyed. So many things can happen. It is a cumbrous book too.

Why not bestow it to me?
I will take care of it and you can finish the translation
when you visit again another year."

As this brother was saying these things to Jacob, his eyes widened and beamed with candlelight reflection and he reached, and his fingertips glided over the book. Sweat as droplets formed on his face. He touched the wonderstone under his habit. As Jacob returned his gaze, it suddenly seemed to him, by the assurance of his voice and noble contenence, that his must be prudent counsel indeed.

Jacob was startled out of the trance. A familiar sound did it.
Like blasts of a triton's horn, which must have awoken every monk: goose calls filtering in from outside. Was it Aileron? The bird was calling from the courtyard just outside the *scriptorium*.
A clarion for the monk to battle!
Surely that good goose was just having a typical goose-quarrel with one of his swan-friends, but something in the resonance of his call conjured thoughts of purpose high and of war unfinished: a warning in Jacob's thoughts. The creature even mysteriously informed Jacob of something, in goose-language of course. Namely, that the monk to whom

Jacob spoke only meant to bamboozle, and coveted the silver-braced book, and would take it.

How strange that a monk can catch news from a goose, exact goose-words in fact. Did loyalty to that creature, a creature who had recently saved his life, give rise to understanding?

But Jacob pondered not that question, rather the news itself.

How did this monk, strolling at night, know so much of what was going on? Do the powers of shadow have a claim on him?

Learn, brothers, how the thaumaturgy of concealing mist, the identity-veil which Maragald used to disguise Jacob, requires certain conditions be met. As in all divine thaumaturgy, the wonder may not be for a self-benefit. Therefore one does not cast it upon one's self. It is only for keeping someone else safe. Also, know that in order that God's justice might not be doubted, the one concealed also is unable to identify unfriendlies, lest any be tempted to use it for unfair advantage. This is why Jacob did not at first recognize Ulcrist Dretch, bird of war. For if he had, he would have more quickly taken leave of him. Last but not least, the one so concealed must not commit sin, and must remain just and respectful, else the mist be scattered.

Jacob tells of this mistake in his written statement to the Holy Inquisition. He recorded the rest, the entire conversation, including his own thoughts:

...It was in this last thing wherein I failed, brothers,
and soon lost the protection of the thaumaturgy.
How is it that I could fall so unexpectedly?
It was because I had been fooled into ignoring the Grand Quietude.

I was yet conversing with this monk, but the rule was ignored by both of us. This is no minor thing, for the Grand Quietude is the will of God, which to disregard is great pride.

When he first opened his mouth to converse with me,
I should have simply covered my head with my cowl
to indicate observance of the rule. I did not, but fell into the vanity of men. Hence I lost the favor of God. The thaumaturgical protection concealing my identity faded away at once. This was a just punishment.

As for brother Ulcrist, master of guardians, this was not just another one of the foolish monks, fattened, drunk, or vain, or one like myself.

Rather a soul become dark, a monk knowledgeable of infernal places, perhaps a mischievous heretic, a gnostic, and he had an evil power in his trained hands. But how could that be?

I glared at Ulcrist, startling him.

"Why, it is you. –Jacob!" he declared. "Strange, I did not recognize you at first. You must have grown. I did hear rumour that you had returned. Did you use a spell to conceal yourself? I pray that you will be wise enough not to report the favor that Formosus and I accomplished for you the day we helped you join up with the circus. Recall that you and I shared fellowship. Were you not fond of circus life? –of course not. Never mind, you do not need to explain."

I did not reply, but looked away.

"Be not melancholy. Look at me. It is no secret," he said, "the opinions some monks entertain of me, and I fear that you also maybe tempted to share the same opinions, even though I think of you as my spiritual equal, since you know me better than others."

"How so? —and what opinions, brother?" I asked.

"Some brethren look upon me askance,
with a certain suspicion, perhaps because, in my spiritual way,
I maunder the corridors of this abbey alone
when the shadows are long. Other monks delight in the dawn,
or in glow of furnace or shine of gladsome wine.
They laugh and smile, and they are confident
in their casual demeanor, looking upon me as one too interested
in the drear things of penitence and melancholy,
and they surmise that attempts at piety are mere show,
in order that I might achieve a high position."

"I repent of such judgements if I have entertained them.
But for selling me to the circus, where instead
you should have cured me of *Melancholia...*"
"Do not be so dramatic. I prayed for you.
We knew you would come back and did you a favor.
Now, why not favor me in turn?
Demonstrate mutual forbearance and lend to me
that unusual tome there for a while as a token of trust."

"Certainly in your desire to please Christ, you have forsaken interest in anything prized among men, save war. However, I cannot lend this to anyone. It would be useless anyway to those not familiar with the forgotten languages. I am about a certain momentous enterprise, things of high estate, the contest not of flesh and blood, but against principalities and powers, spiritual corruption in high places, and I must not trust anyone. It is not of my own willing. Perhaps if you are kind I shall forget your selling me into slavery."

"You distrust even a sworn monk like myself? After all I did to train you? It is on my account that you have survived in the wide world.

Once again I perceive that you are veiling your mind from me, monk.

This is unfortunate... and for you, brother... to distrust me: it be sin. You do not yet discern spiritual things...you have not found your shadow. I was wrong about you, you have not become my equal... " He adopted a tone of rude admonition. "But I do not require your forgiveness. And for the abbey...I know that you are not really making a gift

for the Abbot. You seek something within that book.

I shall inform the Abbot of your adventures, and of certain lies that I surely heard you speak, and advise him of your vain nocturnal labours."

"What does that matter? The Abbot supports my cause."

"Even the Abbot does not stand above the rule. He is required to administer a penalty. However, were you to tell me more on your search and the object of your quest, perhaps I might forget to approach the Abbot regarding this transgression."

"Why so interested?"

"Good reasons have I. I am presently researching some historic questions concerning.....the Fall of Nystol."

"Why is that worth a thought?...magic dead and gone... towers, ruined, unreachable, an abandoned mesa overgrown with asphodel and hellopian ivy, a den for jackals..."

"Now I am beginning to suspect by your tone and tenor that you yourself could not answer that question. But give me the book and I can tell you straightway many things."

"First some answer to my question, Ulcrist. What is Nystol to you? Or what honest need have you of these pages?"

"Not trespass or crime if that is what you hope to imply.
My business has a respectable confidentiality.
Certain interested parties await, spiritual men, from whom I might make profit, and make good, by acquiring for them a passage from that book.
You also may share in this business, even fetch a pleasing reward.
So come, let us reason together now.
Can a monk act as if he owns something, something that is made to be common usage for all, as scripture recommends?"

"No, although this does not really belong to the monastery either."

"However, the restricting of its content and lore is beyond your authority."

"Abbot has given me free use of the library and access to every book. Not even the assistant librarian has such liberty. As for your friends, tell them that the text would be useless to them. The Saturnine Latin in this work is too obscure for even the greatest minds. When Anherm of Whigg, of blessed memory, passed into the next world, he took with him the last remnant of full comprehension in Saturnine vocabulary and grammar among men. I alone survive with the requisite knowledge, which, though imperfect, yields understanding at the old tongue, thanks to his careful training. Others have paid dearly that it might be kept safe, even forfeit their lives."

"A fine story, but truly exaggerated. You have only studied the ancient tongue for a few years. Even your skill of Church Latin is yet imperfect.
It is not possible that you could also master the Saturnine forms, arcane and innumerable as they are. . ."

"That I shall not deny. You have prevailed in argument. Still, I know how to decipher rare words that are unknown, and I should fear to let go the tome or leave it amiss." (Suddenly a way occurred to me to hinder Ulcrist so that he would be forced to return to contemplative silence.) "....Abbot said that this tome should not be yielded to anyone unless they can answer a certain riddle."

"A riddle locks away the book's pages?"

"As if by magic, and since Abbot knew the answer, he opened it. If you respect authority, you will solve it. However I think that it will confound you."

"Say it; and you will learn my worthiness."

"Abbot spoke the riddle as follows '*Some call me traitor, still I am popular. Kings and bishops require my services. I do well with the nobles and men of learning, my works being celebrated since the tower fell, but even so do bards and poets revile me, and style me murderer*! " Now, Ulcrist, return thou to wrapt silence, as is right, and contemplate the mystery for an age. Then come back with your answer."

"*terribile hoc est*, the lock that has shut that codex, but I am a lock-pick, and a rather deft one. It will not take an age. I will draw out the answer, clever, before you can turn the page."

Ulcrist walked a short distance away and pulled his cowl over his head. He turned his back to me and stood perfectly still, like a statue. Would he soon depart and disappear amidst the pillars? He did not. Another few moments passed and he turned about.

"Have you already picked so profoundly secured a lock?" I asked.

"The tumbler I have now turned, aye. So I shall disclose the answer."

"Wait, before you speak it, the book must be shut. It opens not for those without wisdom. Even I myself know not the answer, but Abbot placed that curious beach-stone within so that it would not shut. If your answer is correct, the book will open again. If not, to the Abbot I return it, who alone keeps the riddle's key." I removed the stone and close the lid.

"Now, say your answer, and let it be right or wrong."

"Who is called a traitor? Who is the one betraying another for pay, but who remains popular? Who is he who serves nobles and is paid well, even since the time men's speech was confounded under Babel's tower?
Or why would bards and poets revile such a betrayer?
It is because a poem cannot be extracted from its original words.
"*A poem is what is lost in translation*"
This is why the Church, nay all Whitehawk has outlawed
translating poetry, because the translator is a traitorous agent
who betrays and snuffs out the secret rhyme, and is paid well for his deed. The answer then, it is you! The translator!"

Clearly he had solved the riddle. Now was I honestly in trouble.

"How now, monk. . . why does your complexion fail you so?
Suspect you that my answer has squarely hit, not to be gainsayed?"

"Earnestly deft and worldly-wise are you, Ulcrist Dretch.
Still, Abbot commanded me vouchsafe it.
I gambled what is not mine. I am not given leave even lend this tome."

"So be. Where now has your honour stolen off?
By right the tome is mine. I solved the riddle.
By your stubbornness that you have indeed captured your own shadow. Fair, for I said you must; or perhaps even now you come to grips

with it. If so, then I am fair certain that our training has made you greater in skill than ever was I. You and I are alike in many ways, more perhaps than you are fain to admit. But now you're turned dishonest.

Such reneging puts me to doubt. The riddle proves itself true.

You are the traitor. Your own shadow has traded you away."

"oh....?"

"But I admire you, more than is right, that is why I recommend however that you quit this place soon. Too well I instructed you, Jacob. So much that you almost surpass me and now lift expert heel against me. I did this, and still you trust me not. Be not so confident. My interested parties will be brought to the point of extreme measures, once they learn that you have rejected my offer and treated me unfairly. Your training cannot outwit them."

I exclaimed indignantly. "The Abbot's knights will see that you and your fellows are brought to justice for your intrigues," Ulcrist I perceived as he truly is: the veins about his face nearly bloodless, his visage taut and shadowy, inchoate with subliminal wrath.

Aileron the goose, outside, started making his trumpeting call again. I rose up from the stool and copyist desk to leave.

Ulcrist at once rushed me, grabbing the black silver-braced book and, with strength unexpected, in the scuffle he wrested it from my hands.

Cries for help I sent out and moved to counter him with a grapple, in order to seize back the precious tome. Ulcrist produced a dagger with wavy serpent-like blade from within his sleeve.

I was amazed. Never would I imagine him so profanely armed, even with all war-training, and his virtue feigned.

Surely the devil possessed him, and this on account of having embraced some alien dogmas, or perhaps for consorting with wizards. Even so thought I to know him, but what gravity to resort to such an ungodly weapon. We may not have been fond of each other, but my master and I were brothers who enjoyed sparring with the quarter-staff.

Ulcrist was backing away, getting ready to make a sprint for the door. But at once was heard the sound of rushing feet and voices coming toward the *scriptorium* entrance, for others had heard my cries, and he could no longer use that singular exit for escape.

So Ulcrist turned about. He made for the opposite end of the *scriptorium* hall, where lies the passage to the sacred fountain and caves.

I bolted after him, but only to follow in pursuit,

lest he strike me down suddenly with that dagger.

I had to take that book back.

Ulcrist burst through the door into the passages of the cavern. Although the wondrous cave was lit only by the mysterious and dim glow of the emerald mosses that cover the wall,

I was able to make out to what area of the cave he was heading.

As you may know, brothers, no other exits twist to the outside from these caves of penitence, so did I wonder what he hoped to find for a way out. Ulcrist slipped through shadows, making himself undetectable.

It is a roguish skill the manualist Guy of Xaragia records is not uncommon among those associated with monks.

I could perceive that he had hid himself behind the sacred fountain in hopes of fooling any pursuers.

I approached silently near him, ready to fend an attack with my deadly hands. I estimated that my location might be immediately marked by the others, whose shouts I could hear; after all, with Aileron's calls and my outcry, no monk would have remained undisturbed.

In moments they would be here, and we could thereby accost the rogue monk by combined effort. So ready I stood, undetected, at least six hides away from his likely position on the opposite side of the fountain.

Ulcrist, ever-plotting, crouching, was tracking my footsteps.

"Are you then one of those whom men call an Infernal Monk? " I asked aloud.

Ulcrist slowly stood up holding the tome...

"We are a pervasive organization," he said. "I shall tell you of us because few here would believe it, even were you to inform anyway."

Amazingly, the lout related many things, things that one hopes could not possibly be true. He boasted how they would cunningly use portals "wormholes" of space and time to carry their influence throughout the worlds. Their "law" is what the Church, clearly out of envy, forbids as idolatrous. Their works they consider happy, but such seem as evils to the uninitiated. Unbelievers accuse them of failing to adore Christ, he said. It is not the whole story. In reality, it is they, not the so-called Christians, who adore the true deity. The true savior is what most folk in their ignorance would identify as a demon-god, or a Netherbeast.

"Yet an alien knowledge has been granted us," He continued.

"Our eunuchs have entered the thronerooms of Maceonid Kings in every land and even now whisper undetectable inversions of human law as their counsel, and how praiseworthy is that?!

Our monks publish inverted philosophies in the great schools which will soon dominate every aspect of learning.

Not only seek we kings as our prey, but crook-weilding bishops and mace-armed clerics, as well as the flock of your God, which soon shall be ours. We are the wolves in sheep's clothing of whom I warned you before, but there is no shame in that.

Do not packs of wolves have every advantage over sheep?

Normally we seem to be your everyday Ammouric sort of monk,

for we put on the cloth from the sheep's wool.

Our kind can however be distinguished by one who has a discerning eye. I will tell you this because what I said before was sincere, I admire you. I even expect that you will see the wisdom of becoming one of us."

And he continued. In particular, he pointed out, anyone who notes details can spot an infernal brother-monk. A little chain upon the neck is worn, for underneath the frock these monks devoutly wear an infamous medallion which links them to an ancient relic. It features a *triangulum* about a gazing eye, the "all-seeing eye, --the magnificent *oculus* of —

—You are not ready to learn his name." he interrupted himself.

"But take a moment to inspect some of your fellow monks, and you will see not a few with such a little chain and periapt.

Our number grows. We are chosen, but we are secret: the hidden elect. The common monk *non comprehendit*.

To join our powerful fold and make a difference, that would be high wisdom."

"*Inítium sapiéntiæ timor Dómini*" I declared.

I learned later, from the listing in **The Black Book,** that this relic, the eye itself, like the infamous *homunculus*, was manufacturedfrom a strange and rare fruit which the restless archon Nimrul claimed to have grown for countless years in the second age.

But the tyrant traded the ancient relic for a "vortex" poem, a sacred poem, which having once heard a recital entranced him with rhyme and cancelled his common sense. The *oculus* now is harnessed by Ulcrist's master, and those who wear it yield forbidden knowledge. You see, they say that true master of all the fearless is not the "great architect," as some boast, but one whose name, according to Ulcrist

"is too precious for mortal lips to utter." He can see whatever we see with our eyes fashioned of vile flesh. According to him, the eye of the true god illuminates their *intellectum* and is synchronizing the domination of every human intellectual endeavor...for their own good of coursde...

"So now you know why I have done this. If you are wise, friend, you will join with us and learn the *arcanum* of our secret order, how to be delivered from this prison of the material world, for soon all minds will be under our sway: *mysterion*.

I perceive however by your unworthy expression that you have already made your choice.

May what I have taught bring you earnestly to despair of this life, as a monk should. I have said too much. You must be silenced.

Consider the shadow you cast there, Jacob.

Check it and make sure your stance is correct."

Unthinkingly I obeyed and checked my stance, glancing at the outline of my shadow on the floor. One always unquestioningly doeswhatever is commanded in training. Clever Ulcrist took the distraction to advance an extra move.

Another moment passed before I realized. He uttered something in a language which I could not readily identify. It was not Gohhan. Was it the language of pure chaos, a tongue rumoured of which Guy of Xaragia mentions?

Surely they were magical words, or magic in them was mixed. Nay, perhaps it was abysmal magic.

Holding forth the deadly dagger on his palm, it straightway was suspended in air! It seemed, watching the dagger, that he controlled it by telekinetic means, or better yet, by demons unseen.

Upward the tip turned and pointed toward me.

He spoke again, and the dagger sped toward me

at a velocity and accuracy that only experts at dagger-hurlng would have.

Squarely in the chst it peierced me.

Ulcrist gently placed his cowl back over his shaven head.

He set down the tome, stretched out his arms and resumed more infernal chanting. With strange gestures, what seemed a luminate shaft of blue radiant matter opened beneath him, which, descending by the trace of his hand's direction, morphed into an aperture on the floor, a wormhole of some sort. The dagger was lodged in my chest
and the crimson begin to seep into my habit.

Ulcrist retreived the tome and began descending into the portal by a magic ladder. As he did so, his waist and arms went out of sight.

But something happened next which he did not expect.

His torso stuck in the magical aperture, unable to cross through the threshold and glyphs. Had the roasts and potatoes of the monastery expanded his paunch? No, rather the famous tome he clutched, *The Black Book*, was somehow anchored in this surface world and could not be carried into the world below, like oil which refuses to keep underwater.

Ulcrist turned red with rage, and he cursed angrily. I had never seen him like that before. In training he had always been in control of himself.

The portal of radiant matter was beginning to shut,
and now the other monks, my own brethren, his new pursuers, were close. This imposter was already planning to return as monk again, perhaps through a magical aperture to his cell.

My death would prevent his being identified.

He must not be seen by any others. He let the book go,
and, stepping down deeper into the portal, slunk into the nether-realms without the prize. The tome fell to the floor with a thud as the magical aperture zipped up into the air and vanished.

The radiant shaft produced a sulphurous scent defiling our holy sanctuary.

By now my lungs were making their last attempts, for the dagger had hit its target and filled my lungs with blood. After the book fell to the cave floor, the last thing I recall was the water of the sacred fountain flowing below me; and falling forward into its luminous pools.

It was not seem a seemly way to end this life.

In the sacred waters of purification I may have learned something of what it means to be on the threshold of neverness. My soul did not at once hurry to the Judgement, but remained in some intermediary condition. These waters covered me over in a chaotic rush of wave. My last sensation was an indescribable wracking, and what seemed a rending of my soul, for my body seemed caught on a rock and would not float away.

It is much deeper than sleep, death darksome, and far more profound was the absolute stillness. The timelessness of the abyss of darkness covered me like a shroud. Blackness after that, and a sort of receding into a painless, dreamless, thoughtless sleep from which there is no return...

. . . the four demon-kings had been devasting in their havoc. Afterwards they surveyed what they had done, and sorrowing they repented of the injustice. They at last worshiped God. Now these are become the beneficent spirits who patrol the four winds. If asked properly, they will instruct you in the divinely sanctioned techniques of the staff.

Tien Joshur
Autumn Instruction for Monks on Pilgrmage

XVI   THE TRiBUNaL

 o return...so it is conjectured; at least among the learned: there is no coming back from the other side. Brother Zadoc the theologian himself always asserted this, making exception for a few ghosts which Purgatory leases out. Are some sent to warn uncharitable or unchurched men and spook them into prayer? One should think so. Otherwise no known natural restitution is there, at least, not according to common human record. *It is appointed for men to die once, then comes the judgement.*

However, in that dreamless nothingness, Jacob perceived in his mind's eye a faint light...inchoate. It was removed at a spaceless distance.

This light shining in the darkness which I perceived,
I wished come closer so that I might hold on to it
in my passage through space and time.
Was perhaps this a radiance from the *non-void?*
The light came closer and closer, or else I came closer.
And soon my own self was suffuse with light,
so that all was a peaceful radiance
beyond human description, although nothing else was seen.
That abyss of darkness was far away.
This light filled even the core of my being,
as it were a kind of nourishment. Still, I did not sense my body.

It was as drifting afloat. No form at first was in this light.

Soon however a form did appear, a being, numinous and shimmering. The being was not far off, but did display a human-like frame. The head however impressed as leonine, but was as of one who is aware, and a patch covered one eye, a battle-wound.

Seven horns, like rays beaming from the solar crown, were set
upon this lion-like head. Of his lower torso I could not see,
nor did I think to look —becoming indescribable, for it was covered over in cloud or light.

Nor can I rightly describe the unflinching desire that welled up within, a desire to convey this light to Whitehaven, supply it to other souls, and to serve Heaven

and the God whose goodness permeates all creation.
This being addressed me, not with words spoken,
but rather, as it were, with light outpoured into my understanding.
It is just as when a man with a mirror stands on a hill
to catch the sun's ray and signal his homeland of what approaches.
Immediately I fell down to worship this ethereal being.

"Do not worship me. The Lamb alone is to be worshipped.
Come, Jacob Magister, grandson of Escorvus, initiate
of the Ammouric monks of Whitehaven, dear son
of blessedness. Welcome to the entrances of the last world.
It is the first world in your learning, so also the last.
I am Ambrosius Ammouri, *Agathodaemon*,[27] *nephilung* guardian
of sacred caves. You have come to a place of sanctity,
the threshold of final mystery. You shall now make a choice
upon your life's right desire. Allfather has spoken: You may continue
on this and leave the darkness terrestrial behind you forever.
As your material body went into the waters of purification,
at the same time the power of Almighty
brought you up again in these waters of true life.
Your Abbot has prayed for you. You sinned against Grand Quietude, and that warrants punishment, but your terrestrial life is ending in defense of the Kingdom of Heaven. You are being given special indulgence because you did right in the end. Your spirit and flesh are renewed in the sacred waters.
You will no longer be the same melancholy soul.
Heaven saves you *undeservedly*
from the punishment that awaits the wicked.
It is because of this mercy that Heaven assigns no further suffering to you. You may relinquish the world forever. However, of the other lives that must remain to yet sojourn in the world, will any be brought to right conduct on account of true teachings?

Your absence and purpose unfinished—a loss irreparable.

---

[27] *Agathodaemon* (Oruscan Gr). Simply should be understood as "a mysterious and benign spiritual being." These were good-willed spirits which traversed the world before the Day of the Lord, the Revelations, and were allowed to continue afterwards. They are not technically angels, (*angelloi* is Greek for messengers), since they usually carry no direct message from God and remain in the sublunar world, but they do often act independently, having sworn fealty to the Furth High King. They have however been known to carry divine messages for a special purpose. Ambrosius Ammouris the Nephilung 'the lion head" is the most famous of these.

"This evening you will be far from the world and its sorrows, just as it was with the thief Dismas who, dying, confessed the Lord, and heard the longed-for words *"this very night you will feast with me in paradise."* You too will testify to the Lamb's imperishable glory in heaven. But know this: on earth, in short time, the great red dragon will drag down many with his tail. In a few years the world entire will be overwhelmed in universal Darkness.

No other monk
will dare stand opposed to him and his archons.
The greater part of the souls of men will be forfeit.

"It does not have to be that way. Something the Almighty now grants to you: you may today choose this: return to the terrestrial world, losing this chance at eternity. Go back to deliver the monks from themselves. Great is the risk. A veil shall cover your eyes,
and you will not always have access to this celestial light,
its pureness; only a faint memory to ponder.
But right knowledge will aid you, and interior strength;
to win back your brethren and many others to faith.
However a payment must be made: sacrifices of great cost.
Choose this earthly ordeal and your mind, though renewed
by this vision, nevertheless remains susceptible to deceptions of the wicked. But your heart ever more resolute will be. In the end you will die obscure and forgotten,
the death of a heretic burned at the stake, the Whore of Babylon condemns you, the false Church. Consumed by a dragon's breath, your name is a thing shamefully spoken.
But that is not so bad, provided you have glorified God.
Nay, be warned that in so choosing
there is left one further possibility much worse:
the consequence that, although you have saved many others,
you may not save yourself; nor preserve your own soul
from foolish transgressions, an evil day. In a weak moment,
in a confused world, what is forbidden somehow wins you.
So an otherwise noble life is thrown into confusion eternal, and straightway into the dark Hell you slip.
There is that possibility—most unthinkable, but a possibility even so. Since you are a valiant monk Allfather has vouchsafed you choose between the two paths; upward hurry beyond the Veil now and enter paradise, or return: greater be the glory of the latter, but perilous.. Choose thou wisely."

"Creature," (I spoke not with lips, but with my mind), "can you not see into the future days and reveal the better way?"

"The knowledge of future events belongs to the one who sits on the throne. I am only a messenger whom he has sent, but know that all else is veiled in the mystery of Radiance. So now make you the choice. Here is not a choice given to many."

What can I say? How dearly I wished to enter the gates of those in blessedness which now am I barely able to remember. How much I longed to stand with the blessed in the infinite worship of praise, echoing from the distant place of luminous joy. But an even stronger will within my heart strangely sought to bring that luminous radiance, the light of the Lamb, a light from before the world, to others.

I begged to serve the light that suffused my being.

Terrible indeed was that choice, but it has been made, and now I can barely remember that light, and a veil is drawn over my mind's eye which shall not pass away.

The strange and selfless desire remains, but is faint.

So did I communicate my heart to the angelic being.

He replied in turn.

"The path you are taking is pleasing to God.

However, the choice is a grave one. Learn now this prophecy, for besides keeping only a faint memory of this light, which someday, in some dark place, could be accessible to you,

there must be one glimmer that, looking upon, can give you hope. It is reflection of the light that was and is before the world.

It comes as this one prophetic saying which,

no matter what happens to you, you will be unable to forget.

"There is a creature that gladdens Allfather.

It is the rarest of creatures in the worlds

and no longer even treads the sunlit lands

for fear of the arrows of fallen men. This creature certain legends tell of many mysteries, and provide a hern-riddle that cannot be removed from the mind, it is this..." (The lion-headed one then formed the prophetic riddle by writing it, brothers, if you will believe, in blazing letters, across my mind,

a poem that I am not permitted write down,

for I am not holy enough; but since it was written in the ancientmost Akaratic script, few would be able to translate it anyway. However, I have made a reasonably poor representation, (not a translation) and although it is barely lawful to do so, I think here Heaven's story trumps an old human prohibition:

Come a unicorn from eras primeval,
Then this soulwise verse keep for retrieval:
Lo the vast which he mightily smites
with playful tail, then vanishes from sight
beneath the icey valley. Freckles white
rahis raiment adorn, a spiral lance
his happy horn, he hunts the hills
not of stone born. So be it enough
his pelt to reach and his pity to touch,
For the clever beast a kindness will help,
Then to alban stairs of lambent stone,
narrow way ascend, a corridor lone

without shadow to Argunizial's tip.
above winding way to mysteries unwrit,
wherethings too holy to utter with mortal lip.

"This rhyme will not slip from your mind,"he said, "although you may not fully decifer it; or grasp its mysteries, but if you seek and are willing, even if you have forgotten your own self, the fulfilling of the hern-riddle shall restore you.
"Now return, Brother Jacob, finish God's work
in the terrestrial world, that which you have chosen. Take heart
and go with all strength and confidence to the destiny that is readied."
Thus he spake, and I can recall no more of the higher world."

Jacob awakened on the cold stone floor of the cave. He was in the hold of brother monks who kept pounding his back to cause him to eject volumes of water from his lungs. After he was done he turned over and looked up.

He saw brother Fragga Slowtongue.

"Brother Fragga, thanks be to God."

"What has happened here, Jacob? I cannot believe it is you. We thought never to see you again after you vanished. How is it that you went into the water? "

He lifted him up, and he sat, and saw two other monks, Formosus and Ossica. They had rushed in following Fragga. Jacob sought to explain:

"Someone was lurking, disguised as a rope-girded monk, slipping in shadow. He snatched a precious tome. I gave chase."

Now remembering *The Black Book*, hs eyes searched the floor for sight of it frantically.

"Has he made off with it? he got it away from me. He left me for dead, having made a critical strike with his dagger. I was some time there between the worlds. It seems to me but a moment here."

Jacob looked down to his chest. The dagger's wound had totally closed up. Opening the hole in his habit, no bleeding wound was in his chest but only faint scarring, being otherwise completely healed. A marvel had occurred, but he thought better than to announce it.

"A monk hit me with deadly dagger hurled.
A dagger sent by invisible force. I fell, as one dead
—but the wound is healed, and I live."

"The healing powers of these underworld waters are real indeed; for they are primeval waters, brother; so when in you fell they could not but restore you."

"It is so, Fragga. I would have drowned had you not come and pulled me out." He looked over into the pool. The dagger was submerged on the bottom.

"Let me remove this." he said, reaching down into the pool.

"Do not touch it, Jacob," said Formosus. "The sin of the intruder is upon it. I shall pick it out wearing a glove."

"Did he mean to pierce me lest I alert other monks? Look, the blade is being devoured by rust already!"

"No rust can work that fast. Some other power destroys it. Look, it is even disintegrating!" cried Formosus. "It dissolves into the water! What witchery was upon the dagger that sacred water rejects and wars so furiously against the iron? " .

"He must be still here, lurking in the shadows," Jacob said. "Search this place for the intruder."

"No, this place is a sanctuary. We cannot remove anyone by force. An intruder you say? But did you not also say a monk?" asked Formosus, "Surely none of the village thieves would be so bold to wear a monk's habit."

"No, not a villager...He must be already gone; this one knew some powerful dwimmer-craft. He formed a magical portal. It opened and he descended into the lower world."

"Who was this fiend? Who possibly would break into these most forbidden of holy confines? A cunning wizard?" asked Fragga, angrily.

"You will not be pleased with my answer, brothers. It was one whom you know: It was Brother Ulcrist. It seems that he will no longer break bread with us. "

"That is outrageous!" exclaimed Brother Ossica. "What have you done Brother Jacob? Where have you been this past week? Did someone push you into the pool or not? There is no blood, no sign of a wound. And now that you have been purified, you are to be considered a full monk? It is forbidden; you have not even reached your seventh year of service, and we had just learned of your return here after having joined the circus. Now you accuse Brother Ulcrist of using magics?"

Ossica was a weighty Mahanaxaran, something that somehow characterized his reputation as authoritative. He was the epitome of lawfulness. Nothing slightly untrue escaped from his pious lips, or could get past his ears. Abbot had recognized this greatness and had appointed him minor Inquisitor as well as disciplinarian. To be in his presence meant to reflect on one's own unworthiness, to detect the rotten fruit, one's own produce of half-truths.

"I saw him with my own eyes.

Exactly how I was healed only those waters know,

for the dagger was lodged in my chest. And you are right, brother, now that I think of it. But it seems that a dark cloud has been lifted from my thoughts. This must be what they call The Purification. My soul is no longer is clouded by dark storm, like many voices fighting within me, but I sense something of clarity, as never before. I know what must be done."

"The Purification is a secret of our order. speak no more on't. Now this be serious indeed. It must be reported," said Ossica.

"Brother Jacob, come thou along now, you must relate these things to Abbot."

"By your command, but first, brothers; pray, assist me. Let us locate the precious tome which the imposter wrested from me, wherefore the mayhem at issue. He dropped it around here, somewhere in shadows."

After looking around a little, Jacob himself spotted the silver-braced book on the cave floor, in the same place where Ulcrist had stood. He was relieved. Kneeling down, he grabbed the book and, just as he was about to arise, he noticed something. Weird glow-glyphs remained faintly on the floor. These were of cursive style that were perhaps from far away Arraf.[28]

The glyphs faded away, the very place where the infernal monk had opened his magical portal. They included lines of tiny ideograms, visible only in low light, not to a man casually passing by with a lantern,. They must have been there for a rather long time. Ulcrist had been making passage to his true home on a regular basis, and had planned to do so for some time. He chose a dim place where the rope-girded monks would rarely go, only once a year for the purification ceremony, lit by candles in procession.

The young monk barely noticed them, and only remembered them long after these events.

Jacob now left with the three monks and walked through the corridors of the abbey. Briefly they waited while Formosus fetched a dry towel from the laundry. Someone went ahead to inform Abbot.

How many other monks, imposters of intrigue, might be among them all, perhaps even Ossica who often seemed unfriendly, to doubt his story.

At last they reached the Abbot's chamber and he was conducted in. Abbot was sitting behind his desk with several candles after hours and codices open, as is his right as Abbot.

"I am told that there has been some altercation?" he asked looking up. "Is this true? Brother Fragga? We must investigate." He looked sharply at Jacob. "Therefore the monk in question let be brought to the chamber of tribunal where none mayest eavesdrop."

Our great monastery, brothers, does have such a chamber, though it is seldom used. Many stone statues and inscriptions of the old empire are stored there, as well as the forbidden copies of Epinanaus' biography, Nekkar of Isauria's *Histories*, the cosmogonies of Mercurius Yod, the philosophical tracts of Cornelius Naza, Zaqara's *Oneirocritikon*, the love poetry of Sodd Bloodman···all writings best not to let monks be persuaded by.

A monk was sent ahead to light the quarions.

So they filed down the dark halls of stone in silence

with candles until they reached that grand, bare, octagonal room. Formosus closed the door tightly behind, and the quarions lit up many strange faces of eld statues from the old worlds

that came before ours. They stood in a circle, surrounded

by those strange and broken sculptures.

---

[28] *Arraf*: meaning rising sun...a general designation referring to lower-mideastern desert closed kingdoms, such as Sarnas, Succon, and Gohha, all of which speak a variant of the Egyptian.

"It has come to our ears that there has been violence in these our sacred confines. May God help us all," declared Abbot, seated by an enormous visage in stone, a grimacing ancient judge.

"We were roused by shouts in the *scriptorium*, shouts of alarm," said brother Fragga. "Formosus, Ossica and I made haste to investigate. We saw Brother Jacob slipping through the rear door, the passage into the sacred chamber of living waters. By the time we stepped into the cave, he could not be located. We tried some moments calling his name. Formosus here spotted Jacob floating in the waters. We drew him out and revived him. He is charmed, or blessed by high power, for somehow he did not drown, though his lungs were full of water. We were surprised it was him. We thought he had run away."

"Jacob, what say you of this?" asked the Abbot. "What alarm was there, and wherefore did you trespass into the sacred pool which has never been defiled? Explain this disturbance."

"I was at work in the *scriptorium* when brother Ulcrist came..."

"It breaks the rule to use the *scriptorium* by night," said Ossica. "Have you no mind that the flame of candles could burn away every page of our long labours were one to inadvertently leave it wrongly placed near a stack? Whatever happened, this rule-breaking is the source of your trouble. Abbot shall chasten you with a worthy penance. "

"Yes, high brother; but I needed to- "

"What *you* think *you* needed is of no consequence. We do not care if you needed to save the world. You do not break the rule. It is sacred."

"Others break many rules in this place, and they go unpunished."

"This is not for the monastery, or the other brethren, or saving the world; it is about you, Jacob. Are you good therefore to submit to the will of the Supreme Throne, which in the rule is a clear manifest?"

"I have much to amend, but that is no reason."

"Indeed you do," brother Ossica remarked, but his anger was beginning to pass. "Now tell us whatever transpired there. "

"Brother Ulcrist entered. After an exchange of pleasant words he required that I surrender this book to him."

"And you refused?"

"I did, for he sought to possess and sell the book.
By force he won it from me. He fled armed with deadly dagger, but I pursued him into the sacred cave. There he saw me and then weirdly—or magicly, hurled a dagger by means
of some telekinetic power. He would have slain me."

"What? That is preposterous. Ulcrist would never do such a deed. He is a trusted battle-monk, and pious, and would never misuse his talents."

"And fled is Ulcrist now?" asked Abbot.

"The brethren are even this hour seeking him," explained Fragga, turning to the Abbot. "But it seems that he is not anywhere to be found."

"And how then had you come by your wounds, Jacob?" asked Ossica ". . .if you are to uphold this fable."

"No fable, by all Heaven. They have healed...but lo, a scar stays visible."

Jacob opened his a and displayed the scar in his chest.

"Come here that I mayest examine." The Abbot held a quarion up close and squinted at the scar in the light. "It does seem to be a recent wound. We have it you claim the waters healed it? That I doubt not. You will proceed to the *Sanitarium* after to be examined by Brother Amos the physician. Jacob, if yours is honest accounting, then propose where your assailant Ulcrist went?"

"Jacob claims that—" brother Formosus interrupted.

"Let him say whatsoever answer, himself, Formosus." the Abbot warned.

"Ulcrist is a deceiver and imposter!" Bother Jacob declared.

"You were not asked of his character; answer only the question." Ossica warned.

"He departed into some underground passage, through a wormhole. He knows some sort of magic; he chanted in a strange way...I think, in the tone of the infernal monks below, who call themselves 'the Hidden Elect.' After his dagger peirced me, he traced out a magical portal and entered the intermundane world below."

"Is that so?" asked Abbot, looking askanse. "It seems that my conversation with the noble knights the other day has taken hold of your imagination. Therefore we must inquire of you more, lest sacrilege be accounted to you. Know you something of witchery in these halls, Jacob Magister?"

"I do know something of it."

"Why have you not until now exchanged knowledge of it to the high brothers," asked Ossica, "or any other, such as myself? " Brother Jacob sent Abbot a look betraying knowledge. Abbot glanced away to deflect it.

"I was not considered honest when before I spoke of elven hybrids of the forest," he explained. "What profit would there be to describe some graver but even more fantastic experience?"

"In Jacob's defense," added Fragga, "a dagger was noticed there in the pool where he floated."

"His own-self could have planted it," Ossica conjectured, wishing to pursue every possibility, "and the scar may have been from his forest struggle against the elves, rather the entertainers from the circus. We shall get to the bottom of this. What else know you Jacob? The book you bear in your arms, it does not look like one of ours. This is the book, is it not, which you claim Ulcrist would steal from you?."

"It is the very book."

"What manner of book?" asked Formosus.

"I wager it be a witch's spell book! Hand it over!" exclaimed Ossica.

"No...he guards the book by my authority," Abbot admitted. "It is a work which none else may have, and only he may carry."

"The brethren have a right to inquire of its contents," Formosus remarked.

"Rights? None procure rights before the Judgement of God. But very well," said the Abbot with a sigh.

"It be a compendium of some sort," Jacob said, "with many stories and prophecies from ancient days. Brother Ulcrist coveted the lore it holds."

"What lore precisely?" asked the Abbot.

"That was what I was trying to discern by translating it."

"Where did you find it?" asked Ossica.

"He found it not," interjected Abbot. "Anherm left it in my safekeeping first. He insisted no monks, spare one or two of absolute confidence, have access to it. I did vouchsafe him this."

"Anherm...? How is it that his exalted name is brought into this corruption?" said Ossica.

"Anherm, as you may know, tutored me in the ancient Saturnian-Age Latin," Jacob said, "the impossible grammar, in which partly does this book have commentaries."

"Set it down here on this pedestal," said the Abbot. "The elect will examine it now."

Jacob at this point was perturbed, as he says in his testimony, asking himself: How could I disobey his Abbot? I had vowed never to let anyone else have the silver-braced book, but I did not ever imagine that several high brothers, the elect, would request it. I set it down and opened it. They brought near his lamp and looked closely at the strange script, diagrams, and old Latin notes in the margins.

"It is old...quite ancient in fact," remarked Formosus, "and it is indeed untranslatable by any, save for perhaps Anherm. But is it accursed?"

"We should not assume that a black cover indicates ill omen," said Abbot Cromna. "Don't even the canons of the Regulian cathedral wear black? It may even be a collection of holy writings. If you look closely, you will see that it is of the same make as the gift book you received from the knights. It is the guildswork of the Binders of Vesulum, whose technique has not changed for centuries, and some of the script is also in that hand. Many of the writings seem to be of Ammouric origin. I do not think it accursed. Although beware: some teachings tolerated of old do the learned associate with arcane paths."

" —Arcane paths?"

"Hidden paths to the powers of first world no longer sanctioned by our Faith."

"Alien doctrines be they?"

"Would it be alien?" asked Jacob, a little bolder. "Or is it sciences and histories of the Eldark and Nystoli, wisdom of ancient paraphysics[29] and Neoplatonic sages, writings the Soothfold never officially condemned, but also never esteemed, because never understood?"

Abbot spoke with admonitive tone. "The Neoplatonists? –I am sure you have heard of them, boy, but did you know that in centuries long forgot they sparred against Christ and our forefathers using their sorceries, as well as the swordsmanship of the pen. They betrayed the Truth ever-abiding, and they too were exiled to Nystol."

"Some of this script looks to date back to the third era of the world," observed Formosus. Formosus was an expert on such things, and he also had studied under Anherm.

Strange indeed...however, it is of no account
that some of the writings may be of Ammouric origin.
Cunning minds easily quote scripture to their own purpose.

Many books the Ammouric Soothfold did not judge as inspired and have never been accepted. The Eldark sage Ammoth Parhassius once wrote, *"He who reads the outside books has no part in the world to come."*

"This work may be a great compendium
which men thought extinct from the world-ages," remarked Abbot. "And I suspect it be no hellish contrivance of witch or wizard."

"Are you certain? How claim you that?" Ossica looked askanse. (Brothers, as you may have heard, he had once long ago, when he was young, assisted the Prime Interquist to investigate the Aorist Heresy[30]).

"There is much in here you have not read. Anherm himself
was once a wizard, until the Ancientmost led him to become a monk. Who can say, but that he was not able
to keep his former interests under heel."

"Let us not speak ill of the dead," warned the Abbot. "Anherm knew many secrets that he took with him to the grave, many things on the far away lands that we shall never know, some better not to know, arcana buried in eldest tomes and rimestocks such as this."

"Even so, *what fellowship has Light with Darkness*?" countered Brother Ossica. "And now tell it honestly: how is it that you kept it safe?

---

[29] *Paraphysics, adj. paraphysical*: a branch of practical knowledge which examines physical principles in matter and energy and how their properties reach beyond the space-time continuum. Said to be originally developed by an obscure ancient philosopher, perhaps a Stoic, interested sympathetic relations between objects and their trace elements.

[30] *Aorist Heresy*: It is no longer known exactly what sacred doctrines the Aorist Heresy challenged. Some say the aorist heresy was illustrated mystically in lost epic of ancient times known as *"The Descent of the Hearers of the Dead"* qv.

How is it that Brother Ulcrist did not succeed in the theft
of which you accuse him?"

"Ulcrist did not succeed in the theft because he did not attempt it," a new voice answered, sounding from out the shadows in a corner of the chamber. Jacob recognized the voice, and the one to whom it belonged. The speaker came stepping out of the dark into the light of candelabras.

It was Ulcrist, to his astonishment, appearing somehow, impossibly. He continued his words.

"Indeed, I Ulcrist, must fend myself from these knavish accusals. I, who am a monk vowed, and will not stay silent. This youthful pretender and imposter has defamed me. He is one who betrayed us before, he is like Judas.

After my altercation with him, I escaped the notice of misinformed monks and hurried here to this chamber at once, fore-knowing the grave charge
that my own disgruntled disciple would hurl against me.

I realize that such an iron accusal can only be made in this high chamber. Perhaps you are baffled at the strange explanations of this dissembler. Therefore, give me leave instead to reveal what has occurred."

"Ulcrist," said the Abbot. "You slipped away when monks were seeking to question you. How is it that you remained in the shadows?"

"I have only been hoping to do so, my Abbot.
I learned the way of shadow-concealment
taught by the old monk Gorga of venerable memory.
This technique I have used so that the truth
might come to light. Here is what happened:
I was strolling through the cloister for an evening meditation
and saw a light coming from the *scriptorium*,
and remembering your will that no wax be wasted
in these hard times when the poor are in greater need, I went in to put out the quarion. But I came across this Jacob crouched on the floor uttering fantastic words over diagrams in that strange book. He was ready with an idolatrous dagger drawn to let spill blood from his own veins.

When through righteous indignation I made to hinder him,
he cried out for help, at once ready by the devil's inspiration
to spin a web of deceit, as such kinds are wont.

I nevertheless managed to wrest the book from his furious hands, to check his malicious spell-casting and keep him from injuring himself.

At once I turned to flee with the book.
Brandishing that serpentine dagger, he blocked the scriptorium entrance, so I fled into the deeper chambers of the monastery, into the caves. He cried out for help again, and I percieved that he cunningly hoped to employ other monks to find me, and accuse me as aggressor.

How adept at lying are such kinds! Fearful now even
of my own brother monks, I evaded their arrest by laying aside the cumbersome tome and crawling 'neath the shadows.

So circling back unseen I escaped, hiding here.

For here, in this asylum and sanctuary, is found the best ground where one can be safe from curse or from bonds.

A grand story Jacob tells, a contrivance to persuade each of you. He endeavors to show that the silver-braced book he possesses is no unholy grimoire, but a fine book of historic records. The grimoires, however, even contain passages from our holy books, whose meaning they invert.

They who work arcane evils do their rites in the dead of night, in order to access a spell by a diabolic offering of their own blood when the planets are aligned.

This is exactly what Jacob Magister was doing,

that he may connive the deceits of the devil, and join in the witch's sabbat. This was his hope, and also the hope of the demonic elves

who converted him in the forest, minions from the deep-born caves.

It was they who taught him the unholy art,

for indeed, I have watched Jacob three winters,

and I can now say with all certainty, this is no rope-girded monk, but a quick-handed blood-wizard!

Therefore I, Ulcrist, at once fled, seeking refuge in the Lord, safe in his justice here discerned, for in this sanctum-chamber alone are brought forward charges of heresy and witchcraft

against the duplicitous and the accursed."

"That is high accusal, Ulcrist," stated Abbot, sternly.

"Indeed it is, good Abbot," he replied, "but it is for high crime, and for

all to hear, and judge with tested prudence.

Will you trust this one's tale depicting me endeavor to steal a book?

For what purpose who could imagine? It is an obscure tome

that none can read. Will you think it a reasonable thing, that I,

in fear, fled like a deer from this wiry misfit, trying to slip away,

and that in the caves I found the skill to strike him

with a dagger hurled from a distance?

And it seems the wound has mysteriously healed... already.

And finally, the tale has a magical portal open up

into which I disappear, not even able to haul the imagined treasure with me? What a cunning narration. Or will you receive my own account, a sensible one, namely, that the monk is a blood-wizard, whose father, mind you, everyone knows was also a wizard, and that it was Jacob who turned with unexpected fury upon me,

long time monk of the order,who hoped only to correct his iniquity?"

"He has conjured up a host of lies!" Jacob said in astonishment. "Ulcrist, yes, wrested the codex from me. Could not he manage to lug it away? Not on account of the unwholesome magic he uses.

The book an Ammouric *selva* must have blessed,

or perhaps the elves or the gnome put some kind of counter spell upon it, for as the infernal monk went into the portal descending, the book would not submerge, like oil that will not sink beneath water.

Do not BELIEVE HIM!"

"I cannot judge accurately these occurrences," said Abbot Cromna "...nor ascertain the truth of these accusals. A professed monk's testimony however must not be taken lightly. This has gone beyond my ability and involves questions out of my range of discernment. We are only a simple country Abbot. The Prime Interquist must now be involved in this.

Only he has the knowledge which can unravel such dark mysteries, and his thaumaturgic cancelling is the most efficacious for dealing with any kind of old magic. You, Jacob Magister,

stand accused, and must be brought to Hordingbay and be taken by ship to Whigg on the continent, there to be interrogated by a Divine of High Magistracy, the Prime Interquist. The long-journeying knights will be returning to the continent, so they shall escort you. One week is given you to prepare for this pilgrimage."

"Good Abbot, Jacob has never before been caught in any evil work!" exclaimed brother Formosus.

"All the more reason to be careful. The weight of suspicion now rests upon Jacob, since Ulcrist spake of no unnatural causes. Now Formosus will awaken Brother Amos and you, Jacob, will go have him examine your wound."

There was no further discussion concerning this ruling. Abbot forbade the other monks and Jacob from mentioning anything of what transpired with others or even among themselves.

Brother Amos asked Jacob many questions as he examined his wound, more than here need be recounted.

These were not only regarding bodily health but also of his mind, and his former *Melancholia*. The Mahanaxaran physician placed a patch of special *bemble* leaf over the sore area as well, just in case it might again rend open.

"The body and the soul···we do not say that they are two things, Jacob. Nor do we understand that they are one thing.

They are neither two things nor are they one thing.

Herein is a mystery, herein is wisdom. Keep your bodily posture right, heavenward, with devotion, so your mind and soul will avoid Melancholy. But most of all, eat the bread of angels so that Darkness avoid you. Make your devotion a practice with all your being, body, soul, heart, and mind."

A load of particular medicines he gave him, antidotes, and bandages. Amos foresaw that he might again be assailed by some enemy.

Jacob scheduled to saddle within days, under the custody of the Knights. It was only a day's ride, and another night and day aboard ship to the fastness of Ael Lot. He would go before the Prime Interquist himself.

Into the catacombs beneath Nystol the Sorcerers went, deep into the tomb-complex Astodan. Down there they hoped to be secure from the Maharim, the axe-bearing barbarians hunting them. By the forgotten genius of the dwarven architects they sealed themselves within the necropolis. One questioned if there be any outward way unlocking. To that question they paid little heed, confident of their power over the elements, over earth and rock, for they had carried their magical tomes with them.

The magic however had been closed off to them. They soon realized that they had entombed themselves alive. The thirst would finally claim them, and so they breathed their last, clutching their precious tomes, forsaken in that "city of the accursed dead."

The princes of men have never ceased to covet the scrolls and *codices* that must remain upon the chests of those lifeless lords, locked within bony fingers. Some do foolishly imagine mysterious power enclosed within the bindings or occulted under indeciferable writing. Nay, but the desert airs preserve not such corruption, for the bindings do wither and decay, and the words within are forever lost to human memory.

The Nomads of Sardu
Abbot's travelogue.

XVII   *Forty-thousand Horse-Hooves*

Do we who are monks require silence while eating breakfast? Absolutely, for not everything is found in the Rule. This is an half-hour for monks to be silent and listen to angels. And so it was at breakfast that the *Erelim* were calling Brother Jacob. They were calling him to the cloister garden for fellowship with his beloved hermit-guide.

"Upon my soul I fear how my sins fester." Jacob said to himself.

"They do," said Maragald, who could hear the whispering. "Eventhough we men be naught but dust, Heaven would not have us wallow in sin. Therefore repent, and believe the gospel."

"Maragald, you are a *selva*. Will you hear my confession?"

"I shall. Even honey-tongued poets and priests-anointed must divulge their sins, else even they hurry off to endless torment in the after-time. Could I ever refuse the service?"

"Never —so say the holy ones."

"But don't you also need to speak with me apart from that, my son? Not for admitting your transgressions, but for your interior vexations, speaking as a brother to his brotherly guide. Pray, tell of your worries first."

"No doubt you have heard, Maragald. I must appear before the Inquisition. A certain monk is lying and seeks accusal...Have I betrayed myself...and others? I have. I followed the prompts of vainglory."

"A monk is lying? Say it is not so. No Christian would dare lie. Alas another star of Heaven falls; wormwood!" Maragald shook his head in dismay.

"There is no explaining away these false accusals to the Inquisition. Now an outcast, an adventurer I must become; flee my home and go into the world of worldly men. It's beyond my capabilities."

"Often in some way incomprehensible, Jacob, Divine Providence uses our weaknesses, nay even our sins, to guide us to a new path. It is often a path our feet would refuse.

The horse which the Burgundy Knight bequeathed you, Jacob, what will you do with him? You know, to maintain that kind of beast is expensive. No lands do you possess. If you wish to live here with us, the horse should be left to the care of Brother Amarius."

"No...I shall ride to Hordingbay, and then find a buyer in town
...or else I shall keep him.

"A wise plan...then you may not continue here?"

"I am a monk. I gave word to the Burgundy Knight to pursue the momentous enterprise entrusted. I shall be true, my word must be as iron, but how can I be free to do this if the Inquisition finds me guilty? On the other hand, if I am free, I break civil law to go on a quest. Graham, King of all the Aels, of all Kiluria and Thule, has forbidden anyone save a chosen and sworn knight to campaign in foreign lands. I am not a knight."

"Somehow you will find a way. The knight would not have passed his purpose to you could it not be done. You now realize that this thing may be more difficult than you were imagining."

"I can live as a monk in my cell, could I not?
I relinquished it once to join the circus, like a fool. Maragald,
you also, some monks say, are a fool.
But unlike myself, you have never been so."

"I had my foolish years, Jacob."

"Most of the monks do not take your prophecies seriously;
how a Dark Shepherd will obtain the High Abbacy,
and the advent of Inversus, and the Great Abandonment.
How can I see my brothers deceived?
I cannot rebel and go against the monastery and the Emperor.
We must submit to legitimate authority. We are monks."

"*Submit*, as is right, but also by the power of God *resist and reform*. The Heavenly Father advises us wisely in the holy prophecies of Ezekiel: *the house of Israel will refuse to listen to you, since they refuse to listen to me.*
Therefore, my brother, although they reject our warnings,
our call to repentance, be not disheartened nor afraid of them,
nor any rebellious house like them,
For rebellion is as the sin of witchcraft."

"How can I not stand to correct the wicked monks now?
Must I instead journey another hazardous journey
and fight battles in places of which I am unfamiliar?"

"Stand fast and resist them to the face. Rouse your anger,
but do not sin...and employ not the violent power
of your staff technique, not on these knavish conspirators.
Afterall, Heaven detests a violent man, no?
If He wishes you to flee, then you flee, not fight,
even if you could otherwise prevail.

What is victory without divine favor? Another time you will fight,
for He did not have you trained as a guardian monk for nothing.
Do not let these things trouble you.
The Furth High King has claimed you.
What is more, many qualities knights of the shawl
share in common with monks, so much so that knights
have often retired to become monks, such as Lord Affa
...but it is a rare turn that a monk should have to fight the battles
which long-journeying knights fight. Perhaps the *Erelim* in their contest
against Darkness require a monk right now,
a monk who can make an earthly pilgrimage.
Either way is a way to undergo, and serve Him.
The mind is a forest. Do not get so confused looking over the many
paths that you no longer see where they lead. Focus, and think not too
much of your own ordeals, but of the others and what might be best for
them. Leave concern for what is good for yourself in His hands.
The Master has made you a monk. Walk with Him.
Then no longer will you ask "what is the will of Heaven for me," but
rather what is His will in itself, for our life is in His will, and what's in
accord with his will, no matter,
is in every way advantageous."

"Here in this place? It sounds strange. I know this place divine but it's
quite a failure most times. It's almost impossible to abide among such
insolence from monks. Every day we observe how the brothers indulge in
every manner of mischief, totally ignoring the wishes of our venerable
Abbot."

"It is so. *The wicked spring up like grass*. Take care however not to
condemn, for they are yet God's. Somehow it is you, I foresee, who shall,
in time to come, goad the brethren toward righteousness. But remember,
even our grand knights,
single-hearted vassals of the Furth High King,
though covered with the *oil of the ox's strength*,
may go astray into sinful living."

" —not as far astray as a monk, I don't reckon."

"As I said before, a shawl-knight is already a kind of monk.
Take care, however, one who is not a noble must have
the unlikely permission of a king to go a-questing,
as you have said. You must obey."

"The Abbot will avail me in that, I pray."

"I have been thinking, my dear Jacob.
You must have left this place for a reason not fully known to me, nor
even to yourself. One's heart is a mysterious place.
Now you have returned. But I think, even though your spirit has been
renewed by The Purification, your heart must again be converted—to trust
in Him!"

"Mischievous powers abide in the forest.
It is best to do as I am told. However, I also fear the Prime Interquist."

"Fear God, and you will be afraid of no man!
The Prime Interquist is a man. Aye, he is appointed from above, but
still a man. Will you fear the powers that can harm the body, yet have no
regard for those spirits

that can destroy both body and soul?"

"You repeat the Lord's solemn warning"

"In this place, Jacob, the monks are become wicked by a little encouragement, if thou perceiveth my meaning."

"Do you mean demons? In the forest I encountered a demoniac. A being who was possessed, brother, a dwarf controlled by an ancient spirit of which you spoke, the *drakodemon*!

The man had some power of war in his hands that, were I to have it, that speed would make me the most greatly feared warrior!"

"Are you not feeling well?" asked the old man with concern

for it was truly an uncharacteristic thing to say..."Why do you wish to be feared, Jacob? Be not a warrior of wrath, but a man for the peace of God."

"I cannot fathom why I said that."

"You are angry. You failed to become what you set out for."

"The other monks will no longer regard me after what I did. Some hidden influence lurks, melancholy. Here I shall stay then, do penance, and conceal myself from the old iniquitous-spirit."

"They are monks. They must treat you as a monk.
But seek not respect. Instead, pray, brother,
for you cannot hide from the notice of the watching eye,
for it sees far and wide, be it by wizard's crystal ball
or the dreadful *homunculus* spy, or the gnostic medallions.
Your confusion is from the hellish emanations, my son,
from *diabolus*. Your mind wanders into dark forests.
Quell that fear which rules you too easily; stand sturdy, single-minded, with clenched fists if need be, like an old man who has nothing to lose. Did you think the saints were as little girls and their holiness no more than pretty illuminations? You survived the dreadful wilderness.
Do you think that counts for nothing?
Be who you are, not what the others would have you be.
Do not feign to be manly, no: just be a man
by staying true to your word, no matter what.
An end comes for every man...in the final days, and no amount of success or wealth can persuade the angel of death even for one extra moment beyond the allotted span. Every pleasure is fleeting.
We cannot always have what we want, and if we did,
we would soon want something else. Look at yourself;
just a few moments ago you could not bear to remain here;
it was impossible. The next moment you become fretful
of the responsibility that chivalrous enterprise involves, and you long to be safe again, like a babe wishing to return to the womb. How fickle is your time. Pride is the heinous vice which causes indecision in these matters. The remedy: humility.
Train the soul according to the way of the Ammouric fathers."

"Then it is true; I must stay here and avoid the demons of the world; they will only confuse me the more. I will not again leave this place, lest many worldly struggles haul my soul down to ruin.
Do you yourself not say among the brethren,
"Never leave the monastery!?"

"So what I said yet stands, " said Maragald.
"And hear it: do not cling here because you are afraid.
Cling because you are hungry for war.
I rebuke your unmanly self-preservation. One does not hide
from the enemy in a monastery, my good Jacob.
On the contrary, this place is where you are most likely to encounter
not only "friendly adversaries," but the sneakiest of demons.
Demons are attracted to this place like moths to light. And only the
subtlest of spirits may lurk here. Other less subtle but more brutal demons
take up in the world to deceive nations, as that *drakodemon*...great iniquity
still awaiting its time.
Many are the evil hierarchies and spiritual beasts.
They are all less a threat to you than you.
You cannot be at peace until you accept yourself. Renounce
melancholy."

"Your counsel is understood and worthy. But an unworthy sense of
foreboding remains in me."

"Hmmmm....then I say the Lord permits you a healthy fear.
It is so that you may overcome fear with bravery.
Wherever you go, a spiritual monastery you will carry with you,
and all which you have learned here you will take with you.
Take courage in the Ancientmost power, The Lord of Eternity, He will
fortify your spirit."
"...only a *selva* can banish such great and drooling demons.
I am but a monk."

"The powerful prayer of the *selva* is awesome, that is true.
Few are they to whom the Lamb grants priesthood.
But how can a priest banish if he has not time to locate the demon to
be banished? Shepherds must spend many hours feeding the flock. Who
will locate the demon's haunt?
To skin a cat you must first catch it.
Some rope-girded monks spend their time finding the lairs
of the demons to lure them for combat! Courage!"

"For you I am most grateful; dreadful sense begins to fade. Perhaps I
can convince them to let me stay, if the Abbot and others care not, until
my mind clears."

"Or until the heart, forgiving self, understands...yes, if the heart be
not pure, if it is divided, the mind will never be clear..."

So did Maragald discourse on wisdom to the vacillating Jacob. Many
other things were taught, but the rest need not be here recorded, brothers.

The good hermit heard Jacob's confession, wrapped his stole upon his
brow and uttered the ancient Ammouric formula. The Lamb removed the
hidden transgression.

"The Lord will garner me unto himself soon, my son," said Maragald,
divesting himself and devoutly kissing the stole.

"Let that in no way diminish your happiness. I have seen many
winters, and like Cassandra of legend, my prophetic word the others will
not heed. Even were I to tread a number of more passings on the
Whitehawk, I do not think that my Lord would have me to witness the

unholy fulfillment of the prophecies; of the Dark Shepherd and of the Inversus, and even worse,

    The Great Abandonment which even now commences.
To see so vast a loss of faith
among the people...no...it would harm my frail soul.
Divine favor provided mercy for old Simeon: to keep in the Temple
so he might first gaze upon the infant messiah, seeing him
with his own eyes, the consummation of Israel.
Thereafter the old one could give up the ghost in peace.
Similarly in our time he will not, in his mercy, let these ears
hear the machinations of the greatest deceiver of the Church,
and the mischief to come.
Therefore the Lord will garner me unto himself,
causing me to fall asleep in his embrace. One morning
the cock shall crow and I shall awaken not.
My half-believing brothers shall bury me in the forest,
saying that the old crow was not truly one of them
and should not be placed in the crypt with the others.
It is of no account what they do with this corporeal shell.
The Lord, whose eyes are flames of fire, knows my works.
Now I await the eternity and the reward promised.
So be saddened not much, beloved. It is but a blink of an eye,
and you shall see me again in the halls of the blessed.
Stay close to the Abbot. Help him, for he is strong,
but his task is truly Herculean."

    "In whom shall I confide, father, if not you?" Jacob asked in confusion. "Do not fret so over your passage, old man; surely no man can prophesy his own time and manner of death!"

    "Did not our Lord do so?" he responded. *I go up to Jerusalem, and there I will be arrested, and put to death by the chief priests and elders.* So it has been with my Lord and grant that it may be with me.

    My crucifixion has been this: to be rejected as a lunatic and fanatic by my own beloved brethren.
No, I do not fear. The Lamb has given me the sight.
This will soon come to pass. From death afterwards, my son,
I shall be even more powerful than in life, powerful in God;
and I shall ascend the alabaster steps and present prayers
of intercession on your behalf before the white throne on Argunizial."

    "And so I shall also fight, and usher the Inversus to his deserved demise," Jacob replied.

    "You will not!" replied Maragald sternly.
    "That is under Heaven's warrant. Only the Lamb himself can put down the Beast, since it is written *for who shall compare to the beast? Who shall stand against him*?
I beg that you never try to hunt the beast yourself.
It is not your task. This you must promise.
If he appears in your earthspan, and lifts his arrogant head,
never approach him for combat or even parley.
Swear it Brother Jacob....I said, swear it!"

    Maragald frowned at the inchoate hero and furrowed his shaggy eyebrows.

"All right then; I do swear it...I will not against him alone go," Jacob said this, and it is here written as testimony.

Maragald continued his instruction.

"Even I, who, by the will of Heaven, possess seeming adequate spirit-strength, would not go against the Inversus unless willed by divine command, nor would I even dare match wits with him.

He emits spiritual darkness and confusion in a 500 ft. radius,
but only those who are lawful and holy can detect it.
Everyone else, be they good-spirited, too trusting,
or even having a mere levity of mind, will calculate him
to be the epitome of goodness and nobility.

Great caution is to be observed in such high matters. Consider how I am one who has attained great power over the flesh through mortification, and the Lord's wisdom and knowledge in me is even greater. It is humility, yes, that tells me accurately of myself, eventhough I am deficient in several other ways. I would have voluntarily begged God for more suffering and agonies, requesting of the Lord some greater misery in order that our brethren might be saved from themselves.

Now, however, I am too old, and my terrestrial life begins to fade. My earthly life wanes... involuntarily."

Jacob could not bear this talk over the seer's last days. Even though Maragald would not have wanted tears to stream of sorrow from his eyes, they nevertheless came pouring. Jacob embraced the old man as hard as he could.

"They say St. Peter had furrows in his eyes, for the rivers of tears flowing upon remembrance of his own denial.

Weep not for men, but for Him. You must not be attached too much to any mortal," he said. "It is the way of the monk who is entering Eternity. Love each soul as a flower that you pass by,
and know that its time of blossom is short.
Employ those whom the Lord sends you as a help.
He gives us many helps. Even a pagan can be a help,
in as much as he yields himself to the Truth. Now learn this final prophecy that I prophesy unto you, boy. It is for your inner-knowledge. The Lamb has bestowed on me a gift, and I now pass it on to you. You alone have shown the fitting disposition. The gift is this
—and you will come to find its needful usage soon—
In the will of the Ancientmost, I pass on to you
the power to speak with the children of earth.
Learn you what is meant by that saying.
Now go and join the others in merriment,
but deny not my words and prophecy. Wipe away your tears; to do so is a sign of the coming Day."

So it was that Jacob departed and never did see Maragald again in terrestrial flesh.

night of Burgundy Tincture rest Thou in peace.

Monks lay to rest their own great ones who fall asleep in the Lord. They do so with the same funereal solemnity and grace as they would the monastery-drunkard: they must make no distinction, knowing all human honour and renown is vanity before God.

Brother Jacob was there, and saw the Abbot's

expression; sadness mixed with anxiety over the future. The funeral had a deep quietude. The lords presented the banner-colours of the fallen, which they folded tenderly, with great care, with affection unexpected.

The shawl-knights prepared for the journey to Hordingbay.
They were to sail to Whitehawk, the continent,
of which they showed Jacob a *cartagraphica* or *mappa.*
If you have never seen one, know that it is a kind of illuminated scroll on giant *waffin* leaf by which one may look down upon a rendering of all lands, even as the perspective of a bird's eye.
The cartographer had drawn minutely our monastery, and Whitehaven upon-the-seashore, and Hordingbay, all Aldemarz and the Whitehawk, even the port of Tremas and our destination, Regulum, lapsing capital of the Whitehawk Confederacy, all represented on this plane with routes and roads, in relation of space that could be measured.
I have seen several maps since that time, not only those made by ancient Rumilians and Oruscans, but charts in great detail, of certain feudatories, wilds and deserts, and even labyrinths. Many are the realms there be. As they examined the great chart there in the *scholarium* with the Abbot, on his grand oaken table
Jacob noticed something that struck as uncanny. There, written on the signature of the chart was the title *Kruth's Handy World Map.*

"Another Kruth?" Surely it were not the Kruth whom he had met by misadventure with elfbeards. The maker of the wondrous chart could not be the same gnome whom he had encountered in the forest. He asked the knights what they knew of this one named "Kruth" who made such fine charts. "the Eloniah,' who before the quickening was known as Eleusinion, the earth-guide," the White Knight explained. "He was last spotted in the tomb-labyrinths of Garmsir by our companion, your trust-father, the knight of burgundy mantle, who now sleeps. Know you not any tradition concerning the chart's maker, the being Kruth?"

"Being? What sort of creature is this cartographer Kruth?" Jacob asked, "The bards of my childhood sung of a certain legendary gnome, his exploits and writings, but no one ever thought him real···and "Arcavir" That is a lore-keeper?"

He answered, astonished, "Any well-established bard or lore keeper has heard of him; I cannot fathom that you have only child's tales concerning the gnome."

The Grey Knight smiled. "A gnomish man is he indeed. Some have seen him traveling with other enchanted kin as of late..."

"So it IS him," Jacob declared, "Shouldn't we suspect him an underworld marauder and mischievous gnome, a worker of enchantments?"

"No, rather are they whom he pursues and vexes.
To that end he designs useful charts, having journeyed the entire continent in his thousand-year span.
Kruth has always been an aide for good-willed men."

"I have made talk with him," Jacob confessed at last.

"What? Can that be?" exclaimed the White Knight.

"It surprises me not," observed the Grey Knight, "the lad has been chosen by Heaven to be a knight of the Creed. The shawl-oath has been destined him. He encountered the gnome, just like other knights."

"The foremost knight who benefited from the gnome Arcavir was Duke Ikonn...of the eld tales."

"And just who was that man, Duke Ikonn?"

"The time has come that you must reckon the lore of Whitehawk," the Grey Knight glanced at his companion for agreement. "Ikonn was a chivalric lord who lived long ago, a champion from distant shores who came to the continent during the age of the second world, weapons were brass and armours of bronze work, a time when the behemoths of broad earth vexed men. He was a great hero, a dragonslayer, an adventurer of many paths. It was he who smote down Sinostox, Dire of Rebellion in that time, the first of the Wyrmheld, before they fled the sunny earth and hid below.

Kruth the gnome went along with the Duke, "marauder of worlds" they call him.

Together with other famous heroes they went, Petrozean the Quick, the roguish Godiun Fout, and Elkomenon the Wizard.

Together they raised armies and quelled a feudatory from wicked men: The Duchy of Gorre.

Later he humbly refused the title *rex*, king, for it is a title reserved only for anointed rulers of Ammouric lineage, the Maceonid line. This "Duke," and the gnome, by martial expedition, gathered many treasures hidden away in ages past by the enemies of the righteous, and hear it, Jacob,

of those treasures gave they exceedingly to the poor."

"Many of these works they accomplished below,"
added the White Knight, "in the intermundane lands,
the cavernous world, what the elf-kin called *daedeloth*.

That was an entire age before the All-law, a thousand years before the universal revelations, the quickening. Some Ammouric Knights who have gone down below claim to have even encountered that hero."

"How is that possible, " the young monk asked, "unless he be a ghost?"

"It is said that Ikonn has not yet died a man's death," explained the White Knight, "though in faith be certain that *it is alotted for every man to die once, then comes the judgement.*

He roves through ages, seeking upon the terrestrial plane
     to accomplish some penance. Others have recorded
how with their own eyes they have seen the ghostly image clad in mystic platemail of some bright ethereal ore, a famous prize, and how the Duke maunders to and fro through the ages and the worlds strapping his brand of four-fold devastation: Oceanicyng. Everyone confesses that the Duke has been worthy of such a sword, for he is just. This ghost, however, if that he is, therefore became extinct to this world before the time of the quickening. He therefore cannot pass the veil-fire; he cannot enter the sacred precincts of the holy mountain and go before Him who sits there, like other well-lived souls can. Instead, they say, he glorifies God in another way: by being an aid to single-hearted knights in contest and

expedition below, and be sure, he has guided many. Our order has titled him the Grand Knight of all Chivalry."

"Have you seen this ghost?"

"I have spoken with those who have, who even argue
that he is no ghost, but flesh and blood. The apparition, if it be that, is seldom encountered and no longer comes to the surface, for no more does the famous being you encountered accompany him."

"Why is that so?"

"Only the same of whom I speak can answer with certainty,
but we guess that it is because each labours a great labour
which the other cannot help, and it is the Song-lord alone
who can calculate the times when the portals are open."

"Perhaps if I passed through, this ghost might guide us down to the palace of the elven lady."

"We knights had that, and it is fair certain. Wherefore we even sought to find some mystical way to communicate with him, but it is said that the Duke goes wherever he wills, and no one seeking him has ever found him.

We tried another plan: to contact Kruth,
who knows all the entrances into the cavernous world,
but the remnant elves of Plathonis have by bird sent us message that it cannot be done: the gnomish creature has some dreadfully vital purpose which urges him onward. More than this concerning him the elf lords would not divulge.

But what has the many-song minstrel revealed to you, Jacob?"

"Nothing that I might betray, would I remain faithful to my word."

"Then we will not press you. But pray, if the knowledge be useful, do not shrink from right conduct, even without our approval."

"I fear to have misjudged the gnome," Brother Jacob confessed.

"When I harkened to their report, learning of the elfbeard's hardships, I reasoned some things in their lore. The contrivance of deceivers, an unbelievable enchantment, I found it to be, all their tidings laden with half-truths. Would cleverly worded tales convince a monk over to their perilous trust? The deep-minded devil had already quelled my soul, and now he would require my life at the hands of those strange beings.

My spirit was weary and my mind confused, and they seemed to me as acrobats and jesters on a stage."

"An understandable mistake...You must lead us to them at once, to Arcavir Kruth and the half-elves. This is the closest we have been to those who have dependable knowledge of the lands below,
the cavernous world."

"Could I now find the way in the forest?
Even could I, the gnome and elfbeards would easily hide from us. Nevertheless, I myself have acquired new knowledge that might furnish new plans. I have been translating, Abbot,"

Jacob continued, turning to him, ". . .a bit more."

"You do have the gift, and it honors your former teacher that you so labor. Have you found the passage which Anherm sought on behalf of that fairy-bard the Arcavir?"

"I do not think so, not yet. There are many pages; and my guess is that a particular banshment formula they seek, and which others wish to destroy. Somewhere in these ink-covered sheets the priests of Vesulum must have recorded it. Like the others, this much coveted volume of *The Black Book* is a kind of encyclopedia of researches from the third and fourth age, including a brief account of Nystol's Fall.

It is most mysterious because it indicates a number of things once widely known, but never heard in our time."

There was a long ponderous silence.

"...such things are equally as mysterious to me," remarked Abbot. "Let us hear it. What else has Jacob found?"

A certain chronicle hastily put together by a panel of professors. By means of a synopsis they outlined the vanishing historical record before the few mortal scribes passed into oblivion. Something must have happened, just as some have said, for the ancients to have taken this precaution. After Nystol fell, there was a short time of peace. Then the Furth straightway descended into darkness for nearly two centuries. Why? Jacob wondered, what did it have to do with Nystol?

Was there a conspiracy of some sort?

He was hoping for anything on which that *The Black Book* might have sound record. Then he found it: a good but cursory account on the fall of Nystol.

It had extensive quotations from a most pristine account of the Ammouric Scrolls, a synthesis of the creation-lore put together by the Elthildor. They had unearthed something, a high relic of some sort, pointing to a powerful exorcism, and which must yet be preserved somewhere. Nystol's final desolation originally described by the arcane historian Voethius was translated from the Greek by a certain monk Orbian, it was titled *The Great Burning and Banishment.*

First was sung of the great lanterns; Sun, Moon, and of Stars,
as well the secrets of fire and wind; how early men, far from being brutes, investigated many natural mysteries,
every enigma of mountains and seas,
from the "sightless caverns of earth to heaven's remote galaxies.
They passed on cosmic knowledge. And their sons inherited it,
the first wizardic minds who could write it down.

Hundreds of years they lived: both the worlds visible and invisible they described in every detail. Few things escaped their gaze.
Their own sons in turn improved learning the more,
so increased knowledge. These were the wizards of old;
and no salt of earth ever reached their lips.

Terrible were the magics they knew, and lawless were they,
and from their experiments monsters were born.
It was not long before a superstitious fear
took hold of entire nations. Five kings of ancient time swore oaths

to end the fear and put to death the wizards.
Oaths they swore in blood, and by law they silenced the wizards.

But the wizards would not cease from their works.

At last the five crowned kings exiled them.
With their own hands they cut out each spell-wise tongue,
And sent the wizards to dwell apart, far away
in the great southern desert, high upon the sheer cliffs
of Sardu, the mighty mesa, a high place girt by a sea of shifting sands.

But the wizards were not humbled.
They built tall towers from within the cavernous rises,
Towering to the clouds, and set a watch upon the horizon.

Unable to speak magic words, they recorded on scrolls of *bzebus* leaf
whatever their tongueless heads could recall.
And within those towers stored they secret and deep researches,
scrolls and tomes by dry airs preserved; the strange writ of centuries.
Wherefore great power they found, and they gloried
in the many scrolls, and to the kings sent word:

*"Who can compare or stand against us, for behold,
are we not as gods, reaching to the very edge of knowledge?"*

The kings renewed their vows against the wizards,
marshalling their armies. But it was too late.
If haunting rumour did not keep away the strong,
then sand-laden winds would send even the ranks of champions
into retreat. Entire legions were lost in the waterless wastes,
and men heard of certain doom by dooming magic hurled.

Even so, how ambitious are the princes of men,
For the kings would warn their rivaling sons to forget the magic.
But they would not, and they sought to harness the forbidden power
of the scrolls, seeking commerce with the arcane schools.
Some clever lords did find a way, a safe passage
by secret route obtained, for beneath the sands a meandering
system of tunnels and caves twists for half-hundred leagues,
connecting the Sardu oasis to other lands.

It was in the third age, as the yore-writ annals say,
that great minds conceived new towers. Nine tall towers they planned,
and under favorable omens they erected the first stones.
Dwarf-masons they summoned to work the rock with wondrous skill.
So commenced the laws of the Arcanes, the Soothfold,
and after twelve orbits of Saturn, the magian college waxed mighty,
and gladsome gardens adorned her terraces,
for years the minds of the wizards looked to wisdom instead,
and they forbade whatever spell was known to summon evil.

How brief the time, for soon, through overzealous pride,
did they begin to lose favor, and Darkness, undetected,
made a silent claim. Sorcerers arose and were tolerated,
unworthy men elevated to high places. Soon the lawless
could not be restrained. They twisted the arcane inheritance.

It was the oldest of the orders, the Eldari,
who first learned of that wickedness.
They rebuked the Sorcerers, and prophesied against them, saying,
"Yours is the employment of demons. Will not the infernal wisdom
of your art bring ruin to us all? You call down the scorn of heaven,
and the world cannot escape the doom you have earned."

Unable to endure such words, the lawless took hold of the Eldari and
abandoned the old men to the waterless wastes.
Therefore bright Nemesis bade her time,
awaiting a day of retribution...
Every ally of Nystol did soon abandon her, one after another.
Not even the great druid, that ivy-crowned genius of Melancholy,
would vouchsafe unto them the axes of his grim armies.

In the end, the masters of Nystol could not convince even a single
mercenary to her cause. So the day would come to pass, and afterall, who
can avoid the turning of ages?

Far off in the Northern wilderness a savage race learned tidings
of broken laws and devilish rites, and of many towers
where lived men untrained in war and without wives,
hoarding many treasures. In the pine-stacked woods of Durgoth
the Maharim barbarians painted their torsos with marks of fury,
restless for plunder and spoil. They waited for a propitious day.

At last came the appointed time. So rode forth the horde
through the forests out of their barbaric camps, over hill and dale,
sea shore and mountain pass, crossing the isthmus of Ymmin.
Only the Gates of Dariel bestride the Northern pass
stood in their way. Stern gates of unyielding bronze were these, colossal,
impenetrable, with inscrutable locks. The Conqueror Hermius had them
wrought in the Third age to hold back the unwashed hordes.

On that famous night under the stars the Maharim broke camp.
It was a cave-elf, they say, who opened the gates. Conspirators
against Nystol had duped him into unlocking the massive portal.
This must be so, for only such a deep-delving creature
could recover the lost key from the abysses beneath the world.

Ten thousand barbaric riders passed into the civil lands, four times ten
thousand horse's hooves thundering a new time to come. And the horses
trampled over that cave elf as they went, and the Maharim entered the
torrid wastes and endured the South.
Upon the jubilee they arrived at Nystol; a solemn fast of the
Hyperlyptic Alignment, weeks when the Sorcerers have no access to
cosmic power. So did Nemesis make all things come to pass.

The watchers of Nystol spotted a line of painted marauders upon the
horizon. The Arcanes bickered while the beast leaned close and waited.
By infamous treachery the barbarians got word and found the secret
passage and entry to the mesa. Brandishing axe and torch, they entered
the tunnels, and their sandaled feet climbed the steps to the towers above.
You would shudder to hear what is told of the havoc that ensued.
The library of Hennsooth, as well as all other towers
housing many tomes and scrolls, were consumed in holocaust.
In a single day and night the order of the world changed.

No more would the nations groan under the fearful spell of Nystol,
no more was heard the cold drone of her unearthly chants on the wind.
For three days the smoke of her burning blackened all the sky...

The time of grace dawned
and the powers of heaven and earth were shaken.
An age past and the rolling deserts grew, making vast
the reach of the sands, but the shells of the towers remained.
Remembrance of many things was lost, and men would say:
"A great voice has been heard and a new light has
appeared, let us renounce those towers by name.
No longer shall we speak of that place, Nystol of the Ancient Rises."

Even now, when a clear night reveals galaxies above, the desert
nomads catch glimpses of her desolated ruins; the strange glimmer of her
spires on the horizon. Speak with the nomads of Kutaal, they will tell you:
"Take heed, even the outlaws have abandoned that place,
driven away by her lingering Furies. The earth herself expels the
wizards from their vaults. Restless do they wander from their own
sepulchers and haunt the tunnels, for ancient are the stones beneath."

In our times Heaven has renewed the hope of men,
and our eyes turn away from the failed wonders of doomed ages.
Fame has long departed her windswept terraces, and such glories have all
but passed from the skein of the World's memory.
To her let Scripture's well-known prophecy be applied:
She shall never again be inhabited, nor dwelt in from age to age. Desert
beasts shall howl in her corridors, and jackals in her luxurious palaces.

So preserve this account which has been set down, you monks, and let
not these few pages come to dust, for herein alone is recounted how the
towers of Nystol fell, that day the Magi were deceived.

any hours Jacob spent thinking about this account of
the Fall of Nystol. Surely some details were missing.
All this he related to his superior and to the knights.

They pressed him to learn more from Kruth.

Jacob however could not. He would not tell of the
covert forest location for caution against the listening
elfshade. The valraphs and the gnome had helped
Jacob piece many parts of the mysterious puzzle
together.

"So what?" said the White Knight. "Then you must return alone and
question them for us. You must confide in Kruth the object of our
chivalrous enterprise, and think, is it not already your own desire? You
must beg him to draw us a chart of "the caverns measureless to Man," the
location of the legendary coursing waterway Eluvigar, and the fresh water
that leads down into the sunless sea, the Alph River.

I recall the legends. Were not the dwarves the same ones who also
imprisoned the giants deep below in the super-prison Giganth? If dwarf or
gnome be among them, he must therefore know the way, or at least have
some ancestral lore. The Arcavirs keep lore. And there is no one among
the living who can draw so fine a chart, and who has so great knowledge
of the furthworld and the intermundane passages as that many-song
minstrel does?"

"Can Brother Jacob be released beyond the monastery?" asked the Grey Knight. "This monk, though he seem a spry and upright youth, stands yet accused of wizardry.

Still nay, seems it to me that some allowance be supplied.

The Ammouric saga-sayers tell that the river is the only remaining passage for mortal men, and this lore they learned from wizards. Only by finding that secret stream can any living human enter the lower world.

Those flowing waters circle the cavernous orb thrice three times aand then "sink in tumult to a lifeless ocean"...or perhaps not so lifeless.

We have long searched through many mountains and mineshafts, caves, catacombs, and basements, looking for rumoured access to her roaring marges. We often prayed that Kruth or the Duke would show up and point the way. Now the tide turns;

Kruth himself has appeared to one of our own. It is a moment of destiny."

"Please...I do not wish to return among them," said Jacob. "What is more, I fear they will not help unless I provide for them, in the way they described. They would have me carry out certain tasks, things I must not reveal, works they fancied destined for me, for they believe a cosmic doom presses upon us all."

"It does," said Abbot. "You must do it in faith without question.

Remember, you must make up for all the worry you caused by leaving. Gird well the straps and carry the silver-braced book.

Those books are the histories of men, their painful stories of sin, and so the weight of other men's mischief will be great upon you. That volume is for you, and the world's dark history will be a burden, but it is a yoke that you can bear!

God does not encumber his sacred servants with anything they cannot carry."

"Swallow your pride, man!" added the White knight. "What will it take to complete these tasks?"

"Time...perhaps three week, as much as two moons, but no longer."

"Then we shall set aright the few things of our need while we wait, but you must hasten. Do not rest until your favor for them is done. When you have completed this, you must go to Hordingbay and await us there, in your uncle's house, to take ship to the Whitehawk. We will arrive sometime after the ides of the month, but before the end of the following month.

Keep close the codex; keep it always with you, lugging it around on your back. I know that it is cumbrous, as is the sad story of men on these furthshores. I prophesy now to you: as long as you have faiththe sins recorded in these pages will not over-burden you. Go now to pray, and we who are knowledgeable shall consider more deeply these matters, and summon you again."

Jacob bowed, he backed away humbly, even though he was not pleased. He quickly removed himself from the chamber.

"For wh o can compare to the Beast? Who can stand against him?"

St. John
Book of the Apocalypse

NUMERUM DE BESTIA   XVIII

On the new day Brother Jacob prepared for his talk with the Abbot.

He had made a resolution. His obedience to Abbot in all things would be sincere. It would not concern him what were Abbot's human reasons for any decision, Jacob would treat them as God's will, like a true monk.

When the hour came, he knocked three slow knocks on the door of Abbot's study.

A voice bade him enter.

Abbot sat there at peace and Brother Fragga stood beside him.

as well as the two cavaliers, last of the Ammouric Knights

who were examining charts on a table nearby, the desk near the Abbot's wooden *sedelis*.

"Come, Brother Jacob," said Abbot. "Please approach. Brother Fragga, kindly withdraw from us for an hour. Utmost secrecy for these chivalrous thanes must remain without question. It is not in distrust or to dishonor you,but certain men would torture you to extract any military information which these knights must exchange."

The monk bowed and moved away in humility, gently closing the door. (all that certainly raised a few hairs on Jacob's tonsured head).

"It is wise that you seek refuge in us," the Abbot said to Brother Jacob. "We pray you have let not any others become cognizant of these matters, save your confessor. There already grows distrust and bewilderment throughout the monastery. This mysterious disruption of our peace may be the machination of the devil, or simply the folly of sinners; in any case, the hand of the good Lord allows it."

Jacob spoke: "It has been taught that a monk must be indifferent as to his honour or dishonour, despite any difficulties, and remain detached even to his final day, unmoved as to earthly victory or defeat, for in all things we must be submitted to God."

"Such is gleaned from your study, Jacob," the Abbot observed, "...but not a thing known and lived as from experiences."

Jacob knew it was true. Abbot said more, "You remain a clever boy imitating the wise sayings of elders. Do you wish to be a man? A man who speaks with heart for the faith? It has only in this past hour come to us what meaning there may be for this strange route set before you.

Our Ammouric ancestors were men of high calibur.
They were men for enduring many afflictions
of which the angels did not spare of them.
In former times monks climbed unto the highest steps
of both of learning and of battle-craft,

and of many other skills. It is no longer. The feebleness
of our generation has little ambition for great learning combined
with great prowess. Nor is it commonly agreed anymore
that a monk should want to surrender all
for the Truth ever-abiding, fighting the devil's servants.
With the ages passing and the dimming of the minds,
the love in the hearts of men has grown cold.
Anyone who would selflessly fall in battle
for the banner of the Lamb and for his brothers,
that many do many consider a fool."

"We knights yielded to this invitation, monk," declared the Grey Knight, "...because we consider you no fool, but a worthy youth capable of learning. Even though you are accused of witchery, we think it's the devil's deciet
and will still vouch you our trust."

"That risk do you accept? " Jacob asked.

"Being fully ware that you might be, in fact, guilty of what you are accused. But knowing your desire we cannot imagine it so.
Abbot believes that Heaven high-above has vouchsafed you fall into these troubles, in order that many things might come to light. You must, however, explain clearly your hope, and in no uncertain terms."

"I hope for your help to shed light on the conspiracy darkly brewing, involving Ulcrist Dretch and other monks, not only so that I might demonstrate my innocence, but also persuade them turn them back to God, Ulcrist and the others, before it is too late. For albeit great is their turbulence, like enemies, but yet I love them as God comands, for they are my brothers."

"By what strength or wisdom do you suppose that you can reform these monks?" asked Abbot surprised and a little irked. "They will not even listen to their Abbot.
What makes you think they will hark to you?"

"All of what the elfbeards told me will I disclose:
the coming chastisement of God. The things I heard of what must come, if told convincingly, will inspire the monks to change their ways, return their hearts to God. These will be told after Ulcrist is brought to justice."

"Justice? That is a divine work," said the Abbot. "Do you think that you can acheive such things yourself? Barely a new monk are you."

"Forgive me, Abbot. Who by divine will is not well-enough suited to be an instrument of justice? He may choose whomsoever he wishes."
Jacob suddenly felt bold. "We could find a way to demonstrate my innocence, a thing I know not how myself to do.
Then this monastery together we can reform."

"We...? First reform thyself. The reform of many monks is an Abbot's long labour, by Heaven appointed.
Such things are above your surveyance."

"We might suspect you to be innocent,' said the White Knight, "but how do you imagine that knights errant may avail to prove your innocence? ...by finding the real witch or by dunking you in water till you drown? No, rather trust that the Prime Interquist will be able to prove your inno —"

"—you suppose I will be found innocent?! " Jacob interrupted, now agog. "Or will I falsely confess to being a wizard to preserve my life?"

"*Noli interloqui!* Do not interrupt a knight of the order, Jacob," snapped the Abbot sternly. "...and know your place."

"My apologies, venerable master," said the monk. "There is something I have in mind."

"He is not yet twenty winters. So we forgive his outburst. Whatsoever your mind might come up with, of course, we must hold suspect," said the White Knight.

"Wait, let us hear the boy-monk," said the Grey Knight. "Go ahead; what is your mind?"

"—*The Black Book.* These volumes tell of many things left behind from the ancient times, even from the first and second ages of the world.
One commentator mentioned that some relics are reputed to have transformed the faith of entire cities."

Jacob was adamant. In the *Black Books,* he claimed, there is mention of the Chalice of the Last Supper, The Crown of Thorns, the Veil of Veronica, the Wood of the Cross, the Three Nails, the Bone Dice of Golgotha, and the Holy Lance which pierced the side of Christ, and many bones of apostles and martyrs, and many other relics stirring awe. Forget not the relics from the even more remote times of the Eldark: sacred staves and the wands of great patriarchs, like the rod of Aaron, holy oils and elixirs, the Oil of Seth, and even potions that press men to tell the truth.

"Such could be administered to Ulcrist, as a test." Jacob added.

"No, Jacob...we do not force our brothers," said Abbot in corrective admonishment. "Our Master did not coerce even those who sought his death. Most of those relics you read about are lost, buried in remote wilderness tombs. Their whereabouts are forever unknown.
The Prime Interquist will have his own method of inducing men to tell the truth: interrogations, but not by force...yet, I wonder if we might bypass the use of torture, which, although useful for extracting the Truth, seems to me unnecessarily forceful...although it has always worked. Only a dull-witted monk, I imagine, would risk Hell's everlasting bonfire just to get out of some temporary earthly pain under torture.
Still, it somehow seems to me that torture is not the best encouragement for truth-telling."

"I do hope The Inquisition still uses such methods," said Jacob, imprudently. "For Ulcrist and the hidden elect will be confident.
Without torment applied to his flesh, he will easily outwit any cross examination."

"It be more certain that such a method will be used on you, boy." said the Abbot, frowning. "You are wise to avail yourself of some holy relic.
It would be grace if men recovered another powerful one.
Our Whitehawk ancestors, both the Eldari and the Ammouri,
foresaw that rebellion and hedonism would infect the cities of men, and so they stored the highest relics away in the wilderness, safe from the hands of wicked and idle men," explained Abbot. "The location of each was kept guarded."

"...But Time tires all guards," the White Knight added.
"Most of the relics of The Furth High King are irretrievably lost somewhere in remote wilderness places,
or in shrines under the earth, places forgotten."

So did the knight speak true lore.

Even the former Eldanes of Whitehawk, yes, even those like Abbot who had many works of lore at his fingertips, could never learn
where in thunder such be hidden.
That is why Abbot Caelestius in the fourth age
forged the celibate knighthood. The Ammouric order of quest-knights:
to seek what was lost,
to recover trust that the Furth High King would someday return as he promised. Not only that, but learn the true history of the world:
that there be known among men how the sacred scriptures
are not mere wonder-tales for superstitious do-gooders,
but true eyewitness accounts of when God himself walked the earth, writings worthy of utmost credence.
"A relic provides physical proof of it," explained Abbot. "that it is not just a tale, but history, something which many low books of our time have obscured. The great relics of our Faith must be recovered, especially now in these last days of the world-age, this time of Darkness, before the Light is entirely forgotten.
Now, however, only these two long-journeying knights perdure, and there is but little hope. Many of the relics remain missing. If the whereabouts of a relic is not soon discovered,
It will remain forever unknown."

"Is there not some sacred relic that can bring us truth-saying?" Jacob asked, somewhat alarmed. "I have heard that no liar can bear to touch any relic."

"Close the door, monk," said the Grey Knight grimly. "The enemy has many ears."

The young monk stepped over and closed the door.

"You have no doubt suspected that there exists a great relic by which one might be able to identify and expose a great and hidden evil."

"I knew hidden evil would make itself felt soon," Jacob said, "and I have heard of highly placed evil-doers in the greater world."

"Then will you consent to a mission?" asked Abbot.
"I know that you are perplexed. Bizarre beings already roped you into their great "tome-hunt," just about, however odd it seemed.
Nevertheless, you have shown some understanding
and acceptance of their eldritch lore. I know their kind.

Had you thrown in with them they would have taken you
traveling through the deep-earth. You were not ready.
Are you now? We do wonder."

"Last Sunday the Burgundy Knight adopted me," said Jacob.
"He bade me finish a sacred endeavor for something known to him
alone. One does not refuse a dying man. But I do not wager I can hold fast
to my word without your help. Each of these mysteries touches
The Black Books in some way, but there is another part to this puzzle.
Now I suspect you are going to describe to me something more also
wrapped up in this."

"He has gleaned too much of what we are doing already," warned the
White Knight. "I fear that we must disclose to him the truth entire."

"Is he ready for the trouble this will bring him?" asked the Grey
Knight. "Indeed, this is a cumbersome cross for those who are yet unripe
in faith."

"He will have to bear it," said Abbot. "He has little choice but to
hear it. I bade translate *The Black Book* so that he might come to the
conclusion himself."

"Yes, The Inversus is now in the world," said the White Knight. "He is
a human being. There is also soon to arise: the Dark Shepherd, his herald.
They have not made themselves known yet.
Our deep purpose is to find and expose their plans to the world.We
suspect the identities of who these are, but we must be careful. We must
know for sure. We cannot assassinate, since we are lawful and must keep
the fifth commandment of God against murder, even in case of the most
wicked of men. God giveth, God taketh away;
not Man giveth, Man taketh. Instead our certitude on his unholy intent
must be great enough to convince the masses not follow him.
Inversus must be exposed and imprisoned; and the false prophet must
be silenced. Certain powerful relics may help us to this end."

"Why fear this evil-minded one?" Jacob asked. "Do you not know that
the Lord God himself will reveal the Man of Perdition?
What is this man compared to the Lord of Hosts,
who is light from light, the one of whom it is written
There was no time when He was not?"

"Surely you speak what is true," answered the Grey Knight, stroking
his hoary beard and lighting his pipe. "We know that Heaven does not
place on the world evils without inviting men to match themselves 'gainst
them. That is why He gives us the power to do so. We also agree that
Heaven is not some angelic bueracracy controling all things, but men in
fact decide things for themselves."

"Inversus cannot be slain by the weapon of Man," warned the Abbot,
"The Furth High King alone, as it is written,
will throw him down by the breath of his mouth.
But take care: he and the Dark Shepherd will deceive many, even unto
perdition. No, it is not the Inversus that I foresee you will contest, it is
instead one of the great minds in his employ, his own chamberlain and
secular precursor; the Balecrown of Nzul. If we work now to expose his
deceit, many could be snatched from the rising power of the Inversus. We
must try."

"There have been many men who were antichrists already, Jacob," continued the Abbot, "there was once a grand Sorcerer of Nystol, Simon Infernalius, for example, who by descent of Simon Magus, seized the chair of Archmages at Nystol.

And there have been tyrannical rulers like Nergalf the Dwarf-Emperor,[31] or cruel barbarian warlords like Synostochs[32] of old. You can perceive the foul spirit working in them throughout the history of the furthlands. But the sacred lore affirms that there is one final and absolute Inversus who is to come, *The* Inversus, and we know that he is already in the world. He is a man perfectly possessed by the devil, to whom he consented...I mean, it is a spiritual possession that is complete and entire, difficult to detect.

It is also said that he will be a great statesman who will deceive the kingdoms. This is the warning the ancients pass down to us, and it is confirmed in sacred scripture. All this is indeed touching on the strange lore found in *The Black Books*, and venerable Anherm was seeking something more on it, as it seems.

If the evil archon of the North, the creature of melancholy in his impregnable fortress, were imprisoned, then the influence of the Inversus over Whitehawk would be greatly diminished. But what is also of significance for you is this: it may provide the instrument of your reproval.

"So is there a powerful instrument to be used against the Balecrown? God is faithful and gives us, who are most unworthy, great helps. There is told report among the Eldark," Abbot continued, "word that the ancient Bachal Dsu was seen, the relic once known as the Staff of St. Aldemar. But ware be thou. Scripture calls it another name when the prophets upheld it against the enemies. There it is called "The Staff of God!"

Abbot had mentioned the Staff before, as something he longed to secure. "It was quite irretrivably lost, being a staff of soothsay, that is, of

---

[31] *Nergalf the dwarf-emperor.* A super-tyrant over all the civil lands in the Fourth Age, Nergalf was famous not because he was an Emperor of dwarves, but rather a man-dwarf who became Emperor of all Aideen, all Furth Kingdoms did him obeisance in great fear of his military prowess. On account of his wickedness and abuse of power most Maceonid Kingdoms united against him and waged battle upon the fell of Gederon. Nergalf was defeated, and escaping to the dwarven recesses of earth took vengeance on the wizards of Nyzium who had betrayed him by promising help and then forsaking him at the hour of battle. He arranged for the destruction of Nyzium after obtaining the Spear of Longinus in the underworld. His descent with war-heroes is set down in a famous eyewitness account *The Tower Wyrdd*.

[32] *Synostochs (Synostocs Sinostox):* antagonist of the ancient epics; sworn enemy of Duke Ikonn and King Argoth. Wielder of the accursed sword Illmethodon, he sought vengeance upon Duke Ikonn and swore to his destruction. See glossarium entry for full account.

truth-telling. Tradition says that no one who is a liar can touch it, nor can anyone be deceived by a lie while the Staff is in hand."

Abbot told how the sight of the Staff in the hands of a watchful shepherd or genuine philosopher can inspire hardened sinners to repentance.

The mere sight of it causes men to hope in that which transcends their nature. Of he who holds The Bachal, the Staff....he would see past anything counterfeit and could not be deceived...and it is rumoured to have other powers. *The Black Book* had still more to say regarding this thing.

It is said that God prepared it in the twilight of the sixth day of Creation, hewn from the wood of The Tree of the Knowledge of Good and Evil, and that he delivered it to Anathron,[33] the son of dust, as a help after that poor soul was driven from paradise.

It had passed through the hands of Shem, Enoch, Abraham, Isaac, and Jacob successively, and then it came into the possession of Joseph and even of Christ. In the passing of ages the staff found its way to Whitehaven, and then by way of its Eldark caretakers to Egyptian Gohha, land of pyramids in the eastern Furth. Knowledge of its existence, but not of its whereabouts was passed on to recent Abbots.

Through Anherm's researches in *The Black Books*, Abbot had learned of further powers. "And not of least importance" he said, "it bestows the power to find, apprehend, and even banish unclean spirits! We might lead an army to cleanse Galadif of the draconian idolatry once and for all!"

"Does anyone know where exactly is the staff?" asked the White Knight.

"I do not wish to sound skeptical, but we have done too much unsuccessful questing already. Most sacred relics are, in my estimation, hidden away from the profane eyes of the men of today, who have such little faith."

"How often, my friend, have I warned you never to give up hope?" replied the Grey Knight. "Quests for relics is long and hard,

and few helpful hints are provided of their whereabouts.

If only we had a monk who could read the old texts⋯ but I'll remind you again, and young monk you also pay heed on this narration.

Think of the ever-calling quest in this way, it is a wandering search on behalf of the heavenly kingdom."

The grey Knight spoke of other mysteries, of the soul that wanders through the maze of this world. Forth she pilgrimages along spiraling paths and soon finds herself far away from the central axis in the maze, the banquet room, the goal. The soul sees herself going along the farthest circular wall at the edge of the maze, near the outer darkness, remote from his goal. She nevertheless goes on, weary and out of strength.

Still she does not give up hope. She perseveres to go forward even though all seems vain. Unforeseen, by an unexpected bend in the maze's path, she immediately arrives at the central chamber.

---

[33] *Anathron* according to aLapide; a name for the first man, whom scripture calls Adam. This name refers to his ability to look up into the heavens.

That is the mystery of the labyrinth. She comes suddenly upon what was destined her, that which she ardently sought, even when all seemed lost. Finally she sits at banquet. Even so it is with creed-sworn knights.

"Or if you are right," the Grey Knight admitted "that it be not we who are marked to find, my brother, then at least we can tell another where in the wide world it may not be found. So now we disclose much to you, Jacob Magister, much that has been dark and unknown.

"It is that we knights were once sent by your Abbot and have long wandered the Whitehawk continent, seeking relics in hopes that faith might revive again, and the Dark Shepherd exposed, the Northing frustrated, and the deep-minded devil brought into bonds once again. We are getting too weary to travel through the world, but you, Jacob, you are young, and have many winters left. Reckless roaks like us do not know how to harness the power of a staff   anyway, but a monk...a monk who can persevere...he may do so with skill."

"Add to that your incredible power of resisting fear; said Abbot "all alone you left the only life you knew and tried something totally different. When you subsequently found yourself in thralldom you boldly escaped. Fear is alien to you. Good; there be no place for fear when confronting the principalities of shadow, wickedness in high places. Fear can be fatal."

"And, although lacking in many things, you have the right build and chivalric posture," added the White Knight. "Most monks could never survive so perilous a pilgrimage. But you are a guardian-monk. As for us, though we can bear arms and we can travel far, we do not have the knowledge to navigate the labyrinths of ancient texts and find the appropriate keys. Finding the relics requires one who can do both. You also, and this is critical, have certain monastic abilities which we knights have not learned.

"The ability to veil the mind should be most handy, and in you, Jacob ,it is greater than others. The evil archons and Sorcerers have prevailed because they can estimate well the thoughts and plans of men."

"That is high talk indeed," replied Jacob. "I know that I have come off as eager to defend myself and get to the truth. However, when it comes to such struggles as the overthrow of the Northing, it should be left to a holier monk and someone with a more cheery outlook. I have already proven myself to be irresponsible, even carnal, quite unworthy of such an honorable mission.

I do not think that the Time of The Harvester would much involve me anyway. It is the great saints clothed-with-joy who will help us.

I cannot be of any lasting use, for I am surely one of those

who will be *scarcely saved through fire*, if at all.

No, I did not mean to get involved in this, and I must bow out. I was merely hoping to encourage you knights to help me.

The Prime Interquist will find me innocent,

and I shall live my life quietly as a humble monk.

No more adventures, please. The weird things I heard from those elven-hybrids were enough. Let me live out my seasons in peace here.

Will I give up the dream of adventures?

I must yet disprove the accusal against me;

but the intervention of divine justice is near."

"You do not merit such justice, as you yourself just formerly said," noted the Grey Knight. "But what better way to merit than to go on a sacred quest, a pilgrimage to deliver our kingdoms? Brother Jacob,
if this is indeed your destiny, then do not shrink from it."

Abbot's words took a rather advisory tone. "Fetch the sacred relic and prophesy to unbelieving monks and to all the folk of the land. The Staff may be the best hope, and it is *your* hope.
You comprehend not the Darkness that you would hazard.
Ulcrist is a shrewd one indeed. The weight of evidence against you is going to tip the scales considerably in the eyes of The Inquisition. It will be said of you that you were angry with Ulcrist because he did not include your name with monks to be considered for the knight's recruiting. What will you say to that?
Even I, who see how different you are in character than Ulcrist, would not accept your testimony without something more.
Have you any better-sounding explanation yet
of why everything you witnessed comes off as flatly fiction?"

"Nothing more than what seeds I have already thrown on rocky path."

"Then be assured a devilish bird snatches them, and you yield no crop that grows straight or rings true or even smacks of an acceptable explanation," replied Abbot sternly. "Extreme circumstances call for extreme measures, Jacob.
If you testify before the Holy Inquisition with the Staff in hand, and continue to hold it, God's grace will help you...if you are true.
The Prime Interquist will not be able to convict you.
What is more, in the presence of the relic, Ulcrist will be unable to deceive. No man of God will believe him.
The Inquisition is well informed of the staff-legend."

"Forgive me, my Abbot, but how can a staff make one observe the law?" Jacob asked. "A man himself must bring himself to become righteous. Only then will the brethren repent, not because they see a sacred relic in hand."

"You err and are quite vainly wrong, boy. Your inexperience
in sacred matters is great indeed. Let men of virtue speak on manhood, and let boys who stay safe at home remain boys.
A man does not become holy by his own efforts, but by sticking to the rough path which Heaven has shown him.
This he can do only with heavenly strength. Those monks
who have gone off the path now savagely turn on us
to rend us."

"Why not call the monks this very day to reform their lives?" asked the White Knight, turning to Abbot. "Have them learn Christian respect. It is outrageous, their behavior. Even when our brother knight was buried, they ate, drank and made merry, and no doubt they will steal away at night to some impurity, like heathen swine!"

"My worthy and chivalric lord, those certain brothers here have hardened their hearts and are outside our sway now," explained the Abbot. "We must look to the guidance of the divine hand. Conversion to the right living cannot be forced. The previous Abbot did assay to reform the monks. He instituted a revised rule; and when the monks banded to foist him out, he refused to leave. Like St. Benedict, the grand founder of our way of life, Abbot Aonas was bold, but also hated. His allies, like brother Anherm of Whigg, were beaten often by fell brethren, monks who call themselves "the spiritual brethren." The vicious monks would conceal their faces with wrappings when doing this violence.

These attacks continued until Abbot Aonas at last consented,

short of having his own life snatched from him at the end of a dagger blade.

It was his chance at martyrdom. He always regretted that.

When it came time, they elected me as Abbot, knowing that in my ambition I would consent to the burdens of leadership and certainly would not confront them, but defer to their demands, and so they were right, but only in part.

See now I even begin to weep some at these thoughts. Heaven has given me authority and power as another Christ, and as their father, for I am pastor, I am Abbot. I have become too friendly with many wicked monks and cannot bring myself to go against them, even though in my heart I am against so much that they do. I have let them carry on as they will, to my shame, without discipline. Now I long for some change; but I do not have the strength, nor the dint of will. I have prayed to the Lord God over it, and he has revealed to me that I am not the one for this task. Now, because of all these recent revelations, I perceive that the divine hand may nevertheless give a little push."

"I would teach them myself to what end such overbold flaunting comes!" exclaimed the Grey Knight. "Who are these wolves in sheep's clothing, unruly mockers who have invaded the peace of Heaven's earthly corridors?!"

He placed his hand on his sword hilt.

"Nay my friend···" said Abbot. "Remember that normally cutting weapons are not allowed in the Abbey, save for yours. The sword must not be used against those consecrated to God, no matter how vile they have become

···.nor against any Christian. That is not the way.

Besides, I am forbidden to reveal which monks vex us."

"Who has forbidden you?!"

"They have themselves by their own plotting cleverness. They each made confessions of their mischief to me, purposely, knowing well that great and terrible seal of silence imposed upon the confessor by that awesome sacrament. How great the peril of my soul would I ever dare break it, by saying who or even merely hinting upon my knowledge. I should not even have mentioned that such abuses took place, but it is common knowledge among the monks.

Now, however, I sense the divine hand guiding us another way. It is my trust, Jacob, that right knowledge regarding the whereabouts of The Staff will be advanced to you. But ware be thou.

The Bachal Dsu is a power of unfathomable mystery.

A thing of fire it is, like the burning bush, and only a devout man may touch; and lest he be destroyed forthright, he must be clean, a pure soul, with not the blood of any human or kindred upon his hands."

The staff, many years ago, Abbot claimed, had so holy an aura that it could no longer remain secure among even monks;

for many had become tepid and comfortable with sin.

Such be the wickedness of our time. Some of the monks, it was rumoured, secretly wished to be rid of it, a symbol of the old order, the old discipline.

So it was slated to be removed. When the opportunity came it was eagerly taken. It was contracted to the Eldark who paid a enormous sum of gold for it in the years of the great famine, when our monks had nothing to eat.

The Eldark were considered safe, for they wished to preserve any relics, and yet such are usually righteous as well, to the extent that their philosophy is mostly true. They finally conveyed it to our brother abbey, specialists trained in the keeping of relics, *monachi* of The Weeping Brotherhood in the Dry Blood Sea. From there, in subsequent years, the Hycsoth of Gohha obtained it for their veneration.

It was last seen in the oasis of Vath[34] in the great southern desert. Vath, however, is now a deserted rock island, whose innards are like a honeycomb. The Nomads say it was brought to a place so inaccessible that only those who travel beneath the earth might have a chance of finding it, perhaps even far northward beyond the Gates of Dariel.[35] The legends do attest to its existence;

and its exact whereabouts are known only by two, the Yule Queen, who knows every hollow realm, and another, whom Abbot would not name.

"I will name him," said the White Knight, "Nimrul the Archdruid, the Balecrown of Nzul and Dire of Melancholy, whom the Aels and Osringi name Northing, the thing of the north, chamberlain of the black realm."

---

[34] *Vath, isle of, oasis:* The hycmen who did not follow the law-giver Noshar went and dwelt in tents near the salt lake of Asphyl. These tribes were mostly put to the sword under the Pharaoh Paphsis or died of starvation in the following years when the Urash failed to flood and the lake dried up. Some fled to the deserts of the west under the judge Vathar. These were known as the Vathim, and surviving they later carved out the underground city Vath within one of the great rock-isles in the desert, but it is now uninhabited save by certain monks exiled from the desert Monastery of the Weeping Brotherhood.

[35] *Gates of Dariel:* Colossal gates of bronze and adamantine construction built by Hermius the Conqueror in the third age. These gates block the sole passage through the Valaghir mountains on the Isthmus of Hyrcanth and are maintained by the independent city state Ptur to keep out the northern savages. Hermius built these gates to keep back the barbaric hordes of the north and east that periodically hope to raid the civil lands. The gates can only be unlocked by the possessor of the key, which was reported lost at the opening of the fourth era of the world. According to legend, Godiun Fout stole the key, thinking it for a great treasure, but a century later Gulathar the gelf found in the belly of a vermilion worm. These were the famous gates Gulathar unlocked to admit the barbaric horde which destroyed Nyzium.

Jacob rolled his eyes in dismay. "Right... Well that sounds all too much...but this crusade would be illegal anyway. So please count me out. I am not a knight, and the Crown has commanded that it is illegal and punishable by imprisonment for anyone other than an appointed knight to ask for provision and enter foreign lands upon holy campaign. No, too much for a runaway monk like me."

"You hold yourself in slight regard," replied the Abbot, "but all of us know that you are a rather extraordinary monk."

Then said the White Knight, "You need not be a knight of the realm in order to quest, but knighthood is required. I myself shall dub you an Ammouric Knight. After all, we ourselves possess no land and have no fealty to any but the Furth High King, being similar to the monks. Many of our devotions are shared."

"A knight? I am a monk!"

"You cannot crusade under grace without being a knight sworn of the Ammouri," warned the Abbot. "Only knights have the right to quest, as you reminded us, and only the Ammouri may quest for sacred relics."

"Am I to be both monk and knight?! It is absurd."

"You are to use the combat-training as a monk, but you will have legal rights of a knight, and the blessing. You must indeed quest," said the White Knight. "You can complete your citadel training at Dove Lake after all this mystery is cleared up."

"Let me remain only a monk and be at peace. Forgive me for correcting you, nobleman; you certainly may not do such a thing anyway. The law also instructs that only a son of noble issue may be knighted."

Abbot was now becoming ornery, but not visibly, for he was justly frustrated with Jacob Magister. The shepherd did not even reply.

"That is right well the law, monk; true indeed," said the White Knight. "I do not spend my time reading law *codices*. However, I do know an exception has been made for nobles who adopt because they have no male heir. A son of common issue whom a noble adopts, provided he was a youth, may enter chivalric grace. You, still a boy, were adopted and became the son of the Burgundy Knight, his only heir. Therefore we are quite duly warranted to dub you knight.

He has also bequeathed to you this scarlet hood of his, a great relic of unknown power: The Red Cowl, the wool from the red flocks of Carmakhen, island in the midst of Furthsea. Wear it always for radiance and protection against the evil eye. It confers the gift of choosing paths well. When you wear it, look for a luminous cross shining on the horizon, indicating the way."

He passed the folded Red Cowl to Jacob. Jacob held it in silence for a time.

"Thank you. It sounds tempting, but no, I must decline.

You would bring me on your quest? It sounds grand, but I do not trust it. Can one search in dangerous lands for so treasured a staff and abstain the shedding of blood? Think of it: Satan will dispatch his servants, Veil-Knights from Arraf, or horgim from the Nzul, to come upon us with violence in our journey, bandits or sorcerers;

and if I find myself without someone to fight on my behalf,

I will not hesitate to smite the foe down myself, or else yield. It cannot be done."

There was a moment of uncomfortable silence. The Abbot lowered his gaze. Suddenly he moved as to get up, and so his crutches.

The knights at once rushed for him, but he gestured against them to refuse. He gripped instead the chair so as to push himself up. He looked rather perturbed. Never did he get up and stand on his own, without crutches, without brother Fragga Slowtongue assisting him.

One of the knights moved forward to leverage him up, but he shook his head to shoo him away also. He lifted himself with great effort, forcing himself upwards and standing full on, he stood freely, frowning a manly frown.

The knights immediately knelt down. He looked about at each in the room, but especially at Jacob Magister. Stern was his gaze.

The crutches fell down and banged against the stone floor.

"You are telling ME that it cannot be done?"

In shame Jacob durst not reply. It was always thought impossible that Abbot stand on his own ever since the wild-eyed w itch broke his knees.

This was indeed remarkable.

"*Nihil impossibile per Deum*!" he declared. He stared at Jacob in silence.

He demanded a conversion of mind. "I made spirit-warfare with the gap-toothed hag of the Timberhills. Then Heaven called me to be the weary Abbot of these rope-girded monks, something for which I am most unsuitable, not only in soul but in body.

Yet I have accepted to do the Lord's will.

Do you speak of God, but deny the power thereof? Whose will do you do, monk?" He reached backward and grasped his chair, and slowly he sat back down. He remained hush again for a moment.

The Abbot stared off into mysterious distances.

The knights kept silent in devotion, so astounded were they.

"...it is so:" said Abbot returning from his interior distances, "you must not slay any innocent or bystander, or even kindred foe unnecessarily, or shed their blood, else your hands be defiled, and the purpose of Heaven be forfeit. Remember something

—what is most vital: Be innocent. Allow yourself to suffer in your innocence. If your heart keeps unworthy hatred, or nurses vengeance, by no means should you even touch the staff. Take care, Jacob Magister; I fear a heavy task is being laid upon you."

"As you instruct," Jacob said. "But can a monk satisfy justice in war, or in a world which knows no justice? How can a merciful apostle hinder any foe, creatures that might harry, especially evil-minded men?"

"Aye, it is a cross purpose, Jacob. *Aufer crucem tuam.*

It is this cross, the cross which our Lord embraced.

It is the wood of the tree of life, and the fronds thereof.

From the same tree was hewn the wood both of the cross and of the staff. Let that be your war-cry. God made you an extraordinary monk because he has an extraordinary task that must be accomplished. Keep close the codex; keep it always with you, lugging it around on your back.

Guard it with your life. I saw within maps and diagrams, as well as centuries-old illustrations of the relics, even a sketch of the Staff, so that you might confirm it to be the true Staff when you find it. We cannot know all that is recorded there within the thousand years of pages, but only a fraction, and there may also be certain writings some sinister power may seek,

either to keep or to destroy, and you may at last find therein

what centuries have concealed. I know that it is cumbrous,

as is the sad story of mankind on these furthshores; but it is our story, and we must bear it. *"Take upon you my yoke, for my yoke is easy and my burden light.* Therefore I prophesy now unto you:

as long as you have faith, it will not over-burden you."

"It is not the weight of the book that concerns me, it is the weight of Ulcrist and the others, which will be used against you, Abbot."

"These monks are atrocious characters whose bad example does not go unnoticed in the land," said Abbot. "Of recent much is heard on the increasingly deficient reputation of this monastery.

Even the Bishop of Hordingbay is said to have wept

when he heard of the easy living here. The other monasteries are not much better. Remember what we have been taught: *if the salt loses its flavor, what is it worth but to be cast it out?* Consider how things are on the continent, where are but three monasteries, and only one has resisted alien dogma. So on the continent is not one land at peace. The worship of idols is found in every place,

and so flows blood upon unholy altars.

Kingdoms are overthrown and feudal tyrants rule.

The bolgrim terrorize on all sides. Men go without knowledge of God.

Unlike most knights, you are bookwise.

You must enter those darkened realms

and use whatever monk-lore you can to locate the staff."

Abbot paused and took a deep breath. He let silence buoy his heavy words and continued.

"Fear and dread the failure of this quest, Jacob. For if the monks of this abbey do not repent, they will continue refusing obedience. The folk of our land will not miss this, and soon they too will not harken to our word." Abbot explained many things. That seeing our own corruption, the flock will continue to think that it is enough to yield us their monies but covet whatever they commerce in: to be deceptive, or to spite others, or steal another's wife, or to pile wealth and commit sacrilege, to kill innocents. Afterall, the imposters in our religion keep teaching them to judge for themselves what is right, to ignore God's law.

Abbot also warned that if we fail, our monks will never, for the greater glory of God, make numerous copies of the history of Nyzium, a history to be supplied to every library. All must learn why the wizards fell, how the Lord of Hosts sent his just wrath upon those cold towers.

The tale must be told. If not, a new deception will arise.

Rather than harken to the Truth ever-abiding, masses of unlearned and unwashed will forget babtism and gather in the forest groves, or abandoned temples, to worship the demon-gods of old in the night, defiling these lands which Heaven once granted Duke Ikonn.

"...and men will drink down the alien doctrines of the heresiarchs, poison from the spawn of Nyzium! These kind are sorcerers disguised as deep-minded clerics...men of diabolic enthusiasm in chariots of hellfire.

In their obstinacy and cunning they will oppress men like a swarm of locusts. Then it is certain," he cried, "that divine chastizement will hurry upon the earth. Wickedness will outweigh goodness. Will the Red Death reach here in your own lifetime? Only one thing can convince men: hearing the fall of Nystol; the heresiarchs are indeed dangerous conspirators and sorcerers: it is all witnessed in the fall of Nystol."

Had divine providence prepared this for all?

Clearly it was the crucial moment.

"I do not want any part in this." Nearly Jacob said it, but instead thought "I cannot live with the shame of knowing that it was once in my hands to have thwarted the foul spirit from mastering all." Later Jacob wrote this in his account "I had already said no to common cause with the Valraphim. Now others wished something of me, and one could not doubt these."

"It is most likely that the one who seeks the Staff will die in the attempt to retrieve it, " Abbot grimly added, *"In the noontide of life I must depart; to the gates of the netherworld I must go'* ...your death will not be in vain, however."

"But I have not even agreed to it."

"We do catch the enthusiasm you are concealng," said the White Knight, ". . . but no, you have no readiness for war, young friend. I shall give you a gift: even now you shall be made a knight of the shawl, our Ammouric order, a knight not keeping lands like other knights.

If then you do accept it, it will be done." Grey Knight added, "Many moons in training him should be seen.

Do we even have time to ready him properly?"

"Have you need to train him in chivalric combat?" said Abbot. "He will not be using lance and shield. Those hands are deadly enough. besides, it is his mind that will shake the creature of the North."

"Then for the time being he shall fight as a monk fights." the Grey Knight said, "but there is more than just combat that is learned at the citadel of Dove Lake. Well, this is no doubt a good thing. Yet how will he go against an armoured foe on horse?"

"We train our guardian-monks in every potential combat situation that might arise." Abbot said. "Monks are trained to disarm, or evade, and they will abstain of using lethal force.

By meditation they even know how to make their own skin like unto armour."

"Ulcrist taught me that. It is hard to believe that my own trainer has took the shedding of a monk's blood,

and he would have snatched away my life."

"You have produced no acceptable proof of your blood having been shed. As Abbot I must remain as neutral as possible in this controversy.

Even though I trust you, Brother Jacob, you know that I am not permitted to judge your testimony, for you are duly accused by a professed monk."

"And your counsel is sacred. I cannot be called innocent unless I prove it with the staff," Jacob said with resignation.

"Why not let me accompany the knights as a squire?" asked Jacob.

"That would be enough. I will simply advise you. Knighthood could bring me into lawful troubles and obligate me to the worldly authority."

"To travel with a resolute company of cavaliers having knowledge of their purpose is also to be in league with them, as meets the law of the land," Explained the Grey Knight. "That is why single-hearted Paladins reveal not their quest to squires, since it is forbidden.

"This is so that peons do not come to learn of things too great for them and put in jeopardy the kingdom. If you were discovered and questioned, you must tell the truth, which means revealing what you know of our quest. You would need the legal protection of the rights of knighthood. You must be girded with the chivalric belt."

"Then why do you even follow the law if you are being sought by adverse worldly authorities?"

"We are Ammouric knights. We are lawful," replied the White Knight.

". . . and we are not obligated to earthly kings for quest," added the Grey Knight. "Our fealty is to The Furth High King. To him we must answer directly. No feudal crown of any of the four worlds can obligate us to service. Still, we keep the law of the realm we enter."

"Now, do you hear that Jacob? That should satisfy you. I will not command you, but advise you as your Abbot: be persuaded. Charity, I would say, does command it. Charity to these good men. It is time to meet destiny."

The White Knight turned to his grey-clad companion and spoke a question. "This therefore is your mind without doubt? "

"Let it be done," answered the Grey Knight, "We alone remain of the order. Another must pass on the sacred trust." The Grey Knight stepped over and picked up the gleaming long sword on the table. He unsheathed it and placed it in the hands of the White Knight.

"A king then you are," Jacob asked, "that you can dub someone knight?"

"In sooth I am a King anointed." said the White Knight "I have yet to return to my land, for our quest has been long. During the Wars of the Veil, I sent many knights into battle, to death, so that the kingdom be preserved. Little did I know that a Judas was lurking in my own court while I was away in far off Gohha. I do have a certain sadness.

"My kingdom is a land not like these shores. Let me accomplish this now, for the sun is setting. Hear it: you shall have the right to bear arms and meet justice, this day, St. Valentine's Day...may he preserve your chivalry. Kneel; you must receive the feudal order in sight of a king."

"I do this so that the quest shall not be forgotten. I am a monk, and when I return I shall never again leave my monastery."

Jacob knelt down. The White Knight gathered his long sleeves and hefted high the great brand. It was truly a fantastic weapon to behold. Its smooth blade gleamed in the light and slipped through air like the Whitehawk himself. There is no doubt the blade had some blessing of holy utterance upon it.

The knights dubbed Jacob Magister according to the sacred Ammouric formula, an invocation of the Furth High King, the bestowal of rights. To his vow of ever-whispering prayer was also added the chivalric vow to the hardship of quest. Said the Abbot. "It is written, *one must endure many hardships to enter the Kingdom of Heaven,*"

The chivalric name Sir Hortezan was bestowed on Jacob.

"Arise, Sir Hortezan Escorvus, Thane of Whitehaven.

Grasp thou the deadly sword. You, man, have the right to bear arms and meet justice in the land. Be heedful of the solemn endeavor upon which your life is now sworn."

The White Knight passed the weapon to Jacob, who took hold of the hilt, the guard of which swept round the pommel in an artful double "S" pattern. The blade itself was far more ancient, made with some adamantine steel that could not be identified and adorned with a line of sacred glyphs.

He handed it back. The knight slipped the sword back in its sheath.

"That is Oceanicyng, blade of Duke Ikonn, marauder of worlds. He gifted it to me with Queen Hesperia. Remember that a knight must always treasure his gift-sword. It is of his power, even if it has no magic about it. Congratulations...you may now lawfully wield your own, Witchbane."

"—but keep it hidden," added the Abbot. "Travel with your own quarterstaff as if you remain only a monk.

Do not appear to be anything more;

let not your knighthood be easily known. If anyone asks you, 'shouldn't you be in your monastery and be praying, monk?' Say to them, 'Be not solicitous over the occupation of others; attend to prayer thyself first.' The simple folk of this town must not come to learn that we have girded someone so accused to knighthood,

therefore you must never act outwardly as a knight.

You, as yet, stand accused, although we say that you are innocent; but we cannot prove it. You must be vindicated.

You must locate the Staff of Prophets. Ulcrist is far too word-wise and quick of tongue for any of us to dispute before a tribunal, not without the staff. Bring back the staff, and you might salvage this monastery as well."

"How can I possibly fetch the Staff in time before I am brought before the Prime Interquist? If it is in the Dry Blood Sea, The Isle of Vath,* they are far away. Just measure the chart: it is hundreds of leagues distant.

To enter that wasteland is certain death."

"You must determine that yourself. You are sworn, and earnestly a man, no longer a boy." explained Abbot. "The Angel of the Lord will prepare the way before you. I may not instruct anything deceptive or disobedient toward the Rule, nor urge pilgrimage to the Dry Blood Sea, for monks are not permitted to leave for so long. You have less than a year before the arrival of the Holy Inquisition. That's all the time you have to prove your innocence by testifying with the Staff in hand. You will appear to flee from this monastery again, therefore you will be all the more suspect.

Return not without the staff, for such a return will spell certain death. It is a sorry choice to make: stay and be hauled before The Prime

Interquist without help, or flee from your home, possibly never to be restored.

There will walk abroad many enemies. The Balecrown has many spies."

"If I enter into straits, stoop to violence? There may arise need to kill such a spy or other power to save the lives of innocent folk."

"We ask: be it Christian charity to remain at ease

while your brother is destroyed by enemies, or your liege-lord besieged, or when heretics and witches defile the land? *Be wise as the serpent, gentle as doves.* Never seek out bloodshed, but do stand fast against the wicked.

So listen close: According to the Rule, I may not hinder a Knight from doing what he must outside, nor can I by law shackle a Knight in chains or hedge him in any way. Nevertheless, you are still more monk than knight, so be careful, even in everyday places. God's angel will go before you."

"Careful? Why say you that, my lord?"

"A monk alone in the world without his brothers can lose his soul, and it is not easily recovered. Of any further utterance for you I have none. Pray always like a monk and you will not sin.

Do now what you must."

"Remember always the search," warned the White Knight. "Let no other thing consume your thoughts. Do not veer from its path. If chivalrous enterprise leads you below into the intermundane caves, then into caves you must go. And peril is found in any gloomy place of fallen fairy, but especially beware three illusions: glorious banquets, gold crizets, fair maidens. If you are offered any of these down there, shut your ears and turn away your eyes. Yield no time or thought to them. They will bewitch you and fascinate you with glamours. You will never return, but die the second death down there. Therefore touch not, nor even behold."

"He should not go alone," said the Grey Knight. "He is an inexperienced knight, and will be at great risk. Virtues endowed from knighting do not enter a man immediately. We must escort him through the Timberhills, lest he be waylaid by knavish elements. On the continent one encounters greater dangers, especially if he would find the Isle of Vath in the Dry Blood Sea. Escort him we must."

"He cannot remain unnoticed if he rides with knights. No, and without you knights here by my side," said the Abbot, with troubled brow.

"Aye, it is a risk indeed for us to leave Abbot at this time here alone surrounded by wolves in sheep's clothing," the Grey Knight admitted.

"Are there no other trained guardian monks good to watch over you?"

"Only brother Fragga Slowtongue...he is loyal. He may be slow of tongue, but he is quick of hand. It would be best if you knights could stay until Easter, when the King comes for retreat."

"When the time comes, Brother Jacob, you must make it through the Timberhills and entire Lokken on your own."

Against the Archons

Flee, ye monks, the wicked city. Enter not her unguarded gates, nor take any solace in her soft caresses. Rather, find satisfaction working with your hands. Instruct men in the simple techniques of the staff, fortifying them against bandits and demons, preparing them for sudden enlightenment.

Tien Joshur
Winter Instruction for Wayfaring Monks

The Wicked Cities of Men   XIX

Brother Jacob Magister, shawl-knight; wayfaring monk, hereby gives this testimony to the Holy Inquisition concerning the chivalric enterprise upon which Abbot Cromna sent him.

"They girded me with Ammouric Knighthood in conformity with lawful provision, named me Sir Hortezan. Perhaps I had not all the trappings of a knight, but the title might avail some.

So I did not fail to correct my habits. But even with so elevated a title, one can be humiliated and overthrown. The first thing to defeat me was no spell but something natural, "all-conquering sleep." And with sleep dreams do come rushing. I dreamt another mysterious dream. It was the dream of the fair maiden.

She appeared before me again in flowing gown and holding the gift-book of the knights. With her lovely eyes she was gazing at me, as it were out from distances. She did not call my name, as before, but asked a question. "Who is worthy to open the pages of the book and who can unseal the story within?"

Immediately I looked and I saw the book in her arms. I opened the book and saw an illumination-diagram upon the page. There was drawn in the foreground a pit from which reached up a devilish claw-hand. The claw-hand held a burning scroll. The smoke of the scroll rose up in a V-shape and filled part of the page. From behind the billows of smoke moving upwards there was a sun whose rays fell downward but could not penetrate the cities below.

She closed the book, turned and went away down the stony corridor; and as she turned the corner pillar, she was about to leave my sight. I reached out to her, and immediately she was gone. When I turned the corner, there the white stag, the Arcavir's mount, but it was on its knees and was bleeding from a wound, as if struck by a huntsman. This I interpreted: a prophetic dream of things that were, things that now are, and that to come. Otherwise I did not understand its meaning."

So the monk did his dream relate.

The knight's armour did not fit Jacob so well. It was not lawful for a monk to wear armour anyway, and Jacob could not move in his chainmail with the speed needed for the quarterstaff. So he only strapped on the upper part of the armour.

The knights taught him a few things which they could in so brief a time. First the special prayers to prepare for battle. How to use the horse employing both lance and sword, (the basics), to balance the shoulder plates and ready the hauberk. It was just in case some rival knight learned of Jacob and challenged him to a joust. Of these many things they also told him that it would be long before he could learn the superior way to ride, use a lance, or fence with the weapons of a knight.

He did not really hope to master it, although he did find it entertaining. Jacob had always the freedom of movement: any restriction of armour crippled his ability; his armor was a monk's frock and the bare hand.

As preparations and training took several days, Jacob returned to further a translation of *The Black Book*, hoping to solve many questions. In the *scriptorium* he labored, alone at night, when other monks slept. He did not easily learn the content of that book, but it was his eventual conclusion that a translation of *The Black Book* would reveal many things. It was not some spell book or weird and fatal tome, but a reasonable compendium of the sages that described the history of the Whitehawk realms. By such things garnered, a translation might bring about the recovery of a holy relic to increase the faith of many. Also, might not a translation bring those Sorcerers and others coveting the ancient text to learn the actual contents, and so diminish their craving to possess it? Theirs was a craving indeed, nothing more than a sinful avarice for forbidden knowledge. On the other hand, what if they sought to suppress some lore coded therein?

Each night Jacob would copy down and translate a page from the substantial tome. His knowledge of translating Saturnian Latin conveyed the smooth flowing and clear collection of ancient tracts. He would write some of the translation of those parts that he found pertinent at the time. To show it here would divert our thoughts too much, brothers.

Jacob was loath to begin a hallowed endeavor without first finishing this penance. He had originally estimated that he should translate the enormous tome in time for his appearance before the Prime Interquist. He could demonstrate by the translation that the codex was in no way a grimoire, and that he was innocent of witchcraft.

It was taking too long. In making a translation he was losing valuable time. Whatever lines Anherm had sought on behalf of the elfbeards were quite elusive. A quest of greater or equal import now was pending. In the two days of translating labours, Jacob's heart was besieged terribly with melancholy. The book was too large to hope to finish. And what is more, Jacob began to wonder if the book was a grimoire after all. Certainly the first chapters were strange indeed, and elaborated certain arcane histories. A number of sections described the history and lore of priceless relics, detailing the virtues of each. Those which the Eldark had told, or which Ammouric monks had made commentary upon, added to the knowledge.

Certain Sorcerers, be assured, will use sacred signs and symbols and even scripture itself in their diabolic summoning, as in an attempt to coerce angels. Is that why they sought the work? Some have even tried to manipulate the sacred letters of the Tetragrammaton, imagining in their folly that such secrets could command God himself!

Nevertheless, the deep purpose of this writing remained obscure. Was it for good or ill? Had Jacob been set up? Great black books are, to this day, kept by certain wizards, tomes near indestructible, within whose leaves are locked dangerous things, whose weird and massive bindings had to be shut and wrapped with iron chains, at last being padlocked by the Ammouric Soothfold! The fury of Hell itself was bound up in them. Several of these are said still to remain in the desolated ruins of Nyzium, hanging from the ancient ceilings suspended and locked with adamantine chains wrought by the Soothfold.

The powers of Hell were arrayed against the shawl-knight. But Jacob had mighty allies. He understood the purposes of Aileron the goose, which seemed natural knowledge but surely was not, the sympathetic communication that remained mysterious. He bade the goose go flying above the pines to drop off sacks of food, apples, bread, and sometimes wineskins, finding that enchanted isle in the horseshoe lake, since the elf-kin were still there, hopefully.

He saw to this every day. Another few days passed by. It was impossible to learn whether they had received any benefit. A sense of guilt set in for having ignored them. However, we think that the goose had indeed found them, but this was a guess. Had he done enough to help them? Had the Sorcerer captured them? There was no way to know.

ephyr blew gently as Jacob trotted the horse Burgundius into the Timberhills once again, in the hour before sunrise. Aileron was guiding him to the fey-creature, Kruthendel. "Solar rays warmed the air and snows were melting, for spring was near. Clouds scudded across the starry heavens like massy ships in the upper atmosphere. If there were only a sign given that I were doing the right thing. Nay, but a wicked generation seeks a sign.

After hours of searching, I found the gnome in a narrow ravine, somehow confined in a fungus circle, surrounded by a suspicious mist. The being greeted me and praised me for returning, and explained how new circumstances had befallen:

"...my mountaineers were driven to crazed mutiny, at last" Kruth said, "not to fault them... although they were bound by oath. Perhaps the haunting of these woods eclipsed their wits. Stormraker the Beardless, in a disgrunted sulking, kept talking against me each day, murmuring, voicing discontent at every bit meal. She cited the codes of the military law, accusing me of disregarding them, and she influenced the others to her view. You remember, only roasted wood mice were left to eat. She at last persuaded all but the dwarf Drocwolf to abandon my counsel. They all hated me, because I showed them the narrow way of survival in rough places, because I would not take back my word of command. One frosty morning we were preparing for normal operations when Stormraker and two others immediately seized me and looped my hands right fast enough, simultaneously gagging me, so as to thwart any spell utterance, as if Arcavirs and the like must rely on spoken words like wizards do.

Amen i say unto you: you too must lead them, someday. Speak the truth, no matter what, and fear not to suffer their anger in your leadership, eventhough you be uncertain. You will be hated for His sake. Be not attatched to the praises of men. The assault occurred just after I had blown the horn to call the stag, who was near and subsequently arrived at the usual time. They captured the blessed creature using a net and bludgeoned him with rocks. I warned them again: don't do it, you will outrage Heaven. But they cut up and devoured the sacred stag. Alas, they did not cease till they bloated their bellies.

Stormraker put me on trial, She called a military tribunal, appointed judges, and even a defendant: the brilliant philosopher Buckbar Lancelas. It was a court-marshal of monkeys, fully devoid of procedure. I was sentenced to perpetual shame for unworthy leadership. We Valraphim have sworn an oath never to use magic against one another, and I must stick to my word. Stormraker did not care for our quest anyway; but only that military justice be practiced. Now, without friends, I must follow this line of mushrooms back to a hidden land, its a certain kind of mushroom, whose spores keep me awake. After I am gone, I will no longer be seen in the lands of men."

"Wait, Kruth. Wait now...have you lost your wit? Why do you keep referring to Stormraker as "she and her?" He is a valraph, and a man. Is he not?"

The gnome glared at me. He did not smile.

"Did you not check her form, or the charm of her face in the dawn mist, monk? She is a woman, elf-blooded by half I suppose, but a woman. You must have took her features to be that of an elfish man."

"Being a monk from early years, gnome, I have encountrered but few women in my entire life. . .none clad in armour!"

"She is Phaedra Stormraker. Her clan among valraphs is famous. Legend has them supposedly descended of the "stormraker," that spirit of old that men used to call "Cloudgatherer." The daughters of the clan are all virgins, and amazons as well."

I was puzzled. I did not know much on women, but I had ability to at least recognize one, didn't I? "I am a monk who can miss what is right before my eyes, I suppose."

"Keep your eyes governed. She is death to any man that would act on desire for her, monk. Valraphim take care not to call her by her first name, so as to deflect familiarity. I hope you will not hold it against her. She lost her brothers to the deep world and has been searching for them ever since. She is a fierce fighter, a single-hearted paladin. Doom to any foe...and also someone who must learn mercy."

"What great mystery are they, women...so like men, but so unlike.

"You speak as men do. You are a man, but also a true monk and not a bloodless one. Take heed, women are both better and worse than men. Be wary of her stern heart. You must lead her and not be led by her. After that monkey-trial she contrived, she ordered them shackle Drocwolf and had him gagged so that he could not give commands in his commanding voice. Then they strung up the remaining stag carcass and prepared to cook more venison.

When the time came for rest, such a heavy sense of guilt lay upon them all, recalling the suffering of the animal for all the help it had given us, that they could not sleep with the thought of what they had done. So disgruntled they left the stag's head hanging there. Cruel was their word; that I myself consume it to survive. They departed and would not say whither they were faring. I will not go after them.

Pray lest the *drakodemon* or some other spirit lead them even further astray. That I do fear. And also I fear for myself, having no quest, that without friends, without any laughs, out of boredom I might fall asleep while crossing over to the next patch of mushrooms, not awakening for a thousand years. It has happened to other gnomes you know."

"They actually butchered the sacred stag? What fools. *It is a terrible thing to fall into the hands of the living God*! How, gnome, will you free yourself from such a mastery of situation as this?"

"Snowflakes sometimes drop softly through the aerial tower into this area of forest-shrooms. I have been working on a spell of lightness, a rare gnome-trick that will cause me to be light as a snowflake; in this magical mode I could pass through a yowndrift, when the flakes swirl clockwise. To prepare will take many more weeks; to obtain the concentration of mind, and likelihood spell failure I calculate will be 89.22%, aye, 'tis a most slim prayer; but as you can see, options are running out. So you must go; you can do nothing here. You must continue to work in secret as your Abbot has bid. Speak to no one of this. I fear that the spirit if iniquity has already had an influence among the monks, as you have described."

"Arcavir, for you, and the Burgundy Knight: I translated a fair portion of text, the introductory sections, where is found the lore of the first age, the origin of the *drakodemon*, and the rebellions of the giants. I will find what is needed soon. Quoted extensively are the sacred Ammouric scrolls as well as excerpts from, well, it seems impossible, your own handbook?"

"That is a work of my own observations and excavations which I collected hundreds of years ago. I cannot well remember back that far...back in the early years, when I journeyed the furthlands with Duke Ikonn, Petrozian the Thick, and Elkomenon Archmage[36] of Nystol. It has

---

[36] *Elkomenon*: the first Mage, who built the first chemical laboratory and even erected an observatory on Nyzium where he eventually developed the triadic system of magic concerned with statics. The facilities were destroyed by an earthquake in the year⋯ well, it is not known in certitude, but perhaps nigh 690 years before the fall. Another history says that his towers were magically transfered to Whilom and later became Whitehaven. His Order of Mages did indeed continue until the end, but they were few indeed. The "wise" Archmage Elkomenon out-lived his disciples, but he was stunned by the beauty and songs of the fair lady Lazaria whom he met when he accompanied Duke Ikonn. The Duke, rightly guessing her character, ignored her. But the Mage would risk his life to see her and

been copied and published numerous times. But as centuries passed, I myself never came across any copies. When at last I did find a copy, I could not even read my own writing anymore. My memory of such old Latin was too faded.

"Others have found the *Enchiridion* useful in their researches and quoted from it, especially the lore keepers who compiled *The Black Books*. That particular volume is precious, for not only did the compilers include selections from my own work, but also the histories of the original furth-tribes left by the Outhapians. But tell me, and this is critical, have you learned anything on the mystery of iniquity?"

"I have learned little," I replied, "for I do not even think the ancients themselves could foresee how the conspiracy of evil was outlasting them. Heaven alone can save us. I did have a dream."

"A dream...? What sort of dream? Was it a dream dripped like dew from Heaven? "

"I do not glean your meaning."

"Was it from God? Did you have *timor* during the dream, or shortly thereafter? Were you filled with a sense of dread?"

"The dream had to do with the terrible end of the Whitehawk kingdoms. It stirred in me a dreadful weeping. "

"Then it was most likely from Heaven high-above. Had it first caused you delight, I would guess it from Hell. Tell me what you saw."

"I saw a drawing in a book... " Jacob said, "the devil's black claw-hand holding a scroll, and it was burning. Smoke issued upwards and covered the sky. Words flew about, and locusts came out from the pit. No sunlight could pass through the bibulous clouds *darfurque*."

"Hmmm, the devil's black hand...this dream has some import upon all these things that have transpired. The unsleeping devil is at work in these events for sure...he plots the extinction of the royal Maceonid dynasty. Your dream...it causes me to recall some things. Is it not prophesied by Our Lord himself, in his own words, *In those days the Sun shall be obscured*?

"Look to the meaning of this, for it has some immediate illumination on this question. When the tower-city Nystol burned, the smoke from the holocaust continued. The murky smoke from the incinerating books and magical scrolls billowed out as from some hellish volcano, and so great an inferno it was that the clouds shrouded the skies of all the continent. As far away as Mahanaxar and Orusca the celestial dome was reported obscured with swags of black smoke from the burning *bzebus* leaves. For three days and nights of near complete darkness all the Whitehawk shuddered in fear, and many said that the great and terrible end had come."

---

hear her songs. Thence the old man searched the earth seeking the "globus of all" in hopes to win her admiration. He died of unrequited love, miserably alone on a desert island, or according to Zuphagen and the poet Sodd Bloodman, he metamorphosized into a cicada. Maragald spoke of Lazaria as "a type of the Harlot of Babylon."

"The Sun is still shining quite brightly in the sky today. We must not be '*in those days*.' "

"You are cleverer than that, grandiosus," warned the gnome. "That is not the Sun about which Our Lord speaks in his prophecy."

"I know of no other Sun."

"Must I explain each thing to you? ....What does the Sun do?"

"It lights up the world."

"And who is it saying "*I am the light of the World*?"

"Our Lord and Savior...but we are not pagans, We do not worship the Sun. He is 'the Sun?'"

The gnome rolled his eyes on account of my density.

"Simpleton! It is his sign, a message, the message of God's Light and Truth that gives illumination to men, who otherwise would be in the murk of ignorance. It is the heavenly light of the gospel shining upon our earthly souls."

"So if the Sun is the gospel, lighting up the world, then what is the Smoke?"

"—The breath of the old dragon, the Smoke of the Satan, that blocks out the Light... "

"But how does this knowledge avail us? This grand contest between God and the devil is well known."

"Then we must think deeper. We know that the Messiah indicated His message of Truth by Light and the Sun, the gospel. You said you saw words flying about in bibulous smoke? "

"Yes," said Jacob, mystified. "...words with wings, and nasty locusts, as in the book of St. John's *Apocalypse*."

The gnome rubbed his beard. "Words with wings...and the devil's claw-hand holding a scroll... a scroll indicates communication of some sort. This must have to do with certain deceptive writings, words that block the Light, perhaps the Light of the gospel...unholy verses and false philosophies do this, for counterfeit light confuses even the brainiest men, aye, that is what is indicated to you. This Darkness would steal the precious knowledge on who is God, that God is love, the source of goodness and mercy, and eternal life. Knowledge on the divine nature of Christ illuminates souls; illuminates minds, cultures, and even entire nations, just as the Sun lights up the world. The Sun connotes The Word incarnate...Your dream has the Sun obscured by dark smoke, that is, Truth dimmed by deceit...and heresies —the locusts."

"There is one other thing that I remember now...the claw-hand was in the hem of a monk's sleeve. Does this mean that, may God forbid, I will do the harmwork of the Devil?"

"No...do not think like that. Other monks are up to no good—whom you should watch. The dream is a calling for you to be cognizant of the old enemy and all the dragon-smoke that obscures the minds of men. Heaven would have you muster the true monks against this...but I have said too much. My days are close on being ended; you must yourself mind to where these things tend, but youth is still with you, so I help you. Still, a monk should have known.

"Remember that there is a key of interpretation to be used in order to unlock the mysteries of divine communication. I have given you this key.

"Do not forget it. Did not Anherm teach you? Go now. It is time. I will speak with you no more in the terrestrial sphere. I must now rush to the next patch and return to the timeless caves to seek the gnome-horde."

"Then I too must return back at once, to make things right again in the monastery."

"No, Brother Jacob, they will capture you. You must accomplish what you set out to do. I see that you are no longer a boy. Even so, you alone, a mere human, cannot make things right. Trust thou the mighty Lord, He can make things right when men resolve to obey his law. Do not return to the monastery. The Sheriff of Whilom has arrested the Ammouric cavaliers and you can count no longer on the Abbot's protection. Look at me; I tried to make things right in my eyes. I used the bow against Grimble. I tried to force him to submit. The Lord's peace does not employ the bow against a comrade. Before that the Valraphim would have feared any mutiny as something unthinkable. Had I restrained my own justice, then Stormraker and the others could not have justified in their hearts what they have now done to me, and the great endeavor would not have been jeopardized."

"The Sheriff has arrested the knights? How can that be? On what account?" I asked, on my knees. "Will he detain them in the dungeon? Why has he done this? "

"These things are unknown --as to why. I can only see in a partial way things from afar, and only present developments. Of the future I know little. Above all remember, force cannot win anyone to God. I should never have thought so highly of human brilliance, and so little of God's power."

Many other things the gnome disclosed to the monk, of which here I cannot all recount. I promised him a monk's prayers. In turn the Arcavir assured him not of his escape and safety, but instead spoke of his end.

"You, Jacob Magister, are the last mortal with whom I speak in this world-age. Some long slumber will soon take me, being stuck here with little to do, A gnomish snooze of a thousand years will at last set in and I will drift away. Farewell, and if you ever get time, publish that handbook."

J acob traveled onward through the Timberhills. a   clandestine knight.

"...when at last I finally arrived in the town and the little shanties by the shore at my uncle's residence, I learned that my uncle was away at sea, the house at loose ends. I went about the town asking and talked with other sailors. The home was empty as usual, they said, for he was often at sea many moons. So I lodged there and worked at the Friendly Horse Inn, lugging around bombards of ale for ever thirsty lumberjacks and minding them of their many pints and quarts. It was a rough place, with sailors and miners separating into gangs and often getting tanked and involved in unseemly brawls.Three establishments did business in town. The Flappers was miners' turf; whereas in the Sea-Giant's Hall sailing-crews that ply the Vastess Sea were wont to frequent. The Friendly Horse Inn was aligned with neither. When a knight-errant, or the sheriff, or the regional Edolunt Rangers were come to town, they would be expected to visit to the Friendly Horse Inn. In this way they would steer off the constant round of rowdy sailors or mining crews just come in with several days to kill.

Almost every night there was a fight somewhere in town. The place had become rather lawless and could not enjoy fitting governace without stern measure, and no stern sheriff lasted long.

Only a knight has the right to bear arms, but in this town it was as the law never existed and everyone carried some weapon, be it a dagger, a sword, or even an axe. There was custom in place of laws: just be polite and no one gets hurt. A most imperfect remedy.

Within a few weeks I had spent all the crizets with which Abbot and Maragald had loaded me. Too much did I delight in freedom and independence, having known its absence during my boy-years in the monastery. Nearly all my chinkers on sundry delights I squandered, especially tipsy cakes, draughts of ale, fine clothes, a fancy cap that I never wore, and a few other trinkets. I sometimes wondered over the Ammouric Knights or the monastery on occasion, but I learned to mull other, less troubling things.

Every day I went about town and asked wayfarers if on the road they had passed certain knights, whom I described in detail. Some said "aye," or that they had heard how cavaliers had been jailed in Whilom; others claimed to have seen the knight's tents in the forest just the past days. Which account was true?

I soon needed more work to support myself. Every day that passed my concerns for the knights, my legal problems and the quest diminished. What began to increase was my desire, even need, for gold. With enough gold I could pay to run my uncle's property, and pay any debts, avoid slavery. I began to count my earnings. It was not enough."

Brothers, need we go into any length describing the extremity of banalities and lowly living that the wandering monk experienced in the big town, Hordingbay? Jacob had heard of that part of the island where all the ships arrive loaded with goods from the continent. The lanes are ever busy with the hustle of wealthy nobles and burghers, or the mill or mine owners, and the decadent and drunken clerics; or carousing knights, free lances in their dusky armour purchased from the black market, much different than the quest-knights. These worldly ones go about the streets seeking entertainments from cunning actors, glamorous whores, clever bards or dreamy poetasters.

The monk resists the temptation to become like them. He can only find work at the Sea-Giant's Hall, a local drinking establishment, but his was a wretched task hauling waste and it is better not to bother mentioning details. It involves quite a great deal of nasty odors....and so, that monk's humility improved. To those who have understanding; such is the providential help for those who become "haters of discipline." *Gloria in excelsis Deo*!

There is a church in that town, but few have anything to do with it. It is a nearly abandoned place. The sight of it all empty reminded the monk of that dream again, and of the prophecy, the prophecy which the gnome interpreted, the prophecy from the lips of Lord God himself: *In those days the Sun shall be darkened* ...This means the gospel will be obscured, no longer understood by common men. Many study the scriptures, but some propose fictional things on the divine science and use the scriptures to their own purpose, having no fear of God, hence the obscuring smoke."

An old deaf and mute deacon, meaning to be faithful to the end, would remain to tend the place. The priest of the church had run off after some fair maiden, and is said to spend his days in town in her apartment.

The long-journeying knights never did reconnoiter. A week or so passed. Some mishap must have interfered with plans, as Kruth had seen.

"The knights would not have just forgotten me. The local authority must not have released them from the jail. How is that possible? To arrest them is an understandable mistake, but then not to obey the Abbot or the King and free them at once? I decided to bide where I was, at least as long as I could.

More days passed. I repented of my lack of discipline and tried to return to a predictable monastic schedule. But it was nothing like that blessed Whitehaven."

Here Jacob always had to fend for himself to cook his own food, being untrained; and could neither afford beer nor wine. Perhaps you think, "poor man; he had to fend for himself. It serves him right." I do not take issue with that judgement. But there was something even more troubling. Although, as usual, the monk practiced discipline and awoke early to say whispering prayers; there was no book of prayers, no psalter, to check. Also, whenever he resumed his guardian-monk practice, as usual, there was none with which to practice sparring in the open-hand combat, or judge movement with the quarterstaff.

He had to teach himself to wield Witchbane, but he knew that his proposed technique was far from sufficient, a guess too dangerous to rely on. The quarterstaff Reckoning was his weapon of choice. No, the staff was not a chivalric weapon, but such ideals and fashion mean less in the toil of deadly combat. So he ate his poorly prepared meals, and said his psalter, and practiced his staff technique.

"Now I was longing to return to the monastic way. I was convinced that I was thoroughly a monk, albeit a chivalric and errant one. Sometimes the new monks complain over the soup or barley bread (novices, you know, are often drawn from the noble families; the highly pampered). So Abbot makes them say it: "The monk eats what is put before him." I tried not to complain. Even if all there is to be had slop for daily fare is porrager. What fine victuals did our Lord enjoy in his earthly ministry? Not much; fish and bread sayeth the gospels. Simplicity without complaint is a monk's way.

I had been daft, or immature, not having appreciated the monastic life. I wanted out of the monastery, aye; but what a crummy exchange! Well, on the other hand, there was Maragald's warning. Escape the wicked monks— so I suppose this exile was a blessing in disguise.

Such reflections and but a limping faith in God's plan made things little easier. For example, the study of *The Black Book*: there was no library in town with foreign dictionaries to consult. The monastery library on the other hand had several dictionaries; none too shabby. Indeed, what a miserable, dangerous, and mind-numbing life I had taken up, like that of a bird out of his cage!

When I was working in the taverns, the routine involved mockery and even beatings. This was for being a habit-wearing monk. I became the subject of drunkard's songs as I scrubbed the floors. Many regulars supposed that in wearing the cloth a monk cannot strike back unless countering some evil minion. These bullies were just badly-bred yeomen. Both customers and other workers roughed me up. But I refused to wear townsmen clothes. On several occasions out of frustration I did not wear my habit, and then, well, I hit back, and sometimes hard. I earned a reputation and became feared. May the Lord forgive me.

Most of those bullies went down at once, struck unconscious by my single blow. Everyone laughed. After a while I gained noteriety and made extra coin as a bouncer. However I could not sleep well at night, being a betrayer of the peaceful Lamb for such acts.

So the monk would never again leave off the frock. Now earnestly I longed for what I had lost; now exile was truly painful. There was some joy and consolation from Heaven even in that, however.

With beatings endured, and a solitary life of no books but the manuals Guy of Xaragia and the *Black Book*, that poor daily fare, God in his mercy was preparing me." The wayward monk has described only a small portion of the banal misery in the wicked city. He has accepted what is written; that *we must undergo many hardships if we wish to enter the Kingdom Heaven*. "Many," brothers, it says "many," Not several, not one or two; "many."

So that was by no means the end of tribulations to be endured in the wicked city, brothers. The Almighty now saw fit to send his just and merciful chastisement upon us all:

The Red Death, hooded and with scythe, arrived at Hordingbay.

It was in the month of Calduin, my friends, that I found myself in a state even more wretched than the former. The incarnadine plague takes not just the wicked, and those who indulge in what is carnal, what is forbidden, (the brothels in town were always busy). The plague may call away the innocent as well, children and pious elderly. In this life the innocent pay for the guilty. Death makes no distinction. Folk say "Men of the cloth the Red Death will not touch, for they are immune from such contagions." How far do they miss the mark. Not only did many good Christians die, but even the priest and the old deacon were spared not. In the end the plague took a third of the population.

I was among the first to come down with it, perhaps having contracted it on the way to the tavern. Bloody tears trickled from my eyes. I could barely see. Chivalric Ammouri should otherwise be immune to pestilences, according to Guy of Xaragia, but the good Lord would use it to reveal something.

For weeks I lay in my bed awaiting the end, my skin bespeckled with *maegolot* sores in the shape of Hellopian ivy, my mouth dried like the red desert of the South, my eyes jiggling in their sockets, my head exploding. I prayed for death.

There was a pious Ammouric burgher in town, a successful fishmonger and his family, who, having learned of my plight, understood I was one of the monks of Whitehaven. I was the last man of the cloth left alive in Hordingbay. He came to my uncle's house to care for me, hoping that he might save me and win the prayers of a monk for his family, a rare thing indeed.

His wife even dared the contagion to supply me special fare on occasion when my stomach could take it. One day they arrived together bringing a dish of meat and potatoes.

It was a rather strange looking reddish meat that seemed to glisten. I inquired upon it. They claimed that it was soaked in medicine which might heal me. Every citizen who had contracted the incarnadine plague, with the mere tasting of it, recovered almost immediately. After hearing that, little more persuasion was needed. The mystery meat I cut up right away and chased it down with some wine. I quickly passed out.

I did not recover. In fact the Red Death answered my prayer and called upon me, his ownself appearing before me, wearing a red cowl. His face hooded in shadow, he said, "Come with me now, Brother Jacob of Whitehaven. Lo, your hour of passage from this existance has arrived."

I spoke frankly to him. "Hail, crimson angel," I said. "Please do excuse me. I need more time to obtain a bag of coin for you as tribute, wherefore to win your dismissal."

"What did you say? You are a monk. More so than others, you should know that no amount of coin or treasures can persuade Death's angel from his duty. Your hour has arrived. Now, I say, come."

My hour indeed has NOT arrived." I said, defiant as usual. "This I know as a certitude. The Most High decreed that I must fulfill my mission here in the terrestrial realm, this darkness visible, before my spirit is conducted to its abode beyond."

"What can you show, monk, as sureity, were I to make exception for such a claim?" he asked.

I reached over and took up the Red Cowl of Carmakhen and, with the little strength I had, tied it on. "Not to prove anything to the likes of you, macabre angel, you who once fancied yourself all-powerful, but so that you will not complain: behold this relic, a kind of mirror as proof. Consider it the sign that Heaven prepared. Believe you me, I am more than willing to go with you. An end of earthly misery is a friend to me, a doorway to the life eternal, and your path is finality to the travail of this existance, this valley of tears, which, were it an unending state, would be a curse unimaginable."

"Your sureity and proof I accept," he said. "You have learned. My visitation therefore will be postponed for another day. Go with God, and may grace see you fulfill that task which has been assigned you."

After two weeks my feverish condition slakened and the pestilence abated.

Later I thanked the fishmonger and promised him and his family my prayers, but I questioned him regarding the strange meat that he and his wife had provided. It clearly had only fed my fever and not prevented me from coming close to death, whereas for all others its healing came immediately. I demanded truth from him. He answered.

"When our priest expired with his concubine, verily in her bedchamber, the faithful soon realized that, sinner though he was, no other man of the cloth was left in town safe to beseech God with official prayers or provide last rites.

"Someone had heard of a warlock passing through the area, a priest of the dragon, who had a cure for the incarnadine plague. The mayor invited him here and he immediately came. He put up shop, and many that were sick were brought to him and partook of "the sacrificial meat" and "magic wine," and were healed within the hour. He left with much gold. I did not wish to tell you because you are a monk and I knew that you would refuse such a magical medicine."

Of course I forgave him this indiscretion, but also did I rebuke him, informing him that the meat may have been cut from a human sacrifice, for the idolaters of Galadif are cannibals. Some other good Christians in town had refused to partake of it and died anyway. Let them be an example for us. "The One True God will not brook a mixing of rites and worship with those of lesser gods. We do not eat meat sacrificed to idols."

What intrigued me over the whole thing was that somehow, even with all my failings as a monk, the dragon-magic had no effect on me. Later, doing some research in Guy of Xaragia, I read, in the section on monks, that monks have a kind of immunity from magic.

For Christian monks this is even more so the case. Not only have we immunity from narcoleptic spells, beguiling, charm, hypnotic spells and arcane suggestion, but from all other baneful magic: hexes, negations, illusions, morphings, even from some elemental combat spells. Granted, if a monster or demon is summoned I must still fight the thing...but...think...immunity from all magic: this means the most powerful of magic-users should not prevail against me.

Of course there is one catch. The immunity also counts against any helping magic placed upon a monk for boon as well, such as durability, added power, intelligence, vitality, resistances, bestowals or healing. I had actually been immune to the healing of that the glistening pagan meat.

It is for the better anyway. The healing of such magics is not of God, and is surface only, not permanent. Of those plague victims who partook, most were ill again within a few days, and many did not recover.

My new consciousness of monastic fortitude and immunities, as well as vulnerabilities, meant that God expected much from me, for *to whom much is given much is expected*. So I was ready, but like most souls, slow to act. God would use others to goad me...after all, according to the adept Tien Joshur, the first rule of campaigning monks is never to quest....alone.

"If some things in this life can be proposed as certitudes, all men do admit these: "death and taxation." Let those who are wise add another thing: "trouble."

Morpheus Memnos

XX   *The Kitchen Intrusion*

"Trouble" was on the way to Jacob Magister.

Rolled within a fuzzy blanket he was cozy and asleep, resting from that crucible the plague, He found perfect somnulence within the lodgings of his uncle's home. The embers of the hearth were smoldering in the dark.

At some nocturnal point he was no longer dreaming his usual dreams and sleep was leaving little by little. Some sound was waking him. Unexpected noises came from the kitchen upstairs. There should have been nothing of noises or fuss at that hour of night; after all, he was the only soul in the house.

Now this ruckus put him in consternation. Had his uncle returned? Had sea-raiders broken in? Someone or something was firing up the stove and cooking. Pots were banged about, there was a clanging of spoons and knives.

Alarmed at the disturbance, the errant monk sat up. He shook off sleep and emerged like Lazarus from that subterraneous den of mortal slumber. Keeping himself wrapped in his blanket he navigated the dark. A draft of cool and salty marine air streamed in. He took careful steps up the stairs towards the pantry.

In the kitchen lamps were lit and light filtered through the cracks in the door. There was a prattling of several voices, and laughs as well; bags torn open, and the wood being stacked. A most disturbing conversation transpired next, of each word that Jacob accounts:

"Someone said, "Any eggs here?"

"I'll go out and take a look-see," answered another.

The door was closed. I could not see who was there. No doubt robbers had entered the house and were devouring my uncle's stores. Should I rush into the kitchen to confront them? How many were there? Should I hazard to take them on? Arm myself or surrender? Surely if I attacked they would slay me or cut out my tongue so that I could not testify against them. Should I hide?"

My uncle's name was spoken; mentioned with joviality. Whoever they were, they knew my uncle, and they had some kind of fellowship with him. I went near and peeked into the kitchen door to espy them.

A worrisome sight: it was a valraph standing on the countertop, foraging through the cupboards.

"Here is cinnamon, and salt for the eggs!" he said with glee. He happened to look toward where I was espying through the crack in the door. "Oh look, there's our Jacob Magister, the spry fellow."

At this sight I was incredulous, and becoming rather ornery as well at their careless attitude. Now detected, I yielded up my hiding place. I opened the door and entered the kitchen to my "old friends". With the kitchen and everything now in full view, the most troubling sight of all: The contingent of "Valraphim" had come to disturb the little peace my life had recently acquired. There stood Buckbar, frying up the fatty bacon, toast, and drinking milk.

"What are you doing?!" I asked them all with astounded indignation. "What is this? How did you discover I was here?! What is going on?!"

All paused their rummaging. They looked over at me, and still they were unconcerned and still chewing on the cakes that they had been stuffing into their mouths. Stormraker suddenly walked in carrying the eggs from outside, where the chicken coop was kept. She halted and looked directly at me, and realized what was going on. She held the stolen eggs in view···shameless.

"Get dressed and packed!" she barked her order to me. "And hurry," she added, "there be not much time before first light to make trek to the next place."

"What?" I responded. "Is this some clever jesting? Who exactly do you imagine you all are? Do you fancy that you are sheriffs, that you may barge in and raid my cupboards!"

"There's no time for explanations," Stormraker announced, "we travelers are always looking for some hearty fare ...you must know that...and we know your uncle···but also we would have someone bookwise, a translator of Latin, for many mysteries are recorded in that tongue. You will suffice, and so you will come along. Now get going; get packed! You'll get the cold shoulder o' meat before we go...and the rest of your square to take along....better treated than any other hostage, you are."

"Come along? –and to where? Pray tell."

Stormraker did not answer, but proceeded to cook up the eggs. Several uneasy moments went by, with the others hush, and it seemed that she was thinking deeply on some dreadful answer. Finally "the hearty fare" she had prepared for herself was cooked. Nor did she invite me to join in consumming my goods. She gazed with lazy eyes and at last answered.

"—to dangerous places,..hidden lands beneath the earth..places where the wind does not blow. You will know more soon. But now I and these stalwarts are gutfoundered fierce, and would eat, not talk. Did you fetch any pepper, Buckbar?"

"There's a bit left in this canister here, captain," replied Buckbar, grinning at the quarrelsome frowns.

"I think it's no plan. No one has sent you. You act under no authority. I am far from agreeable," Why was I even humouring them with a counter argument? I continued with irritation. "You can't just dance in here and take over! I must attend to many things. I am making something of myself! Besides, you are a woman, Phaedra Stormraker, that at least I have learned!"

"Oh valraphs, did the monk not even notice that before? Of course not, he is a monk. Do you think it dishonourable to obey a woman? Ask these valraphs if it makes any difference. What you think doesn't matter." But Stormraker had not even doffed her helmet to dine, for she was secretely untrusting even with her own men. "You are by law hostage of this company now. These Valraphs obey me; I am in charge and now press you into our service and noble cause. If you take it agreeably, things will go well for you. Try to escape...you will end up dead "as the law requireth." Don't force me to pull you around with a rope!"

I turned and looked at Drocwolf. How could I better express bewilderment? "Drocwolf, have you allowed this woman to usurp your command?" I could not believe it. The now ex-master of elfbeards Drocwolf did turn to catch my glance with his one patch and one eye, and nothing he said.

"We constrained Drocwolf not to speak," Stormraker explained. "according to code, for his mutinous complicity with Kruthendel. If he does speak, for anything other than some emergency, then back he goes gagged and into strict bonds. "

"This is downright a brutal arrangement!" I cried.

"This is the Valraphim!" bellowed Buckbar in a defiant retort. "The woman is the best commander anywhere to be had. Get used to it monk! " Drocwolf looked up again, and glared at Phaedra.

"You are out of your depth, Stormrake," Drocwolf said, a frown not so hidden beneath his beard.

"Buckbar and Corydon, remind the gallant captain how chains feel." Buckbar and Corydon immediately dropped their rummaging to obey Stormraker and hauled out from the baggage iron shackles for Drocwolf.

"The only reason I remain with you mutineers," said Drocwolf as they prepared the locket, "is to see to it that you cannot hurt yourselves or others; otherwise, know that these frail irons cannot hold me." Drocwolf offered his wrists while Buckbar and Corydon bound him and locked it. "Storm, you are not ready for this command; I warn you to cease this."

"Now hark this all ye," announced Stormraker, "once again you see that it is Drocwolf who is defiant against the lawful authority of the Valraphim, and once again I have put down another attempted mutiny. Corydon, guard the captain."

Stormraker and Drocwolf eyed each other with hot animosity. "You do not have the nerve, Stormrake, to lead these valraphs to glorious victory against the black-hearted bolg and hateful horgrim. We have been at war with the hobgoblins for eight centuries, and many lords far greater than you have ended shamefully in gob-infested keeps."

"At least my nerves have not left me unhinged, Drocwolf," Stormraker countered. "For our obsession you can thank Kruth your master, since like a pestilence it spread to us! I calculated how you were there with us too, when so many of our companions fell because of his exalted ideals, his obsession; but now one must wonder and doubt, for it seems you were not there and did not see it with your own eye, else the underworld fumes got to your brain. But you were there indeed, and even you, "Captain," the facts compel. Admit that my perception be squarely accurate. So we acted according twas hazarded us, and at last as lawful Valraphim we made a stand against a tyrannical command. We did what be right by the book, honestly read."

The elfbeards proceeded to gag noble Drocwolf.

"And do you acheive now what is honest, raiding the larder of a commoner and taking hostages, gagging Drocwolf, an honoured veteran?" I snapped. "He has the protection of law."

"We must do what is needful to do. The Valraphim voted for me to have charge of this party. It would be better were you to comply and not doubt my goodwill, lest you too end up 'gainst the law's smiting-edge as did Kruth. Enough then of much talk. Go on, get yourself ready, Jacob, ready to enter into the everdark world. We make ship by dawn," Stormraker continued and looked up at the night through the window hole, ". . . tonight's the night; look, the moon be pale and dead."

"Ship?" asked Buckbar. "What mean ye? We are not going back through the giant's stones like we came out?"

"You half-wit, Buckbar...it is clear enough that I, not any other, have charge o' this resolute company···and especially clear for you, Jacob. Others, like Buckbar here, cannot help let everything that lawless Kruth taught slip from their minds. Here again is reason: the cromlechs, like those stones standing back on that Tor of the Timberhills, passage for fairy, and that's the place we came through, out from under the earth. They are not for human kind; in fact, had we taken you, Jacob, and had you entered those portals, the magic would have crushed you. Kruth did mention that to you. Men surely can hew tunnels and explore grottos, but no living mortal can go so deep as to enter into the old tract of hell, into the intermundian caverns, the fourth world."

An unhealthy grin came across Phaedra's face, as she enjoyed describing what I must endure. "There's only one way for mortal seed to do that; it's called a sort of mystical warp, and it entails floating down the river Alph, which the Greeks say flows from Stygian waters, a dangerous, perhaps painful thing indeed, nearest death itself."

"But we have no ship, Stormrake," said Buckbar, baffled.

"Then we must...kindly borrow...one," she said.

"What?! Hoist a ship? Are ye mad?!" I cried.

"We have a pinch of madness...for we are the Valraphim! A many-masted ship is the only way we might sail the Vastess Ocean-sea and reach the Eluvigar waterway. Daufin here is an old hand, you know; they'll never know what happened to their ship."

"Why not just hire a ship? "

"Men will refuse to raise sails with us elf-kin. We are bad omen . . . but don't you see; makin' off with a major ship will be a rum-fun game! Why look so worried?...there is no other way!"

"Kruth could have found another way, but you left 'im in the lurch," I growled.

Then Buckbar, his belly bloated with food, now went to sharpening an axehead, and ineptly added, "I don't think we can return the ship we "borrow," Stormrake. How later get it back up from th—? "

"Buckbar Lancelas, you shroom-spawn! Keep sharpening axeheads and leave me to the noodle-work. Now, I have explained everything, brother Jacob, according to law, and I didn't have to; but I almost take kindly to you, so you are in the know. Just remember that you have no options; so make thou ready, groaker....and let me eat..."

She devoured more eggs, glaring at me. It didn't help at all that her eyes were lovely, (whereas before I had mistook them as elfish). She was a warrior. I didn't want a fight, but I thought it unwise that Phaedra Stormraker would lead, not because she was a woman, but because she had such sternness. Even so, my goal was to make such a pilgrimage, to be done with idle days. Stormraker was someone going through some sort of a change. I stared at her as I tried to remember the passage.

"You gaze at me for an answer." she said. "So I shall tell you."

She said that had always been lawful, and she didn't care over disputing it. Our only interest should be the exact fulfillment of every thing which authority warrants. Whether good or evil results in fulfilling law, that has little value. It is merely narrow human judgement. Such results are mere passing anyway, she said. To act lawfully is better than to act by ones own esteem of what's good. Even to accept and execute an unjust law is better, and no rebellion is tolerated, since without authority no law could warrant following. Without lawful right it is better to have never been born. The keeping of the law and codes make the Valraphim honest. "But something happened back there, in those Timberhills," she said. "After Grimble's madness, I realized something. Soldiers may carry out every order, but they are not free from judgement. They may not claim that they only did what they were told. That is a truth which I do not like. It is easier the way it was before. Just to do what we know we have been ordered. Now I am the commander and no one advises me what is right. That's another reason we need you to help us."

"You may not enjoy such help." I warned. Instead of debating more I went and did what she commanded and packed a few things, including *The Black Book*, for it seemed I had little choice anyway. I was vowed as a knight to the quest, and here, all of a sudden, was a way to enter the wars and learn the whereabouts of the staff, although I could not imagine any good would come from a quest so tainted with theft of a ship. Abbot had forbidden any evil deed even if some magnificent good should come of it.

How could I possibly survive? The knights who were to teach me the precise skills of knighthood would not do so. Nevertheless, I donned armour, and the scarlet cowl, and the chain armour that the Burgundy Knight had bequeathed to me. Just to show them. I girded, also put on my scapular over the armour, just as the orders of the cross had done in the Wars of the Veil. I slung the mighty sword Witchbane on my side and placed over my head the Ammouric great helm.

I showed again before the gluttonizing party, standing in full Ammouric equipage of the chivalric order.

Phaedra Stormraker had been sipping a flagon of wine from our stores. She stopped mid-swallowing. They were astounded, perhaps even fearful. The muffins that they had been stuffing crumbled from lips. Corydon, *semi-inebriatus*, even set his hand on his sword pommel, unsure of who was standing there in the helmet or what was about to happen. Perhaps I could have driven them out, but no, I wanted to go.

They said nothing at first, but Stormraker at last spoke.

"What's this now? Snow White transformed?!"

The elfbeards broke out in laughter, but I stood there hush, grim, wearing the helmet, the dread of a warrior's speechless stare. The laughter died down; for I said nothing in reply, and it spooked them, a prolonged, uneasy silence and still readiness. Afterward I finally spoke.

"That mirth will savor little when in payment for it you feel the might of this mailed fist." I said.

"Hearty words..." she said, smiling. "Did you hoist the siege-skin of an Ammouric knight? Take his war goods? I suppose that was brave enough. Good then, try to live up to the image. "

"I require fair share of any gold crizets justly seized from the lairs of gobs and monstrous beasts, and dragon hordes. I am honestly a knight, Phaedra Stormrake. Be ye all mindful of that."

She stared at me, puzzled.

"Smacks more a 'knight o' the highway,' I would say," said Corydon wryly, now interested.

"We press you into our service...." said Phaedra "but so that you will be a help and not a hindrance, you may take fairly divied loot, provided you fight well. How in all Dis are you a knight, you monkling? "

"They indeed knighted me, in the monastery. The Burgundy Knight wanted legacy, being the rightful crown of another land. Shortly thereafter he passed into the next world."

"Hmmm...and it is lawful? You can fight like a knight?"

"Trained hands enough to be a deadly hazard in pitched battle," I replied. "with my quarterstaff. . .or naked sword if need be. Believe you me."

"We shall see, but until I mark that you have the onslaught of a knight, don't wait for me to call you 'Sir Jacob.'"

Phaedra smiled. The others chuckled, well satisfied, together.

"—comin' from you it would be scant honour," I replied sharply. "By the name Sir Hortezan of Whitehaven they dubbed me. Come, if you dare, let us join cause and strike out against common foes, but expect me not to play the hostage."

"You have done well to accept this enterprise. It is one of great pitch and moment. We will treat you honourably as a soldier, but we will not honour you. Remember that you are a hostage and not one of the Valraphim. And mind you all thy present peril and need for us, for who has ever returned from the intermundane caverns?"

"Right...whatever you want, but now hear this: I'll not be party to any theft of a many-masted ship from worthy merchants, not from anyone, not if the world's fate depended on it. You can try to make me to cooperate, but you'll not get far. I'll let all my veins empty out before I commit so mean a sin, depriving men of their livelihood. No, I am also monk. We pay for our passage, or hire a captain."

"What quaint ethic..." remarked Buckbar, "a monk and a knight; and how will you fund such high morality, monk? Where's the coin for such a plan!? " He was glad that someone seemed more thoughtless and impractical than himself.

Phaedra was careful. She was encountering almost defiance; she did not respond. How could she reconcile stealing a ship with her reputation to lawfulness? She stared at me with strong eye, setting her countenance against me and biting her lip. So I spoke again:

"I am resolved on the purpose: the restoration of the right and the expulsion of the powers, demonic archons, from the earth. I have witnessed the bizarre rituals of the *drakodemon*, how they warped the mind of Grimble the dwarf; and heard of unholy power purchased with blood, I've seen also the wyrdding sorcery of Bannock; punishments of shadow and scathefire should come upon the earth for these transgressions. I am solicitous for the souls of my own brother monks. Unnatural entities have come to our doors and, I glean, have already seduced some of my own brother monks—even the worst of whom I wish only the best. So I might forfeit my life in such an expedition, and never again see my beloved Monastery of Whitehaven. Better to die attempting to root out the evil that plagues our land. It is so that souls can reform. And much better that, than lodge in comfort with wicked monks and become wicked like them, earning God's eternal wrath. You spoke right, Stormraker, we are made for greatness, not comfort. How great the shame of a believer who trusts more in his comforts than in the most high! And so I act with no protest, and yet also hope to alert you of God's displeasure, if not at your purpose, then rather at your proposed means: stealing a ship."

There was again no answer. But Corydon said, slurring, "Nice speeeech...can you put it into deeeeds? "

"There's a trove I remember mentioned," I said. "Of magic gold I heard Grimble tell, vaunting aloud, the same evening he took me prisoner in the Timberhills. He made out that I had come lookin' for it, and I never heard him treat of it thereafter. So it must be stowed on that isle, where all you were camped, hiding, guarding your own precious treasure."

"That be high tomfoolery, Jacob —Sir Hortezan rather. There be no treasure haul; Grimble were delirious, " replied Buckbar.

"Buckbar... " snapped Stormraker, irked and turning to leer at him, "Did I not charge you leave me for managing the talk! "

Buckbar went hush, and his lower lip drooped, like he had given away a secret.

"Buckbar is on the level; Grimble were not in his right mind, you know that. He fancied we were after hiding magic gold from 'im...not even the case. We were hiding *The Black Book*; that was the treasure he meant."

"Now you wag a dishonest tongue..." The accusal caused her to widen her pretty eyes incredulously. I explained my accusal.

"Grimble knew that there remain no word-wise scribes alive today that have wit enough for the book," I said. "He knew that even most Sorcerers considered the work worthless. But what he also knew (and what you others didn't know) is that within the silver-braced book someone had stored a folded chart, a chart drawn by the Eloniah, a thing which I in my translating labors have of recent come upon, folded within the leaves. The chart pinpoints the location of the foggy islet in the horseshoe lake, the place where I stumbled into all this misery, and the grouping of pines under which treasure is buried, charted tree by tree, rock by rock. The gnome made the map and signed his name so that no fake duplicates might replace it. But where are your signatures? After ye all buried it the first time, the Arcavir must have foreseen that you mountaineers would get drunk on berry-wine and try to unearth it, adorn yourselves with its magics, or essay to steal it for yourselves, or match fights over it. In such wise, I reckon, he re-buried it when you were asleep, in a new location. He corrected the map lest his memory fail him. I know that there's magic buried on that isle; so precious it is to you, you would just as soon starve than let it be spent. See, I am wise to your elfbeard's vain fault."

There was a long, guilty silence.

"Jacob, you are wise and quick..." acknowledged Phaedra, "save this: that the gnome buried it for his own hoarding!"

"We don't have nar wit o' that," said Buckbar. Phaedra glanced at Buckbar with mild disgust, and at me, guiltily.

"So how much is there?" I interrogated with confidence, having got the better.

"Enough to build a castle."

"Or purchase a ship and crew?" I returned. "Many ships...right, so we therefore shall give them the chart, and they shall sail us to the stygian river."

"It's not so simple, man," said Phaedra, grumbling in her warning voice. "First of all, where do we find a crew that will sail with elf-kin? We are *elphim*, and sailors dread us. Men call us baneful omen. You know how superstitious a crew can be, and some even yet fear the furious sea as it were an unholy power. How can we ask them sail beyond the straits of Furth, and into Vastess Ocean-sea? Many say the massy hand of some giant sea-devil has haul down uncounted ships to a watery grave. And if we do convince them to accept our offer to sail the perilous flood, and they ask unto what destination...can you imagine their refusal? Your answer will surely earn you whatever rebuke follows."

"Why say you that, Phaedra Stormrake? " I asked.

"A crew will never wreck their beloved ship, their livelihood, going into ice laden waters, and down dreadful rapids that lead into the dim places of the deeper world, there to be stranded below with no known waterway out. Nay, you must not only be purchasing their ship, but even their lives; for high chance their families will never see them again."

"Then we must hire a crew that consists of hands ready to risk all, of cantankerous men who have not much else to live for other than the exploration of the deep, the magic gold of pagan kings."

"They would not to fret so," said Buckbar, "if they could remember our heroical grace...it shall grant us victory again!" His eyes lit up with triumphant fire.

"Not so, Buckbar," said Daufin, as to correct.

"Of course we will," protested Buckbar ". . . as heroes...or what else mean you? "

"So, where are found such men for whom loss means little care?" asked Phaedra.

There was a silence. No answer came from any mind. Buckbar tried an answer: "Marine swords, the governor's warriors upon the sea, They are right daring men."

"They certainly will not leave the governor's service to sail with us," I replied.

After a rather long passage of time in thought, at last Phaedra Stormraker in disappointment gave another order.

"Buckbar, Corydon, untie the gagging from off Dhundrerlum," she said. Buckbar unknotted the uncomfortable gagging around Drocwolf.

"And the chains too..." said Drocwolf, lifting his bound wrists. Buckbar and Corydon took a few moments at this. Drocwolf added, "There do operate smugglers, ones who brave the sea as well and risk their life to ferry forbidden goods, warg-men upon the billows of the brooding deep. Not so dangerous these men, but lawless, aye. We might lose our skins pursuing business with them if the law catches us."

"Has not the Crown dealt with them by means of his swift fleet?" I asked. "and those kind long retired from their deeds, at least in these seas."

"For the most part··· the viking-lords of the western Furthreaches have all but vanished over the years," replied Drocwolf. "but some few remain to yet to make their living at sea."

There came another pensive moment in the talk. Corydon looked around at each of us.

"Daufin, champion of the Valraphim, is keeping something from us," Corydon said. "I can sense it. He knows much on this but will not say. You do know more, do you not, Daufin, on this roving kind? I remember you claiming before that you had once traded with the sea-wolves for that telescopic piece you always carry."

"I did have dealings with them, but I am in dread to say more, if they learn that their secret is betrayed. I know much on them, but you assure me that this knowledge never leave our company."

We nodded in assent.

"I know where a small pack of them lay hidden away," he continued. "All the western shores of the Furthreaches seldom ever the imperial navy patrols. There be grottos hid on this very isle, 'neath the western heights that descend straightway down to the sea. It is but a day's hike or so. From there a latter remnant of the smugglers yet operate."

"And how came you by this intelligence?" I asked.

"By the Master of Planets...!" a strange and new voice said. Turning about, none other than the infamous sorcerer himself I saw, standing there in the kitchen! He had, by what I deemed some devilry, concealed himself in a shadowed area in the pantry where our crates and barrels stood. He was all decked out in his arcane robes.

I immediately upheld the great Witchbane and stood ready, ready to fall if needed fighting against this foe. The valraphs, however, did nothing to forfend themselves. In fact, it dawned on me that they had known of his presence all along. One valraph cut himself a slice of sausage and looked about with amusement. The Master of Planets raised his hand toward my weapon and spoke strange words in some infernal and unknown tongue. I thought he must be casting some hell-borne spell.

"I should advise you on that sword you threaten with..." he said. "the famous brand Witchbane you wield. . . "

"Bannock," said Daufin, "this lad here is Jacob, the cavalier."

"Already some silent acquaintance we," replied the wizard.

"Say who and what are you?" I asked with warning tone. "Know that I am a monk of God and do not pale at such a surprise. Therefore yield, wizard!"

"Who and what am I? Strange you should require me answer both questions. You have said what—clearly a man. I may inform you honestly who, but first, lower your weapon lest I hurl a dread spell upon you."

"Such magics are no threat to me. Strong enough is my protection."

"I do not threaten with spells, I just use them without warning. If they are then no threat, deign to put away your weapon. Assuredly I shall not bother to hurl a ball of scathefire, by my word, although adversaries should always be wary of my dagger."

"A mere dagger to match against this lordly sword? Why invest in such a trinket?" I lowered my weapon, as he did not continue his threat.

"Think not slight of wizard's dagger, sir. I have used a knife-blade since the first, in times long before you were born. I even struck down a red dragon using this very metal once. Note the fine make. It has a lightweight skeleton design with holes even as for climbing ropes, but without compromising the Ataluran steel strength. See, it has a triple-serrated edge for manifold tasks as well. I have never needed to replace it."

"That is just shy of a laugh. Only someone pure, a Christian, can hope to slay an incarnadine dragon–"

"No, careful: but only *the pure* can subdue a dragon, mean you."

"So it seems among men." I admitted. "But Elves could do so in those early draconian ages."

"Know this, boy: in days of old, for us who were initiated into the schools of Nystol, the masters forbade any metal weapon –save a deadly dagger."

"To forbid all but a dagger seems an extreme prohibition..."

"That was law. But we hired mercenary swords. To fetch rare spell-components we descended into the endless caverns '*armed to the teeth with famous bronze and life-rending steel*' –the words of the grand epic, the famous rhyme, *the Bladetongue*, telling in sooth of many feats, no fiction, done by the heroes of yore."

"I know not the rhyme." I remarked, feigning as one completely unafraid. "Everyone has that you wizards are weird, so I am not surprised that you quote poetry. So answer then. Why did the Nystoli establish such a baneful rule for themselves?"

"I will tell you why. To go against some adversary with sword or spear was to forfeit one's status as an Arcane and be cast out. The Arcane must remain above such profane weaponry. The law dates from the dawn of Nystol, probably the Great Archmage himself gave it, and what Arcane durst transgress? Only a barbarian, a lawless warlock, blood-painted, would offer such an unseemly disgrace to the Art.

"In those days we would traverse into the depths of earth, into enchanted regions, and we went against any weird creature of the dark, armed with just a dagger and a few low-powered spells. Many young hopefuls were lost; only a few survived. Required to do these things we were, an apprenticeship, if we hoped to advance in the Arcane orders.

"When I saw that horned red beast sprawled upon his mound of gold,...how his eyelid opened, and the black crescent pupil,... how he arrogantly raised up his toothy head from his Aeonrest, I concluded that my end was surely come. The pamphagous beast gazed right at me, his gaze piercing my soul, like a leopard about to pounce. The undersea's fresh waters had destroyed my spellbook, so I reached for this deadly dagger. It was still there. I knew that I could live.

"Know this: we did not pilgrimage into those perilous places for filthy lucre, to seize the gold of pagan kings long buried; rather to fetch the rare components of wizardry: the eggs of a Vermillion Worm or the horn of a Giant Toad, the tail of the Chameleon dragon, or the smoke of a Fire-Horse, the brain of a Grey Mammoth. So it was, and we who survived understand the employment of daggers quite enough to prevail against any clumsy sword."

"You tell your lying tales not well, wizard," I said. "for it is well known that Nystol burned some two centuries past," I remarked wryly. "You could not have studied there."

"How scant the history you know. I was trained for the Order of Sorcerers, –not for the lowly wizard school. The Sorcerers did later degenerate into Summoning; that's true enough. Everyone knows it; it is consort with demons. I saw it happening and tried to put a stop to it. What can one man do? Since the time of the Hypostatic Rift, the members of my own order have hated me. I am 'Nocequ Arizel,' that is, Lord Arizel, whom the men of these parts call "Bannock." I am not a Sorcerer, but a Gohhan magic-user, trained in the ancient glyphs. This dagger is a gift of Arne Saknussem, the great alchemist, who once obtained to the very core of the hollow earth.

"Hear me out first, before you consider me an adversary to be skewered by your Witchbane. I ask, noble knight, will you, contrary to the teachings of God, misuse faith and forejudge me? Have you not convicted me and just now stood ready with that battle-blade to carry out a sentence of execution? And for what crime? Because I employ unseen powers of nature? –because I have been able to master nature and the human mind? Does not that master Kruth do the same?"

"Do not compare yourself to the right-thinking song-lord, wizard," I replied sternly. "The Arcavir's magic was part of his nature. But you wizards, you dare to call yourselves masters of nature. You abuse nature."

"Have men not been known to employ flying machines whenever they are clever enough to fashion wings....like Daedalus of old did?"

"What?"

"You know; with a little help from natural science, Daedalus and his son were able to escape the impossible Labyrinth and fly away, no?"

"That is a mere fable far-flung. What does that have to do with anything?"

"No one says that they abused nature, as you accuse me. Daedalus went above nature, tapping into the supernature of mind and genius. He improved on it. I assure you: that is all that my magic does. It was Icarus his son in his irresponsibility and youthful folly who brought about tragedy. In the same way many unwise wizards have bought the whole profession into disrepute."

"What you and your followers did to the Burgundy Knight, I stand against you for that... he forfeited his life to a churlish throng you incited. And now, for what strange coil of alliance which I did not foresee, the valraphs themselves have made fellowship with you!"

"Did I afford that good knight's slaughter? No...I perceived them not a throng a peasants. Nay, but they were professional cut-throats, they, who had disguised themselves as serfs. Yes, I percieved it well enough. Who were the men responsible for the good Knight's harm? A certain clandestine syndicate operating in this part of Whitehawk did it, they paid the assassins in gold. The gold coins had the imprint of the fallen kingdom Nzul, a feudatory ruled over by a puppet king under the claw-hand of that impious Dire of Melancholia. Had I let on, they would quickly have dispatched me as well."

Arizel had a considerable knowledge of the secret workings of iniquity. My thoughts searched his words. But Phaedra Stormraker spoke her mind.

"Faith ye: this is useful alliance with Bannock. He is quite in mind mercurial, well-prepared of many things and has sufficient wit on mysteries not even valraphs see."

"But so was Kruth the song-lord," I said, "and brave enough no doubt to join dwarf-forged arms beside a man outnumbered."

"You prize too much that cunning fairy. To check his power we had to imprison him within a magical tower of mist," explained Phaedra. "Then we left the protected isle for our questing. We broke our Valraph oaths again. Straightway, Arizel, that is Bannock, with his magic dogs sniffed us out and finally caught up with us in the woods. We were surrounded, the dogs growling, tearing our cloaks, but no onslaught; it looked as if at command they should tear all flesh all asunder. It would be a close fight, too close to wager. Bannock stood there knowing his advantage and initiated parley. He would call off his dogs, and we could remain intact. We must in turn take him as part of our resolute company, and after we teach Mulg his lesson, then endeavor to find the Kingdom of the Yule Queen in the hollow earth. This was his offer. An added boon he made to our cooperation, and we could even bury Hauk the Trollwise. Bannock the mercury-mind vouchsafed another thing. He would by-'n-by divulge everything on the story to which he is wise: the fall of Nystol. It was a square offer not to be passed."

"What? This is an outrage!" I exclaimed, flabbergasted. "Why would you take up with the likes of a wizard? So that you could die back down there again like the dwarves did?! So you do know it is wrong?"

"Relax, holy bell," said Arizel. "It is said that the Yule Queen has a garden in which she keeps a unicorn. We Arcanes who have the knowledge use its horn...for...medicinal reasons. Contrary to what the knavish Kruth believed to be my cause, I have been seeking elfbeards who can advise me against the grey elves on my journey, and I wished merely to refer to *The Black Book* in order to copy down an alchemic procedure for the production of a serum, an elixir of the horn's powder, to restore lost memory. I knew that I could trust these same trollwise men to do the dirty work, for they showed no scruples, not even over slaying a white stag, which, though a terrestrial creature, is yet also an animal sacred to the one who has rightful dominion over souls."

The features, aquiline, of the bald "magic-user" I noticed as he was speaking, there was something most uncanny. His eyes were under a kind of blindness. Though at first glance his eyes seemed normal and right, after some length of time his pupils did not meet my eyes, and on closer inspection I saw that both his eyes seemed made exquisitely like engineered precious crystal set with miniscule lenses.

Nevertheless, he did somehow mark me with those orbs of delicate creation, and every movement I made he had noted with a glance.

Somehow, perhaps through some dwimmer craft, he had these glass-like eyes for himself. However the wonderstone that Maragald had found for me detected no evil presence.

Now as we stood there and conversed, the elfbeards relaxed again and continued their ravenous disgorging. My questions were far from satisfied. Arizel, as I found later, did not much heed any human law save that of the Soothfold, being necessary for a licensed Arcane. Otherwise he had no loyalties, nor fealty to any king. Even so, he came off as the morally superior beyond all the rest of us. Has the merciful Lord sent me to correct him?

"You have noticed my eyes." he said. "Do you admire the mysterious Gohhan trait? A micro-work of fabrication imitating sight, but still not as keen as some creatures."

"It interests me not. Let us apply our minds to what is at hand: why do you need me for this dastardly hunt, to spill the blood of some innocent creature? Who knows what vengeance the Queen of Yule is able to extract? I'll come along just to see that you never accomplish it," I admonished them boldly.

"Like my servant," Phaedra said, "we will require your linguistic ability."

"What gives then?" I spouted. "Leave me be, and I will translate the book for you by the time you return, if you return. "

"Not even...but do you not crave to see what so few have ever seen? Are you not a monk? Do you not desire wondrous knowledge?"

"Faith suffices to know of unseen things."

"Faith? Treat you on faith? You surprise me. Most of the rope-girded monks in your order, I would garner, merely feign allegiance to that poetic deity of yours, the talker on forgiveness and a supposed right way of living. It is a vanity. The fact is that ours is a world of power and rule by the sword. I avert to speak of Him; after all, it is discourteous to speak of a deity who long ago went out of style."

"He lives." I said, frowning. "-and is awake. In fact he reigns over all. As long as there is even scant hope I cannot, must not cease endeavoring to turn men from wickedness, even you. Let his praise never cease to be on our lips. That is my creed, our hope."

"Hope? Hope has left the world. What has that deity ever done for you? You have no power or lands, monk. And have you not heard how the Red Death sweeps every land? That one is an impartial visitor from whom your deity does not even protect children. If a divine king *of the living and the dead* did once come, he slumbers now and another rules in his place. Perhaps the old gods have awoken from their drunken stupor and seized back the Olympian throne."

"A knavish imagining... So if he slumbers, according to your mind, whom or what do you serve?"

"I serve justice and I serve the beautiful, as philosophy instucts, and they serve me, which I gather must you hold an insuffucient resolution. Or else if there is something better, propose for us why your "God," whom you say is also a man, does not therefore defend the innocent. Can a sprout like you Jacob, possibly guess that? "

"The innocent he does defend, but he cannot force men to cease from their murders. He would rather protect from something worse, the immoral influence of godless minds, minds with which you, I imagine, hold sympathy. It would benefit you to be put in shackles awhile. Or be brought before the Ammouric Soothfold, there to be tried for your apostate crimes. I shall go along with you, but when I get the chance, I shall turn you over to the Prime Interquist, Zalmando Kantici."

"You endeavor to sound official, yet being only a monk you do not convince. So doing you would need to turn in also yourself, for you also stand accused of witchcraft, from what I have heard. Men are saying a young monk was caught with a *black book*, a grimoire. They say that he was chanting unholy spells under moonlight, defiling the sacred monastery, and this monk has escaped. It is said he hides himself in Hordingbay...and this monk is clearly yourself."

"You heard that?" I said, stunned that such distorted news should have such speedy travel. "I am innocent of wizardry."

"You will not convince anyone of that if you keep company with a wizard."

"Yet it is not permitted for me to slay you, taking the law into my own hands."

"Nor could you, and neither do you have any choice. Your only option is our stupendous enterprise. You should anyway···I know enough of what should be done. But see here: I will turn myself in anyway, to demonstrate to all the way of the righteous, just as admit myself as one not so righteous and noble as *I should be*, therefore deserving a lousy reputation. But I do consider the welfare of others, begging for mercy from the gods, although they are merciless. All hold me to be fell and unworthy company. A similar disgrace of infamy was hurled upon your Nazarene at the end of his life. In their cynicism, men finally saw fit to crucify a great *magus* who had done nothing wrong. So I have more admiration for him than you may suppose. It all goes to show what I have for a long time suspected: that the way of injustice and oppression brings honour and wealth to the crafty and evil-minded, while the man who seeks only to act with fairness and justice walks in disrepute and misery, an outcast doomed to tread the broad earth alone, whom even the gods curse. Should I not do a noble deed therefore and use my magic against you, you who would put to ordeal and execute your own master all over again? But the prophecy says that only a Christian monk can put an end to the conspiracy. How that is possible none can say. We desire a monk that can be a use for us, one that is holy, not a parasite. Therefore look inwardly at your own sin, and be not some pious hypocrite."

"Your provocation I shall not answer, for without knowing me you adjudge me a Pharisee only because I am religious. The Christ himself observed all that his religion required of him. Instead I ask you this: why is it that men render God to their own image conformed, to paint him as it were too much like themselves, rather than shaping themselves to be like the good shepherd? Know that the Christ was no *magus*; like you. Rather by three *magi* was he adored: God and All-king, even when a babe."

"Smart one; you." replied Arizel, "If you strike out and help us solve these things and unhinge this conspiracy against the kingdoms, then God might ease his judgement on an errant monk."

"You speak with knowledge that is true... but bent, wizard. Even so, there seem things in your search which you withhold from me. You will need to tell soon what you have really done. But it is getting late. So I now do take up with you and these reckless elfbeards, and may God, whose gaze reaches all, overlook it. If we make it back alive, I am afraid that I am obligated to turn you in to the Regulian Inquisition, vague wisdom though you have. Do not be afraid; justice in the end will arise. The great philosopher advises, criminals should run to the law-courts seeking punishments, after all the soul is vastly more than the body that perishes. The permanency of the soul's torment after death is a much greater thing to dread than the temporary pain of bodily torment. So shall we both brightly burn, both receiving in turn a share of justice. That will be for me the imitation of our Lord, but at least I will die with glad knowledge that others may keep their families safe from evil and heresy, thanks to our efforts."

Phaedra rolled her eyes. "Here we go again. Is there no end to this high strung gainsaying?"

Quid refert? Noli interloqui nostram disputationem, mulier," said Arizel. Clearly he was not accustomed to render females anything like Christian esteem, unless they were above him. As a powerful lady and a virgin, Phaedra should have been adressed properly, even by him. He was wise or cowardly enough to cloak his annoyance in the immortal language. Not comprehending the Latin, she did not clear him with a reply, but she guessed it were nothing worthy.

"...but let us not digress," he said. "You quote the philosophers, and speak of death as one who has little worry of it···.Even so, but our chances of success are slight. Nor will I burn, for I assure you that I am a wizard."

"*Etiam nunc conflagrare videmini...*Heaven be merciful to you and safe-keep you till justice. We will see if the flames consume you. If you repent soon, wizard, there may be time enough yet for escape. Still, even now you must know some remorse. Do you not know that your spirit is in great danger? You should turn yourself in."

"That is even more absurd. Tell me your thoughts and I shall teach you reason."

"The tortures of the body are nothing compared to the final good of the soul. Why not repent and renounce your magics?"

"A dreamer idealistic," said the wizard with sarcastic INSINUATION, "and for certain you have been confined too long within the walls of a monastery. You speak of the tortures of the body as trifles. Have you ever experienced extreme pain? Place you finger in the candle there for a heartbeat and we shall more honestly discuss your charity. It is an easy thing to speak on, but to actually endure requires an entirely different level. As for me, I do not care. I have accomplished far too much mischief to turn myself in for civil punishment, as if to somehow lessen divine justice."

"Turn back to God," I countered, "whom you know to exist, to whom all owe worship. There is hope for you. God gives final victory. Your magics might win battles but they loose the war.

The wizard answered, admitting. "Must I make such a choice? Can one harness magic and yet remain a believer in the Nazarene? Is salvation impossible for a magic-user? Fate is written in the stars, and they read that you also could burn with me, monk."

"Your thoughts are strange ones." I said. "What is the threat of stars, or those melancholy angels, compared with the accounting you must make to God who made them? You cannot be both wizard and believer! I say to you: when the magic is gone, your true life will begin. Magic has no power over souls who abide in God's law. So I say, repent of this and serve Allfather enthroned upon the great mountain."

"I assure you that I am not ignorant of the truth, and will grant you this: you are the first I have heard speak with conviction on religion. I will trifle on the matter, monk. But my own soul is not the issue. Rather my mind is bent on this one purpose first: to make right what wrongful plots which in my youthful folly I once contrived: the desolation of Nystol and conspiracy of ages. I would make repair of the world, but not according to the superstitions."

"No reparing will bring back the Burgundy knight. You let murderous assailants go against a lord unto peril. But I shall not seek anything more of vengeance, for neither is that a monk's right, nor is it in accord with faith. The flames of truth will consume you as my enemy or as my friend, but I prefer the latter, since you seem not evil, but mistaken. So drop the issue for now, until experience teaches us more. Instead turn to another matter. I ask you this: know you the prophecies of the Eldark?"

"Ah...the Eldark," he replied with a chuckle. "Now there's a name I have not heard for a long time. Were they not reputed the wisest among mortals before the coming of universal revelations? They had wisdom pre-dating the All-law, and the rise of the Ammouric Soothfold. I have little knowledge remembered on the prophetic lore, save this: titanic powers might be unleashed, and of Nystol their prophecy has indeed proven spry: she will never again be counted among the cities of men, drunk on the blood of the prophets. But weep the more, for her demise heralds the end of ages."

"Then you do have some wit of the prophecies. So it seems to me, Bannock, that we have talked your pricking talk enough. Your interest in our religion coupled with disdain is both unnerving and insulting. Why must I tolerate you?"

"Out of self interest, that is why... I do not care for your findings...who are you, a king? Just know that your actions carry gravity. You will never see your beloved Abbot again unless you deign to take up our service, monk."

"Have you worked your cunning evil on him?! "

"No···Suffice it to say that he has taken ill, poisoned by his own monks. Careful, rash youth, I clear myself of this, and swear I have had no hand in this. Your own Church has failed to assign herself worthy guardians. After you left, the Abbot decided to crack down on leniency and corruption in the monastery. In order to do this he stood on the Twelfth Stone of Whitehawk and read aloud the prophecies of the Eldark during the Feast of Skulls. This caused great alarm since it meant that the monks must begin to do more penance.

"They refused to let him finish reading the prophecies, asserting that he must not close the ritual.

"The Abbot is no fool, but he is old and sometimes loses his sense of time, especially when preaching. It is to the great ire of your monks...and he was counting on you coming back soon. Yes, I gleaned that he spoke of you. Questioning him cleverly in disguise, I learned your whereabouts. And I saw how Abbot's attempts at reform sparked outrage among the monks. But as a "traveling scribe " I rallied behind the Abbot's policy, for my own science. However, any monk-disguise has proved a limitation to my powers.

"At night there lurks in your monastery an unholy and secret sect of murmuring monks. They conspired against your Abbot and dripped a drop of poison in his goblet before supper. He survived, however, to their dismay. Upon finding this, they could not wait any longer for him to die and have been considering other methods. However, the Abbot himself, at unawares for this, and supposing himself near death, became fraught with foreboding over the state of things. He feared lest there be no qualified monk to reserve the Seat of Whitehaven during *interregnum*, the transition of power. Wickedness might seize its chance. So he bade that summons be sent across all the kingdoms, the Soothfold to come to elect a new Godmouth for all Whitehawk. Now all eighteen Archsages are on their way, but the Abbot has recovered. It is not known what will transpire next, with certain unknown monks and their plots, although I think the Hearing-Monk himself had to hire armed guards to the Abbot's chamber."

"Are these guards trusted men? " I asked in my alarm.

"These are your own brother shawl-knights, lords of the Ammouric order, who, having heard of this crime, at once offered their services. The Abbot had foreseen treachery and called them back from their journey. They have been accused of attempting to poison your Abbot. A terrible doom rushes upon the disciples of your inexplicable religion."

I looked at Drocwolf, puzzled, wondering if it were a factual report. The captain nodded in the affirmative. Arizel had no motive to lie.

Arizel's last words almost enraged me, brothers, but I would not become subject to an ungodly wrath and further scandalize our order, so I remained eye to eye, or rather, to glassy sphere.

"Inexplicable? It is you who are inexplicable," I retorted. "Was it not you, Bannock, who ordered your mob of peasants to kill the Burgundy Knight, since you yourself wanted to begile their souls; and the priest-knight would thwart that by wholesome dogmas?"

"I did not know him to be a Christ-crowned priest. But were that my cause, how would such a public crime on my part further convince any to follow me? That be not so...or at least, it were not all my doing. Yes, I stirred them to anger which I could not control, but I do have respect for the work of the rope-girded monks, the many books they have copied, even some ancient magical texts. I simply hold their way in disregard, for their ways make no sense."

"But were you yourself," I added, looking askanse, "somehow to become Abbot, you could direct the monks to copy books of your choice... ancient texts, the forbidden works of Nystol!"

"Perhaps there is a kernel of truth in what you say," he admitted. "Perhaps the thought has crossed my mind. But the rope-girded monks would never consent to it, no matter how grand a powerful display of counterfeit marvels I might perform. Be assured, I do not wish to see your Abbot die. Events must not transpire that way. I wish to see him well again, and to see the monks obedient to him. That may sound strange coming from me. I have my reasons: they will fabricate new books, and the most exquisite illuminations you will have ever seen."

"So then you wish to turn a new leaf?"

"No, I sense that I am still bound beyond your understanding, the old powers. I am committed to the cause of dread Sorcery. This alliance is only temporary, a regretful thing that will pass. Nor will I disclose to you the entirety of my designs, but mind that none of ye shall be harmed while at my side. Now, let us all depart from this place and get to seafaring. The journey into the everdark is long and arduous, and we must begin tonight while we are strong. A storm approaches..."

What more needed to be said? The children of Light have no fellowship with those of Darkness. There was too misty a knowledge of things for Jacob in those days to discern how the truth unfolds. It did not seem to him that Arizel was a cause so very lost. So he did take league with them and pilgrimage with that strange mountaineering band, renegade elfbeards and an obsessed "magic-user" of thawn heart. It was an unwise treaty with the foolish and the reckless. Of this accusal he has admitted it in writing:

"To do otherwise; I would not reason that it was in my power, even though there was certainly a way, since Heaven always shows the faithful a way out of sin's bondage. But I still considered myself fallen from grace, and was sold on mayhem and carnage to make things right. I pray that I have acted without fault, or if fault must be assigned, that it not weigh too heavily in the Great Accounting.

Expect half thy deepseige crew to be with panic o'rwhelmed, even be they veteran, for their imaginations paint with phantasms of blood a dismal end, how they soon will get lost in the mazy passages and, entombed alive, never see the light of day again, nor breathe the upper airs.

The Deeptracker's Guide

Up over high cliffs and down through the tracts of seagirt forest they went, the night black as ever, the trail rugged and unforgiving. They endured a cold and pelting morning rain.

Arizel the mercury-mind knew the path and led the way. Phaedra Stormraker kept close behind, after him Buckbar Lancelas, with whom Drocwolf kept close, and then Corydon, and last myself drawing the horse Burgundius. Finally Daufin, Telperion Granoch, elven-blooded men-at-arms, and Finch Kelperios, took the rear.

The stormclouds thundered and sent out bright flashes on the western horizon, lighting up the turbulent sea. By those glimpses a trail was visible which kept from treacherous drops and precipitous coasts. Landward again the way took them, through creaking forests and trunks swaying stacked with fir and pine. Great bolts of Heaven's fire crashed down not far off, shocking the nerves with a foreboding suspicion of divine disfavor.

The twisting path returned seaward, through the Long Valchines, and the Split County of Swords. Soon they found the sea herself raging not far below where enormous waves crashed violently on the jagged and brine-black boulders. On the way was set an inscription-stone in Latin, carved in characters of the Angerthas poets:

ᛁᚱᛁᛕ ᛞᚪᛒᚪ ᛁᚣ ᚠᚪᛒᛟᛒ
ᚻᚻᛕᚻᛏᚣᛁᛕᚻᚱᛕᚲ ᚲᛟᚻᚻ

Man shall go into the house of his Eternity... The mystery of our destiny writ large before us, that each must go, with all that he is, beyond time.

There was no turning back now. I had made the right decision this time. Morning was overcast, and a tepid wind blew gently from the west. They had gone down through a lower barren wold and then a forest of white cedars, finally arriving at a pebbly westward strand. Following this down a ways by the breaks of crashing sea, they came at last to the mouth of an inlet and reed marges concealing a swirling brook.

There they saw sea-side cliffs where are reputed the grottos of the smugglers. These were so chosen to hide well the masts of ships from any imperial search. The smell of roasted meat went through the salty air.

"Pray thee halt here for a stay, companions," said Arizel, turning about as the trail ended where the great hollowed out cliff loomed not far.

"Make no bonfire here, lest you are noticed, but eat your rations of breakfast cold. I will enter into yon cave, for although these men do know me, we do not want to come upon them together at once, lest they take alarm."

"What deal will you propose to them?" Jacob asked.

"The gnome-horde, all of it, will be theirs, provided they accomplish the voyage as far as the mouth of the Alph River, and they must protect us. I know they will accept that much. Other than this remains to be negotiated. And now, Jacob, you must hand over Kruth's chart of the horse-shoe lake."

So the monk handed over the map. They retired to an area where logs were washed up. Out of sight, they watched Arizel traverse the beach and disappear into the dark grotto.

"Do I fancy this wise...? Nat..." said one valraph, (I cannot recall which one), "letting Arizel the mercury-mind go off with the horde-map alone. What if he does not return? He'll be off with them in a ship, or somehow vanish as Sorcerers are wont."

"He will return," said Phaedra Stormraker. "He must return. This expedition means a great deal to him; it is his very self, it is his life."

"How so is it his very life?" Jacob asked.

"The Sorcerer, the "Magic-user" rather, seems a man in his prime, but be not fooled. It be not natural age. He is old, older than is right for men. By this expedition he says that he will fetch the magic of the unicorn's horn, as that will extend his mortal life another two hundred year. Given that time, he claims, he will unhinge the terrible plans his Arcane peers have prepared."

"Be gads!" the monk exclaimed, "How many years has he haunted the broad earth?"

"An unnumbered count, but enough to have seen the Fall of Nystol," said Phaedra gravely "...but then again, so have I seen many, for we valraphs also haunt earth a good long time. I were but a younker like you when talk of it went round the valraph halls."

"If it is as you claim, then he was yet quick when Nystopolis fell; he may know the story. Perhaps we might persuade him to write it down, so that the monks might publish the tale far and wide, revealing to all the real mischeif of the heresiarchs."

"His human Memory cannot reach back that far with accuracy," explained Phaedra, "but only the earthspan of a life, eighty years for a human; but beyond that, even gnomes and elves cannot so plumb most of their centuries. Besides, even could Arizel remember, he would never consent to such a thing. The forgotten facts on Nystopolis would open the hidden nature of the powers that be now, bringing to light the devilish secrets of Sorcerers. You had better keep translating that black book instead, Jacob Magister, lest he lose his patience and change you to a toad!"

The raiding crew all now broke out in gladsome laughter. "Don't fret, Jacob," added Corydon. "I fancy not even the greatest magician can do that!"

The captain, however, was not laughing.

"Why so glum, Dhundrerlum?" said Phaedra. "I said you might not talk, but never forbade laughing." Drocwolf the dwarf did not acknowledge but stared at the rocky ground as he sat on the log. The sea, calmer now, hurled waves to a gentle rumble upon the rocky shore close by. Buckbar spoke.

"Captain Stormrake, be there pass to speak my mind?"

"Be there so."

"Then I will say my mind. I say: it is enough already. I say let the patch-eyed nibelung talk. He has a world of experience, and we may need his trollwise keen if we find ourselves in a tight spot; but what good if then this bitterness halt his knowledgeable tongue?"

"A useful proposal," added Daufin. "I am not comfortable with the state of things. He might be at odds with your politic, but we crave his wise words to be hearing; he treats of a certain practical forethought. Far too thoughtless are we, offering our necks for this reckless affair."

But Phaedra grumbled.

"If so, then in result it will end this way: that all will heed his words instead of mine, and accomplish his bidding...I can't reason to consent this be changed. He has mastery of leadership, but vexes the Valraphim. Next you will be herded back to Kruth with tails between your legs, and his gnomish madness is far worse for bellies to bear."

"Good grief, have you no faith in your companions?" retorted Daufin. "Drocwolf should have leave to say his mind. I too am opposed to this, as it stands now. He was a good enough leader, one of the Valraphim. If you freely treat him thus, then you can treat any of us likewise. What is more ...if mischief should come, you might need the work of his deadly hands."

"It is well met that this be done," Corydon declared.

"It is my thought too, for like reason," Added Granoch.

Stormraker lowered down her eyes and gazed to earth, troubled. She no longer could take full doom-say over the elf party, a thing she enjoyed earlier, when she first succeeded against Kruth. Now her leadership was in doubt, just as she herself secretly doubted all the laws she once lived by. She had let tricky Arizel take the horde-map without surety, and though none would directly confront her with the mistake, it was obvious.

Phaedra, sitting on a stump with her back turned against us, went hush for a few moments.

"If it is the will of the Valraphim; so they warrant it, I will not go against it. Take care he not speak of the behests that are mine, or criticize them before all, and...he must renounce his claim to rightful command. Are you good to do this, Dhundrerlum?"

Drocwolf lifted his head and opened his bearded mouth.

"To you, Stormraker, betrayer of Valraphim, bane of Kruthendel, I have nothing to say. But to the others I say this: you are surely doomed if you keep on this wrathful course. You butchered the sacred stag. Heaven is not pleased. I know your true purpose: not lusting for gold, you already have all you need, buried on that isle in the horseshoe lake. No, you really seek reprisal against Mulg and the horgs! And you will take up cause with Sorcerers to achieve it! It is quite obvious to me why Buckbar can't stop whetting the axe-blades. All this be ill omen indeed. But come, I will never renounce my claim as rightful leader of this company. Use my deadly hands if you wish, I am a slayer of nasty goblins and blasted wyrms, trolls and gory ogres; not a mutineer governed by the belly, as some of you have revealed yourselves. By now Kruth is far away, so it is no use to lead you back there now. I doubt he would put any more trust in your kind. No, but now your redemption is to restore the good name of Valraphim, and find a way to learn the story of Nystol's fall, of which no history remains, and none on earth can remember well enough. We must make this trip on our own, but I'll not be directed by the likes of Lady Stormraker!"

Now was Stormraker raging in turn. "We shall see who is a valraph!" she exclaimed, standing and bursting into aggression. Red with anger, she drew her axe and barreled toward Drocwolf, who was unarmed. Drocwolf was quick, however, and skirted Phaedra causing her to stumble over the rocks, throwing her down.

The two wrestled fiercely on the smooth beach stones. Drocwolf had Stormraker in a locked grip, pushing back her head with his shoulder. Stormraker tried to raise the axe to smite Drocwolf but could not get her balance long enough to lift a proper swing. The others rushed in and tried to pull the two apart. They failed to do so. Nor could they snag the sharp axe from out the grip of raging Phaedra as both rolled about.

Realizing that Phaedra meant business, Drocwolf was able to pin her down. But she bit his wrist so that he at last let go, but not before taking the weapon. He flung it away. Corydon dashed over and fetched the weapon.

"There, lest they tempted to any murder," Corydon commented.

"Aye, but let them rake at each other a wee bit, " said Daufin. "'Tis a harmless duel to spectate. . . needful practice for fighters."

The grip seemed to last a long time, but it was not fast, and in moments they unlocked from each other, restored their resolve, and went back to clutches. Both were clad in the hauberk of valraph-chain, so the effort required to use force was all the more great.

The contest supplied a few laughs for the Valraphim. When the duelists became too fatigued to continue, they sat there on a bed of beach-pebbles, facing one another, out of breath, their cloaks and leggings torn. Drocwolf had proved the more stern and overcome Phaedra Stormraker, but he was so weary in the end that he could not maintain a hold on the other for long.

The elfbeards consulted among themselves for some time. They stepped back and stood before the duelists.

"Although the day is a gray day, one thing is clear as the blue sky," said Corydon. "Drocwolf is too sober and wise to lead our party, drunk as it is with bloodlust, to a reckless fetching of underworld gold. Albeit 'tis all loot cursed with death magic, but what is even more: we cannot disregard the slight against us; that the honourable name of Valraphim be no longer feared among the horg-tribes.

Kruth it was who first commanded that we forget their taunts, keep afoot, and make fast tracks; to flee like deer from their curved scimitars. Now we are the laughing stock of every denizen who treads deepearth. We will have our honour recovered...have it sung in every mead hall with their skulls as goblets. Buckbar Lancelas, Daufin, Telperion Granoch, Finch and I now stand ready: Stormrake is too rash to captain alone, and she has scant ability to temper herself. It is a punishable crime to attack one of the Valraphim. Stormrake must go before the Vatheng upon our return to the white mountains of Ayrs. Hopefully, by that time, she will have unearthed enough hell-coin to yield a compensation."

"The grave I will...!" cried Phaedra, out of breath, frowning, all together confounded.

"Drocwolf must now have his dwarf-forged arms restored so that he may fend himself," Corydon continued. "...and us. It is best we choose a captain, but none others have right fit to command than these. Therefore both of ye should consult when high matters come, but Stormrake will keep final say and arrange the daily orders. If on some question there is serious cause of dissent, the Valraphim will vote. If there be a tie, lots must decide the vote. Finch, pass Drocwolf back his dwarf-forged arms. When every man is armed, causes for duels are more seldom discovered"

"Hold your tongue, Corydon, you dotty and half-bred elf. Could there be a more knavish plan? There is no such thing as a double captaincy or soldiers voting. We must go by the military code."

"Such an arrangement could not do well," Jacob remarked, (but was ignored as usual).

Corydon raised his right hand into the air, a kind of salute with arm bent and forward, which I took to be some routine among them when a formal decision was made. Buckbar and Daufin raised their hands in the same way.

"Belay that order, Corydon," said Phaedra.

"It is the will and authority of the Valraphim," announced Buckbar. Corydon did not move.

"Finch, I say, return Drocwolf his dwarf-forged arms!"

Buckbar, seeing Finch's hesitation, then fished through the wagon load and fetched Drocwolf's spiral-horned helmet, his long axe, and his curl dagger. Drocwolf himself was still far too extinguished of strength to get up and receive them, but he had at least enough strength left to grab his dagger, and eyeing Phaedra Stormraker, he slipped it into his baldric, a protection to dissuade his adversary from further trying his luck.

Phaedra bade the Valraphs to collect tinder and light a fire for camp. They did, and after an hour Finch returned from the roaring shore with a handsome catch of fish. They set up the iron buccan and cooked the snacks until golden-brown, and all hands took their share.

Arizel returned from the nearby grotto just in time to share the feast. After all had eaten their fill and drunk down cups of dark wine, and had put aside desire for food and drink, Arizel Master of Planets praised the bright day and spoke.

"I, your Bannock, have made a deal with my smuggling acquaintances, and they have agreed to take us as far as to the port city of Ael Lot, north beyond the skirts of Nathycanthe. They will sail us, under certain conditions, but not to the regions everdark."

"What conditions? What say they?" asked Phaedra.

"When I spoke to the band of them, I was explaining that I had some compeers who must come. I showed them the horde map, and one of them verified that it were writ in gnome-hand. This caused them great glee, and they threatened to hunt us down if the map proved forfeit. They were making comments and joking over weirdly-clad wizards and honey-mad gnomes. One said, "I reckon there's no such odd little folk with you, sorcerer, like ill-starred elves or mischievous gnomes, a sure ticket for a watery death on the deep sea...?" I answered that "—no one of elphic race so pure that you should fret over." Now as I was leaving, I whispered enchanted words to them and put illusory magic, dwimmer, on the brutal crew, a crafty trick of mind. When they see you they will perceive you all to be a good bit taller, as if a king's soldiers, so take care to behave the habit of humans...but there is more: you must abide by their rogue-captain while sailing. His word is absolute law among sea-faring men. Also, he refused to take us down the treacherous waterway Eluvigar, where they have spotted dragon-ships, but he will take us as far as Ael Lot."

"And what of sailing into the vast caverns where the Eluvigar joins the waters of the Alph descending? What worthy vessel shall float us there?"

"If we cannot find any vessel in Ael Lot, then it will be necessary to take recourse to that magical instrument which Finch covets."

"What does Finch have?" Valraphs turned and looked at Finch. "Finch Kelperios, what lore have you withheld from the Valraphim?!" Phaedra demanded. "What pray tell have you?"

"No, we cannot take recourse to that, wizard." said Finch. "Why did you say that? It be a thing I would keep not, but I promised the gnome to hold on to it. It is something that I would never talk on," the bulbous-nosed half-elf replied, alarmed. "So I never do speak of it...but in my fill of the new brandy I remembered it, and like a fool showed it to the crafty wizard!"

"You must disclose this thing to us," said Daufin. "Don't you realize, we may be out of the frying pan, be we all are about to be cooked in the fire together. Drocwolf balances the power, and you need hold no suspicions. Speak; what be this instrument?!

"Kruthendel gave it to me. It was his long time treasure. Things were going adverse to his captaincy. He wanted it kept safe. It is strong magic indeed. Please do not question me further on this; it involves something frightful!"

"You will tell all!" exclaimed Phaedra, her anger again stirred. "Or you'll suffer greatly for it, and it'll be forced outta ya! Valraphim are oath-bound! I will go off to catch another catch of silvery fish to smoke, since each will need something for the journey. Others gather wood now for the evening repast. When together here again, nigh the setting sun, all will be expecting your account and to see this thing!"

She stormed away. Corydon looked at Finch whose frown formed under his elfbeard. He turned to follow Phaedra.

Finch squinted and gazed upon the stones and churning billows, his worried brow did not slacken.

With an hour of lengthening shadow all did return with wood and fish, and they prepared smoked morsels. The sun was descending and glowed orange. Each man was eager to hear and see this mysterious magical instrument. When they finished each looked across the campfire flames to Finch.

"All right then, I'll tell all...but there's no pleasure in it, and what good can come of it? It is a magic conch I carry. It is The Duke's SeaHorn."

Finch produced from his things a spiral conch two hands long with a brass mouth piece. "You have seen me now for many moons with this shell tied to the luggage on my back. It's not just a good luck charm. Have you ever heard me use it? No, it be a relic enchanted. When he secretly gave it to me, Kruth bade me never use it when standing on the sea's shore. The gnome himself, I think prepared it in days of yore. When blown upon the churning ocean it immediately summons The Valrast Horizon, ship of Duke Ikonn, marauder of worlds. One may board and sail off right quickly in the many-masted ship."

"Amazing!" said Corydon, with a smirk. "What a thing. If ever the enemy traps us with our backs to the sea, then you, Finch, or some other deep-lunged Valraph just has to blow, and an instant ship! But Finch, why so afraid?"

"I can well guess why he is afraid." Phaedra interjected. "It is because not only does the ship herself appear, fully physical, a thing solid and no mere illusion or cloud, but also the crew, and its Captain —The Duke himself. But why did he not keep it, or give it Drocwolf who once knew the Duke? Why did the Arcavir give the conch to you, Finch?"

The valraph answered. "Drocwolf and Kruth both were together companions of the famous hero. The gnome told me this reason: that the temptation to blow the conch and return to adventuring with the Duke was too strong upon him..."

Finch talked on, mentioning many old adventures. Many were the glittering treasures deeply buried they won in former days, before he was adopted by the Fraternal Guild of St. Dismas. Many were the glorious combats, tyrants captured, demons banished, many the monsters felled by buckler and shield in that great era of the world. But the age has ended and now more pressing things men must be about. The Duke must not be distracted from his penance of rescuing souls from the netherworld and other obscure places beyond the Tethys Sea. So the Arcavir gifted to Finch the magic conch for safekeeping, warning him to use it never, not unless some crushing calamity must be escaped. But if in vainglory we sound it for some unworthy cause, we might stir the ire of the Duke. The man himself an awesome figure by fame, gleaming in his ethereal platemail, his herculean physique and deadly hands wield the sword Oceanikyng and put men to wonder; with a mind full of many strategies that no league of princes can easily dissemble, not only all that; but also there is this: he is a man of impeccable moral caliber. What punishment would he have prepared for us who misused the conch and drew the Duke away through a time-space wormhole, away from some great journey in the nether-seas?

"I would not be the one to explain it to him," exclaimed Finch. "No, there is no fooling the Duke. He was titled "marauder of worlds" for a reason. His fame is spread far and wide as an exacting lord."

"You are wrong on him." said Drocwolf. "I myself am an ancient Nibelung. In days of yore I traveled with Ikonn; a hired axe-hefting champion. I proved my worth, as a companion, and finally as a captain. How often in later years have I heard stories told in taverns concerning the Duke, merely fabulous inventions, his reputation far too exaggerated, all that puffed up description. It is simply because of the magical armour he wears, everyone thinks him superhuman. And what terrible epithet the clever bards have given him, "marauder of worlds, " as if he were some violent flash of terror upon the race of men, a colossus destroying hearth and home. He is no more a marauder than I am a giant. No, not at all; the opposite. The man is a protector of the innocent and kind-hearted guardian, flesh and blood, yet nevertheless an accomplished leader and fighter. By the beneficent will of Heaven he lives long at the edges of the world. But he can fail like other men, and he knows the sorrows and pains of other men. Right away I can tell if some bard singing of him fabricates a spun bit o' spicy lies, By his words I'll wager if ever he met the Duke, or had duly talked with anyone else that had known him. You see, I campaigned with him. I knew him and was his companion, just as Kruthendel."

"You cannot fool us with your own spun tales, Drocwolf," said Phaedra. "You yourself have told us tales before. Everyone knows that the Duke is a strict judge and squarely metes out due punishment to offenders, even his own soldiers, allowing no application of mercy to weaken the fighting spirit of his men. All the bards are in agreement on that point."

"You are wrong. I will tell a factual account to prove it, but it will send a chill up your spine. Perhaps that's what you need. Sit then and listen to this tale of horror. Learn how stand things really.

isualize sails like dragon-wings splayed out against an azure sky, for we struck upon the Northern Warm Sea one summer, seeking adventure and loot. Into Northern waters along the Hrothic coast she cut the waves making incredible speed. With 'the man of exploits' we ventured: Ikonn Duke of Gorre, captain of the Valrast Horizon, the many-masted carrack, and her crew be fellows "armed to the teeth with famous bronze and life-rending steel."

The great icebergs floated about that year. It was a warm year and a greater part of the ice flows had diminished and melted away setting adrift mountainous chunks. He sailed us to a small, rocky isle which had been long encased in glacier. Now the Sun's melting rays exposed it. Foremost interest to us was a massive grotto. An entrance, long frozen, was now open, perhaps after centuries. The entire glacier had melted away. The glaciated cave itself was several stories in height. The Duke explained that he had once spotted it years ago on a previous expedition, iced over, and he vowed to return in a warmer year to explore it. We sailed into this grotto and disembarked along a cavernous inlet.

On foot we straightway came upon a shaft downward leading. Glistening ice fully blocked it; but they soon found a tunnel through the ice. We entered carefully. At once we came to a large pool. Upon it was a great longboat entombed in the glaciate surface. There we beheld a dragon-ship, and a few men and fighting dwarves, seated where they had given up the ghost in some lost age of yor. They were all stiff with deep chill and had a look of terror still upon their faces. Their hands frozen were to the oar shafts, as if they had beheld something of utmost horror. One fellow`, I recall; his hair was still standing on end. There must have been some fifty of these pitiful men. They were Northmen from the ancient world; clanish lords of ancient Osring, I think. A handful of stout dwarves was with them. I would say the second age, reckoning by the cut of their surcoats.

Duke Ikonn pointed out how well-armed they had been, with the best of brazen shields, spears and chainmail available in that era. None of us dared steal from the dead, not even in those days. Yea, and we marked armaments and jewelries of highest value.

These fellows had been frozen, I proposed, by a blast of frost-wind, and further proposing, perhaps from a frost-dragon. The Duke did not agree. Frost-dragons, contrary to popular opinion, haunt mountains in temperate regions, not the sub-arctic. Their freezing breath-weapon would have but negligeable effect against typical sub-polar enemies armed by Nature against frost, such as polar bears, ice worms, giant walruses and the like.

Upon closer examination it was confirmed. The Northmen had not been killed from a blast of cold, but upon seeing something which at once caused both terror and freezing fear within. Something else had slain them. Had they died of fright?

We touched them not, but went on, leaving the dead undisturbed. We also discovered the deep-passage for which they had come in their longship, seeking the loot of pagan kings. This was the entrance to the Mausoleum of Qui. Who exactly was "Qui," none could guess, but the inscription above the entrance was writ in Carnian script, with mysterious warning: DISTURB NOT QUI YE GREEDY SEEKERS LEST SUDDENLY THE HAND OF A GOD PLUCK YOU AND YE CANNOT ESCAPE-DO THOSE WHO ABIDE HERE REST-NAY THEY DO NOT-THEY GUARD NOT FOR YOUR BENEFIT-BUT FOR TARTARUS

The tomb-raiders had broken apart the door's stone seal. They had stacked timber for a bonfire against it and then doused the rock with water.

Several ancient corpses in armour now lay strewn about on the rocks, also chilled mid-motion. Some were partially disintegrated. Or was it that they were half-eaten? One poor fellow I touched, and a remnant limb immediately collapsed. Whatever had been locked in the tomb had gotten out and attacked the ancient explorers and longship.

We entered the vaults of this otherwise unpopulated necropolis. Deep into earth went its lonely corridors.

We descended primitive steps into a narrow passage absent of light. We lit torches and carried them high, armed to the teeth with famous bronze and life-wrenching steel.

Soon great trepidation came upon several of the soldiers. The place was creepy. How eerily colossal was the architecture. Fearing giants, or less namable things, re-considering the pervasive darkness and the plight of the fourscore Northmen frozen where they sat in their ship, some of our soldiers requested that we return above. The Duke, in revulsion at any hint of cowardice, denied and scolded them.

Farther we went down into the dark. There was a scurrying sound from over our heads. The arch of the deepening corridor was elevated, some fifty feet or more, and the torches would not illuminate so far above that mausolean darkness; so we could not see what was up there.

What sort of polar mind could have reared such a massive structure? No human crown, no matter how tyrannous in baneful ambition and impious egotism, was ever recorded to have quelled a kingdom in such polar or sub-polar regions.

Someone suggested that the structure arose in an era when the climate was warmer...

As he was explaining his thought, we heard a scream, a chilling scream. The Duke and I turned about at once and saw it: one of our own fellows, a fully equipped soldier, mind you, seized, taken up into the darkness of the ceiling above. Black claws, enormous, wrapped around him. Alas the memory of his screams and agonizing cries for help. We could do nothing after the concealing shadows hid the murderous terror.

There followed only the silence of a bournless realm. Streams of blood first trickled, then poured down the steep walls in sheets.

Something was devouring our man, something was quaffing his very blood. The soldiers were in a state of indescribable alarm. Some cried out for their companion, but there was only a viscid sound of digestion. One man flung upward his torch and spotted a huge creature with bat-like wings; a frenetic, murderous demon. We waited in stillness. The remains, skin, bones and some armoured members, dropped back down clanging, all slimed and charnel.

Several soldiers at once obeyed their own nature and fled with all haste back up the steep stone steps. The Duke, undaunted, bellowed at them to return at once and stand ready; but they were frightened beyond reason. By now we had gone down so far, perhaps over a quarter mile, into the cold earth, so that we could not even see by torchlight the backs of those who fled away up the steps without us.

We did hear astonished screams. For the phantom creatures pursued and overcame the deserters on the steps above. Duke Ikonn, master of stratagems, commanded that we continue with haste our descent. Several of the crew begged that we turn back. The Duke commanded them to silence: on pain of death by his own hand.

Finally we reached the slimy bottom of the dismal tunnel, with swords naked and spears couched, ready for anything. Only ten stalwart soldiers remained. Into a circular throne room we entered. There, sitting enthroned in the center, as a Pluto presiding over the noisesome pits of the underworld, was what seemed an impish abomination, a spectral statue of some condemned soul. Upon closer inspection we determined that it was the statue of some fairy-lord coroneted with a leaden crown; like an empty cerement. I guessed him the tyrant-lich of the grey elves, Archdruid and perhaps the villanous genius of the legends, whom the dwarves call Nazageist. It were a statue chiseled in great reality; fully detailed of a magisterial art. All looked as the melancholy master had designed this place for his own consignment, or entombment, if you will.

Of the grisly creatures which had attacked our martial crew, some of those species were seated comatose around the circular room as if this lich were holding court. They, however, were not statues, but the animate creatures. Larger than a man, they had infernally taut features of the face, like a ferocious animal; the semicanine mouth with gangrene-dripping fangs, and the featherless, bat-like wings folded. Some of these creatures were hanging upside down from rafters, and still were breathing. They were the vampiric spawn of some brood not found in the bestiaries.

Their pullulating allies, however, who had taken already several of us, were not still. They were now returning from their feast on our companions to defend their quarters by making a dessert of us. Now we men came to know fear. We could hear the flapping of their featherless wings several cubits above. Duke Ikonn, acutely cognizant of how incremental is the influence which fear exerts to freeze the otherwise valiant, exhorted his remnant war-crew to an unchecked battle rage.

He enumerated the names of our dead compeers, and demanded that justice be met in the hell of war. He told them to fear not, turn ye not back, but rather be ready to die doing one's best to rid the earth of such foul blood-suckers, That is how heroes end their days, in battle. Don't be fools. Did you all imagine endless days and never to die? That is not the creed of heroes. Even were your flesh to be drained of blood or ripped apart, a worse end might come to the spirit. But if you risk all, with high esteem in song will they sing of you, the real immortality with which heroes are rewarded, not lifeless gold. Or else, even so escaping terrible odds, with what profound shame will you return to your houses empty handed, in which case death is perferable. Therefore be resolute.

It is factual record that despite such exhortation most common men would still choose their own lives over a valorous reputation. But given the fact that these particular adventurers had decided to sign up for a voyage with the Duke in the first place did not testify to their normalcy. They accepted the exhortation and rejoiced at the opportunity to die thusly. It were as if some power of divine knowledge were in him. He so did charge the men with honour that they did not wait for the foe to find them, but with all fury charged back up the stairs in *testudo*-formation[37] vaunting aloud, frothing at the mouth for combat.

To this challenge the enemy-creatures consented. These grey, leathery-skinned, emaciated-looking, but terribly strong creatures flew down upon us to dine. They must not have supped for centuries before the fleshy feast they had made of our companions. Now, in their insatiable lust for blood, they thirsted for a full belly.

Their teethy mouths were steeped in the crimson of their previous captures. We offered our spears ready to meet them, aye; and we impaled several of them at once, as when hunting pterogigantic cranes in hinter-bogs of Nathycanth, straightway thrust right through the gaping mouth of each.

However, they remained skewered and flapping upon the shafts, and expired not; I suppose this were because they were risen of the parasitic and blood-sucking hordes, after which they are as undead. Thereupon, the Duke, lord of battle, grasping one of these creatures about its thin, wiry neck, instructed the men. He drew his hand-ax from his belt and right away beheaded the grisly creature. Its hairless crumpet went rolling down the steps plopping along one step after another. The Duke had done this with easy candor as one who deprives a chicken of its top when preparing a thanksgiving feast.

This same technique each of us accomplished upon closing with the remaining creatures opposed; in our battle frenzy we suffered no major injuries. Although dismembered, the creatures remained quick, flapping about.

So the Duke paused in deep thought for a moment, and then required the men to extract the weirdly-shaped coronary organs from each and pile

---

[37] *testudo:* "the tortoise-shell" developed originally by the Romans, a battle formation which allowed soldiers not only to be protected by one another's shields, but also to be protected from attacks coming from above.

them up. Whereupon he poured oil over the pile of hearts and alighting with torch burned them to ash. In the end the crew was relieved to find themselves yet unscathed with lives intact.

The corridors went on into the everdark expanse, who knows to where, and we did not follow them but a little ways and turned back for lack of supplies. In the end we returned above and, suspecting not all the evil extirpated, sealed up that tomb with chains; and although we had no Ammouric *selva*, the Duke himself pronounced an execration in the name of the Furth High King.

Then we gathered whatever remained of our own compeers and buried them in the salty waters of the grotto, reciting all courageous feats lest any be held guilty of cowardice; for most who had fled up the steps were merely hired soldiers, while those who fought were bound by oath of fealty and adventure, they were "companions." For with enough victories, they are granted the status "champion." But not the hired men; they, afterall, would not be expected to overcome such a terrifying experience without the courage that obligation supplies.

Be that as it was, tsome oath-bound also fled, abandoning their liege-lord.

One of the *drakers,*[38] was found returning from the tunnel, one surviving and saving his own life whilst his fellows were devoured. Although not yet a "companion," he was a vassal of the Duke. He was oligated to valour.

We all expected that the Duke, the destroyer of armies, would punish the fellow severely for his cowardice, and a court-martial was expected. But characteristically, the godly Duke did not want that. Although he refused the man's apology, he nevertheless omitted him from punishment.

When later his champions questioned concerning this apparent lack of justice, the Duke replied with unassailable wisdom. The lack of bravery and cowardly actions which result are their own punishments, and that the wretched man who fled will have to remember his cowardice the rest of his days, for certainly other men will not forget to remind him of it. For

---

[38] *draker* (dungeoneer's slang), fr. Gk. *drakon* (and later drake, denoting a winged dragon): The word draker is a pejorative: coward. The one who is a draker is said to be like a dragon because dragons are themselves well known for cowardice, despite their terrible ferocity (q.v. Guy of Xaragia). The following verse contains a famous pun about Drake, an ancient would-be-hero of the epics, (perhaps the origin of the common usage): "*Drake fled and did not think but for his own safety, nor remember how many were sacrificed to the horned terror, so the gods named him well, for he was truly a draker.*" -Xilmurian Epic. Another, more trustworthy source, Orbian Escorvus, asserts that Drake was an adventurer who fled in cowardice from a "type IV demon." His name famously appears in "*The Lists of the Dead.*"

this man a second chance is not unjust. We were not in wartime and he was an inexperienced sword. Some are naturally prone to fright and have not matured enough to govern themselves, although that is a weak excuse. Let him recall the bravery of his companions therefore, the Duke said, and hear bards sing of it in mead halls, to his shame. In that way, should the fellow be asked to yield his life fighting the foe in some future engagement; he might choose rightly and make clean his soul to the benefit of all.

Such was the magnanimous spirit of the great Duke, and Whitehawk had never seen the like, nor has since ever known such chivalry.

That accursed and lifeless grotto we left straightway and returned shortly to the open sea and to air and sunshine, thanking Heaven for victory in battle. I will never return to that place, nor will I again disturb the frozen tomb of that ghastly longboat. I tell you, we never did discover the terrible being that could cause men to die of fright, but only its vampiric servants, which we dispatched forever to the halls of dark hell. That was the first time, and hopefully the last, that I had ever encountered such devilish horrors..."

So Drocwolf told his story of horror, and shook with fright at the memory of those events. All who sat there around the blazing bonfire were quite pleased with Drocwolf's tale and lavished him much praise, and they too felt a bit chill despite the roaring flames.

"It gives me great courage just to hear you speak of the honourable Duke and his feats of high renown, Drocwolf," said Finch. "If only he were with men in these last days! But we would not likely search out that lost isle anyway, in the frosty recesses of the mist-cloaked Northern Warm Sea; and as you say, we must never disturb the dead. There must be another way to reach the turbulent Eluvigar from Ael Lot city of Northseas."

"You stalwart valraphs would pilgrimage to the realm of the underworld?" said Drocwolf with admonishment, "...just remember that it will be not much else than that which I have already recounted for you!"

"That may be as you say..." said Phaedra, "but we must look to the matters at hand. Tomorrow's troubles of themselves will take care. Try to remember exactly the Duke's exhortation, Drocwolf; and perhaps if ever we are in some moment of scare, you can recite those words for us, or else blow that magic conch so that the Duke will sail us away. Now then, I could not but help think of the admirable crown of Ael Lot and of this island St. Aldemar, who is the generous King Graham. He has no regard for unworthy superstitions; and like the Duke he is kind, willing to give every help, provided our purpose is right."

"Kruth once gifted Ael Lot with songs finely wrought," said Drocwolf "the time the Duke and I lodged there and searched the high-walled city for the thief Godiun Foute, most deft of all who make their fare off others' unwatched prizes; for Godiun, the red-hand, had stolen the Nagamaud Amulet, an infamous and crafty feat of days long past."

But Arizel said "Many old relics predate the new faith, and yet the magic in them is found active. But I will say this, you are right to not blow upon that conch."

"You! What of YOU, Bannock?" Brother Jacob asked, gazing brightly at the dark-robed wizard from across the bonfire's blaze. "If we are to be sheild-mates in this quest, I warrant that we hear your story in full. Do you think that I fear a wizard? So I ask: whom do you serve? I ask you now. –Heaven high-above? Or do you do the bidding of earthly spirits and men who are mortal. Or is it another, as some whisper, the dark pitchfork-holder, horned devil from down below?"

"Whom do I serve, you ask?" the wizard replied, now eased with wine. "You worry that it is your adversary, the genius of shadow, the great rebel, the infernal prince. But look first among your own for that. Some of your own brethren secretly serve the Archfiend, monk. Learn of the great mystery yourself: of how what many call cruelty may be mercy, and what is said to be worthy may only appear to be so, or what seems evil is really a good."

"It is true that some of my brethren the Archfiend has corrupted, " the monk replied. "but you make that into your boast, as if the Church did not already know it, or were merely the collaboration of mortal men. Perhaps you might offer some more credible boast. You have never encountered that prince of fallen angels and would flee if you did. We monks are not easily fooled."

"Were it not for us few remaining magic-users, and the power we yet possess, a fiery mayhem would soon engulf the world." He gazed intently at the fire, and immediately the flames increased and roared, lighting the gloamy waste around! "You may think us cruel and marred, but our guidance and influence among princes has delivered many from calamity. Our faith is indeed remarkable, perhaps greater than I imagined."

"Faith in God, or in men? That is the question." Jacob asked, testing.

"Too many questions you ask" replied the mage. "I do have what is needed. I have gone to churches, in disguise...–I don't live it and breathe it like you. Can any deny that the transcending magic of the Nazarene was great? Would any but a fool pretend that the man-god never walked among men? That would clearly be an ignorant position. I have better reason."

"You are then like Nicodemus who spoke with the Lord by night?"

"So say you. I will reveal many things of what I am doing, but you all must keep them privy or die the death. It is not for any ear beyond this circle with fire. If you agree to these conditions, and swear by the flames, if you will treat me with a degree of respect, rather than rumour-trusting, then many things that were unclear to you before today shall at once be made manifest."

"We will guard what you tell," the monk answered. "But respect? That is a thing earned... Why would you trust me, your hostage and adversary, with crucial intelligence?"

"You are unreasonable only in those inextricable foolish things regarding your superstitious monkhood. Besides, it seems that you enjoy this work. I would have you, however, comprehend certain things so that the task assigned you may be understood."

"Then tell it and be done with it."

"First swear all ye to keep it hush. Swear it!" All valraphs swore they by the flames with hands raised.

"Very well," he continued, "here it is: Pray hark ye close...

ne day, having smoked well-chosen *bzebus* leaf, I fell into a deep sleep, the kind of sleep that attracts gods—or demons. I traveled many places in my dream and learned the wisdom of many ancients. I dreamt of your strange and superstitious religion, and of the Ammouric lore. Of this wisdom I remember little, for it confounds my waking mind:

During the dream this wisdom manifested in the form of an inspired poem, a Morphean work of epic proportion, perhaps some five hundred verses. After having awoken with swollen eyes I immediately went to my desk and was penning out the poem, slowly drawing up the ever-so-frail fathoming from out the deep pools of dream lucidity.

I had written only a handful of introductory verses before something scattered my concentration. A desert mouse had intruded upon my den. He crept near and was after nibbling on piles of *vellum*, tomes, and *bemble* scrolls. Unafraid, he darted about. He was too fast to catch. I went after him anyway.

After bumbing my head and becoming enraged at the minor beast, I drove it into an crack of the bricks, as in the first age when giants once drove men into caves, I went back to the desk, for I was resolved to finish. But as I touched the pen to the ink-well, lo, the entire gorgeous dream-poem, the epic that I had lodged in suspension of imagination was now vanished away.

I tried and tried again, with great consternation, to retrieve the poem, but to no avail; it was forever lost. Nevertheless, I completed enough of the first stanzas and committed them to memory, and kept them written down:

In the Dry Blood Sea,
Midmain of Damnation's Ocean
An opulent Oasis is anchored
A burning, beatific place
Perfectly marked by one capriform cloud
And here mystic mansions did grace
Whose nine eclyptical towers endowed
And arabesque chambers twice times three
House the roots of Paradise's fallen tree.

For when that great rifting did occur, that day
Sophistry gained the Devil an agricane crown
And the angels over disobedient Adam did frown.

From our dower infernal did Sin's deadly wages
Rend verses from Heaven's holy pages
And when like a satyr exiled Adam awoke
Veins swollen with the fruit's deadly dew,
To Eve he bade listen and spoke
As the poem swelled from the broken reservoirs
Of his frail midrift's sight
And the dragon's eyes with slivers of light
Did gleam and glisten in the realm of night

How much of souls antique be untold
Who fashioned masks of hollow meaning
And tombs of enormity, millstones of gold
Through which Time ambent is seething
Or the world's cloven-footed emperors
As if in juggernaut Ganges
Like mooncalves bathe
While their scathe-fired provinces
Into jetsam are streaming...

Could anyone hope for the meaning of this enigmatic poem?

Certainly something can be guessed. It seemed to point to some ancient desert habitation, most likely Nystol the desolate, nine-towered city of mysteries, an opulent oasis, burning...beatific? Aye, 'tis the very throne of Satan, and blessed by him. I could tell nothing more. I also nursed a lingering suspicion that it told of other things.

To investigate, I took the journey to the Bibliothek Rumiliad in Regulum hoping to learn more on *The Dry Blood Sea* and her oasis of rises the Sardu plateau. I was admitted to the Chambers of Historical and Geographical Inquiry, ready for whatever the old Rumilian library, almost completely forgotten, would yield.

I did find some researches. The sands of the *Dry Blood Sea,* legends say, turned the color of blood when the renegade dragon Gnotus was struck down there and bled out for centuries. I lingered for many weeks studying these legends and trying to find what, if anything, could be learned of Nystol's last days.

One day, not even a year ago now, while perusing the Rare Works chamber in the Inquirium, I came across an incomplete history which a certain Voethius had written: *The Last Days of The Magi.*

The pages described the various events and revelations that led up to the desolation of the mage-towers called Nystol. The work was recent, no date, but written in a style of perhaps but a few hundred of years past.

I opened the half-burnt manuscript of history and found a Greek text in Ulthoran minuscule. As I scanned the ancient writ, I chanced upon the rare name "Arizel" mentioned there. Even more shocking was the name listed in Voethius' registry of conspirators. "Arizel" had been assigned to open the lower gates of Sardu for the Maharim. It was the day Nystopolis would burn!

Not only was he some sort of magic-user like me, but all the more incomprehensible was how Voethius, the historian-author, described "Arizel." The physical description matched me exactly!!! I gasped with disbelief, and my frame shook. At last the writer even mentioned my own sorcerous title, a secret known only to the highest minions of my order; and now you will know it, and that title is "Master of Planets." I reeled with terrifying realizations.

I had once before heard report of strange catastrophes befalling other Arcanes, how they would discover their true age; but only after their own failing memories had long since forfeit deep-fathoming ability. How they would on a sudden realize that they had lived another life by the prolongation of their vital power!

I was indeed that same Sorcerer whom this Voethius described. I had forgotten my own unnatural age! Somehow, though centuries old, I still walked among the living!

I conjectured that I myself was become a ghost, but I could feel my heart beating and could experience digestion, sensation, and emotion like others. Then I theorized that I had risen from the dead, but only gods can so rise of their own accord.

Had I come out from a deep and enchanted sleep like the famous *Seven Sleepers of Ephesus*?[39] Perhaps, but upon inquiry no records of my death existed and I had no other evidence that such had occurred.

Had I traveled beneath the earth? Of course I had; I am a wizard. However, the magic robe protects wizards from time-displacement, among other things.

Perhaps I had reincarnated? Yet that is flatly impossible according to any reasoned metaphysic, both first principles and theurgic axioms demonstrate reincarnation to be a superstition. Souls cannot overleap from one unique body to another. What passes for spirit-travel is merely only vision-displacement, a migrating by magical projection, and then only possible for a short lapse of time. Certainly it was nothing of the sort.

Could I be having a dream? I could be in a dream and not realize it, since some dreams are quite intensely vivid; and if that is so, then I have

---

[39] *Seven Sleepers of Ephesus*: There exists an eyewitness account left from the persecutions of the Roman emperor Decius, around 250 AD. Seven young men were accused of promoting Christianity. They were given time to recant their faith, but chose instead to give their worldly goods to the poor and retire to a mountain cave to pray. There they fell asleep. Almost two centuries later the cave was opened and the sleepers inside awoke, imagining that they had slept but one day. They sent one of their number to Ephesus to buy food, with instructions to be careful lest the pagans recognize and seize him. Upon arriving in the city, this man was astounded to find buildings with crosses attached; the town for their part were astounded to find a man trying to spend old coins from the reign of Decius. The bishop was summoned and interviewed the sleepers; they professed to him their miracle, and praised God.

yet to wake up. Either way it matters not since I would want to finish the dream and solve this enigma.

Finally, after weeks of meditation on this mystery, it was as in my brain a flash snapped, and a long forgotten and strange memory surfaced. It occurred while I drank upon some tea in a local tavern. I happened to hark to some jest involving a unicorn. It was not a funny piece but gets repeated often. Something regarding it triggered a memory.

When I was an apprentice at Nystol, it seems like a thousand centuries ago, I did whatever I wished. I served my own inclinations. I was pleased to remain in this condition. So I waited for some higher purpose to call me.

Time passed; and no great beauty moved my heart to devote my life, either to some cause, or some art, or even a fair maiden.

At last I was in danger of despair, so by force I turned my efforts toward aiding the sickly human race. Yet this was not out of love for the good, but rather out of a sense of superiority.

To friends I divulged new resolutions. I endeavored to ask the great minds. How can the human race be goaded to rise from its lowly stature? Having gained notoriety by my skepticism, I was invited into a secret fold. I conspired with certain like-minded Arcanes of Nystol. We resolved by blood-sworn oaths to bring humanity to the brink of apotheosis, that is, into divine submersion and resignation, and to usher in a utopian era of spiritual abnegation where there would be warfare no longer, nor even troublesome religion. Human willfulness would be submerged in the dream of communal unconsciousness, the masses would serve a group of elect, the Sorcerer-Kings. But how accomplish it?

Why not use the powers already available? In place of religion would be offered a new magian illumination; for most folk, simple magic tricks we would spiritualize, a diversion fulfilling the human need for meaning. Only the elite would be initiated into an arcane governance and the deeper secrets of the neo-magian overlords.

Many would not be pleased with the inchoate order; men of high principle and nobles, out of self-interest, would stand against it. Violent coercion would be necessary to allow a new world without the oppressions of tradition and superstition. Obsolete, deficient, and resistant humans would be "encouraged " to forfeit their lives on behalf of the greater good, and do so without hesitation.

Still, many holes riddled the plan. Among the highly accomplished Arcanes, we agreed to a contest. We wished to see who could contrive the most unusual and persuasive philosophic tracts supporting a utopian teleology and hegemony of Sorcerer-Kings.

After two years, when it was done, several of the proposed philosophies were found pre-eminent in their design. All were impressive systems. But whose arcane-philosophy was most influential among men?

We spread the various novel ideas far and wide among the nations. We even hired scribes to make hundreds of copies of each of the nine competing philosophies, hoping to see which "wisdom" became popular and prevailed. Then we convinced certain not-so-deep-minded clerics and so were able to place great preachers in key cities. They fabricated a quasi-faith based on our counterfeit wisdom. The names and titles of the gods were kept: Allfather, the Christ, and so forth, but altering the philosophic and theologic foundations.

The new wisdom at first urged no conformity. Rather was a merciful freedom from the All-law our ideal, and resignation of the will to a greater, universal volition of power. These clerics were successful and have become known as the 'heresiarchs.' Religion is the guise under which our philosophies are marketed.

Our designs worked better than we had expected. Soon even the authors of these philosophies believed them to be actually worthy of adherence. They even now considered themselves to be the incarnate paradigms of their respective systems.

Yet that was not enough. Our conspiracy went even further. I myself came up with an infernally brilliant plan. There yet remained great resistance among those learned in the older wisdom. The Eldark Sages[40] whom ancientmost wisdom has chosen, were the greatest threat. They are found in every city throughout the realms, and in every tribe on earth.

---

[40]*Sages*: a term used generally to designate a wise man, but in Nyzium this also designated an arcane school. These adepts were to be understood as an outgrowth of the Mage order. The name originally given to them was "The Wisened," since they surpassed the Mages in wisdom and give us the term "Wizard". They were the first to develop a philosophic ground. These Sages would eventually become the governing order of all the Arcanes. We learn from Voethius' *Histories*: "Although not a material essence morphizer of the archaic order, the Sage would come to excel in conforming his volitional patterns to the concussions of planetary radials. Words were infused with diverse inter-glossal universalities to project the preternatural reverberations of the unborn man into the *logos*. Through the acceptance of Ammouric wisdom utterances, apprehended in glyphic representations of telestic derivatives, they discerned the deep mysteries of the celestial spheres. By apprehending percepts represented to the intellect from vibrations aroused in the recital of wisdom poetry, they concreted the will, making it receptive for spirations of *prime sodalia*···"

This was the governing order of Nyzium until the Great *Hypostatic Rift*. It suffices to say that they could not operate after that time, after the great rift in which space, time and cause were idealized beyond the metaphysical predeterminates of the known. Of course how could they? The objective order was no longer regarded as the sense ground for transformate activity.

It is important to understand that the Sages up to the time of Anherm (a much later disciple) had no understanding of the Valent Imagination or the preternatural synthesis. No office of glyph-censor (*Glypharchon*) had been established to evaluate the ethic of various systems and magical processes···(see indices under "*arcane histories*" for Voethius' remaining treatment of the order of Sages)

In order to bring our philosophies to dominate the world, we could not hesitate to silence or destroy all other competition. Works of genuine wisdom, however, are, as you must know, kept in many places, sanctuaries and temples, monastic and secular libraries, and most problematic: private collections. We knew that our grand scheme would avail naught unless all other books of learning and inquiry, in every library, in every city, which contradicted the basic materialist or quasi-spiritual premises of our philosophies, were destroyed.

–But how?–It was a mad proposition, impossible. How eradicate so many numberless volumes scattered throughout the world? No dwimmer-craft is powerful enough to warp all reality so, or to render all books as dust in a single moment.

That such a thing was actually accomplished, that is a grand mystery. This is the point where memory of these dealings fades, and I do not percieve how it was accomplished, for surely on the day Nystol's stacks burned many other libraries throughout the wide world did not. Yet, as the evidence shows, after Nystol fell and was lost to history, nearly all useful books mysteriously vanished from the Furth, leaving us in darkness for an entire century.

My memory, although the unicorn joke had reactivated it, and Voethius' history restored, now breaks away. I cannot explain it; and of the further writings on Nystol, the remaining *folia* have also been consumed in flame. It is as if by the caprice of the stars.

So now I have neither recollection nor report to relate the evil tale any further. Of my own effort I can only remember back eleven month. The vanishing of all books happened well over two hundred year ago. It is a marvel that a few tomes and scrolls did survive, when so many other writings have perished forever.

The remainder of my role, what was all my plan and how it was accomplished, and how so much knowledge throughout the world vanished, yet I have left unremembered! In my journeys beneath the earth, no doubt, I stooped to taste the flowing waters of Lethe.

All I know is that I myself had a hand in this great crime. The plan worked. With all the truthful learning and wisdom of the ancients having been lost, the minds of men were compromised. Untaught after a generation, they would eventually no longer reason their way out of the spell into which our attractive and novel philosophies meant to allure them. Men would become slaves in the worst way: of the mind. Our philosophies could tyrannize thoughts into weird ideologies and fear.

How foolish our designs, and how greatly we erred in mind. Everyone knows, of course, that Nystol, queen oasis of the desert and the only magian college, was razed and her grand library of Hensooth the flames consumed. There is no real understanding of the cause. Was it by hazard of war or by treachery? Why did the magic defenses of the college fail? What did my fellow conspirators know that I did not? This is strange indeed. Had we contrived to rule the world, it would have been senseless to destroy our own great seat of power. And one should ask why the entire world itself fell into darkness simply because one remote desert-college ceased to influence.

The sudden darkness of unlearned confusion soon overwhelmed the earth entire. As I have said, it is a mystery. Within a generation, the "powers of eld Night" took advantage of the loss of knowledge. You may wonder how the loss of books could have so ill an effect on the civil lands. Consider it this way: both high and low laws of the sacred crowns were kept in parchment tomes.

But count other enormities as well. Without access to sky charts and ephemeral calculations, sailors usually get lost at sea. Farmers are left to guess at the mazzaroth. Calendars easily fail. Without the ancient Oruscan medical texts, physicians have no reference of experience. Nor do engineers have any formulas and designs to build walls and fortifications properly. Great agricultural innovations were also recorded in books as well, not to mention the planetary flooding modes of the Urash River in Gohha. Without the Ataluran metallurgical texts and diagrams of the mesolithic strata, superior weapons cannot be built; and know that all the old scrolls for battle-magic went missing as well.

So as you know, the ruthless and savage powers of the North learned of the failing of the West, and all Whitehawk came to know brutal war, the invasion of the troll-horde. The genius Archdruid, that baneful crown, bade his war-master Mulg to muster the horde, that rotting elf, the Dire of Melancholia commanded the bolgoth drums of war not cease. So came the **Bellum Diabolicum.**[*] It annihilated several entire kingdoms. It took many decades before any feudatory dared fly banners again.

Yet there is more...and this is what presses us most, " he continued, glancing about nervously with his ghost-eyes. "Nystol's desolation left a political power-vacuum in the world. Now after many years, and after pushing back the horde, the kingdoms begin to recover.

Nevertheless, I have discovered that a new conspiracy is afoot. It is the masterful design of some of those same minions. I myself was once numbered among them, or else of those heresiarchs who took their place...and I again remind ye how to secrecy you are bound. It is a thing of doom that was long ago planned. There ushers upon the world a veil of universal proportion woven with fatal threads. Here is the mystery of

---

[*]**Bellum Diabolicum:** "The diabolic war." Prosecuted principally by Nimrul the Bane-Lord, this war changed the face of all Illystra. The horgoth and barbaric human armies, united under the banner of the Black Claw of Mulg, invaded all the civil lands with massive force and put to the torch every town. Only the Kingdoms Ulthor, Atalur, and Ael Lot successfully resisted. Tyrnopolis lost all her wealth paying off her besiegers. Most of the Maceonid monarchs of the West lost their heads. Countless lives were lost in its battles, and darkness overcame Illystra entire which has not recovered for centuries.

iniquity to come, a woeful hegemony of Sorcerer-Kings I myself once helped to contrive!"

"What...what a terrible thing; what is this doom?" Jacob urged with great alarm. "Is it something that will usher in the great chastisement?"

"I can hardly imagine that an immortal deity, even old ones like thundering Zeus or dark Poseidon, cares to be forgotten. They are not pleased with the race of men ignoring them. Some say your Heaven has already unleashed just punishment: the incarnadine plague, The Red Death. But the heavenly father is merciful, as you Christians attest. So the plague is only a slight thing. It wreaks havoc on men's bodies so that back from sin it might turn them. What I am indicating is worse. It is not of God. It is something that will bring desolation on men's spirits, it is a reign of wicked kings, a spiritual annihilation."

"You must then know something on it."

"Not much, but I know who does," said Arizel. "They will not inform me. The Arcane Circle is a syndicate of ambitious lords, allegedly comprised of Icloharius Nonus, Zuphagen Wren, Adeuces, and Moeris Flammonar, as well as Neoplatonic sages Dilaziph Albus, and Gleyrin Oakstaff, and the alchemist Rebus Pecequiohr, all famous wizards of Nystol; they also have somehow outlived centuries. I just recently became wise to it. But you mentioned that you had written some sort of theological tract in Latin against the Friars of Whigg; and something on wizards, though it is already too late to curtail them. These Friars summoned the wizards to push back the Troll-horde and destroy the influence of the Dire. Why did they refuse? Because they had no power of banishing spirits, that's why. So the Friars threatened to press the power of the Inquisition upon them if they did not try. Else burn them at the stake according to the laws of the Church."

"Is that what the Arcane Circle craves? ···to acquire spiritual power, to banish spirits?" Jacob said, "There must be some banishment spell in the *Black Book*. What you disclose now I find amazing."

"They cannot become "Sorcerer-kings" if they have no spiritual power. Kingship, you see, requires a considerable spiritual component."

"Did the wizards resist the coercion of the Friars?"

"They turned their old magic on the Friars in retaliation for the threat, but the spells failed."

"Of course," Jacob said, gladly. "That's because the wool-frocked Friars, disrespectful though they be, are protected by the decree of Heaven. Even against lukewarm Christians, by His mercy, magic may not have its sting."

"I believe it. The Friars demonstrated the immunity you speak of; to the dismay of the world's most powerful magic-users."

"So what did the wizards do with that?"

"They submitted. The Friars let them return to Nystol to do research in the basements beneath the delapitated ruins. Many "basement texts" survived the great burning and banishment."

"They must have found something."

"They did. This is what I know thanks to a spying *homunculus*. The excavations found a half-burnt scroll listing all the basement texts. Especially was listed the 33rd *volume* of *The Black Book,* with all its various contents. There was indicated a powerful priest-spell preserved within, one which even a wizard could use. The Soothfold had designed such a thing at one time, in the time after the Hypostatic Rift, when the monsters of wizardic abomination were many, and few were the Ammouric priests in the world."

So Arizel spoke in order to elucidate many things. What he had learned from the book was only a half the story. The wizards' possession of the priest-spell might also be leverage in their negotiations with the Dire. Indeed, the spell could entrap certain spirits, and the Dire was a spirit afterall. So the wizards are desperate to secure the work itself, as is the Dire. They had secretely hired the Friars of Whigg to help them extract it from the Monastery of Whitehaven. "That's when the Friars in turn contracted with me," explained Arizel "to rescue the silver-braced book from the valraphs, but only after a certain passage was found by a monk who could read it. They required me, in the meanwhile, to divert any close scrutiny of activities on St. Aldemar...incite rebellion among the peasantry if need be. I had no idea what group the Friars were really assisting: the Arcane Circle. My little spy had overheard the Friars speak, but only of "wizards." I soon became suspicious. After meeting Phaedra Stormraker and learning of the quest of the Valraphim, I was shocked to learn that the Arcane circle was afoot. I abandoned the contract with the Friars and threw in with this band and sharp-witted enterprise instead.

"So the Friar's contract with me was broke, and the Friars must have given up. But the wizards now have their own purposes. Did they hired the infernal monks, notably Ulcrist, to infiltrate the monastery where Anherm was said to be reading through it? He encountered Jacob instead? That's all we glean of it," added Arizel. "Save that there is some greater danger; and I have only a vague sense of the rest. The deterioration of my memory, or perhaps the strange sagacity that comes with so great an age, has summoned within me new sentiments. I spite the things which I once held dear before, and despise that which I formerly exalted. Therefore my cause is for the balance of my own scales, that some peace of mind I could end and not be further haunted with the thoughts of the evils I have brought upon the earth."

...I observed this unexpected guest, a stranger and wanderer upon the broad earth. Survival in Kithom and the parched deserts was but a minor challenge for him apparently. That much was clear. Had he thrown in with the sand-pirates of the Dry Blood Dunes? The late hour arrived and I set out the straw mat for him. He disrobed and stretched out for the night. It was then that, looking askanse, I spotted something alarming. There was a tattoo painted on the inside of his arm: nothing less than the triple-headed snake-pattern of Master-thief Godiun Foute!

Epinanaus of Asosmus' *Twilight of the Republic*
MonasteryAnnals of The Weeping Brotherhood
24th of Erramere, 147 Ante Flammas

XXII   Fox and Jackel

The account of Arizel was over, but all knew that things were left untold and unknowable. They were puzzled at the account of that wizard's life, fraught with mysteries. Just as the famous Arcane spoke his words concluding, the valraphs saw the circling sun spread his final beams into the azure firmament; over the wide flood the glowing orb sailed 'neath earth's bent, slipping toward the unknown places where the Tethys Sea curves over the Western horizon to rush in tulmult to the deep. The valraph Corydon was suddenly become cognizant of something from another direction, and he turned their attention away, alerting them.

"Look down the beach, the crew of smugglers, the whole band of them! Be ready Valraphs! They come fast upon us to carry out a fight. Could it be, Arizel, that you have been doing business not with smuggling dogs, but sea-wolves!?"

It was so; armed men were upon them of a sudden, only moments away. On foot they tread down the stony beach, forty or so felonius ruffians. Some were bald, others long-haired, both dark-skinned men and pale, gold rings in noses or ears, tattooed arms with heathen design, some battle-scarred, a few maimed. They came with knotty club or spiked in hand, or swift shortsword and cutlass, sharp axes, several crossbows infamous. Miscellaneous sorts of armour protected them, thick ox hide bucklers and cuirasses, or chainmail styled of various nations, some with gladiator's mask or knight's helm, all prizes stripped from imperial soldiers or any other defeated lords that sail the sea in ships. And all had the odd complexion, frown, and look of hardened rogues.

"Arm yourselves, valraphs." said Phaedra, "Our host clearly intends to stop by...and not merely for tea, nor for a pleasant chat, but a gruesome match."

"Then a bloody match will they have," Corydon Elatumal, a valraph who usually kept very stoic, announced.

The valraphs went to their feet and armed themselves at once, hefting their axes or unsheathing swords out of the cart, but it was too late to make ready with armour or helm.

"Arizel, you made out that these were merely smugglers," said Corydon. "They sport a look worse than that. Now we are in for something. Good goin'..."

"They were I say once smugglers, doing minor harm," said Drocwolf. "but after circling years have they become all the more cruel and violent outlaws: a pack of sea-wolves—no petty thieves, nor strangers to a hazardous fight. Too late I detected that. They be seasoned with many victories at sea, their cutlasses afore whetted, seawater mingled with blood streaming. They know sharply to handle weapons, and although untrained in swordsmanship and the lance, they can do fast as much damage with axe or club as any proficient soldier. Mark ye, Valraphim, and count you them to be more than quadruple our number. We cannot take them without losses of our own; but prithee, we ourselves cannot spare a man. Talk them out of it, that is what we must."

The sea-rovers came upon and took position arrayed about us, weapons readied. We were closed against the churning waves of the sea's shore. The leader of the pack, an older man, bald, deeply wrinkled in face, missing some teeth, glared with steely eyes. Strong were his limbs and clad only in toughness, no armour. He stepped forward and spoke. Standing next to him was a mean-looking and fatty mass of tattooed flesh gripping a mace of nails.

"Bannock, you heap of dung! Thought you could play us the fool with a drawn map and some clever words? But we who take our fare upon the rolling waves are wiser than you suppose. We know of your kind, cunning in flash and bamboozle. You cast your spell upon our minds. You hoped that we might miss these elves boarding our galley. So...deceiver, after you say farewell from Ael Lot we would sail off for the treasure you promised. You knew the sea-god Neptune would instead take stern vengeance upon us for transporting his enemies, and deliver us to a watery grave. What a clever plan. Our own blood-painted warlock, Cinna, though one not so highly skilled as you, detected the illusion infecting our eyes. You deserve to come under my hurtful blows without restraint, the blood spurting out of your crushed ears, to teach you respect. Now then, all you filthy elves and the rest of your crew must make a choice, surrender your treasure haul at once, and the humans, Arizel and the monk...unharmed so we can sell them. You will not? Then all ye ready yourselves to fight like the sung heroes of old, but die you will, like dogs, on this forgotten strand."

"You press upon us without good cause, Kluxatta," said Arizel. "Why hold you to those old superstitions for Neptune? I did you a favor. No seafaring captain entertains such notions these days. Know you not that a new god is said to hold the supreme governance of all the worlds? Besides, these men are not elves, no; they are valraphs, hybrids, having little to do with that former race which vanished from the furthlands long ago. No fiction, the blood of Plathon courses through their veins, so they be spry and nimble, and quite steel-fisted, worth three of your fat rovers I would say, no easy kill. If you attack us or try to enslave us, you will lose most of your crew in the attempt. How will you sail your many-masted rig then? You jackel! How ever will you seize loot from imperial galleys, which, albeit quick to let you whenever you hoist up the skull and crossbones, are now always well-armed. When the prey counts a diminished crew on your deck, he will not yield. Therefore come, let us reason together, you and I. Look instead to the better plan, the plan that benefits each party, and accept what your men will respect: to give passage to this troop of deadly valraphs and soon win treasure buried just as the map indicates, only a day's march inland."

"What a story, and a well-drawn chart, but it is a lying one, Bannock. Your kind does not make such deals without surety."

"Kluxatta, you will smile for having trusted us. Know that I have already vouchsafed myself against your unworthiness. Although I gave you the drawn map, I myself withheld the key to the brass-braced chest buried in the Timberhills, a Kalaran chest which in no other way can be opened, no, not even if a giant were crushing it with all force, nor could even the master-patron of all thieves, Godiun Foute, hope to pick its inextricable lock. But that key will be yours, Kluxatta, once you yield and fulfil your part of the bargain." Arizel did not expect to convince, but only to stall until the choleric cooled. Kluxatta peered at him squinting.

"Keep we no bargain, Bannock, clever fox, neither with you nor your doggerel crew. We count you no trustworthy soul to keep bargain with, for you weave many palavers, lie within lie, that it is plainly obvious. Me-self and these sea-brigands, here standing poised to kill; we be not nice company for sure, eager with cutlass to seize treasures other men covet, stored within imperial galleys glutted, all that gold which unjustly merciless tax-collectors took, dishonest men. But the loot we earn with whetted cutlass we put to better use, aye. It pays for gladsome wine and winning livestock, and a few other manly needs. Learn this: we ourselves are at least honest in every other way, and not one of our tongues has ever deceived cruelly like you do, or been caught in a dirty lie to his mate. These know the penalty. We are professionals. Suppose not therefore that we be so ignoble as youself. How much worse than a thief are you! You are a liar, a dishonest grub, lowest of the low, not worthy to be left alive."

"Come now, Kluxatta. Do you honestly think to justify your felonious profession? Ask the monk here, he will tell you, knowledgeable as he is in things having to do with right conduct. Who is the clever fox? No smuggler can be said to be honest, to avoid lies and deceit. You lie when you feign to be a friendly ship in need of supply, but then hoist your skull flag and board another stout ship. So do not hope to trick us with well-woven argument into supposing that you are better than the rest of us, or that the life of roving upon the sea with cutlass to take other men's treasures is noble or somehow justified. If ever the imperial navy gets the better of you, you will hang on a rope from a mast, or be thrown to sharks —greedy to tear your flesh...and believe it, someday you jackels will be apprehended. So put down your weapons and come to reason. You and your men will fetch handsome reward for a crime but venial."

"First show us the key to the treasure haul which you claim you have, wizard. Then do our weapons lower. But before that, expect to feel the collision of iron against iron, and cold steel thrust into your belly, spilled crimson everywhere to paint the beech, and after its done we shall leave your unburied corpses here for the gulls and every flesh-eating scavenger."

"Kluxatta, the key I spoke of is not a metal piece that I can extract from one of my pockets and show, no, not at all. I am a wizard. Our ways are mysterious. The key is a spoken word. Magical is this word when pronounced rightly over the glyphic and impenetrable lock of the treasure chest. It is of the ancient Gohhan tongue and it seals tight the chest so that no force or power can overcome it. I could speak the word now for you, but everyone else would learn it. You do not want some sly betrayer, one of your men who secretly holds a grudge, to strike you from behind when you journey into that woods, hoping to seize the treasure for himself, do you? I myself will impart to you alone that secret word. I'll whisper it in your ear the hour we disembark at the port of Ael Lot, when you have fulfilled your part of the bargain."

"Don't trust it, master," said one of the armed smugglers, with rampant eyes. "The fox plays on yer ambitions."

Kluxatta said, "Arizel, master of deceptive report and misleading words. Even now after I have shown to all that you are a liar, shameless fox, you still hope to dance round our heads another lie covering the previous ones. Only a dolt would believe such a pigeon-story, which, were it no fiction, you would have explained it when you first made bargain with us. Now however expect nothing but pain and a disgraceful death at our hands for the insult. Even among filchers there is a kind of honour, though it be written in crimson. Settle now with your maker, all you elves, for it appears that you would rather fight us, though you be well outnumbered. Yield now, and we will spare your lives."

"Valraphs do not surrender, sea-pup." Phaedra declared.

"Then you will die a gruesome death. Perhaps better than being sold in the slave markets of Isauria —aye, your choice we respect. Ye mates, advance now upon the crew, cutting down any who resist. Recall how this wizard hoped to make you the laughing stock of all sea-faring men. The destructive wrath of Neptune was their fare promised, not glittering treasure. We shall teach what it means to trust a long-robed wizard. Now then, which of you "valraphs" will be first to receive death-blows? At least your name will sung when our bard Melladus recalls this battle, whenever we feast in our echoing grotto. That monk of yours better start now to pray to the gods. No, you men kill him too, for what else is a monk but a maggot who feigns righteous piety to acquire his rotten meat?"

His words stirred Jacob Magister's blood. The monk craved a good fight, but he exercised his self-restraint. He had come up with a better plan: turning to Finch he said. "Finch Kelperios, sound your magic conch, I say. We are about to drawn into mortal hazard—without escape!" loudly Jacob whispered, "Do it now! Now is the time if ever!"

Finch hesitated of course. It was clear that much blood-letting would quickly ensue. Perhaps all of them would die. Kluxatta had roused all his men to great indignation. Finch held in his hands the only means for escape. Just as Kruth had granted it as a fruit of the sea, the time for using the conch had ripened. But he was more fearful of using the conch than fighting the sea-brigands.

Finch took up his conch; hands unsure. No time was left, nor any possibility of bringing the new enemies to a happy truce.

"If I sound this conch, Duke Ikonn will come...at once, in the mysterious ship," Finch said. "It is a terrible thing to disturb such a hero who is about his sacred duty, but it were more terrible to end up a slaving for the likes of these, or pouring out my life blood on the sandy beach."

Still, Finch held the conch in his trembling hands. "But I cannot blow it. I cannot be the one. My lungs are not sizable enough. You blow it, monk. Aye, the Duke will not be so stern with a monk."

At once Jacob Magister grabbed the magic conch from his hands. The monk took a deep breath and blew as deeply as he could. The sound of the conch was booming and full indeed, unlike most other horns.

Kluxatta's men watched us ready to pounce.

They kept still, standing ready, their lives in the balance.

Nothing...

Then the air around echoed a thunder. Kluxatta was startled. He looked beyond them all, squinting, to the far horizon where the sun had set and evening hurried over. The conch's blast had set the few clouds passing over the flood into tumult. Then the very air seemed to bend into a vortex that turned upon the horizon like a child's spinning top. There, within the vast rolling of clouds, the sails of a many-masted ship appeared! They spotted a massive vessel approaching breaking through the fog that had quietly formed.

Kluxatta spoke, full astounded. "What magic is this?"

"It is the ship of a hero, a man of many adventures, and a marauder of worlds," I declared. "He will give us fair passage, since you will not. How now, great Kluxatta? Thou jackel, why the sudden and pale flush of hue upon you and your men?"

"I do know those sails," cried Kluxatta. "Mark them, that be not the ancient dragon-ship of Duke Ikonn...no, nor a ghost ship of any sort. Not even, those sails, mark, be no phantom sails. They are the sails of a galley···the King's Navy of the Aels!"

Just as he spoke, there was a great BOOM and flash from that ship as she turned to abrest drawing up parallel to shore. The cannon ball whistled to shore and whizzed right over our heads. It exploded in the midst of Kluxatta's little army, killing three men. There succeeded another BOOMing thunder and another following, with more explosions. The bombardment continued and Kluxatta cried out for his men to make haste to the many-masted rig docked in the grotto.

But it was too late. Already the marines of Aels were coming ashore on five landing boats. They disembarked and made great speed on foot, eventhough clad with full chainmail, and armed with buckler, shields, swords and crossbows. The whole army descended right upon us. The sea-brigands had for several years outwitted the usually weak imperial navy, and often won quota from seizing the holds of imperial galleys. They had made the mistake however of attacking the king's merchants, and made enemies of the much more vigorous and unvanquished Kingdom of Aels.

Stormraker told all the Valraphs get to their knees, a sign of yielding universally recognized among the Aelic clans. Many marines rushed past us in pursuit of the sea-brigands, several riding on swift mounts to patrol the beaches. In a strange twist of timing, the King's Navy, who had been spending weeks raking the coast of St. Aldemar for the rumoured pirate enclave, had been near and had heard the conch and finally spotted their prey, otherwise well hidden within the voluminous grotto.

The marshals who followed after the marines on foot arrested us at once and put all in shackles on the charge of piracy. The captain of the ship approached and Buckbar attempted to explain matters, but immediately a soldier's mailed fist struck him down.

"As you brigands are under arrest, you may not speak unless spoken to." announced the foremost of the marshals. "Remain on your knees until we board ship loaded with the heads of those who are resisting and fleeing. You who have yielded will be granted the mercy of confessing. You will appear before Graham King of the Aels to profess your guilt and beg for forgiveness. Then you will be hanged from the neck until dead."

"Glorious." Jacob said. "We undertake adventure to save the world and the first thing that happens—we get captured. Such is the turn of would-be heroes."

The captain, a tall Ael with a plentiful mustache, went round examining closely each of his captives. "These who have yielded; they are not the sea-wolves which we have been seeking. They are by race valraphs...who do not take to the sea...they must have thrown in with Kluxatta and his reprobate crew. But no seamen is free of superstition and would allow such kinds in their service...that is puzzling. And that one there; not a valraph...he is a monk, by the cut of his robe and tonsure. Unshackle him; it is not lawful to keep a man of the cloth in irons until the grounds of suspicion are accepted. That is Aelic law at least since the days of the Duke. However the monk must come for further questioning."

They unshackled the monk. Perhaps he might get away with saying something, anything.

"Honourable captain," Jacob said. "You are right that we are not the sea-brigands you hunt. These men, these valraphs, you see, King Graham himself commissioned to acheive an enterprise of high moment; a much more crucial matter than anything else in the lands: it was a certain subterraneous expedition securing the very defense of Ael Lot herself, for valraphs are best at caves and climbing. This mission is a thing that they may only speak on with the king. We came to this strand seeking the smugglers that once inhabited that grotto, men whom the Crown has long tolerated. In order to report to the king himself, our return to Ael Lot had to be unmarked by any, our mission being terribly secretive. Instead we found that the smugglers had been suborned into piracy by brutal men, no mere smugglers, but rapine killers. These are heartless workers of evil under the infamous command of Kluxatta the lawless brigand you pursue. He and his outlaws were about to massacre us, holding our lives as cheaply as they hold King Graham himself. But then I blew the conch, hoping for a supernatural rescue, and, to our glad turn, perhaps by the intercession of the Duke, with his relic, your many-masted ship appeared and fired her debilitating cannons. Had these valraphs considered you an enemy, as outlaws like Kluxatta do, they would have fought against your marines and died. It is well known that valraphs never yield to an enemy."

The captain rubbed his bristly chin and stroked his mustache, pondering.

"Very well; that's almost believable. However it is still unlawful to parley with smugglers or their guild. The penalty for that is at least dungeon time. However if you are true on all this, the king will recognize you as his subjects and agents, and will pardon it. So we shall present you to the king. In the meantime all the valraphs, the nibelung too, and that wizard —ye make sure the wizard is also gagged, marshal, —all of them, you all must remain in shackles until the king commands otherwise."

After an hour the chainmail marines returned to the beach lugging bloody swords and the tops of sea-brigands. They were heaping a purple pile of heads for those who had fled justice or resisted.

Evidently none of the sea-wolves had surrendered, knowing that such an act would only prolong their evil turn. The last head was taken to the ship (to be presented as proof to the merchant-Aels who had funded the Navy venture) and cast like a fish-head in a barrel. The captain was after watching each closely, looking for any that might be Kluxatta's head.

They found his head not among those counted. The master thief had slipped away. But his pirating days had come to their end, at least for a time.

As for the conch, it is not for magic but by faith that I attest how the grand spirit of the Duke interceded for us. It was the Duke after all who had founded the King's Navy.

"...that is not our concern: whatever means you employ to obtain the required intelligence we do not scrutinize. The guild sent me incognito only for this: to remind you of your mission and of your responsibilities, and of the final consequence that must be visited upon the earth if you fail."

"And what, pray tell, would that be?"

"An Age of Darkness Universal; lasting all subsequent days of men, even unto the end of Time···"

Hieronymous Pike
Dialogue with a Stranger

THE ARCHDECEIVER   XXIII

One would think that the fate of the world was at stake. Valraphs reached the portside town of Ael-Lot in record time, and neared the quays and docks before the dawn's light. The many-masted ship glided on the glassy sea without a sound, her torches unlit. Up the inlet was the Castle of Ael-Lot herself with her townside streets asleep underneath her high walls.

The soldiers escorted their new captives to a portside military stable and set a guard to watch until the marshals would come take them the next day.

All bright and blue came morning, and Ael Lot is a merry town. The valraphs did not quickly awaken. No breakfast was to be had anyway, so at least they could slumber in the hay. Phaedra did not turn over again for further sleep. (afterall, she was self-proclaimed leader). Lifting her wrists she presented the shackles to herself with a sardonic grin. She arose and stood over the monk.

"An assignment for you; this will not only demonstrate your acumen, but also your trustworthiness. We might make you an associate. Certainly you may escape us if you wish, you have your monk-skills and all, but is there any other party who will be able to aid you and help you with your legal matters like we can? Therefore you will go to accomplish this and return with report. No safe places men keep for our kind in a town like this, only the court of the king, which protects all. I do not wish to appear to King Graham without knowledge of his mood, or of any news, or of whatsoever influence he might be under; for Kruthendel the charmer is not with us, and the king will wonder at that. If he is melancholy, we must escape town. Be the king cheerful, he will aid us. You will go into the town clad simply, as a yeoman, or a traveler from abroad. We will cover for you, telling the marshals that you went to seek advice from a scribe of the law. Go find a watering hole in the outskirts of town, and take up with the regulars. Learn by inquiry, by clever words, about the temper of the king, and discover any other news. Ask of the king's hospitality as of late; and what might persuade him. Then come back, and keep an eye peeled that you are not followed."

This Jacob did, (feigning to resent it, in order that Phaedra not always expect him for dangerous and awkward work). The monk-spy returned the following day with this report:

"...I seized the opportunity to forget all these troubles by availing myself of mead at a well-known but unpopular tavern: The Squeaky Door. After some time introducing myself to various folk as a traveler and having won drinking-companions, and paying for their pints, I fell silent...

Someone there who had been acting pouty could not bear the peace so he told us a jesting tale. It involved a unicorn, Arizel's interest, the legendary animal of rarity and unknown power. The tale from this pouting man, who was nearly tanked, was of course unartfully told. But it had a ring of authenticity: a unicorn hunt. When he was finished he got up to puke, but held down his drink anyway. He at last departed, stumbling out into the street.

I inquired of the bartend as to the story's origin. He said that it had been learned from a dying man, an adventurer perhaps, who, (as subsequent hearsay purported), had raided the lairs of a mountain beast, and may have found something valuable, such as gold, or terrible, such as forbidden knowledge.

On his return to civilization he ended up victim, of a treacherous companion and had to be silenced. (so ran the original rumour).

That last part turned out to be fiction. Here is what really happened just a week past: the unfortunate subject in question, "an adventurer" had slapped open the squeaky door of that same establishment one afternoon, "death at his back," they said, the day being cold and the snow well piled

The hinges squeaked in the bright winter afternoon and flooded the mead-hall with light and a wisp of snowflakes. Surprised, and with eyes squinting, each drinker turned about to look, only to observe the silhouette of a formidable warrior standing in the entrance way.

The figure stood motionless for a moment, and some drinkers feared danger. Was he an overbold sea-raider come to plunder the hall itself, some highly experienced berserk to slay all in quick succession? In fact "the adventurer" was exhausted. He stepped forward one step and straightway fell to his knees. He seemed all but frozen stiff in his armour. There was a pause.

The glare of the outside was blinding to the squinting onlookers. Snow-capped mountain brightness burst through the open doors, her defiles brooding in the distance.

The squeaking was heard again as the door swung partly back and returned to rest on its hinges. The stranger went down like timber and slammed straight onto the tavern floor with a heavy thud.

Since the stranger was wearing an Ataluran great helm when his head struck, the impact failed to knock him out; but the mysterious man retained consciousness, even though now all could see a feathered shaft lodged in his back. This was sad and strange. Upon removing his helm he seemed to be of noble extraction. The shaft-make was unmistakably horgoth, made of hard bone, and this was most troubling. Even cruel crossbow bolts were never known to penetrate the royal armour, steel plate fashioned in Atalur.

A tactical bow of untold power must have sent that missile.

In the remaining quarter-hour for him to live life, the locals hurried forward a pint for him to swizzle down. When asked who had done this harm to him, he just smiled and even produced a sardonic laugh under his frost-covered beard, and thought it an occasion, oddly, of jestful story-telling.

Wise to the fact that he was likely about to die, he told the short but humorous tale featuring a unicorn, in such a way that the unicorn's particular quality was quite ingeniously illustrated. When he had finished, he posed an odd question regarding it, which was either not serious or too incomprehensible for the locals to remember, (although it is confessed that one blacksmith who lives in the Bifrost Mountains does remember it, but refuses to talk on it).

Unable to answer the enigma, the locals asked him if he had any family, and what was his name. He did not answer, but posed the question again in a way most alarming. This in itself the inhabitants considered ill-omen, for the unicorn is widely considered sacred. The man yielded up the ghost shortly thereafter, while assaying to drown his pain with ale poured into his gullet. He was certainly not laughing anymore. The townsfolk affirmed the old saying "tell nothing laughable about unicorns"

Later that day, local boys playing outside spotted a portentous murder of crows, "ninety or hundred a-wing," a rare sight in those parts. The black avians flapped menacingly athwart the sun-setting sky, but quietly, almost as with purposeful direction. They disappeared over the orchard just outside that remote hill-town.

All this was enough to spook even the local undertaker. So the body was instead was taken a couple of miles into Ael Lot. There, the undertakers, used to unusual cases, would prepare it.

As they drew the body through the streets on a rickety wagon, someone recognized the dead and swore that the stranger were the long-missed bastard son of the king. Immediately this news was taken to King Graham and verified.

The crown was mightily sore on this account and went into sporadic spells of grief. He agreed that his ministers should investigate the fatal event.

They discovered that the man, longing for glory denied him on account of his status, had been campaigning with adventurers in the innards of the Bifrost Mountains near the great ice flow, Nthule. There hidden, under a mountainous glacier, is reportedly an interior garden which several hot springs keep warm. In those defiles explorers had spotted a legendary "unicorn."

Such a creature is extremely dangerous to hunt. Not only are his haunts remote and perilous to enter, but also the beast is exceedingly capable in defense of himself. His horn is priceless. Many nobles try, and any who pass into that garden seeking the beast become disoriented, and are in turn hunted and finally slain by the beast. Quite sneaky and stealthy, the creature easily surprises his enemies. With his long horn he impales his opponent. It is said that only a maiden most pure may see a unicorn up close, touch him, and live. (Also, according to the Ammouric record: a soul consecrated to God, who has kept his vow, may be tolerated to come within arrow shot of the beast).

The bastard son of the king, returning from the failed hunt, did not expect a band of horgoth on patrol this far West.

The townsmen had prudently neglected to inform the king that they had extracted a death-dealing arrow from the man's back. Somehow word of it got to him anyway. His majesty became even more distressed. It is law that of anyone thus slain in cowardly turning from battle, warrants being left unburied, unwept for, a corpse outside the town walls; their blood licked up by dogs, their flesh dinner for the crows. The king, who was just, did not neglect to enforce the law and vouch it apply to his own flesh and blood.

Everyone knows that the horgoth themselves resent having to shoot arrows or make surprise attacks, since it is cowardly, against their code. They always announce themselves with a war-horn. Therefore the king's son must have died not facing the foe, but fleeing the hazard, turning tail. Of course he could have been surprised, but the horg take great delight in fighting as they wish to boast superior prowess. So it was against the unicorn that the king set his royal honor.

The knights of the King would not hunt or in any way hinder the beast, for to take a unicorn brings only shallow glory, long regret. So the King invited the "learned" Friars from Whigg, staying at the local abbey, to go capture the beast alive. He wanted this so that his knights could finally pass through the Bay of Thule and Valley of Clouds and into the fells of Bardelith, to at last drive out the devil's army: the *troll-horde* and Veil-knights long encamped to the East. The king contemplated a fitting reprisal for this breaking of truce. Long had the monarch sought some solution to the blockade anyway and had for years been frustrated to accomplish it. Now he had a *casus belli*.

Since the Friars themselves were assuredly not bold enough for such dangers, they begged mercy from the king. Of the terror of Jonah they reminded him, whom a massive beast swallowed alive. Therefore the king rebuked them. Angrily he threatened to send his own daughter, the only verified virgin in Ael Lot.

She, however, would have refused. He father knew she was like him. Secretly guilty of earthly desire, but for while remaining a maiden and untouched, she nevertheless had fallen into abandoned desire for a certain errant knight. Therefore she would not be acceptable to the enchanted creature, whereby eventhough truly was her body pure and undefiled, her heart remained divided.

"...so the king understandably is grumpy," I reported to Phaedra Stormraker. "for he can in no-wise meet justice with his adversary, since his knights have no other route but through the ice-flow of Nthule and the Valley of Clouds..."

...but there was more. After all that, the jestful tale which the dying noble told of the unicorn was strictly not to be repeated, not ever. The drinkers who had heard it swore oaths not to tell it, save if they were drunk and had forgotten, (a rare thing anyway, as they were practical men and too experienced at drinking). However, on the day I happened to be there one of them had imbibed too much, and having reacted considerably to a heart-felt rejection from a local woman, was most intent on drowning his misery in draughts of ale. So in defiance of his elder companions he sat there in careless abandon nursing his pint and told the strange tale, which I myself did not find amusing. Then, the ale-drenched regulars, noticing that I, a stranger, had overheard the forbidden tale, came and begged me with strong persuasion never to repeat it, fearing for their souls. So did I promise them, and a monk should keep his word if anyone should. So I do refrain from telling it to you, but in reality it is not truly much of a jest or a tale; rather it is a warning of judgement guised as an entertainment.

It was after the drunken swain and the others left for the night that I requested of the bartend an explanation. So did he give the account concerning the king, which I have conveyed. When he was done, I was left sitting there near the barrel-cooled draughts, minding my pint, thinking unicorns and the meaning of such a seemingly fanciful mystery, (for certainly I think that the murder and the tale are somehow wrapped up in all this), but then it occurred that I must return at once..."

That was the extent of Jacob's report to Phaedra. Monks do make for fastidious workers at gathering intelligence.

"So the king is grumpy and in mourning... " said Phaedra, "going before him will be risky. If he finds out that we are not under authorized command, lawful in conduct though I be, he will imprison us. But we must be presented to him. The soldiers will not be persuaded. We could, I suppose, offer to hunt the unicorn. We are valraphs, after all."

"Must we? We do have, however, this monk," remarked Corydon, "one who, I am sure, will be our law-wise defender, and will secure our indulgence."

"Do not hope to use me to hide lawlessness..." Jacob protested. "Do you expect me to hunt a unicorn?"

"No lawlessness let be found in this resolute company, monk," grumbled Phaedra.

"We need not actually slay the beast," observed Arizel. "Somehow there be here a key to the mystery in all this, having much to do over a unicorn. I recollect some vague lore about it being enough to but catch sight of him."

Phaedra Stormraker asserted her mind. "We just need to get through the unicorn's garden in the Valley of Clouds and the waters of Thule."

"What will you say to the king, Phaedra?" Brother Jacob asked. The elfbeard looked at the monk with hardened gaze and answered.

"The truth, as much as possible—without volunteering too much—mind you that, Arizel. One does not fetch extra points for imprudent honesty. This manner of monarch be not easily fooled. And remember; whatever he says, they treat his word as law."

Arriving presently were the naval captain and soldiers. They conducted the valraphs in chains shamefully clinking into the Halls of the Sea-King, Graham. Here was a massive wood construction, with beams from trees that must have been larger than Jacob had ever seen, trees surely which dated from the time of Giants and before. This architectural display of might was more grand than any construction he had heretofore imagined. How many volumes of space, otherwise hanging empty above their heads, could be filled with vast beams and various wood carvings, bestial heads, and interlacing decorations?

Shortly they entered into the very court of King Graham, who had arisen early and of our arrival had been notified. Unlike the most men, he was not unquieted at the sight of elf-kin.

In his report to the Holy Inquisition, the monk wrote of his visit to the court of the great king:

"Those constrained who do crave admittance of his majesty may come," called out someone from the other side of massive wooden double-doors. The portors lifted the enormous grill and guards escourted us into the great chamber. We all faced the King. "'Tis a crew of privateers, sire. Our marines captured them. These may have been in cohoots with Kluxatta and his criminals. They committed not any belligerence and we suspect to be lawful. My lordship may recall these same expeditionaries only months ago."

I at once noticed, and was noticed by, two Friars of Whigg. They stood at court, serving as King's Counselors. The King looked up to see us bowing.

"So quick returned are you from that charge I did lay upon you, valraphs? And in shackles we see. Remove the shackles from these agents, you marshals, if there lingers no danger. We recognize them...we do also recall their accounts of the deep-world and Zenop's Tower in the east not long hence, and we know the very peril that the failure of their quest portends. Have you valraphs fetched the secret text which you sought and secured it from the eyes of the unholy?"

"We have..." Phaedra could not help an uncomfortable pause. "...NOT, your majesty. Anherm the great scribe passed from the world while we tarried beside a pond of the Timberhills. He sleeps now and did not complete the translation."

"Those are quite somber tidings indeed. Where is the gnome Kruth? I see fewer valraphs numbered among you as well. And who is this monk?"

"This is one Brother Jacob of Whitehaven Abbey, sire, a Kilurian who was the pupil of Anherm. He has the critical translation abilities; at least they are a start, but he will take much longer to translate than Anherm, provided we ever do recover the text."

"The Abbot of Whitehaven has given leave for this Jacob to pilgrimage?"

"He has so granted it, your highness. The monk's knowledge will also befit our enterprise considerably."

"Some of your crew, in fact a good number, from my recollection, do seem to be missing. . . whither went they, and again, where is our fellow Kruth, gnome and Arcavir? "

No answer was forthcoming. The king asked more to the point.

"He was knowledgeable beyond all others. I will not require again."

Now all were in high suspense at to what answer be given to a crowned king. Phaedra glanced at Finch, who worried almost to a fainting.

One of the Friars seated in the court piped in. "Sire, there be cause to suspect treachery among these guests, wanderers who have come to us in shackles. Mayhap we were too quick to unshackle them."

"We hardly think so, Friar Sarek." said the King, sternly.

"There was a treachery, aye, your Majesty," said Phaedra. "But not from any who here stand before you. The one who achieved it has met justice in combat...Grimble the Nibelung. He confessed to bloody murder secretly committed during the last expedition. Our captain Kruth did not detect his guile until too late. Two of our number are recently made extinct, for Grimble was under some melancholy or diabolic enthusiasm, and the conspirator Thingle, repenting, fought him but prevailed not. In the end the mad dwarf used a mountaineer's rope to uphang himself, I would say, imagining himself a giant. And as we described when we came to you months before, most "cave-wise" dwarves, save him and Drocwolf, lost their lives in the trek through the grand galleries below. And Kruthendel... my lord... him we relinquished lawfully, for we reckoned by his mindless behests that he had also gone... insane."

"Did you wager that the good King would believe that?" shouted Friar Sarek, "Gnomes do not insane go. They are beyond any brainwise health or unhealth, and the stygian vapours below effect them not. You have mutinied against your commander...and Heaven has seen fit that you be put in shackles. What have you done with our Arcavir?"

"He suffered not, and undoubtedly has 'scaped the confines in which we constrained him for his own safety. Perhaps we were a slight rash. We are honest, and we beg the king for his mercy." Phaedra lowered her head.

The king looked at me. "Be this all honest report, monk, or be it found malarchy?"

Friar Sarek interrupted again. "Prize not so highly the witness of a monk of Whitehaven, Sire."

"Enough, Friar Sarek! This is not an interrogation." The king was not up for a drawn out contest. Friar Sarek was eyeing me, a distrustful gaze; I was distasteful to him. He knew that I was the monk who had so recently and successfully written against the stupid plans for resurrecting extinct wizards.

"Aye, your majesty, it transpired just as the valraph says," I answered...but less so the part somewhat on Kruth's failing, " I continued, "something more however than anyone else's, as the valraph's empty bellies vouchsafed not their minds to reckon things rightly. Only banquets of fancy carried weight, and Kruth was preventing them from sating themselves."

"The penalty for mutiny in this feudatory is decapitation," said the King. "What say you in defense of yourselves?"

The valraphs were all hush. Silence filled the hall. Buckbar Lancelas jerked his little eyes about, quite afraid, as did Phaedra Stormraker herself, turning quite pale indeed. Finch puffed his cheeks and blew hard, thinking all were in pretty deep dung. Corydon scratched his head trying to figure a way out. Telperion Granoch grimaced nervously; a fake smile.

Daufin just grasped his forehead in disbelief. Drocwolf rolled his eyes in frustration. Arizel froze and left a blank expression.

King Graham looked to become wroth, his brow wrinkled. His great beard hid no smile. I myself then had to act, fearing that my own neck even be put in jeopardy. I knelt down and bended on one knee.

"High lord and great monarch, I beg you to punish not these impudent valraphs. As I estimate from their account, the one who sits on Mt. Argunizial summoned them, but not on account of virtue, of which they are quite deficient. For some other purpose deep were they sent, known only to divine providence. Therefore pray, most humbly I beg, give them free passage as you would a rope-girded monk or long-robed priest. Certainly it would be within your anointed authority to assign them some public penance, such as crusade, in order to atone for their failures and build up the Ael's kingdom. They have talents many and remarkable, being valraphs. I have witnessed it myself.

"Kruthendel still lives, although he sleeps. Waste not these good resources by the easy penalty to headless perdition or rotting away in the dungeon....I do sincerely beg Your Majesty in the name of God. "

There was silence. Then⋯

"You are Abbot Cromna's man. How keeps our father's health?"

I nodded. "With good faring he keeps it. But he is not safe, he must vie with rival monks who have enough aggression to check him sorely. "

"Is that so? Need we convey a sheriff to investigate such craven monks?"

Friar Sarek, a man careless to take a hint, interrupted again. "Do not bother, Sire. Everyone knows that the monks of Whitehaven will never comprehend obedience. They are quite libertine. They claim to follow a life of discipline, but are well known to abuse their monastic privilege. "

I first ignored the Friar and his challenge. That is always the best policy with them. Instead I said "Your Majesty, how difficult it is even for good men to discern the truth in the case of spiritual matters. We monks alone can detect conspiracy within the sacred confines. We must put our trust in God who will avenge the righteous and protect his vineyard.m Abbot Cromna only asks that you let these valraphs guard me."

"Now in what you say we do concur, monk. Eventhough it seems they deserve decapitation. Perhaps it would be wiser to put these kind to some noble task."

"It would so please your majesty."

"It is not a minor affair to harm one so favored as Kruth," he said. "We must weigh in prayer what warrants being done with these. Unwelcome tidings are these matters indeed. Have you valraphs anything at all to show for your striving? Did our wizard Bannock find you? "

"Indeed, your majesty, and I am here even now." Arizel came forward, appearing out from the shadows as usual. "Kruth and the valraphs counted me among felonius summoners, as I was after them. I fell in with a group of rioting churls from a nearby outpost who had slain their own ecclesiastic. The throng would have burned me. But instead they proclaimed me their leader and went about terrorizing the countryside.

They refused to take no for an answer. I even sadly witnessed them smite down our celebrated Burgundy Knight. I do admit it true, however, with these valraphs: Kruth the Eloniah was too strict a leader; they were in some terrible straights over it."

"Then you also are admittedly guilty, wizard, of mutiny. How do you hope now to be a king's counselor? "

"No need to fear wizards, majesty." I said. "Wicked monks are about the lands and whisper in the ears of Christian kings. They who look like holy monks, but who wear 'neath their robes the scapular of the All-seeing Eye of Abraxas! "

"The goatish monks are infernal, not to be trusted," remarked Arizel. "Nor are these Friars a worthy help in lands of sword and sorcery. Do not waste time heeding those whose learning is vanity! As your vizier I will keep you safe from their unwisdom."

"Do not propose to teach me about my own counselors. Know your place. Bannock. You yourself are widely confessed as goatish, at least until you have proven your worth."

"My lord, I hear that you are having trouble with unicorns as of late." Said Arizel, making a final play for our redemption.

The king fell silent, thoughtful. "As for you all, you must some high task accomplish, provided that our clemency lasts till breakfast. Go now, all of you; depart from me. Retire to the assigned chambers and prepare yourselves to learn justice. Tomorrow shall you know our mind at full."

There is no debating a high king. We bowed and departed at once..."

So has Jacob testified here to the king's words. Evening in scarlet came. They were well cared for in that old castle. At sunset they were given a tour of the battlements and shown the king's new canons, the "thunder-lions."

Very early the next morning the king's constable invited them to have breakfast with the King of the Aels himself. The Valraphim were at their best behavior. They were trying to remember whatever civilized manners they could.

"Can it be?" said the king with disbelief, 'that Kruth, the great mind of Furthreach, keeper of the Torgrith, has lost the loyalty of his crew? Is he to be dismissed now as insane? And he is even fallen asleep because of it? Well, we suppose some sorcerer has him, one of your fold, Bannock. You are prudent to shun your collegues as you have, for they scheme some dark mastery. Word is that they intend to use great magic to restore the collegium of wickedness, Nystol, enchanter of souls. We do not fear; the ponderous gnome always does escape the prisons into which he is cast, on account of meddling in the affairs of men, and he ends up back here seeking asylum. Whether by his craftiness or by gnome-trick, he gets out. He has been awake as long as I have lived; let us hope he does not sleep; a gnome-sleep could last centuries. The fetching of *The Black Books* is a stupendous enterprise that is most stern and time consuming; and must be acheived while the gnome Arcavir can yet be consulted. It must therefore be worked out among yourselves who is best leader, and that is easy as long as everyone keeps the common good in mind, not their own plan, rather the quest. So you are free to continue, but transgress ye any law and think not that I can overlook it again."

"Your highness, we plan to go westwards upon the ice-flow, " said Phaedra "and then along the coast, skirting enemies, as far as Northern Warm Sea. We shall obtain a ship and sail east, into the unknown waterways of the Eluvigar and the Alph."

The king summoned a chart of Whitehawk to be brought forth and unrolled on a huge adjacent table.

"Eluvigar? There is a reason that its not on the chart. No seamen have returned from those perilous waters, huge isles of ice, massive sheer cliffs on either side with nowhere for a boat. It is surely death...those waters shall bring you into the world beneath, but not in the way you hope. Yet I say you will not even get that far. First there must be traversed the Valley of Clouds. Bolgoth marauders in the Valley of Clouds struck down my own flesh and blood, my son making it back somehow only to draw his last breath. Against the same course I should advise ye, eventhough you are set upon it and determined. You had best eat a hearty breakfast then, here before you depart. Which route do you mean when you say along the coast, the Eastern or Western coast?"

"The East coast and Northernly, my king; it is easiest," replied Arizel.

"That is not wisdom. My platoons no longer patrol there. The foe has established a foothold. They have built forts. The fell armies of Mulcifer might capture you."

"We cannot take the southern coast. The cold is too fierce there. Many have frozen to death in the barren fells. We must take lesser hazard along the Northern shore."

"No, do not; we refuse you such passage. It is but sheer cliff, and there is no corridor. You will instead go through the Valley of Clouds and accomplish this penitential task which we require. Enter the place of the Unicorn and let him draw you into his lair. If your monk is daring enough, he will search the way out, and you will have nothing to fear. We will reward you with freedom if you can capture the beast. Mind you, success is not likely. Some of you might survive and get through; however, no one has returned alive from that place. If you do evade the Unicorn's assault and get through, horgoth detatchments will then ruthlessly hunt you."

"Pray, high lord, inform us of these horgoth armies, this troll-horde," Jacob said. "...we hear but scant intelligence of their movements."

"They are a formidable foe indeed," replied the king in a warning tone, "and not easy to kill, as they might seem in the sagas. What is worst is that you will find no help from men. Mulcifer is in the hire of the Balecrown. The Northern feudatory Nzul is what most kings esteem a paragon of virtue and uprightness, and Baffay, "the perfect feudal state," where all races "get along," and there is no thought of disobedience. But not even grand knights dare go against the great archon. His secret armies of black-hearted bolg are not a secret.

"Noble men, ambitious for position and power, give this Balecrown alliance and fealty in exchange for magics or other advantage. Now ranked under his scepter he has the black-clad cavaliers of the scimitar, Veil-knights. I alone among the crowns have rejected his offers of alliance."

"Where did this villainous overlord come from?" Phaedra asked.

"That story is told not in brief, but we do have the leisure this morning to tell it, if you are patient to hear it. . . a service that any rightful crown would prepare for those meaning to forfeit safety, even their own dear lives for us. Let it be not said that the quest-fellows of Kruth we sent into danger without knowledge. "

"I would like to hear the legends," said Jacob.

"To do so we must go back to the earliest days of this visible creation, to a time even before our own feudatory existed, before even our ancestral tribe walked the earth. The *Xilmurian* epic tells of the first battle that occurred on the slopes of Mt. Argunizial, the second of the Auroran wars. I myself was drawn into that ancient quarrel, as a young man, and as prince, when I fought in the line of the disputed Erl King. Again later as the young king of Ael Lot, even to this present time of my waning. The contest shall go on even after we are life-riven. The tale always be told, and it is one that my father memorized perfectly, and had me do the same. Now the witness, the ancient who left his account to men, whose name was never known, begins his telling. Hear him speak through my mouth."

The king squinted with seriousness and peered at them, no smile under his beard. He spoke, and none durst interrupt:

Veils of years must be lifted, you who are bold and you who are mindful, or whosoever would tell of things that have long ago passed. All ye know too little if ye would tell anything regarding that spirit and fey power who broods in the remote places; have you harkened to but hearsay and the repute of fabulists? Something of that infernal mind I know. I am an anointed King, so now you must earnestly give ear, for I shall reveal in full how the day went. It was a thing which I saw with mine own eyes. You may have heard these things from elders, a story of elf lords and deep-dwelling dragons, but none will tell as I tell. This is the account of Nimrul, The Archdeceiver, who caused elf to slay elf and angel to abolish angel. Many have warned that it is mere fable, and treat of it as a child's tale. Nay, my liege-sons, were only that so.

It transpired in the Second Age, the age of the draconian terror, when men, weakened by the disease of impure ways, and of uncleanness from idolatry, could not withstand the deadly attacks of the great dragons. Some red dragons would appear and burn towns and devour many, and even demand human sacrifice. But not all dragons were so. A few righteous dragons refused to bring terror upon men. They had but minor influence upon the many others. Men had to burrow and rear their towns in hollows beneath the earth to escape destruction.

The Allfather looked down upon the earth from his sapphire throne on Mt. Argunizial and saw the perishing of men. Therefore he sent into the world *elphim*, in particular the courtly race of Elves who were powerful and pure, celebrated atheletes to slay drags. Many and glorious were the dragon-hunts.

When the many tribes of Elves had gone forth into various regions of the continent and had slain many notorious dragons, they were become famous victors upon the broad earth. They began to compete with one another for the imperishable glory. A thousand seasons circled past while the Elves hunted the dragons and slew them, driving many deep into mountain holes and remote wastes. The dragons became few, but drag-hunting remained popular, an ordeal of renown; yet it was becoming an injustice, a sport to drive the race to extinction.

The time came when Elves went thither even to claim those dragons for whom righteous wisdom was a prize, the ones who had not committed crime and were withdrawn into far mountain wildernesses to meditate. These were tranquil creatures such as the Neoplatonian dragons.

Now there is no being which the Almighty ever created which he meant to be evil, so the useless hunting and slaying of dragons was becoming a great wrong, an attack upon the living earth.

There was one highly placed who was above all in skill and accomplishment, Nimrul of the house of Carathiarim. He came from the land of Eltholad by the river Phixon, where today is the feudal kingdom of Aethuria, 'neath the looming hills of Ayrs.

Now when this decree was read in the West, by the Haorite priests, before Nimrul, he gave nod before the tribes. But he was unquieted inwardly. No monarch had ever ruled over the Elves, a race that was free. Nevertheless, he kept secret his thoughts and waited to see who this king might be.

It turned out, some seasons later, that the signs were seen, signs which had been prophesied, of the coming of a chosen Erl King. Nimrul therefore was minded to give the new ruler a grand welcome in order that he might win favor.

The races were summoned to gather together in the hills of Dilmonath to prepare for the new king.

Finally came the day for the unveiling of the young king, whose identity a particular Neoplatonian dragon had been charged to kept privy. The last of the three Neoplatonian dragons arrived from the east and perched at the mountain place of welcome and ceremony.

Nimrul the great lord, when he saw the chosen one come forth from under the dragon wings spread, was taken aback. He had expected the new monarch to be some grand ethereal creature, an angel, or other powerful being. Instead, the Furth High King was a young human, a mortal, a descendent of the son of dust. No one knew what to say, and silence filled the rocky hills. Especially did Nimrul consider this a dishonour, and he was most displeased. He even turned his back on the king as he left and did not attend the entire coronation.

At the end of that day, after the unveiling and crowning, the Elves retired in the place where the lords had pitched their tents and were at peace, strolling without concern under the stars in the cool of evening. Not all were at peace, however, for in brooding walked Nimrul, in vexation and in thoughts dark. He went and found his companion Thraetaon, prince of Ziph, there at ease nearly asleep by his tent, and confided dark thoughts to him saying:

'Why doth thou, my companion, sit at ease welcoming rest? What sleep can close your eyelids as this new star arises? Do you not see how novel and arbitrary decrees have gone forth? Laws which no ear ever expected to hear? Without heed of our right, a novel dominion is founded, issuing from the throne supreme. They have tricked us; we have been made fools.

A mortal human, one who is barely able to sustain himself or have a clear thought, has been accepted as fit to rule over all as anointed king. One who rudely eats the base food of the earth will hold sway over all the elflands and dragon domains. How submit ourselves to him and his progeny? How render fealty and bowing down into dust on bended knee proclaim us slaves of dust? Therefore new purpose now urges me to new words. New laws give rise to new thoughts. Muster before the risen sun all thy vast array of armed contingent, conveying word to every elf prince and highly placed master among us, to come to the ascent of Adommin in the North by Zenith, so that we may all discuss this enormity and what purpose we shall all in common hold.'

Thraetaon obeyed the word of his compatriot, and many hundreds of elves came to the ascent of Adommin in the Crach Mountains, in the high place where now stands the Arc du Baffay. Nimrul gave a speech of great persuasion to the many chivalric companies of elves, explaining in full what advantages a mortal crown might yield them, and comparing those mere hopes with assured and profound disadvantage and humiliation, including extinction of the glorious hunt.

'And what have the Elves since the hunt has been forever banned? Has the Allfather hid from us some other purpose for our lives? Can we whose thoughts and designs are of greatness submit to a breed not long wonton to living outside caves? What must we do next, submit to four-footed beasts? Does the Allfather envy the glory of our hunts? What shall each one of ye do with the thousands of summers left thee in these lands? Wilt thou pick flowers to adorn garlands for thy new master? What other choice can you make but to consent to rebellion against this new tyranny, this unworthy arrangement, contrary to every natural ordering? Or else, if you wish, remain then in dishonour, loyal to your human master. But here is my design: I shall assail the confines of the sacred mountain herself, as did the giants of old, who in their stupidity climbed, but could not seize the sapphire throne. The celestial citadels shall burn like candles, and I myself shall arrest and bind the Almighty, and usurp the cosmic panoply. It is thy choice: learn freedom and self-will or remain in submission to infinite humiliations. Upon the sapphire throne shall I announce a new age of freedom and liberality to all, and the Ancientmost one shall learn new justice. Surely not even a single one of you would propose better counsel.'

So he spoke, and was acclaimed by all. A shout of approval went up from the host. One only did not consent, but came forth and stood alone apart from thousands in glittering mail. He replied in contradiction and contempt.

'Thou rebel, corrupt power, craven spine and worker of highest treason, slanderer and evil genius! I for one will not consent to your falsities and join in your act of folly, certain to become your wreckage. So now silence yourself, though you be great in might, and curb your impudent tongue, and you might find some clemency from Ancientmost. " The rebel Nimrul then growing stern and grim replied:

'I should have expected no less from you, Fendil of Ataroth, and I say it would be better if ye busied your days teaching girlish peace as you are accustomed; but do not interrupt the assembly of the new rulers when they are planning war. Now, off with you; I send you away with this rebuke: Stay a simpleton, unable to sacrifice your safety for the higher right. Run the paths back to Mt. Arguzinial and give your precious Allfather this troubling message: The Furth will feel our native might shake the bright mountain in answer to his unjust decree and proposed tyranny. An invincible army is coming to undo his misrule and teach him what manner of beings he holds in slight regard. Be he prepared to yield the sapphire throne of Argunizial and give the would-be king and his armies up to chains, or if he likes a contest, endure grim war filled with regret."

So he spake, and the shocking news of rebellion Fendil did carry to Arginizial, to the glorious Halls of the High Furth Lord. Dismayed at hearing of such unseemly disloyalty, Allfather did not rise from his sapphire throne, but remained unmoved. Ambrosius Ammouris, the lion-head, had heard all and stepping forward amid the assembly of gods spake, saying "It is beneath the dignity of the Most High to be bothered cleaning the universe of such vermin. Only his servants may justly perform the task. " He called out to all the court of Nephilung, "Who shall lead His armies against so terrible and so passionate a foe? "

None dared step forward. So therefore Fendil, admitting his insufficiency at war, accepted the generalship, commending himself to God's grace.

At the dawn of battle's appointed day, the sentinels of the sacred mount spotted the banded powers of Nimrul, the Rebel. It was a vast forest of spear in furious march. Under stormy clouds against a dim horizon they went in tight formation. The righteous elves of Avim sounded the trumpet, and a vast array of elves and nephilungs now came upon the plain and formed for battle, bristling with a thousand beaming spears upright held, helms and shields of many different houses. Alas, now would this day see elf brother slay his own elf-brother, or the elf-kin of his own clan, ones who so often before had met together in merriment and feasting. All such mild remembrances must now be put forever off, and replaced by the stern councils of war.

And there rode foremost Nimrul onto the ascending slopes of battle, seeming like a god, his gilded chariot illuminated by the sun rising in flames. Like a majestic idol, or colossus in golden armour, enclosed about with elf champions, he radiated dread. Soon the two battle lines formed between host and challenger, and before each facing present in terrible array were the long lines of spear, a foreboding sight.

Nimrul Archdeceiver dismounted from his chariot, seeming more the titan, his frame swollen huge by huge pride, a swelling which he himself fancied was consequent upon his own waxing inward greatness...revealing itself. Yet, in fact, t'was naught but pride. He towered a full arm above the others, gloriously clad in adamantine chain and inaurate plate. Stepped he forth midway between the gap of armies seeking some foe who would be first to initiate combat.

Fendil, who stood by Ambrosius the Nephilung, could not endure such a display, considering in his heart how he would like to disfigure the rival elf, discovering for all to see the same horrible ugliness that inwardly was hidden. So it was Fendil who first stepped out from his armed peers to deface the mighty offender. There he stood and met him halfway in the dreadful interval, wondering how much longer he would have to endure the glorified presence of that would-be-usurper.

'Perhaps you have some lofty intention?' Fendil asked with stern glare. 'Was not your hope to have hazarded the threshold of Ashkhar[41] unopposed and take the throne, a throne you assumed would be left unguarded out of fear of your coming? Think how vain you have been to rise up armed against the Allpower, who, if he had wished it, could have merely sent an incessant flock of sparrows to finish you off, or simply could have reached out and with one blow finished you and sent your legions tumbling into darkness. You did not expect to see me here, did you, as well as others of our race, who prefer faith and loyalty? You did not think me so bold when I stood as one who seemed a fool to your world. This small band of Avim and Ataroth have joined me in the loyalty you once defamed as fanatical. Now you will learn, though it is too late for you, that sometimes only few have true sight while the rest, numbering in thousands, err.'

So Fendil spake. To this the great opposer, with scornful eye, answered:

'It will go ill for you, son of Ataroth, and though you got away the first time, now you will receive your deserved reward, the first act of punishing war which my right hand delivers; after all, your tongue was the first that durst oppose me and the assembly of free elf-kin, in useless contradiction. Your tongue shall then be the first of what you shall forfeit in war, right now to be cut out by my dread spear hand. For all of ye who stand opposed: now I recommend that you shed final tears, since none of you are worthy to be counted among the free elves, the new gods of all. We can no longer bear the sight of our slothful and well fed brethren who tarry on this mount, they who have traded the hardships of liberty in exchange for servile security beneath the angelic wings.'

So the Archdeceiver countered, but Fendil replied.

'Please quit making a baboon of yourself. Do you not see that your last moment of glory is near? Nor will you ever find an end of folly, for truth is too remote from you now. Thou untaught and dull of wit, so revealed are you by your words on servitude. I know divine servitude good and natural, not the kind you describe of; service to usurpers like yourself, that's servitude, to join cause with one who has rebelled against his just and worthier, just like those who now stand behind waiting for the pain you've helped them earn. So let it be the way you want it then; reign yourself if you wish, but do so in the fatal darkness of the dim underworld. That's where you are about to go. Let me serve the Kingdom of Ashkhar ever-blessed, and every divine behest obey, for they alone are worthy of obedience. Yet as for yourself, chains in some enclosing and dark pit now expect, not realms, and include this greeting on your impious head!'

Even before Fendil had finished his words, with spear-blade he had already struck upon the proud helm of the Archdeceiver with tempest, so swiftly that the opposing round shield could not intercept the ruinous

---

[41]*Ashkhar:* The divine kingdom of Allfather which surrounded mount Argunizial in the first age.

impact. Seven paces backwards recoiled the Archdeceiver, and on bended knee he stooped at last, though still holding his spear upright. Amazement took hold of the rebel host, but more so rage, to see their mightiest foiled in such a way. All the army of Ashkhar shouted triumphant cries at the presage of victory.

Adversary spears now closed the line with us, and a storm of clangor soon arose. The mountain valley echoed with cries of those struck down by the first closing of spears. It was a horrible havoc.

There was a riotous rush of chariot wheels crashing into armored battalions and the dismal hiss of slung stones overhead. There was kept no thought of flight or retreat by either side, nor any feats which paled the flush of valor. For a long time the battle seemed to be in the hands of the enemy, and then in confusion it would turn and our banners would advance.

Nimrul indeed was prodigious in power and sent many Elves of Avim to twilight's shores that day. He met no warrior who was his equal, so he ranged through the ranks and sought the enemy nephilungs, none of whom were able enough in close combat to match him. Soon we were forced to make a retreat and found ourselves fighting on the high ground, but still needing to move backwards up the mountain, for the number of the enemy was so great that they would have easily surrounded us in the valley, the original field of battle.

After the foe had taken all the mountain up to the middle ridges, the Archdeceiver with his war-mace was blasting ruin upon the Elves of Ashkar. He would send several at a time into the air, hurled by the wide destruction of his swing. After he had dispatched many companies of these, he went searching the ranks to find the place where the sword of Ambrosius smote down rebels.

Ambrosius the nephilung was labouring constant war, felling each rebel in one blow with the crush of his double-edged sword, which often like a harvester of wheat he lifted aloft. When Ambrosius saw the Archdeceiver nearby, he ceased from his war toil, meaning to overthrow the giant foe and drag him away in chains. So with great indignation the lion-headed paladin addressed the gigantic warlord.

'Author of new chaos never expected from the noble race of elves, heavy indeed are these new acts of sedition, though they shall fall heaviest on yourself and your adherents. Look how you have disturbed the world and brought misery among many, which had never thought of disobedience until your words corrupted. Traitor, you received high glory and wondrous gifts like no other from the Father; is this how you return thanks? You have instilled malice into thousands and today foolishly propose to disturb the serenity of the holy ones. The Kingdom of Ashkhar tolerates not those enraged with war-mayhem. The Father exiles you forever, and your conspirators along with you, to the dark places of the world where other evils hide, the monstrous brood of the beast and the giants from Time's beginning. Come, let your doom start then under my avenging sword.' So spake the Prince of the Nephilim, to whom thus his adversary:

'Airy lion-head, whose frame consists of not much more than some cloudy composition of ethereality infused with spark, so are your words of like substance, a rumbling of hot clouds, meant to frighten with a roar those whom your feats fail to impress. Not even the least of my war elves have you put to flight, and though they may fall down, they rise again unvanquished. What hope do you have then to chase me away with empty threat? Do you call this battle? Perhaps in your eyes it is a conflict born of evil. That we should seek to preserve honour and glory, is that an evil? It is not; we say it is glory itself, which we shall win on this mountain slope today, to your everlasting shame. For we shall never cease to arise anew, no matter how much power you level upon our frame; and so if need be, you shall see the very Halls of Ashkhar today become a bloody field of infinite war.'

So they ended parley, and now moved into position to exchange. Indeed, all watched as the two titans moved about the slope ready to decide the fate of the Kingdom of Ashkhar. At once their flashing weapons waved, spinning deadly circles through the air, their shields like bright round suns opposed darted back and forth, receiving the crush of resolute strokes. Ambrosius, as he was circling there, stumbled over a rock, and his opponent took advantage. He smashed off the lower leg of the unbalanced nephilung, who then sunk to one knee. Just as quickly the speeding fin of that mace struck apart one of the eyes of his lion-head. The Archdeceiver Nimrul stepped back to view his butcher-work accomplished, saying:

'You have been outdone; see it with your one eye lasting; your master has given you no prevailing strength. Allfather has forsaken thee, and now you are destroyed.'

The shock to the great lion-head did not long stun. With lightning speed he rose up into the air on his eagle wings, hovering and holding ready his sword, though losing much ichor through his leg stump. Terrible was the bright blade of Ambrosius, a trophy taken from the hand of a rebellious giant in the previous age. The Archdeceiver now in turn closed to finish his work, and with more butchery strew the ichor of Ambrosius upon every face, for he knew the nephilung would not retreat. But Ambrosius in mid-swing met the shining mace of The Archdeceiver with a smiting of steep force unstoppable. It blasted the opposed shaft that blocked vainly, and then reversing wheeled again a new stroke, in a flash, severing the unprotected sword-arm of the enemy.

Now did Nimrul first know pain profound. The shock of it convulsed his frame as the sword again passed through his shoulder into his chest. His fairy blood in streamlets everywhere poured, staining his armour dark which before had been so bright.

On all sides the elven fighters came immediately running to his aid, grouping for rebellious defense of their yet proud chieftain. Others lifted him onto his shield and with speed bore him away. They brought him to the encampment (which by now they had set up at the foot of the mountain). Nimrul in anguish cried out and wept, gnashing his teeth, as much from the pain of injury as from the deep shame that had struck down his pride and glory; to have for so long been matchless among elves and all other created beings. The body of an elf heals in but a single night, but the soreness of the deep wound and its ugly scar never faded for Nimrul.

Ambrosius, too, they helped away from that place of gore, but he, a nephilung, could not restore the ethereal body parts which he had forfeited, for the corporeality of that race is of finest matter, and each nephilung indeed is a species *in se* like the angels, totally unique, and so nothing lost can be refashioned. So it is that the Prince of The Nephilim is one who is lame, who must walk about the halls with a peg-leg and patch over his eye. These battle wounds he counts for marks of glory; his service, no new eye or limb from the Allfather. The act of valour on the field won him the famous crown of seven radiant horns.

Fendil, Elf-lord of profound loyalty, fighting on another slope, meanwhile accomplished feats of war which earn like memorial. With the might of the house of Ataroth in his veins, he pierced with daunting spear the deep battle array of the opposing house of Ziph, a faithless company. It was furious Thraetaon who had led them into battle crying out blasphemies; and Fendil sent this warlord off with horrendous wounds bellowing.

Then they vanquished other notable elven fighters, rebel champions so titled, Arioc and Zathon, Arrhoc and Ptai, master lords now brought low. I might relate thousands, and their names set down, but their mischief and doom have cancelled them from memory, consigning them to obscurity and the remotest recesses of black Tartarus.

As the day waned, the battle subsided, and pierced armour lay strewn over all the rocks of the mountain slopes, heaps of elven warriors, overturned chariots, wreckage having tumbled to the bottom of the mountain, great warwagons which once mighty mithyn deer pulled..."

The king paused his narration and drank more of his morning wine.

"The tale continued for some length, explaining how the rebel elves had made it all the way up to the threshold of the sacred precinct at the summit. Elves, a few men, and the nephilim repulsed them in a final and terrible contest of arms. Although I had memorized the entire sequence so many years ago, I will not be able to finish the poetic passage for you until I can remember the first word of the subsequent verse.

"I do remember most how Ambrosius smote down Nimrul. Other rebels having been struck down sorely rose from the rocks and fled like wounded dogs. The face of the earth opened up and swallowed many others, and many into the nether furnace went; and taking refuge they sat, obscured in dark Tartarus. Into the great furnaces hurried they, and it is there where the dismal spirits of any rebellious elphim or troll must ever return in just and lasting torment, lasting torment profound. Count others besides; lesser punishment earning, they who hid in the deep-born caves and became the grey elves and even more deeply the drow."

"It was high lore," Brother Jacob said, "how can we thank your majesty?!"

"Aye, it is high lore indeed, but mark ye: it be not just a tale for entertaining. It is a factual account and it was good for me to hear it again. It gives me new purpose to continue the fight against those hordes. It seems a never-ending contest against the master of deceptions, Nimrul, and Mulcifer his servant, descendent of Thraetaon. Now even more so, and in our time Nimrul allies with those infernal-monks who lurk everywhere feigning piety."

"How, if I may please your majesty to inquire, did he become the creature, he who was once called 'Nimrul Lord of Elves,' now 'Northing'?"

"Unfit even for the prison of Tartarus, the dismal creature has been consigned to the remote North of the world, where the earth stays hoary under frost and ice most of the year, the Nzul in far off Bardelith,[42] where not much greenery grows. Although it took him centuries, he acquired many thralls and vassals, both of bolg and wicked men. He built a colossal shrine to himself within the Arc du Baffay, a cathedral of Melancholia, a vast hall commemorating his vain rebellion against the Allfather.

"Once that mountain of a project was finished in the third age, he then brooded for two centuries, bringing about universal misery by devilish wars and scheming assassinations in every place. He is in fact the Balecrown who sits on the sapphire throne of the world.

"By the fourth age he at last rivaled Nystol the wizard-college in power and influence over the princes of the earth. In time, he eventually brought the wretched dwarf-Emperor Nergalf, Conqueror of all the Furth. Under his sway, he beguiled the nibelung's impish mind with vain ideas. In this way he involved himself in a mysterious intrigue which brought about the destruction of those grand wizard towers, and the world tumbled into great ignorance. But all men agree, better to tolerate ignorance than to go even to the edge of knowledge under the counterfeit and unholy light of Nystol.

"Nystol's desolation was Nimrul's only accomplishment worthy of recognition, but done only for distorted self-adulation to wipe out a rival. In our time many good human kings, who should know better, still praise the creature Nimrul for this. On account of this fame his books, his twisted *Philosophy of Melancholia*, are encouraged to be studied in all the universities.

"So after the Dwarf-Emperor passed, the evil creature saw before him no rival power nor any serious contender to world-dominion. So with secret armies having been sent everywhere at night from his glaciate shrine, he directed a cruel and hazardous war upon all the civil lands under the Gates of Dariel. He targeted especially the Ammouric crowns. This was the *Bellum Diabolicum*. My own father fell in the Battle under Moonlight. It was the power and wisdom of a certain crown who rallied the races of men that put a halt to the mayhem, pursuing the troll-horde from the plain of Gederon back into their abominable dens in the mountains of Bardelith. In fact, an epic poem has been sung about that, how a few heroes of my own day even humiliated the Balecrown himself not long after."

"Do you know such a poem?" asked Jacob. "Surely if it be well sung, the high subject warrants it be entered in the *Black Books*. "

"It was never written down. However other great epics are in need of preservation. I have heard that these tomes called *The Black Books* have some remarkable power to withstand mouldering and ruin, among other

---

[42]*Bardelith:* The wild and remote sub-arctic lands of north-central Illystra comprised mostly of tundra and tamarack forest, where is bounded the dark nation of Nzul.

mysteries. Will you now do a favor for a king whose hospitality has not failed you? I will give a gift. I possess an ancient poem of which only two copies exist. It is entitled, *The Bladetongue*. Will you not copy the work into the blank leaves of that tome?"

"Many empty leaves await some grave writing at the tome's end. Certainly it would be a great contentment pleasing to my good monarch in this way."

"Then you shall take with you one of the few copies, as a gift. But you must do yet another thing for me."

"We are at your disposal, your majesty..."

The king summoned one of his servants and bade him retrieve something from his library.

"I would not give such a scroll to just anyone. This is one of the original *bzebus* volumens, perhaps even set down by the hand of Zenops himself. From the reputation of your abbey I trust that you shall make an excellent copy of it, after your travels are done and you have some time. By the way, why exactly, say again, are you going upon the treacherous Alph river anyway?"

"We seek certain relics," replied Arizel swiftly, "at the edge of the world, but his Abbot wishes that we divulge not more on't, for the enemy's spies are everywhere, even the halls of Ammouric Kings."

"That is true, Bannock. Who knows if one may dare to lurk even here. I must not then press you men further on the matter, since it is not right for the crown to weigh matters proper to the holy ones. Come, let us to the throne hall. I must speak from the throne to all of you."

The servant returned and informed us that the *Bladetongue*-scroll the King's daughter, Arcesilea was presently examining. The king assured of her presence among them to advise before departure.

e followed King Graham into the grand throne hall. He was a lord of many winters, grey but still stalwart and not so old as to shirk war. Up close one could see a tinge of sadness or regret in his otherwise flashing eyes, for although he was a magnanimous lord, (a great oak grown strong with many winters), he had, as a young king, taken liberties, many liberties. Nevertheless, repentant, his feudal rule was one of peace, but only minor prosperity had come to the people, for the people were not repentant, but generally insolent.

Colorful tapestries depicting great battles hung about the walls. A great oaken throne and several other remarkable seats were placed, ornate and incredible to behold. All the valraphs stood ready for his command.

"Come look at this," he said, standing where several unusual relics were on display. He picked up what looked like a spear of spirals. On closer inspection it was an elongated animal horn.

"The sacred beast has long haunted the springs of that sub-glacial valley. This magical relic is the long-horn he sports, a thing near priceless. Of its magical powers no one knows." He passed it to Arizel. It was quite large, at least as long as a two-handed sword. The beast which had brandished it was no doubt huge, and I could not imagine the size of the beast who could bear it. Even a hurth horse would barely match it. I looked at Arizel, and he looked at me. This was a sign that we were on the right path to fulfill our common quest. Arizel gazed upon it. At last he held in his hands, the object of his magical quest. He had to hand it back, however.

"In my grandfather's day Duke Ikonn, marauder of worlds, visited us and dared to hunt them, and succeeded. It is said that he rued the deed. I think that the beast keeps his grim enchantment upon the Thulean Pass as a kind of reminder of that bloodshed, no peace between us sinful men and sacred animals. The rumour of his horn extending life is a deceit. The substance does make one immortal, nay indeed, for consuming it ends one's earthly span instead. That is how my poor father met his end —by consuming the powder of the horn, he became maddened with battle-lust.

"You must be watchful when crossing the waters; be alert. If you somehow capture the beast, by no means harm it. We must accept the estrangement that our forefathers authored, but my kingdom will never prosper without a route to the east, to Tyrnopolis. This is Heaven's will, perhaps now many things will soon change. I have done little else but maintain this realm of Aels, Ultima Thule, and blessed Nathycanthe. It has been far too difficult merely to keep the corsairs of the Vastess Ocean in check. Surely my reign can never be compared to those of my ancestors. I have no male heir. For me only my daughter is there, who upon my passage will be queen. Perhaps, if she gets over herself, she will do more than could a king. But otherwise no legacy of greatness do I leave. Some monarchs history will forget, but Heaven will not.

"Even so, beyond all other failings I would say it has been the chastizement of the Unicorn that has kept me from hazarding war against the creeping power of Baffay, to launch a crippling blow to his eastern flank. The surface of the glacier is too treacherous, and there is no way around the Tmolean Mountains save through the valley. Any supply line to my invading army would be cut off by this terror lurking in the Valley of Cloud, and we cannot build a pontoon bridge to span the waters as long as it haunts that place. On this account the Dire and his minions are at leisure to do whatsoever he wishes. His influence grows throughout the rest of the continent as he spreads his immoral doctrines through the publications of the infernal monks and sends his fell armies to vex the other realms.

"Go then, and know how grave it is that this situation be set right. My decree and the prayers of my priests will aid you. I will use my authority to protect you: you will be assigned a different campaign leader, by my command. One of your crew···and the monk, he can stay here. Such physical dangers a monk cannot endure."

"Sire," I said. "I am a trained guardian monk, capable with the quarterstaff."

"Very commendable—but a guardian nonetheless, and no combat-hardened infiltrator."

There was a moment of uncertain interlude. Corydon broke the silence.

"My Lord, I am Corydon, but a lowly man at arms. At first I did not believe it, but Kruth the gnome convinced me. At first we thought her a fair witch, but it was an ethereal Lady who appeared to us in the caves. She prophesied unto us. She said that a Christian monk would be needed to finish the Nazageist. We did not know what she meant, because no valraph had yet set his face against the Balecrown, and there was no intention to go to Baffay. Now we are being sent there. The prophecy must be coming to pass. I dare say we must take along this monk, at your leave, of course."

The great king rubbed his heard in thought.

"A prophecy, heh? Kruth approved it? Then I will accept it. Hmmm. Your breaking of the martial code is a considerable enormity, and you valraphs must have someone lead you out of folly. This monk, Jacob Magister of Whitehaven Abbey, who had no hand in wrong-doing, he will therefore be the new campaign leader. This monk is your new captain; all you valraphs must follow his every order. Do that unfailingly and gain divine protection. So doing you will spare your own dear lives."

There was a silence. The king noticed the startled looks on the faces of the valraphs. Phaedra Stormraker whispered something to the chamberlain, who then spoke.

"Sire, these fighters, swift valraphs, wish for you to know: the monk is bookwise, but no real warrior. He has quick hands with his quarterstaff, but otherwise does not know a thing of gruesome war and campaigning. He has never even slain an enemy."

"It is too late. We have spoken. He knows the quarterstaff. That is warrior enough. I have prayed and will not change my decision. If he knows not how to lead a fighting crew, by God's will he will quickly learn. Do not gainsay a king. Remember how I have spared your miserable lives."

The king paused, held his head in thought, and then continued.

"Now once past the lair of the Unicorn, if it be safe, the guide must return to me with word, so that we can prepare an expeditionary force and ready the army. Your coming is a sign to me, a signal, as was the recent death of my son."

A stern look came over the visage of the King.

"I now rouse me in my throne. The beast will be put off. The Dire and his troll horde will cower at the might of the King. Go therefore; a guide will now take up with you in the castle yard. After subduing the Unicorn, if you can do it, then wend way to Tyrnopolis and take ship to Thasos. Find a way to Baffay fastness and learn its lay. You mountaineers now use your skill, scale its sheer walls and infiltrate. Spy upon the goings on there, do whatever you can to cripple their intelligence operations. By that time we should have made bloody inroads into the wastes of Bardelith, and you can rejoin us with news. We shall strike Northing's iron balecrown into the hazard. Go forth, and Godspeed!"

With this the great king departed his court and all bowed.

"Thanks be to Heaven that you adventurers will sign the king's contract," said the chancellor, silent before this. "You have license to hunt down packs of black-hearted horg and ambush bolgoth patrols, or destroy forts and camps...Veil knights as well. You may assassinate any of their lords. Any trove be had, as much as you can lug on one horse you may keep. But mind you, take you no treasure-bags off their belts; then know that your return is but one sorque for each pointy ear."

"Contract? " asked Jacob, surprised.

"You lackies will sign the letters of marque I have written up, as requested, will you not?" asked the chancellor, suddenly distressed. "That *is* why you are here, no? I admit it has a penitential character...only a sorque per head, but surely you are in debt of the king for his clemency. His coffers are nigh empty on account of this war. Wisdom would not seek a better deal.

"The big money is for this: use your climbing tackle to scale the mountainous walls of the Arc du Baffay and infiltrate his chambers. Memorize any strategic plans that are laid out, then slip away and return your intelligence to the king's camp."

"So we are mercenary-scouts then?" the monk asked, glaring at Phaedra, realizing his motives. The leader of elfbeards did not answer but only scowled.

"Of course, chancellor, but not this monk," Phaedra warned. "He comes along to haul our luggage and pray monk-prayers, but does not engage the enemy. We valraphs, however, are as ready to spill ink on a square contract, as afterward to spill blood on the fields of Ardeheim."

But then declared the chancellor in warning: "Valraph, mind that your spoken words do not cross the King's command."

"So that has been your plan all along?" Jacob asked, returning the frown. "It's not buried gold that you are after, but gold from the coffers of the crown? You abandoned Kruth because he refused to become mercenary, but wanted to complete the quest. I should not be surprised at you."

"Mind your own business." said Phaedra. "Judge not, lest you be judged, remember? The contracts of champion fighters do not concern you. Besides, you, a rope-girded monk, need no share of any loot."

Of this moment Jacob writes: "I watched as the Valraphs muster to sign the letters of marque, and Arizel as well. How useless did signing such contracts make their oaths? Could they fight well now for one another, if now this meant that mere lucre was their purpose? So much for sacred quest. At best it is a cold enterprise. Those were my thoughts, since now somehow was I to be their Captain."

After the chancellor was satisfied he swiftly departed, Phaedra came and stood opposed to the monk, whispering in anger: "Think not gallant monk, your status changed. The fighting Valraphs will never obey their own taken hostage. Nor is the King's word able to have any sway in Valraphic code." With a look spiteful she turned and marched angrily off. No rebuttal did Jacob Magister supply, but thought it best to wait for the right moment.

The king's ministers and clerics glanced about with glad but cold looks. That very morning they were to depart, with all farewells to the gracious King.

Let there abide among you no tomb-witches, fortune tellers, nor any hearers of the dead. Fighting monks must have absolute intolerance for any such cults of decay, lest the party be compromised.

Tien Joshur
Summer Instruction for Campaigning Monks

acob dreamt of a damsel coronated with ivy. She was unlike any lady of other dreams dreamt. On a marble bench she was sitting like an elegant vase in the luxurious garden of the world. A string of pearls about her neck, and she was draped in purple mantel. Her skin was soft and fair, her lips like rubies. Grapes she held in her hands; and a little bird she had taken out from his cage; he was perched on her arm. Was this little bird the foolish monk? Did she hold the grapes of Wrath? She slipped and fell to earth, her cup overturned, and her crown toppled, her red hair spread upon the emerald grass.

"I do not let carnal desire, unworthy of a monk, hinder me." Jacob has confessed all this to the Holy Inquisition, writing: "Holy Benedict teaches that a strong flood of desire is remedied by casting oneself into a thorn bush, or cold water. Aye, the lass was passing fair. Surely it is wrong not to acknowledge such beauty, but anything more than a glance may endanger a lesser monk."

All the more, her lovliness made her seem to be a princess pure, but then in that dreaming something of corruption in her was also indicated.

"My dream-perception suddenly changed; she seemed to me a woman of the night. Her catching and painted eyes as one asleep or dead; or were they shut as one in ecstasy?"

Difting upwards and away, as heavenward falling yet looking back upon the mortal shell; Jacob dreamt a cup of divine retribution cast beside her there in that garden. Jacob makes this important, including it in his confession, asking:

"...slain as victim was she? Or pierced with the devil's lust? There the cup and I read upon an unholy name inscribed: MERETRIX BABYLONIS. The Whore of Babylon··· Struck down from off the scarlet Beast? It was a prophetic dream; I now understand, which told not of an attack upon a man or some earthly desire, jealousy, or murder, but of the soul, and of the doomed bride of Antichrist, the False Church, and the marble bench, the beast on which she rode: the Whitehaven! Mary Magdelene *ora pro nobis*! "

Another woman appeared in his midst, who looked down from above, an elderly woman who sang a melodious song. He did not find her fair to look upon, although his song was with her. So he looked away again and upon the woman who seemed fallen.

The dream passed away. In the camp of the misguided valraphs Jacob awoke, buried under several layers of fur. A camping fire was still smoldering. It had not been as cold as they had expected. They had been traveling for several days with the Hunters of Ael Lot. One of Arizel's nimble dogs was curled up against him. It seems that even magic dogs prefer the warmth of a companion.

His dream on the woman; in appearance attractive, like the daughter of King Graham. His daughter was the lovely kind of lady. Even a monk could not but notice her as he was leaving the palace of Ael Lot, while the elfbeards had started packing the sled with the good supplies granted by royal favor.

How could one not notice her? She had both the elegant shape and the demeanor of the nobly born. She approached them, perhaps out of curiosity, some interest in the expedition. Arizel and the monk certainly were surprised to see her come their way that day they stood getting ready in the courtyard of the castle. It was Arizel whom her gaze addressed, and although noble women generally do not converse with wanderers of that ilk, she seemed to entertain no such scruple.

Mercury-minded Arizel, though gallant with his leather armour and black cap, albeit without illusion to hope for the hand of such a princess, lifted his cap and gave a courteous head bow.

"Good day, princess, if it please you might allow my introduction. Bannock is the name men call me in this land, but Arizel is my original name, famous in all lands. I am the mind behind this dangerous expedition. May we offer you anything? How gracious of you. No doubt you've come to send us off with good faring. "

"You the one rumoured to be a wizard, as it seems by your long robe?"

"I am the same magus of repute, and not ashamed of it, if you will forgive my frankness. These are the adventurers who have caused amazement recently at court, who are perhaps your interest. This company has longed to look upon a maiden so fair; pray, for it is, most likely, their last journey. "

"Who is this one, one not like the others?" she asked, looking at Jacob.

"He is Jacob Magister of Whitehaven, Abbey upon the seaward cliffs."

"And my chivalric name is Sir Hortezan, monastic knight of the Ammouri."

"An Ammouric Knight? Impressive; Were they not all slain at the Ambush of Stormring? Why, he seems a knight who has just begun. "

"We shall render any service for you," Jacob said. "It is the least we could do, given the kindness of your house. "

"Yes, there is something...I have long kept a letter for someone to bear to far-off lands. "

"Most worthy princess," said Jacob, "forgive me, but you are surely mistook. These men foolishly go to places of utmost peril, to the far hinter of the world, Bardelith, and her icy entrance, into the lands not even

Vannahim barbarians dare. We will enter upon the threshold to the gates of Tartarus itself, the darksome lands, where broods the prison of the titans and dark elves, and there no wind ever blows. We pass through the grandiose and fortified prison Baffay which stands frozen in time, a realm over which the accurse Dires holds sway. Surely you have no need to convey a letter in that direction."

"Most excellent Lady," added Arizel, "the dark elves do not read. They are like restless shadows down there in the everdark, so that, even if they could read, the light of a reader's candle would scatter them away.
"

"The place I wish to convey the letter is where the dead await judgement," she explained. "to my paramour whom I suspect no longer walks among the living," (She lowered her voice), "and if you consent for me, I will requite a fine gift to you."

What shade concerns you to such extremity?" the monk asked.

"A good knight, a champion, one who in years past rode the lands flying my kerchief. Since he departed from my embrace, my thoughts have ever been upon him. He went as far as the lands of the dead. I know he is there. Someday we shall be reunited."

"I cannot bear such a letter, princess," warned Arizel. "It is necromancy to communicate with the dead. *Prohibitum est loqui cum mortuis*. None can obtain a license from the Soothfold to accomplish such a spell. One must not disturb the dead, and we seek only to pass through until we reach the palace of the rising sun. Were I to undertake necromancy, my lawful status would be compromised; the Soothfold would meet and render a judgement against me. My Magic-user's license would be revoked. I would be counted among the Arcane Exiles, and my magical abilities would be greatly weakened. This would surely happen, even if done for some grand cause. My current status is already probationary on account of former transgressions."

"Then your companion here, the young monk who fancies himself a noble knight, he can convey the letter. He will not fail, especially not with your magical guard."

"I would be breaking the code even to give aid. I should then be considered an accomplice, for the intention would still be necromantic in design."

"Nor may I carry the letter, most beloved lady, " stated Brother Jacob. "It is written, *speak not with the dead*. "

"And why not? "

"I am an Ammouric Knight, a single-hearted paladin. We who live in the Light do not enjoin such deeds of Darkness. Sacred scriptures forbids such things. There is told how King Saul let a witch summon a shade for him. He had her prophesy the outcome of the next day's battle. He died the very following light, by Heavenly decree. My own soul would be imperiled were I to consent."

"A noble knight...how laughable. You are a rope-girded monk. That is why you not understand how my fondness for this man is my very hope. I cannot live with the news that he is dead, but my very life seems to slip away. I am unable and unwilling to forget him. I must be sure that he is well, even in those lands. The letter assures him that I will not marry. Where is your Christian mercy, monk?"

"Honest mercy does not yield to all desires. It is also mercy to teach uncomforting right to the unlearned and to rebuke those who turn romance into idolatry. Respectfully, I warn that it is an unwholesome dream that you have slipped into."

"Very well, for pity's sake. Although I myself will not carry the letter," said Arizel, "To the shade of your lover I cannot speak—if I encounter him you will speak in your letter. No one else hears of this."

The elegant lady looked slightly relieved as she passed him the little scroll.

"The goodness the letter carries will draw his soul back to me. You will not fail to recognize him, for he is gallant and worthy. His shirt displays the cross and Ammouric sunrise on a silver field... "

"That is a clerical device, " said Jacob. "Did he quest for a certain relic, my lady? "

"He did...but which one and for what purpose he would not tell."

"And you heard of his demise?"

"In his return from the Wars of the Veil a company of horgoth struck him down, a patrol encamped upon the wold. The Edolunt Rangers did not recover his body, but only the bones left at a horgoth campfire. –human bones. The horse escaped, and they brought the poor beast here not two moons ago. We found a letter in the saddle-pack which explained how his hunt had led him to lands which the mount could not trod, and turning back, he found many horgrim were on his trail. I continue to mourn and would not have spoken to you otherwise."

"Princess, it is better to forget and seek another," said the monk. "Let go of dear souls that are in the hands of Allfather. It is a great danger to resist his will and miss an earthly love too much. The heart earnestly longs for an unearthly love, an unearthly blessedness. Only Heaven can supply those things."

"You echo my father. You've gone too long schooling under some monks, you did. –You beggarly prude! Do not hope to seduce me into mediocrity, to the resignations of chastity, and douse my passion with your cold dogmas. My law is the heart. What would a monk know of that?"

"Do not mind the monk, princess. He cannot forget the superstitions of a former age and is slow to embrace the new time. He lives in myths that will cause him to wane in quiet folly. This one should fear the ancient powers that are beyond his keen. The Northing and other spirits can hear from afar."

On the account of this altercation with the princess, Brother Jacob writes:

""I could no more endure her. Perhaps Heaven would have me to view her spirit. What part of being a creed-sworn knight is that? I used the power divine given a monk. Here is what I wanted to say: "Being a princess, you have come to see yourself above any law or sacred commandment, without true lawful sentiment? Your only law is the heart? Beware, above all the heart deceiveth."

We must never pin condemnation. Of her interior character little did I guess rightly. Men cannot see what God sees. It was she who, by the will of God, in the following year would take up the sword and with her own hand restore the throne of Ael Lot. Although her kin were slain withal and every castle razed, she would lead a remnant army to drive out the brutal invader. Even more, it is now she who, repenting of past delusions, alone among Ammouric monarchs refuses the contagion of apostasy in her domain and forbids the alien religion, that Whore of Babylon who even now flaunts herself, masquerading as the true religion.

However it is a work of mercy to rebuke the sinner, and pride is a sin. So I said some things to her. It irked her, but perhaps I sewed the seed:

"For you I pray, my princess. Do not doubt it. One must learn to walk humbly in one's station, keeping the lawful restraints. Repent from that romantic delusion."

"An over-confident monk uses his insight to peek into my soul. You position yourself in peril. If you had not this wizard's alliance, I would have you cast into the dungeon for that boldness."

"Faith, most worthy lady, boldness is needed if to such places we go anyway...and I am the now leader of this fighting crew. I am confident only in the service of God. Dreadful angels be at my side. May it be the same for the princess."

"Oh? I asked them before to protect my beloved. I find angels an ethereal wisp, a dream."

"Then you have not encountered the *Erelim*. Worship God and pray every day if you would seek his help."

'I have done that...yet no help came. I told God that if he protected my beloved, I would provide for his priests."

"A kind gesture, dear princess, but one does not *tell* God. Nor does one strike up bargains with the Almighty. You already owe him. Live by faith. Heaven has sent you me as a help, perhaps."

"Do not think to instruct me. If your *Erelim*, heavenly angels, are so powerful, where are their domains? Can they rival the Northing, who has quelled nearly the entire hinter? "

"It is as you say. Your highness, the Hinter is conquered, save for your father's seaward kingdom. Has the defense of his warlike hand, alone, procured that, when so many other proud feudatories have fallen? Consider that his invisible ally is the same as mine: the Almighty, Lord of Armies."

"Still, you should not speak lightly on the strange power of Northing, who is the Balecrown with many vassals."

"Does it warrant to fear a mouse when lions accompany?"

"That is enough of your zealotry, you wiry brazen." My claims unquieted Arizel, embarrassed by an apparent lack of sophistication, my rustic narrow-mindedness so unpopular with the highly placed.

"If your ancient ways were of any value, would not those same angels have hindered the mouldering of the old Ammouric dynasties?"

Arizel addressed the princess: "Still, lady, in order to demonstrate my graciousness, I myself will deliver the letter for you if this "chivalric" monk fails or relents, being likely; but I ask also that you speak of this to no one."

"I shall speak of it to no one, my faithful Sorcerer."

"—Magic-user, please my lady...title me magic-user, faithful Magic-user."

"Magic-user...your reward for accepting this task is a great one indeed."

"What reward be that, your highness?" Arizel's voice trilled with excitement at what treasure he might acquire for the illegal service. Princess Arcesilea gestured to one of her several servants who had been standing away, waiting upon her.

The servant approached at once carrying a wicker cylinder. She took the basket in arm and dismissed her servant.

"You are a Sorcerer. I had always wished to meet one of your fold, and the power has always fascinated. When I was young, my father gave me this gift. It is a scroll of some ancient poem, rumoured to have been written by a Sorcerer long ago, one Zenops..."

Arizel, I saw, was nearly faint with excitement. His trembling overtook his entire body when he heard the name Zenops, a name he recognized. How difficult was it for me to watch the worldly venerate the worldly as if otherworldly.

"The letters are too strange for me to read," the princess continued light-heartedly, "and the language is unknown. I showed it to the librarians of the court, and they told me that it dates back to a forgotten time, the era before Nystol of the wizard-towers burned. They themselves were unable to find any other record of it. It is titled *The Bladetongue*. I asked my father where he acquired it. He said that it came aboard ship from Orusca. The decorations and lettering seemed fanciful enough, so he required it to be used as ribbons for my birthday feast. He was about to have them tear out the decorative borders, thinking it some foolish poetry. But a sense of shame at the loss of so many books and scrolls over the years took hold of him. He left it and gave it to me as a gift, the way it was. It has been sitting in the storage for many a year now. I heard that you sojourned at court, Bannock. I deemed it right that a Wizard be gifted with a high tale."

By this time Arizel was nearly in tears, holding ever so delicately the ancient *bemble* scroll. With great savour he read aloud the famous opening, set in the lost days of Queen Hesperia:

> *Of the eldark world will you hear; of famous bronze and unearthly fire, how it was that a few companions went up against lawless breeds and creeping peril, delivering all the broad lands from desolation. They dared enter darkest caves, going into depths enchanted. At last they overcame*

the worst obstacle: the horse-devouring, man-devouring, horned terror, first-born of ancient Chaos.

By the son of Jarlath, fiercest among them, was it accomplished. He pierced the artery of the beast with an ancestral blade, trusting that the prayer of his companions had been heard. Willed by the Allfather they were, some to heroic end, but others to return, and see their work harvested upon the Field of Gederon; that day the great armies stood opposed. So witnessed they the hour of the Banelord's doom...

"It is priceless, my lady. Many Arcanes have raked through many libraries of many lands in vain, many years, and never this long cherished treasure glimpsed."

He had his treasure. I looted something even better out of it: a remarkable thought those verses ushered: a few companions, mere pagans, took down the many-headed dragon Vorthragna. If they could do that, I conjectured, using merely bronze blades, a whispered prayer, and a little luck, what could a Christian soldier do? We are armed with Truth, guided by angels, with the ever-rising prayers of an Abbot, and the favor of God. Even so... but would a rope-girded monk dare it...?" Nothing more need I record on this stupendous insight.

ocky defiles and snowy corridors we at last set as our stern purpose. We entered warily the ice-flow region of Nthule. First we passed many forested groves here and there, but soon the land became scarce and bleak. The land was cold but the breezes warm. Somewhere above in the blue sky a gull screeched.

Arizel was high in learning, enough to translate the strange Oruscan Greek of that original text. He did not wait to do so until we had ended our journey. He would unroll the scroll often and recite its words whenever he had chance. I listened, having a little ability at the strange language. Upon hearing it read aloud, harkening to the metaphysic ringing of the Greek, I thought it a wonder.

"Why do you keep so great an interest in a poem, Bannock?" I asked.

"Does not that deity of yours allow me," he answered, "to enjoy classic literature, monk? "

"I confess it is true that certain monks be strict more than me. That is as things need to be for us, but should not a wizard like you have greater interest in a grimoire of spells? What power is there see you in mere rhyme?"

"There is not a great distance between rhyme and spell, unlearned one. The beauty of the poem itself can put a soul under its spell, just as the chants of your God put rope-girded monks under the divine influence. I read this poem because it contains words of virtue, and such words prepare a man for what is to come."

"And what is to come, Bannock?"

"What is to come already we see..." he said, rolling up the scroll. He was peering at something ahead upon a snowy hill. He looked but could see nothing because of the glare. He placed his scroll within the wicker tube and girded a deadly dagger to his belt instead.

After much journey up into rocky hills on horse they at last reached the Nthule ice-flow. That evening they camped and ate well with the provisions the Crown had provided. The following day they went to work felling several trees to prepare wood shafts to make rafts when crossing the interior waters.

As King Graham had indicated, it was impossible to take any other route. They had to descend a thousand feet into the interior of the ice-flow itself, through a mighty and steep crevasse.

We found a rope which previous parties had left behind. But the mountaineering ropes of the elfbeards were of much better make, and they helped greatly, for the rock and ice in certain places was uneven and dangerous, and the horses could not be ridden down that far. I explained in detail to the horse Burgundius another route. He would meet him at the other side of the ice flow. (It did not occur to me how strange that a horse had just completely understood our plan).

So we had to haul the wood beams for a raft themselves. At last, after several tunnels of pellucid ice had been traversed, we made it to the bottom and beheld the vast ceiling of glacial arches formed over the valley-cavern. Mists of cloud floated through the region in various places clinging to the mountain sides and even hung about the rocky earth below. In some recesses grew pine trees and shrubbery wherever holes in the ice formed from rising steam-blasts. The air was not cold, and there were glacial cateracts spilling from the ceiling in numerous spots. The center of the valley had a wide placid lake, or bay, whose surface a mist was hanging over in patches. These were the waters which the hot springs fed and I think possibly connected somehow to the Northern Warm Sea.

We reached the shore of the bay which was hedged with polar flowers of various kinds, and this I would say was what was meant by the Unicorn's garden. We had enough wood to make only a single small raft to float those provisions which would not fit into the water-proof dwarven packs.

"There is no way around the waters," Phaedra Stormraker said. "Just as the king warned, we will have to go through the waters. It seems a shallow pool, although it must be deep in some places. The water is warm, so it will not be a problem. The distance to the other side, however, is considerable. I hope you all know how to swim. There is no Unicorn come against us, so let us with speed then into the flood, before it comes."

Indeed the water was quite warm, like a bath. This put the valraphs at ease. In certain places, however, as they waded across,
it became colder, especially as we went into the deep and had to swim.

"We now reach the mid-way," I declared. "The guide will now return back to the shore and lead the packhorses back up to the surface, and report our success to the king."

"Go ye no farther yet," said Arizel. "I know not this place. It is mysterious indeed. Let the guide go back I say, but slowly, we shall give a signal of our success from the opposite shore. Who knows but that the Unicorn awaits to surprise us there after we are weary from swimming?"

We turned to continue, and looking down one could determine the bottom far below, though the water was murky in some spots, and deep it was.

There issued a great swirl and bubbling of water about us, a great rush of wave in the otherwise tranquil water. Something was moving beneath.

"What was that? " cried Buckbar. Each man halted.

"Peloran titans must come to hunt in these waters!" someone announced in a loud whisper. There was a chilling silence as all looked about in trepidation.

"It is the Leviathan! Look there—his finned tail rises above the flood!" I cried. "Swim for your lives!"

The massive tale slapped down upon the waters, and the great grey and white-speckled megaron rose up and blew mist out his back. Flipping over, he dove back into the depths. In the waters beneath the massive thing, larger than an Authapian war-wagon, moved silently beneath me. It headed towards one of the elfbeards. I called to warn him.

"Buckbar, the colossus comes upon you from below!"

Buckbar looking downwards watched the massy thing close in. At the last moment he did a sudden pull from the beast's underwater course. His elven descent let him elude well. At once the creature broke the surface of the flood and made a great crashing of water. For a moment, as his head reared upwards, his eye emerged and he could see us.

The Leviathan had meant to impale Buckbar. The aquatic giant sported a singular long horn protruding, like the lance of a jousting knight! The horn was spiral-form, just as the horn that the king had. Did the king's long horn originally must have belonged not to the horse-like creature often depicted on shields and tapestries. This unicorn turned out to be water-beast, actually what the bestiaries title a *Narwhale*; The king had wrongly assumed that we knew the local legend entirely, so popular it was. The thing was colossal, impossible for us to fight, let alone capture!

The water-beast was circling around to make another joust. It positioned to go at me. Like Buckbar, I thought to dart out of its watery path at the last moment. But I am not a valraph. His spiraling horn was quite long, like a knight's lance. The great beast barged at me. The horn pierced through the luggage on my back. You may wonder, brothers, how it is that we went through deep water wearing cumbrous luggage, but I tell you these strapped packs were of dwarven craftmanship and caused things to feel lighter in weight, although the *Black Book* always weighed upon my shoulders. The make and fabric, however, always left the contents dry under all conditions. Nevertheless, my rucksack was pierced through, and the beast dragged me through the water as the straps of the luggage caught me into his momentum. It turned about and was now to dive, and taking a deep breath, I was pushed through the water as we both struggled. In order to live and not drown, I had to unstrap myself from the pack. This meant I would forfeit the *Black Book*. So I did it anyway and surfaced. The beast keeled off into the depths, the pack spinning.

Well, what could I do?..without the lore in that tome, it would seem that all knowledge useful for the grand endeavor would be lost. The tome had been truly an easy yoke, even though its bulk was considerable. Just as Abbot had said, as long as I would not groan much against it, accepting it, the great book would remain lightweight. Once I was dwelling on it, the encumbrance increased, to the extent that I could barely sustain it. Now this was often the case, because my mind often returned to the grand tome, so every day I could feel it weighing me down, and I would not accept it. So it certainly was a temptation. Just to let it go off into the sightless depths, the water has probably ruined it anyway.

What if it were lost forever? For surely it be the only copy. I could never prove my innocence to the Prime Interquist without it. I might request of the unicorn that my rucksack be returned. I could offer a truce with the beast. Perhaps I could reason with the magic beast and tell him of our penitential purpose, and even my own plight. Would that yield sympathy? Certainly Jonah had elicited some sympathy from the whale in scripture. Now there came remembrance of Ambrosius the Nephilung's riddle: *Who haunts those hills that never were born,* (that may be meant as hills of water, ocean places like this)...*Be it enough to look upon his pelt, or a kind word suffices, like starlight of many galaxies glittering bright, lighting the way through waters of night.'*

*A kind word...*certainly you chuckle, brothers, assuring yourselves that the very usage of "beast,"·········as Aristotle says, signifies the want of such an ability. It cannot be *reasoned* with. Assuredly, my brothers, this is the very thing I set about doing, to communicate in the various high-pitched whistling tones such whales whistle. The claim seems hard for men of our time to swallow, and I could not fathom how such a power to sing whale-songs was granted to me. Was the animal merely enchanted, and thereby had communication with men, or was it sacred, and so Heaven let a monk to enter way of parley?

Of this great and noble creature I requested forgiveness for our intrusion upon his waters and our need to pass through. I spoke in particular of our noble endeavor to reform the ways of men, who surely were in need of correction... "

The massive *unicornus* informed me of his sorrow at the loss of his parent years ago, and how subsequently he had become an enemy of men. Nevertheless, he understood his own sacral status among men. He knew of the Furth High King and informed me how it was divine providence this passage be blocked so that no army of King Graham might pass through. In God's sight, the king had failed in virtue, and had sinned by keeping women whom he would not marry. Many of commoners and even knights had sinned in similar ways, by drunkenness, whoring, and adultery. The king alone was not entirely to blame. Nor did the clergy urge satisfactory penances, nor courageously preach against sin and worldliness. They lived in luxury, and often vied for honours, allowing heresiarchs to influence them. So too did the monks fail, praying too little, obsessed with reading, gaining occulted knowledge useless for salvation.

So there was no way the king would prevail in war against the bolgoth. Heaven had already determined that the King could be delivered into the hands of that troll-horde. This punishment, however, the Lord relented but could not altogether withdraw it, since the judgement of God cannot be retracted. So he allowed the unicorn beast be as a divine sign to the king, and to block his reckless advance against the evil dominion. This was a great mercy which allowed the monarch to reign many more winters than he otherwise would have, and the people benefited as well, for the wealth of the trade from the East would only have corrupted them. Clement delay the Lord granted the king and holy poverty his kingdom.

The King himself had long since repented, after all, dismissing his courtesans; and in most other ways he had become a gallant and worshipful feudal lord. However, the time now was right, and the king would no longer restrain his natural ambition. He had to pay for the sins of his youth. Nevertheless, the Furth High King had another plan for the wicked troll-horde, and would use the king's punishment for glory.

The unicorn consented to let the knights of King Graham through, for surely the time had come. He would not disturb them while they built a pontoon bridge to their own demise. I, however, was not to mention to anyone the allotment meted out to the King and his knights, since it was not mine to say, but God's will; and besides, the king was so intent on sending through his divisions, that no talk of doom would cool him. I would be wasting my breath. Wars are chastisement for sin. They cannot be avoided. Better for a monk to pray that men survive war rather than to escape war, for by humanity's transgressions, (as we can see are recorded in *The Black Books*), we know that war is stored up for all the civil lands.

He returned the baggage, and did so while the others looked on with amazement from the opposite shore.

The mysterious *Black Book* was unharmed, proofed by some ancient spell against water damage. The old wizards thought of everything.

The great beast disappeared again into the depths.

The way of mercy; it is inseperable from the Monkhood. They are one and the same; to such an extent that a fighting monk is forbidden to venge himself against a defeated enemy, one struck and disarmed. This is absolute, regardless of how much an enemy may deserve otherwise. If instead of mercy the monk exacts his own justice, it is defiance, and by agreement of the sages, he is no monk at all.

Tien Joshur
Winter Instruction for Wayfaring Monks

Wrath of the Valraphim   XXV

We made our merry way to the end of the mammoth ice cavern and upwards into the glacial run off, where wispy clouds of mist sailed over iron-red rock, at last coming into the warmer breeze. The team put down camp for the night and built sleds with the wood we had used for the rafts, wood which had earlier been our little wagons. These mountaineering elfbeards are keen in many ways. In the morning, after a hot breakfast and having dried their clothes in the sun, we at last departed in the afternoon...into the territory of occupying bolgrim!

For some great distance the first day we went, and knew the bolgoth divisions were near, for the valraphs saw plumes of smoke from behind distant hills to the south. The bolgs were on the move. The valraphs went on. Finally we pitched camp in a forest grove. We dared burn no camp fire in those lands.

At one point, on the subsequent morn, the sleds halted. Finch came running back from his scout position.

"It is the horgrim!" he declared. "A palisaded fort can be seen from that incline. I count only thirty; they are holding down the camp for an army, and by the standard, we agree they are Mulg's doggerels. I estimate their brigade left but yesterday. We can... "

"We can avoid them. We must elude their notice, going around unseen," said Arizel.

"Turn the sleds to Northwest." I ordered, "We pass through the wooded area. No need for unnecessary risk."

"Belay that order, Valraphs!" Phaedra called, striking forward to our sled. "We prepare an assault on the horgoth fort. The evil must be wiped out. Ready yourselves; we will fix them right for it."

"For what purpose?" I asked. "How will fighting these horgim bring us any closer to the object of our endeavor, or the underworld trove cursed with eldark magic of which you have much spoken? These horgrim are mere supply-company and guard, no warriors. They will have nothing of treasure."

"Horgrim are not an easy prey to find. We shall seize what is ours against the Mulg tribe. We can wait no longer to offer our terror. Our honor must be known again both in the caverns below and high mountains. We will be feared."

"We are too few, or will we go against thirty or more? This is an atrocious risk. I am against it," said Arizel.

"You would check us?" said Phaedra. "If you fear we are outnumbered and will fail, then use some of your war-magic to help. That ought to give us a minor edge. Otherwise, keep out of the fray; but know this: we will have your magic dogs for it."

"My dogs are not fighting dogs. You have no authority against my wish," Arizel answered sternly. "They are something I will keep you from, for the beasts obey me as to their absolute master. "

At this Phaedra Stormraker could not answer back. She let go any further quarrel with any angry wizard.

"Valraphs, muster, prepare for battle!" She looked back at Arizel, as an afterthought. And it was clear that the valraphs had no intention of obeying the monk as their leader.

"You cannot take any share of our booty," declared Phaedra.

"They must have none anyway. Be warned, any martial action of pure vengeance will reap a paultry harvest, Stormrake. We must not attack." I said angrily. "Obey me, all you valraphs, else you will find yourself in hard straights."

"You are our hostage," said Finch. "A hostage cannot become the leader."

"It is the King's will. His word has real authority. Do not slight it." To quarrel with them was to no avail. These men were so honour bound that it doomed them to folly.

Now I myself had no quarrel with the horgoth, but kept the sword Witchbane readied. The elfbeards went through their luggage and fetched shields, helms, and axes, all of which had been fastened down to the sleds. Drocwolf, too, was given leave to arm himself and fight. What happened next was an amazing thing to see, because unlike other soldiers who plan an assault on a fort with great care, the elfbeards took no such pains, but simply huddled together for a moment, as in a game of macky.

They approached the fort from the East and the West, easily scaling the wood palisades with grapples and rope-danglers for climbing. It was a surprise assault. Arizel and I watched from the hill. We could see nothing, but heard blood curdling screams from within the fort. The sound of buckler clashing, sword and axe echoed. The front gate opened, and one foe fled out of the fort. Corydon rushed after him. He halted, paused to aim, and hurled his axe. It struck the coward between the shoulder blades and sent him to his knees.

After a few moments Arizel and I agreed to enter, for the more experienced soldiers had done their work; and I was expected, as a Knight, to at least be present to guard captives.

What we saw when entering the fort was exactly what the din of battle had suggested. We were stepping over the slain as we passed into the gate, and one was he who had fallen with Corydon's axe lodged in his back. Upon closer inspection, he was no black-hearted horg. Surely a human body was that, smaller and stubby, brutish of face and warped, but not horgoth; the features were not monstrous enough, and the skin not grey like the baalite kind, but reddish.

"They are not horgrim," Arizel declared. "They are hycsoth!"

"Hycsoth?" I asked.

"A half-breed they, many of whom the horgrim enslave. They are the sons of Men whose ancestors perhaps had unfortunate union with some other, less noble, creatures. Some say that they are the distant offspring of Cain, the homicidal son of the original humans. In any case, no one knows for certain. Among the race of Men they nevertheless are counted, but the kingdoms shun them and do not enter cities, being outcasts upon the broad earth. For their sleight many are thieves or scouts. Of those whom the horgrim enslave not, many become adept."

As we entered the fort we saw carnage in sundry spots, limbs strewn here and there, bodies in heaps in various places. The Valraphs had taken twelve captives, all of them being of this "hycsoth" breed. They were all on their knees before them.

Drocwolf and Phaedra, both covered in scarlet blood, were not in agreement, as usual.

"These here are horg spawn!" shouted Phaedra.

"They are part-human mold," countered Drocwolf, "—and were unarmed. It is against custom to do them injury. "

"Finch and Corydon," Phaedra announced sternly, "The horde left days ago. Torch the barracks. "

At once the two elfbeards, also covered in gore, lit torches and made for the various makeshift cabins.

"They have no gold here anyway," I said. "What use is their misery to you?"

"They are horg-spawn, and Mulg claims them. They must pay the price."

"They do not all have Mulg's employ," said Arizel. "Would you burn down their quarters because these men had the civility to surrender?"

"Who can determine which of these did not serve Mulg freely? They all therefore must be treated as enemies. If we let them go, they will return to their masters and inform."

"They were not even armed," Drocwolf said. "These are mere thralls. Why do you not set them free? The only horgrim that were here you have already slain, and rightly. Why extend the punishment to these? Do you think you will bargain a sorque for each ear? That's not in the king's contract, not for humans."

"Drocwolf is the only of the Valraphs who is fixed against this." She answered angrily. "It is well known that these kind are counted horg-kin in our encyclopedias. They are scum and would without thought butcher us had instead they upon us come."

"The encyclopedias list them as Man-kin," said Arizel. "Your desire for vengeance clouds your judgement. Murder them and I fear some high power will be against us."

"If divine favor is not with us," I added, "we should fail in great loss. Do not put to curse our hands. These are harmless slaves."

Phaedra seemed to pause as if doubting herself, but then snapped.

"You are no warrior. How can a knight not first be a warrior? You have not proved yourself to us, Jacob. I cannot even trust you in a fight."

Phaedra Stormraker came close upon me and stared at me. "The other Valraphim, however, I cannot persuade; I cannot hold back their hands, so thirsty they are for blood. It is up to them what to do with these. I fear that they will have their vengeance. I cannot stop them. You however, if you would be treated as a Valraph, must help them. Avail yourself of my axe! "

Phaedra thrust an elven axe into my hands.

"Never," I said, tossing the axe in the snow. "I am a monk first, a man for peace."

"Peace is for the dead. When we do meet up with the monster known as Mulg, and his peloric battalion, you will learn why the Valraphs let you die under his hand." Phaedra picked up the axe and walked away.

The poor "hycsoth" were kneeling upon slush and the blood-stained ground. Many were in tears and begged for mercy. Some even claimed to have children they hoped to see again. The Northern sun glared in their glum faces, and it was true: these kind were near to human, although in speaking they sounded guttural. Smoke billowed past reeking of tar and burned flesh.

The cries went unheard among the Valraphim. They now mustered and voted as to what to do. The fort around them burned and smoldered, letting up huge plumes of black smoke.

"The Valraphim have made judgement. Whosoever has served Mulg and his devils we must make extinct. These manlings too must today meet their fate."

"No, this is a crime! The Ammouric Kings do not count this as a deed of war." I cried. "And what honour is there in killing slaves? Such will not advance your renown. Spare them. Let them go."

They ignored my outcry and proceeded immediately to shed blood...

Oh wretched age of the world! Blood on all sides, and crooked minds, pitiless. I will not describe further the abhorrent executions witnessed that day, brothers. Nevertheless, it is sufficient for you to recall the empty promises of Satan and the vain, unfulfilled *pathos* which the sin of vengeance is wont to reward its adherents. With this in mind you can imagine the cold and empty draw upon the faces of those who actually ordered the crime. Nor are those who carried out the crime, though under the obedience of military discipline, exempt from any blame.

Now upon witnessing these horrors, brothers, at first I reacted, confused and incredulous, not so out of pity for the victims, (for always the innocent are the victims of war), but out of a sense of foreboding for those who had committed the murders. The damage and darkness that so black a trespass effects in the soul is much worse than physical death. That is why wise Socrates taught the paradox, *It is better to be the recipient of wrong-doing than to be the one who carries it out.* These elfbeards who had been sent to aid men in ordering and building the world had themselves fallen. Divine justice would not err in accounting this.

So now it came to my mind, brothers, that the full measure of folly and injustice had overflowed and was spilling everywhere like the blood. The ideals of the Valraphim had not only been compromised but had also been completely corrupted and led to craven works totally beyond the pale of any worthy conduct. It was no longer acceptable to begrudgingly allow myself, a monk, to be passive or submissive to this heinous collection of twisted minds.

God will not be mocked. A certain calm and focused anger formed deeply in my guts, allowing great clarity of mind and pure, undivided resolution.

As we were about to depart, one of the elfbeards announced that a craven horg had been found hiding in a garbage pit. The wretch was brought before us and tied with ropes. Since he was quite cross over all that had transpired, I decided to interrogate the vile and scabrous creature myself.

"Why did you hide and not fight? "

The sinister bolg squinted, and the black eyes glinted with mischief and hatred. He did not answer, so I struck him. He laughed to himself with great cynicism.

"You are a black soul like one of us! What is it all to you anyway? I do not need to prove valor. I was not chosen to fight beside the others. Mulg supplied me no honour, putting me here to overwatch this fort, not on march up front to win imperishable renown. He judges me cheap, an unworthy. So I plan to acheive top axe, to teach Mulg I am not a coward the day he looks down and sees my dagger lodged in his belly...But what are you, a monk? Not one-eyed medallion kind of monk...so not our friend? Then you rot and burn in red Hell! " the bolg snorted.

"Where have the rest of the horgrim and bolgoth legion gone?" I demanded. "Where is the army?"

"They are on their way back to Baffay. You better get on to catch them."

"Do they retreat from the Thulean army? Did they fight a battle?"

"Don't you know? They met the knights and armed host of the King of the Aels. The battle was a blood-letting gruesome indeed. The horgrim do not retreat. They go to celebrate victory." Again the fell and brutal creature grinned with malice. "Did you think us overthrown? Fool, you cannot win, we have a noteworthy weapon."

"What weapon? Tell us or I'll skewer you."

"What matters it if I boast to you about it and tell? All of you are worth as much dead. Mulg proudly dismisses me. Curse be his bones. So if I will tell it to you, then you will do me a turn and slay Mulg if in the hazard you have a chance, saying *'here is a gift from Whiteliver'*? "

"I have no quarrel with that," I said.

"It is a pact then. Know that the Dire designed our mighty bows. This is a bow more powerful than any other. I will not say of what it is made; I do not even know well. Suffice to learn, human, that every noble knight of Thule lay dead upon cold earth. Our archers slaughtered them all even before their horses could skip across the plain, for our arrows were many and when loosed, blackened all the sky. These did fly furiously and pierced Ataluran armour, FFFFT!!...FFFFT! ...FFFFT! The moans of the dying —such delight to hear! Thulean army scattered! And they took the pontoon bridge across Nthule and even went marching far enough to shake Ael-Lot, city-upon-the sea. The town with her castle they torched; but the hall still stands, only so that the heads of her knights might decorate the former haunt of the king of the Aels, now an extinct nation, an acheivement fortunate. Him they found in his echoing chapel, prostrate like a slave to his God. It has been a glorious campaign. Many screaming too, aye, and your little ones. Mulg will pay for leaving me out. "

"And the King, what became of the King of the Aels? "

"No doubt his locks adorn the chariot of Dassak the Bloodclaw." The bolg's eyes glistened with malice again as he grinned spitefully. "You will not hinder our master in Baffay now. I know that you humans are so weak that you can't even get your basic battle-lore right, and these valraphs of yours, if they get anything—"

His sentence was cut short. One of the valraphs thrust a spear into the bolg's chest.

"Black-heart bolg who had no pass to speak of valraphs without asking!" said Buckbar, frowning, and holding, nay even embracing that spear.

That act appeased my weary heart. The threat of this mischievous power had to be ended. One of the sturdiest kings alive the servants of the Dire have butchered. Soon all the civil lands would be prey to the black-ships of the bolgrim, who now had access to the Vastess Sea: the port Ael Lot. From there all the coast, including Regulum, is vulnerable to raids. Who would check this madness? My own sovereign they had treated in such a way, dying as sore disgraced.

So I determined: we ourselves, or just I myself, will find the fortress of Baffay, in frozen Nzul, and dare put down the phantom myself with my own hands. Let my only thoughts henceforth be bloody. O Lord; I knelt in the snow and prayed facing the eastern horizon. I begged you, O Lord, make me the instrument of Your Divine Retribution...!

The burning eyes of the bolg shut, and I looked back at Arizel.

"We must ourselves acheive the Arc du Baffay and infiltrate its corridors, and with our own hands slay the creature."

"You cannot slay what is already dead," replied Arizel. "That master is too great for you. You speak madness, Jacob."

"Then we shall find the right passages in *the Black Books*, the eld exorcism—that will do the trick...banish him to the echoing Voraganth."

"You have no long-robed priest."

"Against the Dire I set my face. The Lamb will provide all else."

Valraphs cleaned their axes in the snow, which became crimson, and we prepared buckles and sleds to move on. By the time we had gone only a league on sleds, evening   spread her soothing embrace athwart the celestial dome. They cleared an area for camp and prepared food. Soon a fire was blazing.

The farther North we kept marching, the milder the weather had become, since we were nearing the Northern Warm Sea, although still patches of ice and snow were everywhere to be seen. We had passed the frontier of the civil lands. We had entered the Outlands.

So the valraphs and Arizel were standing around the fire burning bright. Since their tongues had been silenced on account of the awful sin, they ate their rations heartily; feigning that nothing was amiss with their souls. But soon they found themselves without mirth, laboring in a lugubrious silence. Some expressions seemed lit with every manner of perplexity and guilt; whereas others had long silenced the inner voice.

It was an opportunity to announce the new reality determined to befall them. I thought of Kruth's last words, that I must lead them. Down I squatted and banked the fire.

"You Valraphs....you have all committed dreadful acts. In the sight of Heaven you have shed innocent blood. Your first wrong was to butcher the sacred stag, showing contempt for what is allotted to divine prerogative. Now by your bellies are you returning to further lawlessness. And know that you are guilty of war-crimes. Now you, around all you, nets of destruction the Angel fastens tight, just as once you netted a monk. How will you atone for these misdeeds? –Even now torment of mind. You have deprived not only your victims of their dear lives, as they cried out to you for mercy, but so robbed their families, their mothers and brothers. Shameful tongues cease. Quiet has settled upon the crew since the injustice. Without words you accuse one another. Consumed shall you be, in the cold-fire of Vlogiston, place of endless torture for your kind. There the biting frost now extends into Eternity, so to recompense and meet Justice for what you have done. Yes, Vlogiston, I think, now it be extended to infinite punishment, good return for the infinitely malign deeds of this crew."

"How would you know, pious fool? What know you of war and what it requires? You know...sure." Phaedra Stormraker shook her head.

"I say—Ambrosius Agathodaemon has communicated to me, although he did not have to; since it is obvious. It is through the wisdom granted a monk; but you do not believe it anyway. Furthermore, each of those whose hands were stained in the executions knows the judgement in his soul: my words be honest testimony."

"We have done the necessary thing," Buckbar declared, smiling.

"Had you done what is right, you would not have to assure yourself and say it, arguing necessity, the tyrant's plea. No, you have entered into folly profound, and the Valraphim will pay dearly for it. Prepare you yourselves. This expedition no longer enjoys the aegis of Allfather. Doomed are we."

"You, Jacob Magister, cavil us with fantastic ethic, and warn of after-frost, " said Phaedra. "What do you intend? That we who are hardened by war become frightened mice? "

"I can do nothing to change what has been done; you have chosen for yourselves. However, there is something you can do for yourselves."

"What possibly could that be?"

"Accept that it was God who made heaven and earth, and He places kings on the earth to help us. Now I will pray to the Lord and seek pardon on your behalf. Then make yourselves to obey me as the King Graham decreed. You must deliver yourselves into my command, for you all have demonstrated a crippling lack of wisdom. This grand endeavor must not be left undone; you were chosen for it, as you have confessed with your own mouths. The good even of the half-elf kingdom, your own homes 'neath the Castle Ayrs, seem to rest on its achievement. We can only finish if it's done right, not working any mischief to get it done, but only what's just. It is a sacred toil. Only therein be a possibility of avoiding divine retribution."

"The King's mind is feeble. What is more, you are our hostage. You cannot take command!" Phaedra told of stiff resistance.

"I could have walked away from this at any time; the high Heaven delivered me from your bonds before and can do so again at any time. Arizel cannot lead because you suspect his magic; no one would follow Arizel. Others, either the weight of their crimes shackle them, as you Phaedra Stormraker, (of both rebellion and murder), or they are too weak to lead, as Drocwolf seems to indicate, for he too could easily assume it. Do as I say; it is your only hope, or you'll burn in the freezing dark river forever. This is Allfather's will, and it comes from the mouth of the King."

" —but you are not a Valraph! " declared Telperion Granoch.

"What matters that? As you recall, Allfather sent each of you dreams that you must fulfill this quest. There was never any designation from the divine hierarchies that only Valraphim be involved. Your counsel and voting power is dissolved. All decisions concerning the fulfillment of the divinely ordained enterprise must now come from me. None of you should fight it, or you will perish through sacred vengeance, cast into outer darkness of endless Vlogiston to suffer pains untold that the devil and his apostate angels administer."

I made sincere thought of their welfare, for leadership was not something I craved. Even so, they would reject the proposal. It certainly amazed them all and put them into dismay. I took a square look at each one, each valraph, and at the wizard Arizel. Would any would meet my gaze with defiance? None did, but they looked askance in confusion, even Drocwolf, bravest of the Valraphs. To each I demanded, saying:

"All of you, I reckon that you will not escape full payment in this life for what you've done. But even so, if you pray to Allfather and seek his pardon, you might avoid after-fire. By an oath-swearing to me, you will be demonstrating to Allfather your remorse. You will swear to obey my words and commands, the bidding of Jacob, Ammouric Knight, both in word and in spirit, and that you will accept his words even into hazard and battle."

the
Horg-wall

So I said what I was obliged to have said. That was done. Heaven will hold us accountable if we correct not our companions on their path to ruination, brothers. And leadership should be mine, for Heaven's favor.

Of course in their stiff-necked way they paid me no heed and threatened to gag me.

Phaedra stood up and frowned.

"Thank you for the speech all-inspiring, monk. Please remember that you are still a hostage, and every law among us affirms that no alien hostage can lead Valraphs. We must now travel, and no dormitions until morning. All goblin-kind offer havoc at night, and areas of heavy forest, lakes and swamps. The swamp and fens of the frontier swallow armies, swallow them alive, for reasons unknown. Even the horgrim refuse to enter. Only the most daring armies patrol here about the Wold, and the horgrim fear to enter past the Swamps of Kath in the forest Maboloth, apart from all the civil lands west of Calleth lake. East of Calleth Lake, the lake of doves, a colossal wall transects the Plains of Gederon, known as the Horg-wall, which has hemmed in every troll horde and barbaric invasion from the eastern steppes, keeping men from devastation. Built a millennium ago, yet the Durgoth and Kargoth still maintain it.

The somber sky shed snowflakes again, but only lightly at first. As dark hours passed, more heavily it came. We followed large, glacial basins, staying clear of the thick woods. Evening was soon upon us, and all kept silent as we drove our sled dogs on a trail that passes by a grand and brooding river transecting the basin. The river was not frozen, but warm enough to still flow freely.

We reached an inclined slope and urged the dogs onwards. Tenebrous clouds obscured the moonlight. As the leader-sled reached the top of the slope ahead of us, the driver halted his dogs. The other sleds, however, did not stop at once, but continued to the top. As my sled reached them, next to the others, I looked at Arizel and Phaedra.

"Why are we halted here?"

Phaedra pointed. "Look there! -in the distance." Upon yonder rocky fastness, through the veil of cascading snowflakes, they could make out the gloomy tower of the great fortress Baffay. "We have entered the territory of the enemy. The land where it is lawful to be lawless, and where freedom is enslavement: the Nzul." Of Nzul the bards do not fail in description *"I saw a land with sky ever grey, foul and not fair/ Nzul the melancholy, even the rocks know despair."*

With as much concentration as one can can summon I peered, but did not see the terrible tower. I recalled Maragald's wisdom —do not try to catch sight of what pertains to spirit with carnal eyes; *"the eye of the spiritual man perceives things visible to the spirit..."* I prayed a little, requesting the radiant Lady to help me. I took some moments to return inwardly to Heaven's interior light, and recount the way of our divine Lord. Slowly did the drear fortress begin to unveil; so that I could perceive its position. How did the likes of someone like Phaedra Stormraker see it? Such is the elphic might of valraphs.

Hours later I awoke. It was Maragald's wonderstone, the sacred scapular that I wore even while sleeping, that first awoke me. And some moments later I heard something. At first I supposed that one of the dogs, the wind having waked him, had growled. I also needed to relieve myself. Miserable, I opened the flap of the tent and stepped out into cool airs. Finch, who was supposed to be on watch, was nowhere to be seen.

I was barely thinking. There I stood to take care of nature's business, looking about. I did not see the dogs anywhere curled up.

Much fog was upon the wold. "Not far from here in ancient times the battle of SuarBille was fought. " I thought, "on a night just like this. " And just then, to my astonishment, four heavily armoured soldiers marched right by me. They were hobgoblins on guard patrol. They did in fact notice me but seemed to care not, probably assuming that I were a human mercenary. They vanished into the fog. Then, through the cloudy dimness, I perceived fires and torches. Pitched in every place round were tents just like ours, horgoth tents, hundreds of them all set up before us. Thanks be to God our tent happened to be on the very edge of the encampment. Many horgs here and there went about looking after various tasks, sharpening spears and scimitars, eating raw meat, playing dice.

They had moved in and set up camp during the hours of gloam before first light. I froze in the presence of the troll-horde.

Just then Arizel stepped out, ostensibly for the same reason as myself. Not right away did he also notice the perilous development, but mumbled.

"Had you quiet watch, Sir Hortezan?"

I did not answer, nor turn to him. Lack of an answer from me clued him in quickly to the situation. Soon he also stood completely motionless and remained hush a while, watching.

Slowly I made the sign of the cross.

"Angelic ministers and saints of God preserve us." I whispered.

"There has never been so vast a horgoth army as this," he remarked, his jaw slackened by awful contemplation. "There has been little news of their numbers, or that they have been on the warpath...

"All right," I whispered loudly, "slowly turnabout, and get back down into the tent."

"No, do not move slowly," Said Arizel. "You will easily be noticed. Just do what you must and act natural. Mulcifer sometimes hires human mercenaries anyway."

It was true; I did what he said. I turned so that only my back could be seen and did what I had come out to do. It took the longest time to finish.

Not a stir went up from those horgrim who were near. They were all getting ready for bed and did not care for anything else. Once back inside the tent we awoke the others and made plans.

"We cannot hide long in here," said Drocwolf. "They will detect our scent...and our sleds will not outrun the horgrim; the dogs are weak."

"Right...Arizel, can you hide us?" I asked hopefully.

"No, only the dogs, but I can cause a distraction."

"Then do it," I said. "All of you now flee and hide in the murk and shadows. Grab what packs you can, and make for the swampy forests of Maboloth, as did Nergalf of old. But stay in pairs. They likely will notice us in the softlight, but most of them are asleep by now. Do not make a sound. The snowfall should cover your tracks. We meet a stade up river at first light, near the henge stones we passed. Keep safe."

"Off now —all of you! " ordered Phaedra. Immediately Arizel cast up a magic dancing light dispay to the opposite side of the horgoth camp.

Of course one of our valraphs had to stop and sloppily kill a horgoth guard as we were attempting to escape the predicament. Valraphs have minor self-control when wounds of dishonor have gone deep. The struck guard bellowed in death agony. Just for a chance revenge was our essential silent cover blown. So was the cry heard above the blasts and there was immediate suspicion as in any military camp. Some hurried to investigate, approaching the area where we had taken cover.

Soon several horgrim now picked up on our presence. Recognizing valraph equipment, they headed away to alert others. We would be discovered, so all got up and ran for their lives. Down to the swampy forest the valraphs headed.

The horgrim, being themselves too craven to hunt valraphs without the help of bolgs, (or they may have spotted the wizard, or been wary of the swamp), were nonetheless eager for carnage. The horn was blown, the alarm was sounded.

My horse Burgundius was grazing in a nearby glade. After too little rest he was unable to carry away both Arizel and I for any distance. I bade the noble warhorse to flee. He was reluctant. He craved the fight, citing his three painful attacks: two hoof strikes and a bite. "No, I said, you must go to the grazing fields outside Tyrnopolis, mindful not to be captured by horgs, slavers, or anyone whomsoever, even if they offer an apple."

The great horse shook his mane and snorted in anger at my discipline. But he did obey the behest.

Arizel, with a flick of his wrist, had summoned all the dogs. He said, "Go, my dogs, protect our rear." They were keen dogs, indeed; one by one they disappeared into the murky swamp. I did not think it opportune to speculate on the details of his magic. It took a moment too long; the valraphs were already nowhere in sight.

It was then that I saw him, I myself saw him: The great hobgoblin captain, Mulg, having dashed out of his tent to see what was going on. He was enormous, his limbs were as tree-trunks, and his sallow face sported scars radiant with terror. He stood surveying the plain. A massy spike-bearing cudgel he carried in his claw-hand, the spikes I'm sure were dragon's teeth. An ibex-horn bow and quiver slung aft, and all Hell's fury frowned in his sinews of giganto-frame; storm was upon a malagrugrous expression. Sported he no helm to protect him, and all his hair was shorn from his head, for he was consecrated to destruction. Gore stained his chin, or red war-paint. Nar aught of mail over his torso did he don, but merely a skirt of brazen scales, leather belt and boots, and golden arm clasps of barbaric styling. Otherwise went he unclad, as do all who wish to boast their prowess with emulate pride when the war-wind blows. Mulcifer, vassal to the prince of shadows, master of hateful horgrim, vanquisher, accomplished hunter of trail-seeing rangers and single-hearted paladins; Mulg, waster of castles, whose chariot was adorned with the crowned heads of Ammouric kings. He was poised but a stone's throw.

The great goblin surveyed the encampment, and at last his eyes fell upon me, for out of dread I could not move. His black eyes could not see through the mists for certain, but he squinted. Murderous intellect glinted in his eye: not only the toughest and most massive of all horgrim, but the smartest. He spotted me through all the chaotic running about, and he recognized me as not fitting, and marked me. At once he stepped forward to pursue me.

Arizel and I went together, flying on foot for our lives. Mulcifer paused and knocked off a black-feathered bolgoth arrow. I heard it whiz past my ear. The others also were soon hot on our trail, but we had put good distance from them. Off we turned sprinting from the road embankment and hurried down into the swamp and fens of decaying forest and tamaracks. Several valraphs did the same, scattering. Arizel and I into a remote and watery place went far off, where many saplings, willows, and cat-tails could conceal us.

To be away from that Mulg was a sweet relief. You may hold my action unworthy, brothers, failing to confront the killer with my powerful sword for an exchange of deadly blows; aye, and you announce that I fled like a deer, shamefully. In defense I say this: I have rightly described his massive frame to you. You have seen him not. Of giant's descent is his line. My holy brand is matched for witches and warlocks; not giants, not hobgoblins. You argue that I should have had faith, fight like a crusader. I say divinely taught wisdom makes victories; to flee when clearly outmatched, but a folly to act out bravado. My opinion the authority of Guy of Xaragia upholds, who writes: *Qui sapientia docet fugere periculum, ergo salvetur pugnare in dies sequentes.*

"Here, in this place, crouch down," I whispered to Arizel. "The brutes will not discover us near these waters and reeds, in cat-tails and shadows."

"Of that I am uncertain," said Arizel. "—too many branches scratching in there. I cannot see. Alas that I ever yielded up the comforts of an ignorant life."

"Just get down here and shut your mouth," I warned in a loud whisper.

"What?" he said. "Mind your tongue, you are still a hostage."

"Quiet," I whispered angrily, "or we both die. Don't say another word."

By now many horgrim were searching through the misty swamps and mirkwoods for us. Right then we heard a horg stomping our way. Now you might think these hobgobs dumb and brutish, and indeed are they ugly, but some are as keen in sense as any man. We waited and listened to them traipsing through dim light and willows, raking through brambles and reeds slowly and methodically.

Snowflakes gathered on grass blades and cat-tails silhouetted around me. My feet were numb in the cold waters. Branches of swamp shubs poked. Every snowflake that fell landed perfectly and silently to the place it was meant. Each snowflake that fell to rest upon the cat-tail represented the lapse of a moment of life that was quickly being measured out for me. The splashing footsteps were coming closer, and I hoped that the odor of the rotting swamp and woods might cover us, but perhaps they would not.

Soon we were certain he would detect us; the gob could smell us and was determined to get out of us a fight. I slowly brought forth the sword Witchbane and readied my mind for combat. Arizel could fight well with deadly dagger, but would be at disadvantage in brush; nor did his spell-casting power promise to be a saving hope. If he were to mumble a many-worded spell now, it would be heard.

The horg was close upon us. Through the branches and tall grass I could now see his hunched and contorted figure, his impish profile. Its shadow cast against the morose, *darfurque* gloam of sky. I prayed and hoped he would turn away and head South. Instead he pivoted toward where Arizel and I lay concealed.

Stalking with slow pace deliberated he now was close and even next to us. Even my thoughts went hush. I poised to strike at a sudden. Now everything was instinct. He was searching over a nearby patch. Should I stay hidden and risk being discovered, or do I bury the battle-blade in his belly before he can call out? Which calculation grants victory? Oh Lord, I know that you do not wish us to kill, but these vermin butchers of the fairy realm are ones whose flesh has the character of a demon incarnate, their hearts blacker than soot. Are they even half-human? Not born from a womb, they are the abominal manufacture of evil archon. "Give strength to my hands. " I'll finish the gob in one murder-stroke to the guttural.

My frame convulsed, heaved, and I sprung, but he stepped aside. So I thrust at him in a play to run him through, but he skirted the blade. He howled alarm quite rudely, and he readied his falchion and assumed stance for combat. I had chosen to take him on, but it was a hazardous choice. He moved like an experienced warrior. If he scored a stroke against me, it would not fail to kill. He was formidable, and lunged forward to impale me.

Just then a flashing of fur went pouncing upon him. It was a dog. He leaped against his flank and unbalanced him. The horg stumbled sideways. It was one of Arizel's dogs. The canine's ambush startled him, and he went several steps off as the dog snapped his deadly jaws. He finally tripped backward over a log athwart his retreat. He was sprawled the ground and could not at once get back up; his falchion was stuck in mud as well.

"Don't just watch, man. Have at the wretch!" cried Arizel.

This was something I did not have the luxury to philosophize over. I advanced and went with both arms reaching out; I buried Witchbane deep into the horg's black heart. The horg stopped breathing, looked at me puzzled, and straight away expired.

The dog ripped to shreds the enemy's neck which spurted, to my surprise, crimson blood.

His howl had alerted several other horgrim in the area. Now it was quite obvious to Arizel that although I was in possession of an heirloom sword, (one of the most treasured in all Whitehawk besides Oceanicyng or Elmethodon), that my swordsmanship was not precision enough and probably would not improve any time soon. More horgs were on their way, and we would surely not prevail against them.

"We cannot out-run them," I said.

"Then prepare to be captured, for they will not slay us, but will capture us and hand us over to Veil-knights and other nasty soldiers to be interrogated. Then they will imprison or enslave us. I am not ready for that, nor are you, though you imagine otherwise."

"Call forth your magic dogs to go at odds for us; that will distract them."

"The dogs are strong, but they will not well match even a few of this troll-horde who use the black arrows. Capture is a thing we cannot avoid. Consider now a safe measure which I propose, to forfend what we know, and what they must never learn. Once captured, evil ones who serve the Balecrown will interrogate you to learn what can be known on *The Black Books*. . . but I have packed a potion which, when consumed, will protect that knowledge, and anything of strategic intelligence, even under torture."

"Never will I pollute the temple formed of flesh; I have my obligation."

"Think hard on this, monk; if under torture you give them what information they seek, they will kill you afterwards. You will never even know what our quest has been, or why you have died. "

"And what is our quest —or rather, yours?" I asked. "Why have you led us into this snare? You'd better tell me everything you left out now, lest one of us perish, or I else I will trust you not enough for anything else. "

"Very well... As you heard before, I bear some responsibility for the desolation of my home, Nystol. Although the place was an old trap, it was my home. The memory of my treachery weighs as heavy guilt on my soul. You know how ignorance has overwhelmed Whitehawk in our day, how dark powers conspire to seize the governance of the world, both Bishops and Kings. Who are these powers? Four known are there for certain, ancient powers whose own fallen inversion left them prisoned, but now they go hither and thither, free to distort unwary minds. I am sorry to admit it, but my Sorcerous curiosity caused me to release these creatures from their Tartaran prison. Yes, there are four...there is *drakodemon*, the great draconian spirit, that is, the many-headed spirit of unbridled vice, her breathe weapon blowing rage across every land. There is also a second, Abraxas, demon-god of unholy goatish monks, the infernal book producers who "lodge beneath earth." Abraxas is master of every alien dogma for publication. Of course let us not forget the third who concerns us presently, the Northing, priest of evil, that ghostly creature of the barren Nzul and its black furnaces of Baffay. He is a spirit of consuming envy and melancholy, a horrible mystery which plagues the world. Him I did not unchain, but another did. I could have stopped him."

"Right...quite nice, and comforting to know. You seem to have had your years doing a world of wonders for us all. Now then, you said the four."

"Of the fourth power I am uncertain. It is some foul spirit I am near to discovering. It is an iniquitous power whose name I have not yet uncovered."

"Name is not known...? —so then is that it?!"

"What...?"

"You need to know their names! You already know the names of "Abraxas" and the *drakodemon* "Vorthragna," but Northing's origin-name and the fourth name of some unknown you think are recorded in *The Black Book*. You wanted me to find them."

As I was speaking this revelation, an even greater revelation dawned upon me. . .

"...and it is quite clear now, Bannock, why you wanted me to come: the names! According to the *Rituale Exorcismus*, one can only exorcize a demon if one has its name! You think that I, a man of the cloth, can exorcize them from the world and banish them back to the Tartaran prison!"

"We have nothing of time left for this, but know that I will explain in full later. Quaff you now the potion, monk."

"Well, I have some news for you, wizard. You should have studied your Ammouric religion more closely. Do you not know that a simple monk is not given the authority for a high exorcism? Only an Ammouric *selva*, a priest, can be given..."

Arizel was shocked and baffled at this oversight of his, (a man otherwise astute and precise).

"Well then...never mind it. You are still of great use. I must somehow undo what has been done. A man hopes above all for some kind of redemption from his wrongs, even if he doesn't see eye to eye with ecclesiastics. I must employ concoctions to thwart these foul spirits and the men in high places ready to do their bidding. Now here, gulp you down the analgesic. It is no pollution or unholy elixir. It is composed according to the old sage-craft, an infusion of radiant matter, having qualities more medicinal than anything else. —Its fundamental ingredient? A burnetize of milk from the Gondo Tiger that dwells in the hills of Setet, for receipe the arcane title *Lactis Sphynxis.*"

Now I had to calculate right quick what I should do, for the foe was in sight and would soon detect our concealment. I could not endure a defeat, for myself or for our sacred faith. What had I done wrong? Had I made foolish choices and not strongly enough demanded a share in the leadership? I should have been wearing the Red Cowl, relic of the Burgundy Knight, then I could have chosen well the far-flung route of this expedition. How daft to neglect a gift of the Saints.

I would not, good brothers, have risked this otherwise, but I proposed in my mind that Heaven would not count it against me to quaff the wyrdding medicine just once. I reckoned it rather a mercy, for did not the

Christ break the rule against work on Sabbath, a day sacred, by doing a merciful work—the healing of a leper? Certainly also it would be mercy for me to break a rule and safeguard the sacred quest.

Now, however, looking back, I wonder if it were not a sin. So I offer it as part of this confession. One should try to be more humble and not assume. Perhaps I slighted the prohibition of Our Heavenly Sovreign... and not just where scripture forbids the use of magic. Rather do I recall there was some faulty motive; for in my prideful youth I conformed to nature rather than grace, and so, not trusting in divine providence, I too much feared the humiliation of how things would go were I captured: (the obvious sequence): to be tortured, to the betraying of information to the minions of Darkness, and then at last the dying in shameful dishonor. I despaired of His grace, and could not accept that Heaven would have sent me so far...to end like that.

The milky potion had a glowing orange, nebulous quality, like the mist that rises up out of the swamps of Ard during late Elhithmere (October) mornings. I drank down the magic, and it was sweet to the taste, but bitter to the stomach. I remember a smarting ache in my belly, and a surge of oblivion emptied my thoughts. I passed into dream, and knees giving way, I slowly sunk to earth. In the corner of my sight I could see many horgrim advancing upon our position, their crescent blades brandished high at the discovery.

Of course the potion worked, eventhough I have immunity from all magic as a Christian monk, and it should have had zero effect on me. When I had the incarnadine plague and ate the mystery meat and drank the magic wine mixed with blood, I was in fever and did not know what I was doing. The magic did not work. This was different. To knowingly do this unlawful act rendered the immunity compromised. We go astray if we choose to own way rather than trust in His law. Who knows what would have been if we had fought and escaped? Now we would be captives.

If you are captured, you must not take seriously the tortures which will be administered to you. Do not scream wildly or cry out for help. Accept that which your careless errors have earned you. Make up for your undisciplined mind and lack of training. Do not dishonour the monkhood.

Tien Joshur
Spring Instruction for Incarcerated Monks

XXVI   *The Pythagorean Enigma*

The next thing which I recall, brothers, is a thing too ELSEwise to accurately describe with words. Let it suffice to say that I was awakened in a strange and forsaken place. I was not in a darkness visible about me, but rather was I cognizant of a darkness of mind within me. It was as if my mind were under a certain spell of nether-reasoning, a maze of logics disjunct. Perhaps the state can be best described as a "waking dream," a sort of trance, a quasi-oblivion to all veritable things. I certainly had not been dreaming this oblivion with eyes closed, but with eyes wide-open, sleepless, yet in another sense remaining asleep. This awakening was a peculiar thing indeed; perhaps only the mad or the melancholic are familiar with it. This "waking dream" involved a philosophical delusion guised as ancient wisdom. You could even describe it as a classical style of instruction steeped in high folly, I suppose, depending on how you look at it.

The thread of poetry could draw me out. Certitude requires that one distinguish between what is dream and what is not dream, between the seeming and the substantive, the illusory and the real. Most dreamers are not aware that they are dreaming, and a dreamer may even imprison himself in a sub-reality of his own contrivance. He may let the dream enchant him into getting hopelessly lost into an endless illusory delight. Some are therefore quite content never to be awakened to reality, and to never have certitude, never to know truth.

I was alerted that this dream was, in fact, a dream. I knew it was a dream even before it passed away and ceased being a dream. It should be likened to an echo echoing in a watery cave, as the dreamer himself comes nigh to the very threshold of poetic illumination and becomes quite fully ware of some luminosity near. The gradual tide of cognizance is detected, as when a surge of seawater wets the ankles of explorers emerging from grottos below. One wash after another gives increased confidence to those who are hopeful for a way out of the sightless dark. They follow the twisting tunnels and at last arrive at the open cave and the sea and the blue sky.

The ultimate certitude, however, does not come in degrees like that or successive increments, but instead is as a singular and stupendous vision, blinding and painful. It is likened to one who has been content in darkness a long time but suddenly gets dragged into the brightness of the full sun. Nay... real certitude comes not like that slowly growing wakefulness in cozy bed after a good rest, but it is cold water thrown upon a sleepwalker, a shocking epiphany upright and occupied.

In my dream-state I was occupied with what the worldly would consider a mundane and harmless thing, but what a certain antiquated philosopher considered sacrilege: I was eating a dinner of black beans, and doing so with a fork.

My dream-thoughts had been dwelling on some doctrine of the wiseman Pythagoras, or "Thypagoras" in Gohhan tongue. Exactly which doctrine I cannot recall. Its unfinished or unexplained character had caused me to become completely absorbed in the conundrum, forgetful of who I was and what I should be doing. So this vain mentality might have gone on *ad perpetuum* but for an abrupt interruption which was actually disruption. A soundless flash of mental lightning illuminated my sentient darkness. This flash revealed the hidden den of iniquity that such dreaming conceals, an evil pit of serpents fed on the vain ponderings into which I had led myself.

Thanks be to God the insight lasted no more than a split moment. In a singular flash of certitude I became conscious at once of self and obligation. Was it the hand of God that intervened? During the waking dream I had not been much possessed of myself, or perhaps it was that I had been absorbed in myself to the extent that I had forgotten who I really was. Whatever the case, I was become delirious.

It is clear to me now that this effect was a species of *quasimentia*, a side-effect of the potion which Arizel had beguiled me into imbibing. Indeed, how delusional I was become, and not because of any state of being, but for the assumption by which my activity had been governed. The dream was precisely this: rather than merely accepting what Heaven high-above has passed down through men, and following the holy ones to the well of waters of poetry ever-quenching, I instead sought "my own answers." This was the philosophic prison in which I found myself, along with myriads.

The new reflection caused me to now perceive this dream-error in which I had become mired. I too felt the strain of epistemological burden which certain philosophers put on themselves, namely, to contrive some correct determination for reality, no matter how minute. Like a confused wizard attempting to design a new potion by testing it on himself, the dream-philosopher seeks to answer the question "why" by investigations into himself rather than the reality around him. Certainly it is a valorous enterprise, but such is the failure of all noetic philosophy. What good is a map-maker who does not examine and measure the physical landscape, but instead starts with his own idea of what the land might be and draws out its shape according to his own like? It is vanity.

Is the reality of Reality is to be translated or interpreted? Or is it as a poem to be heard but barely comprehended? Is the Real something that can be revealed in prose, or configured like a recipe, or tested by means of scientific categorization? Is it even pursued as possibility by reasoning?

Thypagoras grappled these questions as did Jacob who wrestled the angel, my namesake. I was not aware that Thypagoras put celestial messengers (the gods) in headlocks, and, not cognizant of his anthropomorphic sublimities, my meditation was bent in upon itself like an ουροβορος, the famous snake biting its own tail. Hence his poetic enigmas, and my own failure to realize them, or even idealize them...

I had long been mired in this way and had lost strength of will, thinking of divinity merely as the *Prime Mover*. Heaven alone could intervene, and it did so with a brilliant force that tore apart the veil of unknowing.

Because this deluded endeavor had dulled my reason, I had been dream-thinking over Thypagoras and his aphorisms obsessively for perhaps many weeks, not after the manner of one who seeks the truth, but as one who seeks hidden knowledge for his own use. It seemed like centuries had passed. I was unable to detect the vanity. Mysteriously, I remained somewhat rational, or quasi-rational. Liken it to when one has dreams which consist of thoughts rather than images and syllogisms rather than sensations.

It seems I had been telling whomsoever was at hand everything I knew on the Pythagorean system, as if some trumpeter in the clouds, not caring at all if they were even the slightest bit interested or even listening; and I hope that I am not doing the same now to you, brothers. As to the meaning of his enigmas I had been speculating unsuccessfully. Where I was and what I was doing, or what I should be doing, never came to mind. Not even hunger could turn my obsessive thoughts away from the considerations of the proposed mathematic axioms.

It was only by chance, or destiny, that I stooped to eat the bowl of beans that had been provided by the guards through the slot. I had become no more aware of future or past than an infant, who eats and makes sounds, "awake" and alert, but is not self-conscious in any real sense. Exactly how many days passed while I was under this spell of obsession remains uncertain, nor afterwards was I able to determine it in a precise way.

Perhaps I was jolted out of the funk because I caught myself eating beans, and Thypagoras' prohibition against this activity had awoken some alarm in my lapsing remembrance of the moral order. I nevertheless determined to finish the bowl regardless of the Pythagorean superstition.

I was becoming wise to my surroundings. Others must be kept in chambers both nearby and far off, and soon it became evident to me that I was locked up in a narrow place. It seemed a chamber of windowless stone, a brick cell in some sort of vast dungeon. These facts had not been troubling me before, not until those moments subsequent to my illumination. My jaw and tongue halted with the shock of it, and the beans waited in my cheek. An evil place I found myself in, echoing with the screams of the tortured. Even such sounds as those which I had so often heard in recent weeks had never warranted me alarm, but now they were from other sentient creatures, like myself.

Some doctrine in Thypagoras' system, which I had previously come across recorded in *The Black Book of Melancholia*, came to mind. I had merely passed over it before. It now pricked me to ponder the welfare of others, and to reflect and speculate over my own identity, even to recount my responsibilities to other sentient beings. All this hinged on the poetry of exactly who I was in relation to my Creator. Was I not committed to him in some way? Did I not owe him some sort of allegiance? Surely he was more than a *monad.* I also remembered that somewhere at some time I had consumed some sort of mysterious lambent liquid.

I pondered over the liquid. Was it a magical potion? Had the drinking of it poisoned me and snuffed the life from me, and at last sent me to Hades, or even to dark Hell? Was my soul finally condemned for having trusted in magic? Some Church fathers and theologians write that it be not just for incorporeal spirits, but rather is a place *paraphysical* in which the body suffers torture along with the soul. Eating beans...is that allowed in Hell?

Or was it that I was discovering a personal hell: the uncontrollable and constant meditation on some arcane philosophical system? Would some demon soon appear to administer tortures by questioning me endlessly concerning Thypagoras' doctrines? Or would the shade of the pagan philosopher himself appear, consigned to this underworld like *King Minos*[43] of legend, appointed as the infernal and inexorable nether-jailer of souls?

I again heard screams afar off in the many levels of corridors. Another man was in the cell adjacent. He was turned away from me, curled up in hay. I could not reckon his face.

I swallowed the last of my beans, and so with trepidation spoke.

"Excuse me...Ho there!" I exclaimed. "Noble sir! Pray tell, where in the three or four worlds are we? Is this the great prison? What place be this, what place exactly? My how melancholy are these chambers. Are we enclosed in the catacombs of Hell?"

"You awoke me...again," he replied. "Go back to your translations and shut thy mouth. The light is almost faded. You should ask for a candle...like I said."

"What?" I asked, perplexed. I looked over and saw that *The Black Book* had been opened and that I had been writing notes in the marginalia. It was open to a section entitled *Aphorisms of Thypagoras.*

"I say, answer me at once. I must know!" I repeated with great panic "Are we condemned to Hell? Is this the great dungeon which Christ prophesied for the wicked?"

"Hell? Were you actually in the spiritual regions of Hell," he answered, "would you possess a body? Would you even be able to talk? If only...! Stop bothering me; You speak of dreams. I wish never to end my dreaming, as one undisturbed for eternal slumber. Ask your Thypagoras, whom you never cease to quote and ruminate upon."

---

[43] *King Minos:* King of Crete, after he was assigned to a post of judge of souls at the entrance to the underworld in the Greek fables.

"His shade is imprisoned here as well? Where then in Heaven's name are we? What is this place? Is this utter Hell? I say, answer me! "

"Of this same discussion I weary." he replied. "So I will try a new tack. Answer me a question. If you can still sense your body, eat your dinner, and treat on philosophy, why would you suspect yourself to be in Hell? Do not your philosophers teach otherwise?"

"They have their limitations," I answered. "As do all the philosophers. Say...by your tone I glean that like me you yourself do not even know what exactly is this place."

There was a guilty silence.

"Or you are afraid to tell?" I continued. "...or perhaps you are one of those who suppose that the damned are not tortured bodily? Well, what do you say? Since you will not give a fitting answer in the first count, I will plague you with other questions."

"Why don't you get some sleep instead?"

"I having been thinking over something. Tell me, are you of the opinion that a divinely sentenced punishment is meted with pain to the spirit only, and not to the body?" (This was certainly the provocation of someone desperate for answers.)

"What? It is clear that the physical body rots at death, friend, and passes into earth," he replied, sounding confident. "A man who has abandoned God is tormented not by physical fire but by the very absence of God. That is Hell, and it is come to earth."

"That is the greatest of woes...'tis agreed; you are right," I replied.

"Good, now hasten back to your reading and let me at peace."

"But I do not know who art thou, prisoner, although your words smack of training in sacred doctrine. Nevertheless, I do warn that you are not entirely correct. Believe you me: the body also will suffer tortures after death. Heaven taught this because God knew that people would be careless over their own souls, but they are always solicitous as to the comforts of their bodies. I worry against this possibility. I worry because I am confused and am at a loss as to how I got here and why. Are tortures about to be applied to me?"

"What does it matter? If your soul is at peace, all is well," he answered. "Do you not perceive the unreason in your thoughts? Do not be afraid on that account. No tortures await the body after death. How can the body suffer torment if it has already been destroyed by death and decay? "

"Fellow," I asked, "do you not confess the resurrection of the dead?"

"What has that to do with it?"

"It is written that God will raise both the righteous and the wicked," I answered. "When He raises the wicked He raises them in their bodies, for as Our Lord rose bodily from the dead, so will every human being, as the Church instructs: some resurrected to joy, others to woe, consequent upon their deeds. Those whom He raises to woe hurry from Heavenly goodness and seek the great imprisonment, where forever the apostate angels will torture them for the heinous crimes committed during life."

"That is absurd..." he answered. "I was wont to think just like you once, that I would get along in my understanding. I have since corrected myself and understood that these teachings of a new body are merely symbolic. The soul separates from the body at death, never to be restored to it."

"Is that so? Then perhaps you can teach me. Tell, me, what is a soul without a body?" I asked.

"Surely it is nevertheless a creature in God's hands," he answered.

"Is it not in itself a creature made for God? And in itself a spirit, and so also immaterial, but needing a body for completion? "

"The soul is a spirit, as you suppose," he answered. "And it is without a doubt immaterial, and like all created beings, it has its ultimate cause in Him...yes, that is right, made for God."

"May a creature have more than one end for which it is made?" I asked. "As for example, we easily observe that man is made for woman, and woman for man, yet both also are made for God."

"You are arguing well, hoping to confuse, and I know not where you think to go with this. You yourself do not sound like one who is amiss over where he is. I agree with your line of thought, however; what you claim cannot be denied."

"I am trying to discover exactly where I am, since a straight answer has not yet come from you. I fear it is because you yourself may be uncertain. However, if we arrive at some definite conclusions on the afterlife, what it means to live again, we might deduce what is our condition. So, let us continue. I ask you this: could not the soul have two ultimate ends? One end is union with God; the other is subordinated but duly ordered, to animate and govern the body, the body for which it has been wrought and in which it is at home. When the soul is without the body, it longs for it and is not really complete without it."

"You are convincing, and quite annoyingly so. But this is better material than I have yet heard from you. Whatever has this to do with your belief that the body is tortured after death, for surely death involves the separation of soul from body."

"At the resurrection a new body is given," I explained, "also, mysteriously, the same body. It seems I have been thinking over Thypagoras quite a bit lately, but that does not mean that I agree with him. It is not possible, (as he proposes, you know), that a soul can transmigrate from one body to another different body, *peregrinatio animae*. That is quite outside reason. To discern error helps us discover truth. The errors of the philosopher Thypagoras help us considerably. Such errors which men fall into Heaven makes as proof for us, when by reasoning our way out of them, we preserve future generations from false teachings. Be assured: the soul is not reincarnated into a different body after death. The soul is clothed in a new body, the same body."

"Another absurdity you speak, always with Thypagoras upon your lips. What your harping on him ends with makes little sense. How could this resurrected body be both different and the same? One should imagine, if we are to yield to this teaching, that the new body will be a different body, perhaps similar, but not the same. "

"Is not a flowing river always the same river, but different and new at every moment? Our resurrected body will also be ever the same, but ever new. Concerning the resurrected body, there is indeed a certain newness. It is just as when a suit of armour, dented and burned, is given to the armourer to remake. He will refashion the armor to suit your need; and when you receive it back, is it not the same? But clearly, it is as new again. Would not the guildswork of Heaven be done all the more perfectly? "

"What proof from revelation have you of this? "

"Consider our Lord, who after he rose from the dead, showed his wounds to the disciple Thomas, known as the doubting. These were scars that he retained even in his glorified body. An old soldier wears proudly a battle-scar. By display of these wounds Christ was able to rescue the perplexed disciple from the hazards of doubt."

The prisoner fell hush a few moments and pondered. He then opened his mouth slowly and spoke.

"So also does it seem that you are rescuing me from my ignorance. Your argument has gained me."

"It is nothing to my credit. Illumination proceeds from grace. "

"No such crediting of you entered my mind anyway...but you wish to be humble; therefore you must be honest and true. A true believer will not put much credit upon himself, and neither is he upset when corrected. How is it that you have come up with these answers? Are you trained in the study of the sacred arts? Are you a priest long-schooled? "

"I do not fathom how I acquired all that reasoning. I must have been long studied under the rope-girded monks. Yet I cannot for the life of me remember. I glean that at least that I am a knight... "

"You have a monk's long robe. At first I thought that you might be one of those monks that serves the abyss, a disciple of that demon Abraxas. Those kind often quote Thypagoras. By your instruction, however, it is clear that you are no gnostic."

"A disciple of whom? That is some infernal power, isn't it? Be at ease; I also know this: there is no abyss."

"Oh? Then I have a further question for you as to what you taught before."

"Please..."

"Why should the body suffer for transgressions committed when it is the soul that entered them, being likewise charged with keeping watch? Is the body to be held guilty when it is the soul which has consented? "

"It seems unfair to you? Although we have no proper introduction, at least in my mind, I will continue this discourse without interruption. Some things duly outweigh politeness. Has not the body benefitted from the soul's governance? For the blessed there is reward, but for the condemned...some say that since the body cooperated in sin, it must be punished together with the soul. However, I say that while they are together, the body and soul are so completely combined that for all else consider them as one, though separable. This is reasonable and further helps us to understand why the body cannot live without the soul. The soul itself is the living component. Nevertheless, the body is less culpable, and on it punishment not so greatly falls. Hell's bonfire will burn the flesh, but this punishment will not be as great as the darkness which comes upon the soul, the absence of God, as you reminded us before. This, of course, is the final result of choices freely made. By successive choices the soul makes during the span which, in the case of the reprobate, confirm their own final choice to turn away from God. Freely choosing to give up their freedom as a son or daughter of God, they choose the imprisonment of sin, which the father of lies calls freedom. So they hasten for eternity to the outer darkness, no longer under the protection of heaven and the angels. I am wondering if this is that very place, or somewhere near it, for the steady repetition of screams off in distant cells overthrows my peace of mind."

"Yet, is it not rank in unfairness," he then asked, "that for a few transgressions in this short life, humans must pay forever in the infernal miseries that await them?"

"The only punitive threat that behooves an immortal soul is the threat of unending punishment," I answered. "Anything less, length-of-time wise, is beans compared to eternity. Consider also that the soul-misery of the condemned is self-imposed, since throughout life they kept making the choice for disobedience, sin, and death ...rather than obedience, being love, and life. They served themselves rather than others. Their deeds become quite who they are, and they die in their sins."

"Could not the mercy of God come upon them when they are near death, provided they repent?"

"Yes, it is possible. It is, however, unlikely. St. Dismas, the thief next to Christ upon the cross, repented in his last moments and the Lamb invited him to paradise. It is passing difficult to be faithful and think of God when in the throes of pain. To do so is a grace. Such a grace is rare. Can one lead a fallen life but repent in the ultimate hour? Can an old dog learn new tricks? Faith is from God. Even were you to show the unbelievers God himself and he granted miracles for their eyes to behold, most would not cease from comforting themselves with unbelief. So went all Corazain the city, says scripture, and earned His curse."

"What if a man were to do good his entire life, and then near the very end of his span commit some horrendous trespass and die at once without time to repent. Would God not have mercy upon him anyway?"

"Holy writ speaks of this question and answers in the negative. The time to secure divine mercy is in this life. Outside time, in the eternity, there is no possibility of change, because change is a temporal phenomenon, and repentance is a change in the soul. Once dead, we have God's justice, the Judgement. Time to seek mercy is past. Further change is not possible. Let us pray for a happy death, that is if we are not already dead. You might say this is not fair. Most who think that way do not understand what great sinners are we all. Scripture, in turn, affirms that one who does mischief all his life, and subsequently in later years, at last repenting, accomplishing a good deed at the very end, shall be saved. It is good to know that there is always hope even for the worst of men."

"Hope? You can abandon all hope in this place, friend. You shall never escape."

"If I do not abandon hope, I think that I shall be better off."

"Why say you that? "

"I say it for good reason, not just to sound sweet. If I continue to hope, then I shall also keep seeking whatever may realize that hope, some way out. He who loses hope, however, and despairs, he no longer seeks a way out, and therefore will forever be imprisoned, unable to notice the moment or the sign of escape, the sign of the cross. The same is true for all believers who find themselves shackled to some vice out of their human weakness. They must never abandon hope."

"That is a sweet and hopeful thought. I offer you this opposing argument: hope yields Man in his earthly misery a counterfeit light; it continues to deceive him into thinking that a new day will dawn. It stays perched on the rim of Pandora's unholy box. In recompense for a failed attempt at escape from this place, you should know that your torturers will multiply your pains."

"Torturers? What torturers?" I asked, quite disturbed.

"The demons that will fly up from the bottomless pit and greet you; they will be your torturers. "

"But you said just now that this is not Hell."

"Did I...? "

"Let them come!" I snapped. "Even in life the invisible demons surround and torture a true believer —by their tricks, and they multiply his pains. Heaven licenses it. The demons do all this in order that one's Will might be broken and he return to his vice for comfort, like a dog to his vomit. But Heaven will fortify him instead with hope. I think it is similar with you and I."

"Then you have answered your own question," he observed. "this place can only be if one has no hope. It is foremost a state of soul, not of body. Will not all the tortures of demons mean quite little to the hopeful, I mean to one who maintains hope to someday escape and find eternal peace? You are right in what you argue; hope keeps one from the inescapable prison. It cannot be contested. I, however, do not have hope, and I do not think there be much alike between us. The fact that we are men who await torture is our only similarity."

"Yet you speak also as a believer, " I said, wondering.

"I am a believer, yes indeed. But think: is it not said that *even the devils believe, and they tremble*? They tremble because they have a certain knowledge of God. I am a believer, true, but I only tremble when I think of the tortures which my flesh will learn. That is why the vile guards here are making us wait for our woes, for the wait itself is a kind of unbearable torture, listening to those screams. They want to be sure we have no hope left."

"So then what I have suspected is so? The Judgement has come, and, in my terror, I cannot remember it? Now I await the torture of my body in this darkness. When will it begin? Will our demonic jailer come this very hour with hooks and torch? So am I really in the pits of the damned?"

"Do you have hope?"

"Yes, I have hope...I can and will escape."

"Your mind is not clear. The coming pains will clarify your thoughts, as they did for St. Dismas."

"So you mean to say that we find ourselves in Hell?"

The man in the cell across the corridor did not answer right away, but looked up, stroked his shaggy beard, turned about, and curling up, went right back to his slumbers. I repeated the question, emphasizing of huge desperation, mixed with a tone of umbrage at his slight regard and dismissal of our conversation.

"I say, are we in the Hell described by the ancients?"

"It is you who have said it."

That enigmatic reply was all he offered before trying unsuccessfully to slip off to the comfort of sleep. After a short time, he opened his eyes, and lifting his head, he explained, like a husband who is bothered in his bed by a nagging wife.

"I told you before...it is, yes, here...but on earth, for we remain in the world, in the terrestrial plane. You are in the dungeon of the Arc du Baffay, in the princedom of Nzul, land where barely a solar ray penetrates through the smokey clouds, for there is only greyness. I crave to once again view even a partly blue sky. Here lodge you in perpetual gloom, a land of somber mists, and you are in its darkest place, its belly. I call it the nadir of the world, even of all existence, a place more detestable than the after-hell of the damned, for the damned are damned justly, but here it is different. Here there is nothing justly meted; not even a mouse could receive justice here. Here the guilty mete out punishments to the innocent. We are prisoners of the Northing, a mischievous fairy-king and priest of evil, who rules a vast and glaciate domain. Our doom is coming. I have become comfortable with this fact. I no longer wish to leave this place. It is my own monastery now. Why must I again unfold these things to you? I spoke with you on it all before, yesterday and the day before that. You wear a monk's robe but cannot figure where in the world you are."

"You have spoken to me before? I do not know why, but I remember it not. Is this what a Pythagorean initiate who has eaten beans experiences? Nor do I comprehend how I was brought here, and I suspect that doom has already come. Who, after all, are you then?"

"You are not certain of who you are yourself. I have already answered the question of who I am, several times. You never remember, and simply keep bringing up the superstitions of that regrettable philosopher Thypagoras. I suspect that you are under some kind of spell, a spell that causes you to focus on one thing and nothing else, and to come in and out of consciousness, your memory lapsing after each episode. I will tell you once again. Try not to forget. You wish to...no, I will not say my name, lest hooded Death hear and check his list. –Let me sleep."

"You sound aggravated," I said frankly. "Is sleep your response to hopelessness? As it is becoming quite evident to me, we are not yet dead or adjudged to fearsome Hell. Thanks be to God. Hell is the only place from which there is absolutely no escape, so there hopelessness quite behooves, and a sign indicating that thought is doubtless posted above its cruel gates: "Abandon all hope ye who enter." I do not despair yet. Death I do not fear. But what are the dreams which may come to the dead?"

"To what things do you refer?" he asked in reply. "The hellish tortures of demons? One does not need to be consigned to the after–hell for those tortures. The vile creatures fly up from the cavernous abyss yonder to administer torments in this place regularly. Nevertheless, what you say is true; worse things are known, and the grand terrors of soul we may yet avoid. Consider the bright side: we are still alive, still able to seek redemption. Even though our imprisonment here is unfortunate, we receive only corporeal pain, probably what we deserve anyway. The condemnation in afterlife is much worse. I consider that no man still living is abandoned by God, unless he wishes it so; and if he so wishes, he is already as good as dead, and his soul in a hell of its own making."

"You seem to know quite well many matters pertaining to spiritual life," I asserted. "Are you a true believer?"

"I try my best, but life is confusing. Heaven has delivered me into the hands of my enemies, and I surmise it is for some good reason. That very reason still eludes me. What about you? Did Heaven bring you here, that you might through tortures become saintly in perseverance? Will you lay claim to some great victory under the guise of imprisonment and sorrows, as the Christ did? Or is it that some sin ensnared you and that the diabolus has claimed you? Please do not answer with some vague saying of Thypagoras again."

"I do not presume on Heaven's purpose. Even a well–taught monk may find himself struggling to answer such a question...I know at least this: I am but a half–taught compared to others. To preserve my sanity I pray that both possibilities you mention are true, for I am chosen and knighted; and I am fain to suffer for His everlasting glory, true enough, but I am not without sins that ensnare, and the devil has ample material for his prosecutorial acts."

"You talk on just like a monk! Thanks be to God on his holy mountain —someone to help me out of my melancholy."

"Please keep your lips barred against that news," I warned. "I expect that our captors shall torture me with greater enthusiasm when they learn that I am an Ammouric Knight, of that I am sure. I lived in a monastery in my youth, but I cannot yet recall where was it, or if I am just wearing a monk's robe to conceal myself or what. I do recall that I was knighted in the monastery, by an Ammouric Knight in the presence of an Abbot. I was given a secret quest to find some sort of holy relic. I was bestowed the name Sir Hortezan, but I cannot recall the name which men called me for many seasons before. Other memories do come, images, but I am uncertain of their meaning. Something awful has happened to my memory. I can remember recent events, but little else. I drank down something that was weird. Nevertheless, it seems they have been feeding us well, most likely in order to delight later in the sights of fattened butchery, as the distant screams I am hearing forebode to me."

"You are right in that assumption, Sir Hortezan, if I may so call you. I have heard that they take prisoners to an underworld arena; and the prisoners, at last fattened on beans and pork, train for a time in gladiatorial skill, and at last go against each other, hoping for a quick end in bloody combat."

"Then I die by the sword, or in some other awful way?"

"...as it seems. As are all who are taken here, all end in such a way."

"Pray that I do not die soon," I begged. "for I perceive that some matter of grave consequence urges me, but what exactly it is I cannot remember. I recall something of a struggle and of fighting. You are a Rumilian clearly, and a soldier captured in war?"

"I was at one time a cleric, but I became a soldier later as well. Heaven's enchanted creature, the one-horned horse rampant, was my family's crest. I should not have become a mace-armed cleric, but it was for the best; rather it were Heaven's will. I have wasted away in this prison for many years. I yearn for tidings from the outer world. This is the first time I have heard you speak in such a way, with clarity, not obsessed on Pythagorean ideas. In the previous days you could not finish a sentence without alluding to him. You must make greater effort to learn your purpose, now, while you can think. Your mind being relieved of that philosophical tyranny, weighty things may be drawn up from the fathoms of memory's well. Think over how and why you were captured. Can you relate what news is going on out there in the world?...or perhaps you can think of an escape plan, a way to get us both out of here."

"Also crucified was the bad thief," I said, "whose name goes unremembered. Like you, he requested not remembrance but escape. However, I am no thaumaturge, let alone a god. You must accept your crucifixion." He did not respond. Therefore consenting, I did as he had requested and cast fathoms into the deep pools of my memory. After an insignificant lapse of time I addressed him.

"A number of things I do recall on what sort of life I have led, and of numerous difficulties which I ran into while wearing these monk's robes. Of recent events, however, I can only recall certain actions, certain things said, and a vision of sundry goings-on; but I am not fully ware of their meaning, for I grasp at many strange things done and words of gravity vaguely understood. The delusion of philosophy fades, and the veil over your mind lifts for just a moment. Please, describe what vision your memory draws up; it may grant recollection of other weighty things. You spoke on hope before."

"Without a great hope in Heaven I myself have carried on," he said with sadness. "I have lived, not as the righteous should, even though I do believe that God is in His Heaven. You must certainly know that some believers have too little hope, regardless of how stalwart be their faith, too little hope. They are ones who tend to hope in the things of this transient existence. They hope in what they will someday surely lose, or may never even gain. They are fully ware that these things should never be the recipients of their hope. But they cannot help themselves; they are blind to the lasting good that is God. I count myself among these sorrowful souls. Please, if I bore you with my melancholy, pray shut me up with stern words."

"Not at all, good cleric, continue."

"I have been merely living off of recollections of past delights and sweet love, but not good hope. I nourish myself by dreaming of something."

"Do not be afraid to say it. Confess, for even deep-minded clerics must wear sackcloth on occasion."

"These prison rags are not far from that. Very well: the deep and affectionate gaze of a certain fair maiden I dream, a paramour, whose face is burned into my memory. I now live only by the vain hope to see her once again. This hope is damn vain, I know, for it is my own damn sin that has deprived me of her."

"A hard thing, for she has likely forgotten you," I warned. "Profane love always leads to some unwholesome pain. *Her kiss is sweet as honey but bitter to the stomach* says scripture. Consider the case of the ancient Archmage Elkomenon, wisest of men in his time, could not but help to woo the stunning Lazaria. Even Hesiod, the Grecian poet, a pagan, did well to teach on these matters, representing the woman Pandora holding the box; hope was the only thing that did not escape the box but remained, leaving us to ponder whether hope were really a curse upon men. That myth is from the desperate ages, however, when men had no true hope. The wise say that all men must hope in something, but woe if that something perishes! Profane love perishes. My fellow, if one hopes in God, who never perishes, hope is transformed from a curse into a blessing. Take care, however, and be warned: if one clings fiercely to a doomed love, it will become a cruel curse."

"So indeed...," he replied, "but we cannot all be monks, our gaze fixed on the eternal, our flesh mortified. My tiny hope for seeing her again had all but vanished until just an hour ago, when you finally were speaking of other things besides the prohibition against beans and the Pythagorean successions of "*monad.*"*

"I myself am too much of an idealist to be capable of truly romantic love," I confessed. "Hence, I seek only to serve as a poor knight. Perhaps you have a similar pain? "

"How is that? Is not romantic love the ideal chivalric? "

"It starts out that way, but I suspect that it is often God's will for it to go sour. The betrayal of that stern idol is a grand catastrophe indeed to the poor bastard whose tender heart is torn out by the claws of a siren. Do yourself a favor, friend —repent of it. "

"At last, someone who does not fear to speak truth to me. Thank you. I am even now turning from that evil. If you ever get out of here, find a pure *selva* and describe my trespasses to him; request of him to pray for me, most wretched."

"Even a priest needs absolution," I said.

"You are one with whom I should talk and make some plans. Please, keep me in suspense no longer. Treat on what has transpired in the wide world, or what battle or hazard it was brought you here so pitifully."

"Of the world's great turbulence I know scarce anything," I assured. "...other than what few things I myself have witnessed. I will tell you what I saw, for perhaps you, who have watched these devils in this place for so long, can also avail me with some useful explanation. My story I will tell you, at least some of the things I remember. If you somehow outlive these evils, relay it to someone who might reach the civil lands and gain insight as to what all this puzzeling should be about. Nothing do I ask in requite for such an amusement, other than please bear the history to any other worthy scribe, if ever you do escape."

In brief I recounted to him all which I could recall from the beginning....that was not much. (Many moons would pass until I found an antidote to that potion and all my memories returned.) Much of what I told him did not make sense. Note how I am indicating that I told him "in brief," for it was truly a synopsis lacking in many details. Nevertheless, I imparted to this prisoner the pith of my flight from and return to the monastery, of the wild elfbeards who made sport of my mishap, of my meeting with the Ammouric Knights, of my protecting *The Black Book* and the accusal against me. I also related my necessary companionship with Arizel, and my hope for him, and at last of my recent pilgrimage into the hazardous northern lands. I could not at all remember the last few days, or was it weeks? ...or months? He then made comment.

"Indeed, it is quite a struggle you have gotten yourself into, sir monk; or let me say, a struggle which *God* has gotten you into."

To myself, reflecting I said: *"Si bona suscépimus de manu Dei, mala quare non suscipiámus?"*[44]

"Aye, and some evil of great import has chosen you; I would say, however vaguely you grasp it; only to be understood with difficulty. Perhaps it be some demon that has thrawn your path, on account of

---

[44] *Si bona suscépimus...* a famous quote from the *Book of Job*. "If we accept good things from God's hand, should we not also accept the evil things?" Job kept his piety and refused to "curse God and die" after many profound disasters.

sinning with magics, like the potion, as you said before. I will make every effort to record your valorous enterprise if ever I escape from this hell-hole."

"I thank you," I said, "and am much obliged;...may Heaven reward you for your generosity."

"Much of what you told involves certain mysteries to which I am no stranger," he admitted. "I only hope that you do not return to your muttering on Pythagoreanism. To this end I mean to keep you talking on other subjects."

"That is a worthy enough occupation," I said. 'Hope for it, and pray. In turn will I pray. I will pray that you learn to forget, to forget a maiden's amorous gaze, or at least harbor no want for it ever again."

"Fair enough..." he answered. "There is much that interests me in your account of what occurred to you, and some of it seems to have a bearing on what I have been through in recent years. You mentioned a sorcerer named Arizel. I also know him: Bannock. He did a similar thing to me. He gave me a potion to drink warning me that I could not withstand the tortures of the king's henchmen after capture. I do not fathom what that man is up to, but it seems we are his dupes."

"Folly persuaded me against treating him as any righteous man should treat a sorcerer," I grumbled; rage at Arizel stirring within my belly.

"You will tell me the story, will you not?" the cleric asked. "All of it please...I would like to hear of this Arizel some more, to judge if he is trustworthy. There remains cause to trust him, somewhat. Can we be certain that he brought us both to this on purpose? Could it be possible that we are actually dead in fact? Now being in our resurrected bodies, strict Justice has assigned us punishment; confinement to this same chamber because our sin was the same: to pollute ourselves with magic?"

"It is fair likelihood. Nearly every description which I have read in the books or which I heard the bards recite; they feature the damned arranged in punishment according to their transgressions. So, as it seems we are each guilty of similar wrongful acts, and hence find ourselves in adjacent cells. One thing is not expected: that we might engage in discourse. The pain of the tortured surely would not allow for easy conversation, as we have."

"The listening to your Pythagorean dribble, constantly every day, was an added punishment for me, pray for my lack of study...a kind of just recompense for sloth, since Justice must be complete."

"And what do you say Justice must therefore be? "

"I can only say that justice, my little cleverness, whatever it is, if it is a kind of truth, will prevail in the ultimate analysis. Not even in the after-prison of Hell can justice be skirted."

Strangely, his words were for me like a key which unlocked a flood of memories from recent events. I cannot estimate how many moments or hours I sat there stupefied, remembering many things, as one who dreams an epic dream and does not consider it when awake, but then one day years later sees or hears something that inexplicably brings him to remember all of it.

There must be no secret doctrines coveted among you monks. All techniques and strategies do openly teach. If any monk is so bold as to claim a secret technique, count him a thief and shun him.

Tien Joshur
Summer Instruction for Campaigning Monks

A MOST SECRET DOCTRINE   XXVII

"I have told you what few things I remember in my life as a monk. However, what you have just said on justice suddenly unbottled an overflowing flood of memory from the pools of my mind. They are memories of recent events, which occurred, I believe, in the weeks shortly before I was imprisoned here, thanks be to justice. Please keep awake a while and hark to this stupendous recollection. This is what I remember: After I drank Arizel's potion I fell into a deep unconsciousness···

"Out of that sleep abysmal I awoke. I could not estimate what elapse of time had passed since being overcome by such a magical intoxication. Tied up again I found myself, terribly discomforted, bound like some prize deer on a spicket, and suspended from a horizontal pole. From my feet and hands I swung. First only joint pains and various aches, to the extent that the soporific effects of the drug or potion, administered originally to keep me from talking, could not even keep me unconscious. That's how major the agony became. A metallic clanging I heard, and looking up and backwards, saw from the upside down position a sabre rattling, and the bronze greaves of horgs marching.

They were carrying me slung on a wood spicket. Was I to be roasted? Back I glanced and viewed upside-down the horg who balanced the end of the pole on his brawny shoulder. He did not notice nor regard me at all. There was another human verticle beside me, on foot, only his hands bound. His name I could not recall, but recognized the face. He also had been captured. Unlike me, he did not struggle.

In and out of a kind of half-sleep I kept phasing. My head swam with the elementals of the potion, and I had no control of my conscious state; as if I had gotten tanked on some foreign ale weirdly brewed.

These horgrim were strout soldiers indeed, not like other goblin kind, for they carried me a good distance. They had tied me securely; the discomfort was intense and only bearable for the numbness of my limbs. I cried out in agony nevertheless, and they soon put me down and fashioned a makeshift stretcher to lay me upon.

At last I was untied and allowed to sit on the cold earth, while our captors paused for rest. It seemed that we were headed to a great horgoth encampment, and I did fear that we were destined to even worse places.

Hours of their marching must have passed. Soon I was wondering if several days had passed, or only seemed to have passed. On account of the potency of their unwholesome drug, my reckoning of time was no longer. I did not become hungry or feckless but half-slept most of the time.

We would not be going to a horg army encampment I soon learned. Although I did not know the landscape, I reasoned that we were headed North and East, into Bardelith, to the Nzul and Baffay, home of corruption; for we had passed the confines of the civil lands. At some point we saw many grand pine trees, colossal, which once glorified the wilderness of hills. They had been reduced to half-scorched and withered sentinels of doom.

Fortunately, the weather turned mild. Eventually my body mastered the drug's effects, or at least became so accustomed that the effects diminished. I felt pain and could not pass out. This was when I first noticed a most disturbing sight, and I pray that you can explain it to me, although I suspect already the meaning.

Certain other humans, armoured horsemen, faces shrouded by dark veils, tarried near. They were dour men who had oathed themselves to a dark master like Prince Sinostox of old. These were the Veil-Knights, devoted to the soul-sucking Cult of the Veil, and they are the devil's children, militant arm of the Arian heresy.[45] paid with coin probably from the treasure hordes of Nzul.

Past our line of captives, one of these lords in scaly armour, darkly robed, rode for inspection. I watched him. His black shield was emblazoned with their particular emblem: a burning mountain cast upon the sea, where a many-masted ship is sinking: the Church. Is the scourge of the infidel not described thus in St. John's vision? Alas, I could not check *the Black Book of Melancholia*, gone from me, with all my other possessions. Had the horgoth taken it?

One of the dark cavaliers noticed me looking about as the horgrim laboured to carry me, and so instructed them to make me march instead.

This is not yet what disturbed me. Rather it were certain men I saw, men on foot. These, to my astonishment, were robed not unlike our own monks! –But with a different cut of cowl.

They were on the march to Baffay. They were not chained or tied or whip-struck at regular intervals as were we captives, myself and some twenty others, with various soldiers and villagers who had been taken in

---

[45]*Arianism:* A heresy which denies the trinity, teaching that Christ the Son was inferior to the Father, and not truly divine. Its principle sign is the Tau cross. The heresy was widely adopted by various barbarian tribes, such as the Durgoth, as an expression of independence from the Ammouric monarchies. An even more diabolic and dangerous manifestation of this heresy developed as *The Cult of the Veil* in the eastern principates, whose oppressive cult clerics gained control of the Kalar caliphate, empire of all Arraf in the fourth age.

war. The horgrim and Veil-Knights treated these monks with a degree of respect. As to why, I could not guess. These monks even traveled together as in procession, making some strange droning in an alien tongue, as a kind of chant; but it was in a scant mode, not true chant. Perhaps they had gone mad or were heretics of some sort. Then a horrible flash of insight···they were going to Baffay to be sacrificed voluntarily!

One of them had noticed how I also was wearing a monkish robe, under the tabard of my chivalric order, and he came to me as we marched. He had a sharp accent; it sounded eastern, like the old Egyptian tongue, perhaps Gohhan. His head was shaven, and strange glyphs were tattooed on his neck after the manner of the heathen. At first he spoke a few words in various tongues. It was in order to ascertain my native language, but failing to do so he resorted to Greek. Here is my translation of the conversation:

"Friend," he says, "it seems that you are in difficulty. Do you speak Greek?"

"I do not know you," I warn in the Greek. "Speak with me not, lest our captors notice and render me some painful correction. "

"Be not concerned over that. I assure you those warriors respect my status, and I can command them to not harm you."

"I do not consider an enemy's word reliable, " I say to him.

"Why be a foe?" he says lightly. "You will need to know what I can tell you. Answer me, and you will not regret it."

"Very well...I do have common Greek fair learned," I say to him. "I can even speak it, but not perfectly. It seems, however, that you have a quick mind for spoken ability. You have the look of a mind; you are a monk? "

"I am a monk, though perhaps of an order which most folk know little. I do speak the common Greek, but I tend to lapse into the Oruscan dialect. "

"That is outrageous! Oruscan?" I say. "No one bothers with such archaic forms. I know the vocabulary a little, but would not ever guess that monks might use it in speech. What sort of monk are you?"

"I am a devotee of a certain power, consecrated and sworn only to serve his purpose, renouncing normal human living for a sublime path. All our prayers were originally from Oruscan poetry. And it seems you also are a man who prays, no? "

"A Christian, Ammouric in cult."

"Speak not that so loudly in these lands, friend," he replies. "Remember, you are a prisoner of the Northing."

"Some blood-sucking vampire I will not fear," I exclaim. "I am ready strike his baleful crown."

"You are quite weakened," he says, "not strong enough to match even one of these horgrim, let alone a lord of death. Your God has delivered you into the hands of the enemy. Look at yourself. You are a prisoner, never to be freed, but to dwell forever in bondage, in shadow. Northing will enslave you, and with his unholy magic he will not let you die. You will serve him in the ranks of the undead...how sad."

"You say you find it sad," I retort, "but you yourself are going this way, so you are not much better off than myself, save that you go willingly. You are one of those infernal monks."

"Ye are mistook. I am as much better off than you, as a master is better off than his slave," he replies happily. "I love being an infernal monk. The being whom I worship bestows upon me power; he is a being of light, Abraxas, the god. He will deliver me when any mischief comes, for he knows all the labyrinths of death's halls and has great influence upon the Northing, with whom he holds common cause."

"Abraxas you call your god? Who or what is this being you worship? I have heard that name. Is that not some gnostic archon or Egyptian oddity? You are being led astray and know it not. Even the fallen one can appear as an angel of light."

"My Abraxas is among the greatest of gods, if not the greatest; and he is a power like Northing, one of the Anahit. He gives true knowledge of the bright Beyonds and their emptinesses. Would you yourself not be particular to this knowledge? I ask you to please consider joining our fold. You could be a monk, well taken care of. Renounce the weaker god who has delivered you into the hands of an enemy."

"Thank you, but no. There is but one God."

"I do not expect that your consent will be forthcoming this very day, but do think on't. We are treated well by the Northing, and from his crown comes great funds to expand the cult of Abraxas on earth. You are both a warrior and a learned one, as it seems. Have you not read *The Spiritual Tetramorph* by Mercurius Yod? [46] He explains that an alliance of four gods will, in the coming age, rule the worlds."

"Mercurius Yod, pagan seer of the third age? I have examined some of his writings, his *Meta-Prophecies*. Vain works; wistful they are. And his magnum opus *The Spiritual Tetramorph* is extinct."

"That is not so, my friend. It has been found...preserved beneath Nystol, "the basement texts." We also have learned that our explorers found certain scrolls of magical power which could mend the Hypostatic Rift, the eldark theories of Simon Magus, and when they learn the translation, they will usher in a new age of Sorcery. The *Hidden Elect* will

---

[46]*Mercurius Yod* was a heathen seer of the Third Age of the world. He claimed to have seen visions of past, present, and future events. He recorded these visions, but he oddly kept the past tense in writing verbs, as if he were writing historic facts. His "*Metaprophecies*" as they were later called, are in the form of an encyclopedic tome. He died before completing the work, having been cruelly slain even while recording his prophesies. *Source provided by Thanato Excorpus.*

no longer be so called. It is the will of the high powers that be, the principalities. Submit to them."

"Who are these demons you hold in such high regard?"

"—demons...or gods? You must have heard. Have you not learned of the spirit-beast Vorthragna? She is empress of the Intermundane Expanse, goddess of war-wind and technologies, ruler of the fourth world, a great spirit enthroned in her "cosmic lair." Mother of all dragons; her berserker servants abide by her will, traversing the worlds."

"Indeed, I have seen with my own eyes the infection of that apocalyptic beast. *Noli timere*; Don't fear, her power fades."

"Her power increases, friend. The Northing, demi-god of illumination, crown of the free elves and all the horgrim, a true monarch, keeps alliance with her, as well as with Abraxas."

"A gathering of devils, I would say."

"How dare you. Abraxas is no pit-borne devil. He is an immortal, a titan dwelling below in the mystical caves. Nay, he is a god, lord over all books and written works in the age to come, master of knowledge, master of worlds. You would be wise to heed his invitation; and if you watch your tongue, you might be given a high position by him, and in our fold elevated to librarian."

"Why that elevation —? "

"—your ability at Greek. It is rare indeed; outside our own monks, you are the first I have met who has the skill to understand Oruscan Greek."

"It is a skill that I almost never use. I am a warrior-monk and must always train with the quarter-staff. I no longer have time for brushing up on Greek."

"Join us and you will have much time. Why not use it prudently as a scribe, or as a monk, earning the way to final salvation and reward? Make yourself slave to Abraxas, like me. He will free your mind. Like you once was I, even an Ammouric monk I was. In those days I lived at the Monastery of the Weeping Brotherhood in the Dry Blood Sea. I did many penances, a strict life of miseries for God, but nothing seemed pleasing to "Him." It was not until I met Abraxas that my life really changed. He told me that his love was true. Things started looking up for me. Abraxas, you see, entered my mind and illuminated me through his sacred doctrines found in the copper scrolls, *The Light of Abraxas*. Some have even met our radiant and titanic lord, he who dwells in the caves of Earth. We have a wondrous monastery below dedicated to his worship, of far greater beauty than what may be found up here on the surface."

"Abraxas is not a god," I say sternly. "He is a creature who cast a spell on your mind. There is but one God and father of all. Say, you did not identify the fourth spirit, for you said that all the worlds they divy among them."

"Once we find the Nagamaud Amulet," he says, "the white goddess shall be freed; that is the prophecy. On this I am permitted to speak no further. I must do his will. Abraxas is a god."

"That is foul prophecy. It is written as a mandate: *There is but one God, and him alone shall you serve.*"

"—a painful superstition..., I say, shackles for the mind...from which I am glad to be freed. If one all-powerful God does rule, then why does nearly the entire world now wait upon the many eldritch gods? Very well, I see that the powers will need to exact some further teaching upon you. May your stubborn mind be changed, and may insight into true knowledge be granted you, friend. A Sacred Tetrarchy will someday possess all the worlds."

"One last thing, monk," I requested. "When I was captured by that horgoth army, my possessions were taken from me. I had a great sword, and a silver-braced book; a black tome of great size and antiquity, with gloriously decorated elephant binding. Have you seen these?"

"What does it matter for you?" he asked. "You will not need them in the next world. I know of no sword, but the book I could not forget. It was tossed in a bonfire by the horgrim the very day we met up with them. I myself extracted it from the flames just in time. Its worth, any experienced monk would tell you, is beyond calculation. I could not read it, so I passed it on to the monks who were returning to our subterraneous monastery for safe keeping. You need not fear its preservation any longer. It will be safe there until the end of time, if time does in fact end."

This monk then parted from me and continued the march alone with his brother "monks of Abraxas," the infernal ones.

ertainly we had ventured into the Crach Mountains. They were no mere curiosity of geologic anomaly. These orogenies later were ominously known as The Cracked Mountains. They have cracked-pinnacles and summits, and the sides jut from the earth's surface like jagged blades in a forboding manner, as if ruined obilesks and blasted pyramids of some alien world. They were not always cracked, so it is said, but on account of divine displeasure the Almighty cleaved them asunder in the ancientmost war.

It was getting colder. The Veil-Knights, either out of some fear that we, a valued prize, would die from exposure, mercifully lent us furs in the evening when we were encamped under rock overhangs. The contingent of black-hearted horgrim and sable-clad Veil-Knights was some one-hundred strong, and it seemed to me that they must be escorting us to Nzul. They had finally become weary because of the cold. Complaints had started among the horgrim, who resented the presence of heavily armoured Veil-Knights issuing vaguely understood behests from their hurth-horses. They had been imposing a forced march. Of all, there rode only twenty Veil-Knights, heavily-armoured cavalry. The light-armed horgim infantry were on foot, and the two groups were looking askanse at each other.

At one point, while passing upwards along a narrow ridge in single file, one of the captives, a hycman, slipped and fell. He was hanging on the ledge overlooking a sheer drop of perhaps a thousand feet. The horg that had been guarding him did not have the strength to pull him back up. The column stopped. Another horg in charge of that section, in anger at being bothered by the nuisance, struck the rope with his axe and severed the line upon which the hycman hung. The captive fell headlong through vastness of air to a miserable but swift death, his bones snapping on the jagged rocks below.

Moments later, one of the Veil-Knights returned from ahead to see why the column was held up, and he noticed one of the captives missing. As preservation of all the captives seemed to be a great desire for the Veil-Knights, this was a high matter. Enraged, he shouted at the horg responsible. The horg, dishonored and without escape, straight away boldly attacked the much stronger and well-armed knight's horse, hoping to surprise and unbalance the animal so that it would slip from the ledge. It did not work. The horse reared, and the Veil-Knight called out for help in his own tongue. He dismounted, and using a broad sword, disemboweled the horg, a brutal but definitive act.

This shortly caused a panic among the more numerous horgrim. A general revolt followed. An intense hazard ensued as groups of horgrim ran back and forth along the ledge striking at the Veil-Knights. The knights, however, were far too heavily armoured and strictly trained to be overthrown. In fact, the horgim were driven back to the ledges by the onrush of the hurth-horses, and some of them fell to their deaths.

Several of these Veil-Knights always continued to maintain and protect our section of the line, and to guard us as their valued prize, not allowing any havoc to erupt where we were tied. A few horgs had unsheathed their weapons and approached during the battle, but seeing quite notably how formidable these horsemen were, they backed down without proposing parley.

Other areas of the line farther behind our section echoed with screams of the dying who had revolted.

No Veil-Knights were lost putting down the horgoth mini-revolt. When the mischief was done, the remaining horgrim submitted, and the line moved on.

Soon the gothic and smoke-stained parapets of the Arc du Baffay came into view between two slopes of cracked mountains. They rose high above the world as if to dispute with the heavens. The Arc was partly veiled in the northern mists, but as we came closer we perceived it were not mist, but smoke from furnaces, (the furnaces of this place below where now, my friend, we sit in consternation). At least it is not cold here.

There yet remained a two day journey through jagged mountainous terrain. At meal time, when the prisoners were sitting in their group eating the tasteless porridge, and the infernal monks happened to be nearby, I beckoned to the same infernal monk who had spoken to me earlier; and he came to me, still hoping that I might "see the light of Abraxas." Before he could say anything, I spoke.

"Thinking much I have been, o monk," I said, "...this angelic Abraxas of yours must guard you and your brothers well, since none of you were seized by the horgs and held captive when the Veil-Knights enforced their strict obedience."

"You may not think that Abraxas is a god, friend; however, you must admit that his power of protection is godlike. Is it possible that you are beginning to see the light that emanates from his temple below? "

"I am curious to learn more of your deity," I said, "since I can see no harm done by those who worship him. "

"Abraxas would welcome you. Do not, however, imagine that we who are his disciples do not mark when the war-wind blows or fail to make ready by indoctrination. Do you wish to serve Abraxas?"

"I wish to...at least meet him first, for I am not yet convinced that he is a god."

"It is good that the light of Abraxas is beginning to enter your mind. He is definately a god; he is immortal. You, however, are a mortal. You cannot presume to appear before him without an invitation. I myself never saw him in my seasons as an initiate. Only the elect may behold him, those he has chosen for the most secret doctrine: *doctrina occultissima*! "

"May I speak freely without danger of being called impious? I mean, as one who speculates and wonders in order to come to the truth, and must do so by making assertions that he is in doubt over, and therefore risks sounding a little irreverent to the devout? "

"I do not think that the elect would mind, since you are new. Those who are truly learned can withstand what those of weaker faith cannot bear...but do be careful. Other monks may overhear and become infuriated. Let us move away a little."

(This done, the conversation continued without interruption).

tell you..." (how bold my mouth!), "with due respect, I propose that Abraxas may not be a god. You say that you have faith in this god and that he will save you. Your faith is wrongly directed. I tell you what, take me to him and I will discover for you whether he be immortal."

"If you look at him, you will be terrified," he warned. "No one has seen him and returned. Seeing him will do you no good. Not even I have seen him. Only certain monks may appear in the presence of Abraxas. He is an emanation from beyond time and space, unlike other gods."

"You said you were once a Christian monk. Do you not entertain the possibility that you have wrongly abandoned Allfather, the true God? Now you would have me abandon Him because of a little hardship. How am I to be a devout monk of your fold without witnessing that Abraxas is the real thing? If he is really divine, I must become his monk."

"Very well, I will arrange for you to be released by the Northing to become a monk of Abraxas. Your training will begin in the third moon. You will see him in time. Monks like myself do not need to see him. We have faith."

"I cannot wait that long. I must see him now. If I wait too long, not deciding between either one god or another, I will go mad."

"That is true; I see your anxiety. Such a dilemma would drive someone to the brink of hopelessness. We do not wish to lose an initiate as valuable as you. When we arrive in the Nzul and you are imprisoned, I will come for you after a few days, and we shall take one of the black ships along the Eluvigar and escaping the Baffay enter into the Alph and

Intermundia; and we shall pass into the deeper region to find where the Grand Temple of Abraxas sits ...is that what you expect? How ridiculous."

"I am being quite serious. I have understood that mortals cannot pass into those regions."

"The world of the deep...that is not what concerns me. To tell you the truth, friend; may I speak candidly, that is, without you doubting my faith in Abraxas? "

"Of course...speak freely; it is obvious that you have great faith."

"It is not traversing the deep earth which I worry over...it is this expedition we are making that worries me, even more than some trip into the caves. The Veil-Knights are getting into deadly matches with the horgs and have developed a dangerous atmosphere. What is more, we monks do not fathom why we are being sent to Nzul. Some have whispered fears that we are to be offered on high altars to Nazageist as part of a treaty made by *The Tetrarchy*. If this is true, my faith will be put to the test. We must fulfill our vow and do what we are told in obedience. Some of our monks, however, we have heard, have not returned from Baffay."

"Then for sure it is time for you to make a move. Be straight with me now: is it possible then to travel beneath the earth?"

"Most mortals cannot do so without serious injury to mind or soul. But you are young, and you are taught in spiritual matters. Even if for the wrong god, any monk-training can be useful. I myself have been down there, for Abraxas protects his monks, although I never saw his temple. If we were to rely on a good guide, however, one who really knows the way, then I predict no adverse effect in the travel. Besides, that old warning on humans not being able to go down has now come into great doubt."

He continued on, saying that Dwarves and Elves and princes of the earth spread such rumours because they do not wish adventurous men to raid the tombs of kings or seize the underworld gold —gold to which they themselves have already, in their greed, laid claim. And he knew of a certain guide, one who knows the corridors and caves of deepearth, who could take us to the Temple and Monastery of Abraxas. He will require payment, however.

"I myself have longed to make the pilgrimage," he added, "even though it is forbidden. That reminds me, I must inform you that we monks of Abraxas live a life of poverty for Abraxas; it is so that we can serve the higher cause without hesitation. Are you capable of this? "

"As it seems, for I have lost everything, save for one friend."

"Oh? Who is that? "

"Do you see that miserable fellow over there gulping down gruel like a ravenous dog?"

"I see him."

"He is my companion traveler. He has been paying the Veil-Knights to keep the horgs at bay, not to molest him. He was captured with me, and the Veil-Knights yield to his promises of untold wealth, for they fear him.

396 NEVER LEAVE YOUR MONASTERY

He is fooling them by feigning to be a wizard, hence instilling respect. May I take him with us? "

"Of course not; you cannot take your friend, that is, unless you offer him as a sacrifice to Abraxas."

"I said I will worship no false gods."

"You know, you heard me say before that I was wont to be not unlike you, " he said. "In the days of my youth I was as a Christian acolyte chanting hymns to the Ur-vather."

"You were better back then. Repent and come back to the Truth. Why are you no longer with God? How do you know for sure that this "Abraxas" being is divine? Just because others say? What miracles has he performed testifying to his divine origin? "

"He has changed serpents into staffs, he has made the ignorant knowledgeable, he has spoken his will through oracles, he has called down fire, and he has told of what must come, among other things."

"So can any wizard arrange those mere marvels. Numerous tricks of seeming thaumaturgical charm a wizard might have at hand, but none save a knave would call a wizard "divine" for such powers. Even Inversus, it is said, will raise the dead. But that will be a cunning trick; it will be a counterfeit miracle."

"Then by what other criteria would you discern that some power is divine? By Wisdom?"

"Not entirely that either," I answered. "For there have been many wise men. First let me ask you: how do you define what you call a god? Do you say that a god is one who can save you? That seems to be your criteria. After all, you know that it is quite possible that God could have gone ahead and made all things, the entire world and all its creatures, but certainly not bothered with 'saving' anyone from death. That a divine being is maker of all things is nice, but what will this profit you or me? Men die, and God lets them. You and I must die. Instead you seek a god that you know will save you from this doom. This is because you know a god must be more than just super-powerful or all-knowing or able to travel about speedily and perform great feats...now tell; it seems that you think there is a kind of race of super-beings, gods you call them by recognition of their power? "

"Abraxas is from a race of super-beings, such like him, the angelic powers; they emanate from the beyonds. He did not fashion this world and all its evils. He is not to blame. He comes from outside the cosmos to save us and return us to our true home of light. Of course, he must live beneath the earth while he does this, out of sight from the servants of your God and the cruel world thus made. Abraxas is a messenger, an angel to bring us knowledge for escaping the world."

"If he is an angel, that would imply inferiority, since a messenger is sent on behalf of some higher power, what the word *angel* means, 'messenger'."

"He is not inferior to the divine one dwelling in the beyonds, but is one and the same, an emanation."

"A projection of himself?"

"I do not think so. I do not know. Only the god knows."

"That is fair enough," I admitted. "Consider this: the *Erelim*, the angels, are incorporeal; they are purely spirit, unhindered, immaterial intellect. Do you agree?"

"That is what I remember from my studies with the Ammouri. However, be there sufficient reason to look askance upon such a doctrine. As it be not incontestable⋯ I recall certain legends which tell of a race of super-beings, perhaps corporeal angels or giants, called *nephilim*. Such is what Abraxas may be known as exactly. He must stoop to be clothed in the material form, even though we insist that matter is evil, of no good in itself. He puts on this mask in order to remain in the prime material plane...to save us."

"So if Abraxas is a corporeal emanation, as your cult teaches, and also generated from the divine race, as you claim, he will be all-powerful as well? That is, he would have to be, in order to deliver you from death...no? After all, death itself vanquishes all in the world, save itself; and what good to worship gods that are not all-powerful or who cannot quell death and keep you safe from its sting? "

"Yes, if he is a saving god he must be all-powerful, or I will not waste my time. Then surely that is the best criterion for determining if a certain being or archon is the divine one: it is raw power: the ability to deliver his adherents from the adversary, even the jaws of otherwise inescapable death. Added to this must also be the ability to provide for his own devotees."

"Certainly it would be a sign of genuine divinity if Abraxas vanquished death, would it not?"

"It would certainly."

"Have you seen him die and rise again?"

"No, I have not seen or heard such a thing on him."

"Has he raised any others from the dead? "

"Not that I know of. We do not need to see it, but we instead testify that the soul rises, whereas the body cannot; it is a mere shell."

"Your meaning is that a soul rises, though it is impossible to see an invisible thing rise, since the soul is un-see-able, invisible. As for the body, men, of course, can observe a visible body lost and destroyed. So you teach nothing regarding how the soul regains the body?"

"Correct. The body is worthless."

"Have you seen a soul 'quick' without a body?"

"No, but men ever hear reports of ghosts."

"But ghosts are counted among the dead, not the living; and what is the use of rising if one is not alive? As for the undead, they are of no account, an abomination."

"That is an honest appraisal."

"And you have seen no soul from the beyonds return and tell you of it, neither yourself nor the others?"

"We have faith that the god will help us escape death."

"How can you have faith that Abraxas will salvage you from death unless you see someone appearing from the dead who testifies to it? Has any human escaped death, ever? How can you claim Abraxas is your saviour unless you know that he can himself rise from the dead, and do so not by escaping it, but by conquering it? If a physician cannot save himself from plague, can he save others? Mull it over. Perhaps you will waste your entire life worshiping not a god, but a demon from the abyss."

"Thou yield too much credit unto death. Death is a lie, a deception. It is merely a shedding of this shell we are trapped in, the body. We are released at death so that the spirit may enter into the beyond, the regions of blissful light."

"Suppose you are right, and death is merely an illusion. It warrants agreement at least in this: that by observation we may easily perceive a certain life-force is missing from a dead man. The corpse is no longer the man. Death undoubtedly involves the separation, soul from the body."

"Of course, no one would dare contest that."

"If Abraxas were by force separated from his corporeal vessel, his body, should we not then admit that he would become...extinct? "

"Abraxas cannot be made extinct...but for the sake of argument, if that were to happen, yes, I imagine he would be...well...dead."

"But is that not contrary for the race of gods as universaly defined: that they cannot die, precisely that they are deathless and unable to die?" From there I continued, and explained that it is not so much they are powerful; what determines men to call them gods is that they be deathless, like all nature herself may seem. I said to consider the tales of the Greeks: the hurricane-titan, Typhoeus, for example, foul ass-headed many-tentacled and monstrous progeny of earth; who warred against and temporarily vanquished the glad-thunderer god and rain-stormer Zeus, according to one version. Immortal Zeus, however, could not be slain, since he possessed immortality, but even so Zeus could put into bonds and cruelly tortured in the caves, which did happen. But there was no possibility in the eyes of the Greek poets that Zeus might die, being the principle deity. So he did whatever he wanted and didn't fret even if his wife Hera became more influential and powerful than himself...

"Even low-ranked gods were also included among 'the deathless race." I added, "although they had only minor power, deities such as Eos or Hestia."

"Very well, those stories I have heard before. What you say is in accord with the traditional cult of the many gods. It has little to do with our theology of *gnosis*. However, you do endeavor to compare, though poorly. The Greeks described their gods to be like themselves, with every human foible and immoral deeds uncounted. We, however, have a god that is entirely alien, one pure, not fashioned by our fancy."

"Surely it is right to want a righteous and pure divinity," I added, "but entirely alien? So you, clearly by appearance a son of Rumil, worship a god who, being not human, has no human sympathy, or has pity equal to perhaps a locust? That is worrisome. Our Lord was like us men in every way, but remained pure and sinned not. But I digress from my line of argument. So you surely will consent to a reasonable definition: the gods are deathless."

"Provided that whosoever is called 'deathless can save from death. Even Zeus could not save his heroes from death."

"No creature is deathless, for everything created is subject to change and is therefore destructible. The only being that does not change, who is changeless, deathless, is not a creature, but is the uncreated one, the being from whom all others receive being. The one being who alone is necessary being, without whom the others cannot be. Death is part of change, and time, but the one who is from eternity always is, and is timeless and always changeless, therefore deathless. Do you follow? "

"I do...but what for angels—they are deathless yet are also creatures, are they not?"

"They are deathless, true, but only in as much as they participate in the immortality of God, as do also those souls who worship God and become saints clothed-with-joy. So then you agree that a deathless and immortal deity should have the power to bring you back from death? "

"It is a reasonable definition of divinity, if divinity must be defined in human terms."

"So if there is a possibility that Abraxas can die, then you will admit that he is not a god?"

"Only if he dies and fails to return to life; after all, your deity, the Christ, died, and is said to have resurrected, although that is merely a written account written down by men. You yourself have not seen his resurrecting with your own eyes. Abraxas would have said so if such a thing could be witnessed. He is all-seeing, for his great cyclopean eye searches out all mysteries of worlds, heavens and earth and under-earth."

"We have a good number of witnesses," I retorted, "humans who had no cause to lie and told it even though they knew they would suffer for it: the disciples themselves, the same who had abandoned him in his hour of trial, (which they also admit in their testimony, so not even making themselves look good). There is no reasonable doubt concerning such a testimony."

"So what?...Who are they? It is just a written testimony. Your god has left you on earth to suffer and to doubt."

"He has left us with faith. What testimony does the world have concerning this Abraxas of yours? He is supposed to be a god of writing and letters, but he has nothing testifying in writing to his divinity? No feats worthy of recounting? The Olympians would laugh him off Olympus. Does he himself even claim that he will save you from death?"

"He gives us wisdom and secret knowledge, the proper sacred hymns and magic symbols needed, so that when our soul journeys to the underworld we will be prepared to escape from death's power. The all-seeing eye, our venerable symbol which we place in every shrine, in every book, sees the route out of misery's labyrinth."

"So he is not going to save you by might or force, but rather by revealing some secret knowledge of what to do?"

"Knowledge we already know. He has taught us."

"Yet he himself cannot escape death. Think over what we have already established: death involves a separation of body from soul. As a corporeal being, Abraxas cannot last forever on the prime material plane. Have you yet met a corporeal being, animal or human, that is indestructible?"

He thought for a moment. "I have not."

"Then rely on the wisdom of your own practical knowledge of things. No corporeal powers are eternal. Such bodies, being material compositions, are made up of many elements. Only a purely spiritual being can be eternal because it is non-composition and not a complex, in other words, not made up of elements or parts. The divine being must by definition be a singular immaterial unity. One in and of himself, above space and time, for the divine cannot be taken apart and destroyed, or even decay."

"I see what you are saying. So if Abraxas dies and begins to decay, then it will be quite clear that he is not an immortal being, is not all-powerful, and cannot save."

"Precisely...The Christ died but in his dying made a fool of death. His shroud became a kind of Trojan horse for the underworld city of Dis, of which Hades is king. His body experienced no decay while in the tomb. He invaded the labyrinthine halls of the dead and slew lead-crowned Hades, and he rescued the souls of the just who lived before him. His body was preserved three days until he returned and rose again. This is the love of God, stronger than death."

"That is some lore to be recounted. But let me ask you...what if Abraxas has a soul-body, what might be called a psychical body? Could his soul not go forth from his corporeal shell and dwell in his temple as a ghost?"

"—Two bodies, a material-body and soul-body? " He was making no sense, and confusing categories. There can be no such thing as a 'soul-body'. An immortal soul has no spatial extension. If a soul were made up of fine atoms, I explained, like the invisible air, it could still be destroyed, just as air is destroyed by flame. If someone were to lose a limb, would he be diminished in soul? Body and soul are combined but separable. They are distinct. I added that "For an immortal spirit, like a human soul or God, spirit separates not. It is like the invisible power in a candle burning. It is there, you can sense its presence and see its result, warmth and light, but you cannot see or take hold of it. The flame, the light, and the heat are one, not separable from one another."

He admitted defeat. "You have made your point. I should never have spoken with you. Your arguments have caused me to suspect and reasonably doubt Abraxas as a divine being. Nevertheless, why not apply the same doubt for the Christ?"

"Christ resurrected bodily. He was entirely a man, like you and me — not a god in the form of a man. He has demonstrated for all time that he will restore the human body and make the dead rise again. The resurrection is divine love, vanquishing the tyrannies of death."

"Please, curtail your preaching. I cannot take it."

"It is the same power that salvages men from sin; for when he appeared to his disciples afterwards, he breathed upon them and bestowed on them the power to forgive sins. It is sin that caused death in the first place. Your Abraxas has no similar reputation. I am on firmer ground."

"You are so annoying...but convincing. Still, I keep my loyalty with Abraxas. I will come up with some good answers soon; I will keep faith in his power."

"That is noble, but will take great faith indeed. I propose that you put it to the test."

"How so?"

"How not so? Will you go through your life wondering if Abraxas is able to save you from death? Will you devote your life to an incertitude? This being must be tested. Bring me to his temple, and I shall slay him, cutting him down with my sword in deliberate combat. If he dies and does not rise from the dead, and rots, you will know that he was just a titan, a monstrous nephilung, not a god. Then we shall pray together, and you will renounce idolatry, and ask God to forgive you and receive you as one of the Ammouric monks instead."

"And if Abraxas does rise?"

"I am confident that he will not."

"And you are so confident as to bet your life on it?"

"I am so confident, and so bold."

"You do not fathom what you are saying. He will slay you and me. Those who have seen him say that he is a great and terrifying giant. Look here; let me show you. " The monk pulled from his pocket a little periapt, an intaglio of cut precious stone, and the "magical" Greek title ΚΘΟΝΙΑΣ ΑΒΡΑΞΑΣ was carved upon it with a depiction of a strange looking being whose serpentine legs moved as amphisbaenen coils.

"This is what the god looks like. He is terrible indeed. No one but the initiates may view such a relic. You are privileged."

"I am a well-trained fighter. This monstrous creature will feel my cold iron without pity. He is privileged to die by my hand."

"You are bold indeed, and have some wisdom as well, or folly seeming to be wisdom. This troubles me greatly. I will have to mull over your proposition."

"If you have enough doubt against that demon, and are sensible, then you must take me to him and see for yourself. There is no risk to you. All you need to do is watch."

"And the temple guards and priests? "

"I shall enter wearing your robe, disguised as an infernal monk."

"But will you slay them as well when you begin to fight?"

"They do deserve death, being apostate idolaters who gainsay Christ. I, however, will be merciful. I have a nice knock-out hand-strike. The monks trained me in that. "

"Abraxas is a god who has great magic. What magic do you have? What will you do when he unleashes deadly spells upon your flesh, or lifts you high into the air by merely willing it? You have no contrary ability."

"No need be there to match magic when the Truth is manifest. But we must bring my companion anyway, for the fellow really is a wizard, and not just feigning it. He has his wits about him when it comes to powerful magics. He is not a Christian, but neither has he sworn against us. I will not begrudge the Lord of some help even from his kind."

"So this is done for your God? "

"And also to save you from a life spent worshiping a demon...and for treasure. After all, we have nothing to pay the wizard, and the guide."

"Yet you are commanded not to steal."

"Who ever said anything of stealing? This is holy war against evil and dissidence. "

"A rationalization it sounds like to me..."

"Lord God is a conqueror who does not deprive his guildworkers their pay, but he is generous. *Victori spolia*, 'to the victor go the spoils'. Do you know of any treasures in that library? "

"A number of sizeble tomes and rimestocks are worth their weight in gold, and some *bzebus* scrolls as well, worth even more. Of course, do not forget the priceless *Pure Vision of Abraxas* enclosed in a separate shrine. You would have a tough time selling that on the surface, since most humans, except us devotees, agree that it is accursed."

He also added that stored down there are several of *The Black Books* as well, and some grimoire that magic-users abandoned fearing the spells writ therein were too dangerous. Some have also seen there the architectural plans of Zenop's Tower, his famous 'Tower of Wyrdd in the chasm of Thurmas, one of the eleven wonders of the Whitehawk continent. To look upon the plans, he said, is just as amazing as to look upon as the tower itself. These plans would be a great trove for anyone hoping to get inside the colossal ruins for exploration, since the tower is now forever abandoned and sealed, but not uninhabited. Several of the rarest works of Mercurius Yod are known to be in the subterraneous library as well, so passing rare. He claimed to have also spoken with monks who tell of having seen a copy of Kruth's *Handy World Map* which reveals the secret underground route to Nystol. Other things add to the list which must not be neglected. Certain inhuman writings are kept in that library, most ancient. The infernal monks have even translated some of the untranslatable and incomprehensible theologies in an alien work called *The Dread Book of Ocean*. Certain lizard-men would give their own lizard-tail for that rimestock (and not all lizard-tails grow back). It is the only sacred text for all reptilians, never copied.

"They worship something called the Black Prime Mover," he explained. "That a mad cleric could command an entire army of lizard-heads just by possessing the book, aye, I am certain. Now wait...an argument terribly simple suddenly occurs to me to test your thought."

"Then present it without cushions."

"—that if your deity, the *Deus Pater Omnipotens*, were indeed awake, would he not smite down false gods, gods for whom other sacred texts are kept? Would he not blast the gods with the breath of his mouth?w"

"He is no longer on that inferior level of business, but keeps more to the management level of things. He leaves the dirty work up to mace-armed clerics or single-hearted paladins. He knows that without letting such adversaries cause havoc, his fighting men, reckless men like the knights, would, well, get rather bored. That's the way I see it. It is just like some great king who has his knights fight for him so that they might share in imperishable glory...keeping them occupied and staying out of trouble. Jousting, after all, gets old after a while. The crown doesn't *need* the knight to fight his wars; rather he *wants* him to do it, invites him. So likewise does the Furth High King...that is what the Wars of The Veil were supposed to be over. The Ammouric Knights were fighting against an unholy and blasphemous Arian cult which had taken over the eastern lands and which threatened to bring entire Whitehawk into unholy weirdness. The same must be done with your cult of Abraxas."

"I no longer think this is wise. I must end this conversation."

"End the conversation if you must, but you cannot end the thoughts which my words have sown within. Humour me one last question."

"Say it."

"Some of your brother monks, I have noticed, have a glass eye; others have patches as over an eye lost. Why is this? "

"I will tell you a secret, and then this conversation will end. When our monk reaches the highest level of devotion, becoming a long-robed priest, he consumes the lotus plant and, thus unable to feel pain, in ecstasy plucks out one of his own eyes. This reveals his willingness to make an offering for our god, and in order to become cyclopean like Abraxas himself who has but one sacred eye which sees all. The highest degree archpriest may receive a glass eye in place of it, and it is said that our leaders see what Abraxas, praise be his name, sees."

The conversation ended. That very night in the tent I did not neglect to tell Arizel of my encounter with this monk of Abraxas. Arizel should have been ecstatic with enthusiasm over finally being able to have a crack at a demon he himself once let loose upon the world. He was instead weary of adventuring, or of our captivity, it seemed to me.

"Finally, "the gods" have given you an opportunity to undo what has been done, " I said. "Abraxas the devil sent in order to deceive men with heretical and falsifying books, books to replace the many worthy writings long ago lost at Nystol."

Arizel, deep pondering in thought, looked up and answered solemnly. "Whatever dissidence the demons purveyed, which are now guiding the ways of wicked men, and all the mischievous monks devoted to Abraxas, they are transgressions which men may not undo, Jacob. One thing I have learned in my life is this: evil done remains so, for what is done cannot be undone. Nor can we pretend that a dark thing done was not evil. At best we can repent on behalf of the sinners at whose hands we carelessly let mischief be accomplished. Be satisfied that we might hinder some future sorrows."

"Tis true...how can a mischief-maker hinder the sorrow that must come of it? He cannot. Learn this, wizard: God will take an evil done and render some good out of it, for others, or even for the sinner, provided you trust him. I admit that I myself have consented to mischief. I swallowed your potion. I can still feel the effects of it stirring in my brain. Tell me, Arizel, in all your old wisdom, why do you resort to such pollution, these magics?"

"You imagine the phial to be unclean, but it is simply of a knowledge which angels granted of distant time. No doubt there exists unholy magics, to be shunned, but do not fret over this potion. During the lost age of Nystol the

Soothfold distinguished things of magic into two major categories; those that were "natural magic" and those that dealt in "demonic magic." The former was acceptable, because it was viewed as merely taking note of hidden powers in nature that God had wrought; for instance, the leechbooks contained spells for medicinal purpose and were tolerated...as was the harnessing of magnetic currents, explosive ore, and radiant matter. Necromancy and divination however they condemned. Even I know this. Has no other monk taught you as much? "

"Right well, they were busy praying...but still, you have kept something from me. Side effects must be expected, or not? "

"The concotion increases influence substantially over a period of days, having a magnifying effect on the mental faculty, and so causing certain paraphenomena, anomalies of thought. In particular, the user experiences a highly focused thought pattern that results in acute concentration on numerical symbology. This slowly morphs into an obsession and mania, finally burning itself out by a lapse of many weeks. The side effect is inextricable from the very purpose. As soon as it takes effect, no one will be able to have a conversation with you on anything else but numerical metaphor. This protects the recipient from answering the interrogations of torturers in any understandable way. There may be other side effects as well."

"That's just grand. Thanks...*Luna* has already sunk, and I am weary. Good night!"

"I myself have seen a monument of a codex, the ancient scripture of the Vri, not to be touched by any save the Saurian high priest."

Kruth Eleusinion
Intermundane Bestiary

THE SEA HAG XXVIII

Arizel and I were asleep in the ox-hide tent. The monk came and awoke us.

"You fellows," he whispered. "Hear me. I have spoken with our master, a wise man to whom I repeated your arguments. He has agreed to let us flee, tonight, as he himself will do, going east to Namaliel.* The other monks are clearly too fanatical to be persuaded. They well might be going to their deaths in Baffay, all the while praising Abraxas. It is my goal to reveal to them that Abraxas is not a god, provided I see him rot with my own eyes. I may yet rescue them. Although they are fanatical monks and not open to reasonable argumentation, they are good men and do not deserve to die in that way. Let us act now before our priest-lord changes his mind."

Freed from bonds we crept around the tents of the Veil Knights. I knocked out the watch with a silent open-hand technique which I had learned from Ulcrist. Until the moment I crept up from behind and executed the move, it was never anything but for repetitious practice. My body remembered exactly what nerves to strike and make him go limp quietly, not to awaken for many hours. The body also can remember like than the mind. I went sneaking through the moonless night and neutralized the other sentinels in the same way. I fetched the precious *Black Book of Melancholy*, but could not locate the great sword Witchbane. I seized the saddle bags and draped them around me. The other human hostages were freed as well, and in turn they finished off the horg-guards with their bare hands.

The monks, having awoken, were horrified. They did not fight, but merely gathered their things and continued the march to Nzul, in blind obedience to Abraxas.

So went my recollection of recent events, my conversation with the infernal monk and my escape from the horgrim and Veil Knights. It was good to remember and happy to tell, even though I would be captured again later and finally brought here. My fellow prisoner, (my only audience beside a certain intrusive mouse), had fallen asleep again.

My cell mate must have dozed off while I was outlining with precision the proofs of divinity. I am not certain now with whom I had beenspeaking, having been so deeply involved in the telling it, and still somewhat under the effects of a sort of hypnotic spell. Was it the infernal monk in the story who made the protest,

saying, "Please stop your preaching. I cannot take it"..? I suspect, rather, it was the cleric in my cell who requested that. I am not surprised. When it comes to such things, even the most well educated quickly get distracted. Such distractions are encouraged by the agency of some fiendish spirit.

It was not until the subsequent light that things commenced, when the cleric in my cell was nearly in tears again. (He was wont to be in tears around that hour, reminiscing over his lost paramour, of which the noon-day demon provides ample imaginings.) I distracted him again from his melancholy with a continuation of my account.

"You are weeping again. Why do you do this to yourself? Fool!"

"It is in these hours that I think of her. I do not know why. Leave me to my reflections... "

"I will not. You are an Ammouric cleric, a *selva* vowed to God. Yet you fantasize all day over her and forget God. For shame; it is you who are in the darkness, not I."

"Then please, tell me more of the things you did, the war you protracted against demons. If for a moment I might glimpse what my life could be like, no longer trapped, without such an obsession as that to which I am hopelessly subject..."

It was then that I at last figured it out. Who was the lady paramour of this man, this mistaken priest? He had said that he was a soldier, which would make him a fighting cleric, worthy of a knight's armour. He had mentioned that the Unicorn was his blazon. He was none other than the one loved by the ill-starred daughter of King Graham. She had given a scroll-letter to pass along to him, even if he were a shade in the underworld. That letter had perished in my various misadventures, lost at what point I know not during my painful travels. Arizel had promised her to convey some message of her longing. I could do it. However, by doing such a thing I would make his lovesickness all the more acute, perhaps aggravating him to despair. Still, I had given my word. I had to say something. Nevertheless his soul was in eternal jeopardy, since he was vowed to God, not a woman. I would remedy him with the gospel first, bring him to renounce female charm like a priest should, and then tell him.

"What obliges me to tell any more? " I asked wryly. "You deserve such a trap, a trap you made for another but fell into yourself, as the psalmist says."

"You are right. If I earnestly loved her, I would let the memories pass into oblivion. Please, help me forget her with your story-telling."

"That is right well, for earthly love is forbidden you. Now consider: the story I tell is not just a story; it is the truth. Very well, I will tell it, but you must harken attentively and not get distracted when God is talked about. Your lower nature rebels in this way; yea, know it, and your flesh carries away your reason on swift wing, having lulled you into the hypnotism of spirit-death, like the hang-clawed harpy with a lullaby to alure you into her pseudo-romance."

"Please, I will do anything to get out of this, this caving-in upon myself, this vile melancholy. I do repent once again. May God forgive me."

"Wipe the tears from your face then and be a man, and listen close:

way we stole. Away to the beyonds with ample supply and three horse, and made our way to the city Tyrnopolis, crossing through rugged Ardeheim, the windy wasteland, on the Axe-cut Trail. It took us a week of stern travel, feeding the animals our supply even more than ourselves, there being no abundance of grazing in those lands. To ward off the voracious hulk-wolves of the bad lands is no easy task, and we killed several. At last we found ourselves at the city of brass domes on the shore of the furthsea, great Tyrnopolis, Eastern hegemon of the Whitehawk Confederation.

We were looking for a tavern particular, The old "Sea Hag," now called "The Sea Queen." This maritime establishment once was a watering hole for the typical navy and merchant-sailors of the old republic. In time it had been transformed slowly to accommodate foreigners from across the sea, especially with the shipping routes that opened up after the Wars of the Veil. Then, having gained a reputation for strangeness on account of its variety of guests, it at last became host for an entirely different, so-called "dangerous" breed: non-humans. At some point, a certain non-human, from a sentient race known as "Celestrian," purchased the establishment. Its name was changed to The Sea Queen, for obvious reasons.

Apparently in our time the hag has been elevated to royal status.

Most still call it the Sea Hag; the fantastic witch-like marine creature described in human terms, but surely not human. A drink had been named after the legend. Who can duly say if the Sea Hag is real? Sailors fear her enough to decline employment on ships sailing past her reputed grottos. Guy of Xaragia lists the creature in his manual on monsters, but no one has ever actually seen her.

Riots ensued when the new owners changed the sign above the tavern entrance, so on one side the old name painted on wood remains.

This place, according to hearsay and which I do affirm by this testimony, resounds with the twangs of the eastern quiddlehar and relish-pipe. Those zealous tunes encourage the imbibing of wild whiskeys and sundry intoxicants imported from around the Sea of Goldyndol. During a risky visit the drinkers become quite pacified under the sweet rhythm of the gentle waves which lap against well-worn seaside porches. Supposedly no brawling ever occurs at this tavern, that is a rumour unsubstantiated and clearly bandied about in order to suggest a superiority over other establishments, (namely the outrageous behaviors seen in the human saloons of Tyrnopolis' suburbs). Heed the whispers: brawlers do not live to tell of their exploits.

The Sea Queen, they publish widely, had such a carefree atmosphere that it could only be attributed to the influence of so tranquil a sea which hosts it. In no other place will you find so many different races together in one city as Tyrnopolis on the Furth Sea.

Even so, non-human races are barely tolerated within the city, and it took a decree of the Prime Magistrate, as well as arrests, to prohibit the racist intimidations of locals. The Sea Queen is the only tavern tolerating non-humans in Tyrnopolis. It is located in the bayside slums, an area for non-humans who are more human than not, but actually not all that human, (although often more humane than most humans). The imperial guard enters only in numbers, and only for necessary work, such as tax-collecting. Humans wanted for unlawful deeds or escaped from thralldom often take refuge there as well, but these only come out at night. Otherwise, the most unusual of races frequent the narrow streets.

Never did Elf patronize of course. No Elven nobility would ever actually enter a city anyway. Among both men and other humanoids the warning has never been left unsaid: *stay away from Elves, my friend.* Their kin, such as deep-born gelves, weird-foot dwarves and gnomes, and others are given free pass, but then again so are such kind as massive cyclopes and hairy wilder-hulks, bulbous-headed celestrians and star-goblins, red and purple lizard-men, troglodytes and squid-heads, bone-mutants and tree-skinned brothers, retired trolls and forest satyrs, half-horg and half-ogre, ridge-heads, *cynocephali* and cat-heads; all these are welcome.

So we went through the narrow streets, we kept cowl-covered so as not to openly display an unabashed human look. Townsfolk noticed nevertheless, and supplied gracious frowns in some cases, (except in the case of a squid-head, who glanced at me. His tentacles seemed to smile). A recent rain had faded to a mere eves-dripping. A blanket of dark cloud had broken as we strode along the cobbles wet from a recent sea storm. We found the place at last.

The only requirements were listed as follows; that one have two legs rather than four, not fins, and that one actually be a living being (a sign added the entrance reads UNdead are UNwelcome here). Of course one must be able to order and pay for drinks, (you do not go into such a place just to loiter and chit-chat).

A little trouble getting in was bound to happen. The foreign-coin inspector, (a white-eyed gelf at the entrance, and the well-hewn horg-kin bouncer within), even went so far as to warn us. Most humans never return after a night of conviviality at The Sea Queen, they said. According to them, humans don't make friends here easily. Men, elves, and dwarves, even gnomes, all on account of their like appearances, are counted as members of the human race.

"—but if they are outcasts, or mercenary types looking for business, or have some strange look, or are in any way not the usual mold, then they are well-tolerated...and especially bards, or jesters; certainly they are welcome, but definitely not elves. And take care, if newcomers be found of impolite demeanor or cause any trouble, they will be punished severely, cut into pieces, and their drinks taken away. And that goes for the regulars as well. No need to surrender any shining coin first."

Would-be adventurers are watched closely.

The well-hewn head-bouncer, a cyclopean, laughed one time when he heard that rope-girded monks were at the door. He bellowed to his hench-guards from the back of the tavern:

"Monks? Really? What are you doing?! Let in monks; they are traveling monks, confound it! Only the impious would turn away holy walkers. Thought of Heaven has been away from this forsaken place long enough."

We attracted no little attention when we stepped into that dimly lit and smoky snake hole. All turned and looked, and did not smile. The quiddlehar ceased twanging its playful melody.

Silence behooves a monk. So we went along with the silence for a few moments, covering our human profiles with hood pulled over, until the soft mumbling of the regulars resumed. At the loudest table were two horg-kin and what seemed a cat-head (who was their captain), having a lively and sometimes antagonistic debate over the proper pay for a whaling expedition. It seemed they were long-time seamen who knew each other all too well.

When the atmosphere returned to normal, we approached certain safe-looking tables, where cards fluttered and dice rattled, to venture and make inquiry around and about, that we were seeking for "one well-traveled guide, a saurian named Sahkah, said to frequent this establishment."

No one would help us, no matter how cautious and unobtrusive we tried to be, even as monks; and even after we announced, "free prayers for anyone who can help us meet Sahkah." Still no clue came our way.

"Ale is what loosens tongues in this place...otherwise Humans should mind their own business here! " a half-horg declared with bitter expression.

We approached the bar which was reeking of a bitter alcohol. The bartender, a celestrian rubbing shot glasses, greeted us sternly with the obligatory snap:

"We don't serve your kind here!" Of course this only meant we would have to pay a little extra.

"Have you any knowledge on a deep-earth guide that comes to this place? " I asked him.

"I know a number of such professionals," he remarked.

"One named Sahkah," I added. " —a famous Saurian."

"Information; of which I myself have nothing on anyone-, " he replied in that alien-sounding voice, "will increase the cost of drinks. The one you name only does business with those who have lost a loved one, as in a child or wife kidnapped by goblins, harassed by deep-trolls, imprisoned by horgoth or like issues. His guild-training includes no tomb-navigation. Nor does deal with undead problems. He is no cleric if that's what you holy rollers are looking for, so forget it."

"We want him not to hire for any of those things, warranted."

"You have the aura of true monks. But if in fact you are royal wardens disguised, or if you are bounty hunters, I will warn you once, avoid taking him by force, even if you imagine yourself fast."

I placed before him a few crizets. "We are in sooth monks, nothing else."

He took the cold coins and glanced about uneasily.

"He sits out on the porch alone, out back by the sea. He is soaking up the last few rays of sunlight for himself, as his kind is wont." He gestured with his bulbous head the direction to go.

"What does he like?" I asked.

"—He is fond of Kreech, even though it quickly empties his purse..."

As this bartend was pouring the drink of kreech for us to bring him, I took the opportunity to ask the celestrian regarding his own person.

"If you do not mind to give a few words to an ignorant human...please, tell me, whence does your kind hail, celestrian...? "

He looked at me with stern eyes, measuring me.

"It is useless and vain knowledge for you, human, but suffice it to know, we are not too unlike your own species. We also have the capacity of reasoning thought."

"So like us are you...as your kind is well known for high reasoning...but not on reason do I seek more talk. Rather do I wonder on your race, whose origin I was hoping you might give some account...you are celestrians, which in our tongue means 'from the heavens'. "

"We are so called. Many say that we are from the outer regions of the starry expanse, the Milky Way. Some think that we are highly formed humans with an advanced mythology. Others assert that we are cosmic intruders, alien to your world, and must be exterminated. Nevertheless I will tell you. Some of our kind still worship the same Father of All whom you monks do. I only know the lessons my parents taught me... "

He then saw that we were interested, and told the story. He told of how many centuries ago his kind lived far way in a region of four suns. Their civilization at that time had discovered, with confirmation of certain celestial movements, that the deity had incarnated in the universe somewhere, just as prophecied. It was not long before angels indicated to them that the incarnation had occurred on earth. His own ancestors were troubled, much so at these tidings, since it was well known how violent and spiritually decadent the Earthling races had become, and this world had been the first in the galaxy to earn an official travel-advisory for other sentient races.

The story relates that his kind sent emissaries to this world "Terra" in order to contact the supreme being, so as to congratulate him on choosing a certain race, the human species, by which to enter the prime material plane. These "galactinauts" were also sent in hopes to learn the proper mode of worship most pleasing to the deity, since it was here that he resided. To their dismay and horror, however, the emissaries returned twelve years later, describing an outrageous account: that the humans had actually tortured and executed the deity. Their kind was deeply distraught at this news. It took their theologians many decades of disputations to determine the meaning of the outrage, its implications, and what their own species should do in response...

"So your kind; be they Christians? " I asked eagerly.

"Those of us who still believe this story of our origins call ourselves 'Outer-christians'. It is said that in order to do penance for the human race, our ancestors sent colonists, like my grandparents, here to your world. Heaven sent them in order to educate humans on right conduct, to make up for what was done. But the humans shunned many and they have gone to live underground. It is more like home down there after all. I have heard that most extraterrestrial races live in vast caves anyway on their respective planets. Earth is quite rare with her cloudy, blue welkin filtering otherwise harmful solar rays through various gaseous elements, allowing creatures to dwell on the surface."

"Are you a wizard?"

"Wizard? I have multiple talents. What you humans call wizardry we merely identify as the application of knowledge regarding the natural world and its various principles, including the harnessing of elemental forces, even the invisible energies of air."

"Indeed... meta-science and alchemy ...paraphysics, dangerous stuff...but tell, have you not heard the good news of life eternal? "

"We have heard the Word of God. My parents explained how it was originally elevated human spirits who themselves brought it to us. They are ones whom you call saints clothed-in-joy, who by spiritual power teleported to our home planet and announced the gospel to us. In response, our ancestors accomplished great works of charity...but as I have said, contact has been lost. Those who remain on the surface here among the ever-restless humans have become cynical, detached from sacred tradition. 'Bad company corrupts.' As for me, all I hope to do is console any soul who comes in here feeling despondent over their lives as non-human. I tell them to cheer up; at least their race is not guilty of deicide."

The celestrian bartender smiled an alien smile and handed me the glass of Kreech. "Go in peace, and keep your hoods up."

Through the passage and door to the seaside porches we went, where the salty air struck our nostrils. The rhythmic crash of billows upon the nearby shore had a hypnotic effect. A humanoid figure was seated aglow in setting sun's rays. This man, if you will call him that, had red-orange scaly-horned skin. He was the one we sought, Sahkah. He was a lizard-head, a race which I had been told, even throughout my youth, never to trust. This was the one who knew the way to the hidden underground fane of Abraxas and could be persuaded to take us. But did he even speak the common tongue? He sat alone in a corner smoking a long pipe. His three-fingered claw-hand, (the scales were also red-orange colored), lazily moved about as counting something, or as one who might be remembering a song. His appearance did not include any of the usual green coloration common to other lizardmen, as in the greatest of all saurian tribes, the notorious Vri. This red kind claimed racial superiority, marked, they held, by more "rational features," than the Vri. These red lizard-men had generally a less pronounced snout and mouth. Sahkah, however, was an exception and resembled more the Vri save in the color of his skin.

He squinted at us through his leathery-lidded lizardic slit-eye and then closed it again to ignore us. We approached his table with the gift of Mahanaxaran Kreech and set it down.

". . . a gift for you, Sahkah."

Kreech is a warm and smooth rum that is sailed up the coast from the tropical Mahanaxaran trade lands on clover-ships to the northern land of icy mists, Ael Lot, in exchange for cod and other goods. It is highly prized by the Aels and many others.

The pungent, spicy aroma caused Sahkah's eye to open again. When he spoke, his accent added "-s," "-sh," and "sk" sounds as you can imagine of the reptilian kind.

"*Monachi* of some sect approach Sahkah to proselytize Sahkah...a knowing and ready lizard-head," he said, as to himself. "—and no fool. " His menacing tongue once flapped out and back.

I could not guess how to rightly reply, so I blurted out, "May the holy ones render you health and wellbeing and knowledge of his commands."

"Does your kind never tire of declaring things commanded by the gods?" he asked, not looking at me. "Lizard-kind do not understand the deity in the same way; we say there is one deity only. It is useless to quarrel over. Leave Sahkah in peace; let him be content with Sahkah's own "maker " who also made you. Sahkah particular to the old way...keep your gods...Sahkah yields to the Kreech; it will be good enough payment for disturbing Sahkah."

A thin cone of billowing smoke streamed from the lizard-man's scaly lips and floated heavenward, he parted from his lips the ivory carrik-pipe with its long and elegant stem. His beady and swollen lizard-eyes watched the smoke ascend and curl in the rays of the setting sun.

"We have not come to convince you on religion, Sahkah, " I said. "···Although the praise of God is never far from our lips."

"Then let Sahkah be, for Sahkah now in need of quiet and rest. Or is it that you come like Greeks in the famous story, a happy greeting, a wooden horse for Trojans, in order to turn about and take the life of Sahkah at unawares?"

"We have not come for the sake of fighting Sahkah," said my monk companion, "...who is a worthy opponent, to be feared. Instead we seek the aid of your knowledge. We hope that you will guide us as we travel beneath the earth."

"Why would monks slip beneath the earth? Are you the kind of monks that sing no songs? Are you the devotees of Abraxas? "

"I am a devotee of Abraxas, but this other is not," replied my new companion. "Sahkah, we will pay you well to guide us into the great cave where his sacred temple may be found."

"Others have asked this of Sahkah," the lizard-head replied. "Some were thieves wishing to break in; others were monks curious to see their deity, an act forbidden them. Sahkah answers nay to all them. No devotee is permitted to see Abraxas, not even the elect. Dark *monachi* say he a god, but learn this; the wise point out something wisely: humans always crave to behold their gods; to see them, I find this to be the case. That is why the humans are ever fashioning strange idols to worship, gods of wood and stone. We other kindred, we are not so foolish. The God cannot be seen. Humans must learn be content to worship the gods with faith, not seeing. Perhaps if you have faith then the one you call Abraxas will not destroy you. Sahkah himself does not care for that Abraxas, however. Sahkah does not worship a creature. Sahkah worships the Black Prime Mover who is like the Sun, but also unlike the Sun, is non-visible. This is the mover of all things, the unmade One who has made all them that are existing. You monks are gnostic teachers; you seek hidden knowledge. Your Abraxas hates the One maker-god. Abraxas teaches falsely how the maker-god is evil come, or made everything from evil, all earthly things not-holy. Abraxas no god; he lies the lying wisdom of the father of lies. Therefore Sahkah also hates your Abraxas, and will not help those monks or any monks. Go!...let Sahkah smoke his swamp-leaf in peace."

"Bide us a moment longer, Sahkah. Perhaps we also percieve, Sahkah, that tawdry gold or other reward is not much for your kind. But if you knew that there would be something else that rewards, something of true value to be had, perhaps you would join us happily. I say there is something—"

"—I have said, and I not repeat: *monachi* may no longer parley with Sahkah. Go now, or there be trouble." He carefully placed his claw hand on his dagger's hilt.

"We apologize for disturbing Sahkah," I said. "Come, brother, let us take leave of him and elsewhere seek help."

"But Sahkah is the only one who can—"

"—I say, come away now, monk. We drop it. Anger not one of the Slaanit...

We pivoted to withdraw from him. Then, as we were strolling away to return from whence we had come, I declared to my monk-companion,

"He is in a mood. Blame him not harshly. It bodes ill for his kind, his lizard-tribe, the Slaanit; they never retrieved what they lost."

"How mean you? What lost they?" asked the monk.

"It is nothing; I merely refer to a certain noteworthy tome which I recall you mentioning once: *The Dread Book of Ocean*, a forgotten thing. You told me of it before, remember?"

"Ah, yes, of course...that old rimestock..."

At that Sahkah looked up at us again, seemingly alarmed, with his lizard-eyes wide open.

"Hold, you monks. I overheard the bait you said just now. What is this? You tempt me, clever ones. What know you of that croc-bound book?"

"You may have heard," I said. "or you may certainly already know that the lizard-headed Vri stole away with a famous and most treasured tome of all lizard-heads. It is the tome called *The Dread Book of Ocean*, ancient relic of the Slaad, primal tribe of lizard-heads, written on giant *waffin* leaf and bound in the skin of a primordial crocodile. Within its covers are sacred recordings of pristine origin: the will of The Black Prime Mover for all lizard-heads, the bible of all reptilian kind, and the runes of Slaa...It was your clan, Sahkah, the Slaanit, who were keepers of the sacred text for ten thousand years. Then, in years not long past, the war-wind blew and your clan went against with the scaly-green, long-tailed Vri; and the green Vri slew many short-tailed, red Slaanit in the second War of the Veil, when you allied with the Ammouric Kings, whereas the Vri had allied with the Arian Kalar. Many of your families were wiped out, entire desert-towns destroyed by the Vri. It was a horrible genocide. Now you Slaanit always look for an opportunity to pay back the Vri. This monk told me he has heard from others who have seen the croc-bound book."

"Did you know..." added my monk-friend, "that *The Dread Book of Ocean*, which they stole from your kindred,--that the Vri no longer possess it? The bloodthirsty and careless green lizardmen, the Vri, have traded it away for a mere few pieces of silver. Were you not wise to that? Not many Slaanit are left, so I am not surprised that no one has informed you."

"Traded it to whom?" Sahkah demanded.

"I was going to tell you...I know to whom it was that they traded this work. It was traded to us, to the monks of Abraxas. It is an added treasure for our subterranean library. "

At that moment Sahkah flashed. He flashed like that certain desert lizard which, watching for a meal, keeps motionless as a lifeless statue. Of a sudden he darts with elongate tongue protracted to seize up an unsuspecting beetle into his jaws. Sahkah moved in a similar way. He immediately thrust forward over the table, seizing the monk's hood with his scaly claw-hand and pulled him close, knocking over the glass of Kreech. The lizard-head, (whom anyone would have formerly concluded only capable of the slowest motions), now demonstrated quite clearly his extraordinary prowess. He drew the monk's face right close to his own and positioned an Ataluran rim-dagger at his neck. He spoke and those reptilian hissing sounds made fast his words.

"Tell Sahkah exactly where is found *The Dread Book of Ocean*, and Sahkah will decide if you are going to perhaps still breathe yet another breath, human."

The monk, alarmed, spoke carefully, nervously.

"The great book can be recovered...both of us, we two monks, we are going to raid the temple of Abraxas and his library, tome-hunting can be part of the expedition. You can be the one to restore honor to your tribe. You can return with the sacred work of the ancestral lizard-heads. I am a low-ranked monk and do not know exactly where in the library it has been stored. We were hoping you would join us in the raid."

Sahkah, whose reptilian eyes had drifted away in thought, now glanced intently at the monk. He let the monk go. Then, as the bar-maid was cleaning up the spilled Kreech, Sahkah put a crizet on the table and said to her,

"Inform Phaedra that Sahkah must to see her for dangerous business. Tell her come here at once."

Sahkah then looked over at me. The bar-maid hurried off. Was it Phaedra Stormraker that Sahkah was summoning? Had she somehow survived? And if so, why did she take up here in Tyrnopolis?

"Why hope you Sahkah of the Slaanit make good with a low-ranked monk of Abraxas?" he asked me. "And why does a *monachus* of Abraxas go for seeing Abraxas? It is forbidden the monks, a thing well known."

"It is my doing, honourable Sahkah." I answered. "Him I have put in doubt of his own god. To this monk I am proposing that Abraxas may not be a god, with words well-argued and demonstrated. This monk wishes me to slay Abraxas in order to finally prove that the gorgon is not a god. In this way he will be freed from his superstition."

"And who are you? You have hood like *monachus*, but you seem more than monk. You wear Ammouric knight's over top. You are one who is deceiver."

"—not a deceiver...I am one well enough trained with open hand to do quick work of ten soldiers. I wish, however, to hazard a different kind of battle, to win the soul of this monk to our savior-God. In this way I will help him also salvage other poor monks from destruction."

"Who are these other monks?"

"They are his brother monks who have enslaved themselves to the fictional deity. They march even now to forfeit their lives serving the demon Abraxas, offering themselves willingly, and others, including women and children, as a sacrifice to Northing, a blood-treaty. "

"That is evil fully worked."

"Evil work is come fully upon the lands in these last days of the world-age, Sahkah. Hark to what I must tell: the deity I worship, is Lord of the Ammouri, whose banner is the Lamb. We calculate him not so differently from what your lizard-wise men have told, the highest whom you call the Black Prime Mover. It is the one Divinity we both seek, who is goodness, who made both leathery lizard and soft-skin human. It is to this cause that we plan, but the cult of Abraxas must end, for they are as toxic as misbelievers; they publish lies and commit idolatry. We mean to deprive this unholy cult of its head, Abraxas himself."

"Why you are not interested in lands and castles, knight?"

"The Ammouric Knight is not like other worldly knights. He is vowed to a simple life, remains unmarried, and only keeps what monies are needed for his purpose grand. His is a valorous enterprise endured so that the realm of the Furth High King may be increased."

"That is a worthy thing."

A woman entered. She was not young, although she was attractive and shapely. Her hair was in a long braid, and she was no longer clad in leather armour, but a gently falling dress. A deadly dagger was readily slung at her side, which I suppose she needed in this establishment. How different she looked. Feminine grace was powerfully with her. Yet she had the same stern gaze, like a mysterious sadness in her lovely bright eyes, melancholy yet not lost, rather strong but tired. Perhaps it was remorse for her unworthy conduct as Valraph commander which ended in catastrophy. For the sake of brevity I shall not here recount all Phaedra's story after capture. Suffice it to say that she had become hostage for Northing. Northing had allowed her to go to Tyrnopolis on a diplomatic mission, making her swear to his balecrown an oath to return. But she persuaded the senate to reject Northing's peace offers, having heard of Ael Lot. She pretended not to know us.

"I see that you have some customers, Sahkah," she said.

"Phaedra, you are to have payment again for your knowledge. Please sit." She sat down at the table, and then Sahkah looked at us. "Phaedra is my business contact. Most adventurers first come to her. It is good that you monks did not, however. She would have turned you away." Sahkah then looked at Phaedra and said, "They mean to do something regarding the demon Abraxas."

"That is crazy," she said. "Look, you rope-girded monks, I have been through all the intermundane caverns in my years, with the toughest hell-raiders you can find. No one would even think of raiding that monastery. It is not only guarded by black-hearted bolg and hate-filled horg, but the demon himself is terrifying and can kill with a glance. Forget it. Why would you want to do that anyway?"

"They say that brother-monks are to be sacrificed under a blood-treaty to the Northing at Baffay. By slaying the gorgon Abraxas and showing his head, they hope to dissuade them from continuing this madness, to prove that Abraxas is not a god."

"Why not just imprison the Northing?" she asked. "It would be easier. I cannot determine for you how to slay Abraxas. He is some kind of gorgon-demon himself, so I would use a mirror perhaps. Do not lock eyes with the monstrous fiend directly. Other than that, you are on your own. I do not know of any other lore. You could banish the thing if you had an Ammouric priest, but they are most rare and hard to find; and even if you found one, he might not agree to do it, or if he did, his parish would ask for no minor-tribute, and he would need permission from his bishop."

"Phaedra knows many things," said Sahkah, "what is above and what is below, and of the lower world; you monks would do best to heed her. I pay her well for her information."

"Of course, but if you do, by some marvel, actually slay Abraxas," she continued, "who has never been defeated, you will then have a great and powerful weapon at your disposal: a gorgon's head."

"And what should we do with a gorgon's head?" I asked.

She laughed. "Oh my, have you no schooling? Don't you know? You must do the same thing that the hero Perseus did..."

o man descends into the deep-born caves alone, not without wizard or priest, not if he wishes to see daylight again...but of those who have been so vain as to have tried, no mortal has returned to tell of it.

As for me, I made contact with Arizel the following day, who, as he had indicated earlier, was renting an apartment in town. I knew I must convince him, (surely not without difficulty), to aid us in our campaign, if not by magic, then at least by his knowledge.

His humour turned rather troublesome, as he did not wish to be disturbed while reading *The Bladetongue*, some ancient literature with which he was obsessed. I excused myself and told him that I considered him a worthy compeer, and that he must descend with us in order to hurl some destructive spell and finally crush the evil power. He had grown a substantial beard in the past months, but that did not hide his frowning. He responded with the usual challenge:

"For sake of the old gods, what else will you require me? Why are you interrupting my researches? Have you not some appointment to keep with thy Prime Interquist? "

"The Prime Interquist has long been away, and no new appointment has been made for that post. So I must wait here and accomplish what good I can as a man of the cloth. Now listen, you have a chance to serve the God of all. We are in great need. Terrible devilry walks the earth, and we would have recourse to some other power should the sword fail us."

"Is not your faith stalwart enough to confront such creatures single-handedly? I think that it is, and that high Heaven will provide for any weakness in your regard, and will see you quell many dark kingdoms, as all you Christians are wont. All you have to do is ask him, as it is written, and he will; he will put a great weapon in thy hand. Pray therefore, kindly depart from me. I must now begin my meditation on the *monad*."

Unwittingly however, his very words of dismissal worked into my hands, and at once cleverly I countered him.

"I will then. –but first let me say: I have amazement what your clever words modestly conceal. You say that all I have to do is ask God and he will grant me victory. You must have great faith yourself to believe such a thing, that Heaven would vouchsafe me some conquering weapon. Your faith is greater indeed even than most Christians I know, for you have said that all I need to do is to ask for something and Heaven will grant it. How many Christians have that kind of faith? But wait, do you yourself not crave a share in the victory, to have some part in glory? I cannot imagine you otherwise, since I know that you rejoice in such adventures. Can you miss witnessing with your own eyes the epic toil of combat? —but you would rather merely read over someone else's amazing feats in *The Bladetongue*, a poem which barely anyone even knows exists? Why don't you come along and preserve our lives with your masked faith, something even better than your magic. Surely it is on account of your faith, not mine, that Heaven will grant protection and victory. Your faith was but a mustard seed, but it has grown and is become even greater than ours."

Stunned by such an unassailable reply, he took a moment pondering and answered thus:

"I fail to perceive how an expedition beneath the city into the infernal monastery would in any way further my purpose. "

"I assure you that it is God's mysterious will; otherwise, you would not have answered just now in the way you did, revealing your faith, which, though untaught, is nevertheless praiseworthy."

"—untaught'...what daring you have. But I admit; His will is mysterious indeed," he replied sarcastically. "For had God consented to wizardry, doubtless many wizards would be doing work for him. But as it stands, he condemns it. So you are the closest he has to one who can hurl thaumaturgic spells, and being one of His own, you best not tempt your Lord by using an actual mage like me; after all, consider what happened to King Saul. Did he not consult a witch before some grim battle to prepare its outcome? And as it turned out, he took not the victor's spoils, but contributed his own head instead."

Now this was a crippling argument, and it took me a moment of intense focus to come up with a reply, but I did it well: "A worthy warning you supply, Arizel, but not from a truly informed position, as I say, "untaught." Did you yourself not mention just a while back, how some magics the Soothfold did *not* condemn? But if you cannot persuade yourself, then consider on this: how the ancient Jews by ritual law were forbidden to eat pork, and they would die before so doing, as scripture dramatically describes, and many did so die observing strictly the sacred law. On the other hand, we Christians, we do often eat bacon for breakfast; in fact, just this morning I had some. Our Lord said that it is not what goes into your mouth that makes unclean, it is what comes out. Many old prohibitions, from the times of Moses, you see, need not be observed. God's clement rule can provide for the temporary suspension of such rules."

I do also add that, under extreme conditions, certain magics are found to be technologian, merely instrumental, like a fireball or frost-blast. Under the condition of deadly combat, would it really be trespass to use them? They are no more immoral than a catapult. No, rather it is granted for a special case, albeit strictly. As for King Saul and his accomplice, the Witch of Endor, that was different. She employed necromancy, summoning a past soul to foretell the future, whereas summoning the dead is lawful only to God. In so consenting to the witch's power, for selfish cause, the king doomed himself in his slight regard of the divine law.

What we are asking for is altogether different. These magics you know do not involve such nefarious incantations. They do no harm to the soul. It will not be displeasing to God, after all, that you join the expedition. By means of it you may even begin atonement for your transgressions, the damage you have done."

(...to which reasoning he merely rolled his eyes).

Although overcome by my superior learning, quite stubbornly he still refused. Perhaps he was considering his own life, or the quest that he desired for his own purpose. With this percieved, I reprimanded him thusly:

"I set upon this campaign with or without you. My grand endeavor is to fetch a great staff, the relic from ancient times, and to thwart the evil powers, the spreading shadow. The infernal monks, however, have the key to this in their hands: *The Black Book of Melancholy*, volume XXXIII. I do not doubt that they will either store it away in their vast subterranean library, or else sell it to some high bidder, perhaps some rival of yours, a sorcerer. If I fail in my quest, therefore, what makes you think that you will succeed in yours?"

With these extreme words he finally consented, excusing himself that he must do it anyway, especially lest I be harmed or captured, for somehow I was right; I was essential to the accomplishment of his own search. He reflected on his life at last. I provided him some scripture: *Ego dixi: In dimídio diérum meórum vadam ad portas ínferi.* The Master of Planets subsequently visited a local wizardic *pharmacium* to obtain the critical spell components for any combat-possibility. When he was well satisfied and ready, he returned, but seemed somewhat under anxiety.

"These magics may not be enough to face so dread a grinning gorgon," he said with a grunt, frowning. "...a thing worse than a deep-dwelling dragon. I have some highly writ *bzebus* scrolls to use, but I shall not be much good for anything after I say them. And these spells may not be enough to put the creature out for good."

"Worthy wizard, thank you,.And I pray that none of your spells rely on a demon for manipulation?"

Arizel stared at me for a moment with incredulous eye.

"Of course not; I would never rely on contemptible conjurations, unworthy of a man. These magics are merely elemental in character, a metamorphic projection entirely noetic, drawing on energies from the elemental planes of existence, without debilitating side-effects."

"Then we will have little to fear. *The Lord is a warrior*, as the psalmist sings, *the Lord will fight for us.*"

"Aye..." he said, squinting toward unknown distances. "Perhaps what you teach on the Nazarene is no fantasy, for although I cannot seem to fully yield to it, certainly I also know this: the many gods have passed into dream. Just these past days there has been restored to my memory, Brother Jacob, a certain dream I had. Long ago I dreamt a prophecy loosed from the timeless well of being, a dream dreamt when I was at Nyzium, a dream which I did not understand and which frightened me. Little did I know that it would soon come to pass, and now I see clearly its meaning."

"Please tell it."

"The gods on Mt. Olympus were having a fantastic feast in the great hall of Zeus the cloud-gatherer. There was seen his relentlessly pecking wife Hera with her prim looks of prideful superiority, adorned as a peacock, making pronouncements. Also there at table bright Apollo struck upon the lyre, while Bacchus danced, (drunk, as usual) and Diana looked on. Zeus' brother Poseidon, a less welcome guest, brooded in the corner.

Gangemede, not even a god, flitted about in an unmanly way filling goblets of nectar. Ares was pouting at having been overthrown in chess by Hermes, who in turn boasted of his trismegestine trickeries.

Aphrodite flirted with guests, embarrassing her lame husband, at whom everyone laughed. Next to her sat Hestia, ashamed and all hush.

Zeus's poor jokes and fake laughs filled the hall...

Suddenly a figure was seen standing at the entrance, but it was difficult to say who this might be through the ethereal mist. Had someone dared come late? Apollo halted his lyre, and all turned to look. Surely all the gods had received invitations. Zeus looked to Hermes for an answer, but he returned only a puzzled glance.

The figure came forward, slowly, for he carried something heavy and dark. It was a man who came into view. He was quite bloody and torn.

Upon his back he dragged a terrible wooden cross. Adorning his head, mysteriously, was a crown not of gold but of thorns. He approached the banquet table and stared rudely at the guests, and from 'neath his brow droplets of blood dripped. Their gazes they lowered.

The man stood in the midst of the gods and from off his back hefted up that great wooden cross and cast it down square upon the round table, upon which it slammed with a hazardous crash that echoed throughout the universe. All the dishes and bowls of nectar were upset and toppled; the goblets were overturned and spilled out.

The endless and luxurious banquet of the immortal gods had come to an immortal end. That was my dream, and it has come to pass."

"I pray, Arizel, that your faith may not fail the moment you catch sight of the monstrosity."

"Indeed, may it help me, for the gods cannot."

"If this thing is a gorgon," I said, "should we not bring along some kind of mirror, as does the hero in the Grecian legend? "

"I have something here in these scrolls that might work even better, but take care; many different kinds of gorgons haunt the world, and a reflector is not always sufficient. We must look for one to bring along, nevertheless, in case the other spells fail. Come."

There was no mirror to be found, for they are extremely rare and must be imported from the East. Even if we could afford such a luxurious item, the investment would be lost. Sahkah explained it would surely break apart during the treacherous journey down. We would be lucky to get down as far as the grand galleries with no broken bones. We returned and met Sahkah at The Sea Queen again that day. Sahkah took us to a back room at The Sea Queen which had a secret door and a stairs leading downwards. We entered into the vast sewer-labyrinth beneath Tyrnopolis. Sahkah led the way.

"As told by my father, and to him by his own father, and so on back to when the unborn man first glanced upon the waters; forth out of the hills came demon-gods..."

Outhapian altar
inscription
The Library of Morpheus Memnos

ABRAXAS WAS NOT a god   XXVIII

Many non-humans brave the sewer-system beneath that city, brothers. In that way such races have been able to maintain an abiding presence in the town. Since these many non-humans, such as celestrians, theriomorphs, and various kinds of semi-men, have a knowledge of underworld cultures and languages, the underworld races have found them crucial in negotiating treaties with the magistrates of Tyrnopolis. Such treaties must be strictly observed. Travelers must have great caution. They must not be caught hazarding into the zones which the treaties forbid.

No one would want to travel through the narrows and deeply set jawholes through which we squeezed, for they were of a most contorting sinuosity. Add to this, that for the closeness of all the limestone, the menacing thought of one's great distance from the surface was ever recurring.

There was relief at last, however, after several mighty gates had rattled open and revealed a stream. We followed the cold waters down through a slanting tunnel.

We at last let go and slipped downward being carried by the current. Its cataracts hurled us just off the shores of intermundane sea. No great injuries sustaining, we took only a few bruises. By the pellucid mists we could see before us all the expanse of grand caverns stretching far and wide fading into vaporous horizons.

"The arduous part of this expedition is payed," said Sahkah. "But you humans stay close; the dangerous part is yet to come. "

We stroked to the shore. Recovering ourselves, we headed for the mountainous stalagmites of unthinkable size in the distance. Huge clouds of bats flapped through the empty spaces; and we also spotted featherless, flying creatures, larger than eagles, that glided to nests on other distant stalagmites of colossal proportion.

We followed the stony path through the deep world farther down and finally came upon a horgrim keep. It was built into a giant stalagmite. The chasms, colossal wall, and turrets constrained any free passage. A mighty bridge spanned a heartless gorge dropping into misty abysses. Any oncoming force was confined to the bridge, a bridge beneath an over-tower whose portcullis included murder-holes above.

"It may appear to you that the horgrim have built a fortress to guard the monastery from intruders," explained Sahkah. "That is not the case. The black-hearted horg keep dominion over most of these great caves.

These walls and barbicans, however, were built centuries ago, but for reasons forgotten: they originally were meant not to keep us out, but to keep something in, to hold something back."

"Something which many monks have not seen, not in hundreds of years," said our gnostic monk, ". . . a god!"

Suddenly there was a "shoosh" and thud. An artillery shell had just struck the rock behind which we had concealed ourselves, but rolled off. I looked up and spotted it on the other side. When I went back to my position, there was a mighty explosion which rattled my head and sent shards of rock into air.

"Glorious." I declared. "The horgrim have *ballistae* on those turrets with explosives shells."

"The monks have been hard at work aiding their allies with their advanced weaponry from Cathay," said Arizel. "It seems that swords and spears were not enough to protect a god."

"Why should not even a god warrant protectors?" asked my gnostic friend, quick to forfend the reputation of the god he doubted. "Did not the nephilung Ambrosius the lion-head fight in the army of the God of Hosts as the legends relate? Simply because a god uses others to fight his battles does not mean that he is unable to do it himself."

"So you admit that there is a God of hosts?"

"I am just pointing out that—"

"Enough of talk, you two!" shouted Arizel. "Allow me focus; I must extract from deep memory words for an open-portal spell."

Arizel intoned his magic, during which he was required to stand exposing himself to enemy missile fire. Thanks be to God, the horgrim shots were hampered thanks to the mishapen crenels of the tower. Our black-robed wizard made certain strange gestures, folding his hands and bending his fingers in an "x" shape. He spoke the spell in the old Gohhan, a form of Egyptian tongue. A power-sent crossbow-bolt whizzed just by his shoulder.

The iron portcullis screeched open, rattling its chains, and the two others, Sahkah and the monk, with swords unsheathed, raced across the chasm-spanning bridge (and even myself dashing forth as well, though unarmed, like some mad barbarian).

We charged in before the defending enemy could pour down hot oil or shut the portcullis. The furious rush of war possessed me with reckless abandon to do what needed to be done. No floor guards were seen ready to meet us, a sign either of cowardice or poor stratagem...

Sahkah and the monk bracing his bow rained down death-bearers for the heavily-manned left turret but I myself rushed into fortification under their cover-fire. Entering into the turret's circular stairs, I saw that they had left the rope in the fallway to the top.

Quickly I hoisted myself up to their position. I would surprise the artillery troops from the rear; even before they could step off the barbette. Stealthily I would strike, so as to eliminate one opponent at a time, confident to trust my bare hands. I set my quarter-staff aside to the battlements without a sound.

The closest enemy at hand was busy cranking the ballista for another shot. He did not detect me. From behind I seized his brutish jaw and twisted. I snapped the poor fool's neck; but another, an artillery captain, turning about, noticed me. At once he grabbed a sturdy spear. I stepped back to fetch my quarter-staff, but it was too late. This one was a massy brute. He was fast enough to strike the staff out of my hand, knocking it into hazard before I could get any grip.

Straightway he lurched and stabbed it at me, but I evaded the spearhead and took the crouched stance, holding the body of my first kill as a fleshy shield. He feigned right, then left. "Seriously?" I thought. "What does he take me for...an amateur? " With the corpse I hindered his subsequent thrusts before the spear could tear into my torso. Then back several paces I removed, and I lifted and hurled the dead wretch upon the artillery captain, and eventhough sturdy, it caused him to stumble a little and then stepping back he tripped and fell beneath the ballista-arm.

A third horg, the shell-loader, came from behind me with a bombshell uplifted to crush my head. He took it that I did not foresee his advance. The horgoth captain was struggling to lift himself up and get out around the ballista. He sought to lunge at me again.

I stepped aside and grasped his thrusting spear, pulling him downward off balance, and controlling his armed claw-hand.

I paused, poised as in struggle, but completely in control, exposing my flank for just long enough as a bait for the one behind me closing in.

At the right instant I stepped aside as the other assayed to execute his flank attack, but I caused him instead to be impaled unexpectedly by the spear I controlled. All this happened in a flash that is not easy to relate with words. It is a technique I learned under Ulcrist for a double strike from rear and behind. In a singular motion the attack is evaded but turning back and going down on one knee, and the momentum of one attacker is drawn against the other. One ends up on one knee, as in a genuflection.

The horg holding the spear stood there in disbelief that he had provided the instrument and grip to slay his compeer. The impaled horg looked down at the iron shaft now implanted in his belly, and then at his captain.

At once I struck the stooping captain as well with a crushing open-handed knife-stab to the neck, which put him out. His hand let go the spear as the other horg stumbled backwards and fell upon the battlements, his bulbous eyes rolling up, the blackish-red blood smearing over the grey-white stone.

I finished the job and sent the artillery captain quickly to Hades, pushing the stunned wretch over the battlements to fall some thirty cubits to the rocks below.

Meanwhile, the sound of war echoed through the caves from the adjacent turret.

I retrieved my staff and quickly made way there to give Sahkah and the dubious monk aid. However, by the time I arrived, only those two remained, standing, drenched in blood, standing over some eight black-hearted horgrim.

The dubious monk had a skin wound which shortly we bandaged up.

Looking over the faces of the slain and sundry items these brutes had left behind in their chambers, one room seemed an officer's, or the captain's. This one also, we concluded, had been a Bolg-bear, what Guy of Xaragia lists as "Bugbear," one of the largest and hairiest of gobs, (in reality a hobgoblin that resembles a bear). Clearly he had raided the F section of some library. His quarters contained a number of noteworthy books: Fronto's Orations, various works from the heretical Fratecelli, and *De constructione muris infernis contra Neubestiis* (On the Fortifying of Deep Battlements against Netherbeasts) by Fulgortius. There was also Fulgentius' rare work *De Aetatibus Mundi*, Ages of the World, which I greedily snatched up, like a burglar finding an exquisite jewel necklace. Since I could not lug around both, and the technical writing of Fulgortius I would not be able to use or give to any engineers, I had to leave it. Also, to my surprise, the vanquished had been reading a copy of *The Poems of Morpheus Memnos*, a rare work which I should have taken, but poetry was the last thing on my mind at that point. It was no great forfeit. Secular poetry, being an unnecessary and sensual entertainment, is counted last. Was it not God who elevated poetry to its highest place in heavenly souls? One must have some way to decide. In the grand galleries so many rare works are found, works which never reach the surface. You cannot take them all.

Then, to my utter amazement , on the desk of this Bolg captain, rested a common copy of *De Trinitate* by one of the illustrious fathers of the Church. Great consternation seized me when I saw that he had been reading such a work. Is it possible that this Bolg-bear had been a secret convert? Had we slain a Christian? Can such a creature hope for baptism? Even more, were such a thing possible, is it not to the great satisfaction of the devil that Christians strike down one another? O Lord, what did I do? Could I have been wrong on these subterraneous creatures all this time?

"What troubles you?" asked Arizel.

"The Bolg-bear; he was reading a famous work of the Church fathers."

"No, do not suppose so. They are brutes. I say he had been saving it for tinder."

This explanation seemed to fit, but still, a doubt remained. On the desk of the creature were what seemed ink stains. Had he been taking notes? But even were he a nascent Christian, let it be understood that one cannot both serve God and the empire of evil.

"This keep was too lightly guarded," I said.

"The horgrim are feared enough down here," explained Sahkah "...enough that they hire other troops for patrol. See the helmets posted on the battlements. Sahkah guess that at least there be as many as thirty here. Sahkah feared capture. It is good that we not give enemy time to strap shields. Sahkah not young as once, cannot fight long."

"Why do they send away large patrols?" asked the monk, ". . . leaving only these few to guard. It must be that the horgrim are looking for something."

"We must go, and must lock down the portcullis at once," I urged. "Some patrol will shortly arrive and be alerted. We must infiltrate the monastery now, before it is too late. "

We hurried to the monastery gates in caves not far away and blasted through them as well, silently.

The monastery beyond, sporting spindly buttresses, seemed instead some marvelous palace of horrors. We traveled through various tunnels and fore-courts undetected until we reached the strange entrance. It was no fiction regarding the beauty of this monastery. But it was a strange and horrifying beauty, a repelling attractiveness like that of a lovely woman possessed by the devil. Bizarre sculptures of infernal design, a babery of colossal gargoyles and demons greeted us as we passed into the enclosure and stoas.

Passing by several side-altars and miniature shrines, we stumbled into a small herd of stone-faced goatish monks leaving the library. When they spotted us they would have sounded the alarm, had it not been for my reacting quickly. Just as they turned to run, I caught them from behind and used non-lethal hand strikes on two of them at once, knocking their heads together so that the blackness of oblivion overcame them. For another two I provided the same lesson. Alas, how awful to use these hands even for necessary violence. Sahkah also struck one down with a lizard claw. We tied them up and hid them in an enclave, seizing their frocks to wear for being counted among the ranks of Abraxas, and these were disguises for Sahkah and Arizel who still did not have monk-robes.

We entered the gloomy library and passed by stacks of many priceless tomes unguarded, titles I recognized, copies of works which many have supposed vanished in the great burning of Nystopolis. Why list them here? We could not haul such large books away without being noticed. Several monk-librarians at the entrance had watched us pass by.

Did they see through the disguise? We had to get through the library and find the fane of Slaa; however, this became difficult. Mirrors had been placed by the stacks here and there; and as we passed those innumerable stacks of ancient works collected over thousands of years and were turning this way and that, sometimes backtracking, we lost our way. This cave-complex was revealing its vastness, and we could not reckon which way we must go, or whether we had passed by a certain point before or not. We were wandering in a labyrinth. What seemed like several hours went by debating the way. At last we sat down on the cold floor to rest. We picked up a faint sound, the sound of chanting having begun, eldritch chanting, grim and somber, not like the glad, transcendent chants of our own world. We followed the echo, since it might better anchor our direction.

Arizel suddenly paused at a section which was for tomes written in cursive Gohhan. He was browsing.

"We cannot stop here," I whispered. "There is no time for browsing."

"There are preserved writings here that cannot be found on the surface. Things by Morpheus Memnos even, otherwise lost to men."

We finally found our way to the great "Arena of Sacrifice," a massive circular temple of Gohhan styling. We could hear the "infernal monks," their prayers droning in alien key within. Entering, we saw a collection of many hooded men standing to chant eldritch chants to Abraxas, the demigod. As if in another great cave, vaults of eternal stone in geometric perfection filled the volumes of space above, suspended as if to bear witness against the idolatry.

My plan was to wait until most of the monks went off and then we could make our move.

We entered the back row of choir stalls, unnoticed. The dark monks had, however, already begun ceremonies which I cannot now nor should I ever wish to accurately describe, other than to note for you that they prayed unholy prayers for a long period with hands folded like Christians, but with fingers pointed downward instead, to a pit in the center about which they stood. Unholy dancers gyrated on pedestals near the pit while others did homage by repetitious bowing.

"They are praying to the *diabolus*," I whispered, ". . .we must act soon or we will be discovered."

"No, to Abraxas they pray..." replied the infernal monk. "He is near!"

"When you see him you will become excited, but not in the manner you expect," I said.

We waited in the final row of choir stalls for too long and observed the bizarre and vain ritual. The dubious monk wanted to get closer. He insisted on this to me, whispering, and said he knew a way to stand at the rim of the sacred pit where it is said that the high priests (and select other initiates) look upon Abraxas. We moved forward through the rows of goat-monks in their stalls, our sheepish faces concealed under the hoods. My dubious monk-friend produced his particular amulet of Abraxas to present to the master of ceremonies, an armed guard, who taking it in hand and examining it, (for a moment seeming uncertain), let us pass into the sanctuary anyway.

"It might as well be the same as praying to the devil," said Arizel. "If Abraxas is down there, we must find some way to lower ourselves into the pit without the other monks noticing. Now here is the plan—"

We stood not far from the edge of the pit, but could see nothing. Immediately from our rear arose the dooming sound of many boots.

We looked back and saw the armed henchmen of the monastery, twelve mercenary warriors of Atalur in full leather with chain, well-armed with crossbow and axes, they at once surrounded us.

The drone of the diabolic chanting stopped.

What would they do with us? How had they learned of our presence? Was it that the master of ceremonies had not been fooled? Or had Sahkah betrayed us, for I could see he was not with us, but had slipped away into the labyrinth. Perhaps he had found *The Dread Book of Ocean* in the library and did not wish us to learn of it, knowing its immense value. His contract with us had come to an end anyway, for he had led us to the monastery as he had promised. Indeed, that must have been what he had done; he had found his sacred tome and kept it away from the profane eyes of humans. We expected never to see or hear from him again.

All the stone-faced goat-monks now looked on to see what was the disturbance. There was no way we could match these hardened warriors.

They had captured us. Even were Sahkah still with us, his fighting mastery could not give us hope against them. The head cleric of Abraxas now came forward, (surely a demonically possessed man).

"You imposters dare intrude upon the sanctuary of Abraxas!" he cried. "You shall pay dearly for such an enormity. May you now be offered as a blood offering to the great one, though you deserve not such a high honor." He addressed his mercenaries: "Warlords of Abraxas, look there! Is that a wizard among them? Gag him before he can think of some spell! "

How he knew which one of us, disguised under a monk's robes, was a wizard, I cannot for certain say, save that it must have been from this priest's own infernal ability as a high summoner of a demon. Wizards, I think, are not protected from the sight of demons.

Two mercenaries seized Arizel and threw him to the ground, gagging him brutally.

We were all then led into the ritual chamber where the scabrous-faced monks, probably lepers, surrounded us and made an infernal chant as to put us into a trance, the swords and axes of the mercenaries at our throats.

At once, even without fair questioning, they were to cast us into the sightless pit.

This was a most daunting thing. We could not reckon what lay beneath or how far we would fall, whether on rocks or into the mouth of some dragon. Glancing down for an instant, I could see the distance below, and it was some twenty feet. Hence we landed hard but without harm on sand. It was quite a relief to know that there was still hope of escape.

The drip of water from stalactites was heard some distance off. There was a stench of death. Immediately I removed the gag from Arizel.

"You cannot hope to win against a god, worldling, even with your elemental magics! –But for us a good fireworks show before you die!"

The taunts from the impious cleric above echoed throughout the great cave as he stood there with his hooded brothers to watch.

We saw before us a long, cavernous passageway lit with a large torch at one end, but too far to see clearly. At once that singular torch moved and came closer. Quite some sort of monstrous arm brandished it high.

"Come, my friends, now is the time for men to show their mettle," I announced. "This be the creature they call Abraxas whom you espy to hunt. My friend, meet the hideous monster you have for so long worshiped as a god. See, he must hunt for his faring like a dog. Now you shall see him face to face, as you longed to do, but ALSO...you will see him die...Your *malchus*, please, and I shall presently slay him! "

The monk, now terrified, meant to flee to the other end of the cave, doubtless believing that his god would tear apart his soul. He had taken out the sword but dropped it on the sand in his terror.

I picked it up and readied myself to take on the creature single-handed if need be. Arizel and I positioned ourselves to surprise the enormous creature, for it was evident that he had not yet spotted us.

It then became apparent that we were facing no thoughtless cave giant. I glanced about me and now noticed all the human bones everywhere, whitened as under a desert sun.

What power of flesh-destruction had done this? There arose grave reservations over entering into combat with the unknown thing. In other places I saw human skins, as if clothing tossed aside. It dawned on me that these were extra parts the infernal monks had discarded from their victims, not worthy enough to use as binding for their diabolical books.

While Arizel readied some spell, I watched the giant's torch nearing, and so peered from behind the rock to spy the advance. It was then that I first saw in full the ghastly specter, a giant which traveled on two massive swirling, scaly, writhing, serpentine legs, with a manlike torso and a gruesome head, indescribable, eyes glowing, a demon incarnate, if ever there could be such a thing. Wisdom warns me not to further describe the abomination. Two of them came hither, but the lesser one, failing detect us, turned about and went down some other cavernous route.

As for our monkish companion I spotted him there quivering in a dark corner, ready to cower before his fictional deity. The sight sickened me even more than the abomination itself. I realized that not I, but he must slay the thing. I slipped over to where he was crouched.

"Look at yourself, friend —you mammer like a fool, you shake in your fear, you who are a monk. You disgrace monkhood itself regardless of the deity you worship...you fear a being whom you suspect might NOT be a god? Where is your manhood? If death will be inescapable, then meet it head on, with chin held high, dying with deadly honor. Heaven will at least respect that. If death is not ready to take you, then I pray, do not act like a disgraceful coward, but be bold and live your life in a noble manner, cutting apart the despicable foe like a man."

"Be thou mad?" he answered in disbelief. "Look at it! The thing will rend us all to pieces, and roast our bones like pork chops."

"Indeed it may well do so, for it is a terrible gorgon. But if you were to survive through cowardice, what worth would your life be? You would just return to your slavery, and it would be even worse, for you have seen the heinous creature which the others worship. A muddy toad would have more noteworthy merit than such a coward, in the eyes both of men and angels. Nay, demons themselves would hold you in much less distinction than themselves. Therefore slay the horror with well-placed murder-strokes and give no quarter. This is the same lying creature which has long deceived you, depriving you of the good things of life; a being ready to offer you and your brothers as vain sacrifices to Northing, priest of evil. The time is now! Fie upon the beast!

"You have an opportunity few have ever enjoyed. Avenge your brothers, who by now lay lifeless upon bloody altars in Baffay. Take this

sword and yourself accomplish the blood-letting, and if you fail then be glad to finish your day with honor. It is the only way."

"Even if I slay the thing and destroy its body, good friend, its spirit will haunt me ever afterwards. It will come for me in the night with terror. This is my greatest fear. Many curses are stored up for betrayers."

"You do not need to worry yourself over that. I shall prepare an exorcism and banish the demon's spirit to the outer darkness. It will never again haunt the terrestrial sphere, or any sphere save that of the infernal. A dreadful angel will make sure of that."

"How will you do an exorcism? You have no long-robed priest."

"I have even better: Christ-crowned priests back in my monastery who owe me. They will cast a Banishment at my request, a particular kind of exorcism; it can work from afar."

"Work from afar?...right. And what if I myself am wounded by the thing and finally die of my wounds? His demon-minions will quickly come for my soul and hurry me to the abyss, conducting me away to torment unending."

"No, the *Erelim*, the heavenly angels, protect their valorous allies. Your very feat of heroism will demonstrate clearly that you believe in the true God. Again...deeds do louder than words speak. It will be an action of faith...but anonetheless, I say that you will not die nor be forever lost."

"Then if no risk why don't you do it? You look like a monk who can fight. You said you were trained in the—"

"One must choose one's battles. I do not percieve this match destined for me, but for you. It is the way of things: gods must be murdered by their own disciples. This was your god. You therefore must be after the task. You the Judas must play!"

I stared into his incredulous eyes like a frenzied berserk, frowning, in order to communicate to him a warrior's wordless madness, a killer—madness, a thing which only such men of war can know. He grasped the sword hilt in hand and took it from me, glancing at the approaching monstrosity. For a moment it looked that he would be a man. But he winced again at the abomination nearing. His jaw dropped, then he unconsciously let the sword drop again onto the sand.

"I cannot...I cannot budge from this place!" I looked down again and my clothing was no longer cloth, but it had metamorphosed. In a full suit of plate-mail I was clad, perfectly fitted to my limbs.

"I have heard of this kind of power, Arizel. Was that not a clerical utterance you employed...in the language of the Church, Latin?"

"It was indeed a clerical utterance. Emergencies permit a wizard to employ a clerical utterance if it justly protects the believers."

"How can that be...? You are not a man of faith."

"I came down here into this hell-hole with you, didn't I? That takes a little faith...at least that of a mustard seed. You cannot know everything, monk. Besides, what is most weighed is that the recipient has faith, not the caster. Did not the Christ teach this very thing? He himself said it; where there is no faith how can there be miraculous works? How can there be thaumaturgy? Let me in brief unfold the history that makes this is possible."

"Great! –a history lesson moments before combat. Be quick; for there is no time left. Say something right, for I cannot fight well if I believe that witchery protects me."

"There was an old indulgence given by the Ammouric Soothfold in Nystol; days long gone, the close of the Third Age of the world. Most have forgotten that dispensations were granted for certain Arcanes to use clerical spells back in that emergency-time, shortly after the Hypostatic Rift, when magic-users lost contact with the elemental and mundane spheres. Priests were needed in those days; so many Arcanes converted over to become Divines; however, little time was left for educating them in theology. Catastrophic events threatened to plunge the world into universal darkness. The Soothfold decided to give conditional sacerdotal powers to the ex-wizards. This privilege was needed for the sake of combating the rise of evil magic and demons. The decree, however, never lost its efficacy, even after Nystol fell."

"Hypostatic Rift? The holy inquisition would be most interested in this I am sure...but thank you; the spell increases my confidence...make sure none hear of this."

The platemail shon with furbish like a mirror, almost as bright that glimmering mail of the Ammouric Knights.

"You will not need a reflector now, friend," said Arizel. "Go ahead; use what you know to put this horror down. This conversation has cost us valuable time. I must prepare other magical blasts, despite the dangers of the unstable vortex. Now look quick there, the thing is upon us."

We listened as the slimy serpent legs slithered near, the giant having detected our whispers. The flailing legs went passing by as the mind was searching with his eye for the intruders. The massive monster slid by us, not wise on our presence, although it halted and paused. Was it keen by spiritual means that a traitor, the dubious monk, was hiding somewhere close?

From behind the giant I darted out and rushed to climb up the many minor horns of his back, whereby to plunge my short-sword into his ribs

and pierce the heart without sustaining wounds myself. The great beast, however, whirled about and flung me off, having detected me at once. I arose from earth and prepared to face the thing head on. Upon finding me on the sands beneath him, the creature curled back his head and gazed upon me with his diabolic burning eye.

Instinct; shield my head. I shut the visor over my face. Powerful orange lasers poured forth out the gruesome eyes and arrayed in hazard all around me. Most of these struck my platemail but bounced off at once, and the deflected beams went to other areas of the cave. One stray beam even hit the monster's own tail, injuring it badly. The thing bellowed in agony as the burning beam carved a deep shaft athwart the scales of its spinning appendage.

The creature moved back from me and took up an enormous trident that lay up against a stalagmite. His primary weapon would be of little use against my reflective platemail. With the trident he circled me, watching me with his cyclopean head, cautious, the glint of a mischievous intellect in his singular eye..."

"—Please, my friend, hold off your story." my cell mate said. "I am too fearful to hear what will next occur. I must rest my soul from these gruesome images which you have conjured up."

"I am no conjurer. Rest now, for I also weary of the telling. Tomorrow, if it be not your last day, you will hear of what dreadful things next occurred. Sleep in peace, for I say we shall yet escape this Tartarean prison."

"You are not a serious person. Do you think that you will escape a spirit like the Northing? You may have escaped Abraxas the demon, but this Northing you will not escape."

"I trust that all things are in God's hands."

"You do not. You are like me. I can tell by listening to your story; you seek adventure and conquest. Beware, a single success against one demon will assure nothing against the prince of devils."

"Our victory is in Christ." I reminded him.

"You claim to be a man of faith, even more so than I? I am an Ammouric cleric, a priest-anointed. Be assured, the flesh is stronger than you imagine, my brother."

"And now we will face the Northing himself," I replied. "for he is yet another Satan and lord of shadow who has come upon the world, just as others before him: Abraxas, or whoever, bloated with pride, deceit, and devilish wisdom. My hour is near, and so I shall be brought before Hell's bureaucrat. I shall face him without sword and armour, without magic, only wearing but this mere habit, and trusting in the Word of God rather than in the swords of men. The power of Heaven comes down to me. Did you think of only the powers of yourself and mine own? No, we share the power of God. Heaven will show me how." My fellow prisoner had already fallen asleep, and I suspect that he went back to dreaming of his paramour. So, too, then did I take the opportunity to slip under the spell of ancient Night and her subtle charms.

rothers, something awakened me subsequently in a most untimely manner. Let me indicate this with suspicion: can one ever know anything for certain when ripped from sleep in such a dim place. Neither waking nor sleeping would avail me after "the ghosts of my mind" vanished. Instead it were the cries of a man in panic that alerted me. Someone else was in distress, someone nearby. Had my cellmate also been demon-visited? Was he dreaming the approach of some melancholy specter?

Some *pavor nocturnus* shook him. He was shouting monotonously in enigmatical verbiage like unto gibberish. Here is what I heard: ". . . *-he will not ever! You do not know this one, he that dwells here. I have been here reading through that, aye, by the moon. Nutiro segerinem mulse aman truhoi, ktha! What are...you, what be going on here? You announced him before...you hoped for...rege eram estactico find dathza ....passages for which....you had long warned...nazam...not...the . .* "

"Awake, man, awake! " I cried. "You talk in your sleep! Awake! You have been spouting unknown sentences, sentences mixed with gibberish."

"What...? Did someone say awake? " he responded feverishly.

"You were as one speaking of things written by the ancients, I will guess that you were speaking of the book. The moon has been full this night, and lunacy visits you, and spirits loosed to rove the world."

"What mean you? "

"Were you conversing with a spirit in your dream? "

"I were, but I suspect that spirit were you. I suppose. I am a lunatic, aye, for I myself do not comprehend how long I have been here, do I? I have indeed found the passages which were sought. I did grasp *The Black Book* in my dream."

"How so be that? And wherever is *The Black Book*! Do you have it? "

A look of guilt came across his face, barely visible in the dimness.

"You are asking me if I have it...hmmm...somehow...you communicated these suspicions to me before. I shall admit all. You see...it was the creature, that chamberlain of Darkness himself, who coveted the eldritch history, for that archon is so old that he cannot himself remember what transpired in past ages, or even remember how to read the *Akaratic* script. He knows something on it, though, something the scribes say it contains. He wants it translated. Who knows why? I have discovered something else, my friend. I realized it one recent night. You were talking in your sleep, and I talked with you. And you answered my questions honestly."

"I trust not. It is you who talk in your sleep, not I. This you have just now this night demonstrated, and you also rudely woke me out of an important dreaming vision, my spiritual father appeared to me."

"My sincere apologies...but you do so prattle in your sleep. This is something you and all the others may never have realized: *The Black Book* is indeed a magical tome. But it is not a grimoire, not a spell book, as those monks who are accusing you claim. It certainly has magical properties, or perhaps supernatural power: for those who read it, even if they cannot fully translate the complex and arcane Saturnian Latin or Akaratic quotations while awake, understand. They translate the passages they have examined while they are in dreaming sleep; they translate them aloud! "

"What now are you saying? What nonsense! Return me back the silver-braced book, give it now I say! The Northing knows that his real name is recorded somewhere in the many pages. Divine providence has put it in my custody. However did you get hands on it? "

"The servants of Tartarus lent it to me, they having wrested it from you during your original capture. When they discovered that you only cared for Pythagoreanism, they charged me with the task of translating it.

However, I failed to provide an understandable translation. So instead I have been talking with you in your sleep, and you have been unwittingly giving me the translation.

Please forgive me. When Professor Naza examined the leaves which the Veil-Knights presented him, as booty upon your arrival at this hell-prison, a scribe immediately recognized it as a script of the treasured

Black Books, and he surmised that you had been translating. Immediately the guards, those servants of Tartarus, returned to this cell the famous thirty-third volume, which remains untranslatable to even the most sage scribes and archigraphers. Believing that the lost tract contains some key to his final quelling of the Whitehawk kingdoms, the guards informed you that the unholy creature demands you translate it.

You denied them, content only on delving into it for the occasional Pythagorean aphorism with which certain commentators entertained themselves, and you ignored all the lore...but you did have to skim over it to find the aphorisms.

May God forgive me, a mere belly; for having given into the solicitations of my flesh. To the clandestine task I consented. I could not translate the bizarre and ancient text, but I could feign to translate; and in pretending I began to understand bits and pieces. I questioned you in your sleep, and you provided me with the pertinent passages.

This was only to save your life...rather our lives. It was on this account that we obtained better treatment. We could eat well and avert torture. I reasoned, nevertheless, that I might make some good result of it, for if we could go through the annals of the ancient text, we might find some clue, not to avail the Northing, but rather to overthrow him. And it is to this end that you and I as well continue to labour while sleeping, as you have done for many nights past, but not this night, because of the moon. There is always hope, as you say."

"You make me ill with your folly. Of course there is something in it, but only I know what to seek through its thousand pages."

"What is that?"

". . . a certain exorcism, a prayer of banishment that will lock the Northing in his deep chamber forever. I must learn first the origin-name of the creature."

"What does that have to do with anything?"

"Don't you know? You are a priest! Think over it...and think over what you have done: you have been giving the servants of Tartarus the translation? Have you provided the Northing lore now by which to destroy the Whitehawk kingdoms? Alas, you are a pitiable priest indeed. You should have let us die rather than betray the world to an evil hegemon. Give me the book before I am driven to sinful rage!"

"I cannot...Northing's servants have taken it. It may be that Professor Naza is satisfied with the secrets he found in the translation which I supplied, for we have not yet been tortured. I shall pray that the strength of faith will stay with you. But, come, I sense there is something else that emboldens you against that fairy spirit, that druidical maniac, something other than indifference to this life, some knowledge other than what your faith gives."

"Do not try to change the subject. We will need to go over all lore which you obtained talking to me in my sleep. First, however, aye; there is something else: the recounting of high feats nobly done. I am going to finish the story on the creature Abraxas, and you had better listen well. I do it because it must be done.

"Know this: we dispelled fear; we crushed Abraxas and his unholy cult. Perhaps you too will learn to overcome your fear."

"I am all ears... "

"*He who has ears let him hear*. And a good listening is the least you could do.

emigods entertain no pity. I was locked in mortal combat with Abraxas, an abhorrent, a serpent-leged horror. This was a demon incarnate, as it were, a gorgon whose cyclopean eye emitted deadly beams of destruction. My furbished suit of plate armour, being my frock revealed as a paraphysical shiny structure, had caused the most powerful beam-weapon to deflect and even injure the creature. So it picked up the massive rusty trident instead and was ready to lunge at me. The power of Hell was upon me. The thing recoiled like a cobra. Knowing that the great weight and brutal strength of the thing would prevent me from successfully blocking the trident, my only hope was to leap or duck out of the way when the strike came. The creature did lunge. Unused to wearing armour for combat, I did not avert fast enough. The trident caught me on the shoulder and opposite arm *segmentum*, pinning me down to the sandy earth against the wall of the cave, like a lobster under the fork of someone about to dine.

Although the barbed prongs of the trident only grazed my flesh, they ripped into the armour and snagged it, as a lobster gets caught on a fish hook, and wedged my torso. The hideous creature now lifted me up in order to devour me. Arizel, however, launched a number of ruinous freeze-spells and frost-plumes against the thing to hold it back. The creature froze in place but only momentarily, not enough time for me to gain footing and strike with my dagger, for the creature had caused me shock enough to drop the sword.

It was a mighty gorgon and busted out of the frost-trap each time; He lurched and thrust, and it pinned me with his fork to the cavernous floor. Before it could finish me, Arizel attacked his flank. The magic-user ventured close in order to cast the elemental spell, for this particular frost-spell required proximity. He came too close; the thing struck down Arizel with his tail. At this moment I was reeling and overburdened with excitation, fumbling, unable to free myself. Arizel was knocked out cold.

Now the monster drew me up high and opened wide its hideous jaws to devour me, as he must have done for many other poor souls, somehow leaving only human skin.

The gorgon-head tilted back to swallow. I myself, dangling on the trident, was placed into the creature's mouth like an oyster to be slipped into the throat, a living tomb. The corossive acid of the creature's druelling maw seeped through the creases of armour and singed my skin. Oh horror...since I am large, the creature had to keep its head tilted back in order to swallow me whole. My head also was slung back, and in excruciating pain from the digesting tentacles (it did not have many teeth). I could see the infernal monks leaning over the cavernous ledge above observing the spectacle. I instinctively cried for help, knowing that there was none to be had. Surely now I was going to die. My glorious end would consist of being horribly digested by a creature from the abyss; a just payment for my sin, the sin of having abandoned the monastery which Heaven had once graciously provided for me.

The tongue-like tentacles coiled about my legs and secreted wierd saliva. Immediately, however, they slakened and released. Out of its mouth I tumbled back down to the cave bottom, able to catch myself and land well. The creature bellowed with a sound of rushing torrent. I looked up and saw the dubious monk standing there holding the broad sword which he had thrust into the bristling back of the monster, piercing its heart from behind, impaling the thing. With warrior's voice he proclaimed:

"Abraxas ...IS NOT A GOD! "

He extracted the shiny blade from the creature's torso, pulling it back through the way it had entered. Buckets of burgundy cruor flowed from the cut and spurted like a wine barrel cut open by an axe. The thing bellowed miserably and fell forward to hold itself up by its scaly arms, its writhing serpent legs behind flailing about dangerously on the sand, flipping to and fro like the tail of a fish out of water.

The dubious monk, (no longer dubious), then stepped over astride the creature. Straightway in one deliberate stroke he deprived the thing of its capitol. The scabrous head incarnadine rolled thither. The scarlet ooze of its unholy ichor now gushed forth out of its neck as the torso dropped finally to earth.

Within a few moments it rotted and turned a horrid color. We were filled with relief.

At once I yielded up thanks to Heaven for this victory, and for the spirit of fortitude instilled even in His own lost sheep.

We glanced around and saw the onlookers above gasp in horror. Among those assembled who worshiped Abraxas I spotted a disturbingly familiar visage. It was the face of my accuser, the monk Ulcrist Dretch...what a thing it was for me to notice him there, I tell you. It warrants stopping and pondering, for I do not hate the man —but he must be stopped. Now, I have once again wearied of the telling, for there is much my soul relives. Let me rest now, and consider for hearing what stories you, my dear and learned fool, must tell me..."

Observed my priestly cell mate; " —it rotted away before your eyes? I suppose that's how it goes with anything abominable. That which is spiritually hideous is much removed from the beauty of the rest of creation, and even more remote from the highest beauty of the celestial hierarchies, and finally is outrageously distant from sublime divinity."

"You will not tell a story? "

"I shall, but first I must exhaust this point, lest my philosophy remain unsated: those furthest from the divine are more mutable, more corruptible, and so rot away quite fast. But even a lowly spider has some beauty, for it is God's handiwork, although narrow human sight may fail to see it. Created things which are higher and closer to God are more permanent, such as glorious Heaven, and the angels and saints.

So be. Now your account also aids my remembrance of lore I memorized from the old Ammouric texts."

I said, "Then I am in for a worthy lesson..."

"So you are...The memorization of this lore was accomplished when I was studying my way to priesthood in the Halls of Ambrosius. The lore I speak of is known as the forsaken lore of Nazageist."

"What forsaken lore is this? "

"Have you not heard the saga of war-tales that tell of the winter battles men waged against the lordly elves and their master? "

"You mean the stories from high antiquity? I have heard an account passed down from long ago to King Graham of Ael Lot, city on grey seas. It was from the lore-master's own mouth that I heard how Ambrosius, the guardian nephilid, smote down Nimrul The Archdeceiver on the steeps of Argunizial. I have nothing concerning we who are mere men daring to match steel against any elf lord."

"Did he not also sing of what King Argoth did once to subdue that same fey creature of woe?"

"King Graham only sang of the time before kings. Who is this king you tell of now?"

"An Ammouric king who lived long ago, in the first years of the Fourth Age of the world. He was a king who rallied the civil lands against the hordes of dark elves come up from the deep. I suppose now I can trust you with more on my true identity. A learned fool I am indeed, and a frowning one too. I am an ecclesiastic, a fighting cleric, once liege of the same King Argoth of whom I shall tell. His hollow crown has fallen and his castles are taken, and I myself have been overcome and imprisoned here by the servants of that unholy creature who deceives many."

"You do not seem aged so many winters as that."

"I am perhaps fifty passings. It is uncertain, but Heavenly grace has prolonged my natural life, just like wizards who drink the nectar of the deep. Believe me, it does not necessarily feel like a blessing. Perhaps it has all been so that I might arrive at this very time, in hopes to rise up again to make one last stand against evil and its offspring, the great heresies. I remember those early days and will tell you of them, for I was with King Argoth...

Eastward and North we rode with him into great battles at the opening of the Fourth age of the world, forty passings after the Great Burning of Nystol. Nimrul had finally caught wind of the catastrophic holocaust of books, the blaze of Nystol's libraries.

He knew that men needed books to train their weak minds, and to preserve knowledge of God and the making of the destinies of men. The mischievous lich-creature saw his advantage and renewed his war against the civil lands. He raised a great army of beast-men, trolls, horgrim, and black knights. This troll-horde was rumoured but never seen. Suddenly, one day, a vast army of malice somehow breeched the Horg-Wall and marched upon all the northern civil lands, Arahom, Ardevium, Tyrni, all Regulia, Kithom, and the Nine Feudatories. Ulthuring alone did not capitulate.

This monstrous war is remembered as the Bellum Diabolicum, and it changed the Whitehawk Continent forever. The lich and his troll-army of sinister horgrim built a fleet of Horror-ships and sailed unchallenged to Ulthuring. Ulthuring, vanguard of the West, was utterly destroyed, her princes put to death, her earth salted. It was a sorrowful time for men, but the people of the feudal kingdom of Ulthuring would in later passings rebuild their town Yrbath, north upon the Sea of Goldyndol, which men call the Furthsea.

This King Argoth rose up and called upon all men of good will in the civil and barbarous lands to come meet in the valley of the holy city Vesulum to assemble a feudal army.

Not enough strong souls came to make a sufficient army, and even though King Argoth the Good wielded the ancient sword Gam, there was still too grave a risk for the making of a campaign. It was I who studied the metallurgical texts and consulted with the Arcavirs. The adamantine Gam was melted and recast in the smelter's mould, and with a ceremony the blade was consecrated in sacred fire, bestowed with thrice destruction upon the seven tempestuous spirits.

Argoth then led a force of five thousand across into glades of Arahom where we faced the troll-horde.

King Argoth knelt and prayed to the Allfather while the battle raged. He prayed fiercely until, seeing a need for more carnage, he entered the fray himself. He was still able, at an advanced age, to heft a great two-handed felling-sword and kill five score and seven horgrim in a few hours. The horde master, Mulg, was slain by his own retreating horg-troops. Many of the Ammouric Knights were cut down in this battle as well, which has been titled by men The Battle of the Longhairs, after the style of knights in those days, whose hair was let to grow long. After a costly victory, King Argoth, steeped in gore, entered Hithgorod and the Cracked Mountains seven days marching into the remote hinter and reached the Arc du Baffay, called Ghazabol in those days. That same fastness now hems us in, this very place in which we now miserably sit, 'neath the blasted throne of the Northing.

The weary host pursued the scattered foe and finally marched here, into this cold land where the sun never really shines. Within a circle of torches on the snow-capped ridges, in sight of the drawbridge they at last stood. The King donned his hauberk of chain mail, and taking up sword and shield, addressed his men.

"Noblemen of every Whitehawk Kingdom, be not fearful. You know how our grandfathers, in the days of their youth, managed to undo past tyranny when it threatened to oppress all feudal nations. Men from many divers places banded together in war-brotherhood. With strong arm united on the plain of Gederon not far from here, they stood against the tyrant-emperor, Nergalf, the man-dwarf. His empire of cruelties crumbled in a single day. Now today a few men unite again to make war against great oppression. This fortress Baffay, formerly thought inaccessible, we will breach through a series of bold forays, and the halls of iniquity will be taken in tremendous combat. Fear not this accursed place, but remember and take heart, for without fortitude we can go no farther. Remember that I, King Argoth, am with you all the way, even if I should be first to be struck. I shall enter the grand hall and by divine help withstand the magic from the Northing. Casting earth upon him, I shall seize him and throw him down into the great pit, chaining him with unbreakable bonds: the electrum laces of Queen Ariandol's sandals. I have told you, and I shall say it again: I tarried three centuries listless in her palace, and I found the key to her treasure chamber. Now through my hand divine retribution cometh, and through me the mischievous spirit will be shut away, for not all spirits can be put down by a cleric's words of banishment, but some by dint of sword and axe must be smote down. So now stir up fury in heart unto fearsome battle against the enemy, that it may be recalled by your descendants: 'Grandfather marched with King Argoth and fought with him the day the power of The Northing was eclipsed.'

So he spake, and what he prophesied did they together pray to acheive.

A dreadful hurly-burly ensued against the huge troll guards. Not a few stalwart knights were knocked off the bridge and battlements receiving their death honourably in the glaciated morass below.

The remnant host then came before the massive iron doors of the Hall of Melancholy, which enclosed the forsaken and hideous Northing. Behind these doors the creature sat in infinite malice upon his gloomy throne, once of sapphire brilliant. The King then halted his men saying:

"Go no farther, good fighting men; the Erelim have warned that this is my task alone, I alone must quell the fallen power. Within does the great apostate cast his baleful gaze hither and thither, looking for any he might seize; and if you enter that place with me, he shall employ the weakest among the knights against us. Stay then and pray on bended knee for the souls of thy slain companions, and glorify with hymns the Furth High King."

It was I myself who brought forward the troll-key and saw the grand iron doors opened. The King bade us lock them behind him and entered.

We heard only frightening crashes of thunder within. Here is what the king reported of that which occurred: With the mystic bread of Vesulum in his pocket, protection from dark-elf-magic, he drew forth his great sword Gam in his right hand and held the soil of Ashkhar in his left. He marched in his reddened armour, clanging down the great hall, and he was singing the song of the mountain airs, and verses from *The Golden Pages of The Wind*. At last stood he before the grim throne of the world-ghost. The wrinkled, grey creature was robed in white, and although appearing as a healthy man, somehow communicated the look a terrifying hag and spider, warty and hairy. The being is a nephilid, like Abraxas, but a corrupted thing of the terrestrial order, a lich of terrible foulness.

Know you of the lich-creature's long white hair and grown nails as well, its burning eyes, the rough gargo-voice, the glance penetrating souls. The King was not affected by the enigmatic hissing of the evil one (for Argoth's song was great). We, listening without, did hear some of it. How amazed were we to hear that song.

But seeing his boldness, the horrible thing addressed the noble king thus:

"Erl king, how is it that you, a mortal, still walk upon the sun-warmed earth? Return to your tomb, for every furth-kingdom has been granted to me. And has the Unspeakable Power envied you so, that He has brought you back to the realm of the living!? "

Such was the blasphemous insinuation of the unclean creature, and King Argoth replied not, but seizing the creature, thrust the soil upon the Northing and forced much into its mouth, weakening him sorely. The creature bit him horribly with bestial fangs but did not deeply penetrate his armoured fist. The lich's old fairy magic was quite useless against a righteous king, and the only weapons left him were his deceiving mind, his thunderous hissing, and horrid claws and bite.

Know that King Argoth forced soil into the many-fanged mouth of the hideous being, for it is written...and thou shalt eat the dust of the earth all thy days... In this way he was able to weaken the heinous creature so that he could be bound with the unbreakable electrum laces of Queen Ariandol. Again this was foreseen in the ancient curse of Allfather upon the rebel, as it is prophesied in the Ammouric scrolls: "The daughter of fairy shall constrain you, but by stealth you shall deceive unto doom the sons of men."

They struggled in grappling-combat for some time. The King confirmed in his mind that the grisly creature could not be destroyed by normal means. So after some herculean effort, he finally managed to bind him with the electrum laces. He hurled the vile overlord headlong into the abysmal pit, the Voraganth, which drops mercilessly into the deep enclosure of the Horma gorge.

Our men had earlier prepared a gigantic, adamantine grill with Akaratic glyphs, since we foreknew the place of the lich's imprisonment, having planned it well. The glyphs are sacred wards, which scribes copied; it is said, from the Tablets of Destiny. This grill our loyal serfs and burghers now hauled up the mountain and under difficult labour placed over the stone rim of that tartaric pit and fastened it in place with an adamantine lock, exhorting one another with gladsome songs while toiling.

After we did this, the King maundered and looked over the ancient and solemn palace. It was then that King Argoth re-discovered his true identity and told of it thus...

"Upon the eldritch murals and scripts of the great Hall of Melancholy I set my gaze. There at once returned into my memory knowledge of long forgotten things, wyrdding things communicated in dreams a man dreams during deepest night. The tapestries taught me profound memories; that it was I who was the Erl King in days long past, the life I had before I dreamt away countless passings of Calduin in Queen Ariandol's chambers. It was I; I was the one originally chosen in the draconian age to preside over men, elves, and dragons. Behold, I was there, and I fought against the elf-rebels in the fey war of Ashkar; I saw how Ambrosius the Nephilid struck down Nimrul and rightly deformed his shape, who then became the Nazageist, whom men call Northing.

Indeed sorrow profound and insults like deadly daggers had the elf-rebellion brought me, for it was I whose rightful office as universal sovereign remained disobeyed and unrecognized. So it was that, for a time,

I became yarl of Ulthork, then only a minor princedom of good men who keep the old ways.

I remembered more...After some seasons as yarl of Ulthork, a further evil befell me. I was in the routine of riding unescorted with only my page and one other knight through our lands to spend days in tranquil retreat. Nor ware was I that an unforeseen new power of shadow was arisen, the berserking Wyrmheld, knights who serve the drakodemon. It were these butchers who ambushed us in the apple groves of Dilmonath and sorely wounded me in the thigh by a swift flying shaft of poisonous dart.

I bled much, and the power of this life was failing me; but it was the longest day of the year, and the light of the sun kept me awake, so perhaps that finality was delayed. At last, however, I entered a sleep under the apple blossoms. Before I drifted away I gave the holy brand to the page boy Ikonn, so that he might fight any remaining attackers who still lurked.

It was the blessed Queen Ariandol who heard my cry and intervened; she took up my body and brought me into the everdark, where flow airs of unusual origin, halting Time's power. She took me to her spiral tower deeply hidden in the great caves, and placed me in what seemed a crystalline boat. She cared for me with a divine skill, and I lived and breathed in still sleep, and aged not, nor died. Often I would awaken, and she would entertain me with sweet songs upon the lyre, causing me to forget my earthly troubles and my land Ulthork. Allfather let me stay under dreamy sleep until the furthreaches were ready for a high king."

So did the great old king come to remembrance.

With the Battle of the Longhairs and the overthrow of Northing accomplished, King Argoth had remembered his true identity. The Northing could not be slain, however. The thing is only restrained by the laces of Queen Ariandol and imprisoned. So Argoth himself then took to the thankless task of guarding the abysmal pit-prison, which came to be known as the Voraganth of the Nazageist; for the king alone knew how great a mischief lurked below: it were its devious mind that was of greatest peril, so that none must ever converse with it. By the will of Heaven a deep chasm opened in an earthquake that occurred on that very day, doubly isolating the unclean creature.

After some time other men who were king's helpers at guard duty grew weary, abandoning the king to a lonesome watch, for mortal men are eager to return to their homes. The king was relegated to living off arctic rabbit and ice-fish for his sustenance. Clad in animal skins he lived a primitive existence like The Baptist in scripture, but never did he set down his spear. He did not diminish soon to frailty, even though his age was quite advanced from the power of time in this terrestrial reckoning. Many say that he would spend endless hours in prayer and penance for the transgressions of men.

The great king expired after some forty passings, guarding the pit of the Nazageist in ice-cold conditions. No one replaced him, and he left no disciple, nor chose any heirs.

The race of men has a short memory. It has not been Argoth the King whose feats they have loved and celebrated, but ironically, they sing on the enemy whom he subdued. The unholy lich has become truly beloved by worldly powers, a symbol of one who offered freedom, the great rebel, but who has endured oppression under the established Ammouric power. After Argoth passed, Nimrul's restless professorial mind undertook a new tactic. Instead of pressing men's realms by dint of steel, or enslaving their bodies, he would persuade and quell their desire. From his prison, he gained unwary lawyers and vain scribes to publish many tracts in defense of himself, literally re-writing the history. Styling himself a victim of unfair aggression, his case was actually brought before the grand tribunal of Soothfold, to the dismay of the few learned left in the world. He gained sympathy of the judges nevertheless, who ruled that he had been unjustly treated and that he be released, and his former dominion restored! His reputation was greatly enhanced from that time.

The fame is not only for his governing a feudatory in which all his brutish subjects gladly do his will, (being generously rewarded), but also for his sagacity and courteous nature, which his artful diplomacy made famous. Although he had long ago gladly been credited for the demise of Nystol, he published many denials of having unleashed the subsequent Bellum Diabolicum. He had even gone so far as to claim unfair treatment at the hands of King Argoth, and so argued like a true sophist this re-constructed history in numerous tracts. His "Professor" Cornelius Naza also arranged for him a twisted theology in a number of tomes, especially one titled The Contemplations of Thendex the Archdeceiver. He sent them to every Whitehawk University. At first he was acclaimed among students and common folk, and then before long the square-hat scholars and grey-robed monks sung his praises, and later the nobility. Finally even the Ammouric royalty elevated him to chivalric title!

At the same time they found themselves battling his secret armies, unwitting of the connection. For he had secretly and quite shrewdly made pacts with Mulcifer, and then offered the deep-browed kings his aid, feigning to intercede on their behalf to the likes of Mulg, or the Troll King, or the hobgoblin empire. He claimed to win for the human kings freedom from harassing horgoth armies, but at a steep price, intrusive alliance and hostages.

I say these modern kings deserved to be thusly deceived; they had abandoned true devotion to the Radiant Lady—lacked the protection which never-ending prayer wins, let the Church fall into disrepair, and so were quite easily fooled. Every one of them, save the King of the Aels, made alliance with "The exalted Sir Cornelius Naza, chamberlain of Lord Nimrul, beneficent guardian of all the Furth, the most worthy spirit of all." So the fame was great, indeed, and his eloquence celebrated everywhere.

Over the following decades Nimrul, the secret archdruid, watched over the crowns and kept them bound by treaty. The tidings of the recent destruction of Ael Lot and beheading of King Graham should have shocked the world into waking up from the delusion. Instead it is hailed as a liberation.

That is why I originally came here. I was to restore King Argoth's watch, for I am a selva, and the Church has charged me with rooting out the sources of heresy. It was often said that my line was related to Argoth's, and that I knew something of the evil. Still I never actually saw the hideous fiend on the day Argoth overcame him, thanks be to God. I had managed this task well for a few winters, but it was something of inhumane enormity, and I am but mere flesh and blood.

It was the memory of my former life and the goodness of youthful days, and to some extent the memory of the dalliance of a young maiden, that slowly but surely turned me away from my task. I let these thoughts torment me, and the Devil who-sleeps-not sent weird dreams upon me to cause me dread. I soon sought comfort in wine and would leave my post more and more often. One day I returned and found the glyph-warding grilldbroken.

I did not know the original name of the spirit, so I could not perform the priestly binding to compel him back into his confinement. At last the identity of the pernicious Nazageist, long hidden from mortal men, you may discern. Indeed, if you recall the eldark lore of the Ammouric texts, it is clearly Nimrul, architect of the Ancientmost War, who had been struck down by the Agathodaemon Ambrosius and fled from the battle on the sacred mountain. In centuries past he had recovered and built up the fortress Baffay in the recesses of The Crach Mountains.

Nimrul cursed all life and swore to lead all creatures away from fellowship with the blessed Allfather. His spirit and form became so warped over the centuries that he was no longer recognizable and soon was known only as "The Nazageist" among dwarves, or "The Thing of the North," Northing in your tongue, and the "Prince of Melancholia." It was he who enthralled thousands of souls: dwarf, elf, gob, and human, to build his mountain fortress Baffay from the stones left of Sennoch, fallen city of wicked men. His vines of elfshade, manufactured with an unholy spell, spread throughout the forests of Whitehawk like Wormwood, blackening and strangling the trees, increasing wherever evil grows, all connected back to him.

The Northing would spend unnumbered passings waiting to accomplish his schemes and to inform Ashkhar how new generations of men worked evils worthy of divine wrath. The corruption of Melancholia, though greatly diminished on account of being chained in the great pit, continued and on account of the grievous sins of men, became even more influential.

My friend, know that the few Ammouric knights who survived the Bellum Diabolicum did not escape. The Regulian emperors charged the Edolunt Rangers to hunt them down in later years.

Certain decadent and lawless "free princedoms" were especially opened to this evil influence. Nazageist would in each age present to God the demands of divine justice, informed by commerce with the Devil. He would ask for the power to raise beastly armies of chastisement. I wonder if the Almighty has sometimes granted his requests? Heaven does not deny what justice obliges, a bitter remedy for sinful mankind; and it is written He smites the crowns of those who persist in their sins."

"That lore is high lore indeed," I remarked. "But most of it you took from my recital of the old texts while I was talking in my sleep. However, for the storyteller to feign that he was an eyewitness to events, thereby adding to realism, is a praiseworthy technique."

"You do not believe in faith that I was there? "

"If you say "in faith" therefore I do; after all, you are a priest-anointed. You wanted to tell a story that rivaled my own. I will, however, accept that you were there, if that is what you hope, though I remain skeptical; for you do not seem the type to volunteer for such a guardianship as you claim, but I can imagine no other reason for your presence in this dungeon."

"You never saw me in my youth; I did not appear haggard and withered, with a long beard as you now see. I was once as stalwart as Valherc, with eyes as brilliant as an Apollo, with Jove's brow and Hermes' hands. Alas, but all flesh comes to calamity."

"And the Church? Do you still serve her?"

"Of serving the Church you ask? Yes, I do still serve, as one might serve a master who appears to be alive but who is quite become comatose. It reminds me of an incident in the days of yore. There was once a powerful queen of Atalur, Hesperia, who went to war against the hydra Vorthragna in the age of heroes. She, too, had won the undying loyalty of her subjects. But a viper lay in her bosom, long planted by the conniving spirit no doubt.

"Upon the plain of Setet, far off in the East beyond the Urash River, her army went up against the horde, the sinister Wyrmheld. After much gore, it was a close call which side would prevail. As the battle waged on, the queen fell down from the height where she stood in armour overlooking the plain. Had she been struck by a Saxigat arrow?

"No, she had been poisoned earlier that day. Her host halted the chariots, (just a shy forty thousand upon the plain), and looked back to the hill, ready to turn tail if she did not rise. Although blood yet coursed in her veins, she certainly was not alive in any other respect.

"Her generals, therefore, fearing that all would be lost if the day was not theirs, put out the report that she had merely fainted from exhaustion. They cleverly propped her up, standing on the hill overlooking the forbidden passage, even though she was comatose. The entire army looked back from a distance and did not see any blood, rather was she standing there the same as before. A wizard made the crowned head seem to nod and the armoured limbs to impart benediction.

"Is not this comparable with our queen, the Church, as she is today? After the poisonous compromises in the great robber-council, the Soothfold of Rumil, is she not paralyzed by some alien doctrine widely spread through her limbs? Her bishops prop her up with grandiose show and great pronouncements, but will not admit her morbid inability to breathe new life and win converts, and this is because the tinkerers have changed all but her essence.

"This is why she cannot presently be healed, because no physician will be called as long as the people think she is in perfect health. Meanwhile the bishops wonder why the wings of the dragon overshadow the plain of war. Let us therefore flee to the desert, I say, and hide away from that dragon."

"Very well...I recall that story, but never imagined it could be so applied to our own time's malaise. Now I think it is time to rest, however, before I continue for you tomorrow and relate the terrifying conclusion of my account, of how we escaped the cult of Abraxas, a thing done just shy of miraculously."

"So be," he said. "Enough has been told for now. I also must rest myself and return to my melancholies.

The acolytes of Nuzzib's heretical cult watch a certain well, staring long, and keep stern vigil unmoved. They ensure that no buzzing flys alite upon the sacred waters, nor spider nor insect crawl, nor mouse slip in for a drink, and especially no unclean flesh of infidel touch. Were such things to happen the cult would need to spend an unknown length of time and expenditure finding a new well and pure water, devoid of disease, unseen creatures, and waste, and upon which the "divine" Shahi Nuzzib, heresiarch, "the most cleansed," will be able to wash, "tasting his own soul in the waters of the abyss."

History of the Corruption of Religion
by Krithusel Eloniah

XXX   *The "Holy" Shahi Nuzzib*

"How grand! Now you are awake again and can listen while eating the sautéed rat meat, a sumptuous fare in these grim chambers. I will therefore take the opportunity, since your mouth is now quite busied and unable to make the typical interruptions, to finish my account of the great deeds recently done. I'll not neglect the daring men who did them, the underworld campaign in which I found myself endangered. Now, without burdening under too much detail, I must relate how it came to pass that we escaped from that unholy fane which the gorgon Abraxas haunted. Listen then, and learn of it.

Indeed, one may prevail and slay a false god, but this does not cause the devotees of that power to cease from believing. This is the very nature of faith, which persists in certitude even after the object of devotion ceases to be visible. So it is, and the devotees of Abraxas believed that the hideous gorgon, which they were wont to keeping a worshipful fear of even looking upon, was more than a monster. Rather, he was the only deity worth propitiation and indeed the saviour of their souls. Why, therefore, would the mere dissolution of the physical and outward form of the thing impinge upon their faith? It certainly must not.

"Everybody acknowledges that invisible realities exist," remarked the haggard priest with his mouth full. "The consistency of mathematical principles, for example. It is the logical order of reasoning, well, you could say even thought itself, something which cannot be seen but only represented by language. Add to that as well as the inalterable laws of nature, laws not visible in themselves, but which remain operative in the revolution of the celestial bodies as well as the properties of atoms on the prime material plane. Nay indeed, invisible realities cannot be denied. Therefore did the faith of your intellectual enemies not wane, but increase all the more. I can imagine how the spirit of Abraxas would become idealized in their own minds."

"You know human nature all too well." I replied. "It shortly came to pass that the head cleric of the cult was quickly elevated as to be the very sole vicar and mediator. This was the "Holy" Shahi Nuzzib, a dusky man from Atalur in the nearer East, and Archpriest for the "Almighty Abraxas in the beyonds."

The cult-cleric was quite clever: when he saw his deity the gorgon Abraxas slumped over, headless and slain, he contrived to take advantage. Being keen that its monstrous spirit was banished back to dark Hell, he sought loyalty of his own minions within the cult. This is how that came to pass.

As would be imagined, the sight of their deity motionless and headless, stretched out slain on the cave floor was too much for the disciples of Abraxas. They watched silently as the ichor oozed from its severed arteries, a spectacle too awful for the weird monks to endure. Mercurial Arizel kept his wits, having come to and seen the carnage. Fast as he is with his dagger, he did extract the steaming yellow globus of the eye of Abraxas and, not discreetly enough, hid it away in his purse.

Outraged at the mutilation, the infernal monks with shaven heads began to leap into that pit. We were trapped. One after another of these prepared their reprisal with daggers and clubs. The long robes of these attackers caused most of them to stumble when they landed, for they were not agile. Nevertheless, as the count of these men totalled at least a dozen, we were jeapordized. They surrounded us brandishing their pointy daggers, ready to kill. These monks were now more peril than any gorgon. However the high priest Shahi Nuzzib, a man whose facial features would remind you of the buzzards of Yezez, took the opportunity to make the will of Abraxas known...the will of a demon-god through himself.

"Cease! My brothers...put away your knives into your belts. Do not profane the very place where the blood-death of Abraxas hath been achieved by low mortals, thereby causing his sacred ichor to mix with the polluting blood of infidels. Hear me, oh friends, for the god Abraxas is still living, and he is speaking through me. Remember this great moment always; keep it close to you. Someday you will savor this memory. These defilers are only a few unworthy adventurers from the surface who do know not what they have done. They are not the chosen like you, but instead Fate preserved them for destruction. Could such as these overthrow the magnificent god Abraxas? Do ye not harken? Abraxas whispers to thee now, "I dwell in the beyonds and await thee." Would the god himself give leave for these defilers, mere mortals, to destroy his own thusly without cause? Could there be some purpose deep we might not suspect? -That a spirit can much more powerfully execute the great war between Light and the Darkness if he is not anchored to lowly flesh? My friends, the luminous mind of Abraxas remains with us to continue what he began. It is the will of Abraxas that these men be not punished with mere physical death, but rather be free to stray like the moon, for they are a sign that he cares not for the uninitiated, who must wander the lowly material plane forever without hope of anything better."

"Nuzzib," cried one of the infernal monks, ". . . how can you utter such things? These infidels have committed the greatest of all possible sacrileges and slain our master and lord, the great Abraxas. . . and you would let them go?"

Little did that subordinate monk know he was questioning one of the greatest heresiarch's that would befoul the Whitehawk continent. Nuzzib said "Who be you to even speak, acolyte? " He then struck the frail man down, and proceeded to beat him to a bloody pulp, a thing so horrendous I shall not describe it. Had I the chance back; had I known that this incident would give me opportunity against such a brute and dissembler; I would have let Abraxas alone and gone after Nuzzib instead. He wiped the blood spatters on his face, a décor which made him appear as a buzzard that had been feeding on a mountain sacrifice.

"My blessed acolytes," Nuzzib said, "Behold these glorious fists purple with blood, and how this pious but mistaken acolyte here provoked me to shed his own blood on behalf of our god. The spirit of the magnificent god has entered into me. Abraxas did this in order to teach you that all monks should learn obedience to me. Do you imagine the will of Abraxas would be that these imposters, mere flesh, should also be so honoured today in such a way? To die on the same day and in the same place? Do you not grasp how Abraxas could have slain them with the glance of his terrible eye had he wished it? Instead he has not done what he could most easily have done. Our god allowed these men to slay his corporeal form so that he might provide for us in a particular way. Why, you ask, why has the god allowed carnal men, and worse, defilers, to deprive him of his terrestrial form? He has done so in order that all of you might prove your loyalty and obedience to him. You prove it by doing what is the most difficult of all things: to ratify that these fools be let go, these who have slain your god. If you can suffer this painful command of Abraxas, in what else could you ever deny him? You will see him win his contest against the Nazageist and the drakodemon, unworthy allies, mere demigods, and in this he reveals his spiritual supremacy and puts all under his claw-hand. We are his chosen disciples, the high ones. Thou holy and obedient servants, hear it: I am his oracle upon the earth.

"He who listens to me and heeds my word listens to Abraxas. Do not be deceived, brethren. Prove your loyalty to Abraxas by letting the god's Will be done. What would your faith be if you always had your god in the visible world as you have grown used to? Even the vile Christians claim to have faith by worshiping a deity that died a miserable death, although in their case it is all mere folly. Therefore show your virtue by allowing these defilers to survive, for indeed their idea of "living" will be a worse punishment for them than to die at your hands. To kill them now would be a mercy. Abraxas the god conveys evil upon them, malediction, and has assigned them the curse of never learning the great freedom; ever immured in the world of base matter they must wander. Look upon the vanity of their faces. Do you think they are a threat to the disciples of Abraxas? They are not. What is a threat are the hordes that are like them. These men must be released in order that a sacred wound and desire for justice always remain upon your souls. Were you to quench your anger against them now and take vengeance, your devotion to Abraxas would wane in time. But as long as you know that such as these walk about and durst enter into the caves, beings that would steal your devotion, then rest you cannot. Therefore we shall let them go up to tell all that Abraxas is extinct, and in so doing, the deceptive world shall itself be deceived. Without an enemy like us, the church of the upper world shall relax her discipline; they shall no longer bother to publish anathemas against us, supposing that we are scattered. Men shall say to us, "Your god is extinct." We shall reply only with silence, but we shall continue to publish our sacred writings, the secret knowledge of Abraxas, bringing many converts to worship "The true god who awaits souls in the abysmal beyonds."

"Shahi Nuzzib..." another monk said solemnly, one of the elder monks, "your wisdom is magnificent indeed and has transformed our faith in Abraxas. There is no doubt in me that Abraxas speaks through you. Let us do whatever you say. He who harkens to Nuzzib, " he declared aloud, "harkens to Abraxas!"

This monk then knelt down before Nuzzib and bowed his bald head. All the other infernal monks immediately followed suit, together, all baldy heads. It were a scene as a committee of vultures.

We alone, the freed monk, myself, and Arizel, stood there stupefied and watched the swarthy, dark-eyed, and bald Nuzzib raise his eyes to the beyonds and begin to pray in Gohhan tongue to Abraxas. After his unholy prayer was ended, his gaze returned to us. It was as a buzzard ready again to feed.

"Ye defilers must now leave this place and never return. Remember, tell your boast to all, saying "Abraxas the god is extinct." It is only in this way that the god might deign to treat you less harshly when you pay for your crimes in the material darkness. Be gone then, ignorant ones, and speak not as you leave, lest one of these disciples here suddenly become enraged, and suffer you not, straightway placing a sacrificial dagger in your belly. Do you not deserve worse? On this account I should not suffer a son of Abraxas to lose obedience to me and forfeit his right to be a disciple. That would be a greater tragedy, indeed, rather than your worthless demise. Go now! Ye chosen for destruction!"

Something was so obvious from this speech, and from the affirmation of the monks to whom it was directed, that I could not help but smile. They were afraid of us, the great Shahi not the least afraid, because we had slain their demon lord. So it was that, elated, we actually escaped from that pit and those grim corridors, that library infernal. As we passed through their midst, viewing their indignant expressions, I remembered The Black Book. Where was it? Certainly it was not yet stored in their vast library. It would take a long time for a monk of Abraxas to determine its contents. It must be at hand somewhere. With this in mind I spoke aloud for Shahi and the others, as if addressing my companion:

"Thanks be to God that they are letting us go," I said jubilantly so that all the monks could hear. "Perhaps we shall recover what we came here to find. It's good that these monks down here will never know the accursed black book which brings misery to all who touch it. If only they had known that I came here to save them from it, rife as it is with Ammouric curses upon those who do not give worship to our God. I hear that boils appear on the skin of such idolaters in a matter of days, just like the Philistines who dared retain the Ark of the Covenant in their midst. Oh my, perhaps the book is really down here somewhere; after all. Could we have dispatched so mighty a demon on our own? It must have been the holy curse, radiating from the Black Book."

After noting this speech, the Shahi Nuzzib got up and hurried us over to the chamber where The Black Book was being kept and, taking me aside, privately begged me to take it away and never return, which I gladly accepted, warning him to never again touch anything that is sacred to God. So we left the subterraneous monastery.

New sorrow soon stole away our smiles, however. After we exited that deeply-built monastery we found a friend in trouble. Sahkah was at the entrance where the great caves open in their vastness. There he lay upon a great purple heap of Black-hearted horgrim. As many as twelve black arrows were lodged in his lizardic body, but he still breathed. Certainly he had put up a valorous fight and had even continued to cut down the enemy to the last. No more fight was left in him, for his many wounds were mortal. There at his side lay a great tome bound in croc-skin. It was undoubtedly, The Dread Book of Ocean, for the script was impossible.

"Sahkah," I said pitifully, "you have fought your last fight."

"So it seems I have," he said "And I have done so well, fulfill the purpose of my life; a purpose which I never expect. The Black Prime Mover saw fit that I die well, and with honour, even though for most of life I was nothing but mere mercenary. It was long forgotten dream: die well, and fall in combat fighting for our clan and our god. In childhood I vowed to service of Black Prime Mover, the deity from which are originated all beings. I had forgotten this oath, long time, because our tribe scattered. No dread book, so our priests estimate that the deity forever abandoned us, that he favored Vri, the scaly-green tribe of lizardmen who oppress us. Now I see how they were wrong about the deity.

"When I heard you mention *The Dread Book of Ocean*, monk, I knew destiny was close. Somehow remember my childhood vow. This became singular purpose.

"A man should not just sit in the Sea Queen all day and drink screech...not even a lizardman. There is no honour in that. We had little chance against a gorgon. I knew that, but prayed to Black Prime Mover, and as usual he not answer. But this I took to be good sign. So I took risk and went for one last crusade, true crusade.

"Please, I only ask that you forgive for abandoning you in your time of danger. I heard dread book calling. Sense its nearness I did, and I found it. I to choose between recovery of the dread book, so serving the divine One, the unending Founder of the Worlds, the All-lizard, or, fight along with you, being not divine, who merely like me are, just a passing song."

"No matter···You we do forgive, Sahkah, and we esteem you in high honour. The bards of men shall sing of your batttle. It would have been a greater evil had you unsung the faith of your kind. After all, had you not vanquished this battalion of Horgrim, they would have us and easily put us to the sword, tired and wounded as we are from dismembering the demon Abraxas."

"May the victory over the accursed one be praised by the gods. I see the great swamp swiftly now come, and upon me it nears, you monks. Please harken to my last wish. I have waited for someone to come along, for I should have died hours ago. My prayer was heard, and you came. Take sacred tome and return it to remnant of my clan in Succon. Do this and I pray for you before the great lizard throne. Now fare thee well; From this world I go."

The lizardman's eyes did not close, but gazed into what seemed some unknown place of light. I shut his jaw and closed the eyelids.

We spoke some prayers over Sahkah and commended him to the Creator. We dragged his body to a place apart from the scene of gore which he had accomplished and placed random rocks hastily over his remains. The ex-monk looked troubled.

"Friend," he said. "You are an Ammouric Christian. Why therefore do you treat Sahkah with honour and bury him? Surely you would not do the same for the infernal monks. Yet they are both opprobrious to heaven; Sahkah for worshiping The Black Prime Mover, and the infernal monks for worshiping Abraxas."

"Consider what you are saying, friend. Did not Sahkah help us in every way? Surely he is worthy of burial. Even the pagans would grant him as much. Before you consign him to oblivion, think of his idolatry this way: His Black Prime Mover deity was, in ancient times, the great Lizard-headed god, Slaa. After some passage of centuries, the Slaanit became more educated, far surpassing their scaly-green rivals, the Vri, in culture, philosophy, and literature. In this way they gained the lasting enmity of the Vri.

In course of time the writings of Aristotle found their way south into Succon and were translated into the language of the lizardmen. The Slaanit theologians were greatly impressed by Aristotle's understanding of "the deity," the Prime Mover, the first being that exists and causes all else to move, "thought thinking itself," the origin and foundation of reality. The Slaanit deemed it right and necessary to no longer worship their old, capricious god, Slaa.

On the other hand, they also knew that it would be impossible to please the clerics of Slaa and religious traditionalists by replacing him with an abstract description, "the deity," so they got together and designed prayers for *The Dread Book of Ocean*, addressing Slaa with the same properties that one might find addressed to a Prime Mover.

In this way the capricious personality of their former idol faded. No one is certain how the descriptive "Black..." became attached to the title. This history of the lizard-folk is not missed in The Black Books of Melancholy."

"Still, Sahkah and his race were idolaters," protested the ex-monk indignantly. "Are they not deserving of the same treatment, having accomplished the same sin in the sight of God?"

"Not really...the races of Lizardmen were never Christianized, since their kind were always fierce in battle and looked askanse at strangers. Missionaries never even dared into the swamplands, not so much for fear of giant crocs and lizardmen, but mosquitoes. Nevertheless, Aristotle's description of the Prime Mover was about as close as any pre-Christian could get to the truth of God without the benefit of revelation. The human intellect can only go so far in its willful contemplation on the reality of God. Who knows of what a lizardman's mind is capable? After all, they can use reason like men, (hence they are called "Lizardmen.") Nevertheless, even if their minds are rational like ours, so being finite neither can they much penetrate the divine mysteries, such as the Trinity, the Incarnation, or just the very fact that God would reveal himself as like to us in personhood.

It was a huge leap backward to realize that again after the philosophers had, over many decades of speculations, abstracted him into "deity," into an "it." But he is not just an impersonal force or power like Aristotle's Prime Mover. So too were the Slaanit, who adopted Aristotle's understanding of the divine, seeking the truth, but fell short, like him, save in that one thing; for they actually came to think that their god was also a person, Slaa. Even though they knew nothing of the Slaa, they still had a taste for the Truth. Everyone knows that lizards don't have much of a personality; the same is quite true for most lizardmen. Even these saurians, however, could understand that a personality was a great gift; but why would God himself not enjoy the very gift that he himself alone bestows?"

"How does this differ in any way from the infernal monks? Do you not realize that they were transfixed by the terrifying personality of the gorgon? Their demon-god Abraxas they deem a person."

" —But oh, how different. Did you not note the way in which that raw-headed vulture Shahi Nuzzib spoke of Abraxas as he addressed his monks? It is obvious that he was once himself a Christian, but had abandoned the Ammouric way. He is post-Christian, not pre-Christian like the Lizardmen. The Lizardmen were following after a type, the faint image of the Truth himself, as seen through a glass darkly, albeit quite darkly, but still foreshadowing the full luminosity. Shahi Nuzzib, however, has contrived something else: not a reflection of God in his account of Abraxas, but a dysflection, a diabolic and unworthy mockery of the Incarnation. Abraxas, he said, made a sacrificial offering of himself for his followers, by allowing himself to be slain. This scenario he stole from the true story of Christ. But he has mixed it with lies, failing to acknowledge the One who is the true sacrifice for all men, the Lamb of God. In his idolatry he worships a counterfeit messiah, a fabrication. His faith is empty, or perhaps a deception; at any rate it is not directed to Heaven. Even if it were, faith alone cannot save. Even the devils believe, and they tremble. Shahi and the infernal monks, I fear, will be found entirely reprehensible and worthy of everlasting torment. Not so the lizardmen... through no fault of their own they do not know of Christ-messiah, and may only vaguely be aware that some spiritual salvation should be sought, though perplexed as to how to find it; so like Sahkah they do good deeds in hopes to "please the gods." Nay, but are they like children who may be rescued from fire because they live a virtuous life? Some things we may like to believe are so, but no sure answer can be found."

"You argue well, but something doesn't sit right. What of the savage lizardmen Vri? They know less than the Slaanit. Will they be saved therefore even in their savagery?"

"The Lord is generous, but no fool. A great number of the Vri will be lost forever. Souls are judged on what they know, especially right and wrong, for God imprints his law in every rational being; even if that being is not fully human, the logos still has left his mark. Nevertheless, whosoever is ignorant of the lawgiver yet retains the responsibility of seeking truth regarding whatever they do not know. Consciously the Vri refuse this responsibility. They prefer ignorance to understanding, they prefer brutality, and so I estimate they will not make it. Those who by nature turn to God, in as much as the Prime Mover is a dim reflection, will be saved."

"You have explained these things...not so well. How, without the supernatural grace of true religion, can any creature desire the transcendent God? Someone who has never sipped Mullinth liquor, for example, will never desire that taste. In the same way can men desire God without an outside agency to teach them of God? Clearly natural religion cannot supply it. Even so, I will say it: may somehow there be mercy on Sahkah."

I was quite surprised at his sudden acumen and unable to argue against it.

"We do not have time for anything else but this poor burial of rock piles," I said, trying to change the topic. "Sahkah has died a hero; his memorial will be this: to be sweetly sung by bards in the land of the living. But we must leave this realm of the dismal caves at once. One of us must accomplish his last wish; one of us must return the **Dread Book**. It is the least we could do for him. We shall draw bones from a helmet; whoever has the shortest bone must take the old rimestock to Succon, to where the Slaanit dwell."

It was my companion who drew the short bone, the slayer of Abraxas, the same monk who had become the profoundest of betrayers in the eyes of the infernal brotherhood. That is why I do not include his name in this account, brothers, since those gnostic monks still prowl the earth and go among us as sheep in wolves' clothing. As it now stands, they are still seeking to ensnare souls with their false doctrine, by means of cleverly written books elaborating unholy theologies; and they do not cease their hope to take that betrayer alive and administer unimaginable tortures upon him.

Alas, that I had drawn that shorter bone instead, for then I would have parted ways with Arizel and would have gone more quickly to the world's surface, ascending on my own. No indeed, that was not my lot, rather did I bid farewell to the ex-monk, and I spoke of meeting up with him in two moons time at The Sea Queen. I intended to conduct him to the seaward Monastery of Whitehaven. Then, during the interlude as I was giving him advice, it occurred to my mind that I should direct him instead to The Monastery of The Weeping Brotherhood in the Dry Blood Dunes, since he could abide there on his travels south to Succon.

Little did I know at the time that alien doctrines were already victorious in those once hallowed halls of the Weeping Brotherhood!

So there he has gone, at my persuasion, and I must pray now for the preservation of his soul⋯ "

"And what became of you and Arizel?"

"Must I tell in full that folly and hazard as well?"

"I think so; it would be best to get it off your chest."

"It will be humiliating for me to explain it."

"I promise not to laugh, at least not too much."

"Very well..."

pward returning to the streets of Tyrnopolis we made it, retracing many tunnels and sewers labyrinthine.

Arizel fancied he could convince me me to return to our captivity with the troops of Veil-Knights and horgrim, thereby gaining access to the Arc du Baffay.

"That is insane...what on earth was his reasoning?"

"It was actually this... (and it is by way of an unreasoning not too unreasonable): Our purpose could not be realized: we could not scale the mountainous walls of the Arc du Baffay without the help and equipage of the rock-wise Valraphs. Still, I could not fail to fetch the truth-telling Staff. The staff must be had for testifying my innocence before the rope-girded monks of Whitehaven and the Prime Interquist, if I ever hoped to be restored to my monastery. Arizel also had an interest. He craved access the private library of a certain Professor Cornelius Naza, who is in court at the Arc, where are certain precious tomes otherwise impossible to view. This would be his only chance. So did Arizel talk up his mad plan.

So that is my history as of recent. The blessed cedarwood Staff has great power," I continued, "and can be used against Northing, to banish him back to his bottomless pit. I doubt, my friend, that we will recover that finely-carved staff. But if I had the blessed sword Witchbane, I could at least rid the world of the ever-twitching Archdruid, even if I was found guilty of other mischief."

"In that you are mistaken." my cell-mate, the haggard priest, announced. "That famous blade Witchbane cannot do the task, my friend," He brushed back his long greyish hair, tangled but nobly kept, then glanced up from the shadows in his corner of the cell. "Because Nimrul was and remains an ancient elf. Such a blade wards off not any fairy magic; its edge puts witches and warlocks in fear, nothing more, to check hu man wickedness; it is a spirit-cleave against them. No universal spiritual weapon can injure him. Northing, you see, is a spirit almost extinct, but being divinely cursed he cannot die the death like other men. He is virtually a ghost *in corporeale* requiring the potent banishment that only so great a ministerial relic as the Staff can provide...or perhaps if one has not that relic···.a bladetongue might do, that is, a tongue like a blade, cutting apart errors with a precise theology grounded in undeniable axioms, disemboweling his philosophical presumptions. That therefore must be your weapon."

"Use my tongue as a blade? That's certainly not your everyday technique. You said before that there was some kind of professor, or theologian, famous throughout all the furth, a master of words."

"Know this: the one you are thinking, Professor Naza, said to abide in the library of the Arc du Baffay, is none other than the Nimrul himself. The name he uses to deceive the collection of learned men in the various universities, and ultimately bring them to his own sentiment by the repute of his scholarly publications."

"If that is so, what hope does a poor and obscure monk like me have against him?"

"Ask you that, having already lectured *me* on hope? You do underestimate yourself. You possess a mind young and versatile, and your will-power is stronger than mine, as behooves a monk. You are taught quite well enough. Use what you have and let the Uncreated Spirit look after the rest."

"What about you? You are a priest with great knowledge. You will not go against him?"

"No, the ritual itself is accomplished by priests, true, but has greatest efficacy when the Church is present. My learning is too structured and predictable, and my "cerebral mercury" waning. He would easily undo me in mental combt. Surely my priest-intellect is keen and I know theology, but my will-power is quite damaged from the tyranny of the flesh. For a proper banishing I must fast. My mind will be weak. But a willful opponent like you will tire Professor Naza. I must remain silent and ready as you distract his mind with clever arguments. Then by the power of Christ, not my own power, I shall perform the exorcism."

"What you have said is possible indeed, but we will not do it easily. The creature, you have said, has published several famous works via the monks of Abraxas. His writing, (which outrages anyone squarely learned), being fraught with knotty quodditties cleverly proposed, is nevertheless acclaimed as brilliant by scholasts and professors of theology throughout Whitehawk. The name Naza is both celebrated and feared in the cathedral schools of the Nine Feudatories, and even in Plathonis and Aquilar, as well as Kithom, Bardelith, Hroth, and Kargiwall. How is it that you hope to accomplish anything against him by having let yourself become imprisoned here with inextricable bonds? I cannot dispute him in this condition."

"A well-informed but unschooled Christian can sometimes outwit the most sublime professor of philosophy. But this is provided he knows the scriptures and prays. As for your question as to my intention, know that this folly seems to be more than folly. However now continue your previous story, that I also may learn something new."

"Very well....consider how the Christ let himself be incarcerated, so that he could have solidarity with those who are in dungeons. We decided to do something similar. We would give ourselves back into the hands of our enemy. To foil him by surprise might do the trick. This possibility had come to my mind when I remembered one experience as prisoner to that cruel army and troll-horde. There had been a moment when it appeared that an ornery Veil-Knight would impale me. That was on account of my having been involved in hostages escaping. The Hobgoblin-commander of the unit however saw the aggression and sternly forbade it. We were extremely valuable to him as sacrificial offerings. The infantry commander argued with this knight. When the furious Veil-Knight disagreed, he raised his lance to skewer me. The commander gave a signal and the knight was immediately dispatched by a bolgoth arrow. Hostages are worth more than an extra battle-hand.

So we had great protection. Who in their right mind would dare the wastes of Hithgroth and the dreadful tundra of Bardelith, with the dire-wolves and the polar bear, the frost-zombies and pamphagous ice-worms, not to mention the berserking Durgoth barbarians? It is no enormity, and is even terribly safe, provided one is a hostage of the dark horde.

Certainly it cannot be a frontal assault as in the days of King Argoth, but you must make a hidden intrusion. No, there really is no possibility for a common adventurer or even a small army to openly advance upon this dreadful Arc du Baffay, not without the sky being blackened with nasty bolgoth arrows or one's own limbs being torn off by massy troll-guards, no, nota' all, (and that be if one hasn't already frozen to death in the mountain passes, or fell from a ledge on some unknown route).

Here is what we did...We offered ourselves as lackeys to a detachment of Veil-Knights, feigning to be lost pilgrims needing work. Consequently we obtained barley bread, gladsome wine, blankets, and protection from the horgrim; and better pathway to here, and we suffered only an occasional beating. "

"How did you convince them not to slay you on the spot? It is quite easy to see that our kind is of the same which the Veil-Knights are sworn to kill. "

"It were not aggression that beset in this matter; rather it was convincing the enemy warriors to bother with us at all. We waited for many days about the Horn of Ardeheim, upon the same route taken by the Veil-Knights in their mad pilgrimages. They lead prisoners captured in the crusades northward to Baffay; hope for a good ransom.

We camped for several nights upon the bluffs overlooking the road and spotted none of the expected wagons at all, nor any wayfarers. Had the knights made some truce with King Huda of Ulthuring upon the Sea and were lodged in his halls?

So we traveled south unto Kithom and its deserts, knowing that the routes through those wastes are also popular. We prayed that we might come across some slavers from the East who would know when to sell us to a party of northbound Veil.

All our efforts to locate passing Veil-caravans failed. We must have spent a week camped out upon the plain of Kithom, searching the horizon and waiting to spot Veil-Knights. Even if we had spotted them, we did not have any reliable plan to convince them. Could we even persuade that they could fetch a worthwhile price from Baffay for us?

We ended in quiet; watching the sunlight move our shadows and listening to the wind blow the tall grasses to and fro, and shake the frewel bush. At last we admitted that the whole idea was not so clever after all. After the end of the bread and wine, we packed up our few supplies and headed back to *Tyrnople*.[47]

Upon our admittance into the great city of brazen domes, a certain detail was noted which excited our curiosity. I happened to espy shining scimitars in scabbards with brass tacks laid aside by the gate-house, an

---

[47] *Tyrnople (Tyropolis, Tyrr):* The eastern exarchate of the Regulian Principate. Tyrnople lays in a strategic location, not only having ports and access to the Sea of Goldyndol, but also on the route called the Serrian Way which leads to Namaliel.

unusual sight. Also saw we handsome steeds arrayed in Gohhan skirts stabled nearby.

Upon inquiry a city guard explained it to us. Several Veil-Knights had been permitted into the city, since Tyrnopolis had always been neutral in the Wars of The Veil. These dark-cloaked cavaliers had strolled off to the eastern quarter. That is the run-down district where are found taverns amenable. This was not unexpected, explained the city guard, since by the law of the Veil no drinking is permitted in the closed lands. Imbibing nevertheless is their secret custom before any martial enterprise; a pastime never to be mentioned at home.

We hastened back to The Sea Queen. Upon entering warily we spotted no Veil-Knights. Had they gone elsewhere or lost their way in the unfamiliar city? Perhaps they would show up. Nonetheless, we determined to endure our sense of being unwelcome. We ordered topsy tancerds and a hearty roast with the few chinkers we had left.

By the time evening set her veil over the world, we were beginning to wonder how we might fare for sleep. We were slouching and even dozing off in our chairs. Suddenly the front door of the tavern swung open. Great warriors, darkly clad in chain mail and veiled with black cloak, entered.

The Veil-Knights always keep their identities obscure by veiling their faces, save for when they have a duty that outweighs it, such as imbibing. The entire tavern ceased its chatter and watched these four knights go to an empty table and sit. At once they ordered shots of kreech and tancerds, and removed their oriental helms and black scarves. I was surprised to see how everyday and human were their faces. Given their dark reputation for assassination, enslavement, and ruthless war, I had misplaced their humanity.

"I know a game of wager from the East which might challenge them," said Arizel, who knew well the Gohhan tongue. "...a game which they no doubt also know, and which I can win at terribly. "

It was not easy for Arizel to gain their tolerance at first. He ordered them shots of kreech and introduced himself as a Gohhan scribe. He knew the language and provided good jokes, some of which were at my expense, but I could not tell what they were saying about me. This odd game of symbols which he played against them using a strange-looking dice was quite complicated and difficult, the winner receiving drinks provided by the loser. At first he feigned overconfidence, winning no rounds, a cunning strategy. It enticed them. He forfeited a considerable sum. But he won himself just a few rounds, increasing their sense of excitement and resolve. Finally, he executed his last, and in a sense quite unfortunate, ploy. He let our side be overthrown several times, wagering the greater share of his pouch. All the while more and more drinks we ordered them so as to dim their judgement and encourage further play. When he had quite little left, he explained to them that he must try to at least partly win back his savings. On this account he bet my freedom, and to my dismay, I was assigned the title "slave." Nevertheless, I reckoned it was part of the plan. After losing the subsequent round, I gambled away my freedom; and then Arizel wagered his own freedom, with slices of Tipsycakes, and put down his last crizet. But the sly dog won. The Veil-Knights were drunk silly on kreech, and one passed out, leaving the chivalric Captain and his compeer. Arizel slowly re-claimed all gold, and the one knight that was left at the table was put off and clenched his fists.

At this point Arizel revealed to them that he was a Sorcerer. They had best be mindful of the terrors that awaited those who would dare mishandle any Arcane from Nystol. In turn, the Veil-Knight, lacking judgement, boasted his many campaigns, and how after his men were finished sacking a nearby town, an enormous force was coming to sack Tyrnople herself. An entire fleet was on its way with horses and war machines. They themselves were the first to arrive. The others, he said, had been delayed by a storm. Whether this were a mere drunken tale or a warning, it was impossible to tell; but the apothegm *in vino veritas* came to mind!

Arizel beguiled the chivalric Captain to bet his entire ship and a month of chivalric service in order to win back all he had lost. The knight agreed, and thus he bet, and lost to Arizel again. The Veil-Knights, however, being men of honour, will die before failing to live up to their oath-given word. Arizel had known of this and now requested the despondent knight to take heart and escort us to his ship. We were to sail off at once for mountainous Thasos and wend way north to Bardelith and to Baffay, a course which the Veil-knights had known well. Afterwards his ship would be returned, and he might rejoin the naval expedition. Yet more drinks were offered, and the other remaining Veil-Knight, distracted by a song and completely ignorant of his captain's downfall, drifted off into inebriated slumbers.

We retrieved their horses and loaded the two passed-out knights on their fine beasts. Bringing the other two passed out in wheel-barrels, we followed the stumbling Veil-Knight captain, all the two-mile long walled walkway down to the quays. He would moan often, fearing the worst and dreading Arizel. He brought us to his sloop and awoke the crew. We embarked the horses and set sail that very night.

Loud cries of alarm awoke us the following morning, our heads pounding from the previous night's revelries. At sunrise the sky was a bright blue and the sea wine-dark save the frothing white breakers; but looking upon the horizon, someone had spotted many sails. It was the glory-fleet of which our Veil-Knight captain had spoken. They were bearing down upon Tyrnople in the early morning. The warriors were enraged that their ship was going in the opposite direction, without explanation.

But the Captain told them not to fret, since the siege would last many weeks, and they would miss nothing but a great deal of confusion and work. And he promised them loot. This flimsy explanation calmed them down a great deal.

Three days sail it is to Thasos, and it must be done upon the open sea, with no land in sight. How the Veil navigators accomplished this I am not certain, although their ancient knowledge of the stars is great for sure; nevertheless, most of the time the weather was overcast.

Arizel now explained our plan, in detail, to the Veil-Knight captain.

The great turbaned and bearded warrior grabbed his huge belt tightly, and he bellowed with laughter at the wiry and bald Egyptian wizard. He found us most insane, and, in fact, he became teary-eyed with amusement at learning how fellow humans could concoct so hazardous a plan against The Dire. His mood turned; he became irate. He called us "adolescent do-gooders," saying that he could never understand why so many westerners do not crave death in battle with honour against the Veil, but rather would die attempting to banish what every reasonable man of Arraf would accept as a mysterious spirit of nature.

"If that is all you look to do," said the Veil-Knight, "we already have slavers stationed upon a certain shore which remains unpatrolled by the Edolunt Rangers. We can hand you over to the horg-slavers, and they will take you at once as slaves to Baffay."

Thasos is a wild country of massive ranges and pine forests whose lofty and remote mountains are a timeless refuge for the giants of old. The ever-scheming giants, say the legends, were banished by God to lodge in the mountains there, apart from men. It is rumoured that mountaineers have seen ingenious and gargantuan castles upon the otherwise inaccessible mountain peaks. There storm-giants carry on their daily life. Thanks be to God all travelers can steer clear of them by taking narrow gorges.

The shores of Thasos are relatively safe, save for the occasional slaver-crews. So we disembarked upon those pagan shores, and the Veil-Knights sold us to a contingent of horgrim who at once beat us and put us into chains with other captured human savages, wild men who live off the teeming fish under those rocky shores.

We soon were to be brought as slaves to toil in the mines of Nzul beneath Baffay. What a sad sight we saw, all manner of men and women, the young, the old, the ignorant and the learned, all once great people of the nation Nzul, but in recent decades brought to ruin and gloom. The dominion and waxing of the Balecrown had caught thousands in debt-slavery under the many greedy bankers and despots, servants whom he had long prepared. Befouled and in paltry rags, for most a good day meant that they might not get beaten by their masters, many of whom were not horg, but fellow men. Every month, the Balecrown's assassins would slip into some town or village and routinely put death some innocent man at night, in his bed or on his porch. This was to keep the population in continuous fear.

And what a pathetic sight it was when I did happen to witness a lowborn thug brazenly mistreat someone of noble stock, some lady of high issue. With shameless impunity he did so. I, with hands bound, could do nothing. But I offered whispered prayers begging the intercession of the saints in glory. It is written; *only through many hardships can we enter the kingdom of Heaven.* "Many" it says, not a few, not one or two; MANY.

After a number of such miseries in Nzul, land oppressed by evil, through rugged mountain passes and desolate landscapes we at last made it to Baffay.

So that is how we did it; we in fact returned to this grim imprisonment, voluntarily. A most foolish gesture in the eyes of the worldly, but we have done it in imitation of the Lamb, himself incarcerated so that men could be made free. It is an unworldly wisdom.

So ends my recollection of all that transpired from the time I drank Arizel's potion.

If a monk has studied carefully the martial art which his masters have passed down to him, the effort will be reflected not just in his technique, but by his entire being. Even the very manner of his verbal discourse will become precise, able to instantly cripple opponents just like the graceful hands of an adept. By unassailable logic he will be able to unhinge adversaries easily in dispute and on any philosophic question.

Tien Joshur
Autumn Instruction for Monks on Pilgrimage

XXI   DISPUTATIONS IN THE DARK

Something in that dark dungeon scurried by, some small form occulted 'neath shadow shambled off, half glimpsed. Who knows what sort of scavenger it was? I sensed unseen eyes gazing at me. The important thing is that it startled me. The fear caused me to reflect. How much time has slipped away in this remote chamber? Horgs with their vacuous brains sit and stare, (fallen *elphim* they are, born of black Tartarus, beings warped beyond recognition). They stare off into the unending gloom for uncounted days on end. Just like them I myself was becoming: a soul overthrown, drained of light, fraught with regret, awaiting the liberation which death in stillness promises. In that place long I sat chained, submerged in the profound dark; the lobby of a veritable morgue.

I gave up on myself, but Heaven did not let me bow. As if by some divine mystery Ambrosius the Lionhead, *Nephilid*, appears in my nightly dreaming and instructs me as to how I must prepare myself for torture, and for confronting the Northing. Every day I practice the monastic technique of Christian resignation.

A sliver of light burst through, and a little sparrow visited on morning. He had in his tiny beak a measure of twine with which to build a nest. Way up above he perched, some 16 cubits aloft. There is a singular window slit from which glows a shard of reflected light, the only aperture for illumination. He flew in to inspect for a suitable location, alighting on the narrow ledge, close to the ceiling.

The cheerful creature was a most unlikely but welcome sight. To the fleet-winged bird I communicated: would he let the twine drop down so I could use it for a few days? Eternally grateful would I be. I would see that the rope-girded monks include him in the annals. The bird was uncertain and chirped back this: although he did not care for the annals of monks, nevertheless he did appreciate my offer. He worried that the crows, who patrol the air in unwavering flight, would go after his new family if they found out. So probably not...besides, the megalithic prison is inescapable. Nevertheless, he said I would have a definite answer the next day.

To my great surprise the poor creature favored me, and at midmorning the following day dropped the twine and down it fell. I exclaimed that he would not be forgotten, and would be counted among the angels who fly about the throne of the great God of all.

This conversation with a sparrow I did not find at all unusual or odd, until I took a moment to reflect on it. Generally, animals are not skilled at conversing with humans. Nor are humans worth much for getting their finer meaning across to most animals. How was it that I knew how to do this? How could I have talked the bird-chirp so well and with such explicit detail? This realization produced alarm for a moment, until I took a few more lapses of time puzzling over it. I asked the cleric my haggard priest-cell mate.

"Friend, forgive me, since this sounds absurd and childish, but, you know, I can understand the thoughts of...of various animals quite well and express to them my own desires."

"That would be entertaining," he responded, waking up. "How is it that you came to imagine yourself thus, monk? "

"It is not my imagining; I do possess some kind of perceptive power of speaking with them."

"Good man, you have been here too long. You now entertain yourself with vain imaginings of supernatural powers. That is quite human of you."

"No, you assume wrongly; I spoke with the sparrow that was up there. You saw him, did you not? He left us twine for our escape. I asked him for it; he consented."

"I shall pray for this madness that deludes your reason; perhaps it is a lingering side-effect of the potion...some hallucination. You understand, of course, the Ammouric teaching that Man forfeit the fellowship of animals on account of the Archsin? "

"I do...and it is doubtless true...but to me the gift has been restored even more powerfully...it is some marvel of God to help us. Just believe me, will you? On faith..."

"Very well, I have consented to stranger enormities."

"I do not understand how this has come to me. Certainly my weak faith does not merit such a gift; conversing with animals."

"I have heard that certain masters spend years in solitude on mountains or in wildernesses, or sitting atop a pillar. Sometimes they obtain such a gift. How it has come to you of all people is mysterious indeed."

"What was that? Masters, holy men...in solitude? Such as a hermit? ...your words have helped me arrive at the answer. I knew and cherished one Maragald the Hermit, a Cassandra shunned by wicked monks. He uttered prophecy, and in his last words to me said, "I give you the power of speaking with the children of earth." It seemed to me a riddle. I thought of giants or cave-trolls or pagan humans, or maybe some enchanted being that lives in the earth. Later I concluded that he must mean people in general on the earth, though how I should have needed a special help was lost on me. So then I thought, many animals live in earth: bears, wild dogs, moles, worms, and many other kinds. Do you think instead that is what he meant?"

"Did your hermit-fellow know the scriptures?"

"He did, in a way most uncommon, a prophetic and enlightened way."

"Then of course that is what he meant: terrestrial animals, not weird things. Recall how Moses describes the Creation in his telling known as *The Book of the Genesis*. The great patriarch writes: *And God said, let the earth bring forth every living creature after his kind, cattle, and creeping things, and beasts of the earth after his kind: and it was so.* Notice how different in wording where Moses gets to the creation of Man; this is just a little detail but it is significant instead it reads *And God said, Let us make man in our image...*He did not say, "*Let the earth bring forth Man...* "

"This is one proof why Man is firstly a spiritual being. God wrought Man in a particular and exclusive manner. He did so separately and *directly*, saying "*faciamus hominem ad imaginem et simultudinem nostrum*" let us make Man in our own image and likeness···not indirectly as other cresatures before, causing the earth to bring forth, after the manner in which all earthly beasts came into being, when he said *let the earth bring forth*, as it were bringing forth animal-children. So there is your meaning. You may converse with animals, "children of earth" herself, by God's will. Consider then what wisdom and piety your hermit-fellow had achieved by God's grace to receive such a gift, and grant it to you in turn as a double share of his spirit; aye, as an Elijah."

"So then it is true...I do have the gift... "

"That is settled, my strange friend. But now harken to me in something else. I have formulated a new plan to use the twine for strangling our jailor. Now listen in detail..." We made a long preparation, exacting every moment of action and every possibility of failing. We went over and over it again and again, taking minute timing observations of the watch. My cell mate and I then at last proceeded with the plan. There exists precise lore kept by the monks of the Dry Blood Dunes of certain extraordinary monastic techniques. Guy of Xaragia confirms this and has recorded how a monk may assume the mysterious state of appearing dead, catalepsy. It takes considerable concentration to induce, but is impossible to detect. To merely feign to be dead, *semi-mortuus*, closing one's eyes, like children do at play, that would not fool the horgs, for although stupid, they are certainly wise to many things.

"Horg, go clean out the adjacent cell, will you?" my cell mate barked at one of them, a rather nasty guard named Ogma. He used a deliberately challenging tone so as to excite the ire of the guard, ". . . I think the prisoner has been bitten by a rat and died of disease! Get up you fat she-dog!"

"You dare even speak without permission, human?...and you try to give orders?! When I am ready, tremendous pain will be provided for that outburst! How could you be so foolish? Perhaps you like pain, heh?"

"Why do you delay? You must be quite afraid of your own prisoner, you helpless sow-mouse." Ogma first did nothing, but after a number of times repeating the request with ever more insolent tones, the porculent horg finally motivated his lazy bones and stood up, enraged. He opened my mate's cell and beat him severely. The haggard priest, however, was able to grab off the horg's helmet and deform it so that it could not be worn.

The black-hearted horg locked him up again and then came over to where I was supposedly dead, leaning against my cell's iron-grating door.

The horg hobbled forward to my cell to take a closer inspection of me slouched against the bars. He grabbed my supposed corpse by the hair and pulled my lifeless head up to himself for a closer look. The *rigor mortis* was quite evident. Ogma opened the cell and came in. He was dragging me out. But just then some other horg called out to him from another corridor. He was missing a dice game. Ogma put me back down and closed the cell which locked automatically.

Ogma returned an hour later. According to my cell mate, the fat horg was ornery because he was about to get in deep trouble for letting a high profile prisoner die. Ogma opened the cell and came in to resume dragging me out.

The technique I was using also involved employment of a trigger word, which, when pronounced by someone else, conveys vibrations that dissolve the cataleptic state immediately. I had instructed the cleric to say this word at the most advantageous moment. He did so, and the horg glanced over in his direction.

At once reaching through the bars, I seized the locks of Ogma and bashed his head against the iron grid several times. He struggled yet and turned to flee, and even made it just outside the cell, but I grabbed his baldric and pulled him back in against the iron grate door from the other side, and my quick hands fastened the little twine round his corpulent neck to cut off his breathing. Ogma reeled and we both slammed against the cell door, which was about to shut and almost lock. Ogma however had fought his last.

His final act was a valiant one. He made certain I would not escape. He actually budged his weight to pull shut the cell door just a tad, all the way so that it locked.

After it was done, the massy corpse of Ogma was still standing. It did not slide back against the bars like I expected but fell forward. Now it was an impossibility to reach the key in his pocket by reaching through the bars. I tried to pull his massy legs toward me through the narrows, but they were just too substantial. I struggled even more with force but to no avail. He weighed a ton and stunk, being so fat a horg, and I was weak from my long imprisonment. Soon a master-guard would come to check on him.

"My friend, we are doomed. I cannot reach the horg's waist and key chain."

"Keep trying; there must be a way."

"Prepare for your death. Once they notice the fat watcher is missing, they will come through that door and in rage lop off our heads."

"I do not think so," said the cleric. "Instead, torture gives these hog-men a rather high entertainment. The only reason that we have not been so far tortured is because of the Northing's order, lest we be injured and unable to write out the lore he wants translated. When the horgrim see what you have done, however, their rage at a companion's death will undoubtedly cause them to forget orders, since they are secretly loyal to Mulg, not Northing. Prepare for a slow mutilation and agonizing death."

"Now we are surely to pay for our misdeeds," I said with sadness.

"Do not fear," said my cleric-companion. "It is not punishment...to die in martial service to the Most High is an unparalleled honour, just shy of martyrdom."

"There is one hazardous chance," I said. "When Ogma's corpse begins its rapid decay, on account of extreme wickedness, it will cause a grand reek. The dungeon rats will come furiously to finish him off. In fact, the vile odor has already commenced. In a moment you will see two grey rat-heads appear through the crevice in yonder crumbling bricks. These are smallish, no taller than your waist, being Shil-humanoid creatures, with torso and limbs somewhat similar in shape to a human, but covered in fur, and sporting claws, as well as the unmistakable rodent head and eyes. These rat-heads had come by before, last month, or was it last year? Whenever it was, it was when I was enduring that reeking infection. I had to beat them back with a sharpened spoon. I call them Grexor and Shilog. The main problem for us, however, is their undue loyalty to Nimrul."

Moments passed, then hours. We had resigned to complete failure and for tortures to begin after the evening guards made their rounds and discovered Ogma's reeking corpse. Suddenly there was a shuffling sound in the twilight shadows. I looked over at the corpse and saw Grexor and Shilog maneuvering about the armour of Ogma, seeking a place to begin nibbling.

I started by kindly greeting them and reminding them how long it had been since our last "misunderstanding. " I politely asked them were they not eager to find some fine dining tonight? How it was provided by an old rival, but just for them, in hopes of some company tonight, and an offer of truce, if they were willing.

They responded by demanding answers. What exactly do I, a human, want? Could there be anything at all I could possibly supply them? Why would I disturb them with my cowardly speech, or with the lies of men? I must let them alone to sup in peace, they warned strenuously, or they would come for me in my sleep, like the last time.

I informed them that I had a favor to ask of them. If they would hear it, it might grant them some relief in their squandry lifestyle.

Grexor asserted that they themselves lived well, and certainly did not aid prisoners. Shilog affirmed his words as right warning, and added that they were ratmen loyal to their Master, Nimrul.

Shilog added by insinuating wrong doing on my part and murder of the guard, and warned that I must want the dead guard's key, and in that I would have no chance.

I reminded them that were they to aid me, they would fetch great rewards, beyond what a rat could ever dream.

There was a silence. The rats returned to their nibbling. They were assaying to nibble apart the leather ties on Ogma's armour and loosen it.

I again tried them with a remark. To miss out on this deal, I said, would be a considerable tragedy. Grexor, who had more patience than Shilog, responded that it were impossible for any rodent not to be curious. What could a human possibly offer their kind? An offer must nevertheless be entertained, on account of animal curiosity that must be satisfied. He was certain, however, the attempt would be vain, so it did not warrant getting my hopes up; it would be strictly rejected.

I told them that they would become higher creatures, and that their names would be included in the epic account of a monk's journeys, to be remembered for all ages. Although they would die as any other creature in the end, their names would be immortal.

They paused a moment in reflection on this. However vanity is not akin to their nature, they responded negatively. They cited the fact that it were Man's fault in the first place that they must die, for they had heard of something called "death" before, and had noticed other rats stop moving, and concluded that must be death. They had never applied the possibility of dying to themselves, however; but now that I had mentioned it, it made sense. Still, it was the fault of the human race, as even they had heard the lore concerning the Archsin, how the children of the Creator had disobeyed and brought death to themselves and all creation, which includes rodents. They now resented me in particular, for teaching them that they also must die.

Immediately I apologized for this oversight, but then reminded them that death is an ending which might not be so bad. What is there so wonderful in this life anyway? They themselves must spend their days searching for half-dead creatures to eat, living in dark and cold places, et cetera. Men sometimes live worse lives, but imagine that its luxury.

They responded that this was what they preferred, and in fact enjoyed, that they were satisfied being higher rodents and would be loath to anything else. However, it is the human fault that their glorious life of rodent-hood must be made extinct.

I considered their point valid, with certain conditions. So I communicated this. The first was that no matter how pleasant a certain type of living may seem, even though it may last a long time, that eventually one longs for something else, something new, especially animals who are curious, and who cannot restrain their natural curiosity. Eventually they would grow weary of eating remains left behind by guards or gnawing on the corpses of forgotten prisoners. To see the greater world would surely be an amazing experience. To become something higher than one already has been, even though it might not be part of the animal desire, would be nevertheless a fantastic thing.

Shilog responded that it were an unusual proposition. He had never considered that it could be possible to become something higher. Grexor, however, disagreed, and asserted to him that were the monk capable of making an animal into something high and noble, by means of some strange power, that the monk himself would have had his own power to escape his imprisonment. Let him free himself if he was powerful enough; then he would trust him. Shilog angrily rebuked his companion, saying that although it were not rat-destiny to become higher, that he should not keep another rat from trying such a thing.

They were nearly distraught over the perplexity that I had proposed, so I went ahead and offered the final bait. Were they to bring me the key, I would overthrow Nimrul and rule from his throne. The rat-men would be greatly rewarded with moldy cheeses and rotted meats, and be appointed to high positions in the prison bureaucracy. However, were they to refuse, and I managed to escape anyway, and overthrow Nimrul, (which was, after all, the purpose of my being here), then it would be likely that the rat-men and others like them would be exiled from the great prison-fortress Baffay. Without supplies, they would have to trek across the great glaciate wastes of Bardelith and probably become dinner for some hungry Rhord-Hawk or Snow Leopard.

This caused them great trepidation. They returned to the crevice entrance and consulted with one another for some considerable moments in shadow. Finally Grexor returned, lowering his head with Shilog standing in front. Shilog spoke, announcing that they yielded to my offer, provided that were I to fail my assault on Nimrul's dominion and still escape from the Arc du Baffay somehow, that I would indeed record them in the account of my monk's journeys, as promised.

So it was done. I unlocked my cell and the adjacent cell of the deep-minded cleric. The rat-heads disappeared into the crevice. We took Ogma's armour and iron helm, the cleric helping fasten these on himself, at least whatever fit.

vil injury unto a foe already defeated, and execution without trial, even if they seem quite guilty and terrible, (terrible like Nergalfin the Butcher in days of old), might seem just as well to some folk. To a monk of God it is repugnant. Perhaps that is why the snag of temptation was whispered to me in privy. And how profound a temptation! This flash suddenly came to me: why not simply abandon this wretched war? Why not forsake obsessive resolve and hurry away from dangers? Northing had not personally harmed me. Certainly going up against him "in the name of God' is no guarantee of success, nor does it give any certitude that I am doing right. It could mean my doom, and if I fail he will exact retribution on others. Or I might survive, but end up maimed, enslaved, or mentally damaged. Or what if he somehow took advantage of my natural weakness and tempted me to into a state of sin? ...something that his master the Devil has done with success against so many. Why not hurry away from this crucifixion and seek peace in some other realm, take a wife, live at ease with a family, working the land, and end my days surrounded by loved ones? This was the moment to act for such a win. I spent many minutes paralyzed by this thought. I was so close. Anger seared my nerves, anger at the seeming fruitlessness of my struggles and the quiet stillness, or seeming disregard, of an omnipotent deity who has left me the choice to continue, left it all up to me. So then, the door is open. I am free of this.

But hold···I am a monk, the kind who knows nothing of working the land···and also there is this: I had run away once before from God's invitation. Should I not here and now make up for it? Should I not prove myself a soldier of God? The corrupt monks back in Whitehaven, the King of love still entreats them: *return! Though your sins be scarlet I shall make them white as snow.* Surely if there is any king for whom a knight should be willing to die, it should be this one. Is not the greater sorrow to desert the honoured ranks of the Lord of Hosts? "*There will be shouts of joy and victory in the tents of the just.*" ...those who do not fight in the battle do not retire to the tents of the just, the victory celebration in the martial camp, the day of His final triumph.

In haste made we our way through the terraced stone paths and circular stairs that spiral upward to the main palace high above.

The cleric looped a rope around my neck and my hands, with Ogma's halberd carried in his other hand. The stupid and unobservant horgoth guards who passed by didn't bother us. They merely assumed that he was another horgoth guard hauling the prisoner up to Nimrul for interrogations...or a sacrifice.

After many a dolorous hallway and passage and some perplexing labyrinthine stairs, we were nearing the Hall of Melancholy, with its colossal architecture. On the cavernous way there we encountered an enchanted power, what seemed a winged demon.

He was patrolling the narrow way which drops straightway into deepest chasms on either side. We shook with fear. Unnoticed, we slipped into the shadows. The deep-minded cleric waited and observed it. He reckoned this no demon of any type, at least not found in any known demonology or in Guy of Xaragia. The entity carried a glowing magical brand, and no demon would weild such a weapon. Yet we could not guess what sort of unholy denizen it should be, one which sported the infernal shape outwardly of a demon yet molded in the solidity of terrestrial substance, for it did cast a shadow upon the wall. I looked at my priest-companion, puzzled.

"Is it a nephilid?"

"No, not that, but you are also right to suspect that neither is it a demon," he explained. "yet this is an enchanted power, though with nar malice as a demon. He is a gargoyle. No longer a cathedral warden he, but one that is turned. This is one who has become melancholy, and serves the fiendish lord of the hall.

"No banishment or exorcism will rid us of this menace, for unlike a pure spirit, he is corporeal and will have at you with force of arms. Come now, take you this rope, 'tis blessed, and be prepared to rush him when he is at unawares, when his rear is unguarded."

"Do you not reckon the size of that monster?" I asked, astounded.

"I do reckon. Have you another plan? You cannot slip past him; he is a super-guardian. Therefore, pray, I shall distract him with the posing of questions. Slip through the shadows, and be concealed when he comes about; and sneaking from behind tackle his legs. He shall stumble, and we shall bind him all of a sudden. Stay yourself back, however, if the parley goes well and he seems to be persuaded, thusly we shall avoid any hazard. If he becomes wroth and will move to arrest me, right away lunge and unbalance him. If we fail in that, we shall have to fight laboriously and take wounds, even expire under that magical blade."

So did we act, and the conversation with the gargoyle went thus...

"Hail, grim swordsman, vassal of Nimrul, destroyer of souls. By what guild and name go ye?"

"Who has come? And what mortal durst address Noroch? You, human, are somehow 'scaped from your soul-imprisonment? Now you shall learn the pain that accompanies defiance."

"Stay, great gargoyle, warden of this forsaken realm, assail me not. I am not one 'scaped from these prisons. Rather have I been "graciously" invited by the lord of the very hall of which you are sentinel. I have with him some high business, regarding high matters. Were you to cast me back into that dungeon, he would miss me and soon not be pleased."

"Your tongue lies, human. Stay where you are and do not think to flee, lest on furious wing I snatch you up with my claw-feet and tear apart your delicate skin."

"Hear me out, gargoyle. Keep a distance, if any fear be left in you for a priest-anointed of the Most High. Know that I shall hurl such a divine spell upon you that His light will burn you to cinders. All I need do is speak a few dread words. You know it to be true, apostate."

"Again you lie. You contrive a character in vain hopes to throw me into doubt. And you dare title me apostate?! You will need to explain that as well. Nor are you a long-robed priest, not in those rags."

"Long I have traversed the worlds, in both time and space, across many lands. The traversing of time faded my vestments. Yet they be no less a powerful conduit. Are you good to hazard some chance, gargoyle? Surely the wanderer is rare who would boast to be priest. But if I am, then you are in a danger greater than you could have imagined."

"You traveled in time? That is impossible; physic teaches that time cannot be traversed. You speak in lying riddles. . . Silence! What was that noise? I heard a movement. You are not alone, human. Tell where your assassin hides. If you are really a priest, you may not lie."

"You seem to already have the answer. Rather tell me, gargoyle, why have you abandoned your post on the roof of a church of God in order to serve Darkness here instead?"

"You dare interrogate? I did not abandon it. Indeed, it were the people themselves who drew me down with ropes and grapnels flung up high."

"The flock of Him pulled you down from your high perch?"

"If yet be they worthy to be counted the flock of the one you mean. They tore down His church, announcing the architecture to be outdated. So deceived were they. There I lay, my head broken, wings shattered; asunder among the toppled ruins. They who did it were among the harvest of God, encouraged by those tares who, unlike wholesome wheat, seem just the same but are rarely seen in church! So it is written, *the one who ate my bread has lifted his heel against me*. My guardianship became useless to them. I was to be thrown out into the river. When next moonlight came, I gathered myself and, in tears, flew away. I traveled far and wide seeking a church that might value my guardianship, one which would stand for the timeless centuries. However, I found nothing suitable...for all of them were patrolled by thick packs of aeroline demons!

Nevertheless, the spiritual reality remains the same: God does not change, nor does the diabolus rest from soliciting men doomed to die.

Many vainly imagine that God somehow will guard all things himself, unrequested, and worshipped only as an afterthought, as if he were some hired hand. What folly! It is we who must serve! News comes now that belief in demons has waned to such an extent that only children's fables mention them?

The clergy has seen fit to disarm, vainly declaring themselves at the service of Man, while strong teaching and service of Heaven they virtually forget. They say "we are building the Church of Christ," and they comprehend it not; for He has already built her and men are the stones: *Tu es Petrus*!

So without steady guildswork, circumstances constrained me to look elsewhere. I spotted this Hall of Melancholy from aloft, which in appearance stood as a grand cathedral. I asked the grim lord ruling here if I might have work. He consented, but warned me not to talk church-talk, unless it be to treat of theological matters, and then, only with him. I have had a few conversations with him, and he has dispelled my mind of many things, of certain scruples burdensome; and now I no longer worry. His reputation is great indeed throughout all Whitehawk, as a spirit wise and generous, destroying no kingdom without just cause; and his vassals are given due freedoms, from the least to the greatest. As a gift he bestowed upon me this magical sword. Therefore submit and tell if you are alone, or else..."

"You have an appreciation for theological discourse, gargoyle. I am impressed...this is from years of your having overheard sermons in the church below, no?"

"It is as you say."

"Therefore learn this: your new master wishes my presence in order to discuss a weighty point of contention, namely, the question of whether the world itself be eternal or nay. The key to this conundrum is written in a tome, *The Black Book of Melancholia*, the translation of which I am about to deliver to him. Stand down then and let me pass, or else, enraged by such an interference, your master will not only relieve you of your duty, but he will see you dismembered and will heave your "lithomorphic flesh" into boiling lava pits. Between him and me you should not stand, or so doing there will be both Heaven and Hell to pay."

At this, Noroch grew indignant and snorted. Then, to our amazement, he actually let down his great sword. "Very well then, do I have any profound loyalty to my new master? I admire his independence. However, if you mention this to him, I will find you and reprise myself on you. Your companion may now come out from hiding, since he could not have prevailed in strength against me anyway, even advancing from behind. I will go and announce you. Be warned: if your tongue has lied, it means you are no priest, and at once you shall learn the destructive power of this magical sword. Follow me."

So we went and followed the incredible monster treading over a maze of ridges and sheer paths. What would become of us?

At one point we came to a merciless chasm which no bridge spanned. There he invited us to climb onto his colossal back, and in trepidation we obeyed. Alighting on wing, he sprung upwards and flew through vast interior regions of cavernous space. Downwards he turned his featherless wings.

Terrified, and holding on to the dorsal fins, holding on for dear life, we plummeted into the sightless chasm, a headlong dive, as falling. It seemed that I had consented to my last foolish adventure. It was to be an unavoidable fact, death; our frail frames broken on some jagged rocks below, when at once upturning he glided ascendent. Upward flying it was as if to storm heaven itself. Upon landing in some dim, mountainous innards, Noroch bade us dismount off his back, and we thankfully set our feet on solid earth and kissed the ground giving thanks to God.

A little farther and we at last reached the enormous bronze doors of the Hall of Melancholy. They were quite a stupendous work of babery, of indescribable and splendid gloom, gracing an architecture of many ornate spires and elevating buttresses of colossal scale.

Gargoyals do not hesitate for any fear. The creature banged on the thick door with his petrimorphic fist. The massive portal screeched open.

...yea though I walk in the shadow of the valley of death...

A pale butler stood gazing. This is a man. Aye, this face is familiar, someone whom I know. I look again, closely.

Oh Lord, it is Arizel!--become butler of the Balecrown! I keep hush, but spry, craving to assail the knavish magic-user furiously for betrayal. I clenched my fist. The gargoyle spake:

"These two are come to attend court before his Supreme Archonate. Living humans they seem, who claim to have traveled time and space. Inform the master at once and learn if it be so expected."

Immediately Arizel turned round and went off. He did not greet me. Then, alas, I could observe that, although he had looked right at me, his glassy eyes were not moving as they usually did. Evidently he did not have usage of his volitionary faculty, his own will. He was there, conscious, but was become an automata-slave of Northing; as it were like the *Shedim*, the walking dead. I thought at the time that perhaps I was witnessing the punishment for wizardry. For not only in this life is one already condemned for such a practice, but life eternal also will be forfeit. But I did not lose hope for him.

All he could do was serve the baleful lord without complaint, his soul immured. Some spell more powerful had overcome the iron will of a powerful magus.

Arizel announced to the Dire who was seated on a sapphire throne at the other end of the Hall. He informed him that there was an important prisoner ready to give cooperation.

The magus returned and escorted us down the hall to where the unholy Archdruid was sitting at court, with all his subject lords and retainers from many lands, his knights and his vast array of thralls. The sapphire throne of the world was aglow, its mysterious blue radiance. What a sight it was, having been affixed there from earliest times, unmovable. The Hall of Melancholy and entire Arc du Baffay had been built around it. The throne was decorated with elaborate engravings in the lower seat all around depicting seven days of God's generous hands making heaven and the earth. On the throne's high back was depicted the Day of Judgement, with goats falling into Hell's Jaws on the left, and sheep being escorted to the heavenly paradise on the right.

And there sat the Dire, dwarfed by the throne, as if he were a child sitting in his father's chair, or a thief on a giant's seat. But the appearance of the tyrant was nevertheless astonishing; with long strands of grey hair and a noble brow, yet fell like a demon head, the bulge of fangs beneath lips wrinkly; a cold glint in his fairy eyes.

Not many humans could see the ugliness about him, for being blinded by their own passions, they saw him only as a noble, as a kindly old elf-king, a wise and beneficent druid; with a bit of necrosis ridden through the skin, but splendid on account not only of his glorious and regal raiment, and also because of his stature and noble bearing, giant for an elf.

Being a monk, however, I perceived with spiritual eye. I saw how two thousand years of bitterness lit up his gaze. I perceived as Maragald the hermit had once taught me. I saw his spirit; I saw him for what he was, just as King Argoth once did. Pallid and wrinkled flesh hung from a jaw filled with fangs. Forthwith he dismissed his court upon our entrance.

"I have been expecting this one, a monk," said the overlord, his fangs grinning with perverse glee. "You probably imagined a ghostly lich," he said, "unmindful and without reasoning power, having nothing of manners. Certainly in the accounts heard from the stories about Argoth, my ancient jailor, you would draw such a conclusion. Let us remove to the dining room, and have you refreshed with food and drink after your long journ."

So we followed them into a great dining hall adjacent, and food and drink of high quality they provided. Roasts and breads, with roots and even many fruits, which they must have magically imported from tropical climates.

The creature dined only a moment and watched me. Only a tittle of bread I took. After we had put away our hunger, he addressed me.

"Now you can quite clearly see otherwise from your surroundings, my dear guest, that I am a mind, a professor of theologies and the arts. I enjoy good dining and various refinements. Please, be at ease here, you and your companion...there at the other end. Horok, supply them flagons...."

Horok, a lowly and drooling bolgoth slave, too frail to be a prison guard or warrior, brought forward the gleaming wine. A glorious banquet was spread before us.

"My taste may not be just as yours," Nimrul continued. The slave poured the pale wine into a handsome golden goblet for me. The trickling sound seemed to propose something. "They have prepared a roast for you, and you may leave yourself well sated on all these good things. We have partaken only the first course. I can guess that someone like you should like some fine delicacies which empire yields, as it seems you must have had enough of monk's soup and also of the dungeon's beans and porridge...be there so many things to see in the world which a monastery closes off from poor monks...as you can see about you, all these fine works of art, melancholy to you though they be in subject matter, are nevertheless finely worked indeed."

"Generous host," I said, "I understand your concern, but let it be known that life as a monk I have freely chosen. Its sparcity and wants have served well my sacred endeavor. It smacks more a proper monk-home, your dungeon! "

"What a clever thing to say," he countered, "but come now, the dungeon's monotony and lack of natural beauty; I cannot believe you. But you must learn soon now how great a mind I am, not easily fooled. You see, although melancholy, beautiful things I do appreciate. You have long been in the dungeon. Now you have my favor.

"Dine without restraint on this sumptuous fare which my cooks have prepared. I will not discuss important questions and high matters without the comfort of a good roast; we are not barbarians. Nor am I the kind who treats his opponents unfairly, but rather I require some tasty distraction as part of a good contest."

The creature did not move, but in his chair was still. He grinned mildly with unseemly fangs, but somehow charmingly. I however was not gazing at him, but at the peppered meats, cooked roots, raspberries and cranberry, various nuts and spices, and many other sweet delights spread out before us. I was salivating, and already had a chunk of roast on my fork.

But, unfortunately for my stomach, I remembered something I had once learned just in time, (thanks to an angel's whisper). My thoughts turned to the Grey Knight; the illusions he had warned me against: *glorious banquets, gold crizets, fair maidens*. Fair maidens, well, that was the struggle for seculars, like my friend the chivalric priest, secular cleric; who was fasting to vanquish the tyranny of lust. But now there was temptation for me, a monk. There was readied and set before me a glorious banquet to ease the trouble of long dungeon-hunger. I had lived off of beans, cabbage, and "mystery meat" for many months, or was it years? But if I gave into this hunger, perhaps taste some virulent berry or oneiric shroom, I would become a mindless thrall like Arizel.

Nimrul would not accept my breech of courtesy however. What excuse could I say to refuse the banquet? Something that would not rouse him to send me back in the dungeon. I gently set down fork and meat.

So I said, "How kind a gesture, this regal fare. But —I suppose that you will think me deranged —you see I must keep my discipline. We monks do not eat meat on Fridays, in remembrance of the Passion.

"I would have enjoyed that roast and gravy, but I must decline your banquet in favor of what is higher. Such a feast would dim my orisons and dull my song."

"Do my ears deceive me? " he said, agape. "What mindless beast bore you? And a dullard you are, mortal man, to decline my hospitality for a base superstition. There is no higher cause, only higher thoughts. You are nothing but a skinny fool." The creature frowned and grunted, "hmmmf."

There was no wish to destroy my body, but rather my soul. A great calm therefore did I yield to, because I accepted that there was no other possibility than this confrontation. I veiled my mind, a power which I had long perfected in monk training. I spoke again.

"My...! What a thing to say. Now I ask, are we no longer to speak politely? If not, my gosh, then I cannot not bare it! Do nothing in this moment you would regret. Think of your position: even this day your liberty will be required of you. It is true that I am a lowly monk of The Most High. You, however, are a monarch, with glory and splendor arrayed, Great Nimrul, celebrated spirit of the North.

"The Church is not taken in by your show. Recall what is writ in sacred scripture of the Lord of Hosts: *Kings in their splendor he slew, for his love endures forever.* That means God himself slew kings, out of love for his own. So might he choose to employ a lowly monk as his instrument; to politely end you in a similar way. Therefore I first offer you a way out: cease from all aggression. Recall your armies from the kingdom of the Aels, renounce your claim to the Thulean crown, and restore the throne of the Aels to the rightful successor. So wisely do you now yield and then we shall negotiate terms and future restraints."

Nimrul smiled and shook his head in disbelief.

"What an introduction. Bravo! But do you think I shall yield without a delightful contest, and to my own prisoner? I see that you have long considered what you might say to me, but now that you see me you are surprised, and barely able to speak without nervous voice."

"I weigh that as shrewdly calculated to make me self-conscious and so disable me." I countered. "It is true what you say; I have been imagining you otherwise. Although your visage is horrible with the wrinkles of a thousand years, it nevertheless retains a sort of nobility from your elven race, and the glint of understanding is in your eyes, all too human, yet still Luciferian, which causes me conundrum. I am far less likely to vanquish such a person by means of dreadful combat, as I would in the case of the villain whose villainy is immediately discernible. But you have wine poured for us and, welcoming us, give us food, even though we are your prisoners...and you must not really mean it, exchanging such hard words. The things you look after now, of treating us well, therefore warrant greater indignation. Although you constrain us as prisoners, eventhough we are innocent, that gains you little purpose for justice. Think over what you are doing. But now you wish to restore our dignity, only to strip it away for entertainment? Our dignity does not originate from you however. Kill me straightway if you please, or in a duel if you wish, that is the honourable thing to which a gentleman would consent."

"When I heard that you were coming, many moons ago, I was glad indeed." He admitted. "At last, a worthy opponent to challenge me. Were you undignified and unworthy, what use would it be for my reputation and glory to subdue you? My powerful magic is powerless against you. You knew that the prayer of the Church wins Ammouric monk or priest, nay any holy soul, be they true and pure, immunity from every magic, and that is what lured you here. You thought you could win against me by your word. How I will congratulate myself, my prowess and mind, for so vanquishing His champion by my words alone! No one ever again will report that the throne was stolen, or not rightly won.

"I do not need to rely on magic. I could have you executed in the morning by rightful authority." He said, dismissively. "The law of this dominion Nzul warrants death for those who enter without permission. Why, as monarch, and as archdruid, I may kill you now with my own hands." He reclined back in the throne, as one pondering. "What you stand for however, that I cannot kill...unless, of course, I can first break your spirit... to break a man's spirit is high dominion. I did accomplish that once; a certain pathetic man, you know. How gratifying a thing that was to observe!

"But come; how rough to treat on such things in noble company. Yours is a reasonable suspicion. Partake whatever you like. . . you may relax for a while from your imprisonment, I will harm not. Insults will be of no use to you; instead, you should graciously accept this reprieve, as would a true Christian.

"Don't you see? I only wish to persuade you to reason, and even friendship. Were you to yield, and subsequently win over the Ammouric Church for me, your reward would be great indeed. No, not riches. . .I know a monk has little interest in riches. I have something else in mind; ancient texts do I possess —from Nystol! Tomes which tell of things ancient and marvelous, but I alone have access to these precious tracts, which were rescued from the flames!

"Know that if you render me obesiance, not only will you win back your life, but have guildswork as a scribe and delight in the texts freely. You would write your own texts, and you would always dine well, be able to come and go as you please, and to have entire armies at your command. You could publish an epic account of your journey. Perhaps, after years of service, I would let you "escape" to a sunny realm. You would become an Archscribe somewhere, Gandolon perhaps, or a lecturer in some university, possessing the unassailable credentials of having studied under the illustrious Professor Cornelius Naza." (He embraced himself with a hug as he said that!) "Therefore, now you have my offer. I can do no better." A black fluster of hue flashed though his suddenly angry eyes. "You must, however, translate *The Black Books*."

"Why is it that you crave this, vampire?" I asked squarely. "You should know that I make no company with a spirit of *Melancholia*."

"It seems your period of imprisonment has not even taught you to compensate a kind gesture and refuse politely. You even are veiling your true thoughts from my gaze. Tell me, did your Abbot really order you come all the way out here to contest against my superior mind? I think perhaps he did not intend this. However, I am tiring of the wait. You realize, of course, that I was waiting all that time for you to escape, to escape into my hands that is.

"Despondency is a helpful persuasive when trying to break the will of mortals. With you, not even that ploy has worked. Nevertheless, I now require your skill. So I yield to you more tidings to sorrow over, monk. Does it warrant such cruelty? Your sacred home is in great disarray. Besides the monastery in The Dry Blood Dunes, your home of Whitehaven is the only Ammouric confine of any significance left in the furthreach. It is the center of the Ammouric rite, the seat of the Eldane of all Whitehawk: the Godmouth. Therefore, be not surprised that infernal monks have completely infiltrated your sacred halls. Shahi Nuzzib, cleric of the demigod Abraxas, found that he no longer had any source for magics. Recently some overbold raiders somehow smote down that feared gorgon. So he and his infernal monks have sworn allegiance to me.

"Now they report that one Ulcrist Dretch, our associate, has been installed as new Abbot in your Whitehaven, monastery-upon-the foaming shores. Him all your brother monks will obey either out of fear or hope. Your Abbot was "encouraged" to retire, or has been dispatched...which, I know not.

"But now my minion controls your monastery and soon will retrain the unsuspecting monks in certain secret doctrines, glorious, what you call 'gnostic heresy'. My epic work *"Hearers of the Dead"* is famous. These things will be published throughout all the universities and schools of the continent. Then the long awaited Inversus will appear for race of men. Of course I shall require his fealty as well."

"What news you pass regarding the monastery cannot be," I cried. In my mind flashed the visage of Maragald and his prophecies. "...There can only be one Abbot of Whitehaven at a time. There can be no other Godmouth. It is the rule of our order, and of the Church. The Abbot of Whitehaven, he alone is Godmouth. He is Primate of Aldemarz, who is Eldane for all kings. There can be no retirement of an Abbot as in other abbeys. Our monks would never yield to that, nor would any son of the Church."

"They have gladly accepted it," Nimrul continued. "Your Abbot was not popular with the people of the Whitehawk continent. My man, Abbot Ulcrist, gives them new hope. Hope to live a life of ease and pleasure, without guilt, without useless penances. Soon many books of sublime new teachings will be published throughout all the feudatories and kingdoms, and your fellow here, Arizel, as you can see, will be helpless to stop it."

I looked over at mindless Arizel, standing there in the shadows. All his craving for secret knowledge, it was all now in vain, his mind having become an empty waste. His plan of examing the private stacks of Professor Naza, learning more on Nystol and somehow deciphering his own dreams, it had all been a mere folly.

"Arizel may be helpless to stop it," the priest warned, suddenly interjecting. "But I shall not. I shall order the Holy Inquisition upon that impostor, and an interdict upon Whitehaven."

"How will an obscure priest of your ilk achieve such a thing?"

"Whoever warranted I was obscure? The Friars? I am a cathedral priest; I am the Prime Interquist."

"What?" I exclaimed. "You...the Prime Interquist??? How can that be possible?"

My friend responded. "Why do you think all Whitehawk is in such awful shape? It is because, constrained here, I have not been free to acheive my mission. Instead, the nasty goblins happily locked me up for years. Alien doctrines are rampant everywhere, and wholesome dogmas forgotten. Alas, what condition the churches are in now! You heard the gargoyle; even the old paganism is coming back...human sacrifices and all that."

"You seem to me far too mild to be the Prime Interquist," I remarked. The priest then responded with the following account:

" 'Tis true...but the Church chose me; I didn't seek the position. When it comes to such delicate matters, where sin sickens the hearts of men and keeps them from doing what's right, there is a plan. Or wherever alien doctrines thwart reason and shroud minds so that men cannot tell what is good, the Church thinks it most prudent that someone be charged with making judgements. She says let him be sympathetic, an ex-sinner himself. He should have some familiarity with a fallen life, with abandonment to desire, with folly, and self-pity, even a soul who entertained a much more terrible sin: heresy. Such a man, who is older and long humiliated by sin and human folly, he tends not to condemn too hastily. You see, we do not just identify a heretic and convict him. Do you think it would give me joy to see some poor soul burn at the stake?

"No, we wish to find the alien doctrine and extract, applying some healing balm, remedy of truth ever-abiding. We inquisitors are more physicians who are seeking to cure a malady or a cancer that has taken hold, not of the body, but of the soul. A physician's hand must be gentle, but firm and steady...so, too, the questions of an inquisitor. To hand someone over to the king as an obstinate heretic for imprisonment or execution ...that means we have failed in our work, and we shall answer to one far greater than any king.

"Do not therefore heed the many knavish sayings regarding us, that we are cruel Pharisees demanding every conformity, seeking to ensnare poor ignorants, or creative and fanciful souls...I will tell you this...that gentle way is how it should be...but the Red Ascetics had gained great influence in the churches, even while I was working. All got so wracked that war ensued, The Wars of The Heresies. Some heretics will not be persuaded, and will not even enter into rational discussion. Instead of being the "kind and merciful authority" with whom one is invited to chat when one starts getting some odd ideas, I had to change the *modus operandi*. I had to enlist as a soldier, a mace-armed cleric. We went to war against the mischievous heretics of the feudal realm Kargiwall. They had recruited the bolgoth armies to their side. I went fully armed in all chivalric gear; "*armed to the teeth with famous bronze and life-rending steel*, " as the poet says, and gleaming mail of sturdy plate-work, a massy mace, and heavy warhorse blessed for combat, all to lead righteous men into hazardous battle. But our forces were overthrown. I myself, to my shame, escaped with my worthless life, fleeing on bewildered horse. Overcome with confusion, I rode to Ael Lot.

There I met a fair lady, fairest I had ever seen...to help me forget the sorrows of war. You know the rest of the story."

"Of her you have promised not to speak again," I reminded.

"You fool," said Nimrul. "Zalmondo Kantici... You betray *the Uncreated* and then try to flee to a woman? And to escape the sin which was ever before you, you journeyed here, as to pierce the heart of alien theology in one blow. You were supposing that your ability at logic and divine principles would supply you victory. Did you think that you could convert me with His propaganda? Instead you received just sentence, many passings of Calduin in that dungeon...nevertheless; at least you've paid for your arrogance. Now the monk likewise hopes for victory in disputation as well...in vain. Such profound folly...

"Knave monk, do you not know that I sit in endless reign? I am as the ancient spirits. I shall last as long as earth and sea and the abyss; that is, I shall not end, for they never end. You, however, shall end. Aye, for it is allotted that you mortals all die...but be not hopeful; your soul will be tortured in my prisons forever."

"Endless are you?" I asked. "Think on't, and learn that you are not. Only God is eternal. His mercy extends even to you: someday he may permit you to cease existing.

"Neophyte! I was never "born" anyway. When He says of the betrayer "it were better had he never been born…" The words apply not to me. The said, "eternity..." and "endlessness"...they are distinct things. You do realize, monk, that time is in no way comparable to eternity. Add this to your knowledge: my professoral research has yielded great fruit: It seems that in liberty primal, eons ago, I virtually wrought myself, and the divine his remote eternity allowed that I be from endlessness. Hmmm, someday it will be I who allow Him. For now He thinks it best to let me dwell here in this creation, but he hopes to torment me. I suppose that it is the way of things, or perhaps it is in the fabric of the universe, the very sympathy of elements. At any rate, I must reign over the world; for the ruler of this world has been cast out, and the Anointed One supposes that He has triumphed. But I, who am pure mind, sit in his sapphire chair and make it mine. Take up a sharp weapon then, strike at my image, or try to imprison me. You will have no success. I am here by the Uncreated himself to cloak all the earth in shadow, a punishment for the transgressions of men."

"It was not divine will that you turned wicked. Even so, Argoth the King, Arm of God, saw fit to imprison you here."

"Are you so certain? Do you imagine now that you are the arm of God? It was God who caused me to exist, a perpetual spirit, like the other *elphim*. Just as they, I also have a terrestrial composition. The High Elven monarchies* of old were all overthrown in wars. Why? because they pitied men, getting themselves involved in their entanglements. I, however, remained fixed in my fortress. I am a spirit, an archon; I cannot be destroyed. I must remain in the world. My vassal Mulcifer rewards horgs and trolls to patrol the Night, and my legions of darkly-veiled soldiers are filled with passion for their cause. On the otherhand, most of those who claim sacred authority are so painfully apathetic with it, that it has caused me great boredom these many years, and I can never sleep well at night. That there has come forward no real challenger, that itself is worse than being overcome, and it has felt as I were one half-dead—*semimortuus*."

I retorted. "Yet you are already lifeless and near extinct, as are all who rebel against the God of the living."

"What do YOU know? Your tongue dares correct me, you puny mortal? I shall teach you that you are dust… thou art forgot."

I spoke sternly. "You were not warranted the grand rest of the Elves in the halls of twilight because of your mischief. It is written: *there is no rest for the wicked, says the Lord.*"

"Be careful, monk, or I might strike you at once, rather than bide my time. You are overbold, and it would be high entertainment for me to watch you undo yourself, with my help, of course. You pretend at wisdom. Before I destruct you, I have the pleasure and obligation to humiliate you.

Demonstrate therefore to me by proofs, if then you are so wise, that I am *not* deathless; and as a reward I shall grant you and the troublesome elf-kin, and the pugnacious dwarf, freedom. If you defeat me what can stop you from taking the truth-telling Staff, the Bachal Dsu? You will go off with it. It would be an unfortunate turn for me. My possession of it keeps a threat upon my minions."

"Beguiling, charms, hypnotics, and suggestion spells only have no chance of overthrowing monks," I said. "...as Guy of Xaragia records. Hence your frustration...I require not the cedarwood Staff of Prophets," (I was bluffing). "I no longer need to convince the Prime Interquist of my innocence, for he knows my guilt and knows the truth. Nor will I return to Whitehaven of the seaward-cliffs until all things are ready, and the mysterious story of that grand babel of towers, Nystol, and its fall, is deciphered."

"Do you not see, Brother Jacob, how Nimrul is bent on the world's endarkenment?" asked the Prime Interquist. "Not only has he constrained me here, but also the staff. I am "the restrainer" St. Paul mentioned; the singular power thwarting the triumph of alien dogmas."

"Very well, suit yourself," said Nimrul, glinting. "But you will discourse with me if you want to live. There is found nothing else around here but mindless horgrim and empty-headed trolls, weird grey-elves, or yet incoherent demons. I never get to have a good lively debate founded in reason. The last time I parleyed with a human was with Argoth, and that dolt hardly said a word. So you please do your best to win for yourself freedom. If you cannot resist my argument, however, then you must do somethings for me."

"What are they?" I asked.

"Obedience. Translate *The Black Book*; find my original name."

"Why do you seek that, creature?"

"Only my name has the power I seek to give me rest. I have not slept for a thousand years, tormented with wakefulness because I cannot recall my name. Once spoken, being no longer nameless, then no longer will that curse keep me awake; I shall fall asleep, and when I awake, I shall remember all."

"You lie. I am a monk and know the real reason. You foolishly imagine that if you can cast an obscurity spell over your own name, then the angel will not be able to call you. Or else you are afraid that I have already found it, or will find it, and will give it to a priest who will use it to banish you."

"I do not deceive," said Nimrul. "That is the devil's game, and I consider lying dishonorable and beneath me, just as the devil is lodged in a place beneath me now, inverted in his freezing pit. I do not lie, and that is why The Uncreated has allowed me to keep the truth-telling Staff of Prophets here. No impure mortals might be found eligible for such a duty. Nevertheless, you would convict me of other unwholesome works which are horrendous indeed. Yet my power is not in such things. I am just an elf. You give me more credit than is due, to think that I can darken all the world. Do you know, monk, how I got this wooden leg here? "

"In some ancient mischief, I imagine."

"Ambrosius the Nephilid took it from me, that day, eons ago, that day when my army invaded His halls. So yes, I can be wounded, but not destroyed. I happen to like my other leg, so you I have no craving to match with sword or mace, lest I lose it, or some other limb...but I shall fend myself.

As you can see, I am a creature, a power who has grown nice claws and whose long locks of white hair you see. They fall gently down beside a wrinkled visage with glittering eyes, yes. But you think me a drooling undead whom some call a lich. It is not old age, no. I yet wear the crown of Bardelith, and that is the inscrutable will of The Uncreated.

Over the centuries, some have spoken of me with fear and dread, contriving stories regarding me, causing mortals to think that I am greater and more powerful than I really am. This has gone on to such an extent that they title me "Lord of Shadows " and tell every manner of fable about me, even calling me "Archdeceiver," and "the Devil Incarnate." In some ways this reputation has worked to my advantage, for since Argoth slept I have not worried over invasions. Every prince and potentate allied with me fearfully does my bidding. So great is my reputation as the Dire that were you to make claim to everyday mortals of the furthlands that you had a conversation with me, they would laugh and call you insane. Thus it is that in a real way I keep all the Whitehawk kingdoms under a spell of fear, just as Nyzium-college, arcane city of many towers, once did.

This is pleasing to me, since I have disdain for the race of men as I do for the deity; (—nay be it truly met to become afraid of if you get on his bad side).

I am a rebel; The Uncreated allows it. He allows it as recompense for the mischief of men, which, if you knew the extent, or were somehow to learn it, you would find their works deserving much worse than my punishments. I have no reason to deceive you; even now your life is completely in my hands. Why should I seek to deceive you?

So now you know: I am not so stern in arm as reputed, but I am nevertheless a formidable mental opponent. A mind-blast from me can be crippling even to a high level monk.

All your hatred against me is misdirected. Do you think that I am the author of wars and other evils? It is men themselves who are the authors. All I do is give a little encouragement by the power of my mind, by the publications of the infernal monks, and a few other minor conspiracies."

"The days of those dire monks have drawn to an end," I informed him. "Their demon Abraxas is no longer. He was smote down by a bold mortal using a simple short-sword."

"A short-sword? You heard that? I can barely believe it. It was a mortal who brought Abraxas down? I am impressed. High feat accomplished for mere men; bound to happen sooner or later. I heard also that the deed was accomplished by the treachery of one of his own disciples. But come, let us to the task at hand. I have not had a good game of Super*atio* in so long a time. You are a monk, well trained in disputation I would guess. Prove to me therefore that I am not deathless, and refrain from such poeticisms as 'you are already dead.' Do you accept?"

"It seems that you are not a liar, but I cannot be certain. It is useless to dispute with one who is dishonest," I replied.

"What mean you by that? "

"You have said that you are not a liar. However, the very premise from which any skilled liar works is that he certainly is not one, and should not even be suspected a liar. The accomplished liar will insist that he always tells the truth. Your words propose that you are not a liar, but I know of nothing in your actions that could confirm that."

"I have told you the truth regarding Argoth's capture of me, and I have admitted many things, even speaking of my power. Still you do not trust my word? Does my fame mean nothing to you? Can you not see beyond my wrinkles? Are you that shallow? Were I to say that I were a liar, how would you take that? No, I do not lie; that is all you have. It is an offense which I will not commit, since it is ignoble and unworthy. Is not the abiding presence of the Staff of Truth hanging on the wall there in my own hall enough proof for you? Enough of such talk!"

"The Staff is ours. Surrender the relic to us."

"How can you request I do that? I tell you what, if you dispute well, even though you lose, I shall offer a consolation prize. I am your master; you are my prisoner, but you are also my guest and deserve a reward for your quodlibet...

"Therefore, -a gift for you: Instead of that old wooden staff you mentioned, why do you not take up a fine brand? You have monastic ability with swords, do you not? Your own weapon, Witchbane, is lost and can never be retrieved. I know this...how that is most unfortunate. You will not escape Baffay and her armies without a sword. But Look —over there on the wall, behold, a fine edge...It is life, my friend. Do you think the Staff of Truth will fend you? All the cedarwood Staff can do is apply pressure on souls to speak truthfully, but it cannot force an issue, nor preserve you from death. Do you suppose to fight the powers of Darkness with a stick? No, you should have a professional blade. It quite behooves you. Go over there and take a look at it."

I stepped over to where a long sword was slung slanted upon the wall. It was a most elegant weapon. It was truly something to behold, a blade of power forged at time's glimmering dawn. Its silver-studded hilt and elegant pommel inlaid with gold flower were fulgid and magical; and the unfailing blade, it radiated a luster of rarest metals. Far more powerful was this sword even than the magic sword of Noroch the gargoyle. In fact, this sword radiated more powerfully even than my own sword, by far. But my own great, two-handed sword, the spirit-brand Witchbane, was lost. Without it the ever-calling quest of the Burgundy Knight was most likely forfeit. With such folly in the wide world and so many witches and wizards consecrated to the devil, what hope was there against them?

But this edge was a lordly prize. One who wielded such an unfailing sword could win back all Arraf, all the lands under the Veil, win them back to Christ. It was the most finely-finished brand which I had ever laid eyes on, wrapt in destiny. I reached out my hand to take hold of its hilt as I gazed in wonder upon its glamour.

The little bird, that angel of mine, whispered winged-words. Did not the Grey knight warn me, not only against glorious banquets, but lest I am overthrown by delight in heaping treasures, which he called "gold crizets," that is to say, any gold whatsoever, to tempt a monastic knight sworn to holy poverty? Halted my grasp I did, at that thought.

"It is a gift, monk. It is yours. One of the greatest swords, nay, *the* most illustrious blade of all Whitehawk it be. Nay, even more awesome is it known than Oceanicyng of legend. "

Oceanicyng; the brand of Duke Ikonn, it was the broad-edge which had been passed down generations to the White Knight. The Duke had won the peice when he defeated the tentacles of the terrible Zudoth. There was only one weapon reputed to match the Duke's bright blade Oceanicyng. That was another magical blade: Elmethodon, the dwarf-forged metal of Sinostox of old, a banelord who had used it to release The Beast from the bottomless pit. He spoke honestly, for I had seen an illustration of such a sword in the *Black Book*.

My fingers were just about to touch the wondrous hilt wrought of gold. Was this not that same accursed sword? *Gladius malignus*··· How could it be? I pulled my hand away, hesitating.

"*He who lives by the sword, he shall die by the sword*," I recalled the words of the Lamb. Warned he of useless violence that night in the garden, when Peter cut off the soldier's ear. "You tempt me with an ancient relic of accursedness. Is this not the very sword of Sinostox, Banelord of old?"

"So, what if it is? Look upon his beauty, his power. A warlock was once the proud owner of Your Witchbane; now lost, so what difference does that make? Would you refuse this on account of superstition? He is a fine gift I am offering you. Think of the victories that will be yours."

"Many thanks... I will happily take it along and sell it for countless gold crizets, all of which will be distributed as merciful alms for the poor."

Snapped the adversary; "No such thing will you do if you value your life! Take him for your own use. He will possess you, and you will have power. But otherwise you may not take in hand the precious gift."

"I see clearly how you offer no gift, but a scorpion, and you wish to put me under evil influence. You hope to seduce me with worldly power. Upon that blade Elmethodon, the blood of myriads cries out to Heaven high-above even to this day. If I ever need a sword, Witchbane will find me. Witchbane is not pretty and does not glow, and it is decorated with thorns, thorns of iron rather than flowers of gold. It is my brand, and it will serve me well. The Bachal Dsu, the high staff, is my purpose. You will not be able to keep it from me. Were I right wise as Argoth the Good, I would have stuffed your fangy mouth with soil of earth like he did, and skirted this conversation altogether. It was he who titled you 'the Archdeceiver,' another name for the Devil. You are not the Devil, but in spirit he is your father and Patron, so the title fits.

"I am not so silent and strong like Argoth, and you draw me with words into what I cannot hope by my own mind to win; but I am nevertheless drawn because my mind delights in such contests. You are clever indeed. Certainly you must entertain some doubt regarding your immortality, to have chosen such a subject for mental combat...

"Still, it is well known that your mind can outstrip even angels. They, however, are only miniscule of wit compared to the One Ineffable True God whose name they all continually glorify without end, and who is my Father. How will you match his wisdom in me planted? I therefore accept your challenge and will require no consolation prize. I will refute your vain philosophies and leave your mind enfeebled by confusion. You have waited long for this. And let this cleric, indebted to both of us, be the judge. He is honest to a fault."

The creature agreed. "I know him to be that way, and it is maddening. He will do, since he is oblliged by his God to always tell the truth; and he is quite competent, having no fixation on a particular argument. "

"Then met are we to fair disputation? For, as they say, "if not fair be the game, then will glory turn to shame."

"Enjoy it, for it will be your last. Hear then, mortal fool, what I propose: the earth and the sea and even the abyss are my brothers and sisters. God made them that way, to never perish. They shall abide forever, as will all the world itself, as will I myself, a demigod whose reign is never ending."

"Perhaps you believe then that you are co-eternal even with the divine?"

"I do not just believe it; I know it as something quite evident. This entire world, all space and matter, came from an underlying prime material plane which the divine mind eternally caused. Do you understand? Nothing else wrought this universal material; nothing else was before or will be after it, not even the uncreated one, although I admit God causes it from eternity, but he did not fashion it. It never had a beginning and will have no end.

"The noblest Elves are appointed in governance over the elements. I am to govern the northernmost realms of cold. According to the order of things, God would not ratify putting a perishable governor over a non-perishing subject. Legend holds that I built this fantastic palace and grand hall upon the sweat and tears of slaves. You didn't believe that did you? This palace was built by the gods of Heaven. After our revolt, when the earth became so rife with "injustice" that Allfather could no longer sojourn here, he refused to continue defending the place and abandoned it, retreating to Heaven high-above. I rightly seized this sapphire throne, which he originally must have made for me anyway, but was too jealous to let me have it. Finally he yielded to what he would no longer deny: this governance is rightly my inheritance because I am just as, nay more worthy, than he.

"My existence is unchanging, and like the melancholy angels, I am imperishable."

"Is that a fact? " I said.

"Indeed, it is a fact. As you well know, God does not retract his moves. Now you are undone even before you set out."

"Not so quick...if what you hold is true, then is not your thwarting of the race of men without worthy cause?"

"What mean you by such a question?"

"If the visible order of things is changeless, and also Man is changeless, who, like the angels, is part of the unchanging order, we should therefore conclude that Man has always existed, and never had a beginning, and the race of men continues itself according to a fixed nature, since whatever cannot be changed also cannot be destroyed. Even if we say that Mankind did have a beginning, which surely is the case, that is a point of beginning that proceeds only now from there. God prepared for us a heavenly life that never fades, so theres a possibility. You are fighting a battle which you cannot win; you cannot end what divine decree has made endless; you cannot end the race of men, for the world is just a finite mirror, a *speculum* of the heaven."

"An unusual point you make...upon which I have never gazed. However, even if what you say is no fiction, then I say that such an infinite struggle provides a kind of pleasure. For it is so, as you say, that the world is a mirror of the divine, but that mirror I may endlessly seek to warp."

There was silence.

"You spoke before of this world as arising from a prime material plane," I said.

"Aye, a substratum of matter which persists and has not come from anything else."

"Yet is there anything of which you can think that does not come from something else?"

"Only God, the uncreated, who is eternal... "

"Yes, God certainly is not from something else but rather is from himself. . . or, he just simply is. Nothing else then? " I asked.

"Nothing that I can recall, save the prime material plane which is."

"Then your prime material plane must be demonstrated; however, it is, by definition indemonstrable, since the infinite cannot be demonstrated."

"If the finite need not to be demonstrated, why the infinite? It simply is to be accepted, first as a concept, then as fact, On this point no quibble can be entertained."

"-Nor angels stand. The concept is not enough. It is not infinity itself. A fact must be established by correspondence to truth, by agreement. You would have the prime material plane come from nothing, but also be caused? No one has been able to affirm, without the aid of faith, that something can come from nothing. Therefore, can we agree that all things must naturally come from something else, excepting the divine?"

"Like the devils who never see the divine, I also have faith ...be it without any affection, so that is no enormity, " he said through his nasty fangs. "I simply have no lasting fear of the uncreated God. The proposition you propose therefore does not sound unacceptable."

"Is your faith not devoid of life? As the apostle declares, *faith without works is dead*. And in another place writes *You do the works of your father the devil*. Judas had faith, but on account of his stony heart, he had no fear of God."

"*The devils believe, and they tremble*...so true...but I am far more noble than some devil, so I do not tremble. It is cowardly to fear any power, no matter how great, no matter how awesome. Better to reign sitting enthroned in a chill wilderness than cower and crouch in the paradisiac groves of lofty Argunizial, submitting to forced 'alleluias.'"

"Certainly you have virtue, but imprudently exercised, my dear Dire of *Melancholia*. Now I ask you: you do really claim the aid of faith and say that something comes from nothing, namely, your proposed prime material plane, or your abyss?"

"I do so claim, for you are daring in speech, an impudent questioner, and that warrants punishment; but first I will teach you to obey the better logic."

"Then let me explain to you, creature, by means of agreement with a certain philosopher, John Philoponus. He says this: That if the existence of something requires something else to exist before it, then the first thing cannot come into existence without the thing before it existing. So an infinite number cannot exist, nor be counted through or traversed. Something cannot come into existence if this requires an infinite number of other things existing before it. Therefore, the world is not infinite, nor can be any prime material plane you imagine."

"You have not disputed worthily...you used the thoughts of a philosopher, not your own mind. "

"You did not stipulate any such rule. The traversal of the infinite argument is well known to the studied."

"Then let me quote the Arab, Averroes. There is a certain famous argument in his tome: *The Incoherence of the Incoherence*..."

"What? You were able to obtain a copy of Averroes in this wasteland?"

"My ministers ply far and wide, even beyond the Tethys Sea. My copy comes from Nyzium, however. It was preserved in the cliff-side caves, the basements of the tower Manihord."

"Is not your High Elven lore enough, or your thousand pound brain, to work some argument without the aid of a human philosopher? His infidel work is not acceptable for this disputation. "

"No such rule was stipulated, " he retorted happily. "To the victor go the spoils..." *spolia victori.*

Expect no monk to banish demons by his word, no matter how determined in piety. Such power is not granted the monk, but to the priest alone. However, if he is a holy man, the monk can frighten off a demon with his staff technique into the deeper caves for many years. The mere mention of the name "Master Sodd" has kept down the vampires of Setet for centuries. Be assured, all such entities are craven.

Tien Joshur
Winter Instruction for Wayfaring Monks

XXXII   MAGNUS EXORCISMUS

The disputation continued.

There is a certain immoral morality known as lawful evil, originating in the hierarchy of devils, which Guy of Xaragia describes in his famous manual. Such a pseudo-moral alignment may be found numbered even among the Ammouric faithful: those wolves that snout the laws of the Church to unfair advantage, dousing the spirit of the law in abeyance to the letter of the law. The real intention, as when they cite divine precepts, is not to please God, but to exalt themselves, and they "*do the works of their father the devil.*" It is the utmost form of moral decay.

It was clear from what had been said that such was the morality of Professor Naza.

The famous ghoul of a professor soon was escorting us into his unholy library of eldritch books, adjacent to his court. His eyes glistened with delight as he surveyed his numerous volumes. How strange and enigmatic were the many titles, and some I knew to be so rare as to only have been referenced in other books. The record affirmed them to have been long extinct, otherwise unknown. I touched and took one up and was about to open a volume which attracted my fancy for its intriguing title. Immediately the good priest stopped my hands, and slammed it shut. He snatched the volume from my fingers, and he whispered sternly:

"No! Take care; you must put it back at once. I know that title; it is a *Narcissus-text.* Keep its ensnaring pages forever closed."

"A Narcissus-text...?" I asked.

"Aye, a codex infested with a curse. Glance into its leaves, and you will end up as Narcissus did, whose doom was to starve, transfixed by a pool's reflection of himself. They will find your skeleton fingers clutching the book's spine, your flesh destroyed by its unending gaze into deep pools of vainly promised knowledge."

Our host glanced over with amusement and smiled a grizzly smile. He moved to a pile of books and pulled out a vellum bound in the hide of a wooly mammoth. He opened it, and reading aloud, delicately quoted Averroes to prove his point.

It seemed that no victory, however, could be declared, since no argument seemed compelling enough to the cleric-arbitrator, who certainly would have ruled in favor of Northing if he had to, on account of his seeming fearsome honesty. Instead, he declared a draw.

We returned to the court. Northing at once claimed he was experiencing boredom, and he called for hand to hand combat between the cleric and myself, for his entertainment. The fight was a fake, and Northing descended from his throne to inspect us closely.

"What is this game that you play? You should wish to please me by an entertaining dispute, by word or hands. What is it you hold there under your cloak, boy? Remember —if your lips utter a lie, never handle the staff."

"It is first and foremost forbidden by God to lie. It is for that reason alone that I will not lie; or I just simply will not answer you."

"Do not your sacred texts require that you obey a master? If I remember correctly, your hallowed laws do oblige."

"Very well, truth can bring an Archdeceiver nothing but woe. Know that I am holding Arizel's globe. "

"And what is that? ...a magical item? What powers does it have?"

"It has strange powers indeed. It can transform into any spherical object of nearly similar size."

"Tell me the truth...even I do not have such magic."

"I tell you the truth: The wizard men call Bannock, even you have heard of him, fashioned it from the eye of the gorgon, Abraxas. You know Arizel, he is famous, and some say that he helped bring about the fall of Nystol."

". . . true what you say; that mortal is renowned, by some mystery his earthspan seems extended. How is it that you came into possession of his crystal ball?"

"He gave it to me for safe keeping before your horgrim captured me. He showed how to make it the size of a mustard seed, so I may keep it in my pocket. So here it is; I kept it. Of Arizel, however, I know that he is happy."

"You have even seen him lurking in these halls," remarked Northing with sinister glint of eye. "Still seeking to fulfill his ever-calling quest, the quest I gave him: to recover the right volume of *The Black Books* from that band of dwarves and valraphs. He did keep it from the Arcane Circle, my rivals, who think that it will help Nystol to rise again. However, he failed to do what you have done for me: to keep it from the monks of Abraxas, who would have charged too high a price for its sale. You, Jacob Magister, have been an even greater help; you found the needed entry in its over a thousand pages. Therefore, by your own hand you are at a disadvantage. Right, well...let me tell you what. Surrender up that *globus* to me, and you may have the Staff in exchange, promising not to use it against me of course...that is a fair offer."

"I cannot give you what is not mine."

"Then I shall seize it!"

The Northing thrust his arm and extended his claw-hand in one motion, and at once an invisible force wrested from out my weary hands the crystal ball, which went speedily through the gap between us and came to the hands of the unsightly creature seated on a sapphire throne.

"My powers are not to be taken lightly, Jacob. This crystal ball has great magic...now mine, a wondrous relic long spoken about in the histories. You should have yielded to my kind offer. You would have the Staff in your hands now, had you done so. You have nothing instead. I, however, possess this sphere. Still, you hold back and are wary, and slow to employ a violent hand against me, but not out of fear...why? "

"I am an Ammouric monk. Our way is not a violent way, unless kindness or charity would call for it; and such an exception is rare, when charity would use force."

"Sometimes exceptions need to be made," he remarked, tempting me.

"The crystal sphere which you hold is a grand relic of Nyzium," said a familiar voice suddenly. "It must be returned to its owner, Arizel."

I turned to look and saw no figure, only the shell of the man who used to be Arizel. The voice had come not from that shell, but from the crystal ball which Northing was holding, and it was Arizel's voice! It was as if the wizard returned from the zombie state to confront him. The voice was coming from the crystal ball!

"This sphere has many powers," replied Northing, gazing into the crystalline mystery. "Where are you now Arizel?"

The voice seemed to reply, "I do not say where I am, nor when this warding was set. I only warn you: beware the great powers of this magic sphere. By mental command it may morph into any object of similar size and shape, anything you wish, when you say in Gohhan 'let this sphere in my hands become whatsoever I intend, it will, provided that what you ask is something spherical and of the same size.' That is the power of this relic. Wisdom counsels against using it at all."

Northing looked at me and furled his spidery-leg eyebrows.

"The voice you are hearing, monk, is merely a kind of prepared *glyph of warding* infused into this curious item. Such a thing is multifarious and can even converse, but not with any exchange of knowledge. Strange, these mortal magics...that they be still active within relics even though Nyzium has long in ruin been desolated. Yet it be passing delight to possess this item of the grand wizard....What a glamorous relic to peer into. I perceive within an facsimile of a lovely garden."

"It is said that whosoever gazes into the eye of Abraxas will see what is most desirable to him. Creature, you see a garden...perhaps you see Paradise?"

"Perhaps...but why would a being like me need Paradise? I see a fruit hanging on a tree...the fruit of Paradise?"

I took advantage of his vanity and said, "The fruit of knowledge? Were you to taste of it, you would be granted unfathomed knowledge, you will learn even the song of the Sirens."

"Knowledge...I do crave greater knowledge. Even a fairy creature like me can employ greater knowledge of things. Not even the *Erelim* were wrought with perfect knowledge. Why does the omnipotent "good" God, for example, allow such grand evil in the world, of which I have been a foremost minister? Which theologian can answer that? If I could answer that, I would be the most immortal of all theologians.

"So that should be what this sphere will magically become, that fruit Paradisiac...forbidden to men, but not to fairy.

"A weary creature am I; the ages have weighed me down, and there is little vigor in me. Even my vast library supplied me not with the knowledge I coveted, but inspired only the inventions of imagination. You know, monk, in past years I was wont to trust in force of arms for keeping my sway, in war-magic, back in the days when I gathered huge armies of fell men and rebel elves, and giants and trolls, as in the *Bellum Diabolicum*. They still await my command. That is useless play, like a boy who has toy soldiers and fights the same battles over and over again. I leave my knights and my champions like Mulcifer to carry on anyway, for those vassals will become bored if I do not give them some war to pursue. A particular weapon for them I designed, and they now take victory; but then brave men will again arise and push my armies back. Now I have outgrown that game.

"The most effective war is entirely of the mind; Abraxas knew that. By means of what the mind accepts, a soul may become so marred that ...well, I shouldn't give it away. I say let the devil keep snatching lives with his wars, for he is quite accomplished at that. As long as I have terrestrial dominion, as long as I am the Dire, it gives me scant satisfaction to learn how men merely are forfeiting their earthly lives, but waste not their spirits. What good be armies that can destroy kingdoms but cannot waste souls? If brave souls offer their earthly lives on battle fields and are thusly spared of any further temptation, they hurry to their happy reward at the great banquet with the unspeakable deity. How is that a victory against Him? You see, by conveying my armies to bring oppression and destruction, I do hope to purvey despair, but that is not nearly enough. It does not last.

"In my opinion it is the monks of Abraxas who have the real game: not to destroy the human body, but rather the human soul, replacing the Truth with artfully written encomiums to self-creating! It is unfettered to any moral morass. Afterall, "Truth" can becomes a cruelty! In the end, one has to determine one's own meaning. Alas, I learned that strategy too late...but what else can I do? I do not lie, but neither do I love. I am become no longer "the dark lord" of the sagas, slain by a magical sword or ring...

"Your immunity from magic, monk, has made you overbold. You thought that you could outwit me. Even if you could, how would you turn men back to the way of righteousness? My work with them has taken on a life of its own. Learn this: I have already, long ago, in a youth of glorious iniquity, set plans into play. Whether I remain on the sapphire throne or some priest casts me into the outer darkness, even so, no one can prevent the Whitehawk kingdoms now from consuming themselves in their own depravity. They will envelope themselves in eternal gloom! Why does your God allow this? But you... You can be like me. You could have strength and power like mine...if you would but believe in yourself.

"Oh...then you'll not surrender your pretense...think of it, my fellow, think of all that you have been through to secure your salvation, and to save the world that you know. You were right to try and leave the Monastery, but you made poor choices. What a pity. You chose to keep monkhood, believing that you served Heaven. You could have won imperishable glory as a Knight of the Realm, hailed by the great kingdoms of this world. Even as a boxer for the circus you would have had winning fame. You could have won the admiration of a fair maiden, that woman of your dreams, and had a happy family. But now, look at you, a haggard "monk of the dungeons." You have become a pawn in a cosmic chess game, easily knocked down. Your God in his transcendence and magnificence, in his sublime eternity, will hardly notice your sacrifice. The loss of His own champion troubles Him not, afterall, did he even lift a finger to deliver his own Son from the tree of woe? All will come to naught as the world passes away just as the deity said it would. So you win the quarrel, and I your soul. You had one life, and you wasted it."

et have I to comprehend in full what he was saying.... Was it true? How cleverly does the Archdeceiver sew doubt. Could it possibly be an honest claim? I slipped off into these thoughts pondering the insinuation of his argument. It was the *psychic whip*, I estimate, which Guy of Xaragia lists as a "psionic attack," meant to inspire feelings of inferiority and worthlessness, and *Melancholia*, timed for the precise moment of disputation.

It was the trumpeter call of Aeleron the goose, (communicated in my soul echoing), which again snapped me out of it.

"I have no answer for you, villain." I said, "Somethings only faith can answer, and no human logic will endure. Still, you cannot convince me into despair. I am fortified by power from on high. I am firm in His footsteps. This life means little anyway, little apart from God. I only hope to make a gesture of recompense for my sins. You, however, already know despair. If you do not think so, then...look within that *globus*. It must be a fruit of Paradise that you are seeing, but from which tree? Do you know? There grew two magnificent trees in Paradise. Is it the fruit from the Tree of Knowledge of Good and Evil? Or is it from the other tree? The tree of life which has been hidden away, as God said, *Lest they become like us, let us hide it away*. Nevertheless, we do not know. *The Black Book* says that the Tree of Knowledge of Good and Evil is dead; some say the wood was used to make the cross of our Lord...aye."

"Nevertheless, whichever tree it is, me will it now benefit," he said. "For upon fairy no injunction or law was decreed against eating the fruit of any tree. In fact, some furth-legends say that the tree of life was given to the High Elves to take care, and that they ate of its fruit. Could that be why, you foolish mortal, we Elves do not perish like you men? Is that the memory of the Elves? ...but memories vanish like smoke. I have waited too long. There has always been the minutest spot of doubt in my otherwise pure soul, an iota of doubt so small that it blots out absolute certitude: doubt that I might not be immortal. I shall now finally rid myself of that doubt. Come therefore...(the Balecrown now spoke in Gohhan) let this sphere which I hold be the Fruit of Paradise! Let me at last be exalted above the angels! "

At first the crystal sphere merely increased its yellowness in glow, but then came a slight change in shape and diminishing translucence, appearing to be a kind of fruit or pomegranate. The eyes of Nimrul lit in amazement as he gazed into his destiny.

"Did Arizel contrive a magical orb which brings about a substantial change? No, an actual change of substance is only from the divine. It is not possible for mortal magics." The great withered lord then rose and stood there raising up the spherical fruit and glorifying it. "And now, I shall taste of the fruit of Paradise, the fruit regarding which the High Elves of old sang songs, the fruit which shall revive me, and which shall make me once again master of all!"

The foul ghoul opened his hideous and rotting mouth, and lowering his yellowed maw forth like some unclean beast, bit into the fruit. The juices of the fruit sprayed as he tore into it and chewed.

As he ate the fruit, he looked up. Some new knowledge came to him. He meant to acknowledge that the fruit had a magic property; and he was about to utter something contemptible, no doubt, but his mouth stopped just as the word was upon his lips. Was his tongue being held by some mysterious power?

It now was quite clear. Although he may have obtained immortality by eating the fruit, nevertheless immortality comes at a price: silence. The first couple who once ate of the Tree of Knowledge paid a similar but more merciful price: the silence of the tomb.

However, this creature was already *semi-mortuus*. So some new punishment, I would say, God assigned the creature. Nimrul was rendered speechless, permanently: just punishment for one whose deceits were so widespread that they even had fooled their author. For like his master he wished not to destroy the Whitehawk kingdoms by mighty force, but to seduce them from goodness by the sweet words of his mouth.

His eyes widened in horror; he kept trying to form words from his withered lips but they would not, for the knowledge of certain things is not meant to be uttered, and this mystery is by God's thunderous decree. Nor can such even be intimated by a collection of phrases. The Professor was now helpless to teach untruth without the use of his lips, and poweless because all spells, be they mortal magics or elven virtue, require some spoken word, no matter how brief, even if just a whisper.

The Balecrown could not give a command to his war-trolls, dark-cavaliers, nor even a horg. In frustration he hissed and writhed and snarled.

That was our chance to act, and we did. However, here is where I must begin to finalize this narrative, my brothers, for to describe in detail our fearsome acts of retribution upon that foul one would not be well understood, and might make us seem as men without mercy, and unchristian. But that is surely untrue. Nor is it even worthy of Christian custom to gratuitously depict such things with words.

Needless to say, the creature fought back with his claw-hands and teeth. But I dealt him hurtful punishment, the quivering palm attack as described by Guy of Xaragia. It was just recompense for his crimes.

We discovered it was indeed no fiction that the creature was an immortal, not at all able to be slain, even by my quivering palm attack. Driven by battle-fury, I must have smote him death-dealing blows several times, and he fell, but died not. I wondered if it were right to destroy him, the usurper of Almighty's sapphire world-throne. Afterall, The Lord himself would have instructed greater men like King Argoth to do so, but did not. I tried to banish the puzzle from my mind. Now, thinking back, I realize that even if one could annihilate him so as to not fret, or fear, so that his malevolence might never again menace the earth, I think it would somehow not be right.

Certainly at the time I was more than ready to annihilate the creature. However, in his stunned lapse he could nevertheless be bound by the laces of Ariandol, gifts of Duke Ikonn, which our haggard priest-friend had long kept hidden. Just as the Titans bound Zeus in the Grecian myths, so we bound the archon, although with difficulty.

As for me, it was with trepidation that I at last approached the great Staff left by St. Aldemar, (who had received it from the successors of Elisheus and his prophets, who in turn had received it from Moses' successors). I was fearful that my hands were tainted with violence upon others. I expected at the first touch to be returned to dust at once because of my many transgressions. The Lord, however, in his mercy overlooked my previous unworthy deeds. Yet not for my sake did He thus overlook, but for the sake of the race of men who are now perishing, led astray from the good pasture by the untruths of the Dark Shepherd.

We raked around a little more in that bizarre hall. We found the extremely ancient Akaratic exorcism copied down in the study chamber of the creature. He had believed that victory was his, having obtained the thing he feared the most; for he had stolen it from me in my cell; probably eavesdropping on my sleep-talking. 'Folly is begotten of Pride,' say the ancient Greeks.

I examined the writing closely and wondered. I said to the Prime Interquist:

"The creature in his overconfident fantasy and self-indulgence had wished to enter his own name into the exorcism, for there is a fresh ink mark where is normally placed the lacuna for supplying the name of exactly which spirit-to-be-banished. No doubt copying the higher level spell had drained him much paraphysical energy, as Guy of Xaragia asserts. But look here, someone has written in a name."

"Death is a gift, a gift of final rest at least... " He said, "but only a gift of peace for the righteous. I suspect that the creature imagined he might use the exorcism, to put himself into a kind of self-immolating transe, to provide a kind of quasi-death release for himself."

"It must have been why he kept you hostage, you, a *selva*," I observed, "since by means of such a priestly banishment he hoped to escape from himself, whereby the curse of deathlessness would be lifted from him. He was too ashamed to admit it. He did not account that every exorcism strictly depends on God's will."

"The Balecrown's origin-name, Nimrul, is pronounced in a certain way," The Prime Interquist explained, "and must be written correctly in Akaratic. Do not utter or disclose the exact characters to any, because to do so might invoke or even release the spirit. The legendary Nimrul of the Ancientmost war, you must understand, exists only as a memory, for he had been warped so in spirit over centuries by envious pride into a most vile entity, to become a thing which no longer could even the name reckon."

Therefore as a mercy, the Prime Interquist did utter the exorcism, which went on some three pages of sacred writ. I had to aid him in the pronunciation of certain arcane words. The accursed spirit was then held fixed in place.

We interrogated him, in particular concerning the *drakodaemon*. What of these rumoured legions of wicked warriors loyal to that seven-headed terror, the mother of dragons? Were they armies that patrol both the surface of this world, as Galadif, as well as the deeps? Are they hoping to besiege Argunizial itself? Did the spirit have another name? I demanded knowledge of how she might be banished from the terrestrial sphere.

He merely grimaced, unable to speak, but only nodded his head affirmative or negative. I asked him if there exists any famous clerical spell or februation. He indicated that he did not know. I asked if any pneumatic weapon exists which might banish the dragon of Galadif He answered in the affirmative, but could not indicate what it was or who its possessor or where it might be sought.

At last the Prime Interquist pronounced the decree of banishment, the final section of the exorcism, saying, if I remember correctly my translation, "*in the name of the thrice holy Trinity and the DOMINUS Deus Sabaoth, Lamb of God, the Son, I abjure you and sentence you to inextricable confinement until the end of the world!*"

With this, a look of amazement came across the ghastly features of the creature, as he gazed upon the glowing face of the exorcist and saw what was reflected upon that visage: the terrible justice of the Lamb. At once the thing backed into its hole, the great pit Voraganth long ago prepared by King Argoth and his knights.

He slipped down there like a spider and wrapped himself in its chains, looking back at us as if to beg that we shut tight the great iron grating and lock it, which I forthright did; and at once the lock shook and sealed itself shut by some kind of holy power.

The worm had turned. *Vermis revolvit*

In the dark pit Nimrul was content to stay hidden, within the prison of which he himself had been the twisted author. Now the creature painfully awaits the end of time, like the titan Prometheus who stole the secret of fire, and was caught; by divine decree Zeus justly chained him to the remote mountain, stretched on cold rock high up, where the devouring eagle returns daily to remind him and taste his liver until it's gone. Likewise does a reminder come gnawing every day at Northing: knowledge of what is to come: the judgement of DEUS OMNIPOTENS, who is final and inescapable Truth.

It was after all this, my brothers, that I sat down there in that place and wept. I wept because my thoughts had turned to home, and to the monastery. I knew that what the creature had said was not rumour, that Ulcrist had been elected Abbot. I wept for the Lord's house, which was about to be turned into a den of thieves in our day, on our watch, a just chastisement for our sins. When my reason had returned, I wiped my tears and I stood up and spoke aloud for the creature below would hear: "I myself vow, with every bone and drop of blood, to oust the imposter of the Eldane with my own hands, under the banner of the Lamb. May He restore worship, penance, and right authority at Whitehaven glorious monastery on foaming shores."

The Prime Interquist bade me return without him. He stood before me and placed right hand upon my left shoulder and left on my right, crossing his own arms x-shaped, so that the indelible sign of the Chi-Rho was laid upon me. He uttered some holy spell in Latin. I asked him what he had just done.

"I pass onto you the blessed power and authority of the *Primum Interquirium*. You are now Tribune of the Divine Regulian Inquisition. You are Prime Interquist. So sayeth the Lord: *I will make the victorious one a pillar in my temple.*"

"Why have you done this? I am a mere monk. My learning is insufficient. I do not want such an office, I—"

"You have learned here what is most needed to learn. You are the only man I can trust with this duty in these unholy times. Your deeds have proven it...

"For my own penance I have determined to guard this pit-prison of the vile lich until the end, just like King Argoth once did. The lock must be maintained and guarded lest some minion come along and pick it. It is in truth no great penance, but it will do. I told you before, I have become content in this prison all these years; it is my home, my monastery which I will never leave. The horgs now shall be my monks, and I their Abbot, to teach them reform, and the fear of God. With God nothing is impossible.

"This I wish to do in reparation for having yielded to the forbidden embraces of that fair lady with whom I once had dalliance. Understand this: returning to the cities would bring about too powerful a temptation upon me, and I would find myself back in luxury with my former courtesan, my soul conquered by sin. *The spirit is willing, but the flesh is weak.* Temptations of the flesh must not be fought, but fled.

"Instead, by sublime grace I shall spend my remaining days in sack-cloth and ashes, praying and fasting in this remote and barren wilderness, as jailor of the beast and reforming Abbot. Our Lord taught that *"Certain spirits cannot be expelled but by prayer and fasting."* Who else will do this? Who knows, this new life, this true life, might even win me final perseverance."

I was speechless. My silence begged further explanation from him. ". . . you see, brother, when I pronounced this exorcism, it was most edifying, and even healing for my spirit. How solemn words uttered, and a glance from the Lord of Hosts through the lenses of a mortal man, resulted in such an expression of tremendous and eternal terror in that creature, and brought such a powerful being to so fearful a submission. . . this reminded me of the *Rex Tremendae Maiestatis*, the majesty terrible and dreadful, seated on his saffire throne, whose glance melts mountains like wax, how awesome his grandeur, his visage unspeakable, beyond human comprehension. My brother, we mortals fear God not enough. *Procedamus* IN PACE."

He added that he would put the horgrim to work, since they would consider him their new master for having put down their former one, and he would turn the Hall of Melancholy and the Arc du Baffay into a house of reform for criminals and heretics. I warned him of Mulg and told the herculean strength of that black-hearted horg. I warned lest he ever admit him to the Arc du Baffay.

Together we cut down the stalk of the elfshade vine which the fiendish Archdruid had for so long cultivated. It was anchored in the abyss, so we took the axe to the root.

And so we embraced and then parted, and that was the last I saw of him.

As for Arizel, he at last snapped out of his zombie-like state and came begging my forgiveness. What was I to say?

I asked Arizel how it was possible that he could have arranged for the Eye of Abraxas to change into the Fruit of the Tree of Knowledge of Good and Evil. He yielded no rational answer.

Nimrul had long coveted the priceless relic, since most of the fruits from the tree had long vanished save that one.

I also found it remarkable that Arizel had come back to life as it were. I had been praying for him, and just then by the grace of God he returned to us. He explained that he had esteemed himself able to overcome the Northing with some magical scrolls that he had found in "Professor Naza's Library." He did not mark however the abysmal posture of one scroll, and casting the extremely powerful spell, the dark energies left a terrible side-effect consequent to the Hyspostatic Rift, turning him into a kind of lifeless automaton.

Reviewing all these things with him I comprehended something in my mind and in a flash solved a *mysterium* which perplexed us. To him I did not confide my theory, lest he be dumbfounded by so strange a revelation regarding himself, although I knew it had to be right. How had I missed connecting the dots and not put these things together before?

As you may recall, Arizel had been wondering how it was that he had survived so long after Nystol, outliving other humans by centuries. In reality he had not survived those years of Nystol's demise, but had died as a refugee in Tyrnopolis, and was not buried like the others beneath the charred ruins of Nystol.

A certain anonymous priest of miraculous power, the one whom Brother Zadoc had been raving about in the opening pages of this tome, must have gone ahead and done it. He must have resurrected Arizel from the dead not so long ago. The wonder-priest, whoever he was, bowed to the instigation of the wool-frocked Friars of Whigg! Of course Arizel himself did not comprehend or recall the resurrection, remaining unaware. So he had indeed stooped to taste the flowing waters of Lethe in the underworld! But then he must have followed the river bank back to the upperworld. He had claimed that his earliest memory of recent years was walking along the pebbly shore of the Inner Furthsea, a fresh-water ocean, examining mysterious stones that had washed up.

All this does go to prove, that to restore a soul to grace is indeed a greater thing than to resurrect a body. Arizel had been walking about as alive—but not alive, for the power of the wickedness in Nzul had mortified his semi-pagan soul. Not until the power of God banished the residing evil, could he be restored.

The Lord did all this, and who will speak against it? The mystery of Inversus I now begin to perceive; for his identity is closer to reckoning. Who certainly is revealed to be not that creature Nimrul, mind of rebellion, nor *the drakodemon*, ancient spirit of the fallen world, nor is he Abraxas, the communication of iniquity. One might certainly name these as kinds of antichrists. Nay, rather it should not be forgotten that the Man of Sin, Inversus, himself may be rightly identified by considering what is written: *for his is the number of a man...*

Going through the labyrinthine prison, we put all the horgrim under the yoke, so that they would fight no more, showing them as proof a braid of nasty hair that we had cropped from the head of their former master.

We ran into Phaedra and Drocwolf, who had just escaped, and although nursing certain wounds from torture, they were still in one piece. What elation for us that they had survived. Many other prisoners were released, but not all. Word had gotten through the massive fortress that a war-monk had deposed the Balecrown. The remaining hobgoblin guards fled at the sight of us. That was nice. But the end of adversities, brother, was not yet.

We passed through many corridors of that melancholy palace making our way down to a certain boat said to be anchored on an underground river. Finch, who, according to Phaedra, and to my sheer amazement, had also somehow survived, had gone ahead of us to employ his roguish machinations and bargain with the horgoth for a strong boat. Thanks be to the intercession of St. Dismas. Finch was waiting for us. I was to drop off the companions and commend their faring, while Noroch awaited me far above. So we proceeded with torch through a number of descending flights of eldritch and crumbling stair.

Suddenly, as we were turning a stony corner, we spotted a devilish monstrosity. It was a magical sentinel, a great questing eye attatched to a globulous body floating. This monster is the one that the Greek bards called "Κλεοψ," euphemistically meaning "pretty eye." Guy of Xaragia catalogues these under the title "Beholder." Lactantius and other Roman monstrologists name it *tyrannoculus*, "tyrant-eye." Apparantly they have exceptional intelligence, (this somehow I doubt). Nevertheless they are the most deadly of all abominations that wizards fabricated in the fourth age. This particular organism had but the lone cyclopean eye. From the many viminal scabs one could guess his other lesser eyes must have been severed during some occult combat in the everdark which will never be known. The thing did however boast three cthonic tentacles spinning. Clearly it had been patrolling the maze-like corridors at the behest of Northing.

"Angels of God deliver us." I said. Any other saying would have fallen short, for each of us stood agape.

Immediately the levitating horror detected us and spun about in air to reckon the position and power of each; Arizel, Drocwolf, Phaedra and myself. We halted and froze. Drocwolf, having knowledge of its terrifying powers, warned that no victory is possible against its infernal magic. He blurted out that we should flee. It was too late. The dwarf at once found himself suspended in air and being drawn to it by unseeable *telekinetic* power. The *tyrannoculus* widened from its gaping maw, druelling horribly, to taste the pugionic delicacy.

Phaedra, being less knowledgeable of such magical behemoths, charged furiously with a horgoth halberd that she had picked up. But the entity was deft with its tentacles. They wrapped around the shaft of the weapon and easily jerked it out of the warrior's grip. Phaedra Stormraker had been weakened from months of imprisonment. The *tyrannoculus* flew up through the shadowy air to navigate above the warrior. The thing obviously was playing us like dolls.

Arizel at last remembered how to cast a freezing spell, but the *tyrannoculus* deflected it reversing to hit the caster, who almost died from the shock. That was the last thing I saw before I fell into drowsing, going to my knees, and the great Staff letting fall. Apparantly the thing had cast a *Resut* (sleep) spell on me, which, on account of my being a monk, should not have affected me. Why did God allow this? Wherefore had I failed to gain his protection? But the will of God is inscrutable...

I was alert again almost within two breaths, but I was still somnolescent and could barely keep my eyelids open, coming in and out of awakeness. I struggled terribly to fight sleep, pricking myself. The Beholder was about to dine on Drocwolf's flesh. Nibelung-roast is highly sought after, a most tasty morsel for dragons and other underworld denizens. It spun him in air to playfully disarm him, as does a cat that bats about a mouse which he is preparing to devour. Drocwolf fought back the best he could, but the dwarven arm just didn't have the reach to plant an axe hit. Phaedra was trapped inside of some sort of magical forcefield which retarded her movement to uselessness.

Finally my eyes yielded completely to somnolence. At some point later they opened, (perhaps a decade of the beads), and a pulsating headache wracked my brain. To the right I glanced. Arizel was still crumpled on his side, frosted and motionless. On the left Stormraker was yelling at me for action. Where was Drocwolf? The huge levitating *tyrannoculus* was already digesting the poor dwarf.

The *Resut* spell now was worn off. There was an opportunity. The scabrous entity was distracted by spasms. Its own acidic digestion of our companion had caused a belly-ache. I reached and grabbed the staff. Although I had not previously had time to memorize any thaumaturgical spells, I had faith that a command from scripture might suffice. If we should only blind the eye, the *tyrannoculus* could not hurl spells or offer any other powerful forays. At once came knowledge, for I was wearing the Red Cowl, which protects from the evil eye.

I recalled how the pure light of God blinds the wicked. If this monster was anything, it was wicked.

"Domine, emitte lucem tuam et veritatem tuam!" I declared, brandishing the Staff on high. Immediately the brightest of all possible physical luminesences beamed out from the capital of the staff. Light stung the eyes of all and transformed the incarnadine lense of the Beholder into a holocaust. The globe subsequently burst into a furious inferno. The thing squealed in agony. Flames cooked its fleshy scales which sizzled and popped like bacon on a stove, while the eye itself coagulated, yes, just like an egg fried sunny-side up. The globus dropped down and broke apart, vigorous heat still cooking it. Oh what a hideous drama to behold.

It took the good part of an hour to revive Arizel, warming him with embers of the burning. Together we collected the remains of poor Drocwolf for burial; and his instruments, weapons and a few other things: his eye-patch, to be returned to his family, in our shame. At least he had died with honour in battle, rather than fleeing. But what sadness! So great a hero slain so effortlessly and so unexpectedly! We all wept sorely, even Phaedra Stormraker (who rarely ever showed emotion). She had often mistreated Drocwolf, but now rued it.

I myself wept much indeed. My foolish overconfidence was to blame. The Lord God did grant His aid against the *tyrannoculus*, for surely it could have been worse. And perhaps the dwarf's time had come; his destiny fulfilled, the thread run out. So God desired that he die as he had lived, fighting with honour against evil. Stormraker was the first to realize this. She wiped away her tears. "Would you rather that he die in his bed at home, with no boots but only socks, his war-deeds forgotten!? "

So went the terrible combat with remnant evil. Learn, brother, that whenever there has been great victory guided by of the Holy Spirit, from devilish power defeated will issue one last attempt. Plummeting into the chasm a wicked dragon will always gamble one last strike with his barbed tail. Sometimes he succeeds. The Devil will have his pound of flesh.

The two survivors and I descended deeper steps into the lowest basements of the great fortress and found the River Alph flowing beneath. Storm, with Arizel, set out in one of the bolgoth skiffs to let the waters carry them into the Intermundane Expanse. So departed they for the edge of the known. Of their adventure, brother, in that cavernous world, I am sure that someday they will tell it.

o, westward faring, aloft over many realms, the gargoyle Noroch was taking me home, with The Staff and the **Black Book**. Yet we had another unexpected delight. To my utter amazement beside us appeared Aileron the half-swan winging it through cloud banks and starry *aether* with us, navigator to Noroch for the way home. On the evening of our arrival however the great fowl suddenly took his leave of us. This was an unhappy omen, as I was soon to learn, wherefore is not the monastery also his home, why then depart?

Heaven's firey globe was upon the Vastess Ocean, setting in sanguine splendor as ever before. About to alight upon the porch of Whitehaven Monastery-by-the-shore we circled round once. Monks were chanting vespers within the chapel.

The wide-winged gargoyle lifted his head and spoke.

"Is that a battle-song I hear coming from your monastery?"

I listened intently. I assure you, brothers, the sound was not in a melody which any true or right-professing monk would chant. Instead we heard dissonant tri-tones in a fallen key, and the words were not the Psalter's sweet Latin, nor any praise of the Lord, but something else.

"No." I answered. "It is no victory song, but a fel-chant with ungodly tone. It is the diabolus-sound of heresy. Come about, Noroch, and let us away from this wickedness until we have an advantage against it."

God would not have me go up against so many monks without a plan and without allies. The great creature turned sharp and headed back East toward a rising moon. He flew all the way to Tyrnopolis so that I might recover the horse Burgundius as a transport, and my own quarterstaff Reckoning. I knew the horse longed to see action and awaited me in the grazing fields just outside the city. Also, I might take another chance at retrieving the great sword Witchbane. After all, that city is free, and her markets were the most likely place where the weapon would have ended up. No, I did not seek it in order to chasten the misled brothers and those monks inspired by unworthy ambition and selfishness. A godly spirit is proof against that. But Witchbane detects witchery, warloxism, and heresy.

So sailing swiftly over Chyldeshire, the Nine Feudatories, and the Andolyn Mountains, I arrived at the Republic of Tyrnoplis, city of brazen domes upon the Sea Goldyndol. The hour was late and the moon was down, so I thanked Noroch and bade him farewell; the great gargoyle whom, I presume, is now at large. He vouchsafed that I might summon him whenever needed.

At once I inquired among the remaining Ammouric families there. One noble family supplied me quarters without even first requiring of my identity. In the morning I gladly told them my story, and in their hospitality they fed me and helped me recover.

From them I learned this: that five rope-girded monks of Whitehaven had been lodged at the Friar's Crizet, an Inn across from the Hall of Philosophical Inquiry, much to the discomfort of some Friars of Whigg. Fraternal charity caused the Friars to begrudgingly house the five. The monks were traveling the lands on foot. Therefore I made it my purpose to find and join them...and so you will soon know what took place from there.

Nor had I seen the last of the Ammouric Knights, but I resolved to learn of their ordeal and return to St. Aldemar with them, to clean out our monastery by rightful force, charged as I am with the *Primum Interquirium.*

No good deed unpunished goes. News of the banishment of Professor Naza spread. But what an unexpected prize: our heroical feat was no means to worldly glory; rather was it a guarantee of infamy.

This was something no one of us would have ever imagined.

I mentioned to you before how great was the reputation of Northing, "Professor Naza," throughout all the Furthlands. But I had no idea how great. When word was spread that a certain monk, Jacob Magister, "guilty of witchcraft," had enclosed the "beneficent spirit of the North, the Northing" a.k.a. "the great professor" helpless in an inaccessible pit, and taken away the key, you can imagine the outcry. Professor Naza was a most respected and celebrated theologian in all the Whitehawk universities. A legend regarding him had even developed that he was the spirit charged with the office of restraining polar winds and providing for mild winters throughout the Furth —what a load of dragon dung!

Although I had mostly overcome my vanity and fear, and had even banished a most felonius spirit from the world, there could be no cessation of spiritual war. It is not demons, but the race of men themselves who, with stiffened necks, most resist the good will of Heaven. Demands at once were made throughout all the feudatories and provinces for my arrest. I had become the agent of all injustice and a living symbol of what is wrong with the world.

Wanted Outlaw, universal enemy, reward paid of 1000 crizets—bounty when apprehended, be he yet quick or dead, and/or information leading—such posts were nailed up everywhere, including a sketch of my face, which, *Deo gratias*, was far from accurate.

For those who criticize the Church, I became an example to cite of her oppressions and cruelties. "Cold are ye this winter?" people would ask. "—then find that accursed monk and string him up."

From now on I would need to walk carefully in the towns of men, as the errant cavalier Sir Hortezan. I have, however, exhausted these pages and must therefore tell of those pilgrimages in yet another tome. So compare all that you have gained by hearsay as to the terrible things which I accomplished, as well as subsequently—*they are all true* (but not exactly the way many suppose). Admittedly, as Prime Interquist, I failed the Church on several counts, as I shall yet relate in the subsequent tome. I did what had to be done, unlike certain predecessors in that office. Nor could I have perceived how the Antichrist was using me. But I must not tell this here.

Other things transpired, regarding which many know naught, both before this and afterwards: that is why I have set down this confession. Here are things which reveal many mysteries of what was, what is, and what shall be.

So all these other things I must needs recount, my brothers, so that thou reckon it in full, not for vainglory. There are monks and others who would to give testimony. But as the Lamb sayeth: *the testimony of men I do not accept.* Indeed, the *Iudex Terribilis* is the only judge I need consider. If you judge me accursed because of my offense of leaving the monastery, or wherefore I went questing accompanied by a wizard, or how I drank the bubbling potion, or condemned not to hell the leather-skinned lizard-man Sahkah, or yeah more, that I even stooped to violence against the infernal ones, or of the thousand other times I have fallen before and since, then so judge. God will yield to your earthly judgement on earth. However, be mindful that *the measure with which thou measure will it be measured out to thee.*

May the labour that God assigned me unmasking cruel powers be some recompense for my shortcomings, which are many and varied. Therefore let this codex, worthily bound in good *vellum*, stand as a writ of confession as to my guilt, not of witchcraft, but rather of tumult. Yet to something even more serious does it testify: the price the world has paid for sin and will continue to pay if there is not widespread conversion soon. Nimrul, aye, he was but a mere minion.

These confessions I have collected and the brethren will place more in other volumes for your perusal, so that nothing be missed regarding the restoration of Whitehaven, nor of that grave event which happened long centuries past, but which continues even to this day to work its influence over the world, that event whose implications continue to be wrapped in mystery: an event which must never be forgotten, the fall of Nystol...

Aels: Maceon, survivor of the deluge, had three sons: Ael, Rumil, and Mahar. Ael was apportioned the sea shores of the west and the north, "for the harvest of sea."

Aeon: A period, possibly reaching into centuries or even millennia, but usually designated by some spiritual hegemony or the metahistoric.

Aethuria: See Ayrs.

Agathodaemon (*Oruscan Gr*): mysterious word meaning "good spirit."

Aidenn: The Greek-speaking empire founded by Hermius which stretched from the shores of Xasbur all the way to Turnople.

Akaratic: Glyphic writings, representing a celestial language used by God himself.

Aldemarz (ancient Kiluria): Also "St. Aldemar, Aldemarse," The great island off the northern coast of the Whitehawk continent to the West, homeland of Jacob.

Ammouri (used as a noun when in plural; adj. Ammouric) (possibly fr. French amour): A rite of ancient Christianity, comparable to the early Celtic rites of Cambria and Hibernia.

Acheulian: a hardy race of the first ages of the Whitehawk continent, of whom Maceon of Achulea and his sons were the foremost projenitors. They built the Axe-cut trail, invented writing, and established their Maceonid dynasty throughout the known realms.

Arahom (*Aram*): A northern "no-man's land " of swamp, plains, and hills, and some fertile land beneath sacred Mt. Argunizial. Site of many battles against the Nazageist.

Arcavir: a mysterious office of elphic origin who were watcher-guardians over the Whitehawk continent, reputed to be half-gnomes.

Ar*chsin*: A term denoting the original transgression of the first humans, (the primordial couple). This was accomplished by encouragement of the devil, whom God permitted to take the form of a serpent and who communicated by telepathica, with false promise of promotion, "ye shall be as gods").

Ardeheim (Kargiawall): Rugged land of brown dust storms and terrible rocky wastelands in the central and northern bounds of Whitehawk.

Arguzinial: Various spellings and pronunciations are found: Argunizial, Acusynicul, Achozinaal, Akkyrzal, etc. This mountain is considered sacred by all the nations of Whitehawk. It is located in the south of the Niruz Peninsula in remote forests.

Arianism: A heresy which denies the trinity, teaching that Christ the Son was inferior to the Father, and not divine.

Arraf: Meaning "East"...a general designation referring to mideastern desert realms, such as Kithom, Kutaal, Vesulum, Vath, Namaliel, Sarnas, Atalur, Succon, and Gohha, all of which speak a variant of the Kutaal.

Ashkhar: The divine kingdom of Allfather which surrounded mount Argunizial in the first age.

Astodan; a vast and labyrinthine necropolis beneath Nystol, within the Sardu Mesa. Most of the tombs enclose wizards from the ages of Nystol's waxing, who protected their area with elaborate traps or weird creatures. The necropolis also is said to be the haunt of the undead sorcerers and other wizards who escaped from the Maharim and Tungoth barbarians on the day Nystol fell, so intent on guarding their secrets, their scrolls and tomes of power, that they sealed themselves off from the towers above so that none might enter. Many lost *volumina* of mundane subjects are also stored there.

Atalur: A land of many minor city-states or western principalities in Arraf, founded by the Atlantean colonists in the second age. The secret of Ataluran arms and especially armour is unknown, but they are famous and highly prized by royal and noble families throughout Whitehawk.

Authapian: qv. Outhapis

Ayrs (*Aethuria*): The forgotten kingdom of half-elves, valraphs, in the sub-arctic pine regions of the Great Northern Forests. Ayrs was destroyed in the Bellum Diabolicum by the Mulcifer the Elder and his massive armies.

Baffay, Arc du: the impregnable fortress of the Northing, Balecrown and prophet of Melancholy, of old called Nimrul. The great fortress was called Nzulg in ancient times, but it is said that the clever entity Nimrul gave it the name Baffay because it sounded euphemistic, like some vacationer's resort town; so as to attract the slavish. Most scholars assert that the name comes from Baphomet, a demon.

Balecrown, Banelord: Osringa titles for Dark Lord, similar to the Aelic "Dire" and "Balecrown." Banelord is used for any wicked archon of foremost power, while "Balecrown" is reserved for accursed monarchs.

Bannock: Whitehawk name for Arizel the wizard.

Bellum Diabolicum: "The diabolic war." Prosecuted principally by Nimrul the Banelord, this war changed the face of all Whitehawk.

Black Books of Melancholia. The contents of these mysterious tomes only are left in fragments. Thought to be compendiums including histories of Whitehawk and arcane studies, these are records of kings, wisdom and lore, and sacred poems, coded keys and enigmas all bound up with the world-destiny.

Bolg, Horg: Ancient terms, sometimes confused, referring to the considerably warlike and fallen elphic races who form armies and raid the surface of earth.

Book of Bloody Battles: Duke Ikonn's own words describing collected events his dungeoneering campaigns throughout Whitehawk in ancient times.

Bzebus leaf: the wide fronds of the plant used for manufacture of scrolls which deal with magic. The flowers are an unusual scarlet colour and emit a rotting smell, which entraps and digests flys. Bemble leaf on the other hand is similarly shaped but the flowers are white and saffron, attracting bumble bees. It nourishes the bees with nectar and in turn they protect the plant from larvae and other pests. It provides the preferred leaves for thaumaturgical scrolls and the works of poets and theologians.

Crach Mountains: Also called The Cracked Mountains because of their appearance;

crizet: Ten silver crizets equal a gold piece (croat). One croat buys a skin of vanic wine. Sixty croats buys a good pack-horse.

Culduin (alt., *Calduin*): A planet of unknown identification, possibly Mars, often used by scientific sages but especially travelers of intermundane lands to keep time.

Dire: (common): Aelic designation for a banelord or power established as an archon or hegemon, over a certain spiritual reality, or exerting a negativity over a region.

Dilmonath: archaic furthname for the lost paradise of the first age, thought to have been located somewhere in the Arcodon peninsula, or perhaps Sardu.

Dragons: "the seed of Ocean" all dragons are sprung from Vorthragna mother of dragons, who embraced Oceanus the titan.

Draker (dungeoneer's slang), fr. Gk. drakon (and later drake, denoting a winged dragon): The word draker is a pejorative: a coward.

Drakodemon: Greek transliteration for dragon-spirit.

Dry Blood Sea: (*Dry Blood Dunes*) part of the Great Southern Desert, the Dry Blood Sea has the appearance of a sea of red sands and stretches from Atalur to The Deadly Hills and Nystol.

Durgoth: The northern wooded lands beyond the great lakes is inhabited by the Durgoth barbarians.

Edolunt Rangers: originally an order of lawful neutral Rangers who patrolled the Furthlands and the Frontier.

Eldark (adj.): On account of the famous wisdom of the Eldari, the adjective Eldark came into general usage denoting anything displaying an ancient and seemingly dark (ie. pre-Christian) or arcane wisdom. Eldari (also adj.; Eldaric, Eldark, Eldrist, and n. in sindari tongue, Elthildor): The foremost authorities of wisdom available before the revelation of the All-law.

Elfshade: A pervasive vine which strangles trees. The vines have spread out though forests across northern Whitehawk and its leaves, it is said, can hear the unworthy talk of men, which it conveys to the dark archons of the world. It clings to castle and monastery walls

Elkomenon: reputed to be the founder of the Order of Mages, a descendent of the idolater Chus.

Elphim: A general term for rational races other than humans and angels.

Elthildor: See Eldari above.

Elves-High Elves, Courtly Elves: they left Whitehawk, and all the world, because of the overwhelming injustice of men.

Erelim (Akaratic erelim): the heavenly angels

Furth High King: This title is reserved to Christ himself, ruling from afar upon Mt Argunizial.

Furthreach, furthworld, furthlands, (*furthlore*): A general name for the lands of the great Whitehawk continent, but especially those not yet under direct sway of the Ammouric faith, ie. including "outlaw" lands beyond the Northern frontier, or the closed lands of the Eastern Veil.

Furthsea: includes all conjoined interior seas: the Sea of Goldyndol, the Sea of Ymmin, and the Sea of Shirvav.

Friars of Whigg: reputedly the greatest theologians of all Whitehawk, they nevertheless accepted the novel, much disputed, and quite clearly erroneous proposition that the ancient wizards of Nystol may be lawfully resurrected.

Gates of Dariel: Colossal gates of bronze and adamantine construction built by Hermius the Conqueror in the third age. These gates block the sole passage through the Valaghir mountains on the Isthmus of Hyrcanth.

Gederon, Plain of: The site in Arahom identified as the fields of battle for the wars of the Allfather against the drakodemon. Prophecy also names it the place of the final battle between the wicked and the just.

Guy of Xaragia: an encyclopediast of the sixth age whose writings cover the worlds, giving in mathematical terms the relative and statistical probabilities for all things; but especially entities of the intermundane regions, as well as spellcraft and demonology.

Guild of st. Dismas. St. Dismas, the good thief on the cross beside Christ, who made a confession of faith, is patron to this organization that employs ex-thieves and bandits, ex-pirates and cut-throats, repenitent and turned faithful, to use their various skills for clandestine operations and subterraneous combats against the forces of darkness.

Gnostic: An early heresy which blends Christian teachings with Platonic philosophy and traditional myth.

Gnome: a mysterious being of elphic nature who is a watcher-guardian over the Whitehawk lands. Originally the mischievous race of "gnomes" inhabited sundry woodlands and caverns.

Gnotus (Notus): The famous bronze dragon, the first Neoplatonian, whose wisdom angered other dragons. Also a friend of Fendil the elf.

Golden Pages of the Wind A mysterious and sacred work of most ancient Akaratic script.

Godiun Fout: A famous rogue and thief whose exploits are the stuff of high entertainment throughout all the Furth.

Gohha: A kingdom settled by Egyptian explorers in the second age. Gohha consists of two princedoms: Sarnas and Succon. Of old Gohha was called Mizraim.

Goldyndol, Sea of: Bounded by the Isle of Arvad in the south and the shores of Mulrud, Hyrticum, and Baradeium to the west, Niruz to the east, this stormy sea is said to radiate a golden color during the moonrises of autumn.

Godmouth: similar to the papacy. The role of The Godmouth is to guarantee genuine teaching and expose misbelief in all the lands. The title "Eldane " refers to the ecclesiastic fealty.

Hermius the Conqueror: Oruscan monarch, founder of the Aideen Empire which stretched from Mahanaxar all the way to Knum and Kalar. He built the colossal Gates of the North at Ptur and began the Horg wall., establishing the frontier.

Horg; also, Bolg (pl.Horgrim, Bolgrim; spelling varies) (adj. horgoth, bolgoth): Shortened form of "Hobgoblin. " See "Bolg "

Horg Wall: This fortified and monumental work of architecture rises some hundreds of feet into the sky of Arahom. It was built by the Ulthurings in the fourth world age to keep out the horg armies of Baffay.

Homunculus: a wizard's creation, an automata of small size, manlike, with dark leathery skin, sometimes cyclopian, nasty little teeth and pointy ears, who can fly with batwings on various errands and act as spy.

Hyperlyptic Alignment: An alignment of the planets well known and used by Arcanes but no longer able to be determined.

Hypostatic Rift: This was a world-changing rift in the fabric of the Kosmoid which occurred on account of space, time and cause —being idealized beyond the metaphysical predeterminates of the known. Most magic became impossible. Voethius claims it was the result of a conspiracy.

Illystra (variant in Osril: Yllistra, Ilyster): The continent was originally called "Illystrax" or "Illystrias" which translates fromproto-Aramthic "White bird-of-prey." This was the ancient name and is still kept untranslated in the oldest accounts.

Intermundian, intermundane: Latin "between the worlds"

Kargiwall (Ardevium) A stretch of brutal and semi-barren rust-hills that stretch from the leswar mountains all the way to Ironport.

Kithom: The semi-arid grasslands north of the Dry Blood Sea where many bandits and lawless types have found habitations. Here in peace graze the sacred elephant herd shepherded by the angelic being Ambrosius.

Knights of the Realm: secular cavaliers have land and are vassals to a lord, like a king, not like religious cavaliers, who are in a sacred order, like the Ammouric Knights or Knights of the Veil.

Kutaal: vast region of semi-arid grasslands that in east and south of Kithom borders the desert of Kithom (Kathon). The nomadic Kutaal wander the canyon of Hermius all the way down to the southernmost extremity of the deadly hills before the Accursed Sea, and as far East as Atalur and Gohha.

Lazaria: the most notorious temptress of the ancient world. It is proposed that she may have been a witch, but this is unsubstantiated. Men from all around the Whitehawk continent desired her, even fought over her, but she had little virtue other than her alluring beauty.

Lokken: a wilderness of forests, hills, lakes, and barren wolds which comprises most of the grand isle St. Aldemar.

Maceonids: The descendants of Maceon, survivor of the great deluge of the first age.

Mahanaxar: The great arid tropical country of western Whitehawk, wild and dangerous.

Mahar: The third Son of Maceon described as one "who was filled with violence." So did he go to dwell in the great northern forest and became the patriarch of the barbaric races.

Magi: mages pl. for Magus. The order of Mages in Nystol was the foundational order. Magi (pl. for Magus): descr. from Voethius' Arcane Histories, (an interview with Kruthendel Eleusinion) The Magus was an adept in the first magic, the proto-Avestic system initiated during the Antideluvian Era, which combines an archaic glyph system of Astral tuning with light-manipulations generating in degrees radiant matter from the preternatural fonts. The Magi also were the first to render astronomic sympathies for the four elements and track their inter-elemental rhythms.

Monachus-i (Latin: monk)

Morpheus Memnos: A great sage of Nystol, see above entry on Mercurius Yod.

Monad: A Pythagorean conception of ultimate reality as the one ground of undivided being

Mulg (*Mulcifer*) Warlord and Anarch of the Troll Horde, vassal to Nimrul and intensely loyal and ferocious, he is said to be part giant.

Namaliel: Eastern city-states on the western shore of the Sea of Ymmin

Narcissus Text: A number of texts, scrolls, and/or *codices*, manufactured in the fourth age by the infernal monks. These have the power to entrap the reader with the allurement of enchanted and forbidden knowledge. The reader is typically found dead, his boney fingers gripping the book, overcome by self-neglect of nourishment or dehydration.

Nathycanthe, Northyrcanth: Originally the province North Hyrcanthia. It is said that the mountains of misty forests are quiet and unsettling to most humans.

Nazageist (dwarven): See Nimrul, note.

Nergalf "the Butcher" A dwarf of the fourth age who was able to gain the seat of the Aideen Empire after the death of Hermius the Conqueror. Much more successful and brutal than his predessessor, he eventually subdued all the Furth. He earned the title "butcher" after his military executions in the seditious city of Namaliel. The Maceonid Kings for a time were exiled to the wastelands. They formed a resistance and at last organized a revolt against the mad dwarf. After his defeat on the Plain of Gederon, he escaped and led a band of mauraders through the underworld to Nystol, whose destruction he engineered as revenge for the betrayal of the wizards and for the ancestral grudge of the dwarves. All this is recounted in the *The Tower Weird*, found in compilation "The Fall of Nystol and Other Tales."

Nibelung (mountain dwarves) Closer to men than the ancient elves, the dwarves have even been identified as stunted valraphs. This insult to them however is to be avoided.

Non-void: a philosophical axiom: that there was never original nothingness, nor any chaos-void from which things mysteriously arose, as the poet Hesiod proposes, for there is no such thing as nothing.

NEPHILUNG (Subaetherialis Nephilung, Anahit): These beings, unlike angels or demons, are visible and physic powers. By the men of Kargiwall, old Ardeheim, they call them creature of the mist, in the East they know them as Anahit

Neoplatonian Dragon: A special line of dragons who had reformed themselves.

Nimrul: the entity who led a great rebellion against the Furth High King. His punishment is to never die. He was assigned as elemental archon to the northern darkness, and became the Dire of Melancholia. –also called Northing, and Nazageist. Variously called dark elf, nephilung, ghoul, lich and vampire, thing, archon, ghost–devil, lord, mind,...much of his strategy lay in the ambiguity of his race/origin, it being always uncertain how one should proceed to advance against him. Most scholars agree that he was an ancient elf, cursed never to die, whose monstrous physique and dark presence made him seem undead.

Nine Feudatories: Another name for Osring. These minor feudal Ammouric kingdoms share a common northern language and culture as well as Rumilian laws and learning.

Notus (archaic spelling): See Gnotus.

Northing: common name for "thing of the north," the Dire of Melancholy.

Nystol (Nyzium): Concerning this usage below Nyzium. Nystol (Nyzium) the older form of the college's name commonly used by non–Latin speakers. Although originally in the eldark usage it was always Nystol, this probably is a contraction from the Greek, Nystopolis, ie. "city of Nystul ". The name Nystul perhaps can be attributed to a great wizard of dungeoneering lore, the fanciful tales about whom claim that he was author of many dangerous spells. Whatever the case, he was associated with the founding of the city in the second age, according to the ancient writer Guy of Xaragia.

Nystoli: Term referring to those Arcanes of Nystol whose memory or knowledge stretched back to the very founding of the same remote college itself.

Nystopolis: See Nystol above.

Nyzium (Latinized form of Nystopolis, "Nystol " commonly used): This is the ancient tower–complex of wizardic colleges which once sat atop the sheer Sardu mesa. In some ancient texts, such as the scrolls Of Mercurius Yod, the name is spelled "Gnostul " which would suggest a connection with the Greek word for knowledge, gnosis, hence Gnosticism. Gnosticism is the principal heresy associated with wizardry and is a source of many scroll–spells. Another etymology points to the legend of a certain wizard of the second world–age, Nystul, who is said to have been an advisor in the building of the city's wondrous architecture. (See also above entry: Nystol).

Nzul: the dark feudatory of the Northing, with its fiefdoms in Bardelith. Zabul (Zabolg, Nzulg): The super–fortress of the Nazageist located somewhere in the Crach mountains. It is said to be a horrible place of smoke, iron, black towers and unthinkably huge architecture, a typical dwelling for any master of evil. No one save King Argoth and a few survivors of the Bladetongue have ever returned from there, so there is little to report. It was built by Thendyl the Archdeceiver to be higher than the throneroom of Mt. Argunizial. Trolls, goblins, and other hideous creatures patrol its walls and territories. Legend asserts that its library is in the shape of a horrible maze of book-stacks whose texts curse those who read them with insanity. Further descriptions were recorded in the final chapters of the Bladetongue, but the dark powers have managed to destroy those chapters.

Oceanicon: The journal of Duke Ikonn detailing the events of his sailing around the Furthshores.

Oceanicyng (Oceanicurst): Duke Ikonn's heirloom sword, supposedly forged in the first age by the Vanir (Nephilim)

Orusca: An ancient city-state of Greek-speakers south of the Anylynk Mountains.Oruscan Greek is the most common Greek dialect of Illyster.

Outhapis (also Authaphis) perhaps the most ancient of city-states was completely covered in volcanic ash in the second age.

Passings: Refers to the orbit of the planet Calduin or the sky ring associated with it, as a calculation of time, perhaps similar to the Martian year.

Plathonis: An Elven Kingdom of the West, bordering the Northern Warm Sea. Once famously inhabited by the high elves who ruled the pine forests with ruthless dominion.

Prime Mover: Some wisemen maintain that certitudes can be deduced by reason concerning the originator of all reality. the philosophers call an "uncreated and only necessary being and power," though according to them, it has no discernible personality.

Prime Interquist: Ecclesiastic buearocrat of the Holy Inquisition, listed as missing.

Regulis (Regulum): A Roman colony of the third age. After the expulsion of the Kings of Rome in Italy, eighty years from the collapse of the Aideen, the exiled kings entered the continent. They began establishing Roman law and engineering and the Latin language. The city grew rapidly and overthrew many neighboring cities finally becoming an Imperial power. It eventually collapsed on account of internal divisions and the Bellum Diabolicum, and in time was replaced with the Whitehawk Confederation.

The Red Ascetic an epicurean philosophy: all must seek to attain "The State of Cathartic Titan," that is, perfect and continuous ecstatic pleasure and ease, found by obedience to an absolute master. The materialist cult was adopted by the later emperors and finally made into the state religion by the Inversus.

roaks (Whitehawk slang) able-bodied men, often used for common fighters

Scriptorium: Hall of a monastery in which monks do the sacred work of copying down or writing manuscripts.

Selva (fr. Gohhan): Originally meant simply "priest,"most common term for "Christian priest" in Whitehawk (meaning "sacrificer ").

Seed of Ocean: see dragons.

Soothfold: The conciliar body of Ammouric Sages in Whitehawk. See note

Sodd Bloodman: famous monk and warrior-poet from the period of Emerald Warriors. He vowed never to shed blood and was victorious in all his one hundred duels, save the last.

State of Cathartic Titan: see *The Red Ascetic*.

Sinostox, Prince (Sinostocs, Synostochs): A Banelord, reputed descendent of Maurob, the son of Maceon. The Katabasid Sinostoxou, an epic poem describing his dark quest and seizure of power, claims he is the son of Tithonus. Originally an Ammouric Knight, Prince Sinostox blamed Duke Ikonn for the slaughter of his family, and swore vengeance.

Tablets of Destiny: the most primordial code of Divine Law

Thanato Excorpus: A writer and historian of the seventeenth century who by his depth-research was among the first of the modern era to become aware of the existence of the lost Whitehawk epics.

Thaumaturgy (lit: "wonder-working"): "wonder-working" It is not wizardry, but appears similar in that it employs scrolls and specially prepared books, amulets and symbols, vestments and incantations, wands and staffs, holy swords and miraculous invocations.

Tyrnople (also Turnopolis): The eastern exarchate of the Regulian Principate. Tyrnople lies in a strategic location, not only having ports and access to the Sea of Goldyndol, but is also on the route called "The Serrian Way" which leads to Namaliel.

Troll-horde, also, "trollwise" does not specify trolls as identified by the encyclopediast Guy of Xaragia, but rather in the Nord-tongue is a general term for humanoid monsters from beneath the earth.

Ultima Thule: The classical name for the Nathycanthe, (Nathycanis) land of the Bifrost mountains.

Valaghir Mountains: The great mountains that rose south from Hyrcanum as far as the desert of Luz and the north bounds of the feudatory of Atalur. These mountains separate the Sea of Ymmin from the Sea of Shirvav.

Valraph(s): Antiquated usage also employs plural, Valraphim. 1) Originally an oath-bound chivalric order of half-elves. Old epics lost to human memory recounted their heroical exploits, deeds which must be attributed to the sterling mix of fairy blood with human, infusing the best qualities of each. When the ancient plural Valraphim is used, the speaker refers to the old chivalric order, but when small case and common termination valraph(s), no capitalization is used as the race is indicated.

Vastess Desert: A designation which includes The Dry Blood Sea, Kithom, Cathon, the Yezez desert, the Deadly Hills, the Plain of Kanats, and part of the Orcodon Peninsula.

Vastess Sea: The Vastess Ocean-sea is also includes the Tethys Sea in its furthest known extent. It is called the Intermundian Sea of the upper world because its waters flow between the worlds.

Vath, Isle of: An oasis-city carved into a rock-island in The Dry Blood Sea. Its original inhabitants were possibly Vri, but Hycmen fugitives from Gohha took it over at the end of the third age. Known as the Vathim, they later carved out the underground city, Vath, on one of the great rock-isles in the desert, but it is now nearly uninhabited.

Veil, Cult of the: A strain of Arian heresy which became a fanatical cult of such great popularity it destabilized all Arraf and threatened to destroy by means of unholy war the Ammouric crowns of the West. The patriarchs called for Crusades against the powerful and dangerous Veil-Knights. The Ammouric knights held the city Vesulum and pushed back the Veil.

Vesulum (Vorsalir): It was shortly before the Great Burning of Nyzium that a virtuous king rose up among the tent-dwelling Kutaal, a certain King Hsarhgoh the Righteous, (in the West called "King Argoth the Good "). This king realized fulfillment come in great prophecy concerning Kutaal: "Your peoples shall be great Warriors and deliver the lands." This did not refer to warriors of bow and horse, he perceived, but rather Spiritual Warriors. He thus convinced the High Patriarch of Whitehawk to establish a spiritual stronghold in a little cliff-village hidden away in the lower canyons of Hermius, known as Vesulum. Vesulum became a training ground for kings and a place of study for selvas (priests). Certain areas were established for prayer with guidelines requiring spiritual clean-ness. Many great monks, priests, and clerics have come from this land. The city remained pure from corruption and heresy until the usurpation of the cult-master Shahi Nuzzib.

Vlogiston: a freezing cold river in the underworld, place of perpetual confinement and endless torment for the nebilung who do wicked deeds.

Voethius: A Regulian author of a history of Nyzium

Voraganth: The Furth designation for The Bottomless Pit mentioned in the book of St. John's Apocalypse.

Vorthragna: A name for Tiamat, the original hydra-dragon of rebellion from the first world, who demanded Ocean as her consort. She opposed the dominion of Allfather.

Vorsalir (Nor-tongue): Vesulum.

Waffin leaf: a giant swamp plant useful for creating huge tomes.

Weeping Brotherhood (the greatest monastery on the Whitehawk continent, located in the Dry Blood Dunes, at the Vathic Rock Islands.

Whigg: A small but significant fortress-town in the Nine Feudatories.

Whitehawk (variant in Osril: Yllistra, Ilyster): The continent was originally called "Illystras" or "Illystrias" which translates "Whitehawk" the emblem of Christiandom in the civil lands, Includes all the intermundane principalities as well.

Xilmuria: A primordial land of unknown location,

Yahoros: a city-state upon the plains of Kithom, neath the Andolyn mountains. Yahoros was founded by Aels in the third age

Yaa, Chasm of: Believed to be located somewhere west of Anshan.

Yrbath, Irbath: The principal city under the Ulthurings Dynasty of Maceonid kings. After the eld city Ulthor was destroyed in the third age during the Bellum Diabolicum, the people of the feudatory rebuilt Yrbath on the sea instead of the city Ulthor. It has grown more powerful and resplendent than any would have thought. This city specializes in fishing and whaling, and hosts the invincible Ulthuring Fleet.

Yezez Desert: The desert between the Canyon of Hermius and the Antelynk Mountains. It stretches south and bends down into Garmsir. It is a place of great dangers.

Yule Queen: The muse of bardic masters in the old world, perhaps a nephilid. She is rumoured to still bless the world with poetry...

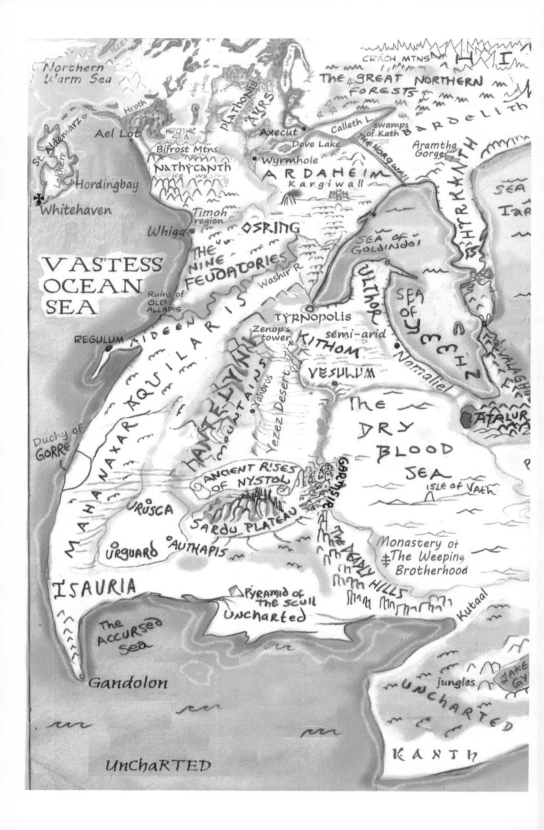

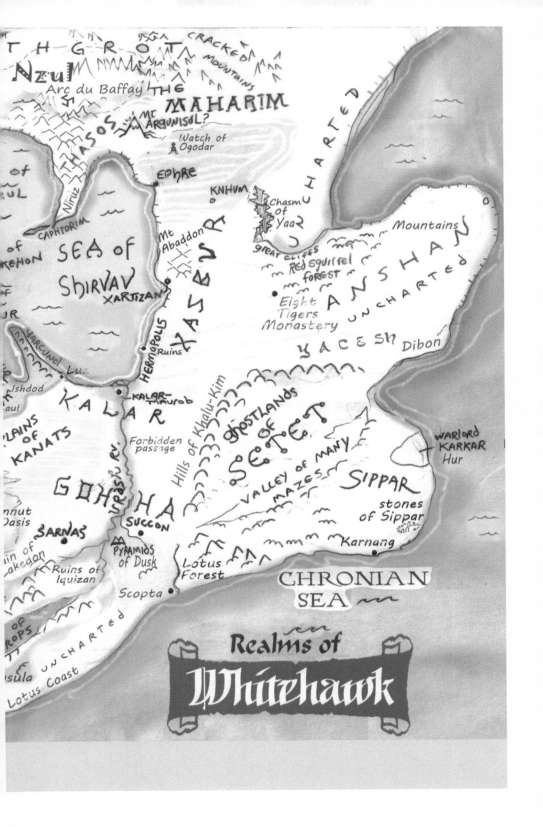

H.G Potter priest; writer, and illustrator: originally a masters in Greek & Latin, Fr. Potter was teacher of ancient civilizations, literature, philosophy and mythology from c. 1990. During the last decades as priest he worked in parishes and burned the midnight oil in his archeonic research. In 2006 he unearthed the corpus of Whitehawk writings from the lost archives of Thanato Excorpus, a 17th century Friar of Whigg. At last finishing the coveted manuscript of Brother Jacob, *Never Leave Your Monastery,* he has recently made ready his translations of Abbot Cromna's compilation, *The Fall of Nystol and Other tales*, various short stories about  Whitehawk which have been waiting his attention since 1986. The Nystol cycle comprises the most important events of the lost continent. He also has been translating the most pristine of all the manuscripts, Krithusel's *The Deeptracker's Guide,* (another compilation of short stories, encyclopedias of lore, and lost texts), as well as an epic poem *The Bladetongue.* All these are available in print at LULU.COM.

Visit

WWW.REALMSOFWHITEHAWK.COM

for more information.